JUST THE MEMORY OF LOVE

PETER RIMMER

ABOUT PETER RIMMER

∾

Peter Rimmer was born in London, England, and grew up in the south of the city where he went to school. After the Second World War, and aged eighteen, he joined the Royal Air Force, reaching the rank of Pilot Officer before he was nineteen. At the end of his National Service, he sailed for Africa to grow tobacco in what was then Rhodesia, now Zimbabwe.

The years went by and Peter found himself in Johannesburg where he established an insurance brokering company. Over 2% of the companies listed on the Johannesburg Stock Exchange were clients of Rimmer Associates. He opened branches in the United States of America, Australia and Hong Kong and travelled extensively between them.

Having lived a reclusive life on his beloved smallholding in Knysna, South Africa, for over 25 years, Peter passed away in July 2018. He has left an enormous legacy of unpublished work for his family to release over the coming years, and not only them but also his readers from around the world will sorely miss him. Peter Rimmer was 81 years old.

facebook.com/PeterRimmerAuthor
twitter.com/@htcrimmer
instagram.com/PeterRimmer_writer
bookbub.com/authors/peter-rimmer
amazon.com/author/peterrimmer

ALSO BY PETER RIMMER

∾

Cry of the Fish Eagle

Vultures in the Wind

Bend with the Wind

Just the Memory of Love

Second Beach (Novella)

All Our Yesterdays

∾

JUST THE MEMORY OF LOVE

Copyright © Peter Rimmer 2017

First published in Great Britain in September 2017 by

KAMBA PUBLISHING, United Kingdom

10 9 8 7 6 5 4 3 2

ISBN 978-0-9957561-3-7

PROLOGUE

ZAMBIA 1994

*T*he Reverend Hilary Bains, male Caucasian, sometime missionary, watched the orb of the sun sink into the upper reaches of the Zambezi River, silhouetting the Phoenix palms and the big acacia trees clutching the banks above the flowing water. The clouds in the heavens were aflame and painted the oily flotsam and the flat surface of the moving river, a blood red. The reverend wore long trousers and well-laced garters around his ankles to keep out the mosquitoes. It was October, hot, and the yesterday-boiled weir water in his whisky made the drink insipid. The insects screeched from the surrounding bush and on the other side, opposite where he sat on his rickety veranda, an old elephant drank the rushing waters which glowed red from the last rays of the dying sun. It was the missionary's sixtieth birthday and the celebration of his forty years in Africa. He was alone in body and spirit, more lonely for the lost, useless years than for any wife or children. Africa. Everything had changed and everything stayed the same. The brave words of freedom, the effort of missionaries, had been defeated by Africa. When the rains fell the people ate. When the rains stayed away they starved. The few elite enjoyed the fruits of freedom and the people lived in the same daily, miserable, hungry, diseased, mind-destroying poverty. Hilary Bains was quite sure he had wasted his life.

By the time he had finished his whisky the light had gone, night coming to Africa like a cloth placed over a cage. To light the oil lamp would bring the bugs. He tipped the bottle into his glass from habit, adding the thick river water, and drank a drink to the long years of his life. He could not remember whether he had eaten that day, but it did not matter. The old wicker chair had moulded to his body over the years and he was comfortable. A comfortable man with a case and a half of whisky. A hippo grunted forty metres down in front of his veranda, in the still pool away from the tug of moving liquid, oozing its way to the big drop of the Victoria Falls one hundred and eighty kilometres downriver... He had done it in a flat-bottomed boat, through all the rapids, but many years ago. That was when the white man dreamed of a Federation of Central Africa to rival the economy of Canada. And then came Harold Macmillan and the winds of change blew it all away and the kwacha, the currency of Zambia, formerly Northern Rhodesia, dropped over the heady years of independence, from two to the pound sterling to one thousand and thirty. A brave wind it was, the cold brave wind of poverty, nations born to be beggars for the rest of their natural lives. Everything had changed and everything had stayed the same. Hilary shivered in the heat.

Two hours passed. The old Labrador that slept at his feet pulled up its scarred head and cocked an ear, the new moon washing their corner of the front veranda. The screeching cicadas, along with the cacophony of a thousand river frogs, drowned the night in noise but Hilary knew there was something else. They were both going a little deaf but the dog could always hear better than his master. Tensely they waited. Something big splashed in the river upstream and still the dog's head was up, ears cocked. Then he got up and turned to face downriver. Hilary stood up with difficulty. A long searchlight was playing over the river, cutting the north bank, and then he too heard the engine noise of the riverboat and the thought of people passing so close and yet so far made the loneliness sink him back into his chair and with morbid interest he watched the powerful light probe the darkness of the riverbank, flicking enquiringly between the gaps in the tall trees. And then, suddenly, harshly, like a World War Two bomber pilot caught by the searchlights, it found him in his chair and stayed, holding him like a big, old and worthless moth in the light. And then he heard the riverboat's hooter beep a friendly tune and the craft, a two-decker raft of a boat, headed for the calm waters of the hippo pool where a small, pathetic jetty was the reverend's only contact with the outside world. His spirits lifted and he stood up to wave. The old dog gave a friendly bark, and the light moved down to search out the rickety jetty and the thatch-roofed house was back in its all-embracing darkness. The engine of the riverboat cut.

"Hilary Bains?" a voice shouted. An English voice.

"Who wants him?"

"Happy birthday... Will Langton... How are you, you old bugger?"

"What on earth are you doing here?"

"I've come to take you home. You want to give a young man a whisky?"

The young man was an old joke as Will Langton was only three years younger than the man his parents had adopted during the war, the refugee who had come down to Dorset to be away from the German bombs and stayed.

Hilary went into his lounge and lit the paraffin lamps around the walls and over the stone fireplace. They all smoked a black plume that rose up to the open ceiling and the neat underside of the thatch. He looked for a clean glass, found a dirty one and washed it under the tap, a luxury created by his windmills. When Will Langton, youngest of the pre-war generation of Langtons of Langton Manor in the county of Dorset, climbed up to the house with a cool bag full of ice, he was ready for a guest, the first in five months when last the supply boat came up from Kasungula. They had not seen each other for more than ten years and as they shook hands, smiling into each other's eyes, each was appraising the other, shocked at the ravages of age. Hilary's hair was white and long, down on his shoulders for lack of a barber; his sunken eyes, dark brown and brooding above the sharp nose, had deep crow's feet etched into their corners from decades of being held half closed against the African sun, while deep lines cut down from nose to jaw. He was thin, overly thin, the result of too many years of toil and malaria. Hilary Bains was now an old man and he read the message in the violet eyes of his childhood friend.

"Hell, you look good," said Will and meant it for the being of the man. "Here, have some ice. The captain said you don't have ice and he's not coming up as he doesn't like the climb. Seventy-four steps. Only man they said who'd bring a boat this far and you can't live here alone, Hilary. Come back to England. You're retired now."

"Thrown out. They want black priests, Will." Then he laughed with a touch of apprehension. "You said you'd come and dig me out but I never believed you would. Now, sit down in that armchair and I'll bring in the one from the veranda... You'll stay a day or two. You're busy I'm sure. But a day or two. We have our compensations... That old leg still give you trouble? Remember the day you tore the cartilage?... Hope you had supper? Not much of a cook. I think I had breakfast. You'll forgive me gabbling, old boy, but when you don't talk for months you gabble a lot when you find the chance. England's all right but I don't have the money. London Missionary Society like to give things away to the deserving and they don't think old white priests deserve very much. Here's all right. Student of mine from the sixties owns three thousand acres on both sides of the river. Sort of compensation for his part in the struggle. No one lives on the farm anymore, except me who could mend a tractor if it broke down out here. This place was a tobacco farm when I first visited. Now it has gone back to the bush. Sit down. Sit down and tell me everything. You can't say in a letter what you can say to a man's face. Now, how's your mother? Our mother as she wanted me to say, but I was never a Langton, you see. Never a Langton. No, never that. You can't be what you're not. Now sit down, Will, and I'll mix you a drink. Didn't by any chance bring any water? Roof water dried up in the tanks two months ago and it won't rain again till November if it rains at all. Terrible rains and all the people gone to Lusaka and nobody plants. Please, sit down. Prefer squatting in squalor outside the cities. The blacks, I mean."

"Let the ice melt." Will was smiling, a hundred memories turning in his mind.

"Right-oh, old boy. Doesn't take long in this temperature. Suicide month, October, before the rains break. Always called it suicide month. But you know that. You did have suicide month in Mongu?"

"It was very hot but I don't remember anyone killing themselves."

"And Randolph, how's big brother Randolph? And Jo, still as fiery as ever? She would have invented the Labour Party if it wasn't around. What do they call them now? Politically correct, that's it. Good old Jo, always politically correct and no damn good to anyone. Priests shouldn't swear but I'm not sure whether I am a priest anymore. You know the most terrible thing, William? I'm not sure anymore if there really is a God." They both thought about that in silence. "And Byron's still making money. That will never change. I could never make up my mind whether Jo's politics were more twisted to suit her cause of the moment or Byron's business antics to suit his pocket. What an unlikely set of twins... I was very sorry to hear about the group captain. Now there was a good man."

Will sat down with his drink and raised it to his old friend now perched in a faded green wicker chair with an uncertain front right leg. The dog was next to him, the oldest black Labrador that Will had ever seen, the liquid and slightly rheumy black eyes watching him intently for any mistakes. A small bat crawled out from behind a picture frame, the one holding a very amateur painting of the Victoria Falls, probably the work of Hilary, and flew round the room at considerable speed looking for insects with its radar, Hilary and the dog taking no notice. Twice Will ducked and once slopped his drink, changing hands and sucking the whisky off the back of his hand. He made up his mind to sleep on board in his cabin. He had been out of Africa too long to bed down with a colony of bats. By the time he had sipped half his drink three more bats had joined the food run. He would talk about the family in the light of day and for the moment enjoy his whisky in the last outlandish outpost that still housed an Englishman, washed up and left behind by an empire whose flag had flown over one-fifth of the world's surface when the man in front of him had been born in 1934.

It had been a long journey from London. Flight to Johannesburg, because Air Zimbabwe were having a ground crew strike, then South African Airways to Bulawayo and the overnight train to the Victoria Falls. Then the trip upriver, the river high and flooding from early rains in Angola, the old riverboat captain, the only man with the skill to navigate the endless rapids, keeping the screws of the big diesel motor off the rocks and in the water, the steel tubes that made up the floats grinding the rocks, searching for deeper water, the double-decker canting. He had said he was coming, so he came and ignored the images of crocodile and hippo. They did white-water rafting for fun downriver from the Falls and with many a spill, no one had been taken by a crocodile... They had seen nothing on the river and little of human habitation on the banks. One village the captain said had been killed by AIDS. Empty. Not even a long-legged chicken. Most of the hut roofs had fallen in. Hilary was still talking, not seeming to expect answers. Will listened, equally conscious of the night sounds of Africa outside. Maybe Hilary talked to himself alone at night... Will got up from his dilapidated armchair and poured them both another drink. Africa and booze went together... Old animal skins from the original white owner still graced the stone floor and from one window hung the tattered remnant of a curtain, that once upon a long time ago had boasted yellow flowers. Rats had eaten most of the curtaining. The fly screen for the door and the open windows were flyblown but of a newer vintage. It was obvious the reverend could not afford servants. Will looked back at his friend and tuned back in to the conversation.

"It's not as bad as it looks," Hilary was saying. "I grow vegetables and catch fish in the river. Tomorrow I will show you my windmills and my bathroom and you won't believe such luxury in the middle of the bush. I have some fowls, a constant battle with the genets. Nasty little creatures. Just eat the heads off and leave the rest. Oh, don't look at me like that, Will. I'm all right. Sort of the last remnant of the British Empire. Left behind but not quite forgotten... What would I do in England? I'm quite happy. I have found that I enjoy my own company. Live in the past. Enjoy the small triumphs and ignore the faux pas. I keep myself busy keeping myself and this old dog alive. There's a bucket outside with a hosepipe connected to the middle of its bottom with the long end of the hosepipe in my shower room with a tap and nozzle. I fill up the bucket at ground level and hoist the bucket and length of hosepipe to the top of a tree with a rope pulley; cold water in the summer and hot on a winter's morning. Then turn on the tap. First time it worked I ran around the house with nothing on, I was so excited."

"Don't you get lonely?"

"Yes, of course. Sometimes. But you can be lonely surrounded by people… Those bats won't get in your hair. Old wives' tale… You'll have to sleep on board, old boy. This is a one-bed family. Do you think they ever thought the empire in Barotseland would come to this? We must've poured millions down the drain in this part of the world, but you'll remember. Not to say the lives."

"You think they would have been better off without us?"

"Of course. Nature would have kept its balance, it was fools like me who rushed in with our one and only God and upset the balance of nature."

"Would you do it all over again?"

"If I was young, brainwashed and pumped up for man's salvation. If you ask me if my life was worth it I would say no. Do-gooders should mind their own business. It's something we westerners don't do too well, minding our own business."

"Can you leave Africa to its own devices?"

"Well, you either do that or run it properly. You can't feed nations that can't feed themselves because their lifestyle has been shattered by overpopulation. No, you either come back in and run the place or get out and let disease re-establish the balance of nature. Africa is overgrazed and you can't keep sending in fodder from the other side of the world. I told that to my black bishop, but he's one of the new elite who live very well thank you on foreign aid. Never tell a bishop the truth, Will. Probably best thing is never tell anyone the truth. And if you and I don't find our respective beds, we will fall asleep in these chairs and both of them are too uncomfortable for that. We will never solve the world's problems so what is the use of trying?… You want to tell me all about the family? Tomorrow. I can wait. I do a lot of waiting these days."

Waiting to die, he thought, but didn't wish to sour the evening. William could do all the talking in the morning. He was tired and a little drunk.

WILL Langton found it difficult to sleep when he found his bed on the lower deck of the riverboat. The decrepit old man in the neglected house on the African river, the friend of his childhood, had once been going to make a difference. Will could see it all in his mind's eye. All the education and study, working to the limit of a schoolboy's ability. Struggling at every stage to succeed, to be better. Growing up and being one of the winners and it had all come to this! The windows in the cabin were open and screened against mosquitoes. A slight breeze wafted damp air across his naked body. The pillow was wet from his own sweat. He was probably trying to sleep six feet above a family of hippopotami. Once he heard a leopard cough and then he was asleep, never remembering the moment.

Birdsong, glorious, rejuvenating birdsong woke him to the dawn, and he pulled the sheet up and over his nakedness. The big cabin windows showed him the rising sun and when he leant up on his elbows, he could see the wide expanse of river, oily, impenetrable to the human eye, flowing endlessly on to the distant sea using its millions of years of experience to know where to go. A black man was fishing from a dugout canoe, a floating, hollowed-out log, crude and dating back into the ancient past. The man looked content catching nothing and Will wondered where he came from and what he thought, if he thought at all. What a blessing not to have to think. Through the opposite window, the low thatched bungalow looked cared for from a distance, huddled between the tall acacia trees – fever trees they had called them once, before man knew malaria came from the water that nourished the mosquitoes. His Africa was a long time ago and he remembered the excitement. Everything seemed better. The question he asked himself in the first light of dawn was simple and complicated. If he left Hilary in his tumbledown house on the river, how would he survive? And then again, how would he survive at Langton Manor, cold and damp and nothing much more there for Hilary to do with the rest of his life? The Church of England was contracting, down to two million churchgoers from a time when every Englishman went to church, his religion a deep part of his life. No one was looking for a worked-out missionary in Langton Matravers any more than they were anywhere else in Europe. It was the new age of television evangelism, a euphemism for ripping off the public in the name of God... Will smiled. Maybe that long white hair could raise a fortune, the sunken eyes still burning from the African toil...

Will hung his feet over the bed. First, he would make himself a cup of tea and then he would go up to the house and tell Hilary Bains what had been happening in the family. Maybe he would have a better insight into the years of his own life, of Byron's and Jo's, Randolph's, his brothers and sister. They say with age grows wisdom, he told himself, but Will was not sure. Man seemed never to be getting anywhere if you discounted his fancy cars and all that modern science provided, thrusting him skyward to a concrete home. Hilary was right. Everything changed but everything stayed the same...

When he had drunk his tea he would go up and ask Hilary again about his God. The man must still believe in his God? Hilary was a missionary. Hilary was a priest... He put on his underpants and a pair of shorts. A couple of wild geese, spur-winged geese, flew low, rushing over the flowing water.

The river captain was still asleep and the two black crewmen had taken the small motorboat they carried to go fishing. He had heard them go and even understood a little of what they had said, the language of the Lozi, the indigenous people of Barotseland, still echoing in the back of his mind from somewhere in his distant past. Will climbed up to the deck above, an open platform with an open, canvas roof, camp chairs and wooden tables bolted to the floor to stop theft in port as much as going overboard in the rapids. In the front was a bar with an insulated metal cylinder for hot water which he checked before lighting the gas. The sweet smell of the morning river, moisture swirling half a metre above the flow like lace, brought more memories from the past, good memories that drifted him on to a sharp jab of bittersweet pain.

He could still hear the old riverboat captain snoring down below and when the water boiled again – the crew had made theirs earlier – he dropped a teabag in a mug and made his morning tea. There was no sound or movement from the brooding house on the high bank of the river, not even sight of the dog. Old noises from the bush tickled his memory, asking him to give them names, and when the tea was cool enough he drank and it tasted good, better than the whisky. Memories as clear as the morning sun... Trying to do another man a favour was a foolish thing. No one knew the real thoughts of another person, no matter how much they spoke. That which he thought he wanted from the last of his life, did Hilary? Peace and serenity, were they not above material comfort? The older he had grown, the less he had understood... There was not a sound of man, the motorboat long silent, the crewmen fishing for river bream, probably content with their world. Maybe he needed Hilary more than Hilary needed him, his carefully thought-out altruism really selfishness. Was he more probably the lonely man in a sea of people, family and friends? Was he looking back to Hilary for his youth that had gone? Even his own mind changed with the constant flow of his thoughts. What had been the point of it all, or did there have to be a point, just the struggling pace of the ages?

"Water hot?" He had not even noticed the captain cease his snoring, let alone get up and mount the ladder.

"Yes, oh yes. Just boiled... Morning to you... Sleep well?... Lovely morning." Loudly, Will ran out of trivialities. The old captain was spare with words, probably never concerned himself with polite conversation. "We'll be here a few days if it's all right by you?"

"Your friend all right?... Suits me. You pay by the day... Nice place he's got," and the old, craggy man with the captain's cap firmly on his head nodded up the bank. He said it in a tone that indicated there were few places like that in the world.

"Bloody crew buggered off. No sweat. Fish for breakfast. Those two are good, man. Very good... Wouldn't mind parking the old girl here forever."

His name was Cookson, second-generation African. Father had come up with the pioneer column as a kid. Ox-wagons. With Selous and Johnson. He had told some of his story on the journey upriver, how he had taken a load of maize meal upriver in the '92 drought, risking his boat, heavy in the water with food for the starving, sacks of maize stacked everywhere, and when he got where he was going the authorities wanted him to pay for the unloading so the old man had gone back fully loaded and some of the people died of starvation. The African thorns were not all on the trees. Will wondered how much British aid reached further than the new political elite, yesterday's politically correct, yesterday's great men of Africa. Will watched the captain make his tea and sit down to watch the river and say not a word. Half a tree, mostly submerged, floated down in midstream and from the bank a voice began to sing, perfectly in time, and the tune was a hymn Will had first heard at his public school, the same school Hilary had attended, paid for by the Langtons. Searching the bank between the trees where the sun was seeking out the inner sanctum, Will made out the reed-walled, roofless enclosure, the shower bucket on high, the white hair of Hilary, and sensed the perfect happiness of his friend enjoying his shower in the African morning, the yellow sunrays that bathed a man in light not sweat, a welcome sun to be enjoyed and sung to in praise of God or the joy of living. Will got up and took himself down the ladder, across the rickety jetty and up the steep steps to the thatched house. The old dog stood and watched him, wagging his tail. It was a very beautiful day.

BOTH CHAIRS WERE on the veranda, waiting for a guest, but Will stood with the dog, enjoying the flowing majesty of the Zambezi River down below. He could see Captain Cookson smoking a pipe and smell the harsh tobacco, raw on the sweet air of the unspoilt bush veld. The back door clanged. The plaintive call of a fish eagle echoed down the river.

"Good morning, old friend," said Hilary, putting a tray of coffee on the veranda wall. "I trust you slept the good sleep of the just. May I offer you coffee from our own trees? I will show you around in a while."

"You were cheerful under the shower."

"I was. And so I should have been. What more could a man of my age want for? You see, William, before you tell me about the family and all the plans they have made for me again, with all the love and goodwill of wonderful people, I want to show you my life. When you left last night I sat and thought, something I am good at with all this solitary practice. Maybe some of us reach a point in life where we wish to be alone, free of having to interact pleasantly with our fellow man. I have done my work, they have told me that in no uncertain words. I have lost my own family twice and been away from my adopted family for forty years... How do you take your coffee, William? Better put in your own milk powder and sugar."

The old dog sat down next to Hilary and closed its eyes, taking no more interest in the visitor.

"I am a lot more organised than you imagine. Behind the trees down there at the river is a windmill and pump I salvaged from the Carters. My word, I wonder where they are now? They ran cattle as well as growing tobacco, maize and a few coffee trees. The cattle needed water away from the river and the windmills pumped up water from boreholes. By the time my pupil agreed I could live in the old house, the tobacco farms had collapsed, the borehole pumps had stopped working for lack of a squirt of oil and everything else had gone to pot. The joke is, William, the new government are offering these farms to foreign owners as no one else is willing to work them, but that's digressing. With the first expedition – and that it was, Livingstone would have been proud of us and envious of our four-wheel drives – I brought in cement among my provisions and some old friends from the mission who had some concern for their old teacher, something lacking in London among the new generation of theologians, we moved three windmills up here. One we put near the river to pump up to an intermediate concrete reservoir which I use as a swimming pool, the second to pump to a second reservoir and the third to pump up into my header tank and give me running water and waterborne sewerage. *Voilà*, we have luxury! The whole job took four days. I have a wood-burning stove for my cooking, paraffin for light and mostly I sleep when the sun goes down, or more rightly, lie in bed and think in the dark with the wonderful sounds of Africa all around me, and rise with the dawn... Please, help yourself to more coffee. I salvaged a few old coffee trees and run water to them from the overflow of the header tank which waters the rest of my kitchen garden. Here I live with my memories and, largely, I am content, as content as man ever finds himself."

"But are you happy on your own, Hilary?" asked Will Langton.

"The question is, would I be happier surrounded by a lot of people? You and I, William, would come to each other as strangers, for a while chewing over common memories, as I would with Jo, maybe Byron, even old stick-in-the-mud Randolph, but that would last a week. Don't you lot worry about Hilary. When you have been through the little ups and downs of my life, this is paradise. Come on, put down your coffee and I will show you something."

Walking back through the lounge, free of flying bats during the day, Hilary led the way through a door in the corner across from the big stone fireplace. It was the most beautiful room of the house and ran some sixty feet along the side away from the river and the damp swirls of early morning river mist. There were big windows along the length of the room and outside an equally long veranda which brought light into the library but stopped the rays of the sun damaging the books. Along the inside wall, from floor to ceiling, were row upon row of books with a sturdy iron grille, that slid open in sections, guarding every one of them.

"I regret to say my pupil was more interested in politics than books and when they took out the Carters' furniture, they couldn't get at the books and left them alone. I had been in the house with the Carters and knew where they kept the spare key... I may spend hours of my time with dead men but some of them talk more sense than the news magazines they bring me with my provisions. I have been making a great study of the evolution of man, from Darwin onwards, and it has disturbed my faith, William. Maybe we have not evolved long enough to understand whether man made God or God made man. Science can make a lot in the testaments smack of fiction, well-meaning fiction, but stories disguised to improve the acceptability of the religious. I think that is where a lot of the Church's mumbo jumbo comes from. I wonder whether much written in the Bible was not for the good of the Church rather than the glory of God."

Hilary walked down the row of books. "In all my life I could never absorb all the wisdom in these books... Yes, of course, there are times when I would like to discuss what I read with the likes of you but then again so few in your world have time to read, let alone think about what they read. They are prisoners of the television set, caught in its beam as I was last night by the beam of your light. The fear I have is millions watching the same picture, everybody impregnated with the same thoughts, unable to search for truth on their own. Come, let me show you round my estate. Then, when all that has been done, you shall tell me of your family. Maybe the good captain will join us for lunch, a vegetarian lunch as I have no meat at present. Come, good William Langton, white knight come to save me from the dark truths of Africa, let me show you my kingdom on earth and introduce you to some of my friends, all animal, but friends."

They walked and talked for two hours, visiting the fowls, the well-fenced kitchen garden roofed with wire mesh, the flourishing coffee trees and tea bushes, the nests of numerous birds without disturbing them, a throwback to their boyhood, and the rest of the small territory of a few acres that made up the life of Hilary Bains. They sat on the edge of the improvised swimming pool, the early sun growing hot on their bodies.

"You might say swimming in the water you drink is unacceptable. Well, I share this water with a whole range of animals and birds. There are no crocodiles in my pool to drag the animals to their deaths. It's a kind of friendly place for everyone, and well used... Randolph has had a good life, a normal life if there is such a thing, and I hope and pray the cancer is not too painful which I know it will be. There is something to being killed by a bullet," and Hilary leant forward and stared into the water for a long time, Will leaving him alone with his memories.

"Take a wife," Hilary said, still staring into the water. "You can have some children. People do anything in this day and age. Will, I appreciate you coming all the way to one of the remotest places on earth. You can rest at home with a clear conscience if that is what you want. I don't think I wish to return to England and the reason has nothing to do with the lack of my own money or the acceptance of your charity once again." Will tried to speak but Hilary raised his hand and went on, not permitting an interruption. "I don't think I could condone the society in which you westerners live. I think the hypocrisy of social democracy would make me an unhappy man. Any society that bases itself on the ability to lie successfully is one that a simple old priest would prefer to leave alone.

"I am a hermit and have been these past few years. Not a recluse, a hermit, a man who has taken himself away to think. My hope was to find my God again who had been lost to me by the Church, by a Church that practised liberation theology and provided guns to kill men in the name of their righteousness. In the process, created monsters that then dined off their fellow humans' flesh... I came to think, not for a brief moment of doubt, but for hours and days and weeks, and I hope I have made some sense of it. The most simple truth, the very pains of Christ's teachings and those of Socrates, is that it is better to do that which is right as opposed to that which is wrong. I began the pursuit of this truth when I left the Church and I asked everyone I met with a grasp of my language, 'Is it better to do that which is right as opposed to that which is wrong?' expecting simple, quick answers. To my surprise, no one gave me an immediate answer and when they did the most common response was 'Well, it depends'. And, when I probed, the real answer to my everlasting horror was 'Everything is right if you can get away with it'. The crystal definition of right and wrong had gone from the world. No one knew, let alone practised, the difference between right and wrong and if we cannot start our lives on that most basic of premises, then we are doomed to destruction and there is no God in his mystical heaven who will be our salvation. The goodness of God lives in ourselves, and if the people have been brainwashed so they know not the difference between right and wrong, how can God be inside any one of them? We alone among all the animals on earth have the power to reason. We have the power of understanding the difference between right and wrong and without exercising that power, all the comforts of modern life will come to nothing.

"Ever since man came out of the forest, he has looked for a way of conducting his affairs in mutual benefit and he has looked for a god, and when he finds either he inflicts his great prize on everyone around him. And because of this, and because the premise on which he built his authority was false, he has failed. At my seminary, we were told to believe in every word of the Bible as gospel, the truth, not to be argued with but to be used as the pillar to spread the word of God. Believe in me with blind faith and everything I say. Believe that God made Heaven and earth in six days as we see it now. That is not true and we know it's not true and we have proof that it's not true. We came out of the primeval swamps, we evolved and are still evolving, and so now the theologians argue that God created the life that came from the primeval swamp. It is a fact that the matter, the original substance that makes up you and me, is as old as the universe, so they separate the body from the soul and tell us the soul is eternal... People just don't know what to believe anymore, ecclesiastical or temporal. I mean, what is the point of being good if there is no spiritual reward? We might as well be bad and enjoy ourselves, proving that it's better to be wrong than right. But right has its way and the bodily comforts turn to mental misery as they drink and drug and fornicate to enjoy themselves, having lost the harmony and peace in their souls.

"Your social democracy is based on the pillars of the majority always being right. Sadly, it's the other way round. The majority are usually wrong when it comes to government as they will always vote for a man who will give them something for nothing and the man who warns them that they are borrowing from their great-grandchildren to pay for their unworked-for lifestyles is swept away. The great-grandchildren cannot vote. Hurray for democracy and its human right to do exactly what we want. It is the human right of a man to spill his seed into the bottom of another man... It is against the laws of nature and therefore, if I believe in God, against the laws of God as God created nature, man and woman, and he did not create a third sex somewhere in the middle. But the gays have political clout in the new democracy and therefore they are right.

"In your society you are not governed by the best man, who will always govern in the way that is right as opposed to that which is wrong, you are governed by the most accomplished liar who has five years to reward himself, mainly his ego, before he is thrown out where he can think of some new angle to lie about to keep him and his cronies in power. One minute they are sweeping into power on the back of a gullible democracy by nationalising everything and then sweeping in to the same seat of power on the waves of privatisation and not one of the politicians could give a tinker's cuss as to which one was right because it no longer matters provided you win. Would the Americans have gone to war with Nazi Germany if the Luftwaffe had won the Battle of Britain? Of course not. They would have watched happily while the German army crushed Russia and lived with Hitler as easily as they lived with Stalin. The European Union would have been in place in 1940 without the destruction of people and property. Do you think the Americans would have applied sanctions to Nazi Europe? Refused to do business with an all-powerful Europe still in control of its colonies? What American business, American trade, required was the Europeans to destroy each other and benevolent America to pick up the pieces. Even then the right and wrong of German National Socialism was not the issue, the issue was trade and the war goes on. We are quite capable of giving everyone on earth a comfortable, material life but we don't. We can fly to the moon but we cannot govern ourselves any better than the city states of Ancient Greece. In most parts of the world we have retrogressed. It is the way of man, the make-up of the animal that often finds it difficult to live within himself, let alone within a community. The confusion is righteousness and the gullibility of people so easily manipulated by their own stupidity. We are sick in body and go to the best doctor our money can buy. We are sick for good government and yet we elect people without the slightest skill to perform the job in hand. Can you imagine if we ran a business with every decision subject to the whim of people unskilled in the art of management? No, there is too much in your new democracy, a word with as many meanings as love, which leaves my heart sick so I will stay and live in my heritage, with my books, and see if by chance I can make some sense out of the whole nonsense of life, the eternal and endless why, what was it for, what was it all about. There is nothing else for me. I am sure I will die in ignorance like the rest of mankind, but I won't be fooled by a charlatan masquerading as a good man, clothed in the camouflage of social democracy. No, let me alone."

They heard the motorboat return and watched the fish being handed up to Captain Cookson while the river flowed on, pocked by flotsam, on its tragic rush to the sea. Will had no immediate answer but instead of feeling sorry for Hilary in his solitary isolation, he felt the beginning of envy, a yearning for the way out into a world untroubled by anything other than one's own stupidity. It made his own life seem worthless and his present more uncomfortable. Priests were meant to make you feel better in yourself, not worse! He began to think back on his life, like a gravedigger digging up bones. There had to have been something in his life that had made it worthwhile and slowly, carefully, he began to sift back, searching for the reason for one William Langton, his family, his friends, and the disillusioned priest dangling his feet in the water next to him. It did not take him too long to feel better and some of the answers to Hilary's despair formed in his mind. He turned to his friend.

"I still say you must leave this miniature paradise and return with me to Langton Manor, and not only for you but for me. We are two old men without wives and neither of us would wish to go out and search for a wife at this stage in our lives despite what you suggested. There is a library at home every bit as magnificent as the one you have here and when you have read your fill during the day, the two old boys can sit down round the fire and have a drink, talk about the things you have been reading and the comings and goings of the farm. Randolph may even be dead by now and Byron cannot live in England as the tax would kill him and he means kill him, the old miser, and the estate has to go to the eldest son of the eldest son by the law of entailment. So Gregory will inherit but he hates sheep. I have nothing much to do now and the idea of caretaking the family home appeals to me... The younger son who went off to the colonies, which promptly disappeared, now has something constructive to do. I probably need you a lot more than you need me but having seen all this I would find it difficult to stop the picture of you being helpless on the floor with the old dog whimpering. You said yourself we should leave Africa to the Africans. As a colonial power we tried our best and was told it was not good enough, we were exploiting and not fairly administering the territories. The new order have done a lot worse for the people but that is for the people to find out and do something about. You may be right about politicians but I think it was Winston Churchill who said democracy was a bad form of government but he couldn't think of a better one. And if the London Missionary Society are paying you a pension on which you are unable to live, we will go and see them and sort out the mistake.

"One of my more cynical friends in London says the Gay Movement is a wonderful thing, it keeps them together, stops them breeding and thereby keeps down the population. One fallacy I have found in life is judging other people by myself. I have no tendency to be a queer and I have liked women far too much in my life, but if a man loves a man or a woman loves a woman and physical contact gives them comfort, so let it be. They are doing no one any harm and if they find some happiness, good luck to them. Your God, I can't help you with. I have been agnostic for all my adult life and nothing has happened to change my mind. I simply don't know if there is a God. I personally think that when we die, we are as dead as mutton and the thing that lives on is the species with its ever-changing evolution and through that evolution and its by-product science, we will generate more wealth in the world to repay our grandchildren. Sometime in the deep future of our evolution we may even understand the reason for our existence. England is a far fairer society than it was when we were born. We may not have an empire but the man in the street has no fear of want. We may all look and think a bit like each other but that can make us homogeneous and stop us fighting with each other. And quite frankly, Hilary, I never fancied living under Adolf and his Gestapo and I think the vast majority of Germans would go along with me. Evolution and man have always taken ten paces forward and nine paces back. Africa has been doing a lot of going back in the last thirty years, and when they work out what they really want – a rural subsistence living or a modern economy, warts and all, one or the other – they will go forward again and find some national happiness.

"The older I grow the more difficult I find it to define your right and wrong. As a kid it was easy, whatever Mother said was wrong, was wrong and no argument; and mostly, looking back, I find her definitions correct. But then I surmise it was a simpler world, a lot less people for one and words like pollution, which they called smog, ecology, which was the countryside, had not been used along with a thousand other disturbing words we use in our daily life. Politically you were Conservative or Labour and the two were on opposite ends of the same, long pole. Now they each change their philosophies in mid-sentence if they find themselves disagreeing with a crowd or the popular opinion on a chat show. The simple clarity of our youthful right and wrong has gone forever. The world is a far too dangerous place to be naïve."

"Then you also don't know the difference between right and wrong," said Hilary, sullenly.

"I know it is better to be right than wrong. I don't say the right is wrong if you can get away with it. What I find difficult is applying the old principles to determine whether something is right or wrong. Yes, buggery is against the laws of nature but creating happiness is not. Science has developed more in the last ten years, man's knowledge has increased more than in the whole previous history of the human race. We just can't keep up emotionally or politically and the mental trauma is tantamount to the industrial and post-industrial revolution all in one and overnight. Our thinking is way behind our scientific achievement. We grew too big too quickly and the body politic is skinny and gets tired easily; growing pains of a global village where once four generations back we didn't travel further than twenty miles. We have experienced, you and I in our lifetime, the great leap forward in history and the compounding energy that it has generated will be even more staggering in the future. I personally don't believe we will blow ourselves up or ecologically destroy the world as the first and strongest instinct of man is self-preservation. The 'wrong being right if you can get away with it' syndrome doesn't apply if you destroy your enemy in the full knowledge that you will destroy yourself. The political Tower of Babel may find some sense and eliminate poverty from the face of the earth rather than mankind. For every megalomaniac shouting his mouth off there are millions of quiet people getting on with their lives who are not activists, gay, lesbian, anarchist or drug peddlers. They are the majority and, though I agree at present that social democracy is controlled by the activist fringe, the swing vote that every politician panders to, there will come a time when more rational thought will prevail. We all discuss the wrongs of the world and never the rights because we are presently confused as to which is wrong and how wrong; the grey shades of understanding. Soon we will go into space, very soon in terms of man's span of evolution, and we will find there are other people in the universe and then the argument between black and white culture will look very mundane. We evolve, Hilary, because we keep thinking as you are doing. Maybe you should publish your thoughts of a one-time missionary in Africa. But do it in England. All you will do here, alone, is go round and round in the same circle, even with all the wisdom in your books. Maybe you have thought long enough in isolation and your untainted thoughts will be of value in the ongoing process. Look, you were always the brains in the family and I tagged along. I probably don't know what I am talking about but I can say your company at the manor would be a lot more beneficial to me than chewing over childhood memories. We can visit the pubs in Corfe Castle, swim in the sea and talk. Just because we are past the age when men procreate children, it doesn't mean our brains are dead... Now, I've said more than I've probably ever said and it's getting damned hot. Come on board and you and I will drink a glass of cold beer with the good captain, eat a fillet of fresh Zambezi bream and try and work out how we can make the last third of our lives as pleasant as possible as you and I, Hilary Bains, are going to live to ninety and by then they will have found a cure for old age and we will live forever just to find out what happens. Give this dog here some food and we will adjourn to the top deck to discuss the more frivolous things of life, and I am not talking about my ex-girlfriend."

"When a society reaches the point where everyone is permitted to do exactly what they want no matter how it affects their neighbour, when moral decay has reached the stage of purification, all your new wealth will be unable to save the goal of that civilisation and it will destroy itself. When righteousness and honour, duty, just reward for hard work, sensitivity to the feelings of others and so many other attributes that were once good in man, once they toss these on the rubbish heap of their rights, most of which are not right at all because they don't know the difference, you have a classic civilisation in its death throes. Churchill also said that if you wish to find out what will happen in the future, look into the past. All the great civilisations fell when they indulged themselves, when discipline collapsed and the free for all of good living took its place. When they morally collapsed, they collapsed entirely. When the comforts of the body were more important than the soul. When a man is surrounded by a problem, he finds it more difficult to see the wood for the trees. Creeping disaster is much more difficult to comprehend... First, I am falling into this water and then I will join you for a cold beer, something that has not passed my lips for a very long time... Poor Randolph. It comes to all of us. One day you think you are going to live forever and the next you have cancer. When one's own generation begins to die, death is indeed close. Good old stick-in-the-mud Randolph. I often envy people with small emotions. England from this standpoint is a long way away... Last in is a fool." Ripping off his few clothes, Hilary Bains, ex-missionary, beat William Langton, ex-rover around the world, into the water by a fraction of a second, both laughing hysterically at the old game they had played so often as children.

"Will you think about it?" said Will, back on the side of the pool.

"It's good to talk to someone, that it is... Skinny-dipping at our age! We should be ashamed."

"Why?" And again they both laughed.

PART I

1937 TO 1950

1

William Langton was born in an exclusive nursing home twelve hundred yards from Buckingham Palace. Ethelred Langton, his father, was not taking any chances with his family. For years afterwards, William thought he had been brought into the world by the same man who delivered the future Queen of England but like so many other things in his life, he would discover from Jo it was the assistant; the twins and Randolph had been delivered by the gynaecologist to the then Duchess of York who became Queen of England the year William was born. His three elder siblings considered him inferior, the youngest child and delivered by the assistant. He was an afterthought, six years younger than the twins and eight years younger than Randolph. Byron, shown the baby in his perambulator when he was first returned from the London nursing home to Langton Manor, asked if he could flick him. Byron was at the flicking stage and when Adelaide Langton, mother of them all, was out of the way, Byron gave the baby his first flick right on the baby's left ear and ran into the bushes when the two-week-old William howled his discontent. Byron, William was to discover, started most of the mischief in his life but was only around to receive the rewards, never the penalties. The pram had been put on the well-cut, sweeping lawns next to the rose garden, and the nurse, seeing the baby asleep in the spring sun, had gone off to visit the chauffeur and nobody heard the child screaming. It may have been the cause of William distrusting his brother, a subconscious knowledge of what Byron was all about.

No one was sure whether Langton Manor took its name from the nearby village of Langton Matravers or the Langton family, or even if the family name had given birth to the village; most people thought they had probably evolved together with the arrival of Angles, Jutes and Saxons in the fifth century and afterwards. The family were definitely Anglo-Saxons, not original islanders, and had probably conquered the land they farmed with the sword, killing or chasing off the original owners. The Germanic tribes landed along the coast of England, beaching longboats dozens at a time before pillaging and raping their way inland where they settled down comfortably, the Anglo giving England its very name. The Langtons, along with so many Anglo-Saxons, were proud of their history and gave their children the names of kings and poets, the great men of English history. William's father had to shoulder the unfortunate name of Ethelred throughout his life, called after Ethelred the Unready, Saxon King of the English. William was never sure whether he came from William the Conqueror, William of Orange or William Shakespeare, but he hoped it was the poet.

1937 was the last summer in British history when the flag of the empire flew without threat or hindrance. The King was King of England, Scotland and Ireland and all the dominions, Emperor of India, Defender of the Faith. Germany, defeated years earlier, would not dare to challenge the empire again, or so they thought.

After a few minutes of howling William gave up and went back to sleep. Being the fourth child, his purpose was to inherit or marry money and as an Englishman it created most of the advantages when looked at in perspective. The snag of inheriting was handing over the inheritance to the following generation. Even William was to find there was no such thing as a free lunch.

Ethelred Langton, Red as he was known to friends and enemies, was one of the many in the island who were not secure in mind when they contemplated Hitler's Third Reich eating up large parts of Europe with no one telling them to stop; but then he had more information than the man in the street, having taken up with aeroplanes in 1924 at the age of seventeen. Red would have preferred a life with aeroplanes but being the eldest Langton son it was his responsibility to run the family estate. Like his middle son Byron, he considered sheep to be the most stupid animals on God's earth. Duty was duty and once he had finished his extended tour of Europe, university and its academic pleasures giving Red as much of a thrill as the sheep, he came home and buckled down to learn the estate business. Appreciating the importance twin lambs were to the estate accounts, and that sheep were as good as the grass they ate and that Harold Langton, Granda to the kids, was primarily a grower of grass, good grass with all the legumes a sheep needed for strength, growth and good wool, Red soon found the secret to every success was knowledge and not the luck of being born into wealth. His father, like his father before him, drummed in the old adage that a fool and his wealth were easily parted. In 1936, Red had joined the RAF reserve squadron based at Boscombe Down in Wiltshire and once a month he was away for four days where he flew to his heart's content and learnt that Hitler was a menace that one day would have to be reckoned with, which was why he was not ecstatic about another child that Adelaide had set her mind to and which arrived in the person of William in May 1937. They had an argument, he and Adelaide, one of their few. Given the memory of the last war and the toll it took on their class of Englishmen, Red was not sure of the future, potentially a war more bloody than the last; he was a bomber pilot and he knew it would be. Her argument, one with painful logic, was that if a war was imminent, they needed more sons not fewer to protect the entailment of Langton Manor and the way of life of all those who lived and worked on the estate. Adelaide won her argument, and William was conceived with all the problems a life on earth was to entail which started with Byron giving him a flick on the ear.

All the same, that first summer suggested his life would pass in sunshine and happiness, as cross words were something rarely heard at Langton Manor. Will sat up in the pram in the same spot next to the roses, vaguely aware of the herbaceous border further down the lawn and the trees, and then the Downs and beyond, the booming sea when the English Channel was angry, a sound young William accepted along with the chirp of the blackbirds and thrushes and the smell of sweet blossom on the evening air, before they put him away in the nursery and his parents came to look at the last of their sons for ten minutes. There were a lot of things happening at the manor and William was only one of them, a fairly insignificant bystander to the greater event of so many lives welded together to go forward through life with a common bond. A sick, expensive sow that earned income, received considerably more attention from Red Langton than his youngest son. Everything had its place and a baby or a small boy was expected to be seen and not heard. Will found early on in his life that he was on his own, that real survival depended on Will Langton and not the patronage of a family responsible for umpteen other individuals who relied on the manor and the good management of the Langton family for a living.

Autumn and winter came and a good fire was lit in the nursery where Will spent his days with the young nurse who thought more of the chauffeur in his fancy uniform than the child crawling around the floor, very often smelling. Will's brothers and sister never came into the nursery as if, after Byron's perfunctory flick, they had all lost interest; Byron found more fun in teasing his twin sister while Randolph followed his father around the estate with consummate interest. Even at that age the only thing they had in common was a mother and father and the same roof under which they all lived. Will was sure, looking back, if he had been loved as a baby, his path would have been different.

The first thing he ever remembered was sitting in his high chair in the family dining room, strapped in, with a bowl of food that came in a warmer, as William was never to be a fast eater and the surrounding jacket of the warmer was filled with warm water to keep the mushed up food hot. As usual no one was paying him any attention and if it were not for the nurse's day off, he would have been up in the nursery all on his own. Will's first, vivid recollection of life was being ignored with the spill-proof warmer of food and himself in the high chair feet away from the long dining room table. Will rebelled, picked up the warmer and dumped it on the floor, waiting for a reaction, and watched his mother get up from the table without interrupting her conversation, pick up the warmer that had landed flat on its bottom and not spilt a morsel, and put it back in front of her son as if she had retrieved a bone for an errant dog. The bellow of rage and frustration that Will had ready to burst with the first smack died, stillborn. No one, not even his mother, had taken the slightest bit of notice. He was two years old.

Four months later Germany marched into Poland. England and France declared war on Germany and Red Langton went to live at Boscombe Down permanently. That week, workers came in to build a large air-raid shelter among the oak trees some seventy yards away from the manor house. Will took no more notice of the comings and goings than the rest of them took of him, his thirty months of wisdom unable to grasp the gravity of the happenings that would totally change the comfortable prospects of his life. 1939 turned into 1940 and the British fought their last great battle as the power that controlled the world and in the process exhausted themselves for the foreseeable future.

From the nursery window, high on the second floor of the manor house, high on its hill, young Will could see over the Nine Barrow Down to Poole Harbour where a squadron of German Heinkel bombers had mistaken it in the dark for Southampton. Will stood at the window, his soft pillow under his left arm feeling the soft material between his left forefinger and thumb while he sucked the thumb of his right hand in peaceful contentment. The searchlights of the ack ack regiment scoured the night sky for the elusive bombers and the sounds of the guns and exploding bombs reached Will through the open window and, as he was unable to comprehend what was going on, he enjoyed the distant spectacle of sweeping lights and bangs. Down below he watched people run out of the house in their night clothes and disappear into the trees not to come out again. Over in the distance, across the estuary, big bonfires were springing up and the wailing noise of the sirens echoed amid the booms of the big guns and the exploding bombs. Down below they had stopped running into the trees and if Will had turned round from the spectacle, he would have seen his young nurse hiding under her bed too terrified to make any noise. Will watched for quite a while but when the big lights searching the underbelly of the clouds were turned off and all that was left was one big bonfire, Will grew bored and took his pillow back to bed. He was still contentedly sucking his thumb when he fell asleep and when the Germans came back at three in the morning, attracted by the fires, he did not even wake up. He often wondered in the years to come whether anyone had noticed he and the nurse were not in the air-raid shelter with everyone else.

Shortly after the start of the Blitz, a good part of it aimed at London and the London docks, the government sent children out of the danger areas into the country, appealing to the country folk to take the young refugees into their homes which was how Hilary Bains first came to Langton Manor with twenty-two others. Will's nursery became a place of joy and laughter, filled with youngsters of his own age. When the warning sirens blared they all rushed down and into the trees and the questionable safety of the extended air-raid shelter which, as the bombing of Southern England increased, became their ignoble home. Everyone was pushed close together under the warm feeling of shared, exciting danger, with duckboards down as the concrete floor underneath sloshed with water, wooden bunks up the concrete walls, two children per bunk, and dripping candles that were always falling over in their saucers constituting as big a danger to life as the German bombs which, distant and soundproofed by the breeze-block walls, fell on the small port. When an air raid was in progress the grown-ups started a game of *I-spy-with-my-little-eye*, to comfort themselves despite directing their energy at the children and, if the children were lucky – which was quite often as old men liked to reminisce – they would listen to Granda Langton tell them wonderful stories of his war, the war on the highveld of Africa, the Boer War, which he had fought with a good horse between his young legs, in the days when a man could see his enemy. There were only old men and boys in the air-raid shelter, the rest having gone off to fight the Germans. It was a great levelling of the classes, the air-raid shelter, all the

Langtons still at home, the servants and the twenty-three refugees from the poorer parts of London.

Hilary Bains's father was a tail gunner in Echo-Bravo-Foxtrot, a Lancaster bomber powered by four Rolls-Royce Merlin engines captained by Squadron Leader Red Langton, which was how Hilary the refugee was directed to Langton Manor, air crews becoming as much family as blood relations. Hilary had been at Langton Manor for seven months when a badly shot up Echo-Bravo-Foxtrot returned to Boscombe Down on two engines, the pilot subsequently receiving the Air Force Cross (AFC) for superb airmanship in bringing the plane home. They had been attacked twice by German night fighters who always came in from the rear, taking out the tail gunner and rendering the aircraft defenceless from behind. When the ambulance collected the wounded, which included Red who had taken a bullet through his ankle and would limp for the rest of his life, the rear bubble was empty, the perspex shattered, and Hilary's father presumably dragged out, presumed dead. The only successful way for a tail gunner to bail out was to crawl through the body of the Lancaster and join the rest of the crew to drop down through the bomb bay while the pilot held the aircraft steady. Bomber Command lost twice as many more tail gunners than any other aircrew. Hilary was six years old. The following summer, during the final Blitz raids on London, Hilary's mother was killed when a bomb hit Charing Cross Hospital where she worked as a night nurse. Hilary's only friend or relation was young William, three years younger but with certain privileges as a son born of the house. It was a friendship that would last them for the rest of their lives as, when the bombing came to an end in May due to the RAF, the refugees went home, all except Hilary who had no one to take him back. His other alternative was an orphanage.

"Can't he stay with us?" asked four-year-old Will, who enjoyed the protection of the nearly seven-year-old Hilary against the bullying of the twins who were going to boarding school in the following term, something William relished as for once he would be left alone.

"This war has turned everything on its head," said his mother, and it was all she had to say on the matter for the next three years. Then one afternoon, tuning to the one o'clock news that talked of nothing but the war, she listened in stony silence to the usual litany about progress in France, advances in the Far East, the brave Russian allies on the Eastern front and the fight up through Italy, until suddenly she heard the one thing she feared most in her day. In clipped tones, as if the newscaster was reporting on a sport that had the annihilation of homes and families as the touchdown, the commentator's voice echoed round the small cosy room in the manor where they now lived to save fuel. "Last night the Royal Air Force flew a thousand-bomber raid into the heart of Germany with great success, destroying a ball-bearing factory. The city of Cologne is burning from one end to the other. Seventeen of our bombers failed to return... And that is the end of the one o'clock news."

Adelaide Langton knew with certainty her husband was part of the raid so she could not concentrate on the children or her home, picturing Red's aircraft burning and crashing headlong into the ground. She looked at Hilary and they stared at each other. She put her arm around the ten-year-old boy. He understood about the seventeen planes shot down and the many more bombers limping home with dead aircrew. What neither of them thought of in their hatred for the Germans was mutilated families, homes and lives destroyed forever as a result of Red's bomb aimer calmly announcing 'bombs away'. It was revenge for the Blitz and they thought it was right. She and Red, who was now in command of one of the three wings at Boscombe Down, had an unbreakable agreement: neither one would phone the other after a raid. 'Bad for morale, old girl. Don't you worry. The experienced pilots bring the crates home. Anyway, the war's nearly over.' The previous night's raid would have made it Red's ninety-seventh operation over Germany. Three tours and two Distinguished Flying Crosses to go with his AFC. But the RAF still kept him flying and Wing Commander Langton, thirty-seven, was tired beyond repair.

The day dragged by and the phone kept silent. She could hear the children playing on the front lawn, treble voices innocent of the crushing weight of the war. She was not even sure young Hilary understood what it meant to be without parents. It was cold outside and she hoped the children were well wrapped up.

Old Harold Langton, veteran of the Boer War and the best storyteller in the air-raid shelter, came in and sat down next to the small fire. He was seventy-six years old and had been running the farm from the day Red went to live permanently at RAF Boscombe Down. They sat in silence, waiting. Harold, named after King Harold II of England who had lost the Battle of Hastings and died in the process, had lost two sons in the last war and to make his misery complete, his wife in 1919 to the flu that killed more people than the war itself. The voices of the children tailed off as they moved further away to play their games. Harold stood up slowly and went to the window. His youngest grandson was jumping from the low bough of a tree, pretending he was bailing out of a burning aircraft, planes and dogfights being preferable to cowboys and Indians. He wondered what future lay in store for William Langton. The boy had already lost too many years of schooling, there being no petrol to drive him to school. The boy couldn't even read. In his day they had a schoolmaster on the estate but the war had made private tutors another thing of the past.

What Harold knew that Adelaide did not was that last night's raid over Cologne was to be Red's last operation before taking up his new job as Commanding Officer (CO), Boscombe Down, with the rank of group captain. They were finally going to put his son behind a desk. Down the lawn, the children grew tired of climbing up and down the tree. He would have a word with Adelaide about William. The other children had stayed on at their preparatory schools as weekly boarders but no one had found the time to think about William or the young boy who would never again know the love and care of his parents. They were always saying they would wait and see after the war whether seven was too young to be away from home and maybe Adelaide was right. Wars affected the lives of everyone, permanently, and a few years later made no sense to anyone on either side. The Boer he had chased in '01 was now a field marshal in the British Army, trusted by Churchill to attend the war cabinets and forty-three years earlier, if Lieutenant Langton of the Dorset regiment had put Jan Smuts in his gunsight, he would have shot him dead and received a medal from the King. The whole thing made no sense, and he was sure this war would make no better sense in twenty years' time.

Harold sat down again in front of the miserable fire and wondered what his life would have been if his elder brother had come back from the Boer War. Maybe he would have stayed out there, even gone up north into the Rhodesias where the game was teeming and a man was only responsible for himself. He had gone up when the war was over to Barotseland, shooting crocodiles in the great Zambezi, but he knew he was running away from a far bigger responsibility than himself. The Langton land had to be nurtured by Langtons, a duty inherited at his birth. After six months, the most glorious six months of his life, he trekked back across the big rivers, crossed the highveld and at Johannesburg took the train to Cape Town and home.

Cowering in the air-raid shelter he had retold the days and the weeks of his big hunt, the candlelight changing to the flickering glow of the campfire, the wail of the all-clear siren, the keening of the jackals. He could taste the water of the Zambezi as he recounted the days and nights, William enthralled, Jo indignant at the crocodile slaughter, Byron probably working out ways of making himself rich and important, and dear old Randolph just being in his bunk at the top, looking at the ceiling. Harold wondered if a thought ever went through the boy's mind... There was one of his grandchildren who would never set the world on fire and probably be the happiest of them all.

As the minutes passed away the picture of Red burnt to death in the wreckage of his aircraft receded and at four o'clock, the old maid came in with a tray of tea and they smiled at each other, old people communicating without the need for words. Langton Manor had been their home for all of their lives, the good and the bad. The old maid left them without saying a word.

Adelaide detected the engine of the motorbike as she was pouring their second cup of tea and put the teapot down quickly on the tray, listening. A few moments later, his old ears picked up the sound, and they both waited. The tension magnified as the light faded with the day and the sound of the engine drew closer by the minute, the volume changing as the motorbike wound its way through the Purbeck Hills. It was a trick of the hills that made the sound travel so far across the countryside. A door banged somewhere in the house. One of the children. They never shut a door, it was always banged. Relentlessly, the motorbike drew closer to Langton Manor until they both knew it had turned up the long, tree-lined driveway to the old house, the messenger of death. The bike ground its way up the hill and stopped. The engine cut and they waited for the doorbell and the old maid who would bring the wire from the Air Ministry. Another door banged, and they waited, frozen to the spot, the fire almost out. Then the door burst open.

"You want to freeze to death?" asked Red Langton. "Put some wood on the fire, for God's sake. I'm frozen. Bought myself a bike. Like it? Petrol goes further."

No one said anything, just stared at him.

"You want to tell me what's the matter with you two? They've given me a week off. Why I'm in civvies and Adelaide, my love, you can relax for the rest of the war. I'm grounded. Last night was my last operation and my wing came back without a single loss of life. They've made me CO Boscombe Down. First reserve officer to command a bomber station. Sort of recognition, I think, for all the young kids who came out of Civvy Street and got themselves killed... Is there any tea left in that pot?"

Half an hour later, Red went out to the woodshed and came back to the cosy room with a fresh basket of logs. It was the end of October and growing cold. The two children had joined the grown-ups and were sitting in front of the fire, warming themselves. He was not sure whether young William understood his father would not be flying anymore but Norman Bains's son looked at him with a distant air of understanding. Adelaide was visibly relieved. Bringing up four children would have been difficult. Granda was toasting bread on the end of a long, wire fork, trying not to burn his hand. As Red dumped the wood next to the fire, one piece of bread fell on the coals and had to be rescued. The old man blew away most of the ash and put it on the buttering plate with a thump that told everyone there was a war on. They were luckier than most, having real butter, making their own on the farm. A small standard lamp was burning in the corner to the right of the fire throwing a shadow of the carriage clock, made by some Frenchman whose name Red could never pronounce, across the room. The curtains had been drawn tight and for the first time in just over four years the war was far away. Red ruffled the children's heads before sitting down in an old armchair between his wife and his father and they were all content to eat buttered toast and stare in silence at the dancing flames in the grate. His ankle hurt when the steel pin took up the heat from the fire. He would not be playing any more tennis but he did not think the wound would stop him riding a horse. Half an hour later the children were sent up to bed and Granda stoked up the fire.

"Young Hilary," said Red into the silence, "can stay on with us. Probably make him a Langton by adoption. Something like that. The crew wanted to know what I was going to do. He's good for William with the others away during the week, and soon for months on end." He was holding his wife's hand and his father had lit a pipe. "There are going to be a lot of changes after the war and most of them are going to be to the disadvantage of landowners. The war won't last another year in Europe, though I'm not so sure about the Japs, and when it's over, there will be a general election. My guess is the socialists will win and Atlee will be prime minister."

"What about Churchill?" interrupted his father, indignantly. "Without Winston we'd lose the war."

"Possibly, but the country has had enough of war and they think Churchill is a warmonger; the ordinary people, I mean, who have the same vote as you and me. During the last thirty years, little over one generation, the country has bled to death. The men want a change and their women something to show for the terrible sacrifice. This time nearly everyone is under fire across the country and they won't listen to the old boys with plummy accents telling them what to do anymore. We will defeat Nazi Germany but Stalin will still be in power in Russia, and communism sounds very attractive to a man with nothing whether he's an Englishman or lives in one of our far-flung colonies. I doubt if we will be able to police the colonies when this is over as we won't have the money, too busy paying back the Americans who waited for us to bleed to death before coming in on our side at the end of '41. Most of my blokes on the squadron reckoned they wouldn't have done that if the Japs had not bombed Pearl Harbor in their backyard. We've got to do a lot of clear thinking at Langton Manor or we'll lose the place. Dad, now I'm off the danger list, you must pass the property into some kind of trust. The adjutant was a solicitor before the war and says we can avoid death duties, and, if we form a company around the farming operation, we can carry a loss from a bad year into the following season and deduct the loss from that year's profit, reducing our tax bill. It won't be just farming land properly anymore, we'll have to learn how to keep our money. The socialists will take from the rich and give to the poor which sounds a winner to me in an election when the majority of the voters are poor. A majority in Parliament can give them the right to nationalise our land. We don't have a written constitution like the Americans so there is nothing we can do but hand over the farming to the bureaucrats and then see how much wool they produce on this farm."

"If it isn't one thing it's another," said Adelaide, and for a while they listened to the fire burning in the grate.

"We must make contingency plans, carefully, and recognise the changes that are coming. They have already promised to give India back to the Indians for fighting with us against the Japanese. Socialism does not believe in colonialism. Anyway, I'm not sure the colonies have been making us money in recent years and the Americans wish to open up our markets to their companies, to say nothing of the Russians. I don't think that we will have the strength to fight them. The island is tired, sick of war and probably sick of policing the world. The empire will wither away as Britain turns inward, more concerned with the welfare of its own people. My guess is, after this war, we will have lost the will to govern the empire."

The clock on the mantelpiece wound itself up and struck seven.

"Even the clock sounds sonorous," said Granda Harold.

"I'll go up and see if the children are in bed," said Adelaide. The two men watched her leave.

"You are alive, son, and that's all that matters," said Harold. "You just stay there by the fire. I want to get you something."

The door closed behind him again and Red's mind turned back to the rest of his aircrew, wondering how they would find their new pilot. There was a superstition about changing aircrew. They were flying again tonight. He looked up at the clock. They would be crossing the French coast, still with night fighter cover. He had long since given up praying for a safe return.

Some lived, and some died. He was one of the lucky ones; or was he? With man permanently trying to destroy everything that existed he could barely see the point. He sat and stared at the fireplace until his father came back into the room carrying two bottles of Madeira.

"One for you and one for me," said Granda Harold. "You and I haven't got drunk together since the bloody Germans invaded Poland. We'll talk of old times and for one night let the future take care of itself. There's one thing an old man can still do, and that's drink. As one of my pals used to say, 'It can't be all bad'. Cheers, son."

ADELAIDE SAT on the end of the child's bed, still shivering with relief. Hilary sat up and smiled. The curtains were drawn tight; black curtains. There was still a blackout. William was fast asleep, his thumb in his mouth.

"Would you like to stay with us after the war, Hilary?" she said, stroking the dark hair back from his brow. "You can go to school with William. You'll both have to start from the bottom... Can you read?"

"No, Mrs Langton. Never been taught."

"Maybe some time in the future you'll like to call me Mother... I'll leave that up to you."

"You think they'll ever find my dad's body?" said the ten-year-old boy. Adelaide turned away, unable to speak.

"I'd like to stay, Mrs Langton, if you'll have me." His voice was very small.

WILL FOUND the rocks at Dancing Ledge for the first time in the early spring. Someone had blasted a hole in the ledge so the tide came in and made a safe place to swim. He had come alone. The winter had been cold and was spent being taught how to read by his mother. Hilary had the hang of it in a month but Will found he couldn't tell which was a 'b' and which was a 'd' and his eyes hurt after ten minutes and his thoughts wandered off outside the room and with them his concentration. It was the first understanding he had of the difference in Hilary's age and, worse, during the winter, Hilary grew and grew and Will stayed exactly the same size.

A late flurry of snow in March had covered the farm with a white blanket and even before the snow had completely melted, the yellow, purple and orange crocuses pushed up through the long grass on the banks that surrounded the tennis court. Growing amongst them were tiny white snowdrops with delicate green shoots. No one had remembered to take in the net after the Battle of Britain at the end of September 1940 and the netting had rotted, leaving the drooping wire pulling the posts inwards to the court. The grass had gone rank and it would take an effort for anyone to get a game of tennis, a game Will had never seen as he was too young to recollect his mother's tennis parties and the luncheon parties afterwards under the elm trees away from the court.

With the small duffle coat wrapped around his tiny body and to avoid any more arguments about his inability to read, or, more correctly, his inability to wish to try and read, he had gone off with two of the dogs for a tramp over the hills. With the need to stare at pieces of paper his headaches came more quickly so whenever possible he got out of everyone's way, especially when his brothers and sister were back from school. They were now all at boarding school and only came home on half-term and holidays. What he heard about the boys' school did not encourage him to read; it sounded a nasty place to go and live, just to let bigger boys beat you with canes and make you run around as an unpaid servant.

When he reached the top of the cliff, he found the barbed wire that ran the length of the coast: there were two lines of tangled hoops that were meant to make it more difficult for the Germans to carry out an invasion. A path led through the wire that led to the pool which was how he came to stand on the edge and look down into the still water. Out to sea, the heads of tall seaweed strands were nodding with the ebb and flow of the gentle waves; above and behind, the big granite cliffs guarded his solitude; seagulls were floating on the water and a strong, good smell came from the sea. For the first time that day he was at peace with himself and forgot that he was still unable to read.

He found a smooth rock nearer the cliff in an alcove that trapped the sun and let the warmth soak into his skinny body. One of the seagulls rose from the sea and lazily flew off round the head, calling plaintively as it went. Will picked up a small stone and threw it exactly into the middle of the pool, which made him smile and hug himself. The war, they all said, was nearly over and he wondered what they would talk about on the wireless that had found a permanent home in the cosy room and dominated their days. There would be no news after the war, of that he was sure, and Daddy would come home and he could go round the farm all day and stop hurting his eyes.

The dogs came back from searching for the stone he had thrown in the pool and shook seawater all over him, making him shout at them to stop which made not the slightest bit of difference. The dogs lay down in the sun facing him and watched with big, soft, brown eyes. They had sprayed him with water deliberately so he threw them another stone and when they came back, he stood on his rock so he would not get wet.

Every day during the summer, if he could give the grown-ups the slip, he came down to Dancing Ledge to be at peace with himself and when it was hot, he swam in the pool with the dogs, learning from the Labradors how to doggie paddle, never once being afraid of the water. When the war against Germany came to an end, he asked his mother what they were going to say on the news.

"Oh, they'll find something, William. They always find something disturbing... Tomorrow, I want you to come with me to Poole. Your father thinks there is something wrong with your eyes so we are going to have them tested. We will walk to Langton Matravers and take the bus."

"Is Hilary coming too?"

"No, his eyes are all right and he can read."

Whatever happened in Will's life it always came back to the fact he couldn't read.

"When's Daddy coming home now the war's over?"

"It's not over in Japan and they've sent Daddy to America."

"Where's America?"

"A long way away. When you can read you'll see it on the map."

There it was again.

A week later, after three long journeys into Poole, he came back with a pair of round glasses in a metal frame that small boys were meant to be unable to break. The world around him was totally new, and he was able to see properly for the first time in his life and once the glasses had settled down, he could look at the pages of the books without hurting his head. He was eight years old.

THE SECRECY SURROUNDING the trip to America for Red Langton and Group Captain Leonard Cheshire VC was extreme. They were not even told the name of the American air force base where they landed or the subsequent staging posts, though both group captains realised they were somewhere in the Pacific theatre of war.

Cheshire, the most highly decorated bomber pilot of the war, was equally unaware what the two British observers were to observe. Only when the B-29 bombers took off on the last stage of their journey were they given any hint of what they were doing.

"Got ourselves a new bomb, skipper," said the American liaison officer who had flown with them from London. "Skipper says we're going out there to make a test and you guys are going to tell Churchill what it looks like.

Told our skipper you two flew some of the first operations over Germany before we came in... You're going to see something today you'll never forget."

"With two aircraft?" said Red. "Over Cologne and Dresden we flew thousand-bomber raids night after night."

"And we finished off Jerry during the day," Cheshire added.

They were flying higher than Red or Leonard Cheshire had ever flown before, their oxygen masks firmly in place. The four-engined bomber made as much noise as the Lancaster. The flight droned on. One hour later the American skipper came through the intercom to talk to the RAF pilots.

"We're carrying an atomic device in the lead aircraft," said the American. "We're going to stop the war in its tracks."

Ten minutes later a large city could be seen looming below which they were asked to observe through binoculars. They seemed to float towards the city above the sparse cloud layer without reducing height. Their own aircraft was equipped with sophisticated aerial camera equipment but they were told to watch the plane just ahead and to the right of them flying at an altitude a few feet above their own. Red watched the plane's bomb doors open and then a fat, large bomb, just one, with a single square fin at its tail, dropped from the open bay and dipped towards the ant-like city twenty-six thousand feet below. For a few seconds Red was able to follow the descent of the single bomb and then he waited for the impact. Neither he nor Cheshire had the slightest knowledge of an atomic device though both knew that British boffins were working on a more powerful bomb.

Below him he saw a massive flash, having been told not to look through his binoculars until the bomb had exploded. It was a flash like Red Langton had never seen in his ninety-seven operations over Germany. When he quickly brought the glasses to his eyes, he saw the buildings below him disintegrate in an ever-widening circle and a cloud rose up to them that, looking back as they overflew the target, was like a giant mushroom ever-seeking the heavens.

"Oh my God, oh my God," repeated Cheshire. "Can man have really done that to man?"

Below them, slightly to the rear, the city of Nagasaki, on the southwest coast of Japan had ceased to exist. It was the second atomic bomb dropped in three days, the first having totally destroyed the Japanese city of Hiroshima.

"We are the worst of the worst of animals," said Red, realising why he and Cheshire had been chosen to watch the devastation. "And what we did to create the fireballs in Cologne and Dresden was no better. It just took us longer with a bit more risk." Next to him, Group Captain Leonard Cheshire VC was praying.

The war with Japan came to an end soon afterwards and President Truman rationalised the destruction of two Japanese cities had shortened the war and saved a million lives. More likely, thought Red when he flew back to England, it was revenge for the way allied prisoners had been treated in Japanese prison camps, only ten per cent of the prisoners captured at the fall of Singapore coming out alive. He had been taken over there to say it was just a bigger and better bang, and the bombing of Germany had been no different. But somehow it was, devastatingly so. It was more like an execution than a bombing raid. There was no defence. Not even a warning. Red always hoped that the women and children of Cologne had been in their undergrounds as the Londoners had been during the Blitz. Surprise attacks on military installations, including Pearl Harbor – which, if the Americans had been watching their radar screens as the British watched their VHF units during the Battle of Britain, would have been no surprise – were somehow acceptable to a man. What Red had seen with his own eyes was not acceptable and gave him a terrible premonition that a precedent had been set and mankind, all of mankind, would pay the price.

WILL WAS unable to make sense out of much the grown-ups talked about but he was sensitive to their feelings towards him and each other. When they hurt his feelings, the ends of his fingers hurt and he went off into the woods to be alone. The laughter had gone out of his father when he came back from the war; everything was serious. For the first time in his life he heard the word 'money' used in a way he was unable to understand. Before the word meant what Dad gave him on Sunday morning before they all went to church. Even Granda was talking about money coupled with the words 'bloody socialist government', all three words being outside his understanding. The word 'Hitler' had been replaced by the word 'Atlee', both being spoken in a spit. Will thought a new war had broken out but there was nothing on the news which came right after *Dick Barton, Special Agent*, the most enthralling fifteen minutes of his day when he and Hilary were allowed to sit around the wireless before being bundled off to bed. Hilary complained to Will that if Will were older, he wouldn't have to go to bed so early, whatever that was all about.

Hilary was going to school with him at the beginning of the winter term but would not be in the same class. Hilary was something the grown-ups called 'bright' and Will was something they called a 'bit dim' which was not true now he could see what was going on. He could see the tennis ball they gave him, along with a small racket, to hit up against the stables wall to 'keep him quiet', words he understood perfectly. Even at eight years old Will understood he was in the way, too young to be of any use to any of them including what had once been his best friend, Hilary. They all told him, the grown-ups, that he would find a little friend when he went to school. If it wasn't for the wireless and *Dick Barton, Special Agent* with the galloping music that started it all off, he would have run away and lived in the deep cave that ran off from the Dancing Ledge... No one else could climb into the cave as they were too big and didn't know the small hole in the cliff. In the cave he had a store of old candles that he had rescued from the air-raid shelter.

The two cars had been taken off their wooden blocks, the tyres having been blown up with a lot of effort from Granda and his dad, and petrol poured into a tube that stuck out of one side. The old batteries he had seen all his life next to the cars on the floor were no good and new ones were brought up by a man in a van and when they were put into the cars and a handle put through the front of the cars and given a lot of turns, both cars started for the first time in five years and to Will's great excitement he was given a ride. After that his father went to the little church in Langton Matravers every day and Granda went to a place called the Ship Inn and was often very funny when he came home. Will's Granda had a friend in Corfe Castle, a retired labourer, who had fought in the Boer War and the two old soldiers found a lot to talk about, according to his mother. Will hoped the old labourer would come up to the house, but he never did and the tension between Granda and his mother grew worse. Will thought everyone was very complicated and then they packed him off to school as a weekly boarder at a prep school in Poole which, they hoped, would make allowances for a small boy who had just come through the war.

The new school lasted one term. Will heard his mother in deep conversation with his father which ended in the dreaded words 'it will do him good'. In Will's life anything that was meant to do him good made him unhappy and the ends of his fingers hurt so much he wanted to hide in the woods. Next term they were going to send him to a new school. He would not come home anymore on weekends to see his rabbits. Thumper, the big Belgian black, would be left alone week after week and no one would clean out his cage and when Big Black's wives had their babies, no one would take any notice. His rabbits, like himself, were a nuisance, and he did not want to be a nuisance or go away to school and not come home and all the other boys would tease him about his glasses. Miserable, Will stayed outside the window, behind the hollyhocks, unable to move, tears pricking behind his eyes.

"The boy's nine years old," his mother was saying, "and he can't read. He'll never get his common entrance and then what do we do with him? Senior school favours boys from their own junior school so he'll have a better chance. He won't listen, that's his trouble."

"The war," began his father before he was interrupted.

"All the other children went through the war and they can read. Maybe he's just stupid. There's something wrong with him. You think it's all my fault he didn't wear glasses sooner? How was I to know? We couldn't run off to Poole every ten minutes and tell anyone who would listen the boy can't read."

"He's not stupid," said his father in defence. "You said so yourself in the air-raid shelter he was the best at *I spy*. Look how well he takes care of his rabbits."

"Damn those rabbits... I'd asphyxiate the lot of them... I'd drown them!"

Outside, Will turned in desperation and ran away to the arbour where he kept his four cages of rabbits and stuffed two of them in his jumper and ran round the back of the big house and through the kitchen where the new cook was preparing lunch.

"What you got there, nipper?"

"Nothing, Cook. Nothing."

He ran on through the kitchen, into the big hall and up the staircase. One of the rabbits had pushed its face out of the top of his jumper, tears were falling on its big ears as the soft eyes looked up. Will couldn't see where he was going.

"What are you doing?" shouted his mother from the bottom of the stairs.

"You're going to drown my rabbits," Will choked out.

"Of course I'm not, darling."

"You said so. You yell at me, you always do what you say. They're my rabbits."

"Don't be silly, William."

"You won't clean the cages every week. You don't like my rabbits. I hate you. It's not my fault you don't want me. If you drown my rabbits, I'll go away and never come back."

Appalled, both parents watched the small boy run up the rest of the stairs; they heard the nursery door slam shut. Adelaide Langton burst into tears and sat down on the bottom stair.

"What am I going to do with him?" she said in despair. "What am I going to do?"

"He'll probably turn out the best of the bunch," said Red. "Must have been in the garden when we were talking. I'll go up to him. Any little boy who looks after animals is good inside. We want him to be like Byron, that's the trouble. And Jo and Randolph never gave us a moment's worry and we expect the same from Will. I'll go up. Get Cook to make some tea. The boy's sensitive and we've had too many things on our minds to take enough interest in him. We'll send him to full-time boarding school when he goes to public school, and that's not for another four years... Maybe Granda can teach him to read. The boy loves all the stories about Africa. We'll tell Will there are lots more stories about Africa in books when he can read. That might do the trick... A lot of children are late starters."

"Thank God you weren't killed, Red," said Adelaide, as she wiped across her face with the flat palm of her hand.

"I'll agree with that," said Red, chuckling, then he mounted the stairs. "Tea outside on the terrace," he called back. "The sun's out... And find some lettuce leaves."

---

2

*B*yron Langton found life at Langton Manor generally boring. He was cursed with a younger brother who followed him everywhere and a twin sister who should have been a brother, a brother that played catch and would bowl to him in the nets he had built next to the old tennis court that nobody ever used. None of the local kids played cricket and Randolph was useless. Since his father came back from the war he was distant, preoccupied, and Byron had enough of chapel at school without being invited in to the local church. Hilary might make a cricketer but he was too young and Byron considered him a hanger-on who should have gone back with the other boys when the Germans stopped bombing Poole Harbour.

Uncle Cliff, who had gone away to the war as Uncle Clifford, sometimes came down from London; then he needed his wits about him in the nets but the price was listening to the rubbish his mother's brother talked about. The only way fifteen-year-old Byron could see to get on in the world was to get rich: all the talk of Labour and trade unions was for losers, when he made his own money he wanted to keep it and not be forced to give it away.

Uncle Cliff had been up at Oxford for two years and then the war came along. Byron's mother thought he should have been made an officer but Uncle Cliff wanted to stay with the men and went right through the war as a private. Granda said he was too bolshie to make officer and that he should take off the damn cloth cap and throw it in the dustbin and get himself a proper job, which was why Uncle Cliff did not visit Langton

Manor very often. The side of the matter that puzzled Byron was Uncle Cliff's Military Medal, won for outstanding bravery in the Western Desert when the Allied forces in Libya were being pushed back towards Egypt by Rommel's Afrika Korps in '41. Even Byron's father said Uncle Cliff had deserved a Victoria Cross. Byron had asked his uncle many times how he won the MM but Uncle Cliff would say nothing and change the subject right back to the plight of the working man and how the Labour Party were going to change all that with a welfare state. Byron heard every small detail of the welfare state, from the free doctors to the free schools and universities, right down to half a pint of milk every day for every child in junior school: it all went in one ear and out the other; as Granda put it, the likes of Byron would be footing the bill and when the rich and energetic had been robbed poor the whole thing would collapse. Jo thought the idea of everyone being equal was simply wonderful, to which Granda said there was nothing wonderful about everyone being equally poor. It had been during Uncle Cliff's last visit that Jo had announced she was going to London University when she finished school, to read for a degree in social welfare so she would know how to redistribute the wealth. Granda tersely replied saying that 'our land was going to the dogs' and why had he fought the Boer War, the Great War and his son was fighting in the second war, if all they were going to do was give away the colonies and bugger the poor sods who did the bloody work? He never got around to mentioning the two sons who had died in the Great War before getting into his car and rattling off down the driveway to Corfe Castle and the pub.

The following day, the family learnt Randolph had failed his War Office Selection Board interview and would spend his two years of national service in the ranks, which brought a smile to Jo's face, a smug smile that annoyed everyone else in the room. Byron was working on a plan to fail the medical and avoid two years of his life in uniform, not one second of which would make him any money. Byron had worked out in the early days at Stanmore that rich boys had it all, from pocket money in the tuck shop to special coaching in the hols if they were any good at a sport. Money bought everything. From the age of thirteen and a half, Byron only wasted his time on boys with rich fathers, or the curious few who were popular. Byron hunted with the pack and sucked up to anyone who kept him in the pack. Flattery came cheap and easily to Byron Langton. At school, popularity was everything, but it took skill to be an arse-creeper without the arsehole being crept up realising it was being had. Being good at sport was one of the keys and Byron worked hard at sport, which was why he wanted to practise in the nets and not be annoyed by a twin sister with a fringe, fat legs and a face full of pimples.

"Will, why don't you go away?" he said to the nine-year-old with the ancient junior tennis racket and the moth-eaten tennis ball.

"Show me how to hit the ball properly?" pleaded Will.

"No. Go away. Go and play with your rabbits or, better still, pester Jo."

"She always talks about Labour, whatever Labour is, and that's boring... Can't you teach me to ride a horse?"

"No. Mother said you'd kill yourself... Where's Hilary?"

"Went to church with Dad... Why does Dad spend so much time in church, Byron?... He must like God very much."

"You'll find out twice a day when you go to boarding school."

"Do you like boarding school?"

"It's all right if you know what you're doing."

"Will you teach me?"

"Can't teach that."

Will looked up at his big brother through the round little lenses that stuck halfway down his nose.

"You'll understand when you're older," said Byron.

"They all say that."

"Maybe I should have flicked you harder."

"What you mean, Byron?"

"Knock some sense into you... Can you read?"

"Some... Not really. Granda's trying to teach me."

"Go find Granda."

"Gone to the Ship Inn to see his friend who fought the Bittereinders."

"What are Bittereinders?"

"Don't know... It's going to rain. What are you going to do now?"

"Look at my stamp collection. I swapped a pretty stamp that was worth nothing with a new boy and got a penny red that is probably worth a fortune."

"I want to see."

"Go away and irritate someone else."

Will slowly turned away and half put his thumb in his mouth.

Behind him, Byron kicked a stone and looked up at the sky. He would be glad when the hols were over. At school there was something to do, and he hoped last term's new boy would pinch a pile of stamps from his old man's stamp album. The little creep wanted the big, worthless picture stamps the French and Belgians printed in their millions. It was a fair swap. No one could say he was stealing. The excitement was back again. Every time he thought of easy money he had a tingling feeling in his toes.

The summer holidays dragged on to a boring end. Jo went off to her public school outside Eastbourne, complaining she preferred the secondary modern school in Poole. Granda had given the twins ten shillings each and their mother had given them a pound. Byron knew rich children at school came back with ten quid or more. The big problem at Langton Manor was money to pay the new taxes imposed on the rich by the new Labour government and to maintain the farm. Most of the produce from the farm was subject to a fixed price; there was no way of increasing the income. As the pound dropped against the dollar, costs rose in England. Byron, at fifteen, understood the mathematics, a subject he found as easy as riding a horse. England brought in raw materials which now cost more because of Uncle Cliff's trade unions and the Americans sold the same product cheaper from a longer assembly line that didn't go on strike. His dad was faced with a government-controlled milk price, a wool price in competition with the Australians, rising costs, and a tax rate that took no account of the farmer needing new equipment to compete on the world market. When Byron left school, he was going to find a business that the government could not control. He was definitely not going to be a farmer.

Stanmore was settled in a large tract of the Surrey countryside with the old buildings housing the chapel, the quadrangle, some of the classrooms and the bogs. The original buildings had been a grammar school with a strong Church of England influence, the masters mostly priests, the headmaster always a priest, all under the direction of the Bishop of Dorchester. Fifty years earlier, the priest had been invited to the Headmasters' Conference. Fees, small at first, were introduced by the church and the new dormitories, house common rooms, classrooms and science laboratories were built, opening the school to boarders and the title of an English public school. By the time Randolph and Byron attended the school it was one of the most expensive in the world, but as Langtons had been educated in the same place for five generations, Red found the money for the fees by selling the small dowry Adelaide had brought to their marriage from her family, the Critchleys, family solicitors of Poole. Red had hoped one of his children would win a scholarship, but with the war interrupting their education none of them had taken the scholarship examination. What he was going to do with Will only time would tell and if Hilary was to remain part of the family, money would have to be found for him as well.

Half the masters in Byron's third year were priests swishing around the school in long black skirts with big pockets and tight belts. He was sure two of them were queers, inviting the prettiest little boys for tea on Sundays at their bachelor houses in the village. Two of the prefects in his own house were playing around with juniors who if they did not want to play were subjected to the most vicious bullying. Byron had been lucky, his voice breaking soon after he entered school, which brought on a pimple rash that equalled Jo's. He was a thickset, hairy boy who would grow into a good-looking man but, luckily for him, the hormones found him anything but sexually attractive.

Byron kept a diary of the rich boys who might be of use to him in the future years, quietly finding out the fathers' occupations, especially those in business. Social class was of no consequence, only money, and boys left out of it because of a common accent were courted by Byron. Uncle Cliff, unbeknown, had set him on the right track in his attempt to deride the 'old boy network' that controlled Britain's commerce and industry.

"It's not what you know in this world, Byron, but who you know and that's going to change in a socialist world. The Labour Party are going to nationalise industry so the wealth will be owned by the people."

Byron had thought about this for a day and then asked Uncle Cliff who was going to run the industries when they were owned by the government.

"The people," Uncle Cliff had answered. "Everyone will be equal."

Byron thought again and asked if Dad would be needed on the farm in the new system if the people were going to do everything.

"We don't need the landowners, lad. They just spend the money the workers make for them. Your father doesn't plough the land or clip the wool. I don't think any of your family have ever milked a cow."

Byron wasn't sure about the farm without his dad as if the labour did everything so well, why did his dad get up every morning at five o'clock and come back to the manor house at night dog-tired, with only enough energy to eat his own supper and go to bed? His only time off during the day was the hour he spent going to church. His dad could tell a cow with fever a day before the animal looked sick, pick out an infertile ewe, and he always sent the milk to market on time, something that rarely happened when he was away at the war unless Granda got out of bed in the dark and read the riot act. Byron thought the idea of leaving a business to people with no interest in the business dumb. There was a catch in Uncle Cliff's new ideas, which sounded all very nice but he couldn't work out why the people wouldn't work harder if they all owned everything, though something inside him said they'd all work a lot less if the likes of his dad weren't kicking arse. His mind was fuzzy. Unlike Jo he didn't think Uncle Cliff's ideas were quite as easy as they sounded.

Byron had played loosehead prop in the previous season's Colts XV and hoped the new rugby season would find him in the third if not the second fifteen. The following year he wanted to play for his school and by the time he left Stanmore to have the colours in rugby and cricket, the two main sports at English public schools. He ignored the minor sports taking no interest in athletics, fives, squash, tennis, hockey or boxing. Even in his youth, Byron understood the need to concentrate his effort. He had little natural flair for either of his chosen sports but when it came to rugby, he was the fittest on the field, breaking from the scrum and desperately trying to make himself the extra man in the line that put his winger over the try-line when he succeeded. In cricket, he was an all-rounder, rarely dropping a catch at slip, always scoring a few runs and able to bowl the odd ball to take a wicket. Every report Byron ever received at school included the word 'dedicated', applied equally to work and sport. Byron Langton was making sure he would get on in life and enjoy the fruits of wealth and popularity.

When anyone important to him, including his parents, housemaster or headmaster wanted something done, Byron volunteered, making a conscious effort to show his superiors how much effort he was putting in on their behalf. Byron worked best in the limelight and if there was any limelight around, Byron could always be found showing off his considerable, hard-won talents. Everyone liked Byron, and he always praised people he thought worthwhile to their face and behind their backs. For a boy at school to hear that Byron Langton thought he was good at something was a sign of having arrived: naturally, they all said what a good fellow Byron was and how well he was liked. He could not have orchestrated his own establishment better had he employed a political manager. He never flattered too much and was always sincere. He never spoke without a reason and never let anyone know the thoughts that ran constantly through the back of his mind. He always told his seniors what they wanted to hear and never started a criticism. With the care of a leopard stalking in the night, he never made an enemy. His days at Stanmore were days of deep satisfaction and no one, not even the most cynical master, saw him as a fraud. Young Byron was always such a nice young boy.

After supper in the big hall where the entire school, masters and boys, ate together in strict seniority, came one hour of prep in the house common rooms. Before supper they had all trooped off to the chapel for evensong, to end the day where it had begun, on their knees. The powers that ran the school took more interest in spiritual welfare, which cost nothing, than food, whose scarcity was blamed on food rationing which was stringent despite the end of the war: having survived the onslaught of Germany and Japan, the time had come to repay the Americans 'for supplying the means to finish the job' and pounds were so scarce the government did not have the financial means to lead the nation. In the dark hours of 1940, Churchill had not been in a position to argue the financial cost of his deliverance.

BYRON WAS NOT a natural scholar and used every minute of the hour after chapel forcing himself to concentrate and learn, conscious of his school certificate examination at the end of the term. What Byron lacked in his brain he made up for in hard work, the goal of wealth and power ever conscious in his mind. Byron had found a seam of gold in his French master who explained that some boys were good at writing exams and why. He knew the piece of paper was only a building block that controlled his upward movement. The mark on the paper indicated how clever he was, how much he had learnt.

"Young man, always think through the question before writing your answer so if you find you don't really know what to say you can tackle another question instead of crossing out ten minutes of precious time and starting again. For weeks beforehand, condition your nerves so the examination room will not feel hostile and impinge on your concentration. And, Langton, if you don't know the correct meaning for the word 'impinge' look it up in the dictionary. When you read French prose, or English for that matter, always read with a dictionary close at hand and use it if you don't know a word. Confidence, Langton, is the key to examination success. Confidence." The French master went away muttering 'confidence', leaving Byron with a point well understood.

Carefully, Byron worked on the system, trying to understand how the examiners thought, how their logic worked for setting the papers, ensuring that his efforts were channelled in the direction most likely to succeed, avoiding the parts of the curriculum he enjoyed if he felt the examiners would not be so interested.

That year, Byron made the second fifteen for two matches, both away, and wrote his school certificate, knowing instinctively his research into the way of examinations had paid rich dividends. To no one's surprise including Byron's, the Oxford and Cambridge Board gave him a pass that suggested a county, if not a state scholarship to tertiary learning was well within his grasp. In the spring term, Byron had his first meeting with the headmaster of Stanmore School in the headmaster's house next to the Speech Hall. A servant answered the knock on the elaborate wooden front door and Byron was shown into the great man's study where he was told to sit down and take tea. Nothing bad ever came Byron's way, so the summons to the presence had left no fear of reprisal and the pit of his stomach was perfectly at ease. The headmaster opened the conversation.

"Now you are in the sixth form and permitted to put your hands in your pockets we consider you an excellent prospect, Langton, for a scholarship to Oxford or Cambridge which will bring us due credit at Stanmore."

Byron took the servant's proffered cup of tea and wondered if the 'we' and 'us' were royal plurals or a reference to the teaching staff as a whole. The cup did not rattle in the saucer nor did a smile come to the surface as Byron waited for the pedantic old bachelor to get to his point. The man had taught him divinity from form four and Byron, inwardly, very inwardly and hidden, considered the man a pompous fool who allowed the senior boys to run the school and terrorise any poor junior who stepped out of line, the head being above the daily routine of running a boarding school for five hundred boys; the great man aspired to loftier things including a bishopric when he retired from teaching which would lead him on to the See at Canterbury. Scholarships were the key to his future, the predominantly clerical board of governors basking in the glory of Stanmore's success.

Byron looked down at his delicate cup and saucer, trying to give the impression he was embarrassed at the thought of such an accolade, meanwhile scheming how he could avoid wasting three years of his life that would not make him money.

"The problem, sir, is money. I don't think my father would be able to afford the extra costs of a son at university. During the war, my father's tail gunner was killed and the man's wife died in the Blitz and we sort of took on Hilary and he's now part of the family and you have him down for Stanmore. And then there's William. William, I'm afraid, sir, is a problem. He can't even read properly."

"How old is the boy?"

"Nine, sir."

"*Nine* and the boy can't read? Must be something wrong with him."

Byron left the problem hanging in the air and dutifully drank his tea. After one year in the sixth form Byron wanted to be out of school, out of Langton Manor and in a position to start learning a profession that would make him money. Time was of the essence as he had no wish to become rich when he was too old to enjoy the rewards.

"My father had to sell my mother's few shares to send me here, sir. If they want Hilary and William to have a proper education, I'll have to sacrifice my last year in the sixth and find a job in the City to start paying my way. We just can't afford it, sir, and I'm by no means sure I would win a scholarship and the one year's fees would have been wasted, better spent on Hilary who doesn't even have a mother or father."

Byron looked up from a bowed head and hoped the last bit had not gone too far but the old fool had swallowed it hook, line and sinker. There was moisture at the corners of the head's eyes. The interview was at an end.

"I'll have a word with your father."

"You can try, sir."

There was even a frog in the old man's throat. Obsequiously, Byron allowed himself to be led away by the manservant and was not surprised to find himself the youngest house prefect in the school a week later, which gave him a pleasant study and the solitude to plan the next stage in his career.

LIONEL MARJORIBANKS, which he insisted be pronounced Marchbanks, was not the type of boy a school prefect with school colours in rugby and cricket would befriend but Byron Langton had his reasons. Lionel wore glasses, was round of face and round of stomach, loathed sport and work and was most happy in the tuck shop. They were in different houses but had gone to school in the same year and Byron had made it his business to befriend the school Billy Bunter. Lionel's father was a partner in the firm of Logan, Smith and Marjoribanks, stockbrokers in the City of London.

When Byron left Stanmore at the end of his last summer term, he was seventeen and a half with a job waiting for him in the City of London at five pounds, seven and sixpence a week. Daily travelling to Langton Manor was out of the question so Stanmore's brightest prospect for 1948 set up home in Kensington with a fat boy the school had already forgotten. Byron insisted he pay for his room, making a big show of his independence each week, and set about learning the trade of money, other people's money and the power of controlling it. All day long he asked questions. He was as happy surrounded by stocks and shares as Lionel was surrounded by food.

Maxwell Marjoribanks, senior partner in the firm founded by his grandfather, was of the opinion that the only good thing his son brought out of Stanmore was Byron Langton, the school fees otherwise having been wasted. When Byron's call-up papers arrived for his two-year national service, the senior Marjoribanks was as concerned as Byron. The boy would obviously be given a commission and a lifestyle that would make it difficult to return to the lowly position of a clerk. He himself had spent seven years with the firm before he was paid a salary that could afford to take out a girl.

In Soho, there were jazz clubs every second street, with the likes of

Humphrey Lyttelton and Ronnie Scott mostly playing traditional New Orleans jazz. The clubs were hot, sweaty basements that smelt of chlorine to suppress the body odour. Best of all they were cheap and every Friday and Saturday, leaving Lionel to eat his fill, Byron took the Tube into Soho. Twice during the intervals he was able to come out for fresh air and half a pint of beer in a Greek Street pub frequented by people with the same aim in life as himself, had he known it. Their accents were strange and interesting and Byron stuck out like a pork chop in a synagogue. The Friday after he received his call-up papers found him lingering in the pub, ordering a second half-pint in succession and thinking through his problem. Down one length of the bar the locals were having drinking competitions, downing half-pints of beer, the slowest drinker paying for the round: harmless fun that Byron ignored, sitting tightly in his corner. The idea of wasting two precious years in uniform for no other purpose than to be ready to fight some politician's war appalled him more as he faced the imminent reality. Jazz and jiving were far from his mind. A half-pint of beer arrived in front of him without being ordered and the barman pointed at the beer-drinking competition.

"Better join in, mate, or get out. Likes of you don't drink here, see. Wrong bleedin' accent."

"What do I have to do?"

"When I shout go, drink it fast and when yer finished bang the bleedin' glass on the bar and if yer last yer pay the bleedin' round. That, or get out. Mr Pike's orders."

"And who may I ask is Mr Pike?"

"You don't know Jack Pike?"

"No, I'm afraid I don't."

"Then get out."

"What about my new beer?"

The barman with a nose that had been broken many times gave him a look which said it all, and Byron knew the right thing to do was leave immediately. He was out of his depth and out of his element and the five men down the bar poised to drink were sneering at him. Byron's arsehole began to tighten and he could not move off the bar stool. The pot-bellied barman shouted "One!" And Byron found his right hand going out to the half-pint glass. On "Two!" he took a grip and on the word "Go!" he lifted the glass without spilling a drop and poured the contents down his throat, thumping the bar counter with his empty glass, followed by a good pause and later five more thumps on the bar. The episode was followed by a heavy silence with everyone looking at Byron.

"Worth a bleedin' fortune," said the man next to him into the silence.

"Bugger's got an open gullet."

"He's a kid."

"Open gullet."

Miraculously, another half pint was put in front of Byron and the schooner race was off again with Byron first back on the counter. He was forced to repeat the exercise three more times with the same result which put three and a half pints of best draught bitter into a belly more used to tea and milk. The barman's face had split into two and a young man about his own age was talking to him in a broad cockney accent he would have found difficult to understand had he been sober.

"I think I'm going to be sick," he slurred and a large tin bowl was put under his chin at exactly the right moment.

"Not used to the booze?"

"'Fraid not," said Byron who had gone white in the face.

"Come back next week when you're sober, cock. Then you and I'll talk."

"What about?" managed Byron as he half fell off his bar stool.

"Yer open gullet... Friday next. Name's Johnny Pike."

"Byron Langton. So pleased to meet you."

Amid general laughter, Byron staggered out into the street where he was sick for the second time. He managed to go back into the jazz club and retrieve his overcoat and was sick once more at the Tube station. He was never able to remember how he got back to the flat in Kensington but when he cleaned out his tweed jacket on the Monday to go to work in his one and only suit, he found a piece of paper.

 Friday night, 28th January 1949. Don't forget. Johnny Pike.

The handwriting was remarkably legible, the work of an educated man.

"You ever heard of Jack Pike?" he asked Lionel as they walked to the Tube station on their way to work. "Has a pub in Soho."

"And every clip joint and peep show in the West End. Tried to do business with the old firm once, but Pater said he would never invest hot money. Man's a crook but a rich crook... Why you ask?"

"No real reason. One of the girls I was jiving with mentioned his name."

"Don't tell Pater you slum it weekends."

"I won't if you won't."

. . .

FRIDAY CAME with the prospect of reporting to RAF Cardington in eight weeks' time, the unseen mind of the state having decided that Byron Langton would follow his father into the Royal Air Force. The two-year period of national service was to start for all but the very few to learn to fly. The only way to get his wings was to sign on for a three-year short service commission: he was totally frustrated. Lionel had been conscripted into the army.

"You must want to laugh, Byron," said Lionel. "Imagine all this flesh wobbling around on a parade ground; and the rules, the glorious rules saying everyone, cooks, cleaners and future tank commanders, shall complete their ten weeks of square-bashing. Even my father mumbled something good had to come out of my obsessive eating. The medical board will reject me, you see. When is your medical?"

"The week before I go. At the Air Ministry."

"They'll pass you A1 with flying colours, sorry for the pun, old boy... You want a ham sandwich?"

"I'm going out... Got a date, sort of."

"With a girl?"

"I can't afford to even think of girls. Anyway, almost eighteen-year-old girls go out with almost twenty-five-year-old men."

Byron had an idea that someone was going to make money out of him as in his short experience of life, no one did anything without an ulterior motive. People did not slip pieces of paper into pockets unless they wanted something and if busting his nose had been the reason, they would have bashed him up the last time. All evening watching Lionel stuff his face again was more than he could take and the meagre weekend spending money had been put aside for a new pair of shoes. Keeping the holes in the soles of his only black pair that went with his black suit from trumpeting his poverty was a full-time exercise and, with the Langton farm sliding backwards to disaster, the barley harvest having failed the previous year through lack of sun to ripen the crop, he knew better than to embarrass his father. The only advantage he could see in joining the RAF was the uniform and shoes that would come with the job but, somehow, Byron was going to fail his medical. Wearing his gym shoes he walked from Kensington to Hyde Park and down Piccadilly to Greek Street. Putting on a face for the likes of Johnny Pike did not seem necessary and if there were no free drinks coming his way, he would simply walk home again and be none the poorer.

JOHNNY PIKE WAS WAITING for him at the bar and seemed pleased to see him.

"By now, my china, you will have asked about my dad. This is how it goes down. My old man has a rival, see. Business opposition, you could say. Well, this bloke thinks he drinks quicker than anyone in London. So you, with all your nice accent, are going to go up against Fred the Miller and we, that's you and us like, are going to stick it to our Fred. You plump up your accent real good when he's had a couple and beaten the likes of me for a tenner and bet him ten quid you can down a half-pint of our best bitter quicker than Fred the Miller."

"Just because I have this accent doesn't mean I'm rich."

"Can see that. Canvas shoes in this weather! Walked to save the Tube fare?"

"Exactly. The family has quite a few assets but no cash. Farming isn't the way to make money."

"Right... Wrong business. Go the way they tell you in this life and you get nowhere. Got to go round the corner, so my dad says."

"What if I lose?"

"Here's the ten quid to pay 'im."

"You trust me with your money?"

"Likes of you are too bloody stupid to be dishonest. Don't know how, see. 'Ad it drummed into you, like... You drink our Fred down three times and you keep the ten quid, I keep the twenty and the side bets."

"Nothing much I can lose."

"Don't throw up again. Barman don't like the smell of puke; neither do I. Now, while we wait for Fred and his hangers-on, tell me a bit about yourself, Byron, and first how you got a bleedin' name like Byron. Don't look the serf, poet or ponce."

Ten minutes before Fred the Miller came into the pub, Byron had reached the problem uppermost in his mind.

"Here you go again, see," said Johnny, smiling. "Your lot always conform. Do what you're told. Look, my lot fight when there's a war on but no one's goin' to give it another bash for a long time my dad says and he's right. Two wars like that in less than thirty years knocks out the stuffing, see. Small wars, there'll be colonial wars, things like that, but no one's goin' to have a big go despite the Russkies and their bleedin' communism. And that won't work, my dad says. Can't 'ave everyone gettin' the same. No one works for nothin'. Their way everyone slows up, see, and in the end come to a bleedin' 'alt what my dad says. No, clever buggers or buggers as want to work 'ard make more than anyone else, see. So they all do as little as possible. You beat Fred the Miller and I will give you somethin' worked for me. Army doctor said me 'eart was workin' so fast I'd be dead before I was thirty. Blood pressure terrible. 'Eart beat ten to the bleedin' dozen, and yours truly is out of the army before 'e got in, see."

"Are you sick?" asked Byron surprised as the man looked at the peak of his health.

"Course not. Took a lot of LSD, didn't I? Just before I went in, I was flyin' ten feet above the doctor when he listened to my chest. Nice trip, too. Well, not bad. Don't do it no more. Bleedin' stuff's dangerous. Once or twice, just to try like, otherwise stick to beer. No one got 'urt by beer, my dad says, and what my dad says is always right... Now, you know the drill as 'ere comes Fred the bleedin' Miller, over there talkin' to my dad."

Byron sat in his corner on his own, drinking what looked like gin and tonic. Every time he ordered, he put on his plummiest accent and ignored the stares. The barman poured water for him out of the gin bottle and filled the glass up with tonic. Byron could feel the ten pounds in his pocket, two big, white fivers. Fred the Miller began challenging all and sundry to drink a half-pint of beer and when the stakes reached half a crown, Byron lurched up from his bar stool and deliberately bumped into Fred the Miller who was halfway towards being drunk.

"Aren't you in the wrong place?" said big Fred, pushing Byron back onto his bar stool.

"Not to my knowledge, old cocker. Frightfully nice place, Soho."

"Push off."

"Not before we have a drink together, old chap... Tell you what. Been watching you. Bet you ten pounds I can drink a half-pint of this pub's very small beer quicker than you, my man."

Fred the Miller squeezed up his face and turned to look at the young drunk on the corner bar stool. "Let's see your ten quid."

After a few moments of fumbling for his wallet, Byron removed the precious notes and placed them gently on the bar, hoping his imitation of drunkenness was not being overdone. Without anyone asking, two half-pints were put in front of them and bets began flying around the bar.

"I 'ate people what spends money they don't earn," said Fred the Miller. "Daddy's little boy or maybe mummy's."

Byron got to his feet and waited for the barman to count. Silence fell around the bar and on "Go!" Byron opened his gullet and poured, slamming his glass down a fraction ahead of Fred the Miller. Neither had spilt a drop, and both glasses were empty.

Byron gave the big man a quizzical look.

"Want to have another go, old chap, or was that too much for you?"

Byron picked up his original ten pounds from the bar counter and left the other man's stake as a challenge.

"Set 'em up, barman," said big Fred, which was unnecessary. The third challenge was more difficult. Fred the Miller had sensed the trap. There were no side bets. When the big man lost again he looked across at Jack Pike. Everyone in the bar laughed except Fred the Miller but when he turned to take a swing at Byron, the bar stool was empty.

"I'll break that little bugger's neck."

"Fair bet, Fred," said the barman, "not a drop split."

"You was 'ad, Fred," said Jack Pike, coming to the bar. "Give 'im a drink on me."

"That little sod's got my thirty quid."

"'Is thirty quid, Fred."

"Make it a double Scotch," he said to the barman.

"There's an old saying, Fred my lad. However good you are at somethin', there's always someone better, see."

"You set 'im up!" shouted Fred.

"We did, Fred, we did."

"Where the bloody 'ell did you find 'im?"

"That was our bit of luck."

"The bugger's got an open gullet."

"That 'e 'as, Fred. That 'e 'as."

The pub closed at ten-thirty. The Pike family had lived above the pub for twenty years and saw no reason to move because they were rich. Their friends were all around them in Soho, a mix of cockney, Italian, Greek, Jewish, Chinese and anyone else who had managed to obtain permanent residence in the island. Jack liked the cosmopolitan atmosphere. Up and down the side streets, below the bright neon signs were girly clubs, peep shows, the Windmill Theatre with its nude shows that never closed, bars, restaurants, whores, pimps, con artists, street vendors, tricksters, showpeople, happy people, drunks: it was alive, twenty-four hours a day. Soho, like the Windmill, never closed.

Two gas fires were burning in the small parlour on the second floor and it was hot in the room. Jack Pike was down to his vest and trousers and young Johnny was yawning, ready for bed. Johnny had repeated the story of Byron as told to him in the bar and Jack Pike had listened to every word.

"Make a friend of 'im, Johnny. We're goin' to need a friend in the establishment. A front, so to speak. Spread our money out of Soho. That lad's goin' places. You think the LSD dots will work a second time?"

"Maybe not in the army, but the RAF doctors won't 'ave seen it."

"Just walked in the pub. Well I never. Just shows, son, mushrooms on your doorstep. You think our Fred saw the funny side?"

"No."

"Then we'll 'ave to watch it, won't we? Walked right in the pub..."

BY THE TIME Byron stood in front of the RAF medical officer he thought he was going to die, anyway. To be sure of success, he had swallowed one dot an hour before the medical and the second an hour later. His mind had left his body, which seemed to be shaking in concert with his heartbeat. The interview was short and Byron was back on the street outside the Air Ministry before the first dot took full effect and the second dot began to work. The office had given him the day off and the spring day sprung to life in a thousand colours of joy and Byron began a game of chicken with the traffic in the Mall. He tried his best to do a handstand on the bonnet of a moving car and ran off down the centre of the wide road, calling to the pigeons. His trip went into full flight when he found himself in Green Park chasing the ducks and then floating in the ice-cold water, fully clothed in his one dark suit, smiling at the clouds in heaven. People kept away, crossing the lawns and the paths to avoid the dripping wet lunatic. For Byron, the day passed in euphoric joy, a happiness so intense he found senses of pleasure he had never known before. The hallucinations were perfect. All the secrets of pleasure were open to his eyes, flooding his enjoyment. Only in the dusk did he trip the light-fantastic home and fall onto his bed, still damp but intolerably happy. The night's dreams were electric, the morning the day after death.

"What the hell did the Air Force do to you?" asked Lionel.

"Leave me alone, I'm dying."

"You want a doctor?"

"Just leave me alone."

"That's some hangover, Byron. I'll make your excuses. Another day at the Air Ministry. They won't let you behave like that in the RAF. Discipline, old boy. You should have been fat like me."

JASMINE BLACKBURN WAS a hedonist who liked men and Johnny Pike had been one of them. At twenty-two she had a good, firm body that she dressed provocatively without looking cheap. Her face was elfin with black hair to go with her name and her skin was rich and creamy with a natural dusting of red on her cheeks. Her nose was long, but not too long, her ears small but visible, but it was the dark, chocolate-brown eyes that did the tricks for her: she could draw a man across the room from fifty yards. She was in life for today and never thought of tomorrow, her wandering spirit inherited from her wandering father, the only man she was ever to truly love. He was her romantic knight from the past who had drifted round the colonies between the wars, coming back to England to join the army in 1939. At the end of 1945 he was forty-one, a captain, out of work and aware that the colonies would soon be given back to the natives. Worse, he was too old to freewheel down Africa, across Australia, up the Indian subcontinent where his charm and youth had brought him the price of everything. Jasmine had been sent back from Ceylon when she was three years old to live first with her grandparents and, when they died, with a maiden aunt who hated children. Her only link to happiness was the occasional visit from her father when the luck had turned his way with the price of the sea voyage back to England. Her mother was Anglo-Indian, very beautiful, more beautiful for her father as the years were spent and the multitude of stories she heard of the empire were spellbinding. As a child she never understood that rolling stones gathered no moss, and when she was old enough to understand she forgave her father his sins. By then he was a dashing lieutenant in uniform, unfortunately posted to intelligence at the War Office as he was considered too old to take part in the fighting.

Neither of them cared about money or permanent jobs and lived largely off their wits, always invited, always included. Jasmine had been told her mother died in India but on that point she had her doubts. Daddy was a roving man and maybe so was her mother.

Johnny put to her the proposition a month after Byron had received the first and only dressing down from his father which only Granda had stopped from coming to blows. According to Red Langton his son had let down the side. At first, Byron had tried to explain and then kept his silence. For Byron, there was only one side, his own, and it had no place for a government or the Air Force. He had left Langton Manor the same day he had arrived, driven to the railway station at Wareham by Granda who gave him a look of pained understanding, a one pound note and the advice to stay away for the summer and write to his mother.

"I don't take money, Johnny," Jasmine had said. "I won't be a whore. How can I take money for something I enjoy? You overpay me for working the switchboard as it is."

"I know, love. It's a nice fit, you could say. We both get what we want and looking after Byron is important to me and my dad."

"Why?"

"'Cause we like 'im, that's why. Double date on Saturday and bring someone nice for me."

"What's wrong with the lot that hangs around Soho?"

"They're common."

Jasmine Blackburn burst out laughing and kissed Johnny full on the mouth.

"What's that for?"

"Everyone wants what they haven't got. Silly, really. If we both want the other, neither can be much good, can they?... Saturday night."

"Buy a new dress. Dad said so."

"You really are very sweet."

"I know."

JASMINE PREFERRED young men as with them she did not have to appear intelligent, put on a pose, be what she was not. Her life was to be enjoyed, not philosophised into depression. They had arranged to meet at a Soho jazz club. The other girl was mediocre to look at as Jasmine Blackburn never introduced her own competition. She knew Byron was of a different class to Johnny, though class was of little importance in her life. She told everyone she was colonial, which kept most doors open.

Byron was an inch or two under six feet and not what she had expected, a public schoolboy wet behind the ears with an accent that pained her ears. The young man that smiled at her was neither wholly poof, as his name had conjured, or athletic, as his record suggested. Johnny had briefed her well on the background of the Langtons, an old landed family being picked apart by the socialists, the old home falling into genteel decay with a bemused owner who had done what he was asked to do to win the war and found himself the target of the new, socialist England which he did not understand. She had given Byron a cursory look before introducing her slightly mousy friend and then been swallowed up by the noise.

She watched him. The hands were surprisingly big with thick, powerful fingers that would surround a cricket ball with ease. She could not imagine them playing the piano. The face that drew her eyes projected a still, unblinking look from almost violet eyes. The face was square, the chin strong and deeply dimpled, the colouring fair with thick light-brown hair that flowed from a right-hand parting in a gentle wave across the top of the head, long and gently curling at the back. The skin had cleared from a spotty youth and in a year's time would leave no trace of his adolescence. For a man so young, still a boy by some standards, he was supremely comfortable and full of confidence. In years to come the well-built athletic body would go to fat but that impediment would only come to him in his forties. Johnny had told her he was a virgin which she found difficult to believe. If he was, then it was by his own choice or plain lack of opportunity. Jasmine was glad when at the intermission Johnny suggested they go as his guests to an Indian restaurant where the owner owed his father a favour. She was slightly impressed when Byron said he had no money, not as an apology but as a statement of fact which said quite clearly, take me as I am or not at all. They left the noise and overpowering smell of chlorine and came up the stairs to the sweeter air in the street. The light was fading from the summer night and she guessed it was more ten o'clock. The smell of lime trees reached them from a side street as they crossed the road to the small restaurant. Byron had taken up position next to her mousy friend which was not what had been planned.

The table to which they were shown was round and small and covered with a big white tablecloth so Jasmine had a man on either side as did her friend. She watched Byron let the others talk, turning his face to whichever one was talking. He gave the impression of listening to every word and maybe he was. Their eye contact was fleeting, polite even, but the brief looks said nothing, not even the silent bite of interest. She leant forward and dropped open the front of her dress but his eyes stayed looking at her face as she spoke. She heard the story of his drinking competition with Fred the Miller but from Johnny. She heard his father was a famous bomber pilot but from Johnny, and from the same source she heard he had turned down a scholarship to Oxford, preferring to clerk for a stockbroker in the City.

"When do you go into the army?" she asked.

"I failed my medical."

"*You?*" and when Johnny burst out laughing she asked, "Heart problems?"

"Exactly."

"With some help from your friend?" Jasmine was smiling.

"I don't have the time to waste."

"Why?"

"I have to catch up with all those people who have started with money." It was the only insight into himself she had heard.

"You intend to get rich?" she asked seriously.

"Oh, yes. There isn't any point in life unless you are rich. The best things in life being free is a lot of poppycock."

"How long will it take you?"

"I don't know yet. I have to learn."

"Do you want to come back to my flat for coffee and talk about it?"

"Why ever not?"

The bastard. He knew he was going to sleep with her all along. She was merely part of his learning curve.

For Byron she was the first and men always remember their first sex and their last. In ten weeks she taught him and not once did she envy the future women in his life. Everything the man did was calculated. If Johnny and his father thought they were going to use Byron Langton, they had better think again. The boot was already on the other foot. The penetrating look of the violet eyes, deep into her secret thoughts, made her shiver and want to bed him, the only place the terms were even. Neither of them were to forget the other.

3

Josephine Langton, Byron's twin sister, was the only member of the family who did not think Byron was wrong avoiding his national service. The forces were establishment, with ninety-five per cent of the officers from public schools swearing allegiance to the King and not the socialist government. Money and power were in the hands of the few and the distribution of wealth and resources was out of all proportion.

Jo cut her dark, almost black hair in a fringe, wore no make-up, not even powder or lipstick, and her clothes were best suited to a nunnery. Her features were as feminine as Byron's were masculine but a man had to have a good imagination to realise the potential hidden under the disguise of her socialist fury. She had told herself from the age of fifteen she was not wasting her life breeding the next generation while in captivity to a man. Uncle Cliff had shown her another world could exist for women, a world where they made their own decisions and led a life that was independent of the whims of men.

By dint of hard work, fuelled by desperation to get out of the trap planned for her life, she had won a bursary to the London School of Economics to study PPE (philosophy, politics and economics), all of which she considered the cornerstones of social welfare. The bursary paid her tuition but not the necessities of life and the typewriter she taught herself to use proficiently was the instrument that paid for her rent and food. Hilary was at Stanmore in his second year; Will at prep school where at last he had learnt to read. Even if there had been any money for her tertiary education, Jo would have refused any help. Her crusade had begun.

The bedsitter in Notting Hill Gate was just big enough for two single beds with a coffee table in between. At the end of the beds next to the door was a bricked up fireplace, a gas heater and single-ring gas cooker. Above the head of the beds was a sash window with a view over rooftops. Jo's room-mate, Sofia Freemantle, was also at LSE, a feminist and a card-carrying member of the British Communist Party. She also affected a severe dress code and was trying to make herself a lesbian in her wholesale rejection of men. They lived off vegetable stew and brown bread and tea and neither of them ever stopped talking. If it had not been for Uncle Cliff leading her into the Labour Party which employed her typewriter at night for cash, she would have joined the communists.

They were as happy as eighteen-year-olds can be in their first flush of independence. They were room-mates, best friends and would have been lovers if their normal hormones had not been at work under their façades. They touched and kissed and once tried to fondle but the minds were weaker than the flesh and the grope in the dark came to nothing.

For Jo and Sofia, every which way the world was being run was wrong. There was enough food production in the world but over a billion people were starving. The world's knowledge was known to a small minority and the colonial powers tried hard to prevent their colonial subjects from learning anything, determined not to create competition. They discussed it all well into the nights. While the rich of the world flaunted their excess, further down the class structure the majority of people were living in poverty. 'A rich man had quick access to medicine, a poor man died.' Sofia argued, in the Third World most of the people died before they were forty. The rich grew richer, and the poor stayed exactly where they were.

The world was unjust, unhappy and Jo and Sofia thought their hours of heated conversation were going to make it change. Through eighteen-year-old, idealistic eyes, the solutions were obvious, simple, long overdue and only required the destruction of the ruling classes to eliminate war, distribute food instead of destroying surpluses to maintain inflated prices, educate everyone and make the world one blissful, socialist, caring paradise. Man had the knowledge, the science and the means to remove poverty and illiteracy from the face of the earth. All the world lacked was good government.

Sofia's dream was one world government run by the people, for the people with wealth distribution according to each man and woman's needs. Everything had to belong to the people, for the people and each individual in the world had the right to take what was needed to sustain physical needs. A nuclear physicist, according to Sofia, would receive the same reward for his labour as a peasant in the fields as each of them worked the same number of hours and a peasant working the fields was more beneficial to mankind than the scientist who had found a way to destroy the history of man in a minute of time. There were all manner of people in the world, she argued, each a vital cog in the greater machine and all deserved the same reward as without each other the machine would stop. 'A factory of bosses produces not a car,' was Sofia's favourite expression.

World communism was the only possible way man could live in harmony without destroying the world. The atomic bomb had fallen and man's time on earth was limited. 'The revolution has to come now!' they would shout, making them feel much better afterwards.

WOLFGANG BAUMANN LECTURED the girls in politics and philosophy. He had left Germany in a hurry in 1934, soon after Hitler came to power on a platform that disliked the communists a little less than the Jews. A hero for a while in England for his outspoken opposition to the Nazis, when Stalin signed the German-Soviet Nonaggression Pact on the 23rd August 1939, Baumann was seen as the enemy and soon after war broke out the following month he was interned for the duration of the war.

When Josephine was first entranced by his magnetism, he was thirty-nine years old, grey at the temples, flat in the stomach from careful diet and exercise, and with not a trace of his German accent or any sign of resentment for the years of his Scottish internment. Being a realist he knew the advantage of being locked away in a safe place while other men of his own age were killing each other.

A university environment suited Wolfgang where his own enthusiasm could be fed and kept alive by the idealistic naïvety of youth. Like the Catholic Church, he liked to catch his converts young. He was at the height of his good looks, peddling the fire to light the imagination of virgin youth. He was not fooled by Josephine Langton's haircut or shapeless dress code, but he was aware of her violet eyes that followed him around the lecture room, drinking in his words and gobbling up anything else she could see. The queer aspect of the girl was that below her right eye was a tiny red birthmark, the shape of a diamond.

In the lecture hall, Wolfgang was certain of the rightness of what he said but when he went home to his barren and lonely flat, he was not so sure. Since the Greeks had given hemlock to Socrates – and before, with the

Persians and Egyptians, the ancient Chinese – men had risen up and proclaimed the way to man's salvation. The whisky bottle was some comfort but expensive, and drinking alone was not the best way to nurture his soul. Dangerously, he understood too much; the task of living was not all the joy he had expected from his years of thinking; 'futility' and 'waste of time' were notions frequently on his mind.

The pursuit of revolution had dominated his youth, taking away the comforts of marriage and children, the normality of family life, for better or for worse. His belief in communism was all he had needed to sustain his life. He was terrified of losing his faith.

She found him one autumn evening at the end of September in Holland Park where a symphony orchestra played to the summer trees and people on the grass, picnicking and blissfully content on a warm dry night, sent their long shadows lengthening across the grass. She had overheard him talking to a maths lecturer.

"I didn't know classical music went with Karl Marx," she said, sitting next to him on the soft grass while the musicians changed their music sheets.

"Hello!" He was surprised, disturbed from his reverie induced by the music. "Not much is free in London. I like the park as much as the music. Soothing, both of them. Why, art is important to man. Art and nature. They soothe his jaded nerves. What are you doing here, Jo?"

"Sitting on the grass."

He gave her a queer look, and the music began again, Mendelssohn's *A Midsummer Night's Dream*. He forgot her next to him on the grass, losing himself in the music and the melancholy of his life. She was only a child, not to be bored with the approaching pain of middle age. His problems were not for youthful ears, if anyone's at all. The swallows were flying high, making him think of their journey out to Africa. The summer was spent. Desperately, he made the music take away the thoughts that tangled in his mind.

FOR YOUNG WILL, autumn brought the magic of the woods. For his twelfth birthday his parents had given him a single-barrelled .410 shotgun, accurate at thirty yards. The dream of his childhood had come true. Across the farm of Langton Manor flew fat wood pigeons that kinked in flight at the sight of a man carrying a long stick. The sloping hills to the cliffs were burrowed by rabbits, the big bucks thumping the ground when Will came looking, sending the kits scampering back to safety in their holes. Seagulls, lazy on the sea-salt air, ignored the boy, turning their wings to dip and dive.

There was freedom in every stride and power in the gun crooked under his arm. A weekly border from his prep school, Will was the only child left in the house. The young hunter strode the woods and dales, the hedgerows, the close-cropped hills above the cliffs and pounding sea, as happy as a boy can ever be, content in his pursuit, bringing food back to the family. Somehow he knew his father and grandfather had done it all before him and the knowledge bridged the gap of age for all of them, the fledgling working for his spurs, the shared and constant joy of youth.

Will skinned and gutted his rabbits and hares, plucked the pigeons and once a pheasant. Everything was eaten, nothing ever thrown away. Even the boy understood the privilege he enjoyed to cull the wildlife on the farm and each new weekend he changed the warren for the woods. He knew the dog-fox and the vixen, the owls and sparrowhawks, the bird-nests in the hedgerows stark from the fallen leaves. He was a part of them as they were a part of him. In the wet, he tramped in gumboots, a black oilskin coat and hat: nothing kept him from the fields after the light came up with morning. He ate his sandwiches in the cave at Dancing Ledge and no one day was ever dull. The boy needed nothing but the magic of the woods, alone.

Winter took a grip on the countryside in mid-November when the first frosts turned the ruts in the farm roads to steel. The preparations for Christmas had begun. Granda had the job of smoking the hogs, young six-month-old porkers, and turning three of them into hams and bacon. He fuelled the big smoker with oak shavings and was as content as Will in the fields. Ever since any of them could remember, which included the repeated stories of Granda's grandparents, Christmas at Langton Manor was the focal point of the year and relatives from far and wide came to the family home. The geese were fattened, plum pudding taken from the cellar and topped with brandy, pickles made and the ingredients for a huge Christmas cake put aside, ready for the big bake with the pies and tarts. It was the period of great and joyful expectations when the year's worries were put aside to celebrate the foundations of a Christian home, part ancestral, part pagan with the Christmas tree, part son of God all blessed in old tradition, giving the family hope for the future from the God proud of the past. The weeks were frantic with Adelaide and Red, Granda, the old cook, more family than servant, two of the labourers' wives who helped at the big house, the dogs, all four of them border collies for the sheep, the cats, six of them of no determinable pedigree for the rats and mice, all scurrying about the big house in constant bursts of energy.

When Hilary came back for the hols from Stanmore, now fifteen years old, he was pushed out of the house by Will to be shown all the new, exciting nests and lairs. Despite the age difference they were still best friends, and it was Will who first heard his friend was entering the priesthood in eighteen months after he wrote his school certificate.

"I want to be a missionary," Hilary told Will. "Go out to Africa, bring them the word of God and true salvation."

"*Africa*?" Will picked up on. "Wouldn't mind going to Africa. All those lions and tigers."

"There are no tigers in Africa." Hilary had been doing his homework.

"Have you told Dad?"

"The group captain won't mind."

"No, don't suppose he will. Dad likes God a lot."

"Don't we all?" said Hilary, serious with his new conviction.

"I like Christmas," said Will more hopefully.

"Christmas is just part of it," Hilary said very seriously, imitating his headmaster. Hilary wanted to say more, to explain the wonderful feeling that had taken him when the headmaster had asked him a few months after his confirmation whether he wished to join the Church and he had answered 'yes', the missionary part and Africa coming later. But Will had gone off behind the hedgerow looking for neither of them knew what.

JOSEPHINE HAD TOLD her mother she was bringing a friend for Christmas which was normal in the Langton family. What Adelaide did not expect when he arrived was a man, and a man the same age as Adelaide and a contemporary of Group Captain Red Langton, father of the four children, all but one of whom was grown up. Granda had chuckled, got into his rattletrap of a car and gone off to Corfe Castle and the Ship Inn: it had mostly been the expression on his son's face at the idea of entertaining a German for Christmas, not the age and relationship to Josephine, that had sent him off for a pint. Old Harold Langton had seen it all and nothing gave him a surprise. When he told his cronies in the corner of the bar, the guffaws of laughter was enough reward for the journey.

"Now don't you go telling the tale round Langton Matravers," he said with a wink, knowing the German up at the big house, right under the group captain's nose, would be the talk of the district by breakfast time.

Wolfgang had known it was a mistake to accept his student's invitation to spend Christmas with her family but he had made so many mistakes by then it did not seem to matter. When they had walked through Holland Park in the gloaming on their way to their respective homes, he had stupidly invited her up to his flat for coffee and a chat, master and student. She had seen the Scotch bottle and suggested a drink, sitting on the carpet at his feet while he talked. Josephine began nursing her only drink and Wolfgang kept topping up his own by the light of the lamp from the street. It had been a Friday, with a long, lonely weekend stretching out before him and he enjoyed talking to an attentive audience. His colleague, the mathematics lecturer, was two years younger than Wolfgang, single, intelligent and more than interesting, but women of thirty-seven failed to excite him, to make him interested in them as a woman rather than a friend. Wolfgang Baumann liked young women and, worse, young women liked him but all the ones he ever met were his students and they were off limits as much from his own understanding of right and wrong as the college rules. If the turmoil in Germany and the war had not kept him apart from women, he would have expended his energy in lustful youth at the right time of his life.

In the weeks to come he blamed the whisky, his loneliness, his lack of family when all he had to do was blame himself. The arm on the shoulder had brought the young lady up onto the sofa, in the process riding up her ugly dress to the middle of young, healthy, surprisingly sunburnt thighs. Wiggling to hear the words of revolutionary wisdom better, Wolfgang giving her what she wanted to hear, had made it worse and revealed a flash of white, virginal panties that made Wolfgang pour himself another Scotch, thereby, and certainly without intention, lowering his power of resistance. When he finally put a hand on the thigh, all hell was let loose, the nights of Josephine's frustration with Sofia finally finding the right object of her desire. Frustration met frustration on the old couch watched from only a few feet away by the street light, and when she cried out in real pain, he realised he had penetrated her virginity and what the Scotch, the lamplight and his male desire had started would not go away in a hurry, especially after they made love through the whole weekend, only going out once to buy two pints of milk and a loaf of bread.

Ever since arriving at Langton Manor, by which time Josephine had moved out of the bedsitter and into his flat in the suburb of Holland Park, and seeing the group captain's uniform in the downstairs closet when he had gone to the toilet, he had been careful not to bring up the war. During his internment, some of the guards had been RAF, so he had known the rank of the uniform arm sticking out from the coats in the closet as he relieved himself, the realisation swiftly curtailing the even flow of his water. His only consolation was the girl being over eighteen, but that would not stop the wrath of the father. As more and more guests arrived, most of whom had the name of Critchley or Langton, he hoped to be less conspicuous. The eldest son was not coming home for Christmas, a fact mentioned once and dropped.

When he asked Josephine she had said, "Oh, Randolph. Army. National service. You know... My twin's coming down this afternoon. Byron's in the dog box for avoiding the army, rigging his medical, Granda says, and Randolph failed to get a commission. Now there's only Will. My Uncle Cliff was in the ranks. TUC, now. You'll like Uncle Cliff. His politics and philosophy are the same as yours. Ma says he's the black sheep of her family which is nonsense... Byron's bringing a girl. Poor Mother. Can't get over we're grown up with minds of our own. You must talk to Father. Make him see socialism is the only answer."

Wolfgang took a path to the left where they were walking in the leafless woods, the trees stark, fingers pointing to a leaden sky. The last thing he intended bringing up in Langton Manor, where the same family had lived for generations, was communism and returning the land to its rightful owners, the people... He was in enough trouble already if her father ever found out.

AUNTY EVE, Adelaide's aunt on her mother's side, and great-aunt to Will, Byron, Josephine and Randolph, took one look at the situation and told Adelaide that Jo was in love.

"Don't be silly, Aunt Eve. She's only a child, he's her lecturer, nothing more."

"Twaddle. The girl's even done her hair."

"She's barely eighteen."

"I was married and widowed by her age." There was a brief moment of silence as both of them remembered the First World War.

"I hadn't thought of that," said Adelaide.

"You'd better. He's far too old. There'll be trouble." And Aunt Eve had a reputation for always being right.

"The hair does look better," said Adelaide, thinking to herself.

"Something good always comes out of something bad. Fact of life. And they're sleeping together. See it in her eyes. Way she looks at him. You don't look at your lecturer like that if you are only listening to his words. Man must be forty, probably a communist if he's London School of Economics... And he's German. Next thing we'll find out he's a Jew, or she's pregnant. Have a word with her."

"You wouldn't like to...?"

"No. I never interfere in other people's business. World would be much better off if we stopped interfering. She's your business and you're mine. Widowed old aunts have a job to do in the family and I've just done mine. Oh, and you're about to tell young Clifford to get a proper job. Trade unions are tantamount to extortion. Extortion or blackmail. I never know which it is but they're just as bad as each other. Can't have the family going to pot."

JASMINE BLACKBURN WAS BORED. She had determined not to be lonely on Christmas Day and was paying the price. Her affair with Byron was over but the offer to spend Christmas at Langton Manor had been accepted weeks before. Everyone was old and family, or too young and family, too young even for Jasmine. The idea of turning a future missionary on his head had crossed her mind during the family silence after Hilary announced at breakfast he was entering the Church when he left school, the surprise even showing on the face of the group captain. Two of the male cousins were just not on and if she had to walk another yard in the country, she would scream. Soggy leaves underfoot and dripping trees were not her idea of fun, the sight of dead birds hanging by their feet turned her stomach, and when young Will with all good intention thrust a dead rabbit at her face she almost gave him a clout.

"Don't you like rabbits?" Will had said, deliberately dripping blood on the girl's shoes.

"Not dead ones."

"You can't eat them when they are alive," replied Will with a small boy's practical logic. "You'll like the look of a leg on your plate."

Jasmine had pulled away, looked at the blood on her shoes and been sick in the bushes, much to Will's satisfaction.

The only possible alternative to boredom was the tall German even though she did not like older men. The fun would be in annoying Byron's sister who was always going off about the welfare state and what the Labour Party were doing for the people. She had even glanced at Cliff but shied away when he took the panacea of socialism a step further than Josephine.

Bored, she had stepped into the conversation. "Everyone getting it all for nothing will soon have the English doing no work at all," repeating something her father had said at which she had smiled as neither father nor daughter were candidates for hard work.

"You must agree with us," Cliff had said, turning to Wolfgang.

"I have learnt never to disagree with a lady." There was even a trace of his

German accent as he spoke. The flash of anger directed by Josephine fried Jasmine.

Tea had been served in the morning room and Uncle Cliff had mounted his hobby horse, encouraged by Josephine. Log fires were burning at either end of the room and outside it was cold – not as cold as the winter of 1947, but the air was wet, blown by an east wind. The dogs were flat on their sides around the fire, interspersed with sleeping cats. The big sash windows rattled with the wind but the room was warm despite the tall ceiling. Old, dark paintings hung on the walls and the furniture was vintage, well tried by the Langton generations. The origins of some of the pieces were only known to the ancestors. It was of some comfort and beauty that had come about by trial and error. At night, the burgundy curtains were drawn against the darkening chill to create a feeling of safety.

Uncle Cliff had finished extolling the many virtues of the new National Health scheme and had launched into the socialist dogma of looking after all the people from the cradle to the grave. As he put it, the vast majority of Britons would benefit from shorter hours, higher pay, guaranteed pensions and equal opportunities. He was clearly expounding for the benefit of the philosophy and political lecturer who was steadfastly refusing to be drawn into the conversation. Every time Uncle Cliff came to a halt, Josephine fired him up again. Adelaide was darning socks and not listening to her brother. The group captain was worrying about four lambs that had been born at the wrong time of the year, the ram having slipped his paddock a morning seven months earlier. Aunty Eve was periodically snorting at so much 'rubbish' being spoken, and Jasmine was trying to catch the German's eye for the third time.

"So everything is going to be done for them?" said Granda ominously.

"The state will distribute the nation's wealth," said Uncle Cliff.

"No one has to think or provide for themselves?" said Granda. "How bloody boring. The only exciting thing in this life is doing things, not being given them. You'll take away life's only incentive, Clifford, my boy, you'll create a nation of bored, dull and uninteresting people whose only interest in life will be shouting for more of where that came from. Having money is not nearly as exciting as making it. When you've spent all the money made by the few makers of this world, your welfare state will go bankrupt. Then you will have to start all over again from scratch, without the entrepreneurs. You'll have dulled them into extermination." Granda stood up and shook himself. "Tea at eleven o'clock is all very well. I'm going into Corfe Castle. Red, you coming?" he said to his son.

"Yes, I'll join you, Dad."

"Byron. Want to come?"

"Wow," said Byron forgetting he was no longer a schoolboy. It was the very first time his grandfather had invited him to the Ship Inn.

The invitation was not extended to Uncle Cliff or the German and Hilary was still too young.

"One of these days your pub will be open to women," said Josephine, "women are just as good as men."

Granda went out shaking his head and said not a word. There were more ways than one to make a point.

Will ate the last muffin and followed the grown-ups out of the room. Something had been wrong which he did not understand. He put on a thick windcheater and went for a tramp despite the damp air. He could hear Granda's car climbing the hill far away, the only sound on the wind away from the sea. Nearer the sea, he saw the gulls, dipping and turning, enjoying themselves. It was the first time he had gone out alone without Hilary: God could stay with Hilary while he walked the woods and the windswept cliffs.

The rabbits stayed deep in their warrens.

Byron was in the back of the car feeling guilty for leaving Jasmine on her own. The invitation to drink with his father and grandfather as a grown-up had been too much for him to think of Jasmine until he was in the car. Why she had accepted to come down to Dorset he did not understand, nor did he understand anything else about her except her insatiable need for sex, something impossible to fulfil at the manor. He knew his mother would never approve of him sleeping with a girl who was not his wife despite everybody saying that things had changed since the war, that people should do what they wanted, not what they were told. For the first time in his life, lying had become easy.

The one thing he was determined not to bring up was his national service. He was learning something of value at Logan, Smith and Marjoribanks. What could have been the point of square-bashing for ten weeks with a rifle on his shoulder? His father had received no reward for fighting the Germans, apart from ribbons and medals, both worthless. The Germans had gone home to a house of rubble. Johnny Pike was right. No one mattered except oneself. Rules and regulations were to be circumvented as the rich were doing to get their money out of England and the clutches of the Labour Party. Only fools were caught in the tax trap. When he made his own money it was going to be offshore, a new word he had learnt and understood to mean wealth that was not subject to the whims and legal theft of governments.

"Didn't do us any good, Red," said Granda. Red was sitting next to him in the front of the car.

"What, Dad?"

"Fighting other people's wars. Even the Boers are now in control in South Africa so all the dead men didn't make any difference. Maybe Byron's smarter than both of us."

"It's either right or wrong."

"Maybe so. But being right doesn't always mean you win... You want to tell your father what you really did at that medical, Byron, and then we will all drop the subject. Lying to your family never did anyone any good."

"Granda," said Byron in a small voice. "Can you read my mind?"

"Sometimes, lad. Twenty minutes of silence had you and your father chewing the same thoughts."

"I took LSD," said Byron and went on to explain what it was and what it did.

By the time they reached the Ship Inn they were all talking normally and Byron could have hugged his old grandfather. The lesson of wisdom with old age was a lesson he was never to forget and many times in the future of his business when he was making decisions without the experience of age, he would draw back and ask himself 'what would Granda have done on this one?'

In the Ship they let him buy his round of drinks and for the first time he felt like a man.

"One word of advice, grandson," said the old man when he had paid, "never go into a pub without the price of a round of drinks. If you haven't got the money, don't go in and that applies to everything else in life that costs money. And work hard. No one gets anything for nothing in this world. Anyone says anything else is a fool."

The old-timer shuffled into the bar when Byron was halfway through his third half-pint of beer.

"'Appy Christmas, Squire."

"Happy Christmas, Ted. This is my son the group captain and his son Byron... Ted and I fought in the Boer War together," he said to explain.

"Better we 'adn't, Squire, what with the Boers gettin' British Natal and the Cape. Don't make no sense of it." He turned to the barman. "Mild and bitter pint. It's Christmas and the Labour Party's put up my pension. You got a pension, Group Captain?"

"No," said Red, taken by surprise. "I was just in for the war. You don't get a pension for fighting a war. I volunteered, anyway. Let me buy you that pint."

"Thanks. Don't mind if you do… You'll be doing your national service," he said, turning to Byron and taking a long pull at his pint.

"They failed me on medical grounds."

The idea of his father fighting for nothing should have made him feel proud but something was sour and any guilt he might have felt avoiding his call-up evaporated. Somewhere, somehow, someone was being exploited but in the naïvety of his youth he was unable to comprehend.

"Lucky lad," said Ted without any malice.

ON CHRISTMAS EVE the weather was dull, the clouds low and grey over the Purbeck Hills. There was the threat of rain but Will had poached two Cox apples from the store in the attic where they had been laid out in rows on duckboards in September, no one apple touching the other, and gone off with his sandwiches wrapped in greaseproof paper. He had again slipped the leash of brothers and cousins to go to his cave. No one else knew the secret place where he could hug his shoulders and be alone in perfect harmony with life and all around.

The sea was angry, a dark bottle-green, thrashing the ledge and hurling the cold icicles of spray, grey-flecked and dirty, at the entrance. Fifty feet above on the cliff, Will looked down upon the fury of the spray. The dance upon the long rock ledge was one of anger, battle, the elements of rock and sea fighting each other, hurling water from the depths with cast-off kelp ripped up by the roots playing in the curling waves to smash upon the granite rocks that absorbed the power of the sea, trickling it back in runnels in the rocks, mocked and tamed.

A monster wave rose up from the depths of the sea, reared up towards Will upon the cliff, up and up, a rising tongue of water, and then it crashed right across the ledge down below, smashing the mouth of his cave, pushing sea water up the funnel making an awful rumbling in the bowels of the cliff that Will could feel beneath his feet, and then the rumbling roar of water rushing back to join the sea.

Quietly, and with due respect, Will ate his sandwiches hunched down upon the cliff. Soon, it began to rain.

The sheep were huddled down together for warmth and watched him pass with fishy eyes, wet and bulging. Seagulls called above the crashing sea and out in the channel a small steamer, belching black smoke that streamed behind, fought the waves and wind for a Christmas port and comfort. Will began to run with joy, the last apple bouncing in his pocket. The sheep broke and ran away, their heads upright, a touch of panic in their flight, the lambs keeping pace with the flock. The rolling hills, short-cropped and emerald-green, dropped back from the guarding cliffs and on he ran down the jagged path. Will ran for five minutes till he could see the dell. High trees rose up and in their safety stood the ivy-clad house, with the small, piggy windows at the back, facing the winter winds. At three o'clock it had already begun to grow dark, fading the grey, low-hung sky above his head. The gulls had not followed him. Now he ran down between the hedgerows, onto the hard road, past the docile cows facing stoically into the wind and rain, tumbling towards the house and Christmas warmth.

Reaching the wooden gate that opened into the orchard, stark and leafless trees well pruned, Will hesitated. Happy to be alive, Will took the last apple from his pocket and crunched it open with his teeth, letting loose the sweet juice of summer.

Will walked round the old house instead of his usual duck through the kitchen and the maid's sitting room. The big oak to the right of the house was all of ten feet across at its base, the home of owls; the family legend had it said the first Langton planted the acorn with the first dwelling in the dell.

The wet path led to the gravel in front of the house where a later Langton had removed the small windows in the family wing, replacing them with the tall sash windows that rattled with the wind.

Turning the corner, with his back now to the great English oak, the wind stopped pulling at his hat and he threw the apple core across the shaggy lawn. The core hit one of the cypress trees, a good distance. Satisfied, Will turned to the house and as he hoped, the curtains had yet to be drawn across the drawing room where the one fire away from the Christmas tree beckoned him inside. The tree took up the whole corner of the sixty-foot room, right to the high corniced ceiling, twinkling with coloured lights and tinsel, piled below the bottom branches with presents, wrapped and ribboned, some with bows; a big star flopped forward on the prickly top; glass balls, reds and golds and sparkling silver, cascading down the tree, clinging by tiny threads of cotton, light as moonbeams. Will stood, looking in on the house with its aunts, uncles and cousins seated on the floor around the open fire, Byron as usual sitting back, Hilary in earnest conversation with Will's father, Will's mother sewing, glasses at the end of her nose. Uncle Cliff looked asleep in his chair, long legs stretched to the fire. Christmas decorations hung from the ceiling, centring upon the chandelier. The big mantelpiece was crammed with Christmas cards. Granda was smoking his foul pipe, content to look; Josephine for once was silent and the lady who was afraid of dead rabbits was talking to the tall stranger, Josephine's friend.

Will stood outside unnoticed in the gathering dark, smiling at everything

he loved, safe in the family to which he had been born. Very importantly
Will Langton reached up and rang the bell at the big front door and waited.
Josephine opened the panelled door.

"What are you doing out here, silly?"

"Waiting to come into my house." Quickly, Will gave her a kiss on the
cheek before running down the hall to change his clothes.

Josephine stood with her back to the closed door for a moment, still
feeling the wet, cold kiss on her fire-warmed cheek. Wiping away the
moisture with a gentle smile she walked back to the drawing room. Even
little brothers could be nice, sometimes.

EARLY ON CHRISTMAS morning Josephine was sick three times in half an
hour. Across the corridor from her bedroom, her great-aunt Eve read the
story as if it were her own. Lying awake for half an hour she decided that
interfering in other people's lives, even with the best intentions, led to more
problems than they solved. Cliff was a socialist who despised his class and
there was nothing she could say, despite her trying, that could change his
mind. She even thought her few words had strengthened his determination.

She went down to breakfast and said not a word when she found
Josephine drinking tea alone in a corner of the dining room, looking out of
the window at the winter's scene. The girl turned and their eyes locked for a
full second.

"Has the tea just been made?" said the great-aunt.

"Yes. It's very nice. Can I pour you some, Aunty?"

"Thank you. That would be very nice... Are you going back to London
before your lectures commence?"

"Yes. Wolfgang has a lot of prelim work. Sort of getting ready. Reading."

"Could you give me a lift? I came down by train but it's tedious alone."

"I didn't know you lived in London?"

"There are a lot of things you don't know about the old spinster aunt."
She took the cup of proffered tea and placed it back on the tea trolley. "You
didn't know I was married. Briefly. He was killed in the Great War. I was just
eighteen when he died."

"I'm so sorry. Mother never said."

"Why should she? There are happier things to talk about. My flat's in
Chelsea. Maybe Mr Baumann would be kind enough to drop me off and
you'll come back later for some tea? It's not far from Notting Hill Gate on the
Tube. Sometimes I get lonely, Josephine. Like most old people, I prefer the
company of the young. Old people are inclined to be negative. Not all of

them..." She left the question in the air and picked up her cup of tea as Byron came in for breakfast.

"Morning, Jo. Happy Christmas," he said, full of Christmas cheer.

"I almost forgot," said Aunt Eve. "Happy Christmas. And me the master, or should it be the mistress, of ceremonies for the present opening. Sharp at eleven o'clock! I'll ring the gong as usual. I've heard that gong every year for over sixty Christmases. We Critchleys have known you Langtons for longer than just your mother and father. There's Langton blood in the Critchleys and Critchley blood in the Langtons further back than any of us know. You see, my husband was a Langton and if he had lived, this house would be his house. Well, not really. Fact is, it belongs to all of us."

Byron was looking at Josephine with genuine surprise.

CLIFFORD CRITCHLEY CAUGHT up with Wolfgang Baumann after breakfast when Wolfgang tried to take a walk on his own. Wolfgang had heard his student in the bathroom for the second day in a row and he had absolutely no idea what to do. Never before had he considered money so important. He had nothing but his salary and that was barely enough to allow him a whisky every second night. The wealth of Langton Manor, despite Josephine's talk of family poverty, had overwhelmed him not by its ostentation but by the family's acceptance of the normality of it all. The history. The past, present and the future. He was an outsider, a foreigner, entertained politely but forgotten.

He had reached the lane that led up to the Downs and the cliffs when he heard footsteps and turned from his heart-searching, almost glad for a distraction until he saw who it was walking towards him with intent.

"You mind if I join you?" said Clifford.

"Of course not," Wolfgang lied.

"I've been wanting to talk with you ever since we met. You are a member of the Communist Party?"

Wolfgang carried on walking. Cliff ignored the silence and carried on talking. "The left wing of the Labour Party is very close to you. If it wasn't party political suicide in England, we would join you outright. Fact is, we can do more to further the cause from within the Labour Party. We are mounting an anti-nuclear campaign to force Western Europe to give up their weapons. But you would know about that?"

"No, I don't."

They had climbed out of the lane where they could turn and look back on the dell and the manor house among the trees. They both gazed down in silence.

"Old families like that are an anachronism," said Clifford. "You could house thirty families where there's one. Just because they inherited. Makes you sick. Our new death duty tax will separate them from their land without a whimper. Democracy is a wonderful thing. You can legislate whatever you like against a minority provided the minority are privileged."

Wolfgang felt a cold shudder go through his body as if a ghost had walked over his grave. For a brief moment he had forgotten that Josephine was pregnant.

WILL WOKE GRIPPED by the excitement of Christmas. At the window he looked down from the second floor at the winter: leafless trees and a white frost but no snow. Standing barefoot in his pyjamas he pulled up the sash window and shivered. The sea was distant, the rough sea gone with the storm. Over towards Poole the sky was clear in the early morning; peaceful. Two of the dogs had followed him up to bed and both were scratching their fleas. The fire was laid in the small grate, with the wood he had collected in a wicker basket. There was no sound from the outside fields. The house was silent and Will pulled down the sash window and ran across to the fireplace and lit one of the big, red-tipped Swan matches which he put to the cold paper in three places, getting down on his hands and knees to blow on the meagre flames, watched by the dogs. When the fire took he jumped back under the bedclothes, ice-cold from his toes to the tip of his nose. The dogs settled down in front of the gathering fire with patient hope, leaving their fleas alone. A door banged from somewhere in the house and Will wondered if his feet would ever get warm again. All he could think about was the bicycle he wanted so much. He had checked every parcel under the tree but none were big enough for a bicycle. By the time the house began to wake, the fire was strong and the painful feeling had gone from his feet. It was Christmas Day, the best day in the whole wide world.

A knock on the door made him snuggle right under the bedclothes, pretending he was still asleep. The door opened wide and the dogs bolted. Josephine saw the fire and the lump under the blankets. In the excitement of Christmas she had not been sick.

"Get up, sleepyhead," she said.

Quietly she moved up to the bed and threw back the clothes.

"Is there a bicycle under the tree?" asked Will, smiling at his sister.

"How should I know?"

"You could have looked."

"We leave for church in an hour. Everyone's going, and that includes the cook, so there won't be any breakfast."

"No breakfast?" Will sat straight up and hugged his knees.

"I'll boil you an egg."

"Thanks, Josephine."

"Happy Christmas."

"Happy Christmas."

"Put the screen in front of the fire before you come down."

THE OLD CYPRESS trees protected the ancient church. The graves were old and mostly neglected, the headstones angled to the weak winter sun that gave light but no warmth. The people of Langton Matravers were filing through the lichgate. The church bells were pealing the joy of Christ's birth and man had come to worship, to thank their Maker for life with all its joy and sorrow, to find their reason for life in God.

Will was well wrapped up against the cold and Granda was coughing, the bowl of his pipe still warm in his greatcoat pocket. Hilary had gone on ahead to join the choir. Adelaide rested her gloved hand through the group captain's arm and was leaning slightly against her husband, her small fur hat well over her ears. Byron walked beside Jasmine Blackburn but neither had talked since leaving the car. Cliff Critchley broke off an animated conversation with Great-Aunt Eve as they approached the church. The tall, grey-haired German, Wolfgang Baumann, walked next to Josephine, happy the family had accepted him even if they had not welcomed him with open arms. Two old uncles trudged along together, widowed and left alone to end their days on earth.

Will had put on two pairs of socks to keep out the cold as he stepped on the old Norman stones that led him into the church, surrounded by bigger people in heavy overcoats. Squashed inside the church it was freezing, despite the puny efforts of oil stoves scattered down the aisles, puffing oily smoke up at the distant, blackened rafters that had watched the people of the village for eight hundred years. The stone pillars were hung with holly; Christmas chrysanthemums that had come from the heated greenhouse at Langton Manor looked splendid around each side of the altar. The organist, who was also the sexton, was playing mournful music to put everyone in the proper frame of mind. After entering the church no one spoke. Will followed the broad back of his father to the left front family pew, the wooden bench worn thin by the sliding bottoms of Langton generations.

Each member of the family knelt and prayed. When the church was packed full, including the folding chairs a churchwarden had set up in the aisles, a few lucky parishioners with feet to the stoves, the choir filed into the stalls and the vicar took his place facing the altar, the whole parish united in the worship of God.

"Let us pray," said the vicar and everyone, from the rich to the poor, fell to their knees in unison, each well knowing his place in the way of things, the allotted lifespan, the allotted life.

"Let there be peace among men," he called up to his God. With a war just finished he had the attention of every man and woman.

The choir began the first hymn, and the congregation joined the singing. Will soon lost the thread and tried to catch Hilary's attention. His best friend was in a white surplice with a black ruffled collar, singing in the third row of the choir and, unbeknown to Will, having difficulty singing the treble notes he had learnt. After fidgeting for a few moments Will gave up and went back to dreaming about a bicycle.

The vicar stood outside his church in the wintry sun, shaking the grown-up hands, everyone glad the sermon had not been long. To Will's surprise, the vicar put out his white, puffy hand and Will found his own engulfed in soft, silky flesh.

"Stanmore next year is it, young man?" said the vicar.

Will looked up at the man in his white surplice and smiled.

"Football team this year, I hear," continued the vicar.

Again Will smiled. With New Year so close, the vicar's years were lost to him. He shuffled forward in the crowd, the people still solemn around the vicar, the less religious nearer the cars and the footpath that led the poorer to their homes.

The vicar stood for a moment when the last parishioner had passed him by. With the war over four years ago, he wondered how much longer they would turn to God for solace. There was Hilary Bains bent on the Church to find his dead father and mother. Red Langton, bomber pilot, with the horror of burning Dresden, the wilful destruction of Nagasaki to live with him all his years, looking to God for the answer why. Maybe some more. But with better times the rest would forget their faith, leaving God to those who were suffering. Stamping his feet, he went back into the empty church to pray alone, to comfort his sadness.

THE LIGHT HAD BEEN FADING for half an hour when Will drew up his new bicycle at the living room window where he propped it up carefully against the red brick wall. It was half-past three and the family Christmas lunch had been over for an hour. A snap of evening frost coated the window panes and Will had to breathe on the thin layer of ice before he could rub a patch clean enough to look inside the long room with the fires at either end. Only grown-ups were in the room, the children having gone to play with their presents. The two uncles were sprawled on the same couch, fast asleep, their jaws open, hands clasped across full bellies which rose and fell. Around the room his family were enjoying the best part of their Christmas, a snooze in the warm room. The dogs were sprawled at the feet of each fire and the cats were asleep on the arms of the chairs. Cracked nuts littered the whole carpet. Small glasses of what once had held port sat on the side tables next to the men and Great-Aunt Eve. Surprisingly, the German was fast asleep in a chair, no sign of Josephine, Byron or any of the cousins. Slowly, the patch in the window clouded and though Will was left outside with the cold, he felt warm and part of it all. They were his family.

THE FEBRUARY NIGHT air was freezing and the lamp post three away was hidden in the London smog, the light a yellow glow. Footsteps crossed from the other side of Greek Street and Byron turned to face the sound.

"This your girlfriend?" asked a cockney voice.

"My sister," said Byron, "my twin sister."

"Have it as you will, mate. Come on, luv, no point waitin'."

Josephine followed him into the smog, Byron left behind with the night. The sound of the traffic from Piccadilly was muffled and after three street turns she was lost, her mind numb. The man stopped and knocked and the door opened and Josephine was walking on a threadbare runner carpet that led up a wooden flight of stairs, a young girl leading the way, the man from the street having vanished into the smog. At the second landing the girl pushed open a wooden door and the pervasive smell of gin wafted onto the landing. Josephine followed the girl into the badly lit room; the only furniture was a high bed with a red rubber sheet covering the top.

"Better take your clothes off, ducks... Don't you worry, been doin' this for twenty years and never 'ad no problems. Want a gin? Better you 'ad. Couple of good ones, I say, and you know nothing, feel nothin'. You can put the money on the table... Whore I was, but you can't make money out of whorin' after forty, you mark my words."

The gin tasted bad and Josephine pinched her nose and swallowed, handing back the tumbler. She took and swallowed the second glass before taking off her skirt, stockings and panties. The room was warm from an old gas heater next to the bed.

"Ships that pass in the night, ducky. What we are." She was counting the money. Satisfied, she put it in a cupboard, in a cardboard box.

"Exactly right... One thing about us English, we never cheat each other. Now, you get up on the bed ducks, lie back and bring your knees up, like wide open. Give me room. Close your eyes and let the gin swill your brains. 'Ad a couple myself." She was mumbling.

The sound of washing hands from the corner basin came to Josephine behind her tightly closed eyes. Byron had made her drink two glasses of whisky in the ladies' bar where she had met Johnny Pike for the first time. The smell of stale gin came nearer as the old woman bent to her work and Josephine felt strong hands on her thighs pushing them open. The old woman's hand groped, pushing into her womb, filling her body and mind. She could feel the woman's fingers searching. Waves of gin were detaching her mind from the groping hand in her womb. A sharp, searing pain made her eyes start open as the new life was wrenched from her body and the gin and vomit spurted from her mouth. The old woman turned away from the bed and went out of the room, closing the door and leaving Josephine with vomit covering her face. A distant toilet flushed and tears of horror began.

The old woman came back and washed her hands in the corner basin, bringing a damp clean towel and a bowl of warm water. Josephine could smell the Dettol in the water over the smell of gin. The gas fire flared and went out and the woman put a shilling in the meter before coming back to the bed.

"You cry, luv. Best thing about us people is memory fades. An' I should know... Never understood what life was about in the first place. Now, let's get you cleaned up and out of 'ere. Life stinks a lot more than this room, ducks. You mark my word. You just startin' down the agony road."

The young girl led her into the street and the freezing cold. The two sanitary towels already felt wet. She was soberer than before the abortion. The smog of smoke swallowed them up as she followed the girl in and out the back streets. After ten minutes she recognised the lights of Greek Street where the evening had begun. When she turned to the girl, she was alone in the street with the babble of voices from the bar muffled by the night and the noise of traffic behind. The theatres would be coming out in half an hour, thought Josephine and pushed her way into the pub and its noise. Byron was waiting for her alone at the end of the bar.

Byron saw she was ashen white, the violet eyes stark against the white, her hair wet at the back of her head. The two sets of identical eyes watched each other for a moment.

"You all right, Josephine?"

"No," she whispered. "I'm bleeding badly. We'd better find a doctor, Byron, or I think I'm going to die. Matter of fact, I feel like dying anyway."

Johnny had been watching from the far side of the bar and caught the nod from Byron. Within three minutes of a phone call being made, Josephine was in a taxi on her way to South Kensington and a gynaecologist who performed a D and C, stopping the haemorrhage. She was driven under sedation to Byron's flat, the one he still shared with Lionel Marjoribanks, where she was put to bed. Byron slept on the couch. Once again he had thought ahead and saved a disaster. Well satisfied, he went to sleep. What he did not know was that his sister would never be able to have children.

FURTHER AWAY IN HOLLAND PARK, Wolfgang Baumann slept through the night undisturbed. He had not seen Josephine after she had moved out of his flat without a word. He was never to know that his child had died that night, the only child he was ever to have.

PART II

1955 TO 1959

_____

4

*I*n 1955, Byron, twenty-four, was convinced the British Empire was heading for extinction and was unable to understand young Will running off to Africa in the wake of Hilary Bains. The young brother had thought himself in love.

Byron had moved out of Lionel's flat the previous year though he still worked for Logan, Smith and Marjoribanks. Johnny Pike was his constant companion. Byron's flat in Knightsbridge, opposite Harrods, was perfect for a predatory bachelor with tax-free cash in his pocket.

Jack Pike, Johnny's father, racketeer, had put him on the right track towards the end of the Labour Party's five years in office.

"They make the rules but it don't make 'em right, see," he said to Byron. "Just 'cause the majority don't 'ave no money, don't give 'em rights to make laws to steal my money. Who ever thought of being daft enough to go into business and pay some other bleeder nineteen-and-six-pence in the pound for doin' nothin', see? Bein' outside the law, so to speak, means bein' outside the income tax act which suits me. Thing is, we got to get the money where the government don't know, which is where you come in, Byron. You watch those money people in the City to see how we can filter our money and whatever you filter for Jack Pike I'll give you two and a half per cent in cash, but it got to be legal when it come out the other end. The government makes all them laws to benefit the politicians, and it's up to us to find the ways round."

For three years, Byron studied the problem while he learnt the trade of merchant banking. Exchange control regulations brought in by the socialists to stem the flight of sterling prevented money being transferred overseas through the banks. Even banking the cash earned by Jack Pike's rackets in prostitution, peep shows and pornography would have left a trail for the taxman. Money collected in US dollars was easy to send out to Switzerland where the bank accounts were numbered and private. The problem was the bulk of the money in British pounds.

Britain under the new Tory government of Anthony Eden, who had taken over as prime minister when Winston Churchill retired for the second time, was determined to attract foreign investment into the country still ravaged by the consequences of war and the constant flow of money and people to America: war debt had mortgaged the empire.

Byron's first exercise was to create a series of dummy companies in England with the shares owned in Switzerland, through the numbered account into which Jack Pike's smuggled US dollars flowed. The dummy companies then imported goods into England against letters of credit paid for in cash from the Pike rackets in England which were then paid into Jack's numbered bank account in Switzerland, less the actual cost of the goods. The dummy companies grossly overpaid for the imports. The fraud was in the certified invoice which overstated the importation.

Should a dummy company be found out by the British police it would have been dropped and the Swiss exporter accused of short delivery. The police would also find untraceable cash had been used to create the letter of credit. The trail stopped with the cash in England and the unbreakable numbered bank account in Switzerland. No finger could ever point at Jack Pike. The gnomes in Switzerland were growing rich under their banking laws of non-disclosure. As Jack Pike said, it was his money anyway.

After the first ten transactions had run smoothly, Byron knew he was going to be rich. His front of legitimacy was maintained at Logan, Smith and Marjoribanks and the word was spread that the source of Byron's new wealth was Red Langton. He earned cash and spent cash and Byron's private life ran as smoothly as the companies that laundered Jack Pike's money into Switzerland.

VIRGINIA STEPPING AND FANNY TRY shared a one-room flat three streets behind Byron and worked as sales girls at Harrods, Virginia in cosmetics and Fanny in lingerie. Emblazoned on the entrance to their flat was the invitation 'Stepping and Try'.

Byron had met Fanny when he was walking down Kensington High Street with a bag of groceries, entranced by a tight, rhythmic movement coming from within a tight pencil skirt. When the young lady turned fortuitously into Byron's street he caught a flash of firm, tight breasts and followed.

The girl turned round and snapped at him. "You following me?"

"Actually this is my block of flats," he said and began to walk up the short flight of steps towards the ornate entrance to Buckingham Court. When he reached the top, he smiled. "And you're welcome to come up for a drink. I'm Byron Langton," he said, giving her a dazzling smile.

She had turned round to look up at him. Flicking her long, brown hair back over her shoulders she gave him a fixed glare before striding on down the street. She had very long legs and the walk of a cat.

Byron shrugged his shoulders and let himself into the foyer of the block of flats.

Not ten minutes later his phone rang in the flat and a strange voice, female, asked him if his name was Byron Langton.

"Who's that?" he questioned lightly.

"Virginia Stepping. My flatmate is a little shy. You just met her in the street... Do you have a friend?"

"The one with the tight..."

"With a chaperone she would be happy to come for a drink, probably several drinks..."

"Johnny will be here in half an hour. We were going out to eat. Seven o'clock. Number forty-seven. What's your friend's name?"

"Fanny Try."

"*Is* that her real name?"

"Checked her passport." The girl let out a small giggle. "What's he like?"

"No girl I ever knew was disappointed."

"We were just saying the weekend looked disappointing."

"So were we."

They laughed and put down their phones. Byron dialled Johnny Pike.

"If the flatmate looks like the one I saw in the street, you're in luck, Johnny boy. Seven o'clock."

Byron disliked jazz clubs or any other place of noise when he was chatting up a girl, believing talk, expensive food and wine were the way to sexual gratification. Two drinks in the flat and a taxi to a small Polish restaurant that kept their vodka in the freezer was followed by more drinks at Buckingham Court. When Fanny helped him fill the second ice bucket in the kitchen, they heard the click of the front door and found an empty lounge, the music playing softly.

"Blind dates don't always work for Virginia," was all she said as she put down the ice bucket, picked up their wine glasses and said over her shoulder, "I enjoyed this evening."

Byron followed her into the bedroom and closed the door out of habit. When he turned, Fanny's dress was on the floor.

"Do you like the lights on or off?" she asked.

"On."

"Good." She climbed into bed and smiled at him. In no hurry, Byron took off his three-piece suit, his shirt and his socks. "Do you want the wine?"

"Not really."

It was a perfect weekend for both of them and they never once mentioned how clever it was of Fanny to remember his name and look it up in the telephone book.

Two weeks later he called for Fanny. She was out.

"Come on over, it's my turn," said Virginia, who was dressed to go out.

"What about Johnny?"

"Who do you think's with Fanny? Good things have to be shared. That's friendship. None of us want to be serious. We still have a lot of living to do. You can take me to that little Polish restaurant. Fanny said the Polish vodka did something strange and nice. One day we'll be old. Come, lover. Let the weekend begin. I'm hungry."

Two weeks later Virginia suggested Byron throw a small party in his flat for fourteen couples. Fanny and Virginia had invited five of their girlfriends and would he and Johnny invite five nice young men. She smiled at him sweetly and he understood.

"You won't be disappointed, lover."

Johnny selected three friends and Byron two, all of whom were making money in the new, revitalised London. The party split up at nine for the guests to pair off and go out to dinner in their separate ways. The arrangement was the beginning of a long friendship with Virginia and Fanny, Stepping and Try.

FOR WILL LANGTON, the best years of his life were not his schooldays. Stanmore had been a disaster. Years later, when Will looked back on his life and the four years of Stanmore purgatory, he told Hilary Bains, the group captain's adopted son who had suffered the same indignations, that the modern reform schools would not be able to get away with the public school system that the wealthy thought essential to their children's careers. The school stuffed the boys fifty-two to a dormitory, half-starved them, prefects beat them for so much as putting their hands in their pockets three times and bigger boys bullied while masters turned a blind eye. If the child happened to be a pretty boy, slight, called the runt, like Will, he was the target of every pervert, senior boy or master.

Will's slight build and bad eyes stopped him playing competitive sport, his work was clouded by the vague theory of wanting to be a painter, but, worst of all, he refused to join in the popularity stakes and say nice things about people he hated. People called him a misfit but Will told Hilary there were some things a boy did not wish to fit into and boarding school at Stanmore was one of them.

The summer after leaving school brought the turning point in Will's life. At last he had begun to grow and the violet eyes, softer and warmer than the twins', were attractive to the opposite sex. He had been almost eighteen and still licking his metaphorical wounds, spending most of the summer days at Dancing Ledge, breathing the clean air of freedom and wondering what he was going to do with the rest of his life. It was a rare warm summer and the tall kelp of the rocks, washed by a gentle sea, nodded their heads in sympathy with Will's mood of relieved contentment. The rock pool that had been carved out of the solid rock for the evacuated kids in the war was perfection.

For most of his time he was alone on the slim strip of level rock that ended at the swaying heads of the kelp, the small, sea-washed pool in the middle sparkling back at the sun with Will's cave, one blind eye, watching all the beauty of sea and sky, rock and gulls and the slim, good-looking boy entering his manhood, tanned to the colour of hazelnut, hair bleached almost blond by the sun.

Byron, for Will, had become an enigma and Will was convinced his brother would become a very rich man or end up in jail. On fleeting weekend visits, Byron told him all about the wining and dining and the name of the current girl; and even Will's mathematics suggested a problem on the salary of a post-war clerk. Will rather hoped his brother was boasting, but that had never been Byron's style.

"Come up to London and we'll find you a girl."

"Who's we, Byron?"

"Johnny Pike. You'll like him."

Everything came back to Johnny Pike.

The conversation he overheard between his father and brother had not been complimentary about the Pikes, especially the father who the group captain referred to as a big-time crook. Everyone had seemed to sense there was something not quite right.

Randolph was now helping to run the farm, plodding along as usual, giving no one even a thought or worry. He had even married, to everyone's surprise, a very nice, very dull girl whose father was an accountant in Poole, and both of them were as happy as if he was the King of England and she was his Queen.

Where Josephine looked miserable, her sister-in-law, Anna, looked happy. Josephine's hair was cropped severely, she wore no make-up, what looked like sackcloth for clothes and maintained a constant outflow of anti-establishment rhetoric that Will found boring. The last time Josephine brought a man to Langton Manor had been the year of his first racing bicycle. Since that Christmas it had been several women, most of them a good bit older than his sister, all of whom gave Will the shivers.

SHE HAD an elfin face and wavy hair the colour of autumn, and she appeared at Dancing Ledge towards the middle of August, just with her parents and then on her own. They had exchanged a flow of glances across the rock but were too shy to talk.

It was the rarest, sweetest moment of his life and he was to take it to his grave. The joining of hands was outside mortal understanding and within a week they had told each other every thought they had ever had. It was the gentlest of purest love, alone in their world.

Her parents found them kissing on the sun-blessed rocks, barely clothed in bathing costumes and tore them physically apart, snatching the beauty and shattering it with filth.

It was all over and Will was never to see her again, except in his mind. In their youthful bliss he had never heard her surname or any beginning of an address. The girl's family had been staying in a farmer's caravan and the farmer had no idea where the three had gone.

"Paid cash, Will. How I like it. No questions. No tax. You lost something?"

"Probably my life."

Then the hope was she would follow him and find her way to Langton Manor.

When winter came he packed two small bags, kissed his mother, shook hands with his father and Granda and followed in the wake of Hilary Bains to Africa, a self-inflicted exile. It was the start of his odyssey through life.

Nothing, but nothing was ever to prove more important than the girl.

Granda gave him a lift to the main road. A shaft of sunlight had penetrated the winter clouds and touched the old car and the men, one old, one young standing awkwardly for a last goodbye. The family had been told a week before that Granda was dying of cancer.

"Life is an adventure, grandson. Some of them good, some of them not so good." The old man was bent and in pain. "And if it were not for this growth inside me I'd have a mind to come along. Now go and take the Langtons with you in your genes. I scraped up five hundred pounds. It's probably all you will get from the family. The price of being a younger son. Now, God be with you and get out of my sight before you see an old man cry."

In slow stages, Will hitched lifts around the coast to Dover. The cross-channel boat to Calais took four hours, the seas heavy, the old boat fighting the strong headwinds. Despite the windfall from his grandfather, the cheapest passage to East Africa was still in his mind, hitching lifts across Europe to Trieste in Italy and taking a cargo boat across the Mediterranean and through the Suez Canal. Two days into France, the excitement of youth had evaporated with the gloom of death and the pain that lay shattered on the rocks of Dancing Ledge.

Back at Langton Manor, while Will was paying his passage on a Greek cargo boat that was tramping around Africa, Will's call-up papers for the army arrived, the summons to his two years of national service. The group captain sent it back marked 'Gone abroad – forwarding address unknown'.

There was no music playing, just the cursing of the Greek captain. The boat was small, with peeling paint and reeking bilges but at least it was cheap. He was more lonely than at any moment of his life.

He was sick for three days from the bad food and water and only watched the stars at night when the boat drifted along the British–French-built canal with the Egyptian desert on either side. There was an eternity in the depth of the sky he had not seen before.

He had purchased a money belt at Dover and with Granda's gift strapped to his skin he walked the streets of Port Said on the Suez Canal and then the boat broke away from Arabia and turned a heavy head for the Horn of Africa. At Mogadishu, in Italian Somaliland, Will felt the warm, soft air of Africa for the first time. The boat had kept out to sea and lighters shifted the small cargo back and forth. When he woke in the morning, they were well out to sea, the shore of Africa distant on the starboard side. His stomach had recovered.

Maybe, he thought, just maybe there was some life after death and the mental vision of her screaming parents took passage with the ship's wake and left him empty and sad.

. . .

HILARY BAINS TRUDGED out to the long drop, checked it carefully for snakes, took down his trousers and sat on the throne. He had grown used to the flies and smell but not the magnificent view from the hill where he sat with his trousers round his ankles and the wide Zambezi River flowing below in constant pressure towards its destination in the unknown, distant sea.

The mission station outside Lealui, Paramount Chief Mwene Kandala III's winter capital, was a desolate affair consisting of two broken-down thatched huts for the priest, a tin shed for the school/clinic, a patch of ground where Hilary tried to grow vegetables mostly eaten by buck, baboons and bush pigs, and an open patch under a spreading acacia tree where Hilary held classes that did not amount to much as his knowledge of Lozi, the language spoken in the British Protectorate of Barotseland, was basic and the children were more interested in the free lunch than the learning.

The London Missionary Society had sent him to Africa to preach the word of God but all he had been able to do was carry on with the rudimentary clinic and try and teach the children. For weeks on end Hilary did not speak English or have any kind of conversation. The few Europeans who lived in Barotseland, in the west of Northern Rhodesia, were eleven miles southeast of Mongu where the British Commissioner conducted his administration. The only way for Hilary to reach Mongu was to walk as the Land Rover promised to him in London six months earlier had not arrived. He was cut off in the middle of nowhere, the previous priest having died of malaria the week before Hilary arrived. His letters to London were sent to Mongu with one of the elder children of the mission who asked at the magistrates' court for return mail. For three months there had been silence. Twice Hilary himself had gone down with malaria and dosed himself to recovery, sweating it out under the crumbling thatch, an old retainer, the mission's only convert, cooking his food. Hilary's belief in God was stretched to the limit. On both occasions, he had thought he was going to die.

THE RAILWAY STATION at Beira was teeming with black people, mostly dressed in rags. A massive steam engine of Rhodesia Railways was blowing smoke and steam over the third-class passengers that were crushed into the three forward carriages. The last carriage, after the second-class coaches, was first class and Will Langton had a compartment to himself with plush green leather seats and two sleeping bunks at shoulder height below the luggage racks.

The Greek boat had sailed on down to Lourenço Marques and left Will on the dockside with his two small bags and no knowledge of Portuguese. Searching the dockside, Will found the largest building and the sign 'Manica Trading Company Limited' and found an Englishman to not only give him a cup of tea but drive him to the railway station and see him into the carriage for Salisbury where he would change trains for Bulawayo and Livingstone.

"Mongu, old chap? Why on earth do you want to go to Mongu?" The Englishman at Manica Trading was rather short and bald together with his all-pervasive helpfulness. "Back end of beyond, old boy. You'll have to go to Livingstone. Did hear once there's a narrow gauge railway to a timber mill near Mongu, but no idea if they take passengers. Could be some kind of trading boat going upriver. Why on earth do you want to go to Mongu?"

"Brother's a missionary."

"Poor sod."

As the guard blew two sharp whistles, the carriage door was wrenched open and a huge man threw in two duffle bags and a leather gun case before turning sideways and pushing himself into the compartment, his head just below the top of the door. Using the leather window strap, the man slammed the door shut, wound down the window to the bottom and looked out at the platform, swearing in a language Will had never heard before. The train lurched forward, and the man collapsed onto the inadequate seat and stared at Will.

Frightened, Will kept his own counsel. The man's hair was a soft, wavy off-blond, as was his full beard. The softness of the hair was in contrast to the rest of the bulk that bulged out of the khaki trousers and khaki shirt, the underarms of the short-sleeved shirt wet with sweat and the sleeves fighting the man's biceps for survival. Will found the age of the man was difficult to guess.

The man took a piece of hard black dried meat from inside his shirt and began to tear at it with fanged teeth, chewing with satisfaction. Will watched him like a spring hare watching a snake, mesmerised. The train stopped and lurched, lurched and stopped, the steam engine belching up its strength to drag the carriages out of Beira across the Pungwe Flats. The big man took another piece of dried meat out of his sweaty shirt and offered it to Will, the girth of the proffered arm bigger than Will's thigh. Again the strange language and Will shook his head.

"I can only speak English," Will squeaked and for the first time the light blue eyes opposite took on a twinge of merriment. The big man put the biltong back inside his shirt.

"Where are you going, *kerel*?"

"Mongu," said Will, apprehensively.

The man laughed out loud. "Hannes Potgieter. Trader. Hunter. Whatever, man. What they call you?"

"William Langton. Will Langton... I've just arrived from England."

The big man laughed again and choked on a piece of dried meat that had stuck in his throat. "You don't say," he said and chewed some more. "How you going to get from Livingstone to Mongu?"

"I don't know."

"Maybe we will see about that," he said to himself. "What you going to do in Mongu?"

"Visit a sort of brother. Reverend Hilary Bains."

"Sort of brother, hey... And then?"

"I don't know."

"You don't seem to know much."

"I'm only eighteen... just," added Will.

"And straight out from England."

"Yes."

"Well I never."

After a long silence Will thought of something to say.

"I say, what language were you speaking when you got into the train?" His voice was light and, Will hoped, free of nervousness.

"Afrikaans." Will looked blank. "Language of the Boers." Will still looked blank. "You heard of the Boer War, Englishman?"

"Yes," squeaked Will.

"Fifty-three years ago. Not so long, really. My grandpappy still has his Boer War rifle. Mauser. Said he killed four Englishmen but I don't know." The man was grinning at him. "Don't think you'd have lasted long."

"I don't think so either," said Will and impulsively put out his hand which was enveloped in a paw the size of a York ham.

The smell of coal smoke permeated the carriage, but it was too hot to close the window. On either side of the train stretched the floodwaters of the Pungwe River, trees half-drowned, water birds scattering from the noise of the train. The big man had closed his eyes and appeared to be asleep. The rhythm of the train and track, iron on iron, made Will drowsy and when he woke there was dense bush on either side of the train and Hannes Potgieter was sprawled uncomfortably in the too-small seat, fast asleep, the half-chewed stick of biltong fallen from his fingers onto the carpet. Threatening, dark clouds billowed above the smoke-spewing funnel from the train engine and the first big blobs of rain were slanting through the open window into the carriage.

The crash of thunder sent Will bolt upright in his seat. Lightning forked far away in the bush, followed by thunderous claps as the tropical storm raged. Will was too frightened to close the window. Solid rain was pouring onto the big man's head and down his beard and still the stomach rose and fell. Three thunder crashes in quick succession sent the rain into a frenzy and Will lost sight of the trees. The sky darkened. A big, pink tongue broke from the big man's mouth and licked to the far reaches of the moustache and beard and then the eyes came open and the right one winked.

"*Lekker* rain, man. If I was in my bush camp and the rain comes like this, I run out naked and make a lot of noise."

"The lightning?" asked Will, fearfully watching the violent display outside the train window.

"What's the difference?... No rain in Africa, we all die."

The storm finished as quickly as it came and the clouds broke open to the clear blue sky of Africa. Will settled back in the green leather seat and watched the Afrikaner sleeping again, the matted wet hair drying in the wind from the open window, the click-clack of the rails lulling Will's mind and the pangs of hunger that had grown with the sight of the half-chewed, dry meat lying on the floor of the carriage at his feet. Then Will Langton slept, to be chased through the dark, primeval forest by a giant the size of a mountain who stood on the top of the trees, plucking at Will running for dear life along the tangled forest path. When he woke, after a long sleep, the big man was standing at the window looking out onto a railway station and the train had come to rest. On the opposite side, the compartment door to the corridor slid open and a swarthy man in uniform asked for his passport. Before Will could pick up his wits and ask for a place to buy food, the train was moving again. The piece of dried meat was still on the floor.

"These trains may be first class but the service is *kak*," said the Afrikaner, watching him with amusement. "You didn't bring no food, did you?"

"No." This time when the meat came out of the shirt, Will took it gratefully and tore a strip off with his teeth and chewed. Hannes bent down and picked up the piece from the floor, rubbed it on the front of his khaki shirt and carried on eating.

"We Boers lived off this when we were fighting you Brits. Why you could never catch us. A horse, a rifle, a few sticks of biltong. No blerry great supply wagons. Twenty thousand Boers and half a million Brits. All because of a few sticks of dried meat. Makes you want to laugh."

They had passed over the border from Portuguese East Africa into the Federation of Rhodesia and Nyasaland, the self-governing British state that encompassed Northern and Southern Rhodesia and Nyasaland. As the sun was setting deep in the highveld, silhouetting the msasa trees that covered the fertile plains on either side of the train, Will watched the first houses of Salisbury, the federal capital, break the pattern of trees and elephant grass.

"You'd better come with me, *kerel*, or you will get lost," was all the big man said at Salisbury station.

Gratefully, Will picked up his bags and followed a man he knew nothing about onto the platform.

"We can walk to Meikles Hotel. First you can buy me a cold beer and then I'll buy you a meal, Englishman."

Like a puppy dog following its master, Will faithfully followed the hulk along the darkening streets of Salisbury, grateful for the protection, expecting a lion to jump out of the shadows at any moment.

The main room through the entrance of the hotel was a vast affair with a high domed ceiling from the centre of which hung the largest crystal chandelier Will had ever seen. Strewn through the room were tables and chairs and off to the left an open door led into a bar. Alcoves fed off the main room with more tables and chairs. All but one of the tables were occupied.

Heads turned to look at Hannes Potgieter, and Will thought it was the sheer size of the man that caused the conversations to falter as he followed him to the empty table on the other side of the room. An old, fat African, wearing a red fez and red sash appeared at the table as they sat down.

"Guru, bring us two cold beers and my friend is paying."

The black man went off and came back in seconds with two bottles of beer and one glass, putting the tray down on the table. Will was handed the slip. One shilling and fourpence for two beers; somewhat cheaper, Will thought, than the Greyhound Hotel at Corfe Castle where his grandfather also drank. Will fumbled in his pocket and came up with one and sixpence which he offered to the smiling black man.

"English money?" said he, giving it back.

"Give him an English pound and he will change it for you at the desk." The enormous hand stretched forward, took up the bottle and within ten seconds the Afrikaner had sucked the bottle dry. Will found a pound note in his money belt, gave it to the waiter and poured out his beer into the glass. The second round was ordered before Will had taken his first sip.

"I say, that is rather good," said Will putting down a half-empty glass. Their bags and the gun case were by then behind the reception desk while the manager tried to find them a room.

The first man to come across to their table was as weatherbeaten as Hannes Potgieter, with a grizzled, grey-streaked beard. The indifference the man showed the big man puzzled Will at first. The second man showed the same manner and by the time the third round arrived and Will had put his change in Rhodesian currency into his money belt, there were seven men at the table, all of whom had been formally introduced to 'the Englishman'. No one thought it strange to find a young man, a stranger, at the table and Will relaxed. Everyone seemed to know Hannes Potgieter and when the manager of the hotel brought them their room keys with apologies for being so long, Will knew he had struck gold. The only round he was allowed to buy all night was the first one. Large plates of sandwiches were brought to the table, followed by wine and more people.

When the big man got him up to his room, he opened the door and then let him go. Still giving thanks with slurred, happy words, Will Langton tottered into his room and collapsed on the bed fully clothed, sleeping the night without a snore or a dream.

The harsh glare of the African sun through the open window woke him in the morning. For the first few moments of consciousness he could not remember where he was and then he panicked, clutching at his money belt, frantically unzipping it to find the blessed money he thought would have been stolen from a drunken boy lying face down on a bed. Then he saw his bags, neatly together on a low trestle waiting to be opened.

Turning over and sitting up he blinked in the sunlight and got up to draw the curtain across the slanting ray of sun. His mouth felt like the bottom of a parrot's cage. The gods had looked after him. It was half-past six in the morning. A door from his bedroom led into a small bathroom, something he had not seen for weeks. Both taps worked, spewing out fresh, clean water, filling his bath in less than a minute. Removing the clothes of his journey, he sank into the warm water and sighed with pleasure, soaping himself clean from head to toe.

With clean teeth and fresh clothes, Will ventured into the new strange world to find himself some breakfast, his sun-bleached hair slicked back behind his ears. The soft warmth of the bath had taken away his headache. A long landing led him to the carpeted stairs, with wooden banisters to guide him down to the ground floor where he found the reception desk.

"Mr Potgieter is waiting for you in the dining room, sir. I understand you will be staying another night."

"I will?"

"Your train leaves for Bulawayo and Livingstone tomorrow."

"It does?"

"I personally made the reservations."

"Thank you."

"My pleasure. The dining room is through the doors over there."

Will followed the instructions and the big man waved him to a seat.

"I think I would like to apologise..." Will began.

"For a lad of eighteen, just, you did well last night, *kerel*."

"I told you my age?"

"That one on the train. She must have been very beautiful." Will looked at him quizzically. "From Livingstone you can come upriver on my boat. You can either join the priest or work for me without pay and learn about the bush... You asked for a job last night, if you remember?"

"After the sandwiches, I have something of a blank."

"You said you could shoot straight."

"That I can."

"Ride a horse?"

Will nodded.

"Which Missionary Society is this sort of brother of yours? Capuchin Fathers, Paris Missionary Society?"

"London Missionary Society, I think I told you in the train."

"Maybe you did, maybe you didn't... *Kerel*... There are more do-gooders in Africa than is good for Africa. No matter. Every man thinks he is different... You see, I lost my wife last year. Bad thing for a man to be lonely. You can mark my word... Went down to Cape Town to see her folks. Came up the coast to Beira by *Bloemfontein Castle*."

Will let the silence drift away.

"Why does everyone know you?" he said at length.

"Done a bit of hunting. The Americans, Germans, British, they all come to my camp to hunt. I've been hunting thirty-five years. Chief Mwene Kandala's grandfather gave me permission. I'm the only white hunter in Barotseland, all sixty-five thousand square miles. I shoot and trade the skins and take out the rich from New York and London. Why my English is good for an Afrikaner... How long this brother been out of England?"

"Six months."

"How long I've been away... Have some breakfast... We've a day to wait."

"They told me at the desk. They seem to have booked my seat on the train, Mr Potgieter."

"Call me Hannes, it's short for Johannes."

THE MOSQUITOES WERE as thick as fleas on a camel. The rain had been continuous for a week. The small hill with the tin-roofed schoolroom was surrounded by floodwater and the mission was empty of children. A small troop of vervet monkeys had taken refuge on the high ground and chattered miserably in the acacia tree that overhung Hilary's hut. Inside, Hilary had been delirious for three days and the old African was sure the white man was going to die. Every four hours he forced quinine into the young man's mouth but most of it spilt on the sodden pillow and dripped onto the cow-dung floor. The old man prayed to his new God and waited for death with the stoicism of his race. He had seen four of them come and die in the hut above the big river. They were strange people, these men of the new God, and he wondered what his ancestors thought of them, the ancestors he secretly spoke to in his dreams. Most of his people had left after the first rains for the chief's summer place at Namushakende where the ground was high above the floodwater of the great Zambezi River. The foolish white man did not understand the ways of Africa.

On the fourth day, as if God himself had come into the hut, Hilary woke from his fever and took the black man's hand.

"Thank you... God has been good to us... Will you pray with me?" Obedient to the miracle, the black man knelt on the dung floor at the bedside and both of them gave thanks to God.

ON THE FOURTH day of Will's journey through Central Africa, the train rumbled over the steel bridge high above the Zambezi River gorge. On the corridor side of the train where Will was standing enthralled, the sun was shining through the billowing mist of water flung a hundred metres into the air by the plunge of the river over the Victoria Falls, eighty metres of cascading green water hurtling down into the gorge. A perfect rainbow beckoned to Will.

Five minutes later they disembarked at Livingstone station, Will having not said a word. The greatest waterfall on earth had been awesome to behold, his young mind unable to comprehend the power of the river.

"Is it the priest or me, *kerel*?" asked Hannes when their bags and the gun case were in the taxi that would take them upriver of the Falls to the flat-bottomed boat that would ferry them into Barotseland.

"If you will teach me, Hannes, I would like to learn the ways of the bush. Hilary will have his friends in the Church and find me a nuisance. I didn't really know what I was going to do on the mission station now I am so close. From England, just going to Africa was enough."

"Good, we have many supplies to take on board and then we face the rapids and in three weeks' time four Americans will be flying into the aerodrome at Mongu. We pick them up in two Land Rovers... Can you drive, *kerel*?"

"Yes, I can drive."

"From Mongu, you visit this Hilary Bains whose parents died in the war."

THE BOAT CONSISTED of two steel pods, ten metres long and welded airtight, the front ends of the pods coming to a point. A steel structure held the pods parallel to each other and what looked to Will like a hut had been built across the pods. At the back were two powerful outboard motors and Will guessed the draught of the boat at less than half a metre. It took them a day and the following morning to buy and stow the stores.

The journey began when the sun was high overhead and even the roar of the main outboard engine could not drown out the thunder of the Falls a kilometre downriver. On the first island they passed, crowded with phoenix palms, a crocodile eight metres long slithered into the water and for an hour followed them upstream. Will saw elephants on both sides of the river behind the tall reeds and elephant grass. Waterfowl he had never seen before were everywhere around the slow-flowing river that pushed dead trees and clumps of grass endlessly downstream, ever questing the unknown sea. It was a magical first experience he would never forget, wellbeing enveloping his mind and body.

For two days they beat upriver and with great respect, Will watched the skill and strength of the big man as Hannes navigated the rushing rapids studded with black-wet rocks, the flotsam of whole trees stuck in the rush of water waiting to twist and drown their pontoon boat. The big man roared with laughter at the challenge, shouting his lungs out above the rage of the rapids until he found the calm water above and switched off the second engine.

At night they camped on the high ground above the swollen river. The sinking sun shot rays of pink light at the tufted clouds behind the trees, glowing red and fading, the light paling duck-egg blue before the orange glow spread from the sunken sun and silhouetted the palms and fever trees. The sounds of Africa were deafening from all around, grunts from the hippos in the water mingling with the last calls of a hundred birds.

Hannes made up a great fire, the flickering flame-light searching for the tops of the acacia tree.

The stars were dominant in the night sky, layer upon layer of the universe crowding the black void of deep space, galaxy upon galaxy, drawing

Will's mind beyond his puny understanding of the meaning of infinity, on forever leaving earth a minute nothing in the great unknown design, the molecules of Will's own body billions of years old from the spatial dust, the matter of himself never leaving the earth but forming the cells of future life in an endless universe.

"Africa makes me feel so small," he said to himself.

"Ja, *kerel*," said Hannes, searching the night sky, "the reason for our own existence is so insignificant. Where we are, I don't know. Why, I don't know. No one ever found out... That 'whoo-oo-hoop' is a hyena calling for a mate, always calling for a mate. Hitch your mosquito net to the tree if you don't want the bastards to eat you alive. We keep the fire going all night or the shumba will be calling."

"Shumba?"

"Simba. Shumba. Whatever. The lion. This is lion country, *kerel*. Keep that rifle ready to fire. You can spend twenty years in the bush without a problem... Never drop your guard. Then you'll grow to an old man."

The big man stood up, and the fire threw his shadow across the river, its surface black and ominous, plopping with night sounds, the surging mass of water pushing at the night and mirroring the stars. "Hell, man, it's great to be back in the real Africa. Makes a man want to be alive. Makes it all worthwhile."

Will went to sleep to the sound of a thousand castanets, river frogs wooing each other in the night, mingling with the screech of tree crickets grinding their back legs, frogs and cicadas eternally calling for a mate to keep the pulse of new life flowing with the river.

BIRDSONG, the joy to dawn, woke Will from a dreamless sleep. The fire was burning down and Hannes was nowhere to be seen. Fear and panic gripped his stomach as he pushed out of the mosquito net, the rifle gripped in his right hand. The bright new sun was heaving itself from behind the phoenix palms, and white fleecy clouds mirrored themselves in the flowing water of the river. Nothing had changed. Fear left him with the balm of dawn, the new dawn.

Ten minutes went by while the sun came up over the trees and the heat rose with the day, the sun burning Will's unprotected legs and arms. Afraid to call, he waited.

The big man strode through the trees from the direction of the river.

"Get out the frying pan, Englishman. We eat like two kings for breakfast. Look at these beauties." One hand holding out two large fish hooked by the gills, the rifle gripped in the other, he chuckled. "Fresh chessa. River bream. Best fish in the world. We scale, fillet and eat in that order... Where's my coffee?"

"Coming, boss." Will was happier than at any time since being chased off Dancing Ledge by angry parents.

HANNES POTGIETER'S permanent hunting camp was on the banks of the river where the waters bent away between two hills in a wide sweep, leaving calm water down below the camp. Here a jetty trod out into the flow giving them landfall on the morning of the fourth day. Three black men were waiting on the jetty to catch the rope Will threw them as Hannes reversed the engine and bumped the right-hand pod against the strong wood of the jetty. Hannes greeted his trackers in Lozi, and the smiles on their faces would have lit a campfire.

"Come, Englishman, I show you your new home... They will empty the boat. Maybe two bottles of whisky will be lost in the river as they unpack but that is good... Every man needs his reward. Maybe they are more pleased to see the whisky than me. Who knows and does it matter? We understand each other. In the bush, hunting, we understand each other very well."

Will followed his first employer up the path from the river, up the hill that guarded the bend of calm water, stopping once to look back at the view over the riverine trees to the endless distance of the bush and the mopani forests, silent, pressed down by the heat of the tropical sun. Sweat was dripping inside his shirt but he smiled with pleasure. The top of the hill showed him a plateau giving a view over the mopani forest from the north bank of the river, over the tops of endless trees running into the distant, shimmering heat haze to a distant range of hills. They entered the gate in the fence of thorn thicket overgrown with sisal plants, making the wide enclosure as impregnable as a fort. A massive two-storey house, open on all sides beneath a single, thick new thatch showed Will an upper deck with cane chairs, a cane bar and the trophy heads of all the big game of Africa.

"For the tourists," explained Hannes, as they mounted the wooden steps to the upper deck. "They like them, I don't. But a man has to live. All of us are killing something. Words have killed more happiness than guns."

Down below, the enclosure was full of tame wild animals and birds.

"Just watch that Goliath heron. His beak is sharper than a razor. The small house over there will be yours, next to the trackers' huts. Now we have a drink to welcome us home, Englishman. You see, I like to drink and I don't like to drink alone. You like it where I live, *kerel*? The ice is in the freezer.

Works on paraffin. Your job, the ice. First we teach you to drink whisky and then we teach you the bush."

Will wanted to say thank you, but nothing came out of his mouth. He turned away from the big man as tears of joy and sorrow flowed gently down his cheeks. He stood for a moment looking out over the endless bush of Africa, then wiped away the brief tears and went to the freezer and cracked open the ice.

5

---

*T*he permanent building at the camp was fifty kilometres down the river from Mongu and by the end of March, a week before the party of Americans were due to fly in from Salisbury en route from New York, the rains had stopped and the floodwaters of the Zambezi were slowly returning to the river. The two weeks of intense training had given Will a new and healthy respect for the African bush.

The three trackers had been renamed by Hannes Potgieter to make his life easy. In order of seniority earned by their knowledge in the wilds, they were called Sixpence, Fourpence and Onepenny, or Six, Four and One in an emergency.

The learning day began for Will the moment he stepped out of his sleeping hut to pinpoint the Goliath heron. The bird, whose snake-like head stood above stalk-like legs a metre and a half from the ground, hated Will with a dedicated passion. The third day the bird had stalked Will, one silent, stealthy foot at a time, the snake-like long neck with the small head and pointed beak waiting its chance for Will to wash his face under the tap, delicious cold river water from the header tank, and then the bird struck at his bent behind, nipping him hard on the right buttock, drawing blood and making Will howl with pain. Will had been naked apart from his underpants. The tame impala ram ran away with the goat and the two Egyptian geese honked in alarm.

"Cheeky little bugger," called Hannes as Will disappeared back into his hut to tend his wound.

The gentle rabbits and seagulls of Langton Manor were as far away as the moon.

The two Land Rovers were needed for the journey to Mongu as the Americans were four in the party.

"Two hunters and two what they call wives," explained Hannes. "The men are mostly overweight and the 'wives' twenty years younger and the macho hunting trip is to show off their masculinity. People have some strange ways of chasing women, *kerel*."

"Hannes, you asked me if I could drive but not if I had a licence. I don't."

"Don't worry, we'll get you a licence in Mongu. That policeman owes me a favour."

The road to Mongu was a game track in and around the tall mopani trees, the track enlarged by the wheels of the Land Rover over the years. The track was wet in many places and they ground through in four-wheel drive, reaching Mongu an hour before the plane was due to arrive. Mongu was the nearest thing to a frontier town Will had ever seen, consisting of the residency, magistrates' court, hospital, the club, police station and a motley crew of bungalows for the seventy British who administered an area larger than Wales. The two Land Rovers drew up at the police station, side by side, covered in dust and mud, with high, game-viewing seats at the back waiting for the passengers.

"Wait here, Englishman," said Hannes and disappeared into the small police station.

Will waited in trepidation, thinking of his driving test, while he inspected the short, single, one-lane tarred road of Mongu.

A man in an immaculate uniform with a black leather Sam Browne and black leather swagger stick, his peaked hat straight as an arrow, walked down the path from the police station, his clear blue eyes fixed on Will sitting in the open Land Rover. The man stopped and looked at him in silence.

"Are you William Langton?"

"Yes, sir," replied Will in quick reaction to the tone of authority.

"Did you just drive thirty miles through the bush from Mr Potgieter's camp?"

"Yes, sir."

"May I see your driving licence?" The policeman's face did not flicker and the inside of Will's stomach dropped on the floor.

"I don't," Will began to stammer, feeling lost in a wilderness.

"You don't have a licence?"

"No, sir."

"Then you had better accompany me to the station."

"Yes, sir."

The policeman kept a straight face all the way back down the path and into his office where Hannes was sitting behind the policeman's desk, his bulk flowing out of the chair.

"This what you looking for, *kerel*?" and Hannes threw a new driving licence on the table. "When you get to Salisbury, whenever, you get a photograph and stick it in the book."

"But I haven't taken a test," said Will, ever more bewildered.

"Hannes says you drive well for an Englishman," said the policeman with a slight West Country burr. "Better than Onepenny."

Then the two older men burst out laughing. Will picked up the licence and put it in his pocket. Things were definitely different in Africa.

The Mongu aerodrome consisted of a flat piece of ground free of trees, a windsock and what looked like a hut to Will side by side with a petrol tank marked high octane aviation fuel. There was a small herd of buffalo and a large herd of impala grazing on the airfield.

They were greeted at the hut by a young man not much older than Will who informed them the Americans were delayed and arriving the following afternoon, and since apart from the weekly run from Lusaka via Salisbury there was nothing for them to do, they should all go to the club.

"You can stay in my bungalow tonight... We look after our few customers," he said, seeing Will's surprise at the offer. "Airport manager for Central African Airways at Mongu is a job of considerable responsibility. My name's Laurie Hall."

"Will Langton."

"How do you do, old boy. Just got out here?"

"Less than a month."

"How'd you find Hannes?"

"On the train in Beira."

"Lucky man. This man has more influence in Barotseland than his nibs the resident commissioner. Probably has more influence than the prime minister himself... His power comes from the chief. That's his secret. Despite what we British think to the contrary, the paramount chief still runs Barotseland. Oh, there's a wedding on here tomorrow. One of the rangers is marrying a girl from Pretoria. The resident commissioner has declared a public holiday but I'll be here to greet your Americans. You're both invited to the wedding, of course."

"But I don't even know the people," began Will.

"What on earth has that to do with it? You're British, aren't you?"

Leaving the door to the only airport building wide open, Laurie Hall climbed into the passenger seat of Will's Land Rover and folded his arms.

"Follow Hannes. Knows his way to the club rather well."

"What about the animals when the planes land?" asked Will, looking across the runway.

"Either my lads chase them off or the pilot buzzes the runway a few times. Tomorrow he'll have to buzz them off."

"The public holiday?"

"Applies to everyone, of course. British fair play. Can't be two sets of rules, now can there?... You enjoying Africa all right?"

"Very much."

"That's good then. Don't miss England myself one bit. Long live the empire."

"The rules of this club are pretty simple," explained Laurie Hall when they drew up outside the Mongu Club. "Every resident Britisher is obliged to join and any visiting Britisher is an honorary member. The third rule states that the club shall stay open provided two members are capable of standing. To my knowledge the club has never closed."

"Do you know any of the missionaries?"

"Most of them."

"A brother of mine is out here."

"Don't know any Langtons."

"My father adopted him during the war. Hilary's father was Dad's tail gunner and his mother was killed in an air raid. Hilary Bains. London Missionary Society."

"No one's heard of him for months. His area was inundated during the floods so it's not surprising. Take a bit more sunshine to dry out that road. Met him when he flew in the first time. Nice enough chap for a missionary... You and I'd better go and drink on our own while Hannes works his way around the club. Everyone will like to buy him a drink. Now, what are you doing in Barotseland?"

"Well, Hilary I suppose... You might say I ran away from England."

"Don't we all. Now what will you drink?"

"Gin and tonic."

"That's the stuff... Hannes teaching you to drink? You have to drink in Africa. Not much else to do. We get a film shown every four months in the African beer hall, one of the few places with a generator. Another excuse to drink, really, as the damn projector breaks down and then they have to keep changing the reels... The only time you see a woman is on trips back to Salisbury and the competition's pretty steep... Cheers, old boy."

"Cheers...and thanks."

"My pleasure."

WHEN THE TWIN-ENGINED de Havilland Dragon Rapide was due to land, Will was given the job of clearing the runway. For all intents and purposes he was still drunk, though he did remember enjoying himself in the club. Despite many enquiries, no one had heard of Hilary since the first inundation and no one seemed that interested in the missionary anyway. Will would have liked to try to find the mission but drinks in the club and then supper and then drinks in the club until the early morning had prevented a dash down the road.

"Don't get out of your Land Rover," Hannes had warned at the airport.

The twenty-minute chase up and down the runway honking his horn at the animals was a lot of fun and he retreated back to the airport building as the biplane came in to land. Puffs of dust spurted three times as the aircraft bounced and then ran the length of the bush runway before turning and coming to where they were waiting beside the Land Rovers.

"Great night. Thanks for looking after us, Laurie," said Hannes.

"My pleasure."

"You come downriver when you want to shoot crocs, *kerel*... Slim's still getting a good price?"

"Well, yes... Can't live on a CAA salary," and he winked at Will.

As Hannes walked with Will out to the stationary aeroplane where the pilot had opened the door, Hannes looked back at Laurie and waved. "Runs his own cargo business on the quiet. Planes are mostly empty when they go back and the pilots stay with Laurie."

"I think the English call it using their initiative," said Will and turned back to the aeroplane to see two young women out of *Vogue* magazine step onto the runway.

"The 'wives'," explained Hannes.

"Wow," said Will. Despite his vow never to look at another woman in his life, Will found his young hormones dancing in the sun.

By the third evening of the American safari, with Hannes, Onepenny and Sixpence in the bush with the two American hunters shooting for trophies, Will knew the 'wives' had come to Africa for another kind of trophy and he was the target. The weeks of hard living on the boat from England, the struggle upriver, three weeks of intensive training in the African bush with Hannes and the tropical sun had his thin body harder than it had ever been before: the boy had turned into a man. His soft warm violet eyes contrasted the rich brown of his suntanned body. Mostly he had worn shoes and shorts and nothing else and the rapacious New York ladies, straight out of winter, were hungry for a healthy young body even if he was only a learner 'white hunter'. Back home in America the 'learner' would be dropped and his age increased by ten years when they boasted to their friends. Hank and Chuck would by then be back with their real wives displaying the stuffed heads of buffalo and antelope.

Will was completely out of his depth.

Polly was the blonde's name and Cherry, appropriately, the redhead. Looked at closer, after the first flush of excitement off the plane, they were, as Will's mother would have said, mutton dressed as lamb. Even then they were twenty years younger than Hank and Chuck who, Will found out later, had sat in the bush camp under the good shade of a tree with the whisky and told Hannes and the trackers to go out and shoot 'their' trophies. Unfortunately for Will it took five days for Hannes to carry out the order and Will was at his wits' end. Byron would have told him to lie back and enjoy the experience but Byron was not around.

There was Will and there was Fourpence who was giving him no help whatsoever, leaving him alone with the women at every opportunity. After cooking the supper on the outside boma with the roar of lions the other side of the thorn and sisal enclosure, Fourpence was off into his hut not even disguising his smirk. He had done his job for the day and now it was up to the young boss. Had there been a telephone, Will would have called up Laurie Hall for some help.

The 'wives' knew exactly what they were doing and played Will as any cat will play a mouse. Late on the third evening they spiked his drink but the Langton head for alcohol together with the weeks of whisky training let him escape into his sleeping hut where he piled all the furniture behind the door and for the second time in a month passed out face down on the bed fully clothed.

The fourth night they were all over him up on the deck before he could escape to his hut, Polly whispering into his ear that the roar of a lion made her horny. Using the last bit of his wits, clutching at the last straw, Will explained he had picked up syphilis in Port Said on his way out from England and before either of the 'wives' could recover he was out and in his hut but with the furniture hard up against the door.

The next night, the 'big-game hunters' came back in time to save Will's virginity. Will listened in trepidation from the safety of his sleeping hut to the Americans making whoopee. It was either Polly or Cherry who called out loudly to the African night that she was coming time and again, and

Cherry or Polly who screamed every ten minutes. Even the lone hyena outside the enclosure stopped baying at the moon. Finally, from sheer exhaustion, Will went to sleep.

At breakfast, Hank and Chuck looked very satisfied with themselves and gave Will five hundred dollars for looking after the 'wives'. With the bloody animal heads in the back of the second Land Rover heading for the taxidermist in Salisbury, Will watched his first hunting party disappear off down the track with Fourpence driving the second vehicle and Will looking at the pile of American ten-dollar bills in his hand with genuine astonishment.

When Hannes came back with Fourpence that evening only the thick bushy beard hid the grin on his face and Will was too embarrassed to bring up the subject.

"How much did they give you, Englishman?"

"Five hundred dollars... Why, Hannes?"

The big man had his back to Will at the bar, unable to answer or pour his whisky into a glass: the huge shoulders were heaving with suppressed laughter. Will began to laugh, and Fourpence downstairs, all three were laughing hysterically.

THEY PUT Hilary Bains on an improvised stretcher over the game-viewing seats of the Land Rover and drove him to the Mongu airfield. The five-foot-ten man of almost twenty-two weighed less than one hundred pounds. His face was gaunt, sunken; yellow cheeks framed a long sharp nose of skin and bone.

After some difficulty in finding the mission school and clinic, the track having been washed out during the inundation, they found the skeleton trying to tend his flock propped up on a door frame the old African had taken from the school. The conditions were appalling.

The doctor at Mongu hospital looked at Hilary and shook his head. "Most likely more than one tropical disease. Get him to the Salisbury General. They have the equipment and specialised knowledge."

Laurie Hall called up a hospital plane against the five hundred US dollars Will had been given by Hank. Will and Hilary flew to Salisbury Airport where Hilary was taken to hospital. He had slept most of the way under sedation and was met by a father of the London Missionary Society.

"Don't worry, young man. He's now in the hands of God."

"I'll see my brother to the hospital, thank you. I want to know what is wrong with him." The priest looked condescending and let him ride in the mission car that rattled to the hospital, Hilary propped up by Will in the uncomfortable back seat.

Only the following morning, having slept fitfully on a bench in the hospital reception, was Will given the diagnosis.

"Malnutrition, Mr Langton. Starvation actually. Left him wide open for malaria despite the prophylaxis tablets he was taking. Most men would have died. Something like this restores a man's faith in his God. I am going to keep your brother here for at least two weeks and meantime write a letter to the Archbishop of Canterbury. Whatever those people are doing at Lambeth Palace they should know not to leave a young lad in the middle of nowhere with no backup whatsoever. If they don't look after their own properly how can they look after others? Total bloody cock-up."

On the second day, with the flight to Mongu via Lusaka scheduled for the following morning, Hilary was sitting up in the hospital bed, gaunt but cheerful. They had talked for half an hour.

"You Langtons keep saving my life. Tell me about the family."

"Mother's fine. Nothing ever seems to get the better of my mother. Dad still has his nightmares. Hilary, Granda is dying, cancer. He sends you his love as do the others... Byron is up to something he won't tell the family and Mother thinks it's crooked. She says he'll either get rich or land in jail."

"Byron will never land in jail. He is far too smart... And Josephine?"

"Bitter...she's so bitter. Hates anyone with money. Despises anyone who has made a success of their lives, saying they are exploiting the masses. Never has a boyfriend after that Pole or German or whatever he was she brought down that Christmas. Byron says just leave her alone to work out her own problems... Randolph's all right. He married Anna but you know that."

"Letters don't reach my little mission. I'm glad for Randolph and hope they both will be very happy... Now, Will, what are you going to do with your life?"

"Don't you start worrying about me. You are the one to worry about."

"God looks after me, Will, who looks after you?"

"Hannes Potgieter at the moment. And very well. Do you want me to tell you about these two American women?..."

"Not really, Will. Not really... Something's happened to you since I left England. Do you want to talk about it?"

"There's nothing to talk about except you getting well. Only strong men do good deeds. Get your strength back. We have a safari on Monday for a week. Tell Laurie Hall to get a message to our permanent camp when they fly you back."

"God be with you always, Will... And thank you."

HANNES POTGIETER'S leather hat was caked in old sweat and dust, heavy with the years in the bush, the lion's claw stitched to the front of the headband a reminder that death was swift and final when hunting the big game of Africa. The client had shot the lioness or rather Hannes had fired simultaneously, allowing the client to claim the kill. The man was standing gun-butt on his knee, right foot on the dead lioness when a blur of maned fury hurtled out of the elephant grass straight at the camera-posing client. Hannes had run in between them, snap-shooting the black-maned lion from the hip, aiming for the heart, and the dead lion landed on top of him. It had taken Sixpence and Onepenny five minutes to disentangle the lion, the rifle and Hannes Potgieter, the client waiting all the time for his photograph to be taken. The English aristocratic had risked his life a second time in one day by suggesting to a badly bleeding Hannes that the photograph would look better with his foot on the black-maned lion.

Relating the story to Will, Hannes had told him never to take his eyes away from the bush. "The old man didn't like his wife being shot, *kerel*, and I don't blame him. Everything is in the food chain in Africa, including you."

They were on their way in the Land Rover to Mongu to pick up a client, a long-time client of Hannes Potgieter who had become a friend.

"Newspaperman. Works all over the world. Anywhere there's a problem. Wife a great socialite. Once a year or so, whenever he can get away from his newspaper editor and his wife at the same time, he comes out here to repair his soul. Hasn't shot an animal for years, prefers to take photographs. An American. One of the best natural shots I have ever seen. You'll like this one. He's a man."

Curious, Will watched the scheduled flight land and one broad-shouldered, sharp-eyed passenger run down the ramp and stamp on the ground. Will could hear the 'yeah, yeah' from where he stood by the petrol bowser, Laurie Hall having gone out to the plane with the mobile stairs.

"Does that every time," said Hannes walking out to greet his friend, leaving Will wondering if three was going to be a crowd. Will watched them coming back.

"This is the young man I'm teaching, Melvin. Will, meet Melvin Raath. You may have seen his byline."

"A privilege, Mr Raath," said Will who read *Time Magazine* and had recognised Melvin Raath's name.

"Melvin, please... You're a lucky man, Will. Best teacher in Africa and I should know... want to write him up for an article but Hannes threatens violence, and that's one man I don't want to fight."

Together they climbed into the Land Rover, Will in the back, waved to Laurie Hall and began the fifty kilometres of potted dirt track back to the permanent camp.

"You mind if I talk freely in front of this young man from England?" said Melvin at the deck bar looking out over the distant bush. The sun would only be down in an hour which had not prevented Hannes from opening the bar. Will listened without interrupting, sipping a weak whisky. Hannes had warned him at the airfield while they were waiting for the aircraft. "Good professional hunters need more than bushcraft. Like a good barman they are part friend, part shrink, part nursemaid and they always listen to the other man's problems. This Melvin Raath will want to drink for two days and then go into the bush. Why I built the fancy house. A trip to the bush is therapy for Melvin Raath. But listen to him. He never talks *kak*. Even when he's drunk."

"Not the same without Danika," was the only time the American spoke of Hannes's dead wife, the shorter man reaching up to put a strong hand on the big man's shoulder. They drank in silence for a while with Hannes going to the open side of the house to look out over the bush.

"Yes," he said finally and came back to the bar and poured another drink.

"Let's get drunk," said Melvin.

"Why not, friend?"

"Can the lad drink?"

"Oh, yes," said Hannes. "A little later, after we eat the best buffalo steak Fourpence can cook on the open fire, when we have studied all the stars in heaven, I will tell you about Polly and Cherry as told by my tracker Fourpence."

Will looked thoroughly embarrassed.

"When he's a little drunk, maybe Will can tell us the story himself," chuckled Melvin, picking up Will's embarrassment.

Melvin drank a Kentucky corn whisky Hannes imported specially, and Will sipped as short a measure as he was allowed to get away with, all the time enjoying the American's range of conversation. The man had travelled to almost every corner of the shrinking world.

"Everyone wants to kill someone. Every jerk knows the best way to run the country. Every politician promises what he can't fulfil and doesn't care and everyone teeters on the brink of Armageddon. Clichés every one of them but every one of them horribly true... My wife wants to wheel me out at her parties like the prize she won at high school and my daughter is looking for the jerk she can nail down to pay for her for the rest of her life. She's pretty so every poor sucker's a taker... Why do men let their balls run their brains? Another cliché but oh so true. Sweet as pie until they give you a couple of children so you can't run away and then they never stop asking for anything they can think of to make them feel wanted. If my wife has had a new thought in her mind for twenty years, she hasn't told me. America stinks, England stinks, the whole world stinks and people make the world stink... Sorry, Hannes. It's been a bad year... You want something so bad and when you get it you wonder why you bothered. And that goes for journalism, wives and daughter... The wife wanted to send me to a shrink so out I came agreeing, wonderful idea, I said to her, 'Best idea you had... How long you think I need? A month? Two months? Make it six weeks.'... She thinks I'm in a clinic drying out having my brain rearranged so it will better fit in with her life... Whatever happened to nice families, with nice kids and people who love each other instead of everyone scheming how to hurt and get one up on each other? Why can't people be happy anymore?"

Will watched the American, puzzled, not understanding what he was talking about. So far as he knew the Langtons had always been happy with each other at Langton Manor, and not only the Langtons but everyone who lived on the estate. They were his family, and it had not once crossed his mind that they were not happy together. Stanmore, the girl at Dancing Ledge were the unhappiness that contrasted vividly the good. If this was another world, the new world they were all talking about, he did not want to know... Leaving the two friends at the bar to become sentimentally maudlin, Will went to bed.

Even though Will knew the Goliath heron slept at night, he watched the earth bathed in moonlight on his way to his sleeping hut. Within a minute of getting undressed, he was sound asleep.

The following day the steady drinking continued with Will watching from the sideline. Hannes let Melvin talk, prompting him to go on when the train of thought meandered off course. It was a sad montage of a life Will knew nothing about with the constant theme of striving for happiness no one found, having trodden on everyone near to them... Will shuddered at some of the bitterness. Even the girl was now part of a beautiful memory, something Will would find again even if the girl had gone from his life forever. They had found a love for each other that had nothing to do with high school conquest but everything to do with the real meaning of life. There were souls, like theirs, that could join together in lasting harmony, in peace with each other reflecting the green trees, bluebells in the woods, gulls above the sea, the crash of waves, the smell of autumn rain on leaves, woods bare in winter, Christmas at Langton Manor, the happiness of family and the joy that was living.

"Kid, you want to join us?" asked Melvin.

"I don't understand most of it," said Will.

"You're lucky, Will," said Melvin. "I hope you never do. The best part of life is being young. Enjoy it before you become an old cynic like me."

The next day they walked out into the bush, Melvin, Hannes, Will, Fourpence and Sixpence. They carried rifles and rations for a week. There was no alcohol in the haversacks. Small waterholes scattered the mopani and thorn trees far inland from the river and the game was scattered over the plains under the burning sun. Hannes and Melvin sweated out the booze in silence, each with his own thoughts. It was Will's first safari with a client. They carried rolled-up sleeping mats and mosquito nets but no tents. Melvin wanted to see the bush, not the shade of a tree. The camera and set of lenses he carried was the most complicated equipment Will had ever seen to take photographs.

Some of the smaller waterholes had dried up and the bush, despite the recent rains, was crackling dry. They walked alone among the animals and by the end of the day when they made camp among a clump of tall, spreading acacia trees, Melvin Raath was smiling. They all collected wood in a big pile to go through the night and then the fire was lit. The sun was ten minutes from setting and Hannes nodded to the trackers.

Just as the sun sank into the far-off horizon of trees, silhouetting the skyline in vivid colour, Will heard a sharp crack behind the waterhole. Hannes had built a spit with forked sticks the thickness of Will's wrist on either side of the fire. He was removing the bark from a long stick of mopani when the trackers came back with the small impala strung between them on a pole. Before the light had gone, the skinned animal was on the spit over the fire, the heart, the liver and kidneys set aside for breakfast.

Using a long-handled spoon that had hung on one side of his haversack, Fourpence basted the venison with oil and herbs, the herbs coming from the surrounding bush. Away from the spit, another fire was made, the flames leaping to the heavens warning the jackals and wild dogs, hyenas and lions, playing firelight far behind the backs of the men lounging in their legless canvas chairs, feet stretched out to the fire, coffee mugs down on the dry earth beside them with the sounds of Africa calling to the night for kilometre after kilometre around them.

They could have been the only people in the world.

That night Will lay awake inside his mosquito net wondering how such luck could have come to him. The mosquito net was hung from a long string attached to the lowest bough of the acacia tree, Fourpence having attached a piece of wood to the end of the string and skilfully thrown it over the bough of the tree. The carcass of the impala had been taken off the fire and hung in the tree. For three hours the carcass had been turned while they sliced thin pieces from the outside with the knives each of them carried in a sheath next to their right legs. The meat had cooked down layer by layer, crispy and better than any meat Will had eaten despite being tough from lack of hanging.

A thin moon, lying on its back, gave a pale light to the bush, and the coughs and grunts and splashes at the waterhole came to him early in the night. The big fire was burning bright a few feet away, and he watched the flames deep in the fire, crashing sometimes and shooting a thousand sparks high up on the draught of hot air. Hannes was asleep and snoring. Across the fire, Melvin Raath sat in his canvas chair watching the flames, the fire reflecting in his eyes. Fourpence and Sixpence were lying on their mats nearby. Sixpence was still awake, the flames deep in his eyes. Fourpence had his back to Will. After consciously trying to stay awake to savour the last of a perfect day, Will fell asleep. Not even the marauding lions woke him in the night.

The morning was cool and the smell of fresh coffee boiling over the fire made him push back the mosquito net to look at the day.

Within an hour the sun had scorched the last vestige of coolness from the air. The liver, kidneys and heart were roasted by Fourpence over the fire and cold cuts of venison piled on a plate on top of the canvas table. Will could smell the herd of buffalo without seeing them in the thorn bush. The waterhole was empty of animals and only the birds, flocks of francolin and quail, tiptoed along the water's edge pocked by the hooves of the night animals. Three mourning doves called from a tree and vultures circled far out in the bush where death had come in the night.

"You know anything better than this?" said Melvin Raath. He had been watching Will for five minutes, his writer's mind noting every expression on the boy's face. 'Pity my daughter can't meet a boy like that,' he was thinking.

"It's so beautiful, it almost hurts," said Will.

They walked all morning to the kill, the skeleton of the cooked impala having been cut down for the scavengers to complete the cycle of life and death, the fire well buried under earth to prevent a bush fire. The heat was intense. Despite the American's enthusiasm Will could see Melvin Raath was glad to reach their destination. A pride of six lions were fifty metres off the kill in the shade of a thorn tree, their stomachs extended. Even the four cubs were flat out on their sides fast asleep. The vultures had settled in the thorn trees with a pair of steppe eagles. Further back the round ears of a small pack of bat-eared fox were just visible along the tall, brown grass. The bush was silent except for the buzz of flies around the half-eaten wildebeest, the eyes already eaten out of their sockets by the birds. Carefully, and with consummate skill, Melvin photographed what they saw, the satiated lions taking no interest in the American. They stayed on the kill until it was dark, jackal and hyena joining the scavengers but keeping back out of fear of the lions.

That night, Hannes, Will and the trackers took it in turns to stand watch over the constant squabbling as the opposing animals tried to feed, the night wrenched apart by whooping and barks, lion growls and the manic laughs of excited hyenas. They had dined on cold venison and a bully beef stew, washed down with mugs of black coffee. The dawn was bravely visible when Hannes led them away, back to the river, downstream from the permanent bush camp where the trackers fished for their supper, turning the river bream whole over the coals of the cooking fire high up on the bank away from the hippo and crocodiles. Again no shot had been fired all day.

The camp by the river that night was peaceful, the river endlessly flowing with flotsam, the bream jumping out of the water to avoid the chasing tiger fish, the moon large. There were three layers of stars in the heavens. Night birds called for most of the night and on Will's shift the river down below the camp broke into a vicious fight of thrashing water he was unable to see in the dark. Whatever it was had died or run away and the night went back to the plopping of the fish, the castanets of the river frogs and the screech of the cicadas.

The tsetse fly struck with the dawn. Hannes Potgieter cursed and flayed the flies with his hat. Will watched from the safety of his mosquito net. Melvin Raath lay asleep inside his net, curled up like a ball. A fish eagle called *weee-ah, hyo-hyo* from an island in the river and a bull elephant went down to the river to drink. The fire had burnt well all night.

Before the sun had gone down the previous night, Sixpence had shot three guinea fowl out of their roost in the acacia trees, gutted the birds and covered them with wet river clay and buried them deep in the ashes of the cooking fire. Breaking open the baked hard clay that pulled the feathers from the birds with the skin, he let out the smell of cooked flesh that woke Melvin from his dreams.

They ate with their fingers, sucking the dark, succulent meat from the bones which they then tossed into the fire.

"I'd give away my camera for a bottle of whisky and the lenses for a cold bottle of beer," said Melvin, looking out down the river. "And I'd give up journalism to stay here for the rest of my life. You, Hannes Potgieter, are the richest man alive and young Will has found his paradise."

For three days they stayed by the river, Hannes shooting up the water so they could swim while he watched, gun ready, from a high rock, searching the clear water of a small bay for crocodile and hippopotamus. Throughout the days, Will listened to the two older men talking, happy with his own thoughts. Then they went back to the permanent camp and opened the whisky.

Melvin had invited the trackers to the deck bar for a drink where Onepenny had laid out a cold spread of green salads, herb wild rice, mayonnaise potatoes, pickled river bream, pickled quail eggs no bigger than a thumbnail and three tall ice-filled buckets, each containing a bottle of Nederburg Cuvee Brut.

Melvin had bathed and shaved for the first time in a week and ten years had fallen from his age. Will no longer noticed the American accent.

"If I thanked you all," Melvin said, "you'd think me sentimental, so I won't. Suffice to say these trips save my sanity. Other people take pills or shoot themselves. Somehow the world has gone off track and doesn't know how to get back again. We want a million things we don't need and lie and cheat to get them. It's all out there, the important things, in the bush. I just hope the new world doesn't destroy this Africa, the last sane place I've visited on earth. Progress, the new progress they sell in every newspaper, magazine and television programme is mostly retrogression. The true value of a man's life is destroyed by his greed and need to compete. If he does not change his ways, it is my humble opinion that life on this earth will not be worth the living. Man was not brought on this earth to live in a concrete hutch, thirty-seven storeys high. He was born to feel the earth between his toes, to be with nature, to love without forethought of gain, to give of himself without calculating the reward. Many generations have criticised their present and most of them have been right. The price of progress is not worth climbing the hill. Thank you all for restoring my faith in the nature of man... Hannes, open that champagne and I'll stop this speech... Thank God we still have booze in America."

The trackers left them after the wine, carrying a bottle of whisky. Laughter carried with them down the stairs and out to the boma where they lit the fire. Hannes told his best joke about an Englishman who had fallen halfway down a long drop, bare arse first, and Will was forced to explain how he had escaped being raped by Polly and Cherry, seeing the funny side for the first time, finding a natural ability to embellish and keep them laughing. Melvin had more good jokes than Will had heard in his life and his stomach began to hurt from too much laughter. Quietly, he prompted Melvin from joke to joke, Hannes watching the performance with approval. The trackers were sent down a second bottle of whisky, Will nearly falling down the stairs in the process.

The lifestyle Melvin described in New York, with nightclub following restaurant, women at every table, music, laughter and success at every corner, sounded appealing to Will. There was a world out there Will had not seen. From the prison of Stanmore to the rural gentleness of Langton Manor to the excitement of the African bush, there was still much more to be seen and experienced. As the evening progressed, Will drank in every word about the good life in America and when Melvin gave him his New York address, he folded it away carefully and put it in his pocket. Melvin had sown the eternal seed of discontent. Even Melvin's wife sounded amusing and the daughter very desirable. Will had never known there were so many parties in the world.

Careful to remain sober himself, Will left them alone to reminisce and sought his bed in the sleeping hut. The trackers had already turned in, the fire burnt to ashes, a soft red glow still visible.

For the first time in the bush it took Will a long time to fall asleep. When he woke late, undisturbed, a Land Rover had left for Mongu and with it the American, Melvin Raath. At lunchtime, to Will's surprise, Hannes appeared from his bedroom, well-slept and clear-eyed.

"Melvin wanted to leave before he cried. You meet them all in the safari business. Fix us a Bloody Mary and cheer me up. Wine, women and song last a short time, Englishman, and then you have the rest of your life. Our Melvin never did know what he wanted and I've known him twenty years. Hell, man, it makes you tired all that listening... Poor old Melvin."

AFTER THE SEVENTH client of the hunting season had been returned to the airfield at Mongu, ten days of serious hunting that had culminated in Hannes shooting a buffalo wounded by the client, Will was surprised they drove straight back to the permanent bush camp in preference to going to the club.

"I'm getting too old," was all Hannes said as he sat beside Will.

The journey took them two hours as Will carefully drove round the larger potholes in the track that wound through the mopani trees. Hannes took no notice of the game they passed, his bulk slumped in the seat.

"You all right, Hannes?"

"Tired, *kerel*. Blerry tired."

They had almost arrived and the big thatch roof was visible between the trees.

"I'm sixty tomorrow, Englishman. Bloody sixty... What does a hunter do when he can't walk anymore?"

Instinctively doing the right thing, Will stopped the Land Rover in good shade thirty metres from the river and turned off the engine. The cooler months of winter brought them a fresh wind from across the water. The bush was quiet in the afternoon sun.

"That buffalo nearly got me," said Hannes. "Circled and waited for me to come back to camp and then it charged. Twenty years ago that would have been the highlight of the season. It's the legs... They always said the legs give out first, not the eyes or the ears... A man needs sons to take over his business and keep him happy in his old age, asking his advice."

They sat in silence for a while, Will knowing it was not the time to talk.

"Maybe that's the way to go, gored by a buffalo... Melvin Raath was right. We are destroying Africa, killing the animals, cutting down the trees, overbreeding with all the good medicine and hygiene from your brother Hilary and his friends. This is the last frontier for new age man to conquer, or destroy as Melvin would have it. They never can leave well alone, always interfering, thinking the other man wants what should be for him... The black man is happier living his old ways, breeding children all his short life with only the very best surviving. Nature's process of selection is far better than man's medicine. Maybe my sons were better not being born. My people first ran away from the Dutch East India Company and then the British. The best of us don't like cities. We like space and the bush and the world's caught up with us again. Even the black man has been fooled into wanting a city life. Everyone wants more years than they should have on earth. A man should die when his strength has gone and when his feet won't carry him anymore. When he is no longer any use. My Danika was the lucky one, bless her. She went at the right time. Sixty, *kerel*. It's too many years for a hunter but what can a man do?"

Will looked at Hannes for a moment. "Have a good soak in the bath, a good meal and a bottle of wine and you'll feel better. It was a long hunt and my legs feel just as weary as yours."

"You're a good lad, Englishman. You always say the right thing. One thing you got wrong. I'll have a large whisky while I'm having my bath."

WILL FOUND navigation the most difficult part of his training, Hannes deliberately letting him lose himself while he was following the spoor of a lion for a client. The lion were decimating the zebra and wildebeest and the culling operation was as necessary to the ecology as the lions killing the weaker animals in the herd to sustain a strong gene pool. Will had run on the spoor, moving around trees and thorn thickets, concentrating on the signs in the red dust. Hannes, holding back, had known the spoor was old. He and the client watched the young Will dash off through the mopani forest and quickly disappear from sight.

"The best way to teach a lad not to get lost is get him lost and frightened. Fear does wonders for the intelligence. Onepenny, we'll make camp here and look for the lions in the morning."

"Baas, you leave him out alone all night?" said Onepenny.

"He's ready."

After half an hour Will lost the trail completely, casting around without success. When he was unable to find the original spoor, he looked from tree to tree, all of them appearing the same. From being a friendly forest, the darkening trees had become a menace.

"Shit," he said out loud. "I didn't think my position before I ran out on the spoor." Desperately, Will looked around for a familiar hill but it was the first time he had hunted the area. As the sun sank deeper into the trees, Will fired two shots into the air and waited. There was no return shot of recognition. With one bullet in the breach and four in the magazine Will knew better than to fire again. The spare ammunition was in Onepenny's haversack. Every sound from the bush became a threat.

"Think, you idiot," he again said out loud.

Slowly, deliberately, Will conquered the worst of his fear and began to gather wood for the fire to burn through the night. He had water in his bottle, a lighter sewn into his belt, and biltong. He would survive. In the morning, he would judge the position of the sun and strike for the river.

"Got himself lost," said Hannes, taking careful direction of where the shots had been fired.

"Shouldn't you fire one shot to let him know?" said the client.

"Maybe."

Onepenny busied himself with the fire. He was not smiling. The night came down dark and moonless and Hannes deliberately kept the conversation away from the man alone in the forest.

"I'm worried, Hannes," said the client before they hung the mosquito nets.

"Don't be. He's going to be good. Better to be lost for the first time when I know where he is. One day he'll really be on his own."

Onepenny was still sitting up when Hannes fell asleep.

Will stayed awake all night tending the fire, his mind alert. Deliberately, he identified each sound from the night. Fear drained away as the night became familiar. By the time the sun came up, giving him the direction of the river, he had made up his mind. Covering the ashes of the fire, he made to begin the long journey through the trees to the permanent bush camp. The others could be anywhere within two miles but he had no idea in which direction. He fired two more shots in the air, heard the return shot far closer than he expected and smiled. Then he struck off away from the direction of the single shot, towards the Zambezi River, covering his tracks wherever possible.

Hannes found the dead fire an hour after answering the two-shot distress signal. They searched the area and found nothing. Two hours later they gave up. This time Hannes Potgieter was frightened.

"You think he teach us a lesson?" said Onepenny in Lozi, not to let the client know they were out of control.

"I'm an old fool," said Hannes in the same language.

The first rule was to fire two shots if lost. The second was the one shot reply which Hannes had broken the night before. The third was to stay put after the answering shot which Will defied earlier in the morning. 'Well,' he said to himself, 'now I really will find out if he has any bush sense.'

"We'll turn back for base," he said to the client lightly. "Will's gone for the river. He'll be all right. Find a lion for you on the way back." For the rest of the day he avoided looking at Onepenny.

ON THE SECOND MORNING ALONE, Will heard the call of a fish eagle and knew he had found the river. The water bottle was empty. Along the way all the waterholes had been dried up, and the game was sparse. The five sticks of biltong had been eaten and Will knew better than to use one of his last three bullets to shoot for food.

He reached the thorn-thicket sisal enclosure four days after firing the first two distress shots. He was hungry and happy. 'Even an Englishman,' he said to himself, 'a pretty raw Englishman can find his way around in the bush.' Will had conquered his fear of Africa.

Towards sunset on the same day, Hannes made it back to the permanent camp with the client and Onepenny. Will was sitting comfortably on the upper deck enjoying a strong cup of tea. He was quietly whistling 'Marching to Pretoria', the favourite song of the Brits in the Boer War. Will thanked Granda for the tune which he hoped would annoy Hannes Potgieter.

"Why the hell didn't you stay put?" shouted Hannes in relief.

"Why didn't you fire back the first time?" said Will and carried on whistling.

"And stop that blerry whistling."

"Don't you like the tune?" said Will with feigned surprise.

Hannes pulled him bodily out of the chair with one hand.

"You stupid blerry Englishman."

For a moment Will thought he was going to be hit. They looked straight at each other.

"You did that on purpose, didn't you?" said Hannes.

"Yes," said Will. "And so did you. Maybe we both proved our points. Now, can I have my arm back again?"

6

_I_t is doubtful whether Byron Langton would have found himself in the music business had Shelley Lane gone to bed with him on the first or second date. They had met soon after Will turned twenty-one, far away in Central Africa. Will had received many letters over three years from the family asking when he was coming home to find himself a job, a professional hunter's licence to Byron being as much use as a man's tits, neither functional nor saleable. His young brother was an enigma; the world was full of people prepared to waste their lives.

Fanny Try with the long brown hair had surprised everyone by going broody and marrying a nice young man of good family who lived in the country. She had convinced her innocent young man that she was a virgin. Virginia Stepping had agreed that 'what the eye did not see the heart would not grieve about'. Very slightly, she was jealous.

The confrontation with Logan, Smith and Marjoribanks had been avoided before Will's birthday by Byron offering his resignation. Someone with a grudge had tipped off Maxwell Marjoribanks, the chairman of the company and father of Lionel, Byron's schoolchum, that the origin of the portfolio they managed for one Jack Pike was suspect. By then, Byron was ready to go out on his own and Langton Portfolio Management Limited was formed the day after he handed in his resignation with a very nice letter thanking the chairman for all the wonderful advice, encouragement and training that he, Byron, had received over the nine years of his apprenticeship. Everybody parted friends. Never to make an enemy was another of Byron's rules of life.

Shelley was nineteen years old and pretty with a figure that matched her face. She wanted above everything else to be a singer, and was realistic enough to know her body was a better product than her voice. If she wanted to hear herself singing on record, she would have to use her more obvious chorus. Her first approaches had been sexually satisfying with a few nights' singing in Soho nightclubs and a few more nights spent in beds that failed to bring a recording contract. She was going around the whole business the wrong way round and by the time she met Byron, through Johnny Pike, she was trying the don't touch first approach.

The gigs brought her enough money to rent a two-roomed apartment in leafy Holland Park where the Victorian houses were falling into decay but the traffic noise was minimal and the rent three guineas a week. Josephine Langton, Byron's twin sister, had known the same lane with the leafy plane trees when she was visiting Wolfgang Baumann in the summer of '49. Nothing had changed in the nine years since Josephine had had her abortion. Shelley's apartment was on the ground floor and French windows led out onto a small patio with its own plane tree and wooden bench with weeds growing through the old crazy paving. High walls protected her arbour of peace from the prying eyes of the world. There was birdsong and butterflies.

Most summer evenings found Shelley in the garden. Her nightclub gigs were at eleven o'clock at night, sandwiched between the strippers, itinerant singers being one behind the strippers who were one behind the whores. In London, there were a lot of good-looking girls trying to make a living.

BYRON HAD TRIED the restaurant and vodka routine on four occasions without any return on his money. The challenge was more interesting than he had imagined, the girl having something about her sexuality Byron had not found before. Byron had enjoyed being teased for the first time in many years.

The old front door needed painting, like most of post-war London, but the brass knocker echoed its message down the corridor while Byron waited, two bottles of ice-cold Chablis in his duffle bag wrapped in newspaper to keep them cold. Next to the bottles was a leather case containing two fluted Waterford crystal glasses, and an ivory-handled corkscrew with the Langton monogram. Byron believed in being prepared. Most women hated disorganised men.

The old landlady, whose family had seen much better days, answered the door.

"Your young lady is in the garden, under the tree," she said.

"I found these for you in the Portobello Road," said Byron, giving her the small posy of summer violets he had intended for Shelley. The old woman reminded him of his great-aunt Eve who had died in the spring, fifty years a widow.

"Surely, they're for..." began the old lady.

"They are for you, Mrs Page."

The violet eyes were looking deep into her past, matching the flowers he put into her old, gnarled hands. For a moment, the day, the week, the whole year had been worth living.

"You know the way."

As Byron moved into the corridor of the house, Mrs Page was smelling the violets. He heard the front door click closed as he followed the open back door into the small courtyard. Shelley, in high-waisted tight shorts and a loose white top, was sitting on the bench. She was not wearing shoes or a bra. Shelley giggled.

"What's that for?" asked Byron, putting the duffle bag on the bench next to the girl.

"The flowers... They were for me."

"They most certainly were not."

"She's very lonely."

"Granda said we all get lonely in the end. Part of life. I hope you missed me."

"Why would I miss you, Mr Langton? I hope you haven't come to try to spend the night with that bag? Mrs Page would never approve, even if you brought her a bucket of flowers."

"Are you singing tonight?"

"Maybe, maybe not... I have to pay the rent. Did you speak to Johnny Pike?"

"They are more into whores than singers. You say you want to be a singer."

"He won't help?"

Byron ignored the question and opened the bag, took out the tooled leather case and put it on the wooden table with the ivory corkscrew.

"Did I tell you my brother is a professional big-game hunter? He sent me the ivory. Asprey's found me a carver."

"You mean he shot the elephant? Ugh!"

"I believe so. He turned twenty-one the other day. Maybe you'd prefer my younger brother?"

"What does that imply?"

"That I am too old for you... You don't like me. You don't seem very pleased..."

"Oh, shut up, Byron, and open the wine. We've been through..."

"What do you want?" He took the bottle out of the wet paper. "Still ice-cold." Little tricks pleased Byron.

"You could manage my career," she said, pouting.

"First you need a career to manage."

"First, I need a manager. Open the damn wine."

Byron thought for a while. "Maybe. Just maybe. I'd need a lawyer's contract and you would need a band... So this was what it was all about?"

"Yes," said Shelley at the same time the cork came out of the bottle.

At last the girl is honest, thought Byron.

The summer evening was warm and behind the high walls, far away, muted, came the sound of London's traffic. From the tangle of weeds and flowers along the bottom of the red brick walls that were crumbling with age came the sound of bees moving the pollen, pursuing their life cycle and producing the seeds of future growth. Puffed-up pigeons cooed from the slate rooftops and chimney stacks. Byron opened the leather case and put the glasses on the rickety table. He was smiling to himself. Gently, he poured the white wine.

"There are rules in business," began Byron as he passed Shelley a glass of wine. "Maybe you should think of them before you decide. Cheers, Miss Lane."

Byron sipped his wine and walked across to the old flower beds, treading through the long, uncut grass of the lawn. He bent to smell the white flower of a tobacco plant that scented the evening air. The little garden was quiet in itself, a haven from the world; brief sanctuary. A child's treble voice echoed from another garden, far away.

"If you work for me, which is what you are asking, there will be nothing but business between us and you will do what you are told. Right now, Shelley, you can't sing. Your body, the lights, sexy clothing are what you are selling. Men are interested in the singers, so gigs are out straight away if you work for me... You could have a voice but it has to be trained. Nothing is easy. Nothing overnight. Nothing of any value has come from this life to my knowledge without hard and dedicated work. Do you really want to be a singer or do you like the idea, the glamour, the centre of attention? Are you using the stage to catch a wealthy man to support you and your future children in the style you would like to be accustomed? You set me up, I see that, but what deal were you really looking for?"

Shelley sipped her wine and followed him with her eyes as he slowly walked around the garden. She did not give him an answer.

"Money," said Byron, "is the only thing about which I am deadly serious. Money carries on if it's looked after and preserved, unlike love. Undying love is the figment of man's imagination. Sad, but true... If you are looking for love, I am not your man. Money, maybe... The rules of business apply to any product and a singer is a product provided she is good enough... You have some of the ingredients; youth, sex appeal, a good body, provocative eyes, good, sexy movement on the stage. But can you really sing, make that deep-throated sound that rings an echoing chord in the male sex organ? The evocative sound that makes men search for satisfaction. The good singer sends the customers to each other's arms, has them dreaming of love with each other. It's somewhere mystical, a further sense that provokes emotion, that strikes the chord in us that is not animal; the artist, the religion, the mystique, maybe beauty in its purest sense."

Shelley waited. Byron was at the back of her bench, behind the mottled trunk of the plane tree. The summer evening was settling gently into dusk, drawing the sweet smell of the tobacco plants. Bending forward, Shelley poured herself a second glass of wine and as she picked it up she shuddered, spilling down the crystal sides of the glass. Bending to the glass, she licked the stem where the wine had collected, her long tongue expertly drinking up the spill. Not a drop reached the grass below. More than anything, she wanted the man behind her to pick her up and take her inside and make love to her until she was lame... She waited through the moments.

"It's your decision, Shelley Lane," he said softly from right behind her seat.

The moment lasted for a long time and neither of them made a move. There was not a sound in the garden, the bees having stopped their quest for food, the light shadowing down with the dusk.

"Have some more wine, boss," she said softly, just stopping the sob.

Byron sat down on the wooden bench with his back to the table. "If you can get that emotion into your singing, you will succeed."

"This afternoon, I wanted to succeed so much there was nothing I would not sacrifice. Now, I'm not so sure... Don't you want me, Byron?"

"Of course, Shelley, otherwise I wouldn't be here. For me it would be just another conquest. A brief moment of pleasure bought with money or the image of money. But, for you, do you want the moment or the future? Do you believe in yourself or is the singer in you nothing but a myth?"

"Sometimes life is not fair." She tried to look at his face.

"Life is never fair."

"Byron, I want to be a singer."

"Then you must work."

"I promise."

"Good. Then you can pour your new employer a glass of his wine. Then your new employer will take you out to a business, strictly business supper, and bring you to your celibate bed. Tomorrow, I will have my lawyer draw up a binding contract... Life does have some strange moments... I'm glad I gave Mrs Page the flowers... Something so simple can change a person's life."

"Mrs Page's?"

"Yours, if you succeed."

Shelley was surprised to see the glasses go back into their leather case and return to the duffle bag with the corkscrew. The wine bottle on the rickety table was empty.

Byron's car, open to the summer night, was waiting for them in the road and they let themselves out of the house without disturbing Mrs Page. Shelley had changed while Byron drank the last of the wine in the gathering dusk. She had not turned on her bedroom light.

The Triumph TR2 drove quietly out of the street into the traffic, heading back into town. He parked outside the restaurant, in the street, and opened the car door for Shelley. Neither of them had spoken since leaving Holland Park.

The table Byron chose was in the corner and they sat facing each other. Without asking, Byron ordered the food and wine. No one he knew was in the restaurant. The oysters came with wine.

"Doesn't make sense," said Shelley.

"Oh, it does. You made a choice."

"What will I live on without gigs?"

"Me. I'll pay Mrs Page and give you an allowance for twelve months. The first three months you will be on probation."

"Do you know what you are doing?"

"Anything I don't know I will find out. The one thing I did find out tonight is you want to sing more than anything else. That's good enough for me. Business is a calculated gamble."

For the first time in her life, Shelley found herself shaking hands with a male escort at the front door to her house. Leaving her standing on the step, Byron drove off into the night. For once in her life she was being offered exactly what she wanted. She had set out to trap a rich promoter and instead had fallen in love. Back in her apartment, in the lonely bedroom, she began to cry.

BYRON'S OFFICE in Pall Mall was next to Cox's & King's bank, former paymasters for the Royal Air Force, a coincidence not missed by Red Langton who had found out through Josephine that his son had changed jobs. Adelaide had once again said the boy would end up making his fortune or end up in jail and the matter had been dropped at Langton Manor where Randolph, the eldest son, was running the farm.

At reception, and acting as Byron's secretary, was a twenty-one-year-old girl almost as good-looking as Shelley Lane. Madge O'Shea was a flaming redhead with a flaming temper and an honours degree in economics from London University where her politics had been wedded to the left. Fortunately, the facts of economics convinced her that governments were unable to create wealth. During Madge's third week of employment, Shelley Lane called at the office to collect her allowance and neither of them liked the look of the opposition. When Shelley left with her money, she passed reception without a word, holding the cheque up delicately between forefinger and thumb. Madge waited less than a minute before making an excuse to go into the boss's office.

"Who the hell was that?" she said to Byron.

"An aspiring singer. I sponsor her."

"You told me this firm was a merchant bank."

"Merchant banks do a lot of things. We have a contract with the lady that just left. Her singing teacher says we may be in luck."

"You mean she can't even sing?"

"Not yet... Don't worry about Shelly Lane. You know perfectly well I never mix business with pleasure."

The outside office opened and closed and to the surprise of neither, Johnny Pike shook out his umbrella and dropped it into the hat stand. Madge walked back to her desk, pulled her typewriter forward and began to type, ignoring Johnny Pike.

"The help not very friendly today," he said and firmly shut the door.

"Leave her alone, Johnny. She doesn't even like you."

"All women like me, eventually."

"Your conceit is only matched by your charm."

"Do you know anything about Africa?"

"Only what my young brother writes on the very rare occasions he puts pen to paper."

"The African empire is about to collapse and with it British control of the mineral resources, some of which, like chrome and copper, are vital to the Western alliance."

"Why this sudden political lecture?"

"We've had an approach from a dark gentleman who tells us the Federation of Rhodesia has the largest copper mines in the world, outside of Chile, and with political change, Anglo-American Corporation will lose control of their mines and their offices in London will lose control of Britain's main source of supply. The man wants money now in exchange for the right to distribute his country's copper. We think he is a communist who intends to install a one-party state. The party will decide through whom the copper is to be sold on to the world market."

"If he's communist, why doesn't he sell his copper to the Russians who can then throttle British industry?"

"The Russians will supply our friend with guns for his revolution."

"If they will give him guns, they'll give him money."

"The man we are talking to has the job of raising funds for the party but he is clever enough to know that post-independence politics in Africa are going to be volatile and dangerous. He wants to place his insurance."

"We are bankers not an insurance company."

"You also know the legal ways of leaving the profit from business transactions in bank accounts untraceable by governments. This man says that the new government will legislate that all minerals will be sold through a government-controlled central selling organisation. We will be asked to finance the sales provided we leave a commission from the proceeds in a party account in Switzerland. The black nationalist movement in Central Africa is shopping for a merchant bank that is not part of the establishment. Someone has told our friend you contribute to the British Labour Party and the British Communist Party. They said your sister is a Trotskyist and a passionate believer in the worldwide socialist revolution."

Byron thought through the implications.

"How did they come to you?" he said, ignoring the accusation against his sister.

"One good rocket recognises another."

"You mean these revolutionaries are crooks?"

"Businessmen. Good politics and good business are the same thing. Dad's checked them out, Byron. Just keep it in mind."

"Has the man an official position in this 'party'?"

"Of course not. The politicians probably know nothing except their need for funds. Most politicians in the world don't wish to know who supports their party. People down the party line bring in the money and pass out the 'pork'. Socialism, capitalism, communism are all as corrupt as each other. All need money to get into power and consider the means justify the ends. Like your Shelley Lane, a little investment up front can bring huge returns. I believe half her earnings go to you if she succeeds?"

"Seventy per cent, actually... How much does this man want up front?"

"Twenty thousand pounds in a Swiss bank account. We'll keep track of him. That will be our insurance... Now do you think that girl outside will let me take her out to lunch?"

"You can only ask. I just won't vouch for the answer."

Byron sat for some time without moving, staring ahead into the morass and trying to make sense of it all. The empire was breaking up faster than his own predictions but business would carry on much the same, only the players and profiteers would be different. With the great political change, opportunities would be available that had been controlled by the establishment for centuries. Political change had nothing to do with the rights and wrongs of a particular system, it was only a means of changing the patronage, of gaining financial control by passing legislation that would require government approval, legislate who would sell the copper... Byron began to chuckle. Without change there was never a new opportunity. For the first time, he began to look kindly at the prospect of the dissolution of the British Empire. A fine-thinking businessman could make a fortune.

GLORIA KENDLE HAD BEEN shopping for a son-in-law for eighteen months and nothing had come of it.

"Mummy, they're all so boring," was the constant refrain from her twenty-two-year-old daughter when another invitation slipped through the letter box. Beatrice, the only child of a rich merchant banker in the City, was the target of mothers with bachelor sons looking for a good marriage, the mothers studying the market with the same concentration their husbands studied the stock market.

Beatrice, unbeknown to either of her parents or any of her friends, was being laid twice a week by an Italian waiter from the Greek Street pub owned by Jack Pike, the smell of cooked cabbage in his one-room bedsitter sending her into multiple orgasms. There was no emotion on either side but the physical satisfaction was mutual and wholly rewarding. Beatrice was as crisp and clean as the Italian was dark and dirty and both of them looked forward to his nights off with equal expectation.

Beatrice considered her parents' marriage as boring as cricket where people played a game for five days without getting a result. She worked in a solicitor's office as prim and proper as her mother expected; high-necked, well-tailored suits, long sleeves, sensible shoes and thick stockings, underneath which was a body waiting to be turned on fire. Her friends whispered she was frigid, a virgin, and were it not for her rich father would certainly end up an old maid.

The last place she expected to see the up and coming merchant banker was Jack Pike's pub on a Wednesday night. Byron was waiting for Johnny to go over some figures. His mind was in free idle, mellow from two double gins when he caught sight of the 'frigid babe' out of the corner of his eye and vaguely wondered what on earth she was doing in Soho. He had just attended one of Shelley's music lessons and was well pleased with his six-month-old investment. The girl's voice had reached a power and range he never could have hoped for.

"No, Shelley, I have a business meeting and you know dating is not part of our contract. But I will give you some good news. I've found you a songwriter and put him under contract. I am now looking for a band so we can take you up north for a try-out. See what the public have to say. Get some feedback. I want every one of your songs to be an original."

"Are you dating that damn redhead in the office?"

"No."

"I don't believe you. She hates me."

"That is possible."

Byron had found out some time ago that tensioning up the staff was good for business. Madge O'Shea was as good a confidential secretary as Shelley was a singer.

Beatrice had known for three weeks that some of the fire had gone out of the waiter and when he politely said he had other things to do on his night off she smiled, patted him mildly on the cheek and turned away.

"You not mad at me, Bea?"

"Why ever? We both used each other to mutual satisfaction. Whoever said an affair had to last forever?"

"Maybe one more time?"

"Your tendency to become romantic is sometimes out of place. Give my love to your mother."

"My mama in Italy. You don't —?"

"You can still give her my love and tell her what a good boy you are."

"You English, I never understand."

"That is comforting. One day, probably tomorrow, I will have forgotten your name. Now, if you will excuse me, there is a friend of mine sitting at the bar who has asked me over for a drink."

Leaving her ex-lover with nothing more to say, she walked along the bar to the corner and sat down.

"Byron, be a darling and buy me a drink. That bloody dago just stood me up."

Byron turned to her in surprise and a moment later they both burst out laughing.

"Mr Barman," he said, catching his eye. "Tell Mr Pike to ring me in the morning. Come, Beatrice Kendle, I've a much better idea. In twenty minutes this bar will be closed but I know a club down the road that specialises in good music. Can't have our aristocracy being stood up by the Italians without a celebration. I mean, why ever did we fight the war?"

"What are you doing here?" They were arm in arm going towards the outside door.

"Mr Pike is a client and he owns this pub among other things."

"There's more to you than I thought."

"My dear Beatrice, if anyone had suggested this morning that you were dating a wop I'd have called them mad... We'll walk the two blocks, so button up your coat."

The club was in a basement and had just opened. Finding a table back from the bandstand, Byron gave an attendant their coats and put the tickets in his top pocket.

"Remind me where they are," he said, tapping the pocket. "You mind if we drink a bottle of wine? Saves chasing the waiter... Red or white?"

"Red, I suppose."

"By eleven o'clock the club will be full and noisy. Trust me. And don't worry, not a soul in your crowd would be seen dead in this club. This is a club where people actually come to hear the music. Jazz, pop, guitar. A couple of big names started off right over there."

"What does a young merchant banker have in common with this?"

"You might well be surprised."

"I can't imagine my father coming here even in his student days."

"I can't imagine your mother dating an Italian waiter."

"Do you mind if I change my mind?"

"You want to go home?"

"Not at all. Make it champagne and let me pay."

"Tonight," said Byron, "the world has turned on its head. The women I seem to meet never offer to buy me a drink let alone a bottle of champagne."

"Then you go out with the wrong girls."

"Not really... Men like to be in control. Or, more correctly, they like to think they are in control... Do you have a flat in town?"

"No. I live in Surrey and the last train has left Waterloo. You see, I was going..."

"And you told Mummy you're staying with a girlfriend."

"Exactly. So you see, I'm in your hands."

Sweetly, they smiled at each other while Byron called for the waiter and ordered a bottle of champagne.

By the time the second bottle of champagne was put on their table the club had filled up and the small dance floor was crowded. After three stiff gins and half a bottle of champagne, Byron was floating, the feeling not unpleasant. A woman he would have run away from in normal circumstances was looking prettier by the glass and had once put her hand on his knee to emphasise a point, making Byron wonder what she was wearing under the stiff tweed jacket and skirt.

When they danced she folded quite nicely into his arms, her body as soft as the clothes were hard. Their eyes met an inch apart, and she kissed the end of his nose before gently resting her soft cheek against his. The music was pure and mellow, the piano melding with a soprano saxophone, the double bass keeping the beat, a mix of jazz and Latin American. There was nowhere else in the world but the spot where they swayed, folded together as one. The music stopped, and they waited, not breaking their hold, ignorant of everyone around. The lights were dim, and the floor crowded making them quite invisible to other people. She licked the end of her finger and touched it to his mouth, their eyes locking, the music playing, their bodies in tune with each other.

And the evening went on, dance after dance, glass after glass.

At midnight, the band changed, but neither took any notice, not wishing to break their spell. Very softly a young girl's voice began to sing with the band, the sound part of the piano and clarinet, each weaving around each other, playing the sweet notes to each other's calls. The music swelled, and the singer took charge, building the song, stopping the talk at the tables. Byron, half-drunk with wine and torpid pleasure, his back to the music, swayed to the melody, his feet no longer moving.

"That girl can really sing," he said when the music stopped.

"The band is taking a break. Champagne makes me float. You should have seen her. The men were transfixed."

"Let's drink the night away," said Byron, and led her by the hand back to the table. "We should have done this before."

"You never asked."

They drank to each other and smiled.

"What the hell did she look like?" snapped Byron, turning back to the empty bandstand.

"What's the matter, Byron?"

"The singer. What did she look like?"

"She's coming back, look for yourself. And she's changed her costume. This time the men will go crazy."

"The bitch!"

"What did you say?"

"The bitch."

"You know that girl? You'd better quieten down. She's going to sing."

This time the singer took control from the start and when she finished, every person in the room was standing on their feet, including Byron and Beatrice. The ovation sounded like thunder, broken by the girl singing again, taking the room and holding everyone in it to listen to her song.

"Who is she?" asked Beatrice.

"Shelley Lane... The best thing you and I can do is get out of here."

"I don't understand."

"You don't want to." Shelley took hold of the microphone.

"This next song is dedicated to my manager without whom I would not be able to sing... And thank you all."

Byron sat down at the table while Shelley sang to him, their eyes locked together.

"She's in love with you, Byron, and silly me, you're in love with her... What a pity. Mummy would have been ecstatic. That girl is going a long way as a singer... This really has not been my best night."

"Don't try and go, Beatrice. This is strictly business. She's a bitch because I told her not to sing in public until she was ready."

"She's ready... So you're the manager?"

"I own seventy per cent of that girl."

In the dressing room at the back, Shelley was in tears.

"What's the matter, Shel?" said the piano player. "You blew their minds."

"What made him come here tonight?... And who was that bitch at his table?"

"Who are you talking about?"

"My bloody manager."

The audience called again and again for the singer until the club manager took the microphone.

"The lady was a guest in the club, not a professional singer, and she doesn't wish to sing anymore."

"Then who's her manager?" someone shouted.

"Sorry, folks, the lady's gone... Boys, take the music, build the night."

"There's one thing about it," said Byron after reflection. "I don't have to take her on trial up north. I put her with the best voice trainer in London and it worked... Did you recognise any of her songs?"

"Not one."

"I'll need to tie up the songwriter... You mind waiting here a minute? Better still, come and give me a hand." Byron caught the club manager's eye and beckoned him over to the table.

"Has Shelley gone, Max?"

"Right out the door. How do you know her, Byron? Used to sing here a year back but not like that."

"Who wrote the songs?"

"She did."

"The bitch. Writing music isn't in her contract."

"Are you her manager?"

"Yes. All the way."

"How much do you want for her? Full-time. Six days a week."

"Not here, Max my boy. Not for money. Maybe a few evenings like tonight but no publicity."

"She'll get publicity whether you and I like it or not."

"Maybe... Can you call me a taxi, Max? Suddenly I'm sober... How did she affect you, Beatrice?"

"As a woman or a singer?"

"As a singer."

"Before she looked at you, she had my stomach melting."

"Come on. There's another bottle of champagne in my flat. You can have the couch in the lounge."

"You mean that woman means nothing to you personally?"

"Nothing at all. Strictly business."

"Maybe Mummy will be happy after all."

The taxi dropped them outside 47 Buckingham Court. The moments of magic had gone with the singer and neither of them knew what to say. Gloria Kendle's advice ran through her daughter's mind: 'If you've nothing to say to a man, keep your mouth shut.'

They walked up the steps to the ornate front door which was opened by the night porter who raised his top hat.

"Why is England so cold in the winter?" she said. Beatrice was shivering as Byron put his latchkey into the door of 47.

"It's late, Beatrice. Two o'clock and I have a meeting at nine."

"You mean the couch?"

"I mean the couch. It's warm. The flat is heated. It was a lovely evening but I never take advantage of a girl who doesn't have the means of getting home."

"A glass of hot milk will make us both sleep."

She was practical if nothing else. 'My,' she said to herself. 'And what was that Italian's name?' The last thing she remembered before falling asleep was having a chuckle to herself.

Byron found sleep more difficult and the dreams when they came were strange and convoluted.

They ate breakfast together before Byron drove her to the solicitors' office before going on to Pall Mall, parking in the basement. At night, he took taxis.

THE PLANE TREE outside the French windows was stark and bare of leaves. A light flurry of snow was falling through the branches and melting on the rickety table and wooden bench. Shelley had the blankets drawn right up to her nose. Deep inside the old house, Mrs Page's grandfather clock struck eleven o'clock. Snug in the warmth of her bed, she counted the eleven chimes as she watched the cold day through her open bedroom door and the French windows.

Her hair, the colour of a raven's wing, blue-black and shining, fell around her oval face on the pure white pillow. Her eyes were dark brown and set in their almond home. Her skin was white, tinged with the down of orange-red. Her mouth was large, inviting, slightly open to the day, white teeth gleaming with the purity of youth. Her small, seashell ears were free of the raven hair. Outside the French window a pigeon watched her from the ground, waiting for the crumbs she threw to the birds each winter's day.

At last, to herself, she had proved she could sing. Twice she turned and looked at the bedside telephone, white-yellow and quiet. Soon it would ring and her life would start again. She had been alone in the world too long. Turning her perfect face away, only her nose above the sheet, she tried to remember the days in her life when she had been happy.

The war had seen her evacuated to Cornwall when she was three. She had known neither of her parents who had met and mated just before the war and given her up for adoption. She did not even know their names. The other small orphans in Cornwall were as bewildered by life and war as much as she. They were pushed from one house to the other, sometimes laughing, sometimes not. The winter days were long and cold, the summer days long and warm.

Three sets of foster parents had followed after the war, all ending with Shelley on her own. At twelve the Jane Lamb in her ration book was changed in a childish hand to Shelley Lane. At fifteen she had left the last home in Croydon and gone up to London. No one, not even the police, had tried to contact her since. She found her first job in a Lyons Corner House, lying about her age. The girls were friendly, cheerful and the little hat sat well on her raven hair.

The following four years tumbled through her mind, a kaleidoscope of shared rooms, girlish laughter, the first boyfriend, crying for her virginity after it had gone and a week later wondering why she had waited so long. The days became short and exciting, never enough time to do all the things that swam before her grasp. Boredom had vanished, lost in her childhood, and all the way through the rhythm of her days played her need to be a singer, to be made someone by herself, to prove the casual mating of her parents was more than one lost orgasm.

One time soon he would phone and the sun would come out in her life forever.

Shelley drifted back into the daytime dreams with the applause ringing in her ears, her man standing up to clap with the others clapping from the dance floor.

By four o'clock in the afternoon, the pace of business had prevented Byron thinking of anything but work. The lack of sleep or Shelley's singing were far from his mind. Even his secretary had not had time to lose her temper. Balance sheets and propositions littered his desk. The job Byron set himself was to find entrepreneurs with good ideas and then match the ideas to risk capital with himself overseeing the financial planning. Where possible he took a small share in the enterprise with the ultimate goal of floating the company on the London Stock Exchange when his profit would be reaped as a non-taxable capital gain. For every feasible proposition, thirty were discarded and Langton Portfolio Management Limited depended upon an eighty per cent success ratio to attract the risk capital that funded the new entrepreneurs.

Madge went home at five-thirty and Byron had not left his office all day, Madge bringing up sandwiches and coffee from a corner shop off Piccadilly Circus. By seven o'clock all he wanted to do was go home to his flat, soak in a hot bath and go to bed. Without going out of the building, he walked down to his car in the basement and drove to Knightsbridge. The first thing he did on entering his flat was take the phone off the hook. By eight o'clock he was sound asleep without the thought of a dream.

The next day, Friday, saw the same pressure of work.

"You need an assistant," said Madge O'Shea.

"So do you."

By the end of the day he was tired and excited. Business was a stimulant for Byron, giving him a high unmatched by any other drug. With the week's work out of the way, he drove to Holland Park with the typed amendment to Shelley Lane's contract.

The night was foggy, and Byron's feet were cold despite the heater in the TR2. Shelley opened the front door with a sardonic smile. She was wearing a housecoat over her pyjamas, her feet in woolly slippers.

"You getting up or going to bed?"

"Neither... What do you want?"

"A signature on a contract amendment."

"Business?"

"Strictly business."

"Damn you."

"Shelley, it's cold out here. You mind if I come in?"

"Why I didn't get up for two days."

"What about yesterday's singing lesson?"

"I don't need them anymore."

"Oh yes you do... I can't get through the door when it's six inches open."

"That's the idea. Why didn't you phone me on Thursday?"

"I have been very busy."

"She looked the busy type. Can't say much for her dress sense."

"You are sending a cold draught all through the house."

"I'd love to slam this door in your face."

"It wouldn't help."

Shelley swung the door wide and swept a hand for him to enter, making the housecoat fall open in the process. Byron winced.

"Please, Shelley, it doesn't do any of us any good."

"That's the idea."

"If we are going to argue, can we please do it in your apartment and not in the hall and inconvenience Mrs Page?"

"You didn't bring any wine with you?"

"Shelley, this is business."

The lady strode down the hall in front of him into her apartment, across the lounge and into the bedroom. Thick curtains were drawn across the French windows. The apartment was freezing cold. Without turning around

Shelley dropped her housecoat on the floor and climbed back into bed, bringing the blankets up firmly under her chin.

"Haven't you got a heater?" he said.

"I ran out of shillings for the water. If you are cold, you can get into bed."

"You really are in a mood. Have you had any food?"

"No."

"Then put on some clothes while I shiver in the lounge and we will go and find a restaurant."

"Is this a date?"

"No it is not a date and we've been through all that before."

"Byron, why can't we be lovers?" Tears began pouring down her face. "I sang like all the world wanted me on Wednesday and I didn't know you were going to be there and the only one I want doesn't want me."

"You're my client."

"Why can't I be your bloody client and your bloody mistress?"

"You can't see it, can you? We start going to bed and in six weeks it will all be over and then what happens to your precious career? It was one or the other... Maybe it doesn't get all over in six weeks and you get famous and I get jealous. I'm not going to put myself in a position where I worry who you're with. You'll be touring the country, the world I hope, and I'm not going to pussyfoot behind you wondering who's getting into your pants. We can run your career as a business or nothing else."

"Then you do fancy me?"

"Of course I bloody fancy you but that doesn't make the slightest bit of difference."

"I won't go out with anyone else."

"Shelley, you're talking to me, Byron, we're exactly the same type, we don't stay with one person. We are not the mortgage and three-kids type. We will break each other's hearts and ruin your career in the process."

"What about love?"

"We don't love people, we use people. That's our price for success. Fame and fortune, but no love."

"We can have both."

"We can't, don't you see?"

"Then I want to start singing straight away."

"I had a talk with your teacher. Not for another six months. Your breathing is still not right and you strain your voice. A year. That was the contract. Write songs. Lots of them. That's what the amendment is about. Now, do you want to get up and have supper?... Shelley, please don't cry. That's one thing I can't handle."

"Why don't you come and give me a hug?"

"Because it won't end up as a hug."

"Well damn you!"

"You're going to be one of the great singers of your generation. You proved that on Wednesday. Find yourself a lover. That piano player has his eye on you. I'll leave the amendment for you to read when you've stopped crying."

"I'm never going to stop."

"You will... I'll let myself out. Shelley, believe me. The other way we'll destroy each other... Find yourself a lover."

"Oh, go to hell."

Quietly shutting the bedroom door, Byron walked through the lounge and out of her apartment, tears stinging the back of his eyes.

"I probably will," he said to himself, going out into the bitterly cold night. Just before closing the door he had a terrible desire to go back. "You can't have your cake and eat it too, you bloody fool," he said out loud.

Viciously, he slammed Mrs Page's front door, sending a shock wave through the house. There was the whole of London waiting for him in the night and nowhere he wanted to go.

7

$\mathcal{W}$ill came home in the summer. The crate of ivory had been taken to Livingstone by road. With Will it travelled by train to Cape Town in South Africa where it was moved on board the *Braemar Castle* bound for the port of London.

The man that went ashore at Tilbury Docks would not have been recognised by the boy who had left the island four years earlier. Will Langton was a powerful man with the physique and look of a hunter. The ivory went into a bonded warehouse where it would stay while Will explored the market.

"Englishman, you take that blerry ivory to England and sell it yourself," Hannes had explained. "Those robbers in Livingstone will give us nothing. Open yourself a bank account but bring me back my half. If the Central African Federation falls apart, I will fall with it but a young man like you needs a few pounds in a safe bank account."

From the moment he landed in England, the face of every young girl was searched for the face of the lady he had run from soon after leaving school. One wore a striped top, black and white, as she had done and his stomach lurched until she turned her face to look at him.

"What are you staring at?" she snapped.

"My apologies," mumbled Will.

"So you should."

Carrying the same two bags he had carried to Africa, Will found the

Tube train to Waterloo and began the journey southwest. It would be strange not finding Granda at the station to run him back to Langton Manor. The mood of false hope that had built up on the boat had evaporated. There would be one last pilgrimage to Dancing Ledge and he would leave it at that.

The train clickety-clacked through the suburbs of London and into the country. Will found the countryside so green after the African bush. He had telegraphed the family his time of arrival, not willing to phone his mother after so many years. Better they meet face-to-face and hopefully save the awkwardness; when it came to letter writing Will Langton was one of the worst.

Randolph, his oldest, dependable brother, met him at the station with the family car but did not recognise the bronzed, big-shouldered, well-thighed man in shorts who stepped off the train.

"The violet eyes yes but the rest of you doesn't make sense. Didn't they call you the runt at Stanmore?"

"How are you all, Randolph? It's been a long time."

"Fine. Anna's fine... Oh, Jo's down for the weekend which is rare for our sister. Considers we live off the sweat of our labourers and stole the land from their forefathers. Never stops talking politics. How is Hilary?"

"Working himself into an early grave, literally."

"Is it worth it?"

"For Hilary or the Barotse?"

"Both."

"If you ask my personal opinion I think they are both doing each other more harm than good. Dad and Mother?"

"Dad still has nightmares about the bombing but otherwise they are well. Mother keeps pestering Anna to have a baby but however hard we try it doesn't work. The doctors say it probably won't but don't tell Mother. Twenty grandchildren would not be enough for her. Jo's going to be a spinster all her life, never has a boyfriend. Byron plays a wide field, so it's up to you, younger brother... Put those bags in the boot and I'll show you what we've been doing on the farm. One thing, don't mention colonialism to Josephine or she will blast you out of the house. Anything that smacks of superiority is anathema to our sister. It's been a good summer so far for the crops. You going to stay in England?"

"No, Randolph, I'm not. If I did, they'd probably want me in the army. You remember, I ducked out of national service."

"I was the only one to be caught."

"I've some ideas for photographic safaris. Want to talk to the travel agents. Brought over a crate of ivory to sell. Better to shoot the animals with cameras. You know, some of the clients don't bother to take the tusks back. Just a photograph with a hero sitting on the dead elephant is enough. Four of those elephants we had to shoot ourselves to protect the customer. There are two ways an elephant flaps his ears. One is to cool his blood down in the heat and another, very destructive way is when he's going to charge. Only then do I use the Sako .458 Swedish rifle. One of the best."

"I'll take your word for it... Oh, just be warned. Jo brought a man down with her this time."

"That should please Mother."

"Not really. He's black. From your part of the world, actually. Paul Mwansa. Comes from Lusaka."

"What's he doing in England?"

"Demanding his country back."

Josephine Langton had not improved her looks with age or make-up and her clothes would have been better off left on the sheep. Her redeeming feature, the violet eyes, with the birthmark below, were her only good feature. They were fixed accusingly on Will.

"This is my friend, Paul Mwansa," she said, introducing him to her brother.

Will put out his hand. "Randolph said you're from Lusaka. I speak a little Lozi but no Bemba, I'm afraid."

"Paul thinks the white man should get out of Africa."

"If you want my opinion, which for what it's worth agrees with Hilary's, Africa would have been a better place without the white man in the first place."

"So you agree with decolonisation with full compensation?" said Paul Mwansa.

"I don't think you will be able to compensate us for roads, railways, bridges, the Kariba Dam and a nucleus First World infrastructure. And you sure as hell wouldn't have built it on your own, with or without your own money... Will you excuse me a moment while I go and find my mother and father? I haven't seen them for four years. If you want to talk colonial politics, talk to my sister. She's much better qualified. And Jo, I want to hear all about the labour movement, what you have achieved and what you hope to achieve."

"I'm a communist now."

"From what I read, which is quite a lot in the bush, there is no difference between social democracy and communism. Maybe you can tell me but not until I have seen our parents."

Randolph took up the conversation in the silence. "Mother's in the kitchen garden at the back or she would have heard the car. Dad's looking at a sick cow. He's been there most of the morning."

Mother and son looked at each other for a long time, smiling, and then they embraced.

"Your father's down at the cowshed."

"How's the sick cow?"

"Nothing wrong with the cows. We had politics for supper and breakfast. Father took sanctuary in the cowshed. I think she brought him down specially to meet you and show you what a naughty boy you are living in Africa instead of working for the cause. It's all Uncle Cliff's fault, but what can you do? If only she would find a nice young man and settle down. She never listens to me. Your father has given up... We've roast lamb, mint sauce, new potatoes and peas for supper. Your favourite. Just hope Jo lets us eat the food before it all goes cold. Everything's changed since the war. Come on down to the cowshed and you can tell me and Father what you have been doing for four years. You children never could write letters, even from boarding school where they made you write home once a week."

That evening before the sun was down behind the big oak, the table was laid outside on the terrace. Red Langton brought forth the leg of lamb on a silver platter that had been in the family for six generations. The smell was delicious. Along the length of the family table were three open bottles of red wine and crystal glasses sparkling in the last of the sun.

As if by a miracle before supper, Will had kept the conversation from being directed back to politics while the men drank a glass of beer and the women a glass of sherry on the lawn under the oak. By the time the lamb had been carried by Red and the wine poured by Randolph, Josephine was no longer going to be gainsaid and came in straight to the point at Will.

"Don't you think it is totally immoral for one people to rule another as master and servant?"

"Well, yes and no, sis."

"Don't evade the question. Nothing could be more simple."

"There is always someone ruling someone. Surely it's better to have a good ruler rather than a bad one?"

"Would you have liked to be ruled by the Germans?"

"No, of course not."

"Then how do you think my friend here likes being ruled by the British and called *boy*. He's a man, isn't he?"

"We didn't want to be ruled by the Germans because the Nazis were fascists, bad people, but we've mostly been ruled by the Germans for over a thousand years. We Anglo-Saxons are from the German tribes who conquered this island. You think we'd better all go back to Saxony and give the island back to the Celts?"

"Colonialism is an affront to the human race."

"Was the Greek Empire, the Roman? Did we islanders not benefit from the Roman invasion? Before the Roman's arrived we didn't even know how to take a hot bath, let alone build a road and travel in comfort... The tribes that make up the human race have roamed over its surface for tens of thousands of years, fighting, merging, conquering, ruling, being ruled. No one can say where any of us come from. The question we British must ask ourselves is do we rule well, fairly, without corruption? If we do, we are doing our job and should continue to do so. You, Mr Mwansa, should remember why Queen Victoria was asked by your people to give them protection and whether the so-called evil of colonialism will not be supplanted by a real evil of fear, corruption and want. Be careful, maybe, that the freedom you seek is not brought to you by the lies of a few people seeking power for themselves. Maybe, just maybe, communism, your world of socialism, will become a name for the worst form of corrupt government in the history of man... Now, may I eat my roast lamb before it goes cold?"

"You talk utter rubbish," said Josephine.

"Probably, I'm not even twenty-two. There are far wiser brains than mine, or any of ours for that matter, and they haven't worked out the answer. Neither, I fear, will we."

"How can some people be so rich and the masses so poor?" she snapped.

"After the dinner, sis, after my dinner. I came a long way to eat supper with my family and I would like us to enjoy ourselves, not argue with each other."

THE DOGS FOLLOWED WILL out of the dell. The new day had come with the rising sun and the call of the birds. The house behind them was asleep as they walked between the hedgerows up to the Downs that swept to the cliffs. Sheep grazed without taking notice. The blue sea came towards them from the folds in the smooth green hills. Will could hear the waves breaking on the rocks with the call of the gulls. His boyhood returned to him as he climbed down to Dancing Ledge and the pool with the dead-eye cave watching behind. Somehow, irrationally, he had thought she would be there by the pool to greet him. The slate-grey rocks were bare. For a brief, short, silent moment he felt her spirit and then it was gone with a bark of a dog.

Checking carefully for summer tourists, he stripped to his underpants and jumped in the pool that had been carved out of the rocks during the war. The balm of time and water washed over him and when he climbed out of the water to let the new sun warm his icy body, the ghost of sadness shifted from his mind.

By the time he went home, hungry for his breakfast, Josephine and the man from Africa had gone off on their way back to London. For a week he enjoyed his family and the only home he had known. Then he too returned to the capital to face the rest of his life.

"A CRATE OF IVORY," said Byron, sitting behind the desk in his office. "That must be quite a lot of ivory."

"Enough to give me a small nest egg," said Will watching his brother. "Do I have to pay tax?"

"Maybe not. You live in England. Did you declare the value of the tusks when you left them with customs?"

"There are some skins, too. No. I said I had no idea. They want a bill of sale but when I said the ivory came from my own hunting, they didn't take much interest."

"First, we will sell the crate sight unseen to one of my companies who will give you a bill of sale. Then we will market the tusks and skins individually."

"Half of the real amount goes to Hannes. How do I send it out of England?"

"That too I can arrange."

"And where do I put the proceeds, Byron?"

"With me of course. You don't think I'm going to all this trouble for nothing?"

"That I would never have thought."

"Life has some risks, younger Brother. You can either be conservative and go through the formal channels and end up giving most of your money to the government, or you can take a risk with me. You may or may not make a lot of money. Risk capital is exactly that. I deal in risk capital. If every venture we ever thought of made money we would all be rich."

"I'm too young to be conservative."

"Good. Now piss off while I do some work and come back at six o'clock. Tonight is a big night. We will go to the show together and then have some supper. You can stay at the flat. You must have grown six inches since you left England."

"Seven."

"I don't think I could beat you up now if I tried... Oh, do you have suit and tie?"

"NICE FLAT, BYRON."

"That's your couch over there... You want a drink?"

"Whisky... I liked the guy downstairs with the top hat. You mind if I have a bath?"

"Have what you like. You staying in England?"

"No. I've talked to three travel agents today and they like the concept of my photographic safari and the price. Instead of taking one customer out to slaughter the animals we take six out with cameras. Guns to protect them. Tell them what they are seeing. That sort of thing. Volume rather than one high-priced customer who is often a pain in the neck."

"People with cameras can be just as much a pain in the neck. Tourism. Going to be the big thing with socialism giving everyone shorter hours. Leisure industries are the growth stock of the future."

"Don't you have a date tonight if it's a big occasion?"

"Not this one."

"The girl in your office. Wow, you dating her?"

"Do you screw the wives of your customers?"

"No. But probably not for the same reason. None of them have ever looked like that redhead in your office." They both laughed.

"We're going to the show and then we are going out to supper at the Café Royal."

"Byron... Not the redhead?"

"You'll see."

"You asked about a suit and tie. I went and bought one this afternoon. The first suit I ever owned. Nearest we get to dressing up in Barotseland is wearing a long pair of trousers... What show are we going to see? One of the musicals, I hope? The billboards are all over for *Irma La Douce*."

The taxi dropped them outside the club at eight o'clock and Max met them at the door. By eight-thirty the invited guests were seated at the tables and the waiters were serving French champagne. The club was closed to the public for the Monday night. The members of the press looked bored. A model agency had supplied the waitresses. The band played a medley of music that no one had heard before. A comedian told some jokes but no one laughed.

Max shrugged his shoulders. It was going to be one of those evenings but the price had been right. If young merchant bankers wished to throw away good money, it was none of his business.

Byron sat back and watched them all. The recording manager of EMI looked the most bored of them all. Magazine editors, all of them women, drank their champagne and ate the snacks. The music critic for *Melody Maker* yawned without putting a hand in front of his face. The comedian went off and nobody clapped. Then all the lights went out. The club was pitch-black for fifteen seconds. The spotlight hit Shelley Lane seated on a high stool, her head bowed down, the microphone hanging by her side. Slowly, she looked up and smiled. The band played softly, the new band, every one of them under long-term contract to Byron Langton. The music swelled and Shelley began to sing, every note as pure as crystal. The power of her voice transcended the band with the opening line of 'If You Want To Be Mine'. The slit dress fell open as one long leg searched for the floor.

Byron watched the audience as the footlights grew with the swell of the music. Shelley slid effortlessly from the verse to the chorus and powered out the line which gave the song its title: *'Try a little harder if you want to be mine'*. For twenty minutes she sang a medley of eight of her songs, strutting the small stage using every ounce of her sex appeal, ignoring the constant flash of the cameras.

Taking up her first number in a different key she sang the songs again. Without a break, she sang for an hour before sitting back on the high stool and lowering her head.

In the silence, Byron went up onto the small stage and took her hand. They smiled at each other.

"Ladies and gentlemen," said Byron, "I want to introduce you to Miss Shelley Lane. Thank you for coming tonight."

He was the first to clap her and then they clapped and the stamping of feet gave way to a standing ovation.

Shelley held up her arms.

"If someone will give me a glass of champagne, I'll sing you another song."

Byron gave her the microphone and a hand from the audience pushed up a glass of wine which she drank in one gulp. Then she sang them 'This One Is For You' while Byron went back to his table.

"Who the hell is she?" said Will.

"I told you, Shelley Lane. She's the lady we dine with tonight."

Shelley's entrance to the Café Royal was a sensation. The dress she was wearing was made of synthetic silk and would have easily folded up and fitted into a man's trouser pocket. The hem finished halfway up her thighs, the slits under her armpits reached the waist-belt, showing she wore no bra. Walking with the power of youth and the knowledge of her success, her long, panther-like strides were followed by every male in the room.

The corner table was immaculately laid for three and in the centre of the middle place setting rested a single orchid, white, flecked with delicate red spots; the small throat was a deep red. The last time Will's legs felt like this was the first time he had been charged by an elephant.

They had left Max's club while the confusion was in full flood with every newspaper and magazine looking for an interview. Shelley, having thrown the flimsy dress over her perfect body in her dressing room, had slipped out the back door into the alley where Byron had been waiting with a taxi. The street light showed her perfectly.

"This is my brother, Will. Climb in."

"Hello, William," she said putting out her hand. Will was not sure whether to kiss the proffered hand. Awkwardly, he gave it a shake.

"They call me Will."

"Well, I prefer William so it will be William in the future." She gave the word 'future' a meaning that extended further than time. Byron looked at his protégée with quick alarm. They drove out of the alley and on towards the Café Royal.

"Where did you manage that gorgeous tan, brother William?"

"I've just come back from Africa." Shelley's bare leg was pressed hard against his knee in the taxi. Will stammered out the words.

"What do you do in Africa, William?"

"I'm a professional hunter with a safari operation."

"Now that is interesting. Over dinner you can tell me everything."

On the word *everything* she put her right hand firmly on his knee and gave it a press. Until they reached the door of the Café, she had not removed her hand.

Byron pinned the orchid corsage onto the yellow-white dress and they sat down to supper. Shelley was having the time of her life and not once mentioned the club to Byron or her standing ovation. The weapon she had been looking for, for over a year had been placed in her hand. Using it was going to be her pleasure and Byron's pain.

Shelley put the oysters into her mouth, sucking each one off her fork with an inner smile, twice catching Will's eye as she swallowed. The band struck up a dance number and Byron asked Shelley to dance.

"It will be my pleasure," she said to him and then turned to Will. "Now, you won't go away?"

On the dance floor she put her hands behind Byron's neck but kept him at full distance, smiling regretfully but mischievously into his eyes.

"What the hell are you doing, Shelley?" he snapped.

"You know your eyes are a similar colour but his have far more depth. Must be all that hunting. Imagine shooting a lion." Shelley rolled her big brown eyes in their almond settings and gave Byron a lascivious wink.

"He's my damn brother."

"I know and he's very good-looking. Nearly twenty-two, he told me; far nearer my age."

"I don't want you making a fool of him."

"I have a secret suspicion that William really would not mind. After all, you did tell me to take a lover."

"But not my brother."

"Why ever not? He's cute. Now, if you had been my lover and not merely my business manager, it would never happen."

"We've been through that a dozen times."

"Exactly."

"You were tremendous tonight."

"I know I was... Now, let's go back to our table. It's rude to leave your brother all on his lonesome."

At the end of the fish course she turned to Will.

"William, come and dance with me. It's my favourite slow number."

On the floor, she immediately folded into his arms so he could feel every corner of her body, one of the seashell ears resting sweetly against his cheek. When the music turned her towards their table, she closed her eyes.

The EMI man found them at eleven o'clock, by which time Shelley had ordered a pen and paper from the waiter and written down her address for William.

"Just come round tomorrow morning when you feel like it. I don't go out very much. Byron will be working so hard. We can go into the park. Holland Park is not very full during the day and there are lots of little nooks and crannies. You might like to buy me a little lunch. There's a pub I know with a lovely little garden and the best pickled onions in London... Now, you won't lose that address?" She tucked the piece of paper into the top pocket of his suit jacket and gave it a little pat to keep it safe.

"Do you mind if I pull up another chair?" said Bob Shackleton of EMI. "Phoned seven restaurants before I thought of the Café Royal. Byron, will you do the honours?"

Introductions complete and an extra wine glass placed on the table, Shelley turned her full attention to the man from the record company.

"EMI wish to offer you a recording contract, Miss Lane. I have it here in my pocket. All it needs is your name and for you to sign. It's our standard contract, the same for all our top artists. I don't suppose Byron has seen one before?"

With just a little theatre he put the contract on the white tablecloth in front of Shelley.

"I don't really want to see it, Bob," said Byron. "Fact is, I also have a contract that just needs your name and signature. By tomorrow I'd imagine we will be holding an auction." Byron offered the contract from his inside pocket. "The manager will find you an office to be quiet."

"Don't you want to read our standard contract?"

"I know every word of it... Shall we say half an hour? You may wish to make some phone calls from the manager's office."

"You planned all this!"

"Just over a year ago."

"What about her band?"

"They are part of that contract. All of us are going to make a lot of money, Bob, a lot of money. And, after all, that is what life is all about."

The contract was signed by all the parties at three minutes to midnight in the manager's office, witnessed by the manager and his food and beverage man, the Café Royal popping a bottle of champagne to celebrate. The upfront payment was twenty thousand pounds sterling with twenty-three per cent of record sales at retail price payable to Shelley Lane, renewal of the contract to be renegotiated each year.

"A negotiable renewal makes all parties perform," said Byron. "Any one-sided contract is a disaster. Congratulations, Shelley, you're on your way."

THEY WERE the only people under the oak tree. Will and Shelley. Wind rustled the leaves above them but the weather held. Neither of them had spoken for five minutes, the euphoria of the night before finding the full glare of the day. Byron had made his phone call at eleven o'clock that morning and she had turned him down.

"The biggest anti-climax in my life," said Shelley interrupting the silence.

"Which one? Turning down my brother or signing the recording contract?"

"Maybe both... Will, you want another beer?"

"The games people play. Sure, I'll have another beer. When something is too good to be true, it usually is. That was you for me last night. Byron and I talked until three in the morning after we dropped you off in the taxi. I made him make that phone call this morning and I'm only sad you didn't accept."

"Did I really make him as jealous as a snake?" she chuckled.

"Jealous as a snake."

"I'm sorry for coming on to you."

"At the time I was delirious."

"We can still go to the park."

"Maybe you are right. You and Byron would never work. Any more than a singer would want to live in a bush camp on the banks of the Zambezi. How do people get together, Shelley? Get together and stay together? I'll go and fetch the beers. English draught beer. Missed it for four years."

"There's always something missing."

"Yes, there is. Oh, and with one exception you are the most attractive girl I have ever met. Maybe we'll meet again."

"What was she like?" asked Shelley.

"The other half of my soul."

HER NAME WAS NOT MENTIONED at 47 Buckingham Court for the next week. The ivory and skins were sent for processing and would be sold for six times the amount stated in the bill of sale which had been accepted for the calculation of duty by the customs.

"Whatever we import into the island is sold again," said Byron. "All we've done is brought the goods into the country as raw materials, arranged for the ivory to be carved, the skins to be made into coats and the profit exported to Switzerland. Perfectly legal and everyone is happy. The middleman always makes the money. The fact we have an interest from the killing to the carving is coincidental. Your friend Hannes Potgieter would be very wise not to have his share sent to Northern Rhodesia. Better we invest for him in South African shares on the Johannesburg Stock Exchange as one day soon he will be going back to South Africa. The colonies are too expensive and there's a better way of exploiting the minerals without having to administer the country and listen to the likes of our sister."

THE CABLE ARRIVED from Hilary Bains via Langton Manor that afternoon. Madge O'Shea, Byron's secretary, had opened the envelope.

"I'm sorry, Will. I'm sorry."

 REGRET HANNES KILLED BY ELEPHANT

Will sat down in the office and stared at the simple piece of paper.

"If I hadn't come over, he would still be alive. His legs had gone. You mind if I get out of here and go for a walk?"

The wooden bench was covered in pigeon droppings and the people passed him by in both directions, unseen, unnoticed.

Will was back in Barotseland in the permanent bush camp and the place was lonely. Neither Sixpence, Fourpence nor Onepenny were talking and the Goliath heron had stopped looking for revenge. The bush was silent and the great river behind the house flowed to the sea. The pontoon boat was waiting for the skipper who would not come home.

Where had they buried him? Would the big man have liked to grow into old age, daily more decrepit? Maybe the elephant knew. Without the big man, would Africa ever be the same?

'The sun's down, Englishman. Have a drink.'

'That's the best idea you've had since yesterday.'

They'd drink listening to the river behind, the bush in front and talk. The most pleasant evenings of his life. There was no intrigue or subterfuge. No hidden meanings. No trying to hurt.

'I've had a good life, Englishman. Danika was a good woman. That's all a man can want. You don't ever worry about me. Worry about having a good life for yourself. You're the nearest I got to a son. You know the bush and years of experience will better your skills... Africa is changing, Will, so be careful.'

The memories skittered in and out of his mind and when he got up his legs were stiff from sitting in the same position. Africa receded and London traffic returned.

"Go well, Hannes," he said and walked to the nearest bar.

When he reached the flat that night he was maudlin drunk and Byron had to sit up listening. For Will, the world had just come to an end.

WILL WOKE with a headache pounding in the front of his head. He had no idea where he was. There was a banging outside of his head followed by bells and the chimney pots outside the window were going round and round. The well of bile-sickness surged from his empty stomach and threw him at the sick-splattered washbasin where he retched and retched until the sphincter at the base of his spine hurt more than his stomach, the opening and closing of the ring round his rectum more painful than the passing of a gallstone. Drunk, Will had wished he would die. Now, he wished that he had. The cold tap gushed and splattered the carpet with diluted vomit and Will got his head down awkwardly to the hard mouth of the tap that rattled his teeth and sucked in water while the spasms around his arsehole continued. The intermittent banging and bells were coming from the hallway and no one was answering the door. It was all coming back to him. With a towel snatched round his waist Will staggered to the bedroom door and down the passage. Byron had gone to work and he was left on his own. After fumbling the catch he had the door half-open and stared out into the corridor. Two tall men in blue uniforms with large, white-banded caps were looking down at his half-nakedness. White blancoed webbing belts circled their midriffs, the brass work gleaming even in the gloom of the corridor.

"Are you William Edward Langton, formerly of Langton Manor in the county of Dorset?"

Will tried to draw the towel tighter and his arsehole clammed up and he was sick into the corridor, a trickle of bile reaching the nearest inquisitor. Will nodded weakly.

"You will report to Royal Air Force Cardington on July the third, by sixteen hundred hours; four p.m. for the likes of you. If you are late, we'll pick you up AWOL, that's absent without leave, and throw you in the glasshouse which is not glass and not a house but a prison cell. Furthermore, in accordance with Queen's Regulations you will surrender to me your passport." The RAF Special Policeman slapped an envelope at Will's bare chest. "We've spent a lot of time looking for you. Your call-up papers have now been served on you in person. The rail pass inside the envelope will take you to Cardington for induction and the issue of uniform from where you will go to a square-bashing unit for your initial training. Your attempts to avoid military service have been noted on your record. At the end of your nine-week square-bashing you will wish you had joined up the first time."

Slowly, the SP Corporal looked down, his eyes half hidden by the peak of his cap, to the bile on his right boot. In perfect unison with the aircraftman 1st class at his side, he left turned, crashing his boots on the tiled floor of the corridor, and marched away.

"Detail *halt*," he bellowed ten paces away. "*About turn... Quick march...* Detail *halt...* Passport?" he snapped.

"It's at Langton Manor."

"Don't try to leave the country."

"No, sir."

"*Corporal* to you."

"Yes, Corporal." By the time the detail had reached the end of the corridor, the towel had fallen to the floor and Will was standing in his underpants, his arsehole still as tight as an oyster, with the brown envelope clutched to his chest.

"THIS IS PLAIN STUPID," said Byron. "Six weeks ago Parliament announced the end of national service."

"Probably for people born after a certain date."

"Total waste of your time and taxpayers' money. Will, we've got to get you out of this one. Two years is a hell of a long time and they won't even consider you for a commission. 'Didn't play the game, old boy'," he mimicked. "You must go back to Africa on the first plane."

"They asked for my passport. Told them it was down in Dorset."

"Where is it?"

"In my pocket."

"Do you have a return ticket?"

"No. But they said I mustn't leave the country. Threatened to lock me up... I have to go back to sort out the safari operation."

"There was a boy at school who joined the Bechuanaland police instead of doing his national service. Perfectly legal. Tell them you're in the Northern Rhodesia police, home on leave. That'll shut them up. Bureaucracy against bureaucracy... What's the name of the chief of police in Mongu?"

"They call him the member in charge. What can he do, Byron? I'll just have to go to Cardington next week. They will hound me for the rest of my life. Problems faced are problems solved. That was Mother."

"Not if we send them official documents. That is, a copy of your police identity document and the leave pass from your member in charge."

"Gave me my driver's licence without a test, did the member in charge."

"Pour yourself a drink. You look terrible."

When the front door had banged, Will sat back with a half-glass of neat whisky and contemplated his options. Forged documents would probably land him in jail but two years as an aircraftman 2nd class was not to be contemplated. Africa was suddenly a long way away.

ON THE FIRST OF JULY, Byron handed a set of documents to Will together with a ticket from the port of London to Cape Town on the *City of York*, a British cargo vessel that carried eight passengers.

"The boat leaves at eleven tomorrow night," said Byron. "I'll deduct the cost from the ivory. Cable me what to do with your friend's money when you get home."

"England's my home, Byron. This is sending me into exile."

"Maybe the whole of England is going into exile. You want to spend an evening with our sister and her friends and just listen. The England the likes of you and I want is dying slowly. Socialism. Democracy. The other side of the equation. You know, when they first voted in the welfare state the contributions were to fund the benefits but the new socialism soon used the contributions as current income and promised the pensions from future tax. Quite understandable. First year economic student will tell you a pension has to be provided for. Very simply they are going to make our grandchildren look after our old and sick and they won't, Will. Social democracy is a tax on unborn children who don't have the vote.

"In the old days the rich were greedy. Now the masses have gone into a feeding frenzy. Wonderful system provided the majority can vote to steal from the rich, the producers, the people who create the wealth. But they won't stand for it either, Will. They won't allow themselves to be punitively taxed. They'll get their money out of the country into a system that is free of currency controls, and free of predatory governments. Between world socialism demanding their rights and the new capitalism running off with the money, the likes of England will probably disappear in financial chaos. Forget about giving England two years of your life. Go and enjoy yourself. What do you think all this free love is about? No one gives a damn about tomorrow. Grab what you can in the feeding frenzy. The sixties will be the best decade ever for the young. They're going to screw what's left of their brains out."

"You're a bloody cynic."

"No, brother, a bloody realist. Ask our father. He saw them drop the bomb and he hasn't been the same ever since. He saw the end of this world and his religion hasn't given him a clear picture of the next. Let's get out of this flat and have a good supper on your last night. You may not be seeing London for quite a while."

THE OWNER of the restaurant on the Bayswater Road welcomed Byron with a broad smile and hands wrung together at belly button height.

"It's so good to see you again, Mr Langton. Are you expecting some ladies?"

"Just me and my brother. That table in the corner."

"Welcome, Mr Langton," said the owner, now smiling at Will in his new suit.

Not waiting, Byron strode across to his preferred table and sat down comfortably. The wine list was put into his hands. Will took a menu that showed no prices.

"There are no prices," said Byron, without looking up from the wine list. "I'm paying."

"Why no prices?" asked Will.

"In a place like this, if you have to ask the price you can't afford to be here... It's your last night. We can go on to a club if you want a girl."

"Where is Shelley singing?"

"Not Shelley. Thank you... A bottle of Château Mouton Rothschild '47. No, make it two and take the corks out of both. And the duck for both of us."

"No oysters?" said the owner.

"What for? No women." Byron laughed, and the owner tittered and left the table.

"Can't remember his name and he wouldn't give a tinker's cuss about me and my name if I wasn't paying... The power of money. Always was and always will be... You owe Johnny Pike a favour."

"Who is Johnny Pike?" asked Will.

"The man that arranged the forgery of your papers. He's a crook. A good one. Trained by his father. They own a piece of my operation. The future growth industry, crookery. When all governments are liars and thieves, no one can tell the difference between a politician and an honest crook. Your documents are perfect."

"And if the RAF check up?"

"Still perfect."

"And the member in charge?"

"He was phoned yesterday."

"You frighten me, Byron."

"You don't think I got rich being a stockbroker's clerk?"

"You'll get caught."

"Nothing I do is illegal."

"Forging colonial police documents?"

"We copied them actually. As from three days ago you were a police reservist in the Northern Rhodesian police. Welensky, your Federal Prime Minister, is having some trouble in Nyasaland with a rising politician named Banda. Your call back letter from the member in charge is genuine. When you reach Mongu, report to the police station."

"How did this Johnny Pike come into it?"

"Someone in the Federal government owed Johnny's father a favour. That's how it works. You may or may not find out yourself. Just depends what happens with your life."

Will found the red wine delicious with the duck. The worry of being found out receded with the intake of alcohol.

"Even though Shelley turned you down, why haven't you taken Shelley out as a girlfriend?" Will asked.

"Because probably I think I love her which is a nice word for lust which mostly lasts a few weeks. Marriage is the biggest single business contract we enter into in our life. Shelley could make me want to get married because of an ancient power that has nothing to do with my brains. Marriage is serious. Shelley and I would be frivolous, sexual and limited, none of which is a basis for having someone around for the rest of my life. Apart from a sexual magnetism we have nothing in common."

"You don't believe in love?"

"Temporary love can turn into permanent dependence which is what they call a happy marriage. Shelley and I will make each other a lot of money. Money lasts longer than emotion."

"Without love, the rest isn't worth living."

"Whoever told you life was worth the living? Most of it is a complete waste of time. There is certainly no final point to it which is why man over the millennia has been so determined to find a religion. And there are as many religious ideas as there are political. Without a God to make it all better and give us a final place to hide, the whole thing is ridiculous and mostly painful. Hence my hedonistic desire to enjoy myself as much as possible and that requires lots of money, brother. The religious and political ideas come and go and leave behind money and sex, in that order for a man, in the reverse order for a woman."

"You frighten me."

"The truth always does. And that's the second time I've frightened you but it won't be the last. The mumbo jumbo they taught us at school was to make us conform to their society. Believe in what we say, do what we say and in the future you will be happy. One superior class, one wife, one religion. Do your duty for queen and country. Load of bullshit."

"How can a family brought up by the same parents be so different? Maybe I should have been a painter and lived in a French attic and thought nice thoughts all day long."

"You want to go to a club?"

"Not really, Byron. If I am to find a woman, she has to have the chance for me of being permanent, I don't think I fit into your hedonistic society of one-night stands. I'm twenty-two and still a virgin and maybe I will leave it that way for a while."

"To the romantic," said Byron, lifting his glass. "Look after yourself, younger brother. Have a good trip."

PART III

1963 TO 1964

8

*J*osephine Langton's flutter with the British Communist Party had lasted six months. The power lay with the Labour Party. Many dedicated to world socialism, where the limitless wealth of the world would be evenly distributed over all mankind, found their political home with Labour. They were patient.

Josephine was thirty-two in the spring of 1963, not married, not wishing to be dominated by any male and using her hatred of the system to hide the awful failure of a mother who had deliberately killed her unborn child. The boy, she was now sure the aborted foetus would have been, would have turned thirteen at the end of the year. She never thought of Wolfgang Baumann, the father, only her son.

Urged on by Paul Mwansa, with whom she had gone to bed twice to prove a point that all mankind was equal, she sat her current hobby horse in the London County Council and screamed abuse at colonialism in general and the Federation of the Rhodesias and Nyasaland in particular. She had won a council seat three weeks after her thirtieth birthday, a birthday she looked back on as the watershed of her life. Finally, she had decided in the recesses of her own mind that she would never now become a dutiful wife with three children deferring to a husband and his career. Brutally, she turned away from the biological function of her life. She was as good as any man and better than most and the only use she made of her female body was to pursue her career – or prove a point. Without her emotion involved,

Josephine found manipulating men pathetically easy, especially the political males, who were generally oversexed and driven to prove it with as many women as they found would oblige. Josephine dressed severely in suits but there was always the penetration of the violet eyes, an unexpected flash, a loose button that showed the soft silk of a bra, the inside of a thigh. Coming from Comrade Langton, the revelation was nothing short of erotic. Paul Mwansa had ejaculated in his underpants before either of them could get them off.

The Central African Federation had been put together by the British in 1953, with the member states entitled to secession at the end of ten years. The economic benefits were monumental, the chance to erase the poverty of turbulent Africa, but the politics remained in the hands of a few white settlers. Northern Rhodesia and Nyasaland secretly opted to secede and travel independent paths on the Westminster system of one man one vote. It was to be the death of the British Empire in Africa and, following upon the aborted campaign to oust Colonel Nasser from his own Suez Canal, marginalised Britain and made her largely irrelevant in world politics. The largest empire the world had ever known began to fold its tents around the world and retreat to the small island off the coast of Europe. The people in the new politics in England who mattered, who were viewing the world from their 'correct' political premise, cheered the loudest.

Byron, being of a more practical mind, had laughed at his sister's rhetoric. "Giving other peoples' money away is easy, sis. The trick is making it in the first place. What do you socialists do when you've run out of other peoples' money to give away? Unsustainable, old girl. It's a one-off like your one man one vote in Africa... Are you sure we are twins?"

When Byron left her small flat in Notting Hill Gate, Josephine was fuming. It was a Saturday night and there were no meetings. Byron had the irritating habit of dropping in when he was bored, stirring her up for half an hour and then leaving with an enigmatic smile on his face. He always had a future scenario to her politics that was the opposite of her intention, with always a ring of truth hanging in the air. First she watered the pot plants and when that failed to take her off the boil she snatched up the phone and dialled Heathcliff Mortimer who answered on the second ring. Josephine always thought he stood over the phone waiting to pounce. The man never said anything.

"Are you there, Heath?"

"Of course. Who do you think picked up the phone?"

"Why don't you say hello or something?"

"You rang, not me. Obviously you had something to say. Why must I clutter up the conversation?"

"Will you come over?"

"Do you have any whisky?"

"No."

"Then I'll have to bring my own."

The phone at the other end clicked and left Josephine looking at a silent hand piece.

Half an hour later Heathcliff Mortimer eased the bulk of his backside into the only comfortable chair and poured himself a large whisky, raising the glass briefly to Josephine. He was sixty and had long given up the fight against his weight, letting his belly grow to whatever size it chose. The sexual monkey had climbed off his back at the same time his paunch grew to a prodigious size but he still preferred the company of women.

"How's the paper?" she asked.

"Spiritually or financially?"

"Either."

"We write the truth but the truth no longer sells. They want bums and tits, Macmillan says they have never had it so good. I was born forty years too late."

"What is Lord Manningly going to do?"

"Look for someone to bail him out." There was a silence as Heath waited. "Thought that was why you had asked me round?"

"No, it was Byron. Accused me of giving away other people's money."

"Nicer to call it a redistribution of wealth."

"Do you think we should give away the empire?"

"Certainly. Damn thing's costing us money and the good parts want to hive off on their own, dump the sterling block and trade in the open market. England's changing. We don't rely on raw materials to manufacture and export back to the colonies. More worry than they are worth, the colonies. Financial centre, that's England. We will sell our ideas, not the product of our factories... So you haven't heard about Byron's latest move?"

Josephine shook her head.

"Are you sure you are twins?"

"Byron just asked the same question. Yes, I'm sure. Opposites can sometimes be alike. What's my brother up to this time?"

"He's made an offer to buy out Lord Manningly. If he succeeds, I will get the sack... Biggest mystery is where he gets the money. Do you know anything about his companies? Something I can use? At my age I won't get another job."

"Byron started young," said Josephine. "Risk ventures that came off, Shelley Lane and his recording company. Byron knows what is going to happen. Why I called you. Says socialism is unsustainable."

"Practical socialism probably is. People always find a way of taking advantage of a good thing. Why does he want to buy a newspaper that loses half a million a month?"

"If my brother takes over, you won't lose money for long. Yes, you will lose your job. Byron has not one jot of sentiment."

"When do you leave for Africa?"

"Next week. Go through the motions. The Labour Party knows its facts when it comes to colonialism. Get out fast. We don't need a fact-finding commission to prove that."

"Don't you have a brother out there?"

"Two, sort of. Hilary was adopted during the war. His father was Dad's tail gunner and got blown out of the rear turret. Hilary's a missionary. Will shoots animals for a living. Rich American clients. Some German. Poor bloody animals. Haven't seen him for years. They tried to make him do his national service. Byron got him out of the country ahead of the Air Force Police. Can't come back, I think. Maybe I should find out."

"What will happen to him?"

"We all have our problems."

WILL Langton's love affair with wildlife photography began four years earlier, after he was forced to leave England in a hurry on board the *City of York*. On his return to Barotseland, he explained to the member in charge, Mongu, why he was reporting for duty in the Police Reserve.

"Glad to help, Langton. Requests to join the reserve are processed quickly, especially for someone with your background. Hannes and I go back a long way. Uncertain times, Langton. Could find the local gentry stirring up trouble and running off into the bush. Where trained hunters like you come in. Glad to have you on board. The RAF sent us a form to fill in so you shouldn't hear any more from them. Once the old files have been processed everything fits into place. No loose ends. I should know. Just between you and me, you joined up here before you went to England with the ivory. Just between you and me, that is, which brings me to poor old Hannes. Who would have thought, a man of his vast experience? Young one, couldn't have been more than a year old, blocked his path upstream of your base camp. Not five hundred yards from your wire. Took his hat off and brushed at the calf and the mother came out of the shadow of a tree and went berserk. Picked up Hannes and threw him all of thirty feet at a tree and then knelt on him. Mercifully from what I saw, Hannes was dead before he hit the tree. Blood and guts splattered all over the place, I'm afraid. Terrible mess. Bloody hell, I had to turn away from my black constable as I wasn't sure whether I was going to cry or be sick and you can't do that sort of thing in front of local gentry. Week before, Hannes gave me a letter for you. Said it contained his will. Had Mr Jones, the resident, witness it with me. Very formal. But it was an accident, Langton. No doubt about the elephant. God has strange ways. You'd better go back to your base camp and sort out the chaps. Sixpence, poor chap, took it right on the chin. The others not much better. We wired the booked clients not to come and waited for you. Fact is, old chap, you own the whole bang shoot now. You want a lift downriver? I'll have one of my men drive you down. Glad you came back to Africa. Sort of has something, doesn't it? Africa I mean, old chap, Africa."

"Thanks but I'll ask Laurie to drive me down," said Will.

STRANGELY IN THE club that afternoon, everyone seemed to know about his brush with the RAF. Mongu, Will rationalised, was a long way from anywhere in Africa, which was a long way from anywhere at all. Anyway, the form had been sent back with all the right rubber stamps.

The airport manager, Laurie Hall, had finally driven him back to the base camp the following day as everyone in Mongu had dropped in to tell Will how sorry they were about Hannes and buy him a drink. They all knew he was Hannes's heir and condoled with him as though he had been the son. Will was drunk and sad and happy in different waves as the procession of people bought him drinks. Hannes had never wanted to grow old. It was not a suicide, and it was not an accident, Will saw with clarity, but Hannes calling to the will of God and God had answered him.

Hilary Bains had reached the club in time for lunch, a pure coincidence. He was thin and wasted, his face-skin yellow rather than tanned. He looked more like thirty-five than twenty-five. He was surprised to see his adopted brother.

"I was going to tell the family afterwards," said Hilary. "How are the group captain and your mother? Fact is, I'm getting married. Mary has been my lay-worker for the last six months. She's quite a few years older than me but looking at us you'd say she was ten years the younger, I'm afraid. Came out to help the mission station and did I need the help! Just don't have enough time or money and Mary is a trained nurse and wants to be a doctor. We both have a compassion for people less fortunate than ourselves. I mean one Englishman and one Englishwoman together in the middle of nowhere isn't quite right. We were eating together and everything else – no, don't get me wrong!" Will had raised a quizzical eyebrow. "Mary suggested it. We both want to stay on the mission so it makes sense. Mary is very sensible. We will have to wait until the bishop pays us a visit but I'll let you know if I have time. Wouldn't it be wonderful to have a telephone, though I can't see that happening in my lifetime. Came in to send a letter to Mary's father in Surrey, asking his permission. Didn't trust anyone else to put it in the post. Now, tell me all the news and about poor old Hannes and why you're back so quickly, Will. Didn't you like England after Africa? Only God knows if I will ever go back. Used up my home allowance to buy medicine. There's just never enough money."

WILL HAD BEEN THINKING through what he was going to do with the rest of his life ever since the boat turned out of the English Channel and headed for the Canary Islands. Now circumstances were driving him back to the base camp as sole owner of an internationally known safari operation, and he had only turned twenty-two on the way up, in the train from Cape Town to Johannesburg.

Sixpence, Fourpence and Onepenny were waiting for him at the gate into the wire enclosure. The black man's ability to know an event before it happened without the aid of a telephone never failed to surprise Will, but after so many repetitions he was prepared to accept that the Lozi, the indigenous people who lived in Barotseland, had another sense that was unknown to the European. The three trackers were dressed in their best clothes, long-faced and formal, and for the first ten minutes refused to show their white teeth in a smile while Will kept his eye on the Goliath heron. Everything looked the same: the high deck above the flowing river, the long bar visible through the open side of the thatched deck. The tame impala buck looked at him with the same soft warm eyes. A twelve-foot python slid out of the shade to have a look at the commotion.

"The white rabbit had eleven babies," said Sixpence, showing his teeth for the first time, "but that python ate them babies and all the rabbits. Baas, we buried next to the fever tree. Bury baas deep so no hyena get his bones. Now you the baas, baas. You one month late for pay. Soon no food. Good you come back."

The conversation continued in a monologue, retelling the small but desperately important details of daily life in the bush. The elephant that had killed Hannes had gone off downriver with the small transient herd. The river was rising from good rains up in the northern region, which Will knew to be the Angolan catchment area. In honour of the baas coming home they had shot six guinea fowl and two Egyptian geese that morning as the sun rose and mist was still curling up from the river to tangle with the fever trees leaning out from the banks of the great river.

"How did you know I was coming home?" asked Will.

"Onepenny had a dream, so we knew."

It was always the same, a dream, a vision, whichever word they chose.

The birds were already plucked and hung in a row out of reach of the heron. The bar was stocked and as they climbed the stairs to the deck to look out over the great expanse of the African bush, Fourpence was bashing a block of ice into drink-size pieces and putting them in the ice bucket.

"Food in two hours," said Fourpence, putting down the bucket of ice.

"You'd better stay the night," said Will to Laurie.

"I think I'd better. Nothing due to land until Wednesday. Fact is, Will, I've been thinking. You can't run this show on your own. What I think you need is a partner. Me, in fact. Don't want to go back to England anymore and the airline is a dead end. Flying, that would have been different. You going to stay in Africa?"

"Not much option even if I wanted one, which I don't. We seem to have washed up together at the far end of the empire while everyone else is going home... I don't want to kill animals anymore, Laurie, or birds or anything. The bush we take for granted is dwindling so fast it won't be here in fifty years. Too many people encroaching on the land. Brother Hilary does a fine job with his medicine with the purest of intentions but the balance of nature will then succumb to man. Kariba Dam downstream, bush clearing by the new farmers, hunting for money. Better we shoot the game with cameras or man will only have the memory of a lion, a rhinoceros, an elephant. You look out over that bush or the big river on the other side of the deck and imagine it without the game, without the grunt of hippo, the pungent smell downwind of the buffalo, the call of the predator birds. Take out the wildlife and you have nothing and my soul and your soul would die with the animals. You think man was really meant to live alone with his own species in a five-hundred-home block of flats with the sound of man permanently beating out his brains?

"I don't know much about cameras," went on Will, "but I am going to learn and anyone who wants to come to our camp can bring a camera. Sure, we'll walk them in the bush and protect them with our guns but the only shots will be fired to protect. I saw a darkroom in London where they developed films and showed me tricks that enhance the photographs. Maybe people will buy the photographs. Imagine getting a fish eagle on film at the moment he takes a fish out of the water while in full flight. Seen those birds sit motionless for hours watching the flowing water, for a fish to swim closer to the riverbank where he can see into the water. Hours of patience for the bird and hours of patience for the photographer. Lions mounting a kill. A cornered honey badger grabbing the balls of a buffalo. That's what I want to photograph. Not take out fat tourists with a drinking problem so they can stand on a dead elephant. Hannes was beginning to understand all this won't last unless we do something. If you want to join a photographic safari operation, Laurie, we can talk a deal. The trackers are great men and I respect each one of them but I have things to talk about other than the bush. Why Hannes let me join his operation. A man's thoughts are important to him but sometimes he wants to share them and my Lozi and their English are not good enough for that kind of conversation. Maybe why Hilary is marrying his Mary. I don't know. Life is complicated. Maybe some of the people bringing their cameras will be young women. We are not the types to be celibate. The rich clients brought whores some of the time, or girlfriends or whatever they liked to call them. Never wives. Never brought their wives, why, Laurie? I'd like to show all this to my wife... Pour yourself a drink. Excuse me just a while."

Down away by the river where he walked the tears were pricking at the back of his eyes. Dancing Ledge and the girl were a lifetime away.

BY THE TIME Josephine arrived in Africa four years later with her fact-finding mission that had long made up its mind, Will was a dedicated conservationist. The photographic safari operation barely brought in enough money to pay the wages, the food and maintain the two Land Rovers, but not one animal had been shot as a trophy. It appeared to Will that if the people of the world wanted to see wild animals to take a photograph, they went to a zoo or the more easily accessible Kruger National Park in South Africa. In the park they could see everything in air-conditioned comfort.

The darkroom had materialised from a shed that Will had draped on the inside with wartime blackout curtaining that his mother had sent him from Dorset, heavy enough to keep out the strongest sunlight. In the summer months, during the rains, the heat made the shed uninhabitable and the liquids that developed the photographs were stored upstairs of the deck, under the thick-thatched roof. Winter nights saw Will bringing his harvest of photographs to light and some made him smile from the pure joy of nature.

Laurie Hall had dedicated his days to hard drinking and was the life and soul of the party when the occasional tourist arrived to be shown one of the last places on earth not invaded by man. The pending visit of Josephine to her brother at the end of the Labour Party fact-finding tour of the Federation of Rhodesia and Nyasaland had kept his attention for three weeks. The letter had been in the mail for Will at the post office in Mongu. When the day arrived, Laurie was sober and drove the Landy to his old airport where the Beechcraft Baron deposited Josephine. The twin-engined aircraft had made three runs to chase a herd of blue wildebeest off the landing strip.

To Will's surprise, the president of the club met Josephine on the grass runway and the shadow of the winds of change brushed once more over Mongu.

Josephine Langton was more important politically than her brother understood. The power of the feminist movement was being felt as much in Westminster as the Civil Rights Movement in America and the demise of colonialism around the world. The women of the Western world were reaching out for the power they would take from democracy.

More of this crossed Will's mind. At first he asked, what the hell was the president doing on the airfield?

"The man's looking after his next job," said Laurie.

"What job?" said Will, not understanding.

"He doesn't know. They're going to toss us all out of Africa."

Josephine was tired and pleased to see her brother and begged off a visit to the presidency or the club and climbed in next to him in the front seat with something close to discourtesy.

"Get me out of here, Will," she said quietly, giving him a kiss on the cheek.

"This is Laurie Hall," said Will.

"Hi, Laurie..." The car lurched away from the official reception. "The fawning protestations of the Colonial Service in its death throes makes me sick."

By the time the Land Rover reached the road, the blue wildebeest were back grazing on the runway and the pilot of the Beechcraft Baron and three passengers were being driven to the club by the new airport manager.

Will introduced his sister to the three trackers and then they went upstairs to the deck, Fourpence following with the ice bucket.

"If it helps your sensitivity, sis, I've tried using their Lozi names but they just ignore me. For them a name, however trivial, given by a white man is an accolade."

"I think I want to keep away from politics for a few days."

"If you talked, I would not understand. Tell me about Mum and Dad."

"First give me a drink."

Laurie Hall listened to brother and sister talk about their family and home. Sometimes they tried to bring him into the conversation but mostly he sat next to them on his bar stool, alone. The group captain was going a bit dotty and Laurie gathered that that was from dropping bombs in the war. Great-Aunt Eve had died and left her money to Uncle Cliff, whoever he was. Uncle Cliff with money had promptly left the Labour Party to Josephine's disgust and set himself up with a young mistress. Great-Aunt Eve had been surprisingly rich, which nobody in the family knew about. All those years in Chelsea had left her nothing to do but search out antiques on a meagre family private income but the old girl had had a good eye and had quietly bought and sold and put the money into property.

Laurie watched Josephine as he drank and by halfway down the bottle of whisky, he found her highly attractive. He had drunk her pretty. Food was served at the table looking down on the river. The night was pitch-black, the moon hidden away from the world. They shot the pot out of financial necessity which somehow to Laurie made the whole thing a bit of a moral balls-up. If they didn't shoot the game someone else would, and they both had hunting licences and the time to get rich in Africa was running out. The venison from a young impala ram was tender from two days of hanging in a tree. Going back to England at the age of twenty-eight without a pisspot full of money was not Laurie's idea of fun, drunk or sober. He had come out like Will to avoid the army and stuck around for the reason he could think of nothing better to do and the booze and fags were cheap in Northern Rhodesia. Making money on safari had been the last idea and that had not worked because Will, over there still talking to his sister, was not interested in making money. Laurie then started on the red wine with the meat which always made him drunk.

The others went off to bed and Laurie gave them a wave from the wrist and went back to the job of finishing the bottle of whisky. Loneliness had him by the throat and maudlin thoughts swirled around in his mind with the whisky. The thought that he had done absolutely nothing with his life came to sit with him on the bar. He looked at the demon and laughed out loud.

"What's there to do anyway, old cock? You make money so damn clever and then what, chum? Not worth the bloody effort... Shut up, Hall, you're talking to yourself again... Your old man was a drunk so join the club. The old man was happy even if the old woman wasn't."

Laurie lurched off his bar stool and staggered to the rail that went round the deck and stared out into the dark. He farted loudly and fanned at the smell behind and then he burped and went back to his drink at the bar.

"Life's a load of shit and then you die so why not have a drink in the middle?"

Then his head came down slowly onto the bar and he was fast asleep, the whisky glass resting on the polished wood still held firmly in his right hand.

His night dreams were better than his day.

TIRED beyond the ability to think, Josephine had swallowed her anti-malaria pill and got in under the mosquito net where she took off all her clothes and let the cool breeze from the river brush her nakedness. Her bedroom was at the far end of the deck, furthest away from the bar but under the same wide, thatched roof. The sides facing the bar and the rest of the deck were screened by river reeds, the one side not challenging her privacy open to the river breeze. The grunts and screeches from the African night orchestrated to a background of croaking frogs and singing cicadas played no fear to her from the dark: her young brother, the big-game hunter, was across the floor in his own screened bedroom and older sister was quite secure. She heard a wild dog bark from a long way off and then she slept deeply. Only once did she dream and briefly. In her dream there was a loud fart and Wolfgang Baumann was Hamlet, soliloquising from the ramparts of a thatched castle.

The dawn chorus brought her awake. Someone was snoring from the far end of the deck and the brief memory of her dream vanished forever. She went back to sleep with the wild geese honking down below while the smell of woodsmoke drifted up from the outside cookhouse tended by Onepenny.

Josephine woke again to the smell of coffee and sausage cooked over the open fire. The yellowing morning sun was slanting up at her room. For a moment she had no idea where she was. Putting on her clothes in the new daylight, she got out from under the net and stood at her private part of the rail looking down on the Zambezi River. Fish jumped and two pairs of hippo eyes watched her, the rest of their bodies submerged. She looked up and out over the bush as far as she could see to the horizon and the hills of the distant escarpment, bush fires hazing the view. The valley floor was flat, not even a hillock. For a moment her primeval soul spoke to her to stay forever in the valley close to the trees and the river.

Will's idea of an African breakfast was plentiful. Two eggs, sausage, two chops, tomatoes, fried potatoes, pumpkin and ample toast. The bread came from an oven cut into an old anthill and baked by Fourpence, the vegetables grown in the base camp garden well protected from monkeys and bush pig, the chops and sausage from the impala of the night before and the eggs out of the chicken run. There was tinned butter and marmalade and powder had made up the milk.

"The shower is outside next to the loo, over there." Will pointed at the river-reed enclosure under a large acacia tree with the full bucket of water already hauled up into the tree and the pipe attached to its closed bottom leading down to a tap above the shower rose. Granadilla grew around the reeds but the monkeys ate them green, the small vervet monkeys with the long tails and black faces.

"Thanks, I'll try it... Where's Laurie?"

"Recovering. Laurie has a drinking problem. Fact is, Laurie has a problem full stop. Across Africa in lonely spots there are many Laurie Halls. There just isn't enough for him to do here. He likes people, lots of people. Photography and the bush are all I need... Hilary, Mary and the kids will be here for lunch... Enjoy your breakfast and I'll take you down the river. Laurie has a hut by the river downstream from the house. Snoring. His idea. Works. That or I'd have shot 'im. Well, not really."

"When are you coming back to England, Will?"

"Not now. Probably never."

"What about a wife and kids?"

"Can I ask you the same question? Poor Mother. Four children over twenty-six and no grandchildren. Poor old Randolph. He and Anna would have looked well with half a dozen. I mean, Hilary's kids are not real grandchildren as much as she says they are in her letters. You haven't seen Hilary for a very long time so don't act shocked and don't say anything. He catches tropical diseases like kids in England catch winter colds. Tough as old boots under the skeleton."

"Byron's buying a national newspaper," said Josephine.

"You didn't tell me that last night."

"And he's up to something in Africa."

"Never been here in his life."

"You remember that black man at the manor who tried to rub you up the wrong way? He wanted to meet Byron. Said I had spoken a lot about him but I don't think it was that. Paul said things about Byron's business that even I did not know and when they got together, they were as thick as thieves for a couple of days. I hadn't seen Paul again until this trip. There is somebody in England paying for party officials of the local black nationalist party to visit England to lobby the cause and what Paul said in Lusaka makes me think my twin is footing the bills. But why, Will?"

"Why don't you ask Byron when you get home? Eat your breakfast. You want more coffee, just yell for Onepenny."

Hilary arrived at lunchtime and the Goliath heron bit him in the back of his right leg making him howl and sending his three-year-old son into a tantrum of excitement.

"Everyone attacks the missionary," said Hilary, rubbing the red mark below the line of his shorts where the sharp beak had broken the skin. "First thing they do. That bird should be locked up. Mary, look out for that bird. It has an evil spirit. Every time I come here I forget the bird and every time it gets me. Is it a male or a female, Will?"

"Does it make any difference?"

"Not really. And my son rejoices at my suffering. Mary, this is my adopted-sister Josephine, so why don't you women go off and talk woman talk with the children so Will and I can have a glass of medicine? Where's Laurie?"

"Somebody mention booze?" said Laurie, coming up from his sleeping hut.

"Certainly I did. How are you? You look terrible."

"So do you," said Laurie with a smile. "The bird get you again?"

"Yes he did."

They all laughed.

Then Will asked, "Are you all happy to camp by the river tonight?"

WITHIN TWENTY MINUTES of the sun going down it was dark, and the firelight was reaching high into the fever trees on the banks of the river. Josephine had expected a twilight. They had camped a kilometre down the river with the intention of spending the night. The three trackers had made their own fire fifty metres away. Both fires were high up on a bank set back from the river under the trees where the sparse grass had long ago been grazed by the animals. There had been no rain for three months.

The two children had gone to sleep on an old blanket next to their mother. Will had his back to the tree, next to his rifle. Laurie carried a gun as did each of the trackers. Dry firewood, hard burning mopani, was stacked next to the fires. A single white, ghostly mosquito net hung straight down, waiting for Josephine. The others had been bitten so many times they took no notice.

Laurie was on his way to being drunk. Once the first 'medicine' found his blood there was no stopping him.

The darkness wrapped around them. A log fell in the fire and showered the night with sparks.

Will let the fire fade away to red coals and then showed his sister the stars. All the planets, constellations, the Milky Way, the layer of stars behind and the inky blackness of the void beyond.

"There's more, if our eyes could see," said Will. "Not even the new scientists know where it ends, we really are a grain of sand in the universe... Is there a God up there, Hilary?"

"Are you asking me that as a boy you grew up with, or a priest?"

"As a man."

Everyone was looking up at the heavens while the children slept. They looked for a long time.

"I don't know," said Hilary. "Without God it makes no sense. Nothing does. But I don't know. We seem to think man is special and deserves a God. Maybe a great concept. Look at it all up there. Did man create God to comfort himself, to give himself someone to pass the questions to that he will never understand? Or did God create man, the universe, all these stars, how they move, how they grow, is there one Great Being out there who controls it all? The Church says God is within each of us. Maybe I have seen too much of man. If there is no God, Will, then our lives are utterly and totally pointless. So let us believe. The alternative leaves us wretched. Without our consciousness, our ability to think, nothing would matter. Who feeds our individual brains with questions? What makes us think? We know how the brain processes thought through electric pulses but who asks the questions in our head? Is the questioner tangible, can he die, is it our God within us? All those heavens above and all we have is a question that man has been asking ever since he could think... I don't think anyone knows the answer, Will."

Beyond their sight the river flowed on its course and Will banked up the fire with three large tree trunks.

First Josephine retired to her bed of freshly cut elephant grass under mosquito net close to the fire. All afternoon and evening she had not once thought of politics.

Mary fell asleep next to her children. She was more happy than any of them: when a life is drying up and then finds its purpose, the joy is greater. She loved her skinny husband with a passion learnt from endless hope and her children with a disbelief that her God could have given her so much. With equal blind passion she loved her God, believed in him as something real around her, within her all the time. In the end, she would show her husband God. With the firelight playing across her children and all that was good in her life, she fell into a dreamless sleep, trusting God and man.

Laurie managed to fight a bout of hiccups by concentrating on the heart of the flames. Then he also slept, away from his bed of grass and loaded rifle. Demons stalked his dreams and his body shook in the reaching firelight. It would not have mattered to Laurie Hall whether he woke or not. The bottle next to him was half full.

Hilary fell asleep on his grass bed struggling with his God as he did every day when the brief moments from work gave him time to think. He was always asking for the vision of the truth which never came.

Will checked his rifle and placed it lengthwise along his bed, the barrel pointing down at his feet. His recurring nightmare, vivid in its execution, was to wake to a rampant lion with the gun barrel pointing the wrong way and not enough time to turn and shoot. Always he woke with the lion bounding through the air.

"Goodnight," he called softly to the trackers around their fire. "Keep your fire stoked."

"Goodnight, baas," came the chorus.

Within a minute Will and the trackers were sound asleep.

For a long time nothing happened. It was the beginning of the night.

THE RIVER FLOWED through the night never changing its course or its intention of reaching the sea. An owl fluffed its feathers and widened its eyes looking for mice, but the night was dark and the owl blinked. The bird called and closed its eyes, waiting for the stars to brighten or the moon to come out. Down below the tree, mice moved cautiously, looked for food by smell in the shadows, hunger chasing their fear. The frogs croaked their mating calls. On the other side of the big river a leopard coughed and still nothing happened; the night world was still, waiting to come out and feed.

The crossed trees burnt away where they met at the fire and a small black hole appeared while the fire spread back down the trunks, shrinking the light and the pool of safety around the bodies sleeping softly near the fires. Even Laurie slept and made not a sound. As the night grew colder the stars shone light that brought back the river, reflecting the heavens in the black oily water as it flowed.

One by one the hippopotamus came out of the water, walking round the hillock where the family slept, to find grass. The big amphibians grazed silently in the night, the mothers close to their calves. All across the valley, buck came out to graze, smelling the wind for danger. At a short distance in the long grass were hyena and jackal, following the night shadows of the grazing herds, and back from the scavengers the leopards came out to hunt.

At the campfires the black holes were large, the tree trunks smouldering away from each other and the glow of firelight almost extinguished.

Will woke and listened to the night, smiling to himself. These were the precious moments around the campfire when the bush was quiet, the clients sleeping. Gently, he slid his hand over the safety catch of his rifle, making sure of its position. Will listened to the night for danger and then he rose from his bed and pushed each of the trunks back into the centre of the fire, sending sparks up into the trees. Brushwood he piled over the stumps and the fire caught and flamed, sending light to the top of the fever tree and pushing the dark away from the sleepers. Will went across to the trackers' fire and did the same.

"Thanks, baas." It was Sixpence lying awake... "God can be found through our ancestors." The black man had spoken to Will's back.

Will returned to his bed of grass and fell asleep.

THE LION ROARED an hour before the dawn, a sound so terrifying to man that everyone in the camp woke, the fear reaching back to their progenitors living in the forest, sleeping in the crooks of trees. Josephine howled, petrified by fear, not knowing where she was and the lion roared again and Josephine tangled herself in the netting as she fought to get away, unable to see or reason, frightened to the roots of her being.

Will ran across to his sister and held her through the netting until the shakes and screams had calmed to sobbing.

"All right, sis. That old lion's more than two kilometres away on the other side of the river and cats can't swim."

"Are you sure?" came a small voice out of the tangled netting.

"Quite sure. Live long enough with the animals and you'll come to love the roar of a lion."

"I want to go home to England where it's safe."

"Nowhere's safe, sis. In England, the predators look like men."

Across the fire, Laurie Hall found his bottle and took a long swig. "I'll drink to that," he said.

Will brought his bedding and laid it next to Josephine's, holding her hand under the netting. Only when he heard her steady breathing and the pressure on the palm of his hand relaxed did he allow himself to fall back into sleep.

They were all woken by the dawn chorus of birds singing the praise of day, the danger past. Soon the smell of coffee permeated the camp.

Josephine watched the children all morning. Malcolm, just three, guarded his sister Penelope, not quite two years old, with dog-like dedication. The void and melancholy detached her from conversation. Josephine watched Hilary with his Mary and Mary with her Hilary and nowhere else had she ever seen such happiness. All the politics and the cause, the righteousness, the great importance, seemed lost in the bush. The meaning of life was here to be seen. The future, man-made utopia was nothing in comparison to the glory of nature.

Back at base camp, Hilary packed the children's blankets in his Land Rover.

"Can't stay away any longer," he told Will. "You know how it is. Well, it's been a lovely stay. Come and visit us on the mission any time. Josephine, my love to your parents and tell your father I pray for him every day. Bombs! Why cannot man shower the earth with love?"

"There never is a right time to say something you don't want to say," began Josephine. "Your charges can wait a little while longer, Hilary. This, everything here, is about to end. I have information, certain information that will change your lives. We are pulling out of Africa, lock, stock and barrel. The British. The days of the empire are over forever."

"Won't affect a missionary," chuckled Hilary, putting the last of their overnight bags in the Land Rover.

"Did you know they hate you?"

"Don't be silly, Josephine."

"I don't mean the people you treat and teach. The politicians. The people who want their own country to rule themselves. A friend of mine likened the missionaries to the most dangerous of front-line troops; people like yourselves, Mary and Hilary, dedicated to goodness and helping others. The concept of believing in our God as the one and only God, our branch of divinity that must be believed by everyone or they will burn in hell for eternity. That's how my friend put it to me. Frightening stuff. My friend said the missionaries told the people of Africa to kneel down and close their eyes and pray to the one true God and when they opened their eyes, they found the Union Jack flying over their heads. He thinks our religious zeal was just an excuse. My friend thinks your good deeds had an ulterior motive, colonialism. In the time of Queen Victoria, Church and State were very close together and the bishops sit in the House of Lords and the Queen is head of the Church. It looked better to have a righteous mission, the honour of spreading the word of Christ. Those churchmen were Englishmen first and being men of God was just their profession. Mostly younger sons. They either went to administer the colonies or into the Church of England. Didn't matter which. You see, like my African friend, I don't think there was even a moral base to colonising people, making them do what they are told. All of you will have to get out of Africa and soon. We have seen what they will do to missionaries and settlers in Kenya and the Belgian Congo."

"What about the Federation?" asked Will.

"It's gone."

"And the white settlers?"

"A minor refugee problem."

"You can't be serious? Why, ten years ago they were trumpeting the future of the Federation, saying it was the next Canada. Over a hundred thousand British answered the call."

"Things change in the world. This part of the country will very soon become the Republic of Zambia. If you say I told you I will deny this conversation but outside of Laurie, we are all family."

"What about the trackers?" asked Will.

"They know. They will run your business, and from what I have seen they will do it well."

"Just dump us like that."

"We shouldn't have been here in the first place. After a few years back in England, you'll forget all about this."

"The RAF will look me up."

"No they won't. I checked up."

"You're very thorough."

"I'm trying to help, Will. Granda always said you can't fart against thunder, if you'll forgive the expression, Mary. What I am giving you is a warning. Take my advice. It's the turn of Africa to enjoy the fruits of social democracy. We can't preach one thing at home and another in the colonies, now can we?"

"From the pre-wheel age to Westminster democracy," said Laurie Hall. "Wow... Should be fun... For a few...a very few... First we bugger up their system and then we leave them in the lurch. We give them medicine to multiply like flies and expect them to go back to gathering and hunting, everyone with a hut by a river. Poor sods, all I can say. Poor bloody sods. Tragedy is, when they've ripped themselves to pieces indulging in mass self-destruction, as there won't be enough to go round, the ones that are left will turn to the likes of Hilary and Mary to bind up their wounds. And the good-hearted likes of Hilary and Mary will do it. The other cheek syndrome. One minute it's the right thing to colonise. Then it's the right thing to not. All in the name of the poor bloody people. The way I see it, the poor bloody people don't matter one poor bloody jot... Better have a drink. Foul taste in my mouth. No offence to anyone. Just man at his selfish best. Last night's lion in comparison was a pussycat."

9

While Will was driving Josephine to Mongu Airport, Byron Langton, six thousand miles away, was again contemplating a major problem in his life: finding a suitable wife. For Byron, everything in life was a trade and if he was going to give up the merry-go-round of a rich bachelor he wanted something equally valuable in return. A man of wealth and position required an heir, a biological impulse almost as strong as procreation.

Outside his office in Pall Mall, the London traffic was relentlessly moving in both directions up and down the streets and round the statue of Eros in Piccadilly Circus. The heart of the empire was beating normally. The discreet plaque at the street entrance to the building now heralded Langton Merchant Bank Limited and underneath a list of subsidiaries that only Byron knew were shell companies that he managed on behalf of his clients, most of whom the financial press had never heard of. Business was plentiful for the upstart merchant bank in the summer of 1963.

On the other side of the entrance, a similar discreet plaque in a different print bespoke London Town Music Limited with three subsidiaries underneath. The one called Music Lane, thirty per cent owned by Shelley Lane, was the cash cow of the whole organisation as it needed no further capital to increase its substantial revenues. Shelley at twenty-four was a very rich lady.

At reception, Madge O'Shea, the flaming redhead, still held court after four years that had seen the company take up any office space in the building that became vacant. The building was four storeys high, thin and old and musty except where the people entered the renovated spaces occupied by the Langton companies. Madge, still his private secretary, had given up trying to date Byron and was genuinely interested in the growth of the company, her bachelor of commerce degree from London University being used to the full. Madge was the first of the new breed of satisfied career ladies with a sex life to match the men; she did not need a husband to give her support.

Byron's mind drifted away from the old matrimonial problem. He had met many girls who would bring money and influence but most of them, he quickly decided, would drive him crackers within a week. Determined not to take second best he banished the problem from his overactive mind and poured himself a third cup of tea from the pot on his desk. The tea cosy from Langton Manor, made by Grandma with her own two hands, kept the tea hot for over an hour. Idly, Byron picked up the model car from its stand and put it back again without realising what he had done; the model was a very nice miniature of an open Bentley 3 Litre. Byron looked at his watch.

"Shit, I'm late," he said out loud.

One rule was to never meet the stooges of the politicians jockeying for power in the collapsing colonies of the empire where Byron would be recognised. The man to be given lunch today was Paul Mwansa and Byron was still not sure whether the man introduced by Josephine was from the same organisation that had approached Johnny Pike for twenty thousand pounds. He was inclined to think not and mentally wrote off the previous investment as premature, too soon before independence, the politicians not having whittled themselves down to the one black nationalist party to face the British.

"Back tomorrow, Madge. Take over for me. Driving into the country for lunch."

"Shelley wants to talk to you face-to-face," said Madge.

"Shelley always wants to talk to me. Give her my love."

"That I won't."

The arrangement began with the coffee. Byron had chosen a small pub on the River Thames just south of Oxford from which they could still see the spires and antiquity of British learning. The food had been good and the weather fine. The willow tree in front of where they sat on the lawn trailed in the water. A stickleback was fussing in and around the green wands of the pussy willow. Out on the river an amateur rower caught a crab, the oar coming out of the water fast and slapping the passenger on the face with a wet paddle, the noise echoing sharply across the lawn. "Sorry, old girl," followed by a fit of giggles. Byron let a half-smile play across his face.

"We can kick you British out any time," said Paul Mwansa.

"You do that, old chap. Nothing to do with me. Don't think I'm the colonial office to badger. You chaps have a habit of thinking you're owed something. You can take control. You can nationalise the copper mines but you won't have sold one pound of copper. You don't exactly have a local market for your product. Forget your politics for a moment and remember the customer is always right and your customer is Western industry, not the colonial secretary. If you get too pumped up with your own importance, you'll inherit a lot of very nice, very dead copper mines. The metal brokers will eat you up, Paul. Just remember, you need me or the likes of me more than I need you. I have a lot of varied business. In your brave new world you will only have copper and very little else. You play around in the copper market and the price can drop in half overnight and all the effort you have put into your politics won't be worth a penny. Political power is the road to money. Money is the road to happiness. I'm not some poor white settler you can bully. Do we understand each other? If you want legitimate and profitable marketing of your base metal, you need buyers who are sure of a stable supplier, continuity, price stability. You need a selling agent who knows the buyers' market. There's plenty of copper in Chile. More importantly, when you find this selling agent, you need a man who will look after your party's interest so that any change in power in your new Utopia won't affect your party's bank account. I can be your legitimate insurance. Now, let's realise we are both on the same side and get down to details. By what you said earlier, this Zambia is only months away. There is a lot of work for my company to do."

"Why did you take over Manningly's newspaper?"

"Oh, that's quite simple. My insurance in a very nasty world. I have a file on every black politician in British Africa. There is no one born in this world who does not do something he or she wishes to forget. Why, I even have a file on my sister."

"Why do I have to do business with you?"

"Because I have a track record and the right kind of track records are very important."

"Can I have two tickets to Shelley Lane's concert?"

"Certainly. I'll have them sent to your hotel."

"I think we understand each other," said Paul Mwansa.

"I rather think we do."

· · ·

ANNABEL'S that night was full. At Byron's first count, London's arguably most exclusive supper club was entertaining two Tory cabinet ministers and their wives, the chairman of the Baltic Exchange, the vice chairman of Lloyd's of London and two well-known British film stars. Obtaining his entrée had required the full force of the Stanmore Old Boys' Association and the pedigree of the Langtons of Langton Manor. The man with him at the table was a South African with considerable copper investments in Northern Rhodesia.

"Nationalisation of the mines won't cause a hiccup," said Byron. "They don't give a damn about making a profit. They want a percentage of sales for me to handle and if the price goes down, they'll dig up more copper and flood the market. If you have any shares in Chilean copper, sell them; they are going to be the losers. You'll get your copper for your American and European factories at a price less than it costs to mine the stuff. Probably bring a run on all base metals and make Western industry more profitable. Drop the inflation rate. Any country who's a primary producer will suffer, Australia included. The new management in Africa just won't understand business and will dump at any price and blame colonialism."

"You think the British government worked this all out beforehand?" asked the South African.

"Don't be silly. They don't know what they are going to do next week let alone think years ahead. What I like is so much money going offshore as we don't leave it in sterling or in any country with exchange control. When the politicians have finished playing around with other people's lives and money they won't even control their own economies. The fund managers will control the movement of more money than governments. You know something, you can always make a lot of money in a period of turmoil. Either when the price is going up or coming down. Stability keeps the establishment in power and the likes of you and me out. If it wasn't necessary to create a fund in Switzerland, they wouldn't need me to launder their copper sales. The real money is in the product that comes out of copper, not the raw material. The new Africa will remain a basket case until it builds its own products and exports them. The Japs are getting rich on the world's raw materials, very little of which comes out of their own soil... You tell your clients that we can guarantee the continuity of their supply at the present price. Later, we will offer them forward contracts. There are large stocks of copper ingots in Northern Rhodesia and my guess is the new administration will put them on the market straight away. Fact is, you can be certain. Your job is to line up the buyers. My job is to get the copper.

"Now shall we go to the Mayfair and meet the ladies? One of my friends from EMI will be joining us. The record business is booming in England. Should be a good evening. The three girls are in show business so you won't be disappointed."

Byron worked on the principle that when a man is middle-aged, rich and has a wife and children the only unspoken bribe that works is young women. It helps if he is away from home. Whores, Byron had found out to his business cost, were no good as the kind of man that went to whores went there on his own accord. But even the most conservative, the most faithful of husbands were susceptible to flattery provided they were doing nothing wrong at the beginning, before the booze took effect. All the hard work, drudgery and wifely hen-pecking seems to need something else when for the first time in many years a young, attractive girl without an ulterior motive takes a keen interest in the middle-aged man's life.

In the music industry, Byron was known as a rich bachelor, good-looking, good in bed and fun to be with; and for the girls in their early twenties who had no wish to settle down he was perfect. Byron, the word said, never grew serious and was always willing to help a friend.

Bob Shackleton, the man from the EMI record company who had signed up Shelley Lane, was interested in keeping Byron willing to renew her contract each year and socialised with him whenever possible. Byron was not sure whether Bob had a wife at home but the subject was never broached. There were always young, aspiring artists more than happy to eat good food and with television, the singers had to be as good on the eye as their songs on the ear. The combination of Bob and Byron for an artist was fame and fortune eight times out of ten. The cross-pollination of Byron's banking and music business was a constant source of amusement to him and one of the cornerstones of his financial success. The staid businessman really thought he had arrived in the world when the young and potentially famous joined him for dinner. The first time the metal broker from South Africa dined with Byron, Shelley Lane had dropped by the table and sat down for a drink.

The three girls were dressed to turn heads in the Mayfair. The dancing partners alternated around the table and the South African had not enjoyed an evening more since he became engaged to his wife. All the talk of famous names made him truly believe he had arrived. The evening was a great success for everyone.

"We'll do this again when we have the papers signed," said Byron, standing up. "Now, Tammy, do you think you could see our South African friend back to his hotel in a taxi?... Have a safe flight back to Johannesburg," he said to the man. "Karen, if you come on over to my office at five o'clock tomorrow afternoon we can look at London Town Music managing your career. My car is back at the office so it's a taxi for everyone. Bob has been trying to tell me something all evening so do you mind if we have a few minutes alone while you ladies go to the girls' room?"

Byron stood away from the table and shook hands with the metal broker, certain they would be doing business. The girls went off together.

"Better get that taxi," said the South African.

"You better do that," agreed Byron.

The man was quickly gone in pursuit.

"Now," said Byron turning to Bob Shackleton. "What's the matter?"

"Shelley. She's burnt out. She collapsed on stage tonight."

"Why the hell wasn't I told?"

"She's in hospital. Couldn't talk in front of the girls. Byron, this one is serious. She's been taking pills to get her up and pills to get her down and the lady drinks. She doesn't have any support at home. She says you've been avoiding her of late and that's not right for a manager. We have a lot of money in that girl and it's your job to keep her singing. We put her in a private nursing home. I've written down the address. Get over there now. I'll say goodbye to the girls. You got to build that girl up again, Byron. You know she loves you. All the fame and money hasn't changed that. The one thing you must never forget in business is that people are human."

The nursing home said the lady had booked herself out a few minutes after midnight and what could they do? A doctor had made a note on the card telling the accounts department to bill the lady for a full day, a house call and a packet of aspirin. All the lady complained about was a headache. It was all on the card.

The night nurse reluctantly called Byron a taxi and twenty minutes later he was running up the steps to Mrs Page's house where he rang the bell. A muffled sound came from the other side of the door. The door opened to a smiling Shelley Lane.

"Bingo," she said. "Spot on time. You'd run to the moon to save some money. I didn't want Mrs Page woken up by the door. Come on in if you still remember the way."

"What's this all about, Shelley?" Byron was thoroughly annoyed.

"Keep your voice down."

He followed her down the passage and through the open door into the same two-roomed apartment with the French windows that opened onto the small garden and the bench under the tree.

"I'd sit outside but voices travel at night. You want a drink?"

"No."

"Don't have to be rude."

"You can't walk out on an audience."

"Oh, but I did. Every performer gets sick some time or another. Mine was rather theatrical."

"Are you high or something?"

"Probably."

"Bob was telling me —"

"Four years is a long time and yes I am sick but not sick in the body as that damn doctor soon found out but sick in the head. You try being the me you have publicised and you'll try LSD and any other damn thing to make you feel good and when the one damn man you care for won't return your calls, you take a damn sleeping pill to make you go to sleep or you get drunk on your own as the adoring bloody fans mustn't see the money machine flat out on her back in public."

"Shelley, I have a big meeting at the newspaper tomorrow and I don't have time for this. There are other people in this world who need some sleep to function properly. They told me you were sick, and I ran over fast but this is plain childish. I can't run around holding everyone's hand who works for me, I can't. I'm sick of other people's problems. Just because I run the bloody company no one stops to think good old Byron might have a problem. I can handle the business problems, I think, but I won't play nursemaid, shrink and everybody's friendly barman. The office girls get pregnant and want an abortion and run to you know who. The air force wants to lock them up and I have to sort out the shit. Some old fart of a journalist who can't write a word any more cries on my shoulder while I pay for the booze, feel sorry though for the life of me I don't know why and only afterwards worked out what to do with the man when he comes back from Alcoholics Anonymous, if he does. They'd squeeze the blood out of me if they could and then smile me a superficial smile that says I'm rich and must be a crook and where's their increase?"

"Have you finished?"

"Almost."

"You need a wife."

"Oh, now you really are out of your mind. You want me to come home to little dots of LSD, Dexedrine in family-size bottles and the smell of pot permeating through the house and then be told it's all my fault because I come home late from work but please buy me a fur coat or whatever bloody bauble comes to mind. I've got enough problems in my life without saddling myself with a wife who takes more than she gives and can't handle life unless she's the centre of attention. Shelley, find one of those hangers-on and have yourself screwed properly."

"You're going to end up a rich lonely old man."

"Probably. And right now I could think of a lot worse things than being on my own. The word 'lonely' has a rather nice ring to it. Now, if you'll excuse me, I'm going home to sleep. On my own. And there's another thought, use some of your money to get out of this dump."

"It's the only place in my life that makes sense."

"Women. I give up. Get yourself a holiday. Cancel this tour. I don't care. But get off my back."

Remembering Mrs Page at the last moment, Byron refrained from slamming the front door. The taxi driver had gone.

"Shit, shit and more shit," said Byron and began the walk up to the Bayswater Road.

INSIDE THE FLAT, Shelley put her hand out for a pill and then fell back on the bed. Nothing ever came up the way she wanted. Her real parents had run away from her at birth. The ones she called Mummy and Daddy she had as much feeling for as a sick headache. Neither had come to a concert, thinking public singers and dancers were one rung up from a whore.

If she had the guts she would shoot herself, but she didn't have the guts. Well, he had given her one good idea. She would cancel the tour. The idea of a holiday, of a holiday as far away as possible, stretched out to her misery. There had to be a point to it all somewhere.

He was right, of course. She'd make a lousy wife just as he said.

"I want someone to look after me," she said to the blank walls and then she began to cry. She felt sorry for herself. When she stopped, she found the brandy bottle and poured herself a tot.

"You're a fool. He's right. You're a fool. Oh, what the hell. Bloody men, who needs bloody men anyway?"

After the third tot of brandy she felt better.

BY THE TIME he got home, he found he couldn't sleep. All the accumulated business problems poured through his mind and Byron tried every position on the pillow but could not fall asleep. He was worried he was going too fast and the muscles in the pit of his stomach tightened up at the thought. Cash flow. It always came back to cash flow, which meant the income to pay the interest to the banks. Every time he bought a new business there were problems as the seller would not sell without a problem. He had too many ping-pong balls up in the air, looking for huge future income. Shelley cracking up was all that he needed in his life but trying to hold her hand and run the business was equally impossible. If he tried the social circuit with Shelley to keep her nicely on the stage, he would never get any sleep.

After an hour of tossing and turning, he turned on the light and went to his desk and emptied the files from his briefcase. At three in the morning, Byron nodded off at his desk with the light still burning. He woke just before dawn and got into bed to immediately fall into a deep, dreamless sleep. At seven o'clock the alarm rattled him awake and the business chase began all over again.

THE GARNET GROUP of newspapers were losing twice as much money as Heathcliff Mortimer had indicated to Josephine just before she went out to Africa. The company was classically insolvent with the liabilities exceeding the assets by twenty-two per cent, even if the old machinery was able to fetch the amount listed in the balance sheet. Byron viewed the machinery as scrap metal if the company were to be liquidated and the greed of the trade unions as the reason why all the staff were going to end up without a job. For Byron to lay his hands on an international newspaper chain there had to be insurmountable business problems as even the biggest fool in a democracy knew the real power rested with the media. People followed like sheep to the polls and did what they were told by the newspapers. Of course the majority voted for their father's party, but they made no difference. The difference came with the swing vote, the plus or minus ten per cent who knew nothing about politics but did what they were told by their favourite newspaper. They decided the government of the day. Byron knew perfectly well that no one bought a tube of toothpaste that his subconscious mind did not dictate.

Byron's problem was to stem the red ink in the balance sheet until the computer industry found a way to do away with hand typesetting and three-quarters of the union-led staff. In the meantime he was forced to live with the unions and his only way out of the morass was increasing circulation, something that television was stopping.

Byron had not gone in blindly when he bought Lord Manningly's family company. He and Johnny Pike had talked for hours. The excitement was the prize, a prize normally guarded with care by the establishment. If they could salvage the company, something no one else in the world was willing to do, they would be able to compete with the establishment. The idea of Jack Pike, Johnny's father and Byron's mentor, the peep show man and peddler of mild pornography, having a say in one of Britain's traditional newspapers was too good to pass up.

The old man, Jack Pike, saw things more simply than most.

"Attention span, see," he had said to Byron. "The bloke in the street don't have no attention span so to speak. This TV makes 'em used to pictures so give 'em pictures. Too many words in the *Garnet*. Cut out ninety per cent of the words and put in a lot of pictures, specially the ones of nice girls with big tits, see. People want to be entertained not bored stiff. All we got to do is work out what the bloke in the street wants and bingo. Keep it simple, Byron, always keep it simple."

With prompting from Jack Pike, Byron had a habit of looking at problems from the other perspective. Manningly had wanted a smart newspaper he could talk about in his club. That was one thing Byron had never done in his life. He had never joined a club of any description that did not have the flavour of 'night'. The exclusive British male club, in Byron's opinion, was where he would find the blinkers to cover his vision of business, his way past the establishment.

HEATHCLIFF MORTIMER STOOD up in front of fifty people and said he was a drunk which was meant to make him feel better. He then proceeded to tell them how he had become a drunk which was a pen sketch of his life, mingling a variety of women, two of whom he had married, with newspaper reporting and booze. Even if his newspaper colleagues had found out his membership of Alcoholics Anonymous, it would not have been news. Everyone knew he was a drunk. Some of his best reports during the war had been sent over the wire when he was three-quarters drunk. For heaven's sake, he said to himself when he sat down to that special blend of 'do-gooder' applause, Winston Churchill was close to a bottle of brandy a day and even with all the cigars he was still alive and the greatest Englishman he had ever known. And more importantly, what was a lonely old man going to do without the comfort of fuddling his brain with booze?

A week after the speech, which had been followed by seven miserable days off the booze, he presented himself to the new man's office and was greeted by an unusual good-looking redhead who vaguely reminded him of someone back in his past. He gave her the best smile and when he was told to wait sank his large backside onto the leather-bound bench that went for a chair. Heath was mildly sweating and ran a finger round his collar. All he wanted right then was a drink as the clock over the door said five o'clock, and that was the time he had his first drink. To Heath's surprise, Byron came out of his office in person.

"Shit, you look awful," said Byron to which Madge O'Shea, the redhead, did not look up. "Come on into my office, Mr Mortimer. When did you last have a drink?"

"Seven days ago."

"I'm impressed. Couldn't last that long myself... Now before we start, would you like a drink?"

"Is that another test?"

"You've passed the test. I wanted to see if you really needed your job. The people I have liked best in my business are those who need something badly. The 'here today' and 'gone tomorrow' are no good to anyone."

"Bourbon. Learnt it from the Yanks during the war."

"Anything with it, don't want to ruin a good bourbon?"

"Just as it is, Mr Langton."

"Byron, please. You're old enough to be my father. And talking of fathers, my father sends his regards."

Immediately, Heath thought of Josephine but that did not fit. He wanted to keep Josephine out of the conversation. Brothers were unpredictable and jumped to wrong conclusions. He took the drink, his hand shaking badly.

"Group Captain Red Langton," said Byron, watching the drink shake all the way to the man's lips.

"He's your father?"

"Yes, he is."

"I covered the dropping of the bomb!"

"After making up my mind, I found out your history and I apologise for my first impression of you which was wrong. You have quite a record as a war correspondent. Dad says you flew with him once on a raid over Germany. You said you couldn't write about it, give your readers reality, without experience. Father's crew were rather impressed. You'd better have another drink with me."

Byron turned to the small bar next to his bookcase.

"I want you to be my roving ambassador in Africa, reporting to me first and then writing for the *Garnet*. There are a lot of wars in Africa and my information has it there will be a lot more. What I want you to tell me when you come back at regular intervals is who is going to win in each of these tinpot countries. Which politicians and which generals. And I want you to make up a file on each one of them. Better, I want you to get to know them and mention my name if they need any help in their pursuit of freedom."

Outside in the street, Heath looked at his watch. It was ten minutes to six, and the pubs were open again at six, the idea of afternoon closing being to stop the likes of Heathcliff Mortimer drinking all day long. The sun was still warm and the rich smell of cooked tarmac underlay the fumes of London traffic. The rush hour had left the City for suburbia, only the wise taking a drink after work while the rabbits scuttled home to their burrows. It was a nice day to be in the country.

The walk to his favourite club in Greek Street, just far enough away from Fleet Street and the newspaper bars, brought him outside the Green Dolphin as the door swung open. Heath smiled. He believed in omens. The door to his life was still open. By the time he reached the bar, Francis the barman had poured a double Southern Comfort.

"You been sick, Heath?" asked the barman.

"Off the booze."

The drinks in the Langton Merchant Bank had stopped his hands shaking, and the drink came off the glass smoothly to join his welcome lips.

"You got to be kidding," said Francis. Francis had been a gentleman's gentleman and Heath thought him probably queer but what the hell, he poured a good tot. Heath gave him a smile and finished the drink.

"Thirsty tonight," said Francis.

The second drink was poured without asking and with Heath staring into space, the barman walked off down the duckboards to the far end of the bar where he began to polish the glasses. There was no one else in the pub. The drink had cleared his head. 'Find out who's backing him,' the editor of the *Evening Garnet* had said. 'What the hell does he want to see you for? Me, I could understand. No one has ever heard of Byron Langton. Came from nowhere but no one comes from nowhere. Find out. Didn't you say you knew his twin sister?'

Heath sipped his drink and put it back on the bar. Red Langton had no money. Neither had Josephine. Josephine was thirty-two, so he knew the boy's age. And why pick on Heathcliff Mortimer for special attention? There were plenty of old drunks in the newspaper business. Heath was sure the connection was not Red Langton, the Lancaster bomber pilot, or Josephine Langton, the social activist. He knew for certain, from years of writing people's stories, that the interview just finished had nothing to do with Lord Manningly or what used to be his newspaper. Looking down the long bar at Francis polishing the glasses Heath had a flash of insight into what it would be like being a manservant and thought the job appealing. There was only one man to keep happy and little need to think. There was a lot to be said for not having to think in life.

Heath thought about the new job some more. What the hell, he thought again. If the young man's a crook, old farts like Heathcliff Mortimer should not be worrying. The trip to the old Belgian Congo might be dangerous but at his age nobody wanted to live forever. The only friends left were Southern Comfort and the odd bottle of good red wine when his liver felt patient. Everything else was a memory. Women were gone and there were no children he knew about. It was fun to be out with a reporter on the town but both of his wives had grown bored with his lifestyle of odd hours and too much booze. Life, he thought, never did come to any conclusion and Africa would give him something to do. Byron Langton would pick up his expenses. Maybe he would lose some weight in the tropics. He hadn't seen his best friend for ten years, except in the mirror. 'Shit, what a life' he thought, and raised his glass. The glass, as usual, was empty.

The bar had filled up while he was thinking.

"Used to know your new boss when he was a kid," said Francis. "You want another drink, Mr Mortimer?"

"Which boss are you talking about?"

"Mr Langton. Came in here often with the gaffer's son."

"What do you know about him?" asked Heath, his mind quickly clear and professional.

"Ask Mr Johnny. He and Mr Langton have been friends a long time."

"Does young Mr Langton know Jack Pike?"

"Of course... You want to pay now or are you having another one?... What's the matter, Mr Mortimer? Did I say something funny?"

"You ever seen a penny drop?"

"Sometimes off the bar."

"Give me another drink."

"You talk to Johnny often when he's in the bar," said Francis.

"I know, Francis... You ever hear of Léopoldville?"

"Can't say I have."

"Or the Republic of the Congo?"

"No."

"They're in Africa."

"I've heard of Africa," said the barman.

THE CONTINENTAL HOTEL in the city centre of Léopoldville had been built by the Belgians in colonial days. Even then the mosquitoes were the size of a half-crown. Since independence three years before, when the whites had run for their lives, not very much had been done outside of fighting. The Soviet-backed President Lumumba had been killed and replaced by the general backed by the Americans. The Cold War was being fought right across Africa with no regard for the Africans. The prize was strategic minerals and the argument between Russia and America, both dirty and vicious. All the ideological claptrap was as misleading in its purpose as the Christian mission in the previous century. The two big powers wanted once again to come up Africa, this time in the name of communism or democracy. Heath, having done his homework before leaving London, saw the same pursuit of spheres of influence that had motivated the old colonial powers. Nothing had ever changed in the world and Heath was not sure it ever would. Only the quicksand shifted position.

Having pulled the chain in his upstairs room and activated a rat the size of a cat that had fallen with a soggy thud at his feet and shot out the bathroom door, Heath had chased the rodent from under his bed and into the corridor. Having checked the skirting boards for rat holes he had taken a shower, put on a clean shirt and taken the stairs down to the bar, the idea of being trapped in a confined lift less appealing than the rat. 'Welcome to Africa,' he said to himself, running the rules back through his mind. Water out of sealed bottles. Anti-malaria pills every day. A big hat for the sun. Salt pills to counter the heat. Not to paddle in the bilharzia-riddled rivers or what was left of his liver would be eaten away by the parasites that lived in the river snails and climbed through a man's skin down to his liver or up to his brain. Never walk anywhere after dark. All wild animals are dangerous.

The bar was down seven steps from the lifts on the left. Fans revolved under the ceiling and the bar was full. The whores, long-legged and delicious to look at, sat at the tables one step down from the bar. One girl wearing a pair of tiny shorts looked particularly beautiful, and Heath sighed for his old age. The girl caught his eye, hers smouldering with a mixture of resentment and commercial need. He would not have embarrassed her with the fat around his body or the whisky breath that soured his mouth. He would have liked to have sat and talked, maybe. There was nothing else left any more, only the memories. She got his eye-spoken message, tucked her long black legs back under the table and turned to her friend, boredom shuttering her eyes. Heath eased his fat backside up onto a stool, adjusting his position for maximum long-term comfort, and ordered a drink. Three of the white men were in mercenary uniforms and speaking French to each other. They were all over forty. The bar was well stocked and the downward draft from the fan pleasant on his shirt, drying the sweat he had made walking down the stairs.

The barman spoke English, which was a blessing. Most of the mercenaries in the Congo, he learnt, were from South Africa. To the white

South Africans, they were on a real mission, holding back the tide of communism. The Americans used them when they thought it necessary.

After the second drink he turned round from his bar stool. The beautiful whore had gone. Looking down the bar, so had one of the French-speaking mercenaries.

"What are you doing here, you fat old bastard?"

Turning back the other way, he was confronted by a Fleet Street writer from the London *Times*.

They got drunk together, having a good time talking about old times.

When Heath went up to his room to sleep he had forgotten the girl in the bar and the rat drinking from his toilet cistern.

In every bar in Léopoldville that was safe for a white man, Heath spread the word. His friend from the *Times* took him on the rounds, day and night. Everybody, including the mercenaries, were waiting for something to happen.

THE THIN, tall black man was smooth, well dressed, and fluent in French with discordant notes. He had tribal scars on his face and a missing pinkie from his left hand. The man was too casual in his approach to be a coincidence. Heath had spoken to strangers in bars for forty years and knew the lonely conversationalist, the drunk wanting company, the whore, young and old. He also knew when a man wanted something.

They got over the preliminaries, buying each other drinks, which was a red flag in post-colonial Africa. The tall, thin man was the first indigenous acquaintance to buy Heath a drink.

Byron had told Heath to tell everyone who would listen that Byron Langton, owner of the *Evening Garnet* with columns syndicated around the free world, and founder of Langton Merchant Bank that specialised in helping the Third World, was a dedicated socialist who abhorred colonialism and was ready to help the new emergent Africa.

Within half an hour the black man was offering Heath uncut diamonds provided the proceeds were paid into a European bank.

"Look," Heath said in French, "I don't know who you are. I expect uncut diamonds are illegal. How do you know the money will be yours to collect in Europe?"

"Merchant banks have ways to guarantee payment."

"Who are you?"

"We have heard Mr Langton is doing business in Zambia."

"Who do you represent?"

"The people who will control the future government. There is no point capturing the diamond mines, the copper mines in Katanga if we are unable to control the flow of money the mines generate. Will you set up a meeting in London with your Mr Langton and our mining commissar?"

"Are you a communist?" asked Heath, casually but very quietly.

"Does it matter?"

"Not really."

Heath stayed on in Léopoldville for two more weeks but no one outside the world of journalism made any contact. He had given the tall, thin man Byron's home phone number and left it at that. Feeling distinctly like a pimp, Heath caught an aircraft to Johannesburg and London, reporting to Byron the following Monday morning.

When Heath bought his copy of the *Evening Garnet* that night he did not recognise his own newspaper. The headline, trivial and of little consequence, was four inches high and right across the page.

 TORY SEX SCANDAL.

There was little else on the subject in the smaller print and the photograph of a half-nude buxom lady on the same page had nothing to do with the main story.

The following week advertising rates went up twenty-five per cent: the circulation had doubled. At the end of the week, the editor announced the paper would be published as a morning tabloid. Heath never knew there were so many buxom ladies in all of England.

By the time the Christmas lights went up in Regent Street, Langton Newspapers were out of the red and Heath Mortimer had made two more visits to Africa while none of his articles had appeared in the newly named *Daily Garnet*.

"Forget about newspaper articles," Byron snapped. "You and I are in a much bigger league. You have analysed Africa as a cesspool of war, corruption and genocide. You say the turmoil will last well into the next century and may never stop without a form of recolonisation. You tell me the only secure places you visited were the producing mines. If I printed what is probably the truth, I'd be accused of being so out of touch the opposition would ridicule my newspaper. The fact that everyone in the world is running in the wrong direction is not my problem. Money is made from the facts, the truth, not wishful thinking. Except when it comes to newspapers. Then you tell the readers what they want to hear and everyone runs off joyously in the wrong direction. Maybe someday when we have used up all your knowledge to our advantage, we will put these articles into a book. You could even write yourself a novel. Oh, and happy Christmas."

"What's this for?" said Heath, taking the cheque.

"Your Christmas bonus. Haven't you lost some weight?"

"Twenty pounds."

"There you are."

BYRON DROVE the car with the hood down. Once past the built-up area of London the Bentley 3 Litre built up speed, the deep-throated roar of the engine vibrating the steering wheel. The Saturday morning before Christmas was crisp and cold, a thin sun washing the grass and trees of Box Hill. The car was the original from which the miniature on Byron's desk had been modelled. Once on the Dorking bypass, the car picked up speed to ninety miles an hour. Byron felt good and put his leather-gloved hand on the knee of the girl in the passenger seat. They were both dressed in thick clothes, only their mouths and noses exposed to the elements.

Lady Fiona Renwick was the second daughter of the Marquis of Bathurst and the fifth cousin of the Queen of England. Through her mother she was related to the King of Norway, the future King of Spain and the last Tsar of all Russia. Her pedigree was exemplary and her father was still rich. She was twenty-two years old, ten years younger than Byron. She had been launched into society four years earlier without any subsequent success. To look at she was a very ordinary girl with an ordinary round face, straight hair to shoulder length that was neither blonde nor brown but, depending on the light, somewhere in between. To her mother and father's mild surprise, Fiona had finished her A levels and, after the season that had seen her coming out at a ball given by her father at their country seat in Scotland, she had taken a degree in English literature at Edinburgh University where she had obtained a First. She had met Byron through his newspaper before it was changed to a tabloid. Lord Manningly had been at Harrow with her father and the job interview had been arranged a week before the company was sold. Manningly, remembering his obligation to an old school friend, had made a telephone call to Byron, recommending the girl for a job.

"Do you know the young lady, Lord Manningly?" Byron had asked.

"Not really but I went to school with her father. First-class chap. Knew her mother before she married Bathurst. She was quite a gal, I recall. If the blood's right, everything else is right, young man."

Byron had smiled, put down the phone and called for her curriculum vitae which gave the girl's pedigree in full detail. The job interview was set with a sub-editor and Byron made sure he was in the building when the girl arrived, watching her at reception through the glass partition. She was what he had hoped to look at, neither pretty nor ugly. No one could ever have guessed her bloodline. Byron made his move.

"Hello. My name's Byron Langton. Your father gave Lord Manningly a call and he passed on the message. Why don't we go out and have some coffee?"

"What on earth for?"

"Because I own the newspaper."

They had stared hard at each other for a brief moment before she laughed. The laugh was pleasant.

THE BENTLEY DROVE through the Surrey countryside into Hampshire where they stopped for lunch before driving on to Dorset and Langton Manor. For the first time in his life, Byron was taking a girl home to meet his mother and father. It was one of the few things in his life for which he required not only his mother's approval but her judgement. To Byron, a man marrying a woman for life that he temporarily lusted over was plain stupid.

Josephine had arrived at Corfe Castle the previous night, alone much to her mother's dismay. Randolph and Anna had met her at the station. All except Hilary's family and Will would be at Langton Manor for Christmas.

Red Langton watched his wife waiting for her prospective daughter-in-law and wanted to laugh. He was fifty-six years old and not unhappy with his life, the horror of the war years sometimes keeping him awake in the night. Adelaide, his wife, wanted grandchildren. It was an obsession. She wanted something more to do than run the house and watch him go to sleep in front of the evening fire, or outside under the oak tree in the twilight of a hot summer day. They were content with each other, deep in a comfortable rut. Red left it to his wife to worry about a generation of grandchildren. The farm was running smoothly, the farmhouse roof did not leak. His favourite bitch had given birth to seven pups. Randolph, his eldest son, was easy to work with and Anna had never created a discordant note from the day she came to live at Langton Manor. Red Langton was at peace with himself.

The morning after Byron arrived in his pre-war tourer, cold but invigorated, Josephine behaved charmingly. She had been to the hairdresser in London and even discarded the horn-rimmed glasses she had taken to wearing to make her look more severe and liberated. She was even polite to

Fiona right through the morning. Christmas Day was to be on the Wednesday.

Before lunch, the family gathered in the lounge next to the fireplace. Red Langton had just shown Fiona the spreading oak tree on the terrace that he told her had been planted with an acorn by the first Langton of Langton Manor. Even Group Captain Red Langton was a little defensive in the presence of the daughter of a marquis of the realm and a little annoyed with himself for showing it.

"Ah, some sherry," he overemphasised when he ushered the young lady in from the cold. Sherry before lunch was a winter tradition.

"I'm glad to see you've changed your politics," began Josephine to her twin brother, putting a friendly hand on his arm. Byron was leaning his right elbow against the mantelpiece.

"What do you mean, sis?"

"Your newspaper has changed sides. Under Manningly it was true-blue Tory."

"But what has that to do with me?"

"Didn't you change the paper from staid conservative to wacky tit and bum?" With the last statement, Josephine took everyone's attention. "And now you support Labour."

"Yes but that doesn't mean to say I've become a socialist."

"Surely you use your paper to put across your views?"

Byron laughed out loud and his sister snapped away her hand.

"Look, Josephine, I'm in business to make money. Yes, you are going to win the next election according to our market research and by a landslide. By this time next year Harold Wilson will be Prime Minister of England and for a newspaperman what does that tell you?"

"That people want socialism."

"Maybe. More likely they've swallowed Wilson's wild promises to give them a socialist paradise on earth. Where he's going to get the money from is another issue but let's leave that aside. No, what it tells me as the owner of a daily paper is the majority want to believe his claptrap and I'm in the business of selling papers. When the majority want to be Tory, I'll switch back again."

"That's immoral."

"Sells newspapers. Oh, and congratulations, sis. You flattened the Federation of Rhodesia and Nyasaland. Long live Zambia and Malawi."

"And Zimbabwe. Nkomo says he's going to call Rhodesia, Zimbabwe."

"Probably. Not for a while. My information says the whites in Southern Rhodesia are going to tell us British to go to hell."

"And whose side will you be on that time?"

"The side in England that has the majority. We don't originate public opinion. All we do is follow and give the public what they want."

"So your paper doesn't have an opinion of its own?"

"Of course it does. It has the opinion of the majority of the people as told to our editor by our market research department. Give the man what he wants. But my word it doesn't mean to say I've become a socialist. When you socialists run out of other people's money to give away, as you will, as will the Russians, even my newspaper will be backing the other side. And more importantly, still making a profit. Darling sister, wealth has to be created before it can be given away. Democratic Socialism is a steal for a politician and a bloody disaster for the rest of us, rich and poor. You castrate a man when you give him something he has not earned. Worse, you make Jack a very dull boy."

"You're a hypocrite."

"No, a pragmatic capitalist allowing the wind of change to make him rich."

"We'll take it all away from you."

"I doubt it. Most of it is held in offshore companies. Socialism says that every person was born equal and therefore must have an equal share of the common wealth. No one is equal, sis, because we are all different, very different. Inability, dedication, physical power, brainpower, likes, dislikes. Until the world stops basing its politics on a fallacy, nothing will change permanently for the better and likely we'll blow ourselves to pieces. It was not long ago the Church insisted the earth was the centre of the universe, that everything revolved around us, including the sun, but science proved them wrong. Similar dogma is putting the Church beyond the logic of the ordinary man. And that is a disaster. Now can I pour you some of Dad's sherry? Mum, it's good to be home... Everyone, a happy Christmas."

10

$\mathcal{L}$indsay Healy lived with her boss during the weekends who lived with his wife and children during the week. She was long-legged and big busted with a finely crafted chiselled face. No man passed Lindsay in the street without turning back for a second look. There were any number of men in Sydney to choose from. Kevin Smith, her boss, suited her plans. She wanted a relationship without the responsibility, and during the week she was so tired from work she wanted to sleep at home without the snores and inconvenience.

Their offices were in Bligh House, next to the Wentworth Hotel in Bligh Street. Kevin Smith Publications was embossed on the glass door that opened into the small suite of offices on the third floor. Lindsay had the office next to Kevin's and they could yell to each other through the thin partition. The month before, Lindsay had turned twenty-one and Kevin thirty-nine. Their birthdays were three days apart.

"Lindsay, you want to come in here?" shouted Kevin through the wall.

"Why?"

"'Cause I say so, darlin'... You want to go to Africa?"

"Sure. When do I leave?" said Lindsay, pulling open his door.

"Tomorrow if you want."

"Thought you were pulling my leg."

"Now why ever would I want to do that?" They both giggled.

The entire staff and Mrs Smith were aware of the relationship, Mrs

Smith having made up her mind to compromise for the sake of the children, so she said, but it was more for herself. She was forty-three.

"Mate of mine in advertising, John Daly, just come back," said Kevin. "Went on a photographic safari for a client. There's a bird in Africa that talks to us humans. Tells us to follow and then goes off through the bush. Waits for you to catch up. They call it the honeybird. For us finding the hive is difficult and getting at the honey for the bird is impossible. Over the centuries the black men out there have followed the call of the honeybird and when they break open the hive after smoking out the bees they leave a piece of the honeycomb for the bird. Now my mate's client sells honey right across Australia and the new campaign will centre around the Legend of the African honeybird. There's a bloke out there, an Englishman, drifted out after school who John says is the best wildlife photographer ever. John tried to get pics of the honeybird in the week and gave up. This bloke gave him half a dozen prints of the bird, with the negatives. I want you to go out to Barotseland and sign up this Englishman on an exclusive. Royalty every time we sell the use of his pictures. Get his story."

"How old is he?" asked Lindsay.

"Didn't ask."

"Don't give me that shit."

"Well if I did I don't remember. Africa's blowing apart so we want those negatives out of the country fast. By the time they've finished kicking out the colonials and carving each other up there won't be any game to photograph and if there is, no man in his right mind will step into that bloody mess to try. Those pics are worth money. Why the bloody English went into Africa in the first place beats me. Now they've got to run for it."

"Same reason they went to America and Australia. Lucky for us they killed off our locals with guns, booze and disease."

"Colonialism stinks. Our blokes are citizens. Take that bloody apartheid in South Africa. Keeps the blacks out of the white areas. Pass laws. You name it. Bloody not right."

"And the white Australia policy?"

"That's different. This is our country."

At five o'clock on the dot the office closed, and the staff went next door to the Wentworth Hotel. Kevin bought the first shout as was the Friday night custom. The bar was downstairs in the basement and crowded. After four drinks Kevin ordered a taxi from the reception desk upstairs. His car was left at home for his wife. Lindsay smiled. The routine never changed. At Double Bay the taxi dropped them outside a house in a tree-lined lane. Eliza's Restaurant occupied the entire house.

They sat at the small bar to the left of the L-shaped restaurant with doors
out onto the patio showing tables under the trees. The food display centre of
the first leg of the room was sensational, along with the prices. A long glass
canopy, well lighted, covered the cold cuts and uncooked fish on ice, the red
snappers and oysters, the lobsters and Queensland mud crabs, the biggest
crabs in the world.

"Don't think I'm flying in and straight out," said Lindsay. They were
seated at a table just inside the glass patio windows. "Two weeks minimum.
Africa. If your mate couldn't buy this Will Langton in a week, I'll need two,
probably more... Don't look crestfallen, Kevin. You've got your wife." She
smiled at him sweetly and sucked an oyster into her mouth.

"You want me to divorce Mahel?"

"Not particularly." Lindsay sipped her wine, a dry white from South
Australia. Kevin believed everything was better from Australia. She had
booked the flight on Ansett from Sydney to Perth with a two-hour delay
before flying South African Airways to Johannesburg. After a night stop she
would fly to Lusaka and catch the weekly flight to Mongu. Three days.

"You don't travel for three days to come straight back again. Mahel
doesn't want a divorce, she told me so."

"When?"

"Oh, weeks ago."

"I don't understand women."

"People don't understand people. What we think and say are very
different." She was excited at the prospect of the trip.

After two bottles of wine and the most expensive meal in Sydney they
went home to her flat in Elizabeth Bay. The flat was high up and overlooked
the yacht basin and Kevin Smith paid half the rent.

Half an hour away by car in North Sydney, Mahel Smith was lying in bed
reading a good book. Two of her children were out at a party and the ten-
year-old girl was fast asleep in the next room. Mahel smiled to herself. Most
of her friends would be waiting for the pubs to close and their drunken
husbands to come home. She was comfortable alone and spared the foul
breath and fumbling hands. Mahel had always been sensible. She needed a
man to give her the children she enjoyed, the home she enjoyed with the
garden her pride and joy: a man with a good income who paid the bills on
time. Sex once a month was more than enough for Mahel and if she never
succumbed again in her life, it would mostly be a pleasure. She had fulfilled
her role and when Kevin recovered from the fact that he was almost too old
to attract the young girls, they would settle down to a normal suburban life.
When the kids left home, they would keep each other company in front of

the television and sometimes remember the good times they had had in the past. Life had its moments. She picked up the book and carried on reading. Regency England; in those days the men were romantic.

By the time Kevin and Lindsay were making love she was fast asleep, content with her own world.

LAURIE HALL, the ex-airport manager of Mongu, was hungover and depressed. His scheme to make a fortune out of crocodile skins was not working and time was running out for the white man in Africa. His need to get rich quickly was an obsession.

Every week he came into the village to collect mail and cables and pick up the week's newspapers. Sometimes Will also made the journey from the base camp on the river but more often than not he drove in alone the night before and stayed in the club where he drank himself into oblivion. He only received a little money from the photographic safari business. He was fed and housed and clothes were a pair of khaki shorts and shirt. He had been wearing the same boots for three years and long ago discarded the luxury of socks. His feet were as hard as the horn on a rhinoceros. To add insult to his depression, it was his birthday. He was twenty-nine, penniless and next year he would be thirty, a milestone in age that boggled his mind.

The rains were over for the year at the end of March and the sky was blue from one horizon to the other with small fluffy white clouds that had forgotten the message of rain. Laurie looked up from the open Land Rover on his way to his old airport. It was going to be a long dry season, the year the Federation of Rhodesia and Nyasaland ended and Zambia was born in the hot bush of Central Africa. There was little point going to meet the weekly flight from Lusaka but those were his instructions. 'Sometimes the cables don't get through in time,' Will said every week: it was difficult to make a living without killing the animals. 'There'll be requests for hunting safaris,' he would tell Will. 'There always are.' On the question of all-important money the two men were far apart. Laurie put it down to the younger age and the security of Langton Manor. Moral high ground was easier when the family was rich.

The two beers he had taken at the club before driving to the airport were wearing off, replaced by a raging hangover thirst. The herd of wildebeest were out on the grass runway and the Central African Airways plane would be late as usual. Even the airline was breaking up with the Federation. He was glad to be out of the airline business and one way or another he would go back to England with big money in the bank. All the national service dodgers had been exempted, according to Will, so there was no impediment to his return.

"Bugger," he said out loud as he drove up to the lone shed building that made up the airport complex at Mongu. There was a small churn of nostalgia at the sight of his work for so many years, the nostalgia for the loss of youth. There was nobody at the one desk next to the window which did not augur well for the plane's prompt arrival, but the door was open and he went inside and took some water from the drum and sat down at his old desk. He took off his boots and looked at his feet; both big toes were slightly nobbled.

"You could be the last bloody white in Africa and no one would care." He had been talking to himself in the bush for years. "The last bloody Englishman to become a colonial." Laurie shivered in the heat at the thought of the rest of his life and looked at his watch to take his mind off the problem. Half an hour and back to camp. He had run out of money for booze. His head fell forward, and he was soon snoring, fast asleep to the world.

He was woken by the pilot stampeding the wildebeest off the airstrip. The bitter taste of gall parched his mouth from the night before, the foul residue of one and a half bottles of club whisky and a bottle of South African red wine. He could never remember after a binge whether he had eaten or not. Professionally, Laurie watched the pilot bring the twin-engined Beechcraft up and around for his approach. The windsock next to the thin-roofed shed, now burning hot from the noonday sun, was limp and Laurie's watch told him he had slept in his old chair for two hours, his discarded boots under the table. A small truck was rattling down the rutted road, pitted by the rains, the ruts baked into iron by the sun. The plane's landing gear dropped as the plane straightened, pointing down the centre of the open piece of veld. Dust puffed three times and then the Beechcraft ran in fast down the grass until the propellers reversed sending Laurie's hands to his ears to block out the noise. The engines made the whole shed shake before they were cut fifty feet from Laurie's old desk.

"Morning, Laurie," said a cheerful voice. "Two pax. Probably for you."

"Probably missionaries come to do some good."

"Hilary would be waiting. Or someone else. Will's right to always meet the plane. Good night in the club last night?"

"Don't remember the end."

"Who cares?" said the new airport manager as he walked over to the stationary aeroplane to do his job.

First a woman with big dark glasses that covered half her face stepped down the steps that had been let down from inside the aircraft. When she reached the dusty grass, cropped short by the herd of wildebeest, she walked with a long, sure stride. Her hair was black, the shiny colour of a raven's wing.

Over to the right of the airfield, the wildebeest were coming back onto the airfield and a crowned eagle called high in the African sky, soaring up on a thermal of hot air, searching the bush below with telescopic eyes.

Laurie's hormones had jumped as he watched the woman walking across to the shed. The airport manager was still at the foot of the steps, waiting for the second passenger. Laurie guessed the dark-haired girl with the large inviting mouth and the small shell-shaped ears to be in her middle twenties. Somehow, Laurie thought he knew the woman. His eyes moved back to the Beechcraft and a young girl with the longest legs and largest bust Laurie had ever seen since running away to Africa came down the steps, her chiselled, clean-cut face free of dark glasses, her eyes almost shut against the glare of the sun. Laurie stood up on reflex and leant forward at the open window to have a better look.

"I'm looking for Mr William Langton," said a voice from the open doorway.

"I'm sorry, I was just…"

"I can see what you are doing." The woman was smiling and when she took off the big dark glasses Laurie was certain he had seen her somewhere before. "She really is rather pretty."

"Yes," said Laurie stopping himself from saying 'and so are you'. It was the kind of day for Laurie that had never happened before in Mongu and not a penny in his pocket and credit at the club a thing of the past. "Will's not here. We always meet the plane."

"They said so. I came on the spur of the moment. The other lady is also looking for Mr Langton. Can you drive us both to his camp on the river?"

"I'd buy you a drink at the club but…"

"Why don't I buy us all one? There was nothing but bush all the way from Lusaka. How far's the club?"

"Five minutes."

"You had a good night last night?"

"Not really."

"Neither did I. I've one small bag and so has the Australian. You must be Laurie Hall. I've known William a long time."

"We call him Will."

"I know," said Shelley Lane, "but I call him William."

"He doesn't know that anyone's coming."

"That was the whole idea."

"You're Shelley Lane," said Laurie, understanding. "Will talks about you."

WHEN BYRON LANGTON'S engagement to Lady Fiona Renwick was announced in the *Times* and the *Telegraph*, Shelley wanted to run away. Her concert tour had finished after Christmas and the new record deal with EMI was still in the talking stage. She had written two of the numbers and liked neither. Her first reaction to the engagement was not to sign the annual EMI renewal of her contract but that would be cutting off her nose to spite her face. Her need was to hurt Byron, not herself. She had finally moved from Mrs Page's in Holland Park to a flat in Chelsea with its own small courtyard and tree. She had moved a bench under the tree, spent a fortune on furniture and curtains, and had never been so lonely in her life. There were people everywhere she went, invitations to this and that every day through her letter box, but all anybody wanted to meet was Shelley Lane the singer. She was heartsick to the point of death and the engagement, though nothing of a big surprise – *Tatler* had been full of them – came when there was nothing in her life but the lonely booze. She wanted to hurt him, make him feel a little of how she felt. It had been nearly five years since Byron had entered her life and left again, except for the business. Cold with fury, she had read of the engagement. Two days later she was booked on her journey to Africa. She was going to bring the young brother out of the African bush and flaunt him in front of his brother. She was going to use her looks, her well-tuned sex appeal, her money and her fame and with them she was going to bring home young Will. The girl on the plane from Australia was a minor inconvenience.

She was glad to hear Will talked about her to Laurie Hall. Byron had mentioned this Laurie Hall who was looking at the Australian from nose to toes.

"Hi. I'm Lindsay Healy. My boss sent me, Kevin Smith Publications, you know? Right. That bag's mine. The airport manager, if you can call it an airport, said you're the bloke to drive us downriver... You always look at a girl like that?"

"Not always," said Laurie quietly.

"He needs a drink," said Shelley.

"Don't we all?... Many people at the camp?"

"Just the four of us now. Then there's Sixpence, Fourpence and Onepenny. Trackers. You mind stopping off at the club?"

"Go for your life," said Lindsay.

Lindsay took the back seat in the Land Rover, the singer and the man with the abundant hangover up front. Lindsay thought him quite good looking in a rugged, sun-scorched way. The crow's feet were deep on either side of his face, stretching out for an inch from piercing blue eyes. The hair on the sideburns was brown with most of the hair on top bleached white by the sun. She was told to wear a wide-brimmed hat but Laurie Hall was bareheaded. The arms holding the steering wheel were hard and strongly muscled, the very British upper-class accent out of place. She felt safe with Laurie Hall. She wondered what he would do when the British were kicked out of Africa.

The drive to Mongu Club took five minutes, the canvas canopy over the Land Rover flapping in sharp, crisp bursts under pressure from their speed over the rutted road, Laurie missing the potholes with unerring accuracy while talking sideways to the singer.

Lindsay had been to a Shelley Lane concert in Melbourne while researching an article on the lack of dung beetles in Australia. Her article had spawned the first importation of dung beetles from Africa to counter the problem.

She had tried to talk to the singer on the plane but the noise from the engines limited their conversation to a shout of names. What the icon of swinging Britain was doing in the bush made no sense but her training in journalism told her here was a story. No one seemed to know she was coming.

There had been few trees along the road and the grass was brown, dry and short. All the way to the club, Lindsay looked for the lions and the elephants. The midday sun pressed everything down into silence and however far she looked from her game-viewing bench at the back of the Land Rover there was nothing but bush and the heat with the red dust billowing out behind. On all sides she looked the bush went on forever.

The club was a single-storey building with a wide veranda overlooking well-cut lawns and a swimming pool. There were two tennis courts to the right of the pool, silent in the heat. In the main room away from the bar, the focal point of the club, long side tables were set with white linen tablecloths and an abundance of side dishes next to the pile of plates and gleaming silver. 'It doesn't take a genius,' Lindsay said to herself; 'curry for lunch.' Above, long-armed fans whirred round and round, three in the lounge-dining room and two over the bar; somewhere a generator beat a pulse that powered the fans. The waiters, barefoot, with white linen trousers and three-quarter jackets, red-fezzed and smiling, stood ready to serve the British.

Lindsay thought it something out of a previous century, the same old empire plodding along as it had done for Queen Victoria. Time had not moved for one hundred years in Mongu.

There was something wrong with the money situation. First, they were signed in as guests of the club and Shelley Lane made an arrangement to run a card at the bar and pay for their lunch. Lindsay saw Shelley hand the club manager, a short, stout Englishman, a five-pound note. The man had given Laurie Hall a less than friendly look and a shake of his head when Laurie had asked to sign in.

"Photographic safaris are not very profitable," he said after the new arrangement. "Maybe you could both talk sense to Will. We turn down a dozen hunting safaris a year and that's money. I have a weekly allowance for Mongu and I spent it all last night. At the camp we don't need money. Sorry about this. Damned embarrassing, I'd say. Five pounds, Shelley, was far too much."

"What about the next time?" said the singer.

'Ah, she drinks as well,' thought Lindsay.

Over the biggest curry lunch Lindsay had ever seen she listened to the new resident talk to Shelley Lane. The old resident, Jonas Jones, had gone to Nyasaland as the last colonial governor. It was all coming apart.

"How many British in Barotseland?" she heard Shelley ask the resident.

"Well, now, if you include women and children about one hundred and fifty."

"How big an area is your jurisdiction?"

"Size of Wales, I'd say. Not for long. Kaunda will be taking over."

"You think it'll work?" asked Shelley.

"Depends who for. Party officials, yes. Maybe even the people for a while. What they won't have is honesty, I'm sure of that, as hereditary chiefs know they are around for life. These new politicians will use power to get rich. You buy and sell influence in the new Africa. We British maintained a disciplined honesty. That will go. Now, you say you are a singer. What do you sing?"

Lindsay smiled to herself, turning back to the food on her plate. It was obvious the British resident commissioner of Barotseland, an area the size of Wales, had never heard of Shelley Lane. The article she was going to write was forming nicely in her mind.

WILL Langton knew the wind of political change blowing down Africa had reached his base camp. He watched the chief drive away in the government

Land Rover that would soon be taken away from the old man. Right across Africa the colonial powers were dumping past agreements, writing Western-style constitutions for Iron Age peasantry, spawning a clutch of lip rants, cut-throats and tinpot dictators. From the spurious moral high ground of 'one man one vote' they left their responsibilities to starve with the peasantry, snug in the furtherance of democracy: it was a great occasion. Africa returned to tribalism with a vicious twist. Instead of the assegai, they used AK-47 automatic assault rifles, landmines by the millions, mortars that fired two kilometres and a disregard for human life not seen in Africa since the high days of the slave trade. The rule of British law was to give way to the rule of the gun and the old chief knew better than any politician in Whitehall that the days of peace, of law and order, were about to change.

Will's dilemma was mixed with an overpowering sadness. From the first days of Hannes Potgieter, the concession to hunt on tribal land had been given by Paramount Chief Mwene Kandala III through his local chief, the old man whose dust trail was still visible to Will above the dry bush and the distant mopani trees.

Still behind Will, the great waters of the Zambezi River flowed on and on, carrying the flotsam of the land: trees pulled down by the floods, grass islands washed into floating pieces riding the flow, dead animals waiting for the crocodiles. That afternoon was the first visit made by the old chief; before he had made contact through his young induna, the village headman nearest the base camp. The chief had been alone.

They had walked away from the house, along the northern bank of the great river, away from the trackers who had left the presence of the chief walking backwards and clapping their hands in front of them, the traditional show of not being armed. Sixpence, Fourpence and Onepenny were in awe of their chief. The chief spoke in English.

"The salary I receive from the British to administer my land in the name of the paramount chief will end with the new government rulers unless I join the party. Chiefs after the British leave will be subject to the whims of the party and their patronage. We will have lost our power. I must protect the last years of my old age and my family. I need money, Mr Langton, and you have the skill to provide me with that money."

"Not the elephant," Will had blurted.

"Not the elephant, no. The crocodiles. In the history of our people there have always been problems with the crocodiles and without a gun they are difficult to kill, which is why the river is infested with so many. I want you to shoot me two thousand crocodiles from the waters that are on my land. I want you to arrange for the skins to be sent to Umtali in Southern Rhodesia where they will be cured and sent on your behalf to London. Then you will sell those skins and pay eighty per cent of the proceeds into a London bank account on my behalf. I want to be sure the money is beyond the grasp of the party. I was educated in London, Mr Langton, for three years. As was my son and my grandson. Officially, I will have nothing to do with the crocodile hunt."

"But I could keep all the money."

"You could but you won't, Mr Langton."

"You think I will be able to stay under the new government? Will they renew my hunting concession?"

"No. It has been sold to someone else. The party needed funds. They have sold many concessions even before they take over. Two thousand crocodiles. You and Mr Potgieter owe me that much. Maybe both of us will once again be living in England. I will probably die in the first winter. The old order, Mr Langton, is being swept down the river. A man must protect himself and his family."

Alone, Will walked away from the house with its open veranda watching silently, sick in his stomach; the ends of his fingers, the nerve ends, were hurting. After eight years in Africa, much of it on his own, he was not sure if he could exchange the animals of Africa for the people of Europe. The crocodiles he would leave to Laurie Hall and the trackers, carrying out the instruction, paying for the years of the hunting concession, himself having no part in the slaughter.

It had been a good eight years and Will smiled to himself. Even at the age of twenty-six Will understood that nothing went on forever. There was always change and rarely was the change for the better. People said it would be better for everyone but it never was. For ten minutes he watched the vervet monkeys watching lion from the tall acacia tree that dipped its roots in the big river.

"They call it the melancholy blues," he said to the monkeys before slowly walking back to camp.

TEN MILES DOWN THE ROAD, Lindsay Healy wished she had drunk at lunchtime. To get into the Land Rover outside the club, Laurie Hall had walked his hands round the bonnet of the car to support himself before slumping into the driver's seat where he was unable to find the keyhole to start the engine. The singer everyone raved about had leant across the front seat and together the two drunks had pushed home the key. No one in the street or from the club thought anything was out of the usual.

The sun was falling behind them with Laurie firmly driving a path that Lindsay would never recognise for a road. The tall-trunked mopani trees were thick on either side and the sinking sun glowed through the bush from the surface of a great river. The brown grass was shoulder high and the bush between the trees green-leafed and partly thick. Too frightened to look for game, Lindsay held on to the bucking back seat bench of the Land Rover watching two drunks singing at the tops of their voices, little concerned with the direction of the road that was more pothole than surface after the rains. Her adventure into Africa had become a nightmare and when the Land Rover ran out of petrol, stuttering its way to a halt in the almost dark, she was not sure whether the blanketing silence and menace of the bush was worse than the crazy drive feet away from the thick trunks of the trees. Their own red dust settled back on the car. Laurie opened the low door and fell out onto the road.

"Shit," he said. "Sorry, ladies... Welcome to Africa."

"Have we got any booze on board?" asked Shelley.

"Nope... Nearest bottle twenty miles down this road. I say, what, could you give me a hand, Lindsay?"

"Get up yourself."

"Ah, the Australian is not amused," said Laurie, pushing himself up the vehicle onto his feet.

"No, she isn't."

"If I pour petrol from the can it will go all over the Landy and blow it up. Be a nice girl."

"You've spare petrol?"

"My dear lady, if I may call you so, today I am drunk but yesterday I was sober and mindful of my own bad habits. Anyway, you never run around in this neck of the woods without water, petrol and oil in that order. Better be quick, Lindsay darling. The light goes in five minutes and then the lions come out and the tigers."

"You don't have tigers in Africa."

"Sometimes I wonder."

"Do you have a gun?" said Lindsay, her mouth dry.

"Yes I do."

By the time Lindsay had emptied the five-gallon jerry can down the funnel into the petrol tank the light had gone, leaving a red glow deep behind the mopani trees that went from blood red to crimson to yellow to white. The frogs from the river were loud, filling the night. There were grunts from the river through the trees. Lindsay could see the first trees away from the last of the light but the rest of the bush was black.

"Can we go?" she said to Laurie, giving him the empty can.

"At your service."

"How long?"

"An hour if we don't hit a buffalo or a tree. At night it's more difficult to pick out the track through the trees."

"You want to sober up first?"

"Then I get the shakes. Worry not, young lady. Alone I do this every week. In Africa it sometimes doesn't matter if you get to the other end. Then I sleep in the car."

"Don't the lions eat you?"

"Not yet. See for yourself."

"May I drive?" asked Lindsay.

"No."

"Why not?"

"Because drunk I'll do better in the bush than you. Make yourself comfortable in the back there and Laurie will get you round the boma before Onepenny serves up supper."

On the other side of the Land Rover, Shelley Lane was being sick into the long grass.

When finally the dark shape of the camp showed in their headlights Lindsay thought her nightmare over. The camp was as silent as a ghost.

"Where the hell is everyone?" shouted Laurie. In the seat next to him Shelley was quiet and still. There had been no singing on the last leg of the journey, just the drum of the engine and the fierce lights probing the black bush shining up trees that quickly disappeared. The gate into the compound was open. There was no answer. The lamps in the house were unlit and the fire at the centre of the boma dead. Leaving the headlights on, shining on the house, Laurie, comparatively sober, followed the beam to the wooden stairs that led up to the big open room under the thick black thatch. Going round the deck, Laurie lit the paraffin lamps.

"Come on up," he called. "Will's gone some place with the trackers. Lindsay, will you bring my gun?... Shelley, what will you drink? No ice for the while... What's the matter? Just watch for the bloody heron. Bill's as sharp as a razor. Bloody bird doesn't even sleep at night."

"A heron?" called Shelley. "Where's Will?"

"Don't know. A Goliath heron. Head stands high as your shoulder... All right, I'll come down."

THE TRACKERS CAME BACK ALONE at half-past eight and made the fire in the boma. Lindsay had drunk three shots of brandy but she was unable to stop shivering. She had been left alone in the bar with the hurricane lamps guttering in the breeze off the river, casting shadows into the night. A hyena had cackled from across the river. Every sound from the night was a deadly menace. She heard them making love from a bedroom behind the bar, the animal thrashing and grunts part of the primeval night. Moths, small and large, hurled themselves at the paraffin lamps, incinerated when they caught the heat from the top of the glass. Crickets screeched at the calling frogs and an owl hooted mournfully from a tree she could not see. The river plopped with fat fish and slowly the stars came out. The moon would not wax until the following night. The constellations appeared in the great universe of heaven and still the shivers raked her body. Too frightened to get off the bar stool, she poured a fourth drink from the brandy bottle Laurie had left by her side. The grunts of copulation had silenced and Lindsay missed the reassuring human sounds.

She was alone in the world for the very first time.

SEVEN MILES downriver Will had the campfire going well and the bream he had caught from the river ready to go on the fire. He had cut the stick from a mopani shoot and sharpened the end to a point. The fat bream was in the shallows when he struck with the light fading in the west. He had covered his tracks after turning back, knowing the trackers would look for him after the night had fallen. Now he knew his life on the banks of the river was soon to be over, each moment was precious. Laurie would be home full of talk from the club and Will wished to be alone with his river and the great black night. His loaded rifle lay on the ground next to the fire and the firelight played down to the river. He was more content than at any time in his life. Looking up, he smiled at the great universe, his own insignificance magnified to infinity.

'It does not matter,' he told himself. 'Life is of no consequence, a pulse of thought in the vastness of immeasurable time.'

They could have his concession. They could have his house. But for as long as he lived, they could never take away his memories. For as long as he lived, all the animals would live in his mind and this place would stay the same. Will could see up, his puny eyes taking in so little. He could see within, his simple intelligence understanding so little. But he was content. He knew this peace in his soul, the being that was him, and this had nothing to do with anybody else. The chief, the British, the moral flagellants.

All night Will stayed awake by the fire. With the dawn he was calm, refreshed and free of any fear of the future. He would go on with the odyssey of his life until he died.

The walk back to camp along the river was more beautiful than he ever remembered. The game drinking with the dawn took no notice of Will as if he were part of them. They watched with a wary eye but took no flight. The tall giraffe squatted splay-legged for the high head to reach the water down below. The birds were singing, hundreds of them.

Will, from Langton Matravers in the county of Dorset, was whistling in the African dawn. By the time he reached the base camp the yellow light of the cool dawn had turned to the white light of a hot day. It was going to be really hot he told himself as he walked up the wooden stairs to the high deck of his house. Down below and behind, the great river, oily and powerful, flowed on and on and a fish eagle on the near bank cried its distinctive three calls to the day. Somewhere behind the house he heard the trackers coming back through the other gate and wondered how far they had gone in the wrong direction. Will was smiling. He had spoilt his own spoor perfectly.

Fast asleep on his couch was a young girl with a chiselled face and the look of sheer exhaustion. On the bar was a half-empty brandy bottle.

"*Laurie*, where the hell are you?" Turning back he looked at the girl on the couch still fast asleep. "*Laurie*?"

Sixpence came up the wooden stairs two at a time.

"Baas!"

"Fooled you, Sixpence. Wanted a night in the bush on my own. Sorry. Chief says we're out of here with the new government. Won't renew my concession or his chieftainship. Where's Baas Laurie?"

"Good morning, William."

"Shelley? Shelly Lane? What the hell are you doing here?"

"Come to visit you."

"Why does nobody ever tell me anything? All right, Shelley, what's that brother done to you now?"

"Engaged himself to marry someone else."

"Who? No one told me."

"Lady Fiona Renwick, second daughter of the Marquis of Bathurst, fifth cousin of the Queen."

"That figures. You had some breakfast?"

"Not yet."

"Sixpence, ask Onepenny to make breakfast at the boma. I'm starving."

"Where did you sleep last night?" asked Shelley.

"I didn't... Wanted to think. Who's the girl on the couch?"

"Lindsay Healy. From Australia. Wants to see your photographs."

"Don't people ever book? What's the matter with her?"

"She had a trying night."

"Morning, Will," said Laurie, shirtless in his shorts and bare feet.

"First, I'm going to have a shower and then someone can tell me what the hell's going on around here."

WHEN LINDSAY HEALY finally woke on the couch there was an extra man sitting at the bar. The singer and her new boyfriend were drinking out their hangovers. All three people seated at the bar had their backs to the couch. The fear from the night before had gone with the heat of the day. Her bottle of brandy was still on the bar, sitting quietly on its own. From somewhere wafted the rich aroma of fresh coffee. From outside men were talking in a language she had never heard before. A soft breeze washed her face and she could smell the river. Tension drained from her body and for the first time since leaving the Mongu Club she was able to relax. Lindsay half listened to a story about the extra man's brother, the man she had come to see, but no one turned round to look down at her curled up on the couch and briefly she drifted back into sleep.

When she woke the man she had not seen before was looking down at her. The eyes were soft and warm, almost violet in colour. The feet were clad in crude leather shoes, brown-red from the dust and the long legs were thick at the top, strongly muscled. The shorts were tight around the high thigh and an open shirt revealed a piece of flesh and a belly button. The shirt was stripped of any sleeves. The skin was tanned the colour of mahogany and when she reached the eyes again, the man was smiling and offering her a cup of coffee. The hair on top was white-bleached by the sun.

"Sleep all right? I'm Will Langton. Coffee. Had a taste of Laurie's driving? You want to camera shoot a safari?"

"Yes and no. I'm Lindsay Healy from Australia."

"Tell you what. We'll leave the drinkers at the bar and go down to the river. I made a spot years ago under the acacia tree. Some call them fever trees. When the whites first got to Africa, many died of malaria by camping next to the rivers."

"Thanks," said Lindsay, taking the mug of black coffee.

"It was the mosquitoes, not the tree that killed them, the insects breeding in the stagnant pools left by the floodwaters after the rains. You can tell me what you want at the river. Onepenny will make you some breakfast."

Shelley Lane had watched the girl's eyes take in Will Langton. She let a brief, rueful smile play on her face and turned back to her drinking companion. It had probably been a bad idea anyway. The younger brother was the antithesis of Byron.

"I'm going to stay here awhile," she said.

"Suits me fine." Laurie was already a little drunk.

"You going to shoot the crocodiles?"

"Been trying to convince Will ever since I got here. Probably get a couple of thousand crocs of the right size. They only use the underbelly for shoes and handbags. Take a few years but the young ones will breed up again. Give the vundu a chance to recover."

"What's the vundu?"

"Big barbel. Stable diet of the crocodile. I want five hundred skins for myself but don't tell Will. My fee for the culling."

"You really think this is all over?"

"You can be sure, Shelley, my love of the night. Once the rule of British law is removed, they have a bad habit in these parts of fighting each other. For a while one of them comes out on top until he's taken out, then the whole process starts over. The man fighting from the bush becomes the president with his hands in the national till and the defeated president's supporters go back into the bush and start a guerrilla war. Tribalism, some of it. Habit mostly. The British gave them peace for a hundred years in exchange for being colonised. The average black man will only find out too late that he never had it so good under the British. Change in world power. Now it's the Americans fighting the Russians for spheres of influence. The Americans think democracy in Africa will give them control of the minerals and the markets. Everyone wants power and to hell with the people. We are not a nice species, Shelley Lane."

The wooden chairs were deep in the shade with the river down the slope not fifty metres from where they sat. Onepenny had put a large pot of fresh coffee on the table in front of them.

Onepenny was showing a lot of white teeth, the great crocodile hunt overshadowing the politics which he did not understand. There had always been a hereditary chief in the same village under the king. If the chief told the white man to go, he had a reason. They would always be the trackers on the banks of the great river and now they were to hunt the crocodile from the long canoes cut from the big trees. It was good work for a man and Sixpence had said they would keep ten skins each for themselves and they would all be rich.

Will smiled at Onepenny's retreating back. He had read his mind without a word being spoken. The bloodlust of the hunt was written all over his face.

"I'll bet they shake out a few skins for themselves," he said.

"What skins?" said Lindsay. She was enjoying the shade and the river. The coffee had taken away the foul taste of the brandy. With Will she felt safe.

"Crocodile. This will be the biggest hunt in a hundred years. Look, you do what you like with my photographs if you think them good enough. A wildlife book I don't know. I can't write a letter."

"But you can tell me the stories of the animals and I can write them down next to the photographs... You think they will really wipe out the game in Africa?"

"There is a population explosion right across Africa. The old diseases have been contained by the missionaries. You'll meet Hilary. He says in twenty years' time there will be twenty million people in the remnants of the Central African Federation. Now, there may be four million. This part of Africa can't sustain twenty million. Not enough rain. The animals will be the first to go; Hilary says we tinkered with the system. Tried to compete with nature and nature has a built-in way of asserting authority. Otherwise the planet would not be able to sustain life."

"What are you going to do when you leave here?"

"Drift down south. The whites in Southern Rhodesia will probably fight for what they built. The last gasp of imperialism. I couldn't live without trees and a river, animals, the bush. To struggle in a big city is against the laws of nature. Stay with us here for a while and you will understand what I mean. Would you like some more coffee?"

"Yes I would... And yes I will. You have quite a place here, Will Langton."

wo months earlier, seven hundred miles to the north-west of Will Langton's base camp, in the high mountains of Angola, sixty inches of rain had fallen in twelve weeks. Every crevice and stream, gullies that had been dry for years, were running with water; seeping, running, rushing down from the high ground in a long pursuit across the breadth of Central Africa joining spruits with rivers, rivers with rivers, all converging on the Zambezi River which would take their waters on down from the high plateau of Central Africa to the floodplains on the coast of the Indian Ocean and the final sanctuary of the sea. The great rains had fallen and the water and word of them would reach Mongu and Paramount Chief Mwene Kandala III at the end of the African winter, the word in time to beat the drums in his palace at Lealui eleven days and nights before he and his people would evacuate the Zambezi Valley and make for the high ground and his summer palace.

The sky was blue, the clouds pure white in the dry of the Barotse winter, the raptors high in the sky above the great river. Below, the mopani forests were scattered with game, while along a fifty-kilometre stretch of the river the slaughter of the crocodiles had begun, the heavy Brno rifles barking from the first light of the morning until the dusk of night. In parts, the river was dull red and the blood of the crocodiles flowed on down with the flotsam and the occasional carcass that had eluded the skinning knives of Laurie Hall and the trackers.

Laurie Hall was in his element and making money for the first time in his life. The crocodile skins, worth one hundred pounds each, were only the beginning. Laurie Hall was going back to London as Shelley Lane's manager. What he knew about the music business was less important than the passion they felt in bed. Shelley needed a man's security and Laurie needed a job. The killings of Africa could sweep right down to Cape Town for all he cared. He was going home with his share of the spoils from the colonies and what happened to them after he left was none of his business. Out of sight would be out of mind forever. He had even begun to limit his drinking. A man needed a clear head to make money. Opportunities never came twice. Once in a lifetime. In Laurie's head, the clichés flew thick, fast and jumbled.

Downriver fifty miles from the blazing guns and the stinking carcasses bereft of their underbellies, Will Langton was camped in a small grove of ilala palms, thin and tall, and feather-topped, leaning at angles to the sky. The island in the river was three hundred metres long and half as wide, thick with bush foliage watered by the constant flow of the river. There were small antelope on the island, hidden deep in the foliage, and the big water-fed trees were the home of crows and a multitude of birds rich in crimsons and yellows, every one of them unknown to Lindsay Healy. Despite the fact that she had still not been able to seduce Will Langton and despite the privacy of their island, she was happier than any other time she could remember in her life. Kevin Smith, his wife and his children, were as far away as the moon. She had removed tomorrow from her mind.

Will was sick with foreboding, knowing they were slaughtering the game for money, money that would be spent and gone with the animals.

The island had always been his sanctuary since the day Hannes Potgieter had showed him the safe campsite away from the crocodiles and hippo, deep in the trees, the smooth glade made by the intrusion of the ilala palms, the seeds deposited by some distant elephant when the river was low and the animals migrated south.

"They don't grow," he told Lindsay, "unless the small coconut, the size of a cricket ball, first passes through the belly of an elephant. Many seeds are like that, spread by the birds. Do you like my hideaway, the heart of the biggest hideaway in the world? There are hundreds of thousands more species of game in Barotseland than people. Why it is so special. Here we are just another animal."

"Are you lonely, Will?"

"Not now. Only sometimes. Yes. Without Hannes. A man needs conversation."

"Will the canoe be all right?"

"It always has been. They cut them out of tree trunks. Took me a while to

paddle without turning turtle. First, we gather wood for the night's big fire...
You're not frightened?"

"Not really. Maybe. Not exactly Sydney. Hard roads and concrete
buildings. Some of my ancestors lived in the bush. We call it the outback.
Maybe this calls to some part of me."

The plucked carcasses of two Egyptian geese hung by their necks from a
low branch of the jackalberry tree next to strips of drying meat cut from an
impala ram. Will's .22 Hornet rifle stood against the trunk of the tree next to
a pile of dry wood that would burn through the night. From the curved
trunk of an ilala palm that had grown sideways before being able to rise up
to the sky, Will had tied the top cord of a mosquito net. There was only one
net as Lindsay had deliberately put the second back in the house before it
reached the Land Rover that took them downriver to the hidden dugout
canoe, the Goliath heron chasing her for her trouble. The first cry of a beast
in the night would be Lindsay's signal to grab fast and hold onto Will.
Shelley and Laurie had left them alone at the base camp with candlelight, a
good bottle of wine and the African night. She had taken his hand at the bar,
stroked his richly tanned arm, pushed her bare knee against his bare thigh,
leant forward to prove her lack of a bra and searched his violet eyes but
nothing had worked. The door to her solitary bedroom stayed shut all night.

"Bloody certain I put two nets in the car. Have to use the one as outside
the wood smoke, the mozzies bite like bastards. There's enough room."

"Good," said Lindsay.

"I'll do the impala's saddle over the secondary fire when we have some
coals. Feed the cooking fire from the main fire. Before the light goes, I want
to show you the sunset reflected in the river. There's a game path through
the trees to a sandbank."

Will picked up the bolt-action Hornet without thinking, the precaution
automatic, and together they walked through the trees for thirty metres
before coming out onto the river. The sky was crimson in the west,
silhouetting the trees along the west bank of the river, sluggish and slow,
waiting for new water, months in the coming. Flotsam passed on either side
of their small island and the distant bark of the Brnos had been silent for
half an hour. As they broke cover onto the sandbank, a cloud of small birds
whirred away into the crimson sunset and an eleven-foot crocodile ran off
on short legs for the water, slithering beneath the reflected glow of the
clouds, red from the sinking sun.

"What were they?" said Lindsay, shivering as the reptile sank into the
black, oily water. Will put a protective arm around her shoulder.

"Quail," he said. "Harlequin quail. They drink in the morning and evening. The crocodile won't come back." Bringing the rifle to his shoulder, he fired into the water a few metres from the sandbank, worked the bolt and fired again. The high whine of the .22 pierced the silent last of the day. "Impact on the water sends shock waves under the water. We could swim if we wanted to."

"No thanks," said Lindsay.

"You're shivering."

"That crocodile was big."

"Yes. He was... They'll come back if they don't get shot up again. The vundu will multiply. That's a big barbel. Main source of food for the crocs. One animal's problem is another one's pleasure."

"How long will they shoot?" She snuggled against him and the shivers began to contain themselves.

"Four days. Maybe five. Depends on how many skins Laurie and the trackers think they can get away with for themselves. Maybe five hundred skins after the chief's."

"Are they worth a lot of money?"

"BNT. Umtali. That's Barotse National Transport, Octavio Goncalves's outfit. They run the skins lightly salted to Livingstone. From there by train to Bulawayo and up to Umtali. Skins don't weigh much. Umtali Leather will pay between seventy and a hundred and thirty pounds sterling a skin but we won't sell, just have them cure the underbelly and Manica Trading will ship them down to the port of Beira, sold to one of my brother's offshore companies. With that number of skins, Byron will probably start a factory making shoes and handbags. That's his style. Hates anyone to make a profit along the way. Don't ask me the end returns for the chief or Laurie and the trackers."

"The bigger the crocodile, the more money?"

"No. The best quality skin comes from a six-to seven-foot croc. The very big ones Laurie will leave alone."

"They're going to be rich from five hundred crocodiles."

"Yes they are. Fifty thousand pounds is a lot of money just for skins."

"Who will make the rest?"

"Byron with what he calls a finder's fee for me. I don't like making money out of the animals anymore. Hannes and I did it once before with the ivory. Byron reinvests the money. What do I need out here?"

"What are you going to do?"

"With the money?"

"No, with your life, Zambia's almost born. Your concession cancelled."

"I've been in Africa nine years. All I know is guns and game photography and this river. I don't want to go back to England despite Byron's offer, wants me to join him in the City of London. You imagine that, Lindsay?"

"Not right now."

"Maybe drift down south. Southern Rhodesia is a colony, not a protectorate like Barotseland, and it's been self-governing since 1923. The British have promised independence but with strings. There's rumours of the white government declaring unilateral independence if the British government doesn't hand over full power to the white government... I don't know politics. Don't want to. I just want to stay in Africa, preferably near this river."

"What are you running away from?"

"What gives you that idea?"

"You."

"Women always try and read in something that isn't there."

"And we're usually right... That sunset makes my heart bleed."

The fire took quickly, spreading new light between the clean trunks of the ilala palms, the limp mosquito net testament to the coming night. They sat round the flames in camp chairs. Half-burnt dry leaves pushed upwards with the heat and smoke, dropping back into the fire. There was no wind. The river smell was sweet mud and water, the sound a constant flow past their island, movement felt more than it was heard. The .22 Hornet rested easily on the ground next to Will's chair and the small camp table. The table and chairs were low to the ground. The silver corkscrew with a cork attached reflected the firelight which penetrated the red wine bottle, showing the third that had poured into their glasses. At the foot of the table, half underneath, was the hamper basket Will had carried from the dugout canoe.

"Are there lion on the island?" asked Lindsay, excited by Will's protection.

"No. Not today."

"But cats can't swim?"

"Oh, a lion can swim all right. Don't like to. They had one up at Mombasa in Kenya that played in the surf. Right there in the Indian Ocean."

"Leopard?"

"They like rocky terrain where they can rest up during the day."

"Snakes?"

"There are always snakes in Africa but they get out of the way."

To the right of the fire, Will had set up a small spit Laurie had made from aluminium tube into two tripods supporting the thin rod welded to a turning handle, three bars welded at the centre to impale the meat. With the small trenching tool, Will moved hot coals under the waiting saddle of impala. Crickets and frogs screeched all around them. From far upriver came the single bark of a .375 Brno rifle and the bush went silent for a moment as everything listened to the intrusion.

"One of the scavengers going for the skins," said Will. "Jackal or hyena. Lion kills its own."

"You think Shelley will be all right?"

"She wanted to go with them."

"What's she running away from?"

"My brother. He's either getting married or got himself married. No one tells me much. She's top-drawer aristocracy, the bride. My brother Byron always has more than one reason for everything he does. She'll make a good hostess and breed him the right children. She may even be attractive, good company, that sort of thing... You want some more wine?"

"Thank you."

"I think Shelley came out here to get her own back on Byron through me but it didn't work as she fell for Laurie."

"Would you have fallen for Shelley Lane?"

"No."

"Have you fallen for anyone, Will?"

"Yes."

"You want to tell me?"

"No."

Will got up from his canvas stool and turned the meat, shovelling coals from the main fire under the spit. He stood with his back to the fires and looked up to the night sky, still faintly blushed by the last of the dying sun. Automatically, Will crossed the pointer stars with the cross of the Southern Cross, finding south even though he knew exactly where to walk for south.

"I'm sorry," said Lindsay. "It was none of my business... Just... Maybe I would like it to be."

"Oh, leave me out of that," said Will, louder than he intended.

"Don't you like women?"

"Of course I do... I find it easier to live with a memory than have someone mess up my life. Oh, don't get me wrong," said Will, turning round. "I've seen enough women out here to understand. In the old days when hunters came out with their wives or whatever they called them they thought I came with the package. A few of the lady photographers thought they could cart me back to New York or London. None of them said they wanted to stay by the river... I'm sorry. That sounds rude."

"Didn't you sleep with them?"

"I've never slept with a woman in my life."

"Shit."

"No, it's not. I don't fancy rutting for the sake of it."

"Why did you bring me here?"

"To show you the bush. You're my client, remember."

The second bottle of red wine went down with the roast saddle of impala and the jacket potatoes that had been cooked deep in the fire covered in clay. Will had made the salad dressing and tossed the lettuce with tomato and cucumber. The coffee pot hung from the meatless spit. The night sounds of Africa were loud. Fish plopped from the river and wild pig snuffled for food not twenty metres from the fire, the firelight not penetrating five metres into the river-fed bush. There was an owl at the end of the island calling to its mate on the mainland. The air was soft and free of mosquitoes around the fire.

"Brandy. I always have brandy with my coffee," said Will, opening the hamper.

"You always treat your clients this well?"

They had not spoken for half an hour.

"I have a theory, Lindsay. Maybe I have thought about it too long alone in the bush. I think we come to the earth to find our soulmate, the other half of ourselves, without which we are eternally miserable. If we don't find that person among all the people and all the lives we are doomed to be born again, time and time again. The rest we call love and satisfaction is only procreation making bodies for the transmigration of souls. We exist on two levels. The physical that eats, drinks, fights and ruts, and the mental that makes us search for the meaning of Soul and God that reaches out for eternal peace. When we find the lost part of our soul, hidden in that other body, we are released from our physical body that gives us pain and unhappiness, that kills and lies and pursues the selfish pleasures. We are eternally free in the ether of our minds. And then we don't have to come back again."

"You found her and let her go?"

"No. I was only allowed a glimpse. Then it was taken away forever. Forever in this life, anyway."

"Then I guess the single mosquito net won't help."

"I saw you put the other one back."

"Why didn't you stop me?"

"It didn't matter."

"Can I still market your photographs?"

"Be my guest, using your words. We'll be friends for a long time, Lindsay.

Let me keep my celibacy. The Catholic priests have their reasons. I have mine."

"I'll have some of the brandy."

"KWV ten-year-old."

"Africa does something to people."

"Let's enjoy the island. It may be the last time for both of us."

"Don't you think people are ever happy in their lives?"

"Only for very brief moments. It's a trick of nature with the strongest trick the act of procreation."

"How do you know? You never tried it."

Lindsay woke with the screeching down alone under the mosquito net, the vervet monkeys fighting in the jackalberry tree to her right. Will was tending a three-legged pot at the cooking fire and the smell of coffee was rich on the morning air. Below the jackalberry tree a family of warthog were feeding from the ripe berries, spitting out the hard, black pips and the skin.

Will finished sucking the sweet pith from his handful of berries and with a piece of stick, lifted the iron lid from the pot. The smell reached Lindsay propped up on her elbows in her sleeping bag, the rich smell of game mingled with herbs.

"Where did you sleep?" she asked.

"Round the fire."

Will stirred the pot with a wooden spoon. "When I put more wood on the fire, I added water to the stew. Been cooking all night."

"You get bitten?"

"Not really. Couple of angry tsetse at the first flush of dawn... There they go again. Laurie's been very active this morning."

"How long?"

"The rate he's going there won't be a live crocodile for fifty miles up and downriver."

"That smells very good," she said.

"It's meant to. Better get up and eat. We're going downriver with the cameras."

They left their small island with the yellow sun of morning bathing the trees on both riverbanks. A flight of pink-touched greater flamingos flew low over the centre of the ever-flowing river. Branches of trees bobbed and flowed. Will's camera caught the birds and their reflection with one shot. He smiled his pleasure and picked up the paddle to steer the log canoe back into the current. The reeds were thick by the bank and small weaver birds, rich yellow with black stripes on their wings, clutched the stems. A honeyguide bird called with great agitation from the top of a fever tree and

Will caught the bird in all its frustration through his telephoto lens. They drifted on into the day.

"Do we paddle back upriver?" asked Lindsay.

"No, we walk. Cover the canoe in the reeds and walk. I have six canoes hidden up and down the river. Hannes Potgieter brought them years ago... Hilary says he's going to stay. You remember me talking of Hilary? His father was my father's tail gunner during the war. The Missionary Society don't want him anymore but he says he will stay. Says we British are running away from our responsibilities, that a few blacks will monopolise a dwindling wealth and the rest will be left to fend for themselves without enough land to go back to their old ways. He doesn't think much of politicians. Told his bishop the same. The bishop is a great believer in liberation theology. Hilary says bad government by the people will benefit a very few. That good government by a benevolent colonial power creates wealth and a future free from poverty. He talks of Africa being marginalised by the rich countries of the world so they can plunder the minerals without responsibilities. Poor Hilary. The worst thing you can ever tell a man with a new idea is the truth, especially the bishop. The words sound good, you see. The new words. Freedom. Democracy. Every man equal... Hilary says it's just a new way in Africa to grab power. He also says the snake mesmerises its prey."

Most of the stories told to Lindsay Healy by men were designed to get her into bed for a brief, mutual moment of satisfaction. The men were either going to be rich or famous or both and the charade of words was understood by both of them.

The man with the paddle, expertly sending the half-waterlogged canoe through the waters of the Zambezi River, was a new experience in her pursuit of men, each one a challenge, like Kevin Smith, to be conquered and, if possible, enjoyed. To come all the way to Africa and find a man on his own who did not wish to take her to bed was an insult. The man was bush-happy, no doubt of it: too much sun and loneliness had cooked his brain.

The guns were still going off upriver, sending messages to her hormones. The slap of the wet paddle on water also sounded erotic.

"You don't think we should get back to your house and see it's all right with nobody there?" she said, trying to change the subject. Politics bored Lindsay to distraction.

"They won't come back tonight."

"The sun's burning my skin."

"You need patience for wildlife photography."

"You don't mind?"

"You're the customer."

Will paddled into shore and tied the canoe to a root of a tree that jutted from the bank. They walked back three miles to the Land Rover along the bank of the river, drove back to collect the hamper, the cooking pot and the bedding, and were back at the empty base camp by eleven o'clock with Will wondering what he had done wrong. The girl was looking at him in a way that made him nervous.

"There's a plane out this afternoon if you want to leave," he said, picking up the hamper basket.

"Oh, I wasn't thinking of leaving," chuckled Lindsay. "Now we are near to ice we can have a proper drink... Shall we go upstairs to the bar? You lead the way, Will."

As she walked up behind him, two wooden steps down, she pinched his bum.

"Hey, don't do that, it hurt."

"Couldn't resist... Were any of your other customers as young as me?"

"I don't know how old you are," said Will, putting the hamper on top of the bar.

"Twenty-one. Must 'ave told you."

"I'll get the ice from downstairs. We make it in blocks."

"Don't be long. I'm very thirsty."

When Will's head had disappeared down the stairs, the first thing Lindsay did was take off her bra and the second was to unbutton the top of her shorts. She heard Will downstairs breaking up the ice while she found the Booth's Gin bottle and two bottles of Indian tonic. She poured in equal tots of gin, half topped up with tonic in anticipation of the ice and cut off two slices of lemon. She thought of taking off her panties but decided there was not enough time. By the time Will came up with the ice, Lindsay Healy was very much enjoying herself. She was young, in the prime of her life, good looking, sexy, and on the pill. What more did she want, she asked herself, handing Will his drink.

"Here's to us," she said, raising her glass.

Will hesitated, not sure of the toast.

"Photographs," said Lindsay. "Money. That sort of thing." Lindsay looked direct into his eyes, winked and smiled gently. Then she saw his eyes drop to the missing button and inwardly sighed with relief. Another celibate night listening to Shelley Lane and Laurie Hall, even from Laurie Hall's small house a few metres down from the main house, was intolerable. Sounds at night travelled in Africa. Most importantly, she had never bedded a virgin in her life before.

·　·　·

WHILE LINDSAY WAS TRYING to seduce Will before lunch, Shelley Lane was having the best time of her life. Her black hair and brown eyes were now matched by a well-tanned skin that had gone from copper to brown in the African sun without peeling. She had touched her large mouth with shell pink. The almond-shaped eyes were touched with dark eyeshadow. She wore a tight, half-shirt and short shorts and was singing. Byron Langton was the last thought in her mind.

The rule at what Laurie Hall had called Crocodile Camp was no booze. The first three days had been difficult but Shelley now felt better than she could remember.

"Booze and guns, old girl, don't mix," he had said when they packed the Land Rover in Mongu with provisions.

Her job at Crocodile Camp was to keep the books. First she packed like-sized skins into bundles of ten, neatly attached a label with a number and wrote it down in a journal. The bundles were then packed in hessian, one hundred skins to the bag, and made ready with an individual waybill for Octavio Goncalves to transport to Livingstone.

At Will's suggestion, Laurie had telephoned Byron Langton's office in London before the big shoot, using the telephone in the Mongu Club. The overseas call had taken two hours to make, person-to-person, Laurie using Will's name as the caller. Byron, always quick on the uptake when there was money to be made, agreed to cover the cost of tanning the skins in Umtali through Manica Trading at the port of Beira.

"There may be an import permit problem into England, Mr Hall," Byron had told him from a voice halfway round the world. "My problem. I will pay you the market price FOB Beira, all transport costs from Mongu for my account. I can recommend a Swiss holding account for your money and this chief's. From my experience of Africa, Mr Hall, the less known about your money the better."

"We'll need cash for my trackers."

"Does anyone else know about your crocodile hunt?"

"Not the numbers."

"On your documents, we may eventually remove a nought from every package on the certified invoice."

"And if customs counts?"

"We made a mistake. I presume Will said I was trustworthy?"

"He did."

"And the chief considers Will trustworthy?"

"Definitely."

"Laurie, if I may call you Laurie. So long as we trust each other then the circumvention of government is incidental. Give my brother my best regards. You can also give him a laugh. Our sister Josephine won a by-election for Labour and now sits in the House of Commons. When's he coming home? Africa's a mess ... You just ship your skins to Umtali Leather and Tanning and we will do the rest."

The drums began on the Friday morning before dawn. They had started at the paramount chief's winter palace at Lealui, eleven miles from Mongu. The drums had spread the message down the floodplains to evacuate the low ground. The beat of the drums was persistent and ominous.

Shelley woke and shivered, listening to the ancient sound of Africa. A lion roared, disturbed by the drums. Hyena were keening from three different parts of the night. A small sickle moon, low down in the east, threw no light across the low plains that spread away from the slow-flowing persistency of the river. The river and tree frogs were noisier than usual. The drums continued, permeating the night. The smell of the waiting crocodile skins was overpowering.

Without waking Laurie, Shelley climbed out from under their mosquito net and threw more wood on the dying fire, sending a shower of sparks up into the fever trees that lined their bank of the Zambezi River. The tinder-dry wood caught and burst into flames, showing the sleeping trackers spread out on either side of the fire. Sixpence turned in his sleep while the drums went on beating into her brain.

Somewhere below her fear she heard the rich notes of music, playing in her mind to the beat of the drums. Going silently to the Land Rover she found her journal and her pen. Back in the firelight she wrote down the notes and relaxed. The words would come later. A thrashing downriver told her not all the crocodiles had died in the onslaught of gunfire. A family of hippo in the pool below their camp grunted, taking in air before sinking down onto the mud. A nightjar screeched, and the fire collapsed into itself, showering the underside of the fever tree's branches. Sitting in the fire smoke, her head just clear, the journal and pen sat quietly next to her. For the first time in many years, Byron Langton was nowhere in her mind.

When the dawn came gently, first blushing the sky, then dimming the millions of stars, and lastly the sliver of moon, three pages at the back of the journal were covered in badly drawn lines. The notes were in between, recognisable. Shelley read back her music and smiled to herself. Cramped from sitting with her arms hugging her knees, she got up and walked down the bank to the river. Many animals were drinking the living water: a giraffe, legs splayed to reach the water; the small buck fearful of the new day.

As the sun pulled itself up from behind the trees across the floodplain, the drums were still beating.

It was a beautiful day.

Octavio Goncalves arrived at lunchtime in a five-ton Bedford truck. Within half an hour, two and a half thousand crocodile belly skins were loaded into the back of the truck.

"Don't you want to check our numbers?" asked Laurie after the Portuguese transport owner had signed for the skins.

"No point. I received a phone call from Will's brother. I have to think they are very different, those brothers. One dreams his life away in the bush. The other very concise. How you say? No frills. We are to take the skins now to Umtali Leather and Tanning. No putting them on the train at Livingstone. You wait in Umtali with skins till cured then go with them to Beira. In Beira you put cured skins on boat to Brindisi in Italy. You go from Beira on same cargo boat. In Beira you receive written instructions from the offices of Manica Trading, shipping agents. I told by Will's brother, Manica Trading subsidiary of Union Castle Shipping Line which is a subsidiary of British and Commonwealth Shipping which Mr Byron Langton is director. Cash for your trackers paid to Barclays Bank DCO, Livingstone, when skins arrive Beira. Maybe one month time."

Laurie looked at Shelley, half-apologetically.

"Shelley," said Laurie, "you can fly out of Mongu?"

"Nonsense, I'm coming with you. Journey through Africa. Boat trip. Lover, just what we need. There's enough room in front of the Bedford. If Mr Goncalves does not mind?"

"To make a journey with you will last in my mind forever."

"You Latins have a very nice way of putting things."

The truck and the Land Rover reached Will's base camp at the same time. Within less than half an hour, Laurie and Shelley were ready to begin on the long dirt road to Livingstone and Will and Lindsay were packing the negatives of Will's photography into his Land Rover together with his and Hannes Potgieter's rifles in their cases alongside his photographic equipment. There was little else of movable value at base camp.

The drums still beat incessantly.

Laurie and Will shook hands formally, their eyes saying more than the handshake.

"Well, William," said Shelley. "This has been quite a trip so far. See you in London." She kissed him lightly on both cheeks. To Will's surprise there was not a trace of alcohol on her breath. He looked from Laurie to Shelley and back again, smiling to both of them.

"One day, Shelley..." he said to her. "Octavio, you'd better get them out of here. We only have two days."

"Yes, that's what the paramount chief said. He not going away on big barge. Big row with resident. When resident use swear word first ever time to chief, chief get fright and give instruction his people leave floodplain now. Message came in Portuguese from Angola which I translate. The gorges up there have walls of water raging down, all flooding into Zambezi. Two days this place go downriver. Mongu safe on high ground. Lealui will be washed away."

"You think the home will go?" asked Will.

"Maybe. Maybe not. Worst floods anyone ever remembers. Stay in the club tonight."

From something so permanent in Will's life, the base camp with its tame animals had become vulnerable and all the time the drums sent out the message, never missing a beat.

The Bedford five-tonner moved away in low gear and disappeared through the mopani trees.

"Funny," said Will to Lindsay. "The sins of the big crocodile hunt will be washed away by the rivers. We'd better go."

"Are you all right?"

"No, I'm not."

The trackers had followed the Bedford in the second Land Rover with all their possessions and the instruction to meet Will in Livingstone on the fifteenth of the following month at ten a.m. outside the offices of Barclays Bank. The bank draft was being sent by Byron in Will's name.

The chief had left his instructions the previous day.

"My money I want in England. My three sons, my chief wife are going to England. We become English. Boys get expensive education."

"You're going to leave Africa?" asked Will in amazement, looking at the grey-haired African in old shorts and a shirt that had probably never been washed. The chief's old Land Rover was covered in dust and dripped oil on the path from under the engine.

"Won't I be rich in England?"

"Very rich, in fact."

"Then I become British. You see. One day my sons speak just like you. Send boys to Stanmore. Buy house like Langton Manor. I remember all you say, Mr Langton. Without the protection of the British Empire, Barotseland no good. Best you go home too... I will visit your brother in his offices for my money. Thank you for address. Next time we will see each other in England."

Will, still smiling at the thought of a Barotse chief living the life of an English country squire, got into the driving seat of the Land Rover and started the engine. He did not look back.

From the corner of the house, the Goliath heron watched the car drive off through the trees.

The Bedford truck ground its way along the twisting road through the mopani trees. The bush was tinder-dry and the elephant grass crushed by the heat of the sun, brown and broken.

The Land Rover, with the trackers, had turned up to the chief's kraal. Laurie Hall had allocated the trackers one hundred skins. The ten thousand pounds sterling would enable them to buy so many cows they would not be able to count them. Each would take a series of wives; each new one very young; there would be many children to herd the cattle.

Sixpence, Fourpence and Onepenny were singing a song of their tribe, an old song of a warrior king. The chief would know from where they could buy their cattle. Even if the chief knew their bonus came from the hunting of crocodile skins, he would still want their money, and it was right that they should go to their chief. Everything in the tribe went through the chief.

THE ROAD from Mongu to Livingstone was a little under four hundred miles. Rarely did their truck come out of second gear. The road had never been graded and when the ruts made by the wheels were too deep, a detour made a new road. When elephant pushed over the mopani trees, the trucks went round the fallen tree trunks.

For the first day they averaged nine miles an hour. It was hot and dusty in the cab and the smell of crocodile skins and the whirr of the tsetse fly never left them. Over their faces they tied handkerchiefs. It was too hot to drive with the windows up and they sweated in the heat. All along the road they saw game, mostly elephant. Twice they backed away from the elephant, driving carefully around through the bush. Laurie and Octavio watched for tree stumps that could cut their tyres. The tall, red anthills were easier to see. It was a journey Shelley knew she would enjoy better in retrospect.

They drove on through the dusk and well into the night, the big headlights picking their way through the tall mopani trees, the bush pitch-black the moment the lights moved on, the big engine roaring at the night. With the dusk, the tsetse had left the vehicle, the circling insects fooled by the moving truck into thinking it was game and food.

When Octavio pulled off the road into a clearing in the forest, they collected firewood by the light from the truck. They were all tired and hungry and alone in the world. The mess of tin foods mixed in a single pot over the fire tasted better to Shelley than any food she had eaten in London.

Within ten minutes of eating they were asleep around the fire, the flames showing the forest of trees and the one side of the truck. Both men slept with rifles by their sides and woke at regular intervals to feed the fire.

Never once before dawn did Shelley move or dream. When she woke the birds were calling.

"Bloody jumbo slept behind the truck all night," said Laurie. "Grass is flat as a pancake. You hear anything?"

"They very silent, elephant, when they want," said Octavio.

Within twenty minutes the truck was grinding down the road in the sweet cool of early morning.

"This is the most beautiful place on earth," said Shelley Lane.

Neither man spoke but both of them were smiling.

They drove into Livingstone after lunch on the third day and then crossed the high bridge over the gorge with the spectacular Victoria Falls on their right, the water cascading over the lip, crashing down into the gorge and sending the spray hundreds of feet up into the blue sky.

"Wait for the big water," said Octavio. "Then you see nothing but spray. Tomorrow morning before the sun comes up, the big water."

They drove to the Victoria Falls Hotel in its colonial splendour looking back at the single span bridge and the cloud of spray flung skyward by the pounding thrust of the Zambezi River.

"I usually stay upriver at the camping site," said Octavio.

"Not tonight, big man. This one's on me. Best rooms. Tomorrow we carry on the big drive. Today we play. My throat can feel the taste of a cold beer. First beer, then bath, then playtime."

"No one can afford this hotel," said Octavio.

"I can," said Shelley in a small voice walking on towards reception. "You two boys go out onto that splendid terrace and order me a very cold beer. Don't pay. I'll sign for it. And lover, don't go away."

The lecherous look from Shelley ended with her tongue licking right across the wideness of her mouth.

After their baths and a clean change of clothing they met under the msasa trees with the last of the sun reflecting richly in the spray from the Falls. A steam engine with a line of goods wagons rumbled over the railway section of the bridge. The night was warm.

For the first time, Laurie Hall saw Shelley Lane in other than shorts and dirty jeans. Her black hair was swept back and the big mouth was covered in chocolate-brown lipstick overcovered with a trace of white. The white dress plunged at the back, showing off her perfect tan. Drop earrings sparkled in the last rays of the sun as she walked towards them on heels two inches from the ground. On her wrists were bangles and on the side of her hair, the left side, she had pinned the single flower of a red hibiscus, plucked from the pathway through the courtyard of the hotel.

A steel band was playing gentle music to the small groups of sundowners savouring the soft beginning of an African night. Every male on the wide terrace and under the trees watched Shelley Lane walk between the tables. There was a hush in the buzz of conversation.

"You ever pick up words, lover?" she said to Laurie as a red-fezzed waiter pulled back her chair and the two men rose from their seats. "Met a girl called Virginia Stepping, old friend of Byron's I think, who was always saying 'lover'. I like it. Better than honey or sweet or my best pet aversion, darling... I think they were lovers," she said.

"Do you still love him?" asked Laurie quietly.

"Not as much as I did."

The lights came up through the trees as the dusk settled quickly into night. The bandstand was splashed with light, the floodlights catching a reflection in the smiling teeth of the African band members. Their medley of African music moved into popular songs, a piano joining the sound. The buzz of conversation picked up with the increase in guests and the flow of alcohol. Shelley was thirty metres from the band, listening carefully to the music, ignoring Octavio's question as to how a young woman could afford such rooms in the hotel. She thought he was trying to say thank you which even his Latin charm failed to bring across without embarrassment.

Slowly, wickedly, Shelley Lane began to chuckle. The man had no idea she sang for a living.

"That tune I know," said Octavio, trying to cover up his gaucheness. He was more used to campfires and the bush.

"Do you really?" said Shelley, pinching Laurie to keep quiet. "Would you like me to sing it for you?"

"Can you sing?" asked the Portuguese.

"Just a little... As a matter of fact, I wrote that song which is why the bandleader has moved into a medley of my songs. Laurie, would you mind? Apart from drunken songs in a Land Rover I never sang to you and this will probably be the most beautiful setting I will ever sing in."

Slowly, she waved her right hand to the band, and the music stopped. The manager of the hotel walked onto the bandstand from where he had been waiting.

"Ladies and gentlemen. Tonight we have an unusual pleasure to have with us as a guest in our hotel Miss Shelley Lane who will sing for you some of her famous songs. Please stand with me to welcome Miss Shelley Lane."

No one moved from the terrace or the lawns for an hour as Shelley moved from 'If You Want To Be Mine' through to 'This One Is For You'.

Stopping the clapping with raised hands, Shelley spoke into the microphone.

"Most singers sing other people's songs. I don't. Everything I sing I wrote myself. While staying with friends for three days up in Barotseland I wrote a new song, the theme of which I wrote out for a piano player. It's to be the first song on an album I will make of African songs from my trip. No one, not even me, has heard this song before. I call it 'Zambezi Night'."

"Sorry, lover," she said to Laurie back at the table where people were thrusting pieces of paper for her to sign. "That was business. Instead of trying to contact my bank in London, I made a deal with the manager. Tomorrow night I do a full cabaret in the dining room. We three get two nights on the house. He'll get his money back from tomorrow's cover charge... You like my song about your river?"

"Best of your songs."

"Had to write the words upstairs. Why my bath was so long... Those musicians are brilliant... Laurie, don't look at me like that. If you're to be my manager you have to grow used to all this. It's not all going to be easy. Fame, lover, has a lot of problems, signing autographs is only one of them."

BY THE TIME they left for Umtali, driving first down to Bulawayo on the strip roads, the river-flood had not reached the Victoria Falls.

Four hundred miles upriver, Will Langton stood next to his Land Rover on the high ground where the road passed four hundred metres from where the riverbank had been. The raging torrent of floodwater now came to within fifty metres of the dirt road. Whole trees, a bloated cow, papyrus beds, rushed on down with the surging, oily water. The base camp had gone, the memory of Hannes Potgieter swept away forever.

They had all gone.

Lindsay had left that morning from the grass airstrip at Mongu, courtesy of the herd of wildebeest. The British resident had gone, courtesy of the new order. The Mongu Club was staying open for one more week, for whatever reason. The member in charge had handed over his police station to a Bemba sent from Lusaka to take control. The remaining members of the British community had left by road. The British Empire had finally ended in Barotseland.

Lindsay Healy had pleaded the best she could.

"Will, you're just bloody crazy. You can't stay in Africa. Place is coming apart. Like the Belgian Congo, they'll be at each other's throats in a week. Come to Sydney. We can get you a residence permit. No trouble. You want to photograph wildlife, go up to the Northern Territories. You don't have your hunting concession here anymore. More likely you don't have a house, judging by the sound of the river. Five miles away and we still heard that wall of water come downriver like an avalanche. We've got something going, Will, even if I did do the seducing."

Will stood looking at the rushing water.

Even his virginity had gone. His belief in the girl from Dancing Ledge had shattered with the destruction of his celibacy. The reality of sex had been brief spurts of ecstasy. His hope for eternal happiness had finally found him coupling in a bed with a girl that wanted sex, a good time, his photographs, money, the next man; her craving had been insatiable.

There was no sign of the Goliath heron.

Will got back into the Land Rover and started the engine.

Three days later, alone, he crossed the high bridge over the Victoria Falls into Southern Rhodesia, leaving idealism and his youth behind in the bush of Barotseland. He was singing badly, out of tune, but louder than his diesel engine. The excitement of a new adventure had overcome his maudlin blues half a day out of Livingstone. There was going to be a new life with new people in a new country.

Maybe Lindsay Healy had done him a favour. Only the rest of his life would find out.

PART IV

1965 TO 1967

12

*B*yron Langton adjusted the dove-grey cravat in the full-length mirror and was well satisfied with what he saw: the dove-grey spats, dove-grey morning suit with dove-grey top hat. At thirty-four, the body was lean and paunchless, the violet eyes, clear and inherently intellectual. He winked at himself. The Langtons of Langton Matravers in the county of Dorset were finally marrying the upper echelons of the aristocracy and his children would be related to the kings of England.

The ceremony was to take place downstairs in the private chapel of the Marquis of Bathurst, father of the bride, on the Bathurst estate seventy miles from Edinburgh. Randolph Langton, the eldest of the Langton boys, was best man.

Josephine, Byron's twin sister, had at first refused the invitation.

"How can a junior minister in the Labour government be patronised by the aristocracy?" The quarrel had taken place in Josephine's London flat.

"Easily, sis. You're my twin sister. What you and I stand for can never alter the accident of our birth. And Fiona's going to be your sister-in-law for the rest of your life and you will be aunty to her children. Now, have you found out anything about Will?"

"Not a word. Once the British resident commissioner was withdrawn from Mongu we have had no communication into the Colonial Office."

"Wasn't that a slip? Didn't you mean Commonwealth Office?"

"Yes, I damn well did."

"Don't swear, sis. Doesn't suit a junior minister in Her Majesty's

Government. Anyway, it's a very small wedding as Bathurst, can't hold any more."

"What about the press?"

"Heathcliff Mortimer only, as a friend. He can take you up to Scotland. You know as well as I that publicity is not my bag. And certainly not with Harold Wilson in power. Even my own *Daily Garnet* will have no mention of the wedding. Now, are you coming?"

"All right."

"There must be someone in the Foreign Office you can lean on to find out about Will. Not a word for over a year. Laurie Hall even had some Portuguese transport man making enquiries. Will's home was swept away in the floods but they don't think Will was there at the time. He has some girlfriend in Australia but she doesn't know. I've told him before he vanished he can have a job with me."

"Maybe he doesn't want one."

"Man's twenty-eight with no career. Doesn't make sense to me."

"I'll try again."

"Thanks, sis. And please, you must be at my wedding."

The guests were milling around in the old garden outside the chapel in the warm sun of summer waiting to be ushered into the old private church. The vicar had arrived from the village and was now resplendent in a white vestment, talking to members of the Bathurst family. The groom's family were left out on their own.

Group Captain Red Langton was looking at the old house and mentally thanking his luck that Langton Manor was small and manageable. The cost of repairing the decaying mausoleum that spread out in four double-storey wings from the central point of the chapel was beyond his comprehension. Even the land was not properly farmed; he had noticed that on the drive through the estate on the way to the big house on the hill, more beautiful from a distance. The empire and Britain were decaying in front of his eyes.

"It took so long to create these estates," he said to Adelaide his wife and Byron's mother, "and so little time to fall apart."

"The world changes, my dear."

"It does. Indeed it does. My only question as I approach sixty is whether it changes for the better. That I question. Are people happier now than before the First World War?"

"Happiness is within."

"Maybe. But malcontent in society affects us all. No one is ever satisfied anymore."

"We are just getting old... You think Josephine will ever marry?"

"No. She's married to politics like a nun to the Church."

"I'd prefer to have been a bride of Christ than a bride of British socialism." Adelaide Langton was irritated. "Bunch of bloodsuckers if you ask me. Parasites. They talk of doing good but the only good they do is for themselves."

"A welfare state has many advantages. Now, promise neither of us will mention politics with Josephine."

"Hope you told Byron the same thing?"

"I didn't need to."

"Do you think Will is dead?" asked Adelaide.

"No, of course he isn't."

"There are lots of wild animals in Africa."

"Will is bright enough. Knows how to look after himself."

"But he hasn't written for over a year."

"Africa is in something of a turmoil," said Red Langton. "Since the British pulled out of Northern Rhodesia maybe the mail doesn't work anymore. It was the Royal Mail, you remember. Months have gone by in the last ten years without hearing from Will. Stop worrying about your children, Adelaide."

"I can't help it. Never have been able... You think he loves her?"

"Why would he marry Fiona without being in love?"

"That's why I asked. Byron is so clinical in everything he does."

"What I want to know," said his father, "is how the boy made so much money in ten years from scratch."

"You don't think the money's been made honestly?"

"I don't think Byron himself would go outside the law. Far too sharp for that. For instance, what's he offered Bathurst in exchange for his daughter? A lot of very rich Americans would like to have a title in the family... Newspapers, music companies, investment trusts, shipping. Where did it all come from in ten years, I ask myself? None of it came from me. Must have either stolen a pile of money or found a backer."

"Byron would never steal. He was brought up properly and he went to Stanmore. A sharp young man with his background is well sought after. I think you call it good management. Can't run anything without good, honest management is what you say, Red. Always what you said."

"I've heard the name Jack Pike mentioned a few times. King of the girlie magazines and Soho peep shows. Byron admits to being friendly with the man's son."

"Even peep show people need good financial advice. Not every one of Byron's clients can be the Marquis of Bathurst."

"Byron does business with Bathurst?" asked Red Langton in surprise.

"Yes. Byron said he'd formed something called an offshore company for his future father-in-law. All sounds double Dutch to me."

"Offshore. Everything Byron seems to do is offshore."

"Told me once," said Adelaide, "it was the only way to keep the politicians' hands off a man's money. Now with Labour in power, Byron says he is doing better than ever before. Says if the government wants to introduce punitive taxation – I think those were his words – then it was his job to protect hard-earned money. Don't ask me, Red. I don't understand things like that. All I do know is Byron is not a thief. I did not give birth to a thief. We'd better go on into the church and have this wedding over with. Women are meant to like weddings but I don't. It's one big pretence that life lives happily ever after. You don't just marry in a church and expect it all to be perfect. You and I still work at our marriage, Red. They look at us old fuddy-duddies and think it was all a bed of roses. There's been give and take every day of our lives... Tried to talk to Byron but I could see he wasn't listening. Young people never listen anymore. Quite infuriating."

"Have we had such a bad marriage?" asked Red quizzically.

"Of course we haven't. We consciously think about each other's feelings. I've never taken you for granted and I don't think you have me... What a mournful sound, a single church bell. Come on. The vicar's gone inside which is always a good sign something's happening. You know where they're going for a honeymoon?"

"Byron wouldn't say."

Heathcliff Mortimer had no idea why he had been invited to the wedding now he saw so few guests making their way into the small church. He had put on a dark suit and even bought a new tie but the old suit was uncomfortably tight under the armpits and he was in need of a drink. The official car that went with Josephine Langton's new job in the Labour government did not run to a cocktail cabinet pulled down from the back of the front seat.

Heath watched the woman with whom he had driven up from London and was sad. She now affected square, rimless glasses which for the life of him he did not know whether they corrected her vision or gave her the feminist appearance she strove to achieve. The square fringe of hair above the glasses, straight across her forehead, straight down over the ears and straight round the back, was matched by a pale face totally devoid of make-up. Any stranger asked to judge her age, Heath mused, might put it from forty through to fifty, and he knew the girl was only thirty-four. What people did for a cause, socialism or feminism, he chuckled sadly. The woman he had once found attractive had no femininity whatsoever.

They had talked little in the car, Josephine aware he was a journalist and he wanting to keep the long journey personal, devoid of politics. Looking at her as she strode through the archway of the church, he wondered what had gone wrong in her life to make her so sour.

The group captain had greeted him pleasantly, remembering their meetings during the war. Randolph, the eldest son, was pleasant if dull. Adelaide, the mother, would have been a good-looking woman in her day.

Something, he told himself, had gone very wrong for Josephine Langton and none of it would bring her any happiness.

He went on into the church.

Heath sat between strangers, Josephine sitting in the front pew with the groom's family. He was faintly surprised to find the bride was beautiful. In Heath's opinion, Bathurst was a rural ass, the type that would have best died out from natural incompetence, nature deciding it had taken a wrong turn in the ways of evolution. Maybe the old goat thought bringing some outside blood into the family, beneath itself no doubt, would rejuvenate the Bathurst species and let it go on living a few more generations. Byron's motive escaped Heath unless the man was a snob. There were plenty of those still in the English woodwork. How often it was that a man never knew what was in another man's head.

During the service, he stood up with the others and sat down with the others but most of the time his mind was far from the small, very beautiful church with its romantic memories of things long past. He had begun his book on Africa, mainly the end of British Africa, and though he was sad to see the era end and find himself writing about some of the most anachronistic characters left in a world where most people were trying to be the same as everyone else – boring, but the same – he was finally consumed with doing something that might just have a trace of importance in the way of things. The cynical side of him knew it was his one and only try for immortality, but whatever the truth he was enjoying himself, happy in his own company for the first time in his life. There was a certain peace coming into his daily routine and he found it comforting to know, as he put it to himself, that the last few years of his life would not be a complete degeneration into pain and depression.

The bridal exit woke him from his reverie and brought him instead the instant need for a large Southern Comfort on the rocks. Even the saliva in his mouth had begun to dribble.

At the long drinks table, Heath stood next to Josephine's Uncle Clifford

Critchley, the reformed socialist who had done so well with the money inherited from Great-Aunt Eve. The man was portly, bald, prosperous and no resemblance to the cloth-hatted Uncle Cliff who had inflamed so much passionate zeal in the young Josephine Langton. Heath was told afterwards about the metamorphosis of Uncle Clifford, his antiques and property business, the second mistress in Pimlico and the shattering effect he had on the life of his niece.

After a search, to Heath's delight he found a full bottle of Southern Comfort. Picking up the bottle where sensibly the guests were able to pour their own drinks, he looked up to catch Byron looking at him from across the room, wearing an enigmatic smile. They both nodded their respect to the bottle in Heath's right hand.

"American liquor in whisky country," said Uncle Clifford, the only words he was ever to say to Heathcliff Mortimer.

Heath, in the habit of having silent conversations with himself at the age of sixty-two, said, 'No wonder that Byron makes so much money. Knew I drank Southern Comfort and took the time to have a bottle on the table. A man could be a slave to such detail. Better still, Heath my lad, what a memory. You only remembered your own birthday last week after lunch when you were half-drunk and once again thinking back over your life. Shut up and pour yourself a drink.'

Guiltily, Heath looked around the reception to see if he had spoken out loud. No one was taking any notice of a fat old man so he poured half a tumbler, dropped in four lumps of ice using his fingers and causing the attendant in a white coat to look disapprovingly. Heath looked up at the ceiling and drank. It was a loft of a ceiling with cherubs chasing round the centrepiece in a dull cream colour aged over time.

Looking round he could see two or three good-looking young girls but nothing high on the scale of ten. He finished the drink and hefted the bottle for the second time. By the time he got to meet the bride the bottle was half empty and life was looking better, the girls prettier and the conversation not quite so dull.

The bride and groom went and came back again, ready to go on their way into life, the place of the honeymoon still unknown to anyone but the groom. Heath sadly put his hand out to pour the last of his tipple only to find the bottle miraculously full again. He was more than a little drunk and more than a little happy. All the bridegroom's family were to stay the night in the old house if they could find their allocated rooms. Now knowing there was life after death, he poured himself a gentler tot, pacing himself. The hard-core partymakers moved out onto the great terrace.

. . .

IT WAS a summer's evening of soft, warm perfection washed by the sweet smell of stocks in full bloom.

The row started at the other end of the terrace to where Heath was happily sitting alone on a stone bench next to the bottle. At first he took no notice and continued to enjoy the rare beauty of the Scottish summer evening. He would probably have left it all alone if the word Africa, *his* Africa for goodness' sake, had not snapped at him from the heart of what had now become a quarrel. When he heard Josephine answer in her newly acquired north London accent that merged better with her political colleagues, he pushed himself off the bench, though not before tucking the bottle into safety underneath.

They had her surrounded.

"The Rhodesians will proclaim their own independence," someone was insisting.

"If they do, my government will retaliate," said Josephine.

"But you promised Southern Rhodesia independence," argued the same man.

"Macmillan may have done that but not the British Labour Party."

Heath had Josephine by the elbow out of the circle and down the terrace away from the drunk with the big mouth who, Heath thought, had temporally forgotten he was a gentleman in the heat of his bigoted argument.

"They just don't listen," protested Josephine.

"People never do. 'Specially drunk... Not you, Jo. Them."

"The whites can't rule in Southern Rhodesia. That kind of thing is dead and buried."

"Obviously not quite. For what it's worth," he said, sitting her on the stone bench, "my information is Smith will declare his unilateral independence and tell Wilson to do his worst."

"He'd be damn stupid. Going full-face against the force of history."

"Maybe. But he's still going to do it. What I hear... Lovely wedding. Have a Southern Comfort?"

"You brought your own?"

"No. Your twin brother. Remembered what I drank. That's what singles out the real leaders in this world. I'll drink to Byron."

"Heath, you're drunk."

"There wasn't much else to do."

Josephine giggled, took the one glass and sipped his drink on the rocks.

"What went wrong, Jo?" he asked.

The reply came after a long pregnant silence. "None of your business," she said, but softly.

"You ever want to talk, you know where to come."

"Thank you, Heath."

"You can't always be the hard-arsed politician."

"I know... Weddings have funny effects on people."

SHELLEY LANE'S *ZAMBEZI RIVER* album went on sale ten days after the wedding, creating music that would be alive long after the lady finished her career. The affair with Laurie Hall had lasted just long enough to complete the record.

Byron had cut short his honeymoon on the Isle of Skye to gather up the pieces in the wake of Shelley's path of alcoholic destruction. Byron himself knew there was nothing more pleasant for the tabloids than to rejoice in the self-destruction of a popular figure. The album topped the charts within the week, fuelled by pictures of a black-haired drunken Shelley mingled with the golden sounds of her voice lamenting the tragedy unfolding in Africa.

'Sunset In Africa' and 'The Day The Animals Died' topped the singles charts by the end of the following week. Financially, it was the pinnacle of Shelley's career and the money flowed into Music Lane, of which Shelley owned thirty per cent, as fast as the floods had hurtled through Central Africa.

With the *Daily Garnet* having the inside story on the singer, circulation jumped ten per cent. Byron Langton was getting richer than he ever imagined.

LAURIE HALL HAD JUST enough money left from the crocodile skins to buy a third-class ticket on the *Edinburgh Castle* back to Africa. There was no way a man could live with a woman insatiably in love with another man, a man in the process of getting married to another woman. Shelley Lane was obsessed with more than alcohol.

It had been fun. He was thirty years of age, single, broke and with no prospects other than going back to what was left of a white man's Africa. The nights of debauchery in nightclubs across London, the passion in the nights when Shelley had drowned her memories of Byron Langton, wanton spending of his money without a care for when it ended, a thousand people met and lost, enjoyed to the full, Laurie the most popular man in London spending money on the fools and thinking them friends, the big-game hunter and the icon of the charts, the beautiful people propelled by alcohol from one riotous venue to the next.

She had never made him her manager. Never mentioned it again. The trip home on the boat with the cured crocodile skins for safe delivery at Brindisi had given Shelley the time to write the songs for the *Zambezi River* album and the recording had taken six months between their bouts of revelry.

When she threw his clothes out of her flat there had been no going back. There was more sadness than fury in his footsteps down the stairs. He could imagine her slumped on the big sofa, crying at the slammed door.

Laurie made one phone call from the cheap hotel found for him by a taxi driver; the album had just been finished.

"Byron? Get a doctor to your girlfriend or this time she'll kill herself... You know where to find Will?"

"No... Can't you stay with her?"

"Threw me out."

"The wedding's next week."

"Your problem... You should have married Shelley years ago. One way or another you've destroyed that woman."

"Who the hell are you to talk?"

"You take and never give."

"Oh, go to hell."

"No. You go to hell. I'm going to Africa."

"WE HAVE BEEN MARRIED A MONTH," said Fiona Langton. "Apart from a honeymoon that was so short it should not have had a name, one dinner out with the directors of EMI, two weeks together in this damn flat and I haven't seen you, Byron. Why the hell did you marry me?"

"Look, the flat is near the office and that saves time and you try and run a business when no one will make a decision without the boss's opinion."

"That's your fault."

"I don't think so. There are millions of people out there who want money and a job but the vast majority spend their lives creeping up people's arses to achieve it. There's one in ten thousand that creates new wealth in this country and when the likes of my twin sister chases them away the rest will bloody well starve. If it isn't the damn unions it's the Labour bloody government with a new rule that gives them more power, and business less chance of competing with the Americans. None of the self-confessed do-gooders ever created a penny's worth of wealth in their lives. Sanctimonious, two-faced parasites that have taken the 'Great' clean out of Britain. They all have a permanent attack of the 'gimmes': give me this, give me that, and then criticise the very bloody people they are stealing from. The fools get accolades while the few producers in this island either go to America or go out of business."

"Sit down, Byron. You'll have a heart attack."

"No one did a damn thing while I was away."

"I'm sure they did... All right, you work hard. But if you work hard I can't sit here cooped up all day with nothing to do. And a string of babies at my age is not on the cards. Kids we'll have but later. I don't want to end up without a new thought in my mind. Why I opted for university. You'd better give your wife a job, Byron, that's what you had better do. Then we can both moan about the paid staff."

"Are we going out to eat?"

"No we are not. Just because my father sits in the House of Lords doesn't mean I can't cook. Fact is, I like cooking and I don't like servants under my feet in my own home. Pour us both a drink and come into the kitchen. But first give me a kiss. I'm sorry I jumped at you. We all think our problems are the only ones around."

Byron gave his wife a kiss and a hug and followed her into the small, bachelor kitchen. The flat at 47 Buckingham Court in Knightsbridge had changed very little.

"Would you like to start a publishing house?" he asked, sipping his drink.

"Would I ever?" Fiona had her back to him, standing over the three-plate stove swishing a pat of butter round the hot frying pan. She filleted fish with garlic and herbs. The side dish of salad stood ready on the small counter next to the bowl of French dressing.

"You like garlic," he said. "That's good. My mother always cooks with garlic."

"She told me... Look, I couldn't just start a publishing company without experience. I'd need a job first."

"Heath wants to write a book on Africa. I think it will sell. The profit margin on books if you get the right one is enormous. Specialised magazines is something I've thought about too. You have the right degree to put it all together. You'd edit Heath's book. That kind of thing. I'll speak to the *Garnet* editor. He'll have a way of getting you in where you'll learn the right stuff."

"You know something, Byron Langton, I'm going to enjoy this marriage.

What was a very big problem for me when you came home has been solved on half a drink before supper."

THREE DAYS LATER, Fiona began her publishing career in the distribution department of Grooms Publishing. Miraculously the following week in the *Daily Garnet* the summer list of Grooms featured prominently for the first time.

"Three months in each department and back to us," the *Garnet* editor had agreed with the Managing Director of Grooms. "Langton's in a hurry as usual. She has a First in English from Edinburgh. Use her contacts while you have her. Pleasure to do business with you."

For Byron, the change in his wife was immediate and the evening homecomings bereft of trivia. After the passion of bed it was pleasant to find the lady in his life had a mind that made him think before he talked. With luck and publishing, he told himself, she will avoid turning into the kind of wife they met socially: made-up, stuck-up and stupid. Without a bleep from his wife, Byron took to leaving for his office at half-past six in the morning, coming home at nine in time for supper, an exchange of each other's day, then bed, both of them exhausted. The nightly sex made them sleep even better.

THE CHIEF from Africa came for his money the week after Fiona started her job. The man was agitated but showed large white teeth when Byron gave him the draft drawn on Langton Merchant Bank's account with the Union Bank of Switzerland in Geneva.

"You bring the money into England as capital," he told the chief. "Normal bank transfer. The only tax that might be payable would be in Zambia but that is your problem. If you require financial help, call on me or my staff. I understand you are staying in England?"

"Your brother is very different," said the African.

"Yes we are. Where is he? We in England have not heard a word."

"The three men who worked as trackers don't know. Took their Land Rover, the one that belonged to your brother, to the Reverend Hilary Bains. He doesn't know too... It is a good way of doing business," said the man, getting up from the chair across from Byron's desk, the draft for two hundred and three thousand pounds in his pocket. "Will, your brother, he say, 'an Englishman's word is his bond'. Thank you, Mr Langton."

Byron showed his client to the door through reception and out to the lift where he pressed the down button.

"How it used to be," said Byron. "How it should be. Not sure how long it will last. You see, the world and its politicians are becoming more and more dishonest. Did you ever meet a politician in your country who did not lie?"

"No, I did not." The door to the lift opened automatically.

"Everyone honest is much easier," said Byron.

"I think we might regret the British leaving Africa."

"The price of progress. Usually rather expensive. People like knocking down what the other system built. Why man, century after century, destroys his capital and has to start all over again from the bottom. And we never seem to learn."

Back in his office, Byron checked the file marked 'Crocodile Skins' and went through the final accounts. In Brindisi the skins had been delivered partly to a shoe factory and partly to a company that specialised in making handbags. A member of Byron's staff had taken the British designs to Italy and overseen the manufacture. The manufacturers received a fee for their services and the merchandise reverted back to Langton Merchant Bank that shipped the goods to the United States of America under the label of a famous couturier, who received a merchandising fee for every item. Within two months, the consignment had sold out in America and the bills to the retailers discounted by an American collection bank for cash, the net proceeds transferred to the Union Bank of Switzerland, the money disappearing as thoroughly as the skins had disappeared from Zambia. The account of William Edward Langton, address unknown, was credited with thirty thousand pounds and re-invested in gold bullion at thirty-five US dollars per ounce, held physically by the Union Bank of Switzerland.

The delivery, tanning process and liaison by Laurie Hall in Brindisi had been executed perfectly.

When Madge O'Shea, Byron's red-headed secretary, came in for dictation, Byron was still contemplating the net profit underlined in the file.

"Better put an extra ten thousand pounds into a holding account for Laurie Hall. These figures are staggering. The man deserves a bonus even if the last thing we told each other was to go to hell. No, put it into gold bullion. My bet is the Americans will want to re-inflate the value of their gold in Fort Kent. Eventually they will allow the market to find the true value for gold. They are the largest holders of bullion in the world and the long-standing fixed gold price has not reflected inflation. We'll buy the great white hunter some gold."

.   .   .

SHELLEY LANE SWALLOWED FOUR 'PURPLE HEARTS' while looking at herself in the mirror. She was twenty-six years old and looked every one of those years. The black hair had lost some of the sheen, the brown eyes some of the excitement and the large, inviting mouth had taken on a slight twist that gave her whole face a touch of melancholy. Her flat in Chelsea had none of the homeliness of the apartment with Mrs Page, and once the front door was shut her world shrank to three rooms, a kitchen and a bathroom.

It would take half an hour for the pills to pick her up again by which time the 'date' would arrive to take her out on the town. It was party time again. If she missed Laurie Hall she was not going to show it to the world and even less admit that 'white hunter Hall' in Africa was not 'white hunter Hall' in London. The man had been magical in his own context by the river and mentally she wished him well on his journey back to the bush.

"Never take a man out of his element," she told her reflection in the mirror.

It had taken her two days back in London to know her lover would never be able to manage her career. The months of spending his money had saddened her but strengthened her reasons for keeping her business link with Byron Langton. Spending his money as fast as he could was part of his inadequacy, his only way to play the game. So many times in a restaurant party, men far richer than Laurie Hall left him with the bill, often with a shrug that only she could understand.

The dress she wore was long and white silk, plunging at the back, her hair done on the side, caught by a small sweet-smelling gardenia, the white of the flower matching her dress. She was the talk of the town, every entrance, every nightclub, causing a stir, people not sure if they were looking at a singer or the stories in the press.

"You don't know your real parents," she said talking to the mirror. "Your adopted parents think you are a whore for singing in public... Your lover's somewhere lost to you in Africa... The man you love is married to a Lady. But who cares? It's party time."

The pills had begun to take effect.

The crystal glass, shimmering the amber liquid in her glass, the gentle clink of ice in the silent flat, were reflected back to her from the mirror as she sipped the soft whisky in the glass, the brown eyes watching her carefully from the other side of the mirror.

"Cheers," she said to herself.

LESS THAN HALF A MILE AWAY, Heathcliff Mortimer was marvelling at the way of things. He was seated comfortably on a bench next to a weeping willow tree. The summer evening was hot and the late sun threw long shadows across the lawn down from the pub. There were customers on the terrace chattering away, the late evening bringing their distant words to the elderly man on the bench, in front of him the dark flow of the River Thames and the ways of commerce taking boats up and down, direct in their purpose. The pint of Worthington's best bitter was half empty on the wooden table next to the wide-brimmed white hat and the silver-topped cane, the head of the cane the face of a lion. Heath was dressed in a cream-coloured linen suit from Africa and his shirt was tieless. He had lost weight in his travels around Central Africa as much from the tainted water and food as the heat and humidity. His stomach was always in jeopardy when he travelled in Africa.

Some trippers waved to him from the deck of a boat and the man with the mane of long, white hair raised the silver lion-headed stick from the wooden table, the silver tip at the opposite end to the lion rising a foot from the table in acknowledgement. The boat and people were soon gone.

The first marvel in Heath's life was the smart flat in Chelsea with the flower boxes over the old mews and the pub a short walk to the river, courtesy of the generous nature of Byron Langton, the bonus cheques for Heath's private reports now exceeding his salary from the *Daily Garnet*. There was never any report back from his contacts or acknowledgement from Byron of the tainted histories of the new heroes, the great, black liberators of the European colonies in Africa. By now, Heath knew, Byron Langton had a file on every leader, present and future, in Central and Southern Africa, from Kenya through Tanganyika and the old Belgian Congo, to the tip of South Africa. There were many men of power and future power who would have wished to burn those files that spoke of every evil known to man's pursuit of supremacy.

The second marvel to Heath was the twisted morality of man, motivated by the angry pursuit of wealth. In Zambia the portion of financial reserves which was the new country's after the break-up of the old Federation of Central Africa, was used by the new government to nationalise the mines and businesses in the name of the people, providing the party with new patronage to dispense to those brave souls who had fought the struggle against imperial power and won. There was a list of worthy fighters for the cause in the order dictated by the deeds of the past and another list of jobs in order of importance that came from the new patronage. The two were joined and the jobs allocated by salary worth. Whether the man or woman in question had any previous knowledge of the job to be done was irrelevant. The Party controlled allocation of government jobs and the Party gave those jobs to the faithful. The previous owners of the mines, businesses and farms drifted out of Africa, never to be seen again, thankfully forgotten by the Party.

In previous years, the world price of copper had been delicately balanced by the producers controlling the output of the mines to match as nearly as possible the demands of world industry. They were equally careful to make sure the price was low enough to prevent the introduction of substitute materials. Mining the copper efficiently was only part of the mining equation. The new government, to retain its popularity with the voting public, whose one man one vote had placed the Party in power, subsidised the price of basic foodstuffs and fuel, using the income from the copper mines.

Within a few months, the insatiable demand of the subsidies required more money from the mines and the new managers quickly sold the strategic stockpiles and told the mine captains to increase production. Combined with the miniaturisation of much of the circuitry that required copper, which was reducing the world demand, the extra Zambian copper flooded the market, dramatically forcing down the spot price. To counter the problem, the Zambian government began printing more money to pay their bloated and largely ineffective civil service, beginning the awful spiral of inflation.

Heath, drinking his beer, marvelled anew. Of course there was a political way out of the quandary which only required words. The fault, screamed the new state, was the old colonial powers who had now manipulated the downward price of copper. The clarion call rang across the new Africa, demanding compensation for the dreadful wrongs of colonialism, which some more strident than the rest called a crime against humanity. The flow of aid to Africa had begun which Heath in later years would describe as 'decanting money down the rathole'.

The sun was almost down when Heath finished the last of the beer, picked up his hat and cane, eased his way off the bench and wandered his way up the lawn to the bar. There was still almost an hour to closing time and then he would go home, pack his bags and be ready for the flight at eleven the following morning for Salisbury, Southern Rhodesia, the last British colony in Africa. He was to meet Josephine Langton with the British delegation at the airport.

"Southern Comfort please, Fred. Make it a double. Lots of ice... What a beautiful summer's evening."

. . .

BYRON LANGTON'S information was quite clear. The British government's delegation would not convince the Rhodesian settlers to hand over power to the black majority. Ian Smith, the Rhodesian prime minister, would declare unilateral independence. The British would not send in the army as it was still controlled by the establishment, ninety-five per cent of all officers having attended a British public school. Over half the Rhodesian settlers were born in Britain, a large proportion from the same upper establishment. Harold Wilson, the British prime minister, would not be able to convince British generals to fire on British people, especially their own class.

Wilson's only weapon was economic sanctions backed by the American white establishment fearful of the black American civil rights movement. The media publicity for the British Labour government and the American Democrats in being seen to oppose colonialism and, more importantly, racism, without any adverse consequence to their countries was a democratic politician's perfect scenario. To be seen to champion the poor of Africa in the United Nations would help stop the communist infiltration into what had been a Western sphere of influence. In the end, Byron knew from his research, the two hundred and seventy-three thousand white Rhodesians would be brushed aside by the tide of history but it would take longer than anyone in Britain or America believed.

There were certain strategic minerals mined in Rhodesia, of which ferrochrome was the most important, that were found in few other places on earth, outside of communist China and Russia. Byron hoped the Americans had not done their homework. Without Rhodesian chrome, an important ingredient in the space and arms industry, the Americans would be forced to turn to their enemies for supplies.

The new movement of copper from Zambia had been disastrous for the Zambian economy but beneficial to Langton Merchant Bank and its clients. The process of channelling funds into numbered Swiss bank accounts had gone smoothly, along with the physical supply of copper to Western factories.

A similar tangle of buying and selling companies with foreign bank accounts had been created for cobalt leaving Zaire, the old Belgian Congo that had been in a state of anarchy since independence from the Belgians. In Africa, the vultures were firmly in power, growing fat from the old colonial carcass. Money or the gun, usually both together, ruled. One man one vote, democracy, had been brief.

ONE HOUR and ten minutes after Heath flew out of Heathrow airport for

Africa, Byron left the same airport on a BOAC Comet aircraft for Hong Kong via Cyprus and India, landing at Kai-Tak airport thirty-three hours later. A helicopter flew him across to Hong Kong Island where the courtesy bus dropped him outside the Mandarin Hotel.

After a good night's sleep, Byron called on the Hong Kong and Shanghai Bank where he had made an appointment with the manager. The manager, not having done business with Langton Merchant Bank, had telexed his London office who gave him the background on Byron Langton. 'African and Swiss connections. Possible major future player. Origin obscure. Probable crime connection for laundering money. Known in market for ability to manipulate funds into tax-free havens. Despite some clients' dubious background has good reputation. Provide full courtesy.'

Ten minutes of polite conversation in the bank's offices led to lunch in Kowloon and only after lunch, over good Brazilian coffee, did the bank manager learn the reason for his guest's visit to the bank.

"I believe the Chinese authorities would wish to buy cobalt from Zaire. Your introduction to a discreet commodity broker here in Hong Kong would ensure your bank handled all our commercial transactions."

Within half an hour of leaving the lunch table Byron had his contact into mainland China.

"You will understand," he said to the Chinese, "all business will be passed through Portuguese Macau. My information is that Portugal, with its Mozambique and Angolan colonies will, along with Switzerland for historical neutral reasons, and South Africa for political, not apply sanctions to a rogue Rhodesia. The chrome when offered to the Americans at a premium will purport to have originated in China. With the Western world suffering a severe chrome shortage the Americans will not be concerned about a Chinese communist origin. Full cargo ore shipments will be made from the port of Beira in Mozambique and the documents switched to Chinese origin when the cargo is on the water. The vessels will sail to Macau where their names and ports of registration will change and they will then proceed to the west coast of America to offload their cargoes. You can bet by the second shipment everyone will know exactly what is happening but more importantly, the buyer wants the chrome ore and the seller wants money. We will provide the system and documentation to make it legal for the buyer. My Swiss company will give your Macau company instructions. No British laws will be broken. Fact is, after today, my name and that of my bank will not feature in this business. Here is a list of American buyers of ferrochrome. Offer each of them small quantities by telex as you do in normal trade."

"Where did you get the list of buyers?"

"From the largest chrome mine in Rhodesia. Those are some of their clients. This UDI may not happen. Smith may capitulate. If he doesn't, we stand to make substantial profits for being in position before the event, ensuring American continuity of supply despite United Nations mandatory sanctions."

"What else can the Rhodesians supply?"

"I will send you a list when I return to London. More simply, you tell me what you want out of Africa and I will see what I can do."

"When do you return?"

"On this evening's flight."

"May I suggest you delay your flight and join me for dinner? It is more beneficial to do business with a man one has come to understand. I believe in people as well as bank references."

"So do I."

WHEN, on Thursday the 11th November at one-fifteen in the afternoon the white Rhodesian government declared itself independent from Britain, the United Nations was in uproar, country after country outdoing each other with abuse for the racist, colonialist, white settlers who defied world opinion and the rights of man, the right of every man to be equal in all things to his fellow man. A week later mandatory sanctions were imposed by a United Nations for once in full agreement with itself. The outrage was to be squashed by placing a total embargo on all cargo in and out of the country and the freezing of all overseas funds of persons residing in Rhodesia together with dividends due to them from their investments. Finally the British declared that anyone furthering the rebellion would be charged with high treason should they set foot on British soil.

THE *DAILY GARNET*, with help from Heathcliff Mortimer's sense of the ridiculous, drew pictures for the readers of a flurry of heads rolling down Tower Hill and the Tower of London being unable to fulfil its traditional commitments from gross lack of space.

In Kenya, it was reported, officers of the rank of captain upwards in the Black Watch regiment flown to Kenya in emergency refused to embark on an airlift for Rhodesia and military intervention. Heath was unable to confirm the mutiny but whatever the facts, the Scottish regiment remained grounded in Nairobi. A more accurate assessment, Heath wrote in his column, was the British high command's calculation that it would require seven British divisions to subdue Rhodesia and control the corridor from Beira inland to guarantee British supplies in a country belonging to Portugal, Britain's oldest ally, who was fighting a small-scale guerrilla war to maintain their hegemony in a country, Mozambique, they had ruled for five hundred years.

The Rhodesian government, by diligence of precaution in their long-standing argument with the British to remove the right of the British Parliament to legislate in certain cases for Rhodesia, and being in full control of their own fiscal matters, had removed their foreign exchange reserves from London six months before and placed them in safekeeping in a numbered bank account in Switzerland.

The day after American factories were denied access to Rhodesian chrome, small amounts were made on offer to them from China at three times the price paid the week before. Chrome being a small part of manufacturing armaments and space material, but without which the whole world would not function, the Americans instantly accepted the offers and clamoured for more. Within a month, the first ore carrier, full to its hatches, left the port of Beira for Macau.

In London, Byron smiled to himself. There was always money to be made from shortages. It was one thing to impose sanctions with words and another to implement them with deeds. There was a risk of which he was well aware, but he also knew everyone was getting what they wanted. The Americans had their strategic chrome, the Rhodesians the same money they would have had in the first place, the British government their righteous indignation at no cost and the risk-takers, the risk of their cargo being confiscated before it was paid for, high compensation for their trouble and ingenuity. The wheels of industry continued to turn despite government intervention.

TOWARDS THE MIDDLE of the following summer, Heathcliff Mortimer received a phone call from his mentor asking him for a drink. It was the end of the week and Byron had left the choice of the venue up to the journalist, who gave the address of the Duke Inn on the Chelsea waterfront. They had not seen each other since the wedding over a year ago, their business conducted by telephone and hand-delivered mail.

Heath had returned from Malawi, previously Nyasaland and part of the old Central African Federation, where he had seen the only candidate allowed to stand in the election become the new president. One or two people had been stupid enough to object out loud and found themselves in jail where the rumour said they would languish for a considerable time without trial. Doctor Hastings Banda, the saviour of Malawi from the British, had no intention of seeing all his hard work go to waste. Heath's article lambasting Banda as a tinpot dictator had been blocked by the *Daily Garnet* editor as out of line with modern political thinking on Africa; the man was a hero for liberating his people from colonialism and the clutch of the white settlers. The press had spent considerable capital on building up the likes of Hastings Banda, the *Garnet* editor had told Heath, and they were not about to find their prodigies walking the dusty earth of Africa with feet of clay. The man was and would be a hero and Heathcliff Mortimer would leave the matter closed.

The phone call from Byron Langton came half an hour after the interview with the editor and Heath wondered, on his way to the Duck Inn, conveniently close to his new flat, whether the owner of the newspaper was going to override his editor or tell Heath to follow the political thinking of a majority socialist Britain.

Byron came into the Duck Inn looking annoyed.

"Give me a Scotch," said Byron sitting on the empty stool next to Heath. "How's the book going?"

"Not bad, thanks," answered Heath.

"You had a good trip in Malawi?"

"You haven't heard?"

"Not a word. That editor never tells me anything. Probably right. The paper makes money."

With relief, Heath ordered a double Scotch and a refill of his double Southern Comfort.

"You seem irritated," he said after ordering the drinks.

"I am," said Byron. "We'll take our drinks outside. It's good to talk to you."

Heath picked up the drinks and followed Byron out onto the lawn and down to his favourite bench next to the willow tree.

"Bloody two-faced Americans!"

"What've they done now?" asked Heath, sipping his drink and smiling over the glass at Byron.

"Breaking sanctions. Buying chrome direct from the Rhodesians."

"You were making money out of that chrome from China! My guess had always been it was Rhodesian chrome. Supplies in that quantity don't appear from nowhere overnight."

"The Americans are hypocrites."

"Maybe, but they were buying it from China, I believe, and at three times the price. The real gripe was the price you and your Chinese friends were charging, Byron."

"If you took American industry's imports of chrome they wouldn't register on any scale but to Smith it's a lot of foreign exchange for his tiny country."

"Don't you worry about this government catching you?"

"My head rolling down Tower Hill? I read that one of yours... Not really."

"How's your wife?" asked Heath, changing the subject.

"She's with her parents."

"Meaning?... Sorry, none of my business."

"No. Everything's fine and Fiona's looking forward to editing your book. The marriage is fine. Just the Americans making me sick. There's not a backbone in their spine."

"You heard from your brother in Africa?"

"Not since he left Barotseland. Vanished."

"I've asked around. Not a word. Laurie Hall too. Vanished."

"I feel like getting drunk," said Byron.

"Good. We'll go back to my place. Walking distance. Plenty of Scotch and plenty of Southern Comfort. It's good for the soul to get drunk every now and again, my son. And I should know. Let us see if we can solve some of the problems of the world."

JOSEPHINE LANGTON'S flat in Westminster was close to the House of Commons and her job as a junior minister in the Foreign and Commonwealth Aid Office, her minister, Andrew Flock, having personally chosen her for the job.

Andrew Flock believed the enemy was the rich, people who had inherited for no other reason than the chance of birth or made it by exploiting the people. Both the minister and Josephine agreed that it was the main purpose of world socialism to redistribute the wealth of the world. Through a member of the Fabian Society, which advocated the slow introduction of socialism, he was in greater agreement with the British Communist Party that believed in the revolutionary process of changing the ways of man's greed. Josephine's brief membership of the British Communist Party in 1959 was known to the minister, though his sympathies for communism were only suspected by Josephine. The fact that he was in direct and regular contact with Moscow was known only to himself and the Russians.

Among the immediate enemy for Andrew Flock were the white settlers of Rhodesia who were the worst kind of bigots and exploiters, men and women who had gone out to Africa to steal the land from the black man.

Josephine's journey to Rhodesia before Smith's UDI had been, according to the press release of the British government, a last serious and genuine attempt to look at Smith's concept of meritocracy, whereby everyone would vote but those with education, position and ownership of land would carry bonus votes in accordance with their position and understanding in society. A high court judge would carry one hundred votes as would the chief of a tribe; an illiterate peasant in the fields, one.

Josephine's instructions had been to ignore the whining of the rich and privileged whites and take notes on anything that would denigrate their position in the eyes of the British public. She and the rest of the delegation had known before leaving London that the British government had only one agenda: to hand over full power to the blacks and to conduct an election on the basis of one man one vote to determine the party to govern the country.

Unfortunately for the British Labour government, Southern Rhodesia had been a self-governing crown colony since 1923 and the civil service, police and army were appointed and paid by the settler government in Salisbury, voted into power by the settlers without one vote from the indigenous blacks.

Josephine's leak to the socialist press, of white farmers with ten servants and a lifestyle out of feudal Britain, sparked the kind of envy and hatred in the majority of Britons that was to be expected from people who had to do their own washing up. The whites that Josephine pictured for the press were swaggering mini-dictators as close to fascism and Hitler as made no difference.

The Labour Party had won the previous election with a slim majority but the popular action of Harold Wilson in throwing every curse at the privileged racist Rhodesians gave his popularity a well-needed boost: better still, it was done, as Josephine was aware, without cost to the British exchequer.

There were two clichés often swimming in the mind of Byron Langton: *If you can't beat them, join them*, and *Know your enemy like your friend*.

Before the last British general election, Byron, through his twin sister, had donated ten thousand pounds to the Labour Party to further their pursuit of power. He did not tell Josephine he had given the exact same amount to the Conservative Party. Both parties were promised the full support of the *Daily Garnet* which caused the editor some concern when the mixed messages reached him from his political reporter. He had thought of phoning the owner of his newspaper but the owner had not phoned him on a vital aspect of editorial bias and the silence, in the editor's words to himself, 'was deafening'. There was a wry smile on the editor's face when he understood the humour.

Byron Langton believed that socialism, in any one of its many forms, was gross over-government and inefficient distribution of charity. Byron's careful and private research had shown him that eighty per cent of the charity money was enjoyed personally by the dispensers in collecting the money from the public and, like anyone handling money that was not their own, they gave it away with careless abandon. In Byron's mind, the altruism of socialism was akin to a professional thief administering the bank.

Since his sister's appointment to the government he made it his business to call socially on a regular basis, which Josephine attributed to his conversion to social democracy and the ten thousand pounds. Being a politician she found her private life lonely. New friends had to be chosen more carefully. Her twin brother was her twin brother who could be talked to without the restraint she applied to her colleagues, even Andrew. The evenings in her flat with Byron were the moments she looked forward to most.

"Why don't you bring your wife?" Josephine asked on a summer evening in the middle of September. They were sitting on her small balcony with its view over the River Thames. Both held a crystal whisky glass in their right hands.

"Oh, sis, whatever for? Just because a man takes a wife he doesn't stop private conversations with his family, 'specially his twin. Had a letter from Hilary on Monday asking for money. Wrote back and told him to come home. No place for a white man. That kind of thing. Goodness, they killed half the missionaries in the Congo. Hilary says the conditions are appalling and most of the medicine and supplies sent to him from London disappear before they reach him. They want to tax donations. Not the government, just every official who can stop the free movement of the goods."

"Nonsense. I mentioned that to Paul Mwansa and he said it's pure rubbish. Paul's with the Zambian High Commission here in London."

"Well, either your Paul Mwansa is a liar or the Reverend Hilary Bains. Take your pick."

"Hilary's been brainwashed by contact with the settlers. The whites left in Africa will say anything to denigrate the new order... Any news of Will?"

"Nothing."

"You think he's dead?"

"No. We'd have heard."

"Why doesn't he write?"

"Maybe he's sick and tired of Mother telling him to come home and get a proper job." They both laughed. "We should go home together one weekend," said Byron.

"We should, but every time I have a little free time I want to just sit here and relax. But you're right. We must make an effort. How is Fiona, by the way?"

"She's fine."

13

*H*orst Kannberg was a rolling stone who gathered very little moss. When he was born in Riga of white Russian parents in 1931, there were more servants in the big house than Kannbergs. Latvia, of which Riga was the capital, had been good to Horst's grandfather. The block of flats overlooking the Gulf of Riga, owned without mortgage by the Kannbergs, were impressive and should have led Horst into a life of decadent sufficiency, a role he would have filled to perfection. His mother spoke German which was the reason for the German Christian name. Horst had remained in Riga during the German occupation but when Germany was defeated and the Russians conquered the Baltic States of which Latvia, the middle one, was the most prosperous, the Kannbergs fled to England and the communists confiscated their properties. From very rich to very poor had taken less than a week. Horst was fourteen, proficient in Latin and ancient Greek, with a passion for Russian literature but in practical terms of no use in a life that would require him to make a living for himself.

The Kannbergs applied for assisted passage to South Africa after three fruitless months in bleak, post-war England. Kannberg senior offered his considerable classical education to teach children in any one of three European languages he spoke fluently, French, Russian and German. The problem was his English, the guttural accent of Kannberg senior being so pronounced that few could understand what he said. But in South Africa, determined to flood South Africa with white immigrants, the impediment of the father and mother was outweighed by the four children who would quickly learn English and Afrikaans and be the material to build a strong, white South Africa, free of communism.

If Horst had been five years younger, like his brother and sister, he might have been saved. What he had was continental charm, good looks, and a cute accent from picking up fluent English during their three months in England by finding a very nice girl of seventeen to teach him the rudiments of language and entertain each other. School in England and South Africa was difficult. Maths had never been his subject but taught in English the process was unintelligible. Horst went through the motions of school but gravitated to the Cape Town beaches and the new sport of surfing. Horst Kannberg was always ready to try something new.

He never quite said that his family were Russian aristocrats, victims of the Bolshevik revolution, but he never squashed the rumours. Colonial Africa was impressed with old money and titles, something usually left behind in Europe. The charm and manners of an old-world aristocrat were the hallmark of Kannberg senior, well adopted by his eldest son. The Kannbergs were poor in money but rich in history.

After two fruitless years of South African schooling, Horst gave up the unnecessary trek to Rondebosch High School and concentrated his talents on Clifton Beach, where he bronzed to perfection as an amateur lifesaver. If there was a Saturday night party anywhere in the peninsula, Horst Kannberg allowed himself to be prevailed upon to accept the invitation and the offer of a lift. The small, rent-controlled flat of the Kannbergs in Green Point was not the right address but, being on the ground floor of an old house converted into three flats with trophies of Riga littered around the quaint old lounge, Horst was socially much in demand.

To become a waiter or barman, two jobs of which he might have been capable, would have destroyed the image built for him by the many people he acquainted himself with in Cape Town. Horst talked to everyone, charmingly, as if every word spoken to him gave his mind extreme pleasure. If the conversation led to a coffee house or, better still, one of the hotel bars where he was known by all the best barmen, he would say before his new friend drove off in the direction of coffee or beer that he was a 'bit short'. After three or four beers at the new friend's expense, Horst would ask the man how much money the man had in his pocket. If he had asked outright to borrow money, the man would have pleaded poverty but, caught in the trap of answering the question, Horst would extract five rands as a loan, noisily buy the man an expensive cocktail with the man's own money and explain he had to tear himself away for a meeting. The man, a little drunk by then, was quite happy to see the remnants of his five rands walk out of the door. He had enjoyed himself and what a nice young man. All the barmen kept their mouths shut as with the exotic cocktail went a good tip.

The first meeting after a successful bar encounter was with the florist in Sea Point where Horst would buy his mother a bunch of flowers. Living at home for Horst was the price of a bunch of flowers. It was said later on in his life that if Horst Kannberg told you to go to hell, you knew you were going to enjoy the journey.

There is a limit to the number of gullible people in any one town and when his father's hints at a job had reached the point of irritation, he left Cape Town and a weeping mother clutching her last bunch of flowers. He was twenty years old, and the world was his oyster. With a small but expensive bag packed with everything he owned and enough money sewn into the lining of his jacket to get him out of trouble, he took a bus out of Cape Town along the coast, getting out at the first small town.

For Horst there was nothing so vulgar as hitching a lift by standing on the side of the road. He waited across from the petrol station, checking the cars and their occupants heading away from the Cape. He knew his type to perfection and when a man or woman driving alone with the right registration plate on the car and the right body language pulled up for petrol, Horst would wander across the road and start a conversation.

"Nice place, Knysna," he would say, translating the CX number plate to be Knysna or Plettenberg Bay, the richest villages on the Garden Route.

If there was no positive reaction, he would move on to the toilet and try again.

He was the right size, not too big to intimidate and not too small to be thought of as short. Once the conversation began, Horst would have in his memory bank the name of an acquaintance in Knysna. The diary he kept was full of names and addresses with careful notes about each person. He always did his homework. If the driver knew his acquaintance Horst would ask to be dropped off at the house, having first casually asked for a lift. Most often, Horst was in the passenger seat, his bag on the back seat, chatting away before the car was filled up with petrol. By the time they reached the destination they were firm friends with the driver wanting to boast to friends of the young Russian aristocrat. The longest Horst managed to stay with a lift was a month.

As it was a large country, Horst was able to spend fourteen years travelling round and round.

By the time he reached thirty-four, he had run out of options in South Africa, his credit having reached an unacceptable low. With the last of his money, he took the train north to Southern Rhodesia, arriving at the railway station opposite the Victoria Falls Hotel on the same day Will Langton rolled across the bridge in his Land Rover, Barotseland left behind. It took Horst Kannberg less than sixty seconds to recognise Will as the perfect target.

BETTY GULLIVER HAD HEARD there were four men for every woman in Rhodesia and the very idea had consumed her for six months. She was neither plain nor pretty and competition in swinging London had reduced her sex life to a dribble. She was twenty-eight, never even engaged and trying to compete with fresh young things ten years her junior. After the six months she went to Rhodesia House in the Strand and made friends with one of the Rhodesian girls who worked at the High Commission. When the subject was Rhodesia, Betty was a good listener and as the girl was homesick for her family, the family farm and the bush. She was ready to talk to her new friend and eventually confirm the four-to-one statistic.

"That's including Salisbury and Bulawayo, the two cities," the girl had explained. "You go to a small village like Victoria Falls where they operate safaris and likely there are no single girls at all and probably forty young men... What's the matter, Betty? You thinking of leaving England?"

"Yes," said Betty Gulliver in a tight voice that almost squeaked.

When Will walked through the quadrangle of the magnificent Victoria Falls colonial hotel, having first cut across the sights of Horst Kannberg, Betty Gulliver, having her afternoon tea in the shade of a thirty-foot mango tree, had been at the Falls for a year, the best year of her life. Not only was she Queen of the Ball, she was the only single girl at the Falls and a film star could not have received more attention from men. Betty was sure at least three men were in love with her and she was working on the fourth. To Betty's disgust, Will Langton did not even look at her when he sat down at the next table which was also in the shade, and ordered himself a hot tea. He then studied the view of the bridge, the cataract and the great power of Victoria Falls pounding the air with sound, crashing spray three hundred metres up into the clear blue sky.

The second insult in Betty's afternoon came shortly afterwards when Horst Kannberg sat down at Will's table, explaining it was too hot out of the shade at the other empty tables. Horst was exactly Betty's type and her table was also in the shade. Why had he not chosen *her*, was the indignant question in her mind. When Will did turn his gaze in her direction, the violet eyes were focused just right of her left ear. He was taking no more notice of her than of the man who had just sat at his table. His mind was not even sitting with him at the table but far off somewhere that had nothing to do with either of them. She guessed rightly he had just come out of the bush. She took Horst for a tourist, the paler skin talking to her of a cooler climate far away from the Victoria Falls.

Betty watched the tourist try to talk to the man from the bush and felt better herself for his lack of success. The man in the bush jacket had not snubbed her after all: he just wanted his tea on his own.

"Are you from these parts?" insisted Horst to Will.

"Not sure really," answered Will.

"Where are you from?"

"That depends on when."

"You staying at the Falls?"

"That depends as well."

Over at the other table, Betty Gulliver was having a good smile to herself, confident that once she opened the conversation, the tourist would be more interested in her than the man with the unfocused stare. First she caught his eye and then waited for the conversation at the next table to peter out.

When the man finally got up and went across to the other table Will barely registered he had even been and gone. He was trying hard to think what to do with the rest of his life.

Will sat for an hour not listening to one word of the animated conversation going on at the next table. He heard neither the words 'bit short' nor 'if you insist, a Lion Larger'. When the small band came out onto the terrace for cocktail music, the same band that had backed Shelley Lane, Will decided a cold beer would be better than another pot of tea. He had still not made up his mind where he was going to spend the night.

Horst, out of the corner of his eye, watched Will switch to beer and, while giving his full attention to the lady who was buying him drinks and talking volubly about her new job, he was sure the man was a target who could prove successful. The man had a Land Rover and was probably local, the girl who said she was twenty-four was to Horst's mind nearer thirty and she wasn't even his type.

The sun began to go down and Horst was on his fourth free beer, resigned to spending the night with the lady, when Will, bored with his own company, decided to join the couple at the next table and buy them a drink. For more than an hour he had them thinking in circles, getting absolutely nowhere.

"Mind if I join you two? Seems silly only three of us on the terrace and sitting at separate tables. My name's Will Langton, lately from Mongu in Barotseland. Can I buy you two a drink?"

For Horst, the offer of another free drink was music to his ears and there was even a chance at this rate he would be able to get himself thoroughly drunk at other people's expense and by then, surely, the girl would be more than acceptable.

"Come and join us please," said Horst in his best German-Russian accent that had taken him so far in his life.

"Sorry I wasn't saying much earlier. Lots to think about."

"This is Betty Gulliver from England and I'm Horst Kannberg. My family are white Russians. We were chased out by the Bolsheviks."

"What'll it be?"

"Would you mind if I changed my drink to a large whisky and maybe a nice cocktail for Betty here? Something like a Pimm's No. 1. I'm sure the famous Victoria Falls Hotel will know how to make a very good Pimm's. My great-uncle used to travel from Saint Petersburg to England every summer and he said Pimm's was the very thing for the summer."

"What did your uncle do in Saint Petersburg?" asked Betty with dewy eyes, the idea of a Pimm's from this Russian aristocrat almost overwhelming.

"Diplomatic service. For the tsar, of course. They were very large landowners on my mother's side, before it was stolen. Of course, after that we went to Latvia and owned half the beach front before that all went as well."

"What a terrible shame," said Betty.

Will by then had caught the eye of the wine steward, ordered the large whisky, which he took to be a double, a Pimm's No. 1, which he knew came with all the fruit, mint and cucumber in a tall glass frosted at the rim with sugar, and thought he had better count his money before he was carried too far away.

"Make mine a Dimple Haig," said Horst imperiously to the waiter, briefly interrupting his monologue to Betty Gulliver.

Will gave a wry smile as he waited for a round of drinks that was to cost him the price of ten beers. 'Bet he hasn't got a penny to his name' he thought, and mentally wrote it all down to the price of looking for a new life. Already he was missing his home on the river, even the painful tricks of the Goliath heron.

Having bought the drinks, Will was obliged to sit through their drinking while he tried to interest himself in the one-sided conversation now being oiled by the Dimple Haig whisky. The man was a braggart and a bore, something he had seen many times when Hannes Potgieter was running the hunting safaris. Then the customer was paying for his own whisky, which was some kind of comfort. Will smiled at Hannes's usual comment when the likes of Horst Kannberg had left the base camp. 'Englishman, they may be phoney but they're rich.'

Will was trying to finish his beer and get back to the Land Rover that he would drive upriver a kilometre or two and find a level spot to stop and spend the night. Over the boxes, gun cases and camera equipment, Will had laid a mattress. His head would be a foot and a half from the ceiling but with the small windows covered with gauze to keep out the mosquitoes he would be comfortable enough. For breakfast he would catch himself a bream and cook it over an open fire and brew a good pot of black coffee ladled with sugar. Will had enough money in the Livingstone bank to last six months. Then he would make decisions.

Downing the last of his beer, warm already from the heat, Will started to get up from his chair.

"Please," said Betty, "have a drink with me. Horst explained when he first sat down he was a 'bit short' and I know how bad that can feel. I don't think I'll be able to run to Pimm's and Dimple Haig but how about three cold beers?" She smiled warmly at Will. The girl was not so stupid after all. Will smiled back. Suddenly he liked Betty Gulliver.

When the new beers had arrived at the table, the conversation turned around to Will and he told them of his home on the banks of the river and the floods that had swept it away.

"What are you going to do next?" asked Betty.

"That's the point. I don't know. My brother wants me to go back to England and join his firm in London, but after so many years in Africa I don't see myself wearing a bowler hat and riding the train up to London every day. I know nothing about Byron's business, so the offer looks like charity to me, probably a favour to my mother. The other suggestion was going to Australia but the girl has a boyfriend she lives with. He would be the source of my income. So here I am with the guns and the cameras, a few pounds left in the bank and no idea what to do next. Somehow, that's quite exciting. There's nothing worse than knowing the rest of your life. You see, younger sons in the old days went out to run the colonies but we're running out of colonies fast. This one's going."

"Not Rhodesia," said Betty, emphatically. "We'll declare UDI and tell the British government to go to hell."

"That's as it may be but it won't last," said Will, sadly. "The Americans have a racial problem with their civil rights movement. They won't allow a few whites to retain power in Africa. They'll use them as a whipping horse to take the pressure off the American government at home. Make their white government look anti-racist. What Hilary says. Brother of mine who's a missionary in Zambia. Says he's staying. Can't leave the flock. That sort of thing. But Hilary knows. He reads. He says in the end it will be a total disaster for Africa, that the building of a modern world in Africa will have to start all over again when the new revolutionaries have destroyed the place and stolen its money... What do you do here for a living, Betty?"

"My boss has a safari company. Takes tours walking in the bush. Customers have drinks at sundown round the fire. Some spend the night under canvas. We have a small office. Me, a phone and a typewriter. Problem is, Roy says, there's not enough to do at the Falls. After half an hour of gaping at the waterfall and getting wet in the rainforest, there's not much left to do. A day and a night at the Falls then down to the Wankie Game Reserve. Roy says we need riverboats that can cruise upriver with tourists. Sundowner cruises. Drinks and food on board. Trouble is, a boat big enough to carry fifty people would be hell to transport on the strip roads from Bulawayo, and while it was coming up nothing else could be on the single-lane road. Roy says once a boat trailer that size was on the strips it couldn't get off. But that's what I get asked for. There's game on both banks of the river. A riverboat could get close without frightening the animals away. You would see that as a photographer, Will."

"Why don't you build a boat right here?" said Will. "All you need is a pontoon with a double-decker superstructure and two big outboard motors. Probably do three or four knots, but what else do you need on a booze cruise?"

"How would we make the pontoons?" asked Betty.

"Out of forty-four-gallon petrol drums. Weld them into a tube and flatten the front one into a wedge. Then weld a frame across two lines of drums. There must be welding gear at the Falls. If not, bring it up. You need two floating decks, one on top of the other, the top for game viewing, and a canopy to keep off the sun. Canvas chairs and tables. Big cool box for the ice and cold beer."

"Could you make something like that?" asked Betty.

"Probably. Take a few weeks."

"I'll talk to Roy... Does Horst here know how to weld?"

"No, but I wouldn't mind finding out. You'd need a host on board to tell the passengers what they are seeing. Now that kind of job would be right up my street."

"What was your last job?" asked Will.

"I've never had one," he said into the silence... "You know, I think that's the first time I've been honest to anyone for a very long time."

. . .

SWEET DAYS BECAME weeks became months by the side of the river. In front of their camp, one hundred metres from shore, the Zambezi flowed around an island of palm trees, the oily, heavy water, flotsam of trees and small beds of floating grass-weed, surging the last two miles towards the lip of the Falls. The thunder of water was constant. The small village next to the Falls had grown used to the crazy Russian who was going to sink a line of steel drums to the bottom of the river. No one knew the depth of the water and the crocodiles made sure no one swam down to have a look.

By the time the riverboat was ready to push from its cradle into the flowing water, Will was sure that Betty Gulliver and Horst Kannberg were deeply in love with each other.

Roy had financed the building of the craft, buying the used fuel drums and the steel floor mesh, the thin girders and the two second-hand outboard motors. In exchange, Will and Horst gave their time for nothing, working on the iron monster from sunup to sundown with two hours in the shade of a jackalberry tree at the height of the noonday sun. Roy had written a small contract that gave Will and Horst a half-share in the craft, Will and Horst to run the boat and Roy to bring up the passengers in his small bus.

Down the slope of the riverbank, Will had designed a wooden jetty. Horst slept in a small tent and Will in his Land Rover. They fed themselves by fishing in the river and poaching at night. No one seemed to own the land on which they camped and no one seemed to care. Only a bad dirt road wound parallel to the river, petering out in the bush a kilometre from their camp upriver from the Falls. They were in a world of their own visited by kingfishers and fish eagles, hippos grunting from the cool pools bypassed by the river, crocodiles coming right out of the river to inspect from a distance the strange structure growing high on the riverbank. And always, Betty who pedalled a bicycle the two miles each evening to bring them the cold beers, their reward for the hard day's work.

Roy, Betty's employer, was not sure whether a ceremony to launch the ten tons of iron was a good idea that could better be changed to a clandestine push into the water one night when the moon was up, so when the sharp point ploughed the water and carried on down to the mud on the bottom, no one would see his money sink out of sight.

To live in the heat and isolation with the constant thunder of the Falls required a sense of adventure. Everyone who would come were invited to witness the launch. A young impala ram was spitted and turned over the fire for nine hours, the beer, whisky and ice were delivered by the Sprayview Hotel. Betty made four different salads and Will, smiling happily to himself, watched the agonised conversations of his partners.

Betty had found an array of flags with the Rhodesian flag flying side by side with the Union Jack. Unbeknown to the launch party ready to push and pull the iron craft over the logs and into the river, it would be the last time the two flags would fly together in peace. Wisely, Roy had himself three stiff whiskies before he named the riverboat *Zambezi Queen*. Most of the guests were intoxicated from the drink and pumped adrenaline. A bottle of beer cracked against the last tight drum at the back of the boat and the ropes were heaved and the ironwork clutched and pushed with hysterical abandon.

When the *Zambezi Queen* reached the lip of the riverbank and tipped down towards the water, the three people either side on the ropes let go for their lives and the back pushers felt the ironwork leap forward out of their hands. There was no need for rollers and the bow of the boat hit the water at ten miles an hour, flushing mud and water high on either side as it tore out into the river, the front under water headed for the bottom at forty degrees. The momentum carried the second deck below water and still the boat was going down. Everyone except Will Langton looked on aghast. The thick rope Will had tied to the stern ran out to its limit of sixty metres and jerked hard against the base of the jackalberry tree and held, jerking hard on the forward plunge of the *Zambezi Queen*. Sensibly, Will had left the outboard motors on shore to be fitted from the jetty. The flags whipped at the back with the change of momentum and the stern settled back as the prow of the boat heaved itself out of the Zambezi to settle high up like a duck on the water. Gently, Will pulled on his rope and edged the craft alongside the jetty.

In twenty minutes, Will had the outboard motors locked into place, the fuel tanks connected, the roasted impala on board with the last of the booze. Betty placed the captain's hat firmly on Horst's head and Roy announced the sunset cruise was about to begin. Forty people clambered on board, both motors coughed and fired and Will untied the craft from the jetty. Horst on the top deck holding the wheel, pushed forward the throttles now connected to the motors and the *Zambezi Queen* moved out into the stream, turning her back on the thunder of the Falls. Sedately she pushed upriver against the stream. The sun was almost down, glowing rich and red behind the fronds of the palm trees etching the banks of the river. A crocodile slid from a sandbank into the water and disappeared. A hush descended on the people, awed by the river and the surrounding bush. Gently, Horst drove the boat to the side of the island not pushed by the river and Will threw out the anchor. Horst cut the engines and let the peace fall down from heaven.

· · ·

FOUR MONTHS LATER, Horst and Betty were married on board the *Zambezi Queen* by the Church of the Province of Central Africa. The Church of England priest also blessed the boat. Roy gave away the bride and Will was best man.

That night Horst moved from his tent by the river into the village and Betty's one-bedroom flat over the office, and Will was left on his own. For a wedding present he had secretly given the bride and groom his share of the *Zambezi Queen*. Horst found the note tied to the wheel saying Will had gone on his way and a month later Roy told them of his gift. For Betty, her dream had come true, a week after her thirty-first birthday. For Horst, at last, he had found a place to rest.

In making his decision, Will had seen the way of things to come in Central Africa. It was not his fight and never would be. The Zambians had closed the border with Rhodesia in defiance of its declaration of independence. The road and rail route out for Zambia's copper had been closed. The kwacha, the new currency that had replaced the federal pound in Zambia, plunged. Men with guns pointed them at each other across the Victoria Falls Bridge.

Will's note had said he was going back to England. The intention had been to drive through Rhodesia into South Africa, sell the Land Rover and with the money fly back to England and look for a job. Will took the road out of the Falls with good intentions, loaded with fuel and provisions.

A few miles from the Falls a sign pointed right to Botswana and without knowing why, Will turned the Land Rover off the strips onto an old, badly kept dirt road until he found the border post and passed out of Rhodesia into Botswana. He drove on through into a country where people were outnumbered by the cattle and game ten to one. At the Chobe River, Will found himself in game country more prolific than he had ever seen before in his life. Great herds of elephant watched him from the mopani trees near the river as he made his first camp. Lion roared all around him.

For three weeks, Will lived with the animals, procrastinating. Indirectly, the decision to return to England had been made for him by Horst Kannberg. Over the months of building the *Zambezi Queen* side by side they had swapped their life stories; Horst's a litany of successful scams to have other people pay the way of Horst Kannberg through life. The man was proud of his stories of coming out of a bar drunk without spending a penny of his own money which he never had. There were so many women who had fallen for his charm and paid for his board and lodging. The end of every escapade had found Horst moving on happily to a new adventure, a broken heart left to be consoled by the privilege of knowing Horst

Kannberg; Horst was always the winner, according to Horst Kannberg. The message came through clearly, the man was going to live off other people for the rest of his life using his charm to earn a living.

Will began to wonder about himself. He had drifted out to Africa to avoid two years in the army, if he was honest with himself. The odyssey had ended with the flood and the new Zambia not wishing to renew his hunting licence. His livelihood had washed away with the river. The *Zambezi Queen* had been a small interlude while he faced up to the facts of his life. A man had to earn a living through life, had to work. The likes of Horst Kannberg were charming parasites. Will hoped Betty's happiness would last as long as possible. Maybe, Will thought, marriage was only a mutual convenience, one giving the other what the other lacked. If she was prepared to support him for the rest of her life, turning a blind eye to the inevitable infidelities, Horst would stay around. Will had understood that under Horst's bravado hid a man on the run. Maybe neither of them, Horst or Betty, had been going anywhere with their lives.

Will was twenty-eight going on twenty-nine with nothing to his name except three guns, a good camera and an old Land Rover. He knew that if he did nothing about his life, carried on drifting, he would end up despising himself. Africa, for the white man, was finished. The ivory money given to Byron would have found its way down the drain by now, the wilder business ventures, Will suspected, a means of milking the investors.

The rains had continued from the middle of January and soon the dirt road would be impossible for a four-wheel drive. The time had come in his life to face reality and find himself a career in England that would take him through life without relying on other people, relying on the likes of Betty Gulliver now Kannberg or the new welfare state.

A man who was a man made his own way through life, Will told himself. Maybe, someday, the new Africa would face up to its own day of reckoning.

Out of Botswana and back on the strip road, Will drove on south, camping on the side of the road, using his money for petrol. His long journey home had begun. Six months later, when Byron was still furious with the Americans for buying chrome ore direct from the renegade Rhodesians, Will arrived back at Tilbury Docks in London. Three times he had been forced to stop and work for petrol money. The airfare from Johannesburg was more than the dealers offered for the Land Rover. The inner cabin, shared with five others, on the *Transvaal Castle*, matched the Cape Town dealers' cash.

When Will landed back in London with three guns and a camera he was broke. Even in August it was raining. Plucking up his courage, he phoned his brother Byron at his office.

"Who's calling Mr Langton?" asked a bright voice.

"His brother."

"Which one?" asked Madge O'Shea, Byron's red-headed secretary.

"Will."

"We thought you were dead."

"So did I a couple of times. I have three guns in nice cases, a camera and a small bag. No money."

"Catch a cab to the office and tell the cabbie to come up for his money. Where are you, by the way?"

"Tilbury."

"Welcome home, Will."

BYRON LANGTON KNEW the biggest problem in a rapidly expanding business was good management. The news of Will's arrival made him think. There were many people in his organisation who would perform when told what to do. Few were able to initiate and carry through on their own. Good management also meant honesty, a creed that was constantly being laughed at by the new generation. The unspoken understanding was if governments could lie, cheat and steal, so could everyone else.

Will had no idea he was a wealthy man and Byron was not sure whether it would be in his own interest to explain to his brother the capital growth in the investment made from the ivory, including Will's inheritance from Hannes Potgieter. Certainly, under the circumstances, Byron had no intention of divulging the thirty thousand pounds' worth of gold bullion stored for Will in Zurich from the bonus he had earned after the processing and sale of the crocodile skins. From Byron's perspective, a man of wealth would not join his brother's firm at the bottom and learn the trade. No one in Byron's company came in at the top without experience, however honest and intelligent.

By the time a dejected Will arrived with his few possessions, Byron had decided to downplay the ivory and not mention the gold; thankfully, not once could he remember mentioning the figure invested after the ivory sale. Too much money anyway could damage a man, he rationalised, thinking of Laurie Hall spending for so little purpose.

Will was seated on the leather-bound bench when Byron came out of his office to shake his brother's hand. It was four-thirty in the afternoon and still wet in the street outside Byron's office in Pall Mall, next to Cox's & King's bank.

"Still raining?" said Byron after the warm handshake. "Come into the office and have a drink. Not quite sundowner time as you would say, Will, but what the hell. Haven't seen each other for a heck of a long time."

"Had to borrow from Madge to pay the taxi."

"Don't worry."

"I'm broke."

"Who cares when you have a family? I've been telling you for years to get out of Africa and come and work here. Africa's a disaster, Will. Colonialism at least gave it some kind of stability. Provided we can get out the minerals we want, it doesn't matter a damn to us. All this nonsense in Rhodesia caused by a bunch of Englishmen holding on to land which isn't worth a penny. Glad to see you saw the light."

"How's Mother and Father?"

"Both well. Why didn't you write to them? Mother was hurt."

"Didn't really know what to say. Anyway, here I am as you see me. I can sell the guns, I suppose, but don't imagine many people in England are looking for an elephant gun. Do you have any money from the ivory?"

"There's something there, have to have a look. Can lend you something now if you want? How about five hundred pounds?"

"That's a lot of money."

"Good. That's settled. You'll come and work here at Langton Merchant Bank. When we've had a drink or two, we can go home and introduce you to my wife. She'll be very happy to know that you're safe. I'm still in the same flat, believe it or not."

THE YEARS HAD NOT BEEN good to Red Langton, Will's father. The war and too many financial worries had left him a year short of sixty looking nearer seventy. Leaving behind Langton Manor in the condition he had inherited was his last ambition. Even Red understood the cornerstone of socialist policy, the demise of inherited wealth.

There was always something on the farm heralding disaster; everything from the low price of meat paid to the producer while the men in the middle ratcheted up the price so the average Englishman found it difficult to afford his Sunday dinner, to the weather and disease. Ruefully he thought it easier to sit in a big London office and buy and sell grain on the international market. Those kinds of farmers grew rich without planting a crop.

Will had not seen his parents since the death of Hannes Potgieter had chased him back to Africa. He found them less than the pictures he stored in his memory. The only thing his mother seemed pleased about was her younger son finally taking a proper job and what he had done was playing around in Africa with guns and cameras and living in the jungle with a lot of dangerous animals.

"It's bush, Mother, not jungle."

"Whatever. You can't deny the dangerous animals. Look at those terrible guns you brought with you. All your father ever needed was a shotgun for rabbits and pheasants. You make sure one of those guns doesn't go off in your room or it will knock down the whole house. You could have written me a letter."

"Yes, Mother."

"Now, when are you going back to London?"

"I've only just arrived."

"I know that."

The second bone of contention was Anna, the daughter of the accountant from Poole who had married Randolph Langton, the eldest son. Not once had she been pregnant even with a miscarriage.

Leaving the barrage of questions mostly unanswered, Will went out the back of the old ivy-covered house, through the dell and the apple orchard and up onto the Downs, taking the dogs. The sun had come out and Will needed the walk after the train journey from London.

England after Africa had looked so drab; even twenty years after the war there were still signs of the devastation caused by the German bombs. And everywhere he looked from the third-class carriage window, wet washing hung on the lines at the back of grey, dirty, semi-detached council houses. The countryside had been better but the mile after mile of houses had made him depressed.

Up on the Downs, the dogs chased the sheep with a merry cacophony of sound, the sheep running together in circles, their heads high and rigid. None of the dogs had recognised Will.

Reaching the edge of the cliff, he looked down on Dancing Ledge with the small rock pool cut out of the bare rock for the forgotten orphans of the Second World War. Across from the pool he could just make out the entrance to his childhood cave.

Leaving the dogs with the sheep, Will walked down the winding path, past short, tufted grass, out across the rocks and stood beside the pool that gave him so many memories. There were three holidaymakers on the Ledge, all from another part of the country and none of them took any notice of the young man with the deep suntan looking down into the depths of the pool, looking for the other half of his soul. After ten minutes Will realised she had gone. There was nothing there in the water except an old and distant memory. All the years of running away had come to nothing.

Will began to laugh with bitter sadness, building to the point of hysteria. Then he turned his back on the pool and ran across the rock ledge to the path which he took like a goat chased by a dog. At the top he carried on running, calling for the dogs who broke off their endless chase of the sheep for a different game to play.

Back at the orchard Will stopped, his lungs bursting from the run. For the first time since meeting the girl on Dancing Ledge he was free to lead his life without feeling her presence.

Circling the front of the house, Will touched the trunk of the great old oak tree as part of the superstition, the oak that old tales told had been planted by the first Langton of Langton Manor.

"Tomorrow I will write to Lindsay and find out if the photos made any money," he said out loud.

"What photos?" asked Randolph Langton, coming out of the house. "Heard you were back, Will. Welcome home... You know something, I think it's going to rain and I haven't stacked the hay... What have you been doing with yourself, old son?"

"Nothing much, Randolph. How's Anna?"

"She's fine."

Neither of them could think of anything else to say to each other so they went inside and joined their parents, the dogs going off on their own.

14

Six months later, Will met Heathcliff Mortimer for the first time. Will had gone to visit his sister in her Westminster flat and found the corpulent newspaperman sitting in a large armchair sipping Josephine's whisky out of a cut crystal glass. Soon after his arrival, Josephine said she had to rush off to the Commons to vote on a bill to extend British social welfare.

"You two stay and have a chat. Heath's spent time in Africa, Will. Got to rush. Back in an hour. Slam the door shut if you want to go."

The thought of going back outside made the idea of drinking with a stranger more comfortable. Will watched his sister dress up in a long raincoat with an attached hood and pull rubber galoshes over her shoes. Outside Will knew the February east wind was howling down the streets of Westminster and whipping up the black waters of the Thames; the street and the pavements were puddled in water.

They both watched Josephine go off to face the elements. A taxi was waiting downstairs but even the few yards to the open door required the raincoat and the rubber boots. Heath got up and found a whisky glass, half filled it with ice cubes and poured on the amber liquid, handing the glass to Will.

"I'm writing a book on Africa," said Heath. "Maybe you could help. Are you enjoying being back in England?"

"No."

The silence stretched for a few moments.

"Not a man of many words," said Heath, refilling his glass.

"Not on that subject."

"Amazing how people love giving away other people's money," said Heath, looking at the newly closed front door of the flat. "It makes them feel so good. Almost like a drug. Totally unsustainable of course. By the time your children's generation go on pension or get sick from old age there won't be any money left and nothing to show for it. Such a pity. A nation of bums and parasites. Our ancestors who created the world's greatest empire must be turning in their graves. I gather you miss your life in Africa?"

"Yes I do."

"Why don't you go back?"

"Sometimes people have to be realistic. I'm trying to be. They want the whites out of Africa. My parents always said you should never stay in another man's house when you are not wanted. Maybe you have to be very thick-skinned to do that kind of thing… If I had never gone out in the first place it wouldn't have mattered. My own fault. Running away from two years in the air force. I never liked taking orders. You obviously know Jo quite well."

"We cry on each other's shoulders on a regular basis with the help of a bottle of Scotch."

"I'm glad she's got a friend."

"Byron says you're not happy running his Africa desk."

"Why would he tell you?… Sorry, that sounds rude."

"I'm the conduit. Rather like the booze supplier during prohibition in the States; never had to advertise but everyone knew where to go. Newspaper reporting is only one of my talents. All those black customers your brother has in Africa first came through me."

"Byron's helping these men to rob their people blind. Makes me sick."

"Funny. Being tossed out of Africa I'd have you enjoying the irony."

"Byron thought that."

"And he thought wrong. Interesting… The title of my book is *The New Rape of Africa*."

"The British never raped Africa."

"But the conventional wisdom says we did. The black leaders say we robbed the place, ah, hah. Most important, the wonderful liberal press of a wonderful liberal world says colonialism was an ogre. So we stole them blind, forget about the roads and railways and the invention of the wheel. Have a drink with me to the end of the white man's garden."

"Did you meet my friend Laurie Hall when he was in England?"

"More than once."

"What happened? Why hasn't anyone heard from him?"

"Spent his money. Thinks he made a fool of himself. Went back to Africa."

"Where?"

"No one knows. I'll let you know if I hear anything on my travels. There are whites in the Congo. Mercenaries for General Mobutu. Keep him in power, probably. No one really knows what happens when the colonial power moves out. Mostly Whitehall thinks it is good riddance to bad rubbish, to quote a phrase I heard as a schoolboy. You ask your brother. Knows more than most. He's making money out of the mess. To businessmen that's all that matters."

Across in the West End of London, less than three miles away, Byron Langton was attending a cocktail party thrown by the chairman of Lloyd's of London, the largest insurance market in the world. Byron had been surprised and pleased to receive the invitation which included his wife, Lady Fiona Langton, who was four months pregnant and happier than she had ever been in her life.

Casually, as if the chairman was doing an outsider a favour in inviting him into the club, it was suggested to Byron that if he approached the chairman again, he could become a 'Name' at Lloyd's and reap untold profits without laying out a penny.

"You just stand surety for the syndicate. Hundreds of years of experience. Safe as the Bank of England. Marvellous institution. Americans have been trying to create a Lloyd's for half a century. Never succeed. Tradition. Once you get the hang of things, Langton, you can put your name on as many syndicates as you like. We account three years in arrears so you'll have to wait for your first cheque. Your father-in-law has been a 'Name' for years. Give my secretary a ring on Monday and she'll do the necessary. Welcome to Lloyd's, Langton. Give my regards to your father, Lady Fiona."

The man put his hand briefly on Byron's shoulder. A king of old England would not have done it better.

Will's first affair had ended with a cheque for ten pounds four shillings and sixpence, a note from Lindsay Healy in Australia wishing him a good life in England and a regret the photographs had not sold better. The Lady, Will surmised without a great deal of regret, had gone on to better things and he had been wise not to rely on other people to make him money. The last years in his twenties were proving that his young dreams had been nothing more than dreams and life's reality was a more commercial world where success had nothing to do with heart and soul but a more mundane product of life called money. People in the world outside of the bush and Barotseland did everything for money and even the Chief had followed his cash over to England.

Sitting in the dentist's waiting room, listening to the drill from the other side of the closed door with fear more real than any lion had ever been able to create, Will picked up a three-month-old copy of the *National Geographic* magazine from the coffee table, his eye caught by the front page with its quarter shot of a fish eagle taking a fish from a river in full flight. More conscious of the dentist's drill than the magazine, he flipped the pages and found himself admiring page after page of animal photography. Some of the shots he wished he had taken himself so he turned back to the beginning of the article and instantly felt sick in his stomach. The writer was one Lindsay Healy, the story the Zambezi River. Will looked carefully from photograph to photograph, page to page, remembering mostly, exactly where he had been when the photograph had been taken. There was even a picture of his Goliath heron. Nowhere did he find mention of his name.

Some weeks later, casually, he asked Heathcliff Mortimer what a lead article of eleven pages with photographs in *National Geographic* would fetch for a freelance photographer and writer.

"Between ten and fifty thousand pounds, depending on the uniqueness of the location. Why, do you want me to write the copy round some of your photographs?"

"Somebody's done it using my photographs."

"Hope you got paid well?"

"Ten pounds four shillings and sixpence."

"He must have seen you coming."

"She."

"Explains everything. Join the club, Will Langton. Women... It's five o'clock. Let's get out of here. You don't by any luck feel like getting drunk?"

"I think I do."

"Good. I like getting drunk. You think that secretary of Byron's would like to join us?"

"No women, Heath. Seems I don't have any luck with women."

Outside on the pavement they turned left past Cox's & King's bank and walked to Johnny Pike's bar in Soho. The pavements were wet and shiny from the street lights but it had stopped raining.

It was the same bar from which Josephine had gone for her abortion.

· · ·

WILL HAD TAKEN a bedsitter in Holland Park which he knew looked like ten thousand others in the poorer parts of London. The floor was three-quarters covered in a threadbare carpet that could have been an imitation Persian when a long time ago it had been new. The single bed sat in the corner diagonally across from the alcove that served as the kitchen. Across the alcove hung an old curtain to hide the kitchen cupboard and the two-plate gas stove that worked off shillings in a meter. The two drawers to the kitchen cupboard stuck at an angle every time he tried to pull them open.

At first Will had hung his guns on the walls to remind himself of better times, but after a week he had taken them down and locked them in their cases which he pushed under the bed. There were no photographs to frame and hang on the bare walls as they had all been shipped to Australia. Will had thought of writing to Lindsay to ask about the article but it had never been in his nature to complain or make a scene. The room had a gas heater, and the bed was warm and any thought of Africa made him crave for the bush so he put it out of his mind.

He was paid seventeen pounds and eight shillings every week and gave just under a third to his landlady for the rent. He worked hard in the office to keep his mind away from the big river, staying as late as possible to avoid the Tube train back to the room and a miserable kind of solitude so different to that which he had enjoyed in Africa, the one open and full of space up to the stars, the other cramped and with a view as far as the ceiling.

Twice Will had brought up the subject of the ivory but Byron had a knack of changing the subject so well, they always ended up talking about something else. Vaguely, Will knew he was a disappointment to his brother but as hard as he tried he could find no comfort in diverting millions of pounds of African money into bank accounts that did not even have a name. Bills of lading and certified invoices of origin became second nature along with back-to-back letters of credit and all the other paraphernalia that went with the paperwork of shipping and commerce. He was sure his brother was growing richer by the day but it mattered nothing to him.

There was enough money to drink three pints of beer in the pub down the road from his bedsitter before going home and turning off the lights and shutting tight his eyes to see the animals of Africa and not the squalor in which he lived, both physical and mental. There was no escape for a man of almost thirty without any skills and the days went by one after the other and with them the days of his life.

It was as if his life had finished before it had begun. Even the image in his mind of the girl on the Ledge had begun to fade, slipping higher up into the sky between the fleece-white clouds to disappear, his arms stretched to heaven and all eternity, for no purpose, the reason for his life gone away with his dreams.

And at night, when he was lucky, he would dream again he was back in the bush with his love for all eternity and he was happy in his dreams, floating up through the clouds with the great bush of Africa spread out below with all its animals and birds. There were many mornings when on waking he wished the waking had never been. Then he wondered if heaven was like his dreams and hell his bedsitter.

THERE WAS something wrong with ten pounds four shillings and sixpence and Heathcliff Mortimer was going to find out what and why. He also had an idea. Armed with a copy of *National Geographic*, he talked to some of his many friends in the newspaper and magazine business. Everyone said the wildlife photography was superb.

Heath could see the problem with wildlife photography in a small-size magazine was the miniaturisation of the picture, giving some but not all the feeling evoked by the bush. Mostly the animals dominated the frame and the background was lost to the readers' imagination. Four of his friends had made the same comment. 'Pity the pictures aren't bigger.'

Damian Huntly was a magazine publisher who also specialised in coffee-table books where the size of the animals would be seen together with their backgrounds. The leopard at a waterhole would be clear down to the last spot, but so would the colours of the harlequin quails that drank alongside the cat, their trail of tiny footprints visible in the mud.

"Can you imagine those photographs the size of one of your books?" asked Heath, sitting across from Damian Huntly in the publisher's Regent Street office.

"Yes I can but what's the point?" asked Damian Huntly, handing back the three-month-old copy of *National Geographic* and tapping it at the same time. "These people will have bought exclusive rights to those pictures forever. They own them, not your friend. Anyway, how can you prove he took the photographs? The byline is Lindsay Healy."

"Will says he took them and he's not a person to tell a lie. He's lived in the bush for years."

The smile that spread across Damian Huntly's face told Heath the man did not believe anyone ever told the truth, especially when it was to the liar's advantage.

"We don't have to use those actual photographs. Will has thousands."

"Where are they? Show me."

"He gave them to Lindsay Healy."

"So she probably owns them legally. *National Geographic* would not print photographs without being certain they had bought them from a legal source. But what are you talking about?"

"A glossy book with photographs as good if not better than these, in full colour, with a brief, backup story written by me. Call it *Zambezi River*. Shelley Lane's made enough money with her Zambezi album just singing about Africa. She's a friend of Will Langton's, the photographer."

"Would she write a foreword?"

"Probably. Though she's not in the best shape right now."

"So the rumours tell. Booze can be a terrible thing."

"Or a pleasure," smiled Heath. "If I can regain the rights to the unpublished photographs will you consider a book?"

"Probably."

Over lunchtime drinks a week later, Heath was pleased to find a young reporter about to go out to Australia to cover the referendum on whether Aboriginals should be included in the census. The reporter had a reputation in Fleet Street of being a stud.

"Can I put you onto something in Sydney?" asked Heath of the young stud.

"If it's good, why won't your paper cover the story?"

"It's a girl. A very pretty girl, from all reports. She likes men I'm told."

"You're putting me on, Heath."

"No, actually. But I want a favour in return. She has some photographs belonging to another young friend of mine and I want them back again. When are you leaving?"

"Tomorrow. Why would she want to meet me?"

"I think she will when you mention my friend's name. Where are you staying?"

"The Wentworth."

"Her office is next door. What a nice coincidence. Her name is Lindsay Healy. Give me a ring when you come back."

The envelope Heath handed to the reporter had Lindsay's address on the outside with inside a short letter from Will Langton.

During Sunday lunch in Heath's Chelsea flat prior to meeting the young reporter, he had asked Will if he wanted to make some money.

"I can't think how but of course. My brother doesn't overpay and the bedsitter grates on my nerves."

"But I thought you had a lot of money?" said Heath, "Laurie Hall told me Byron had given you a substantial introductory fee for the crocodile skins."

"He was wrong. That was Laurie's show. I didn't want to be part of a massacre. Ivory from our safari operation was something I sold without thinking through the implications. When you first get to Africa, you think the wildlife is limitless, but it isn't. The wilderness is shrinking in direct proportion to man's population growth... Even my ivory nest egg seems to have disappeared. Byron won't talk about it; my brother likes to talk about his successes, not his failures. He warned me that not all venture investments make money and I just assume I was unlucky. Everything in England is so expensive. In Africa if I wanted food I put a line in the river. Everything you do in London costs money and seventeen pounds eight shillings doesn't go far. When did you get into journalism?"

"When I was fifteen."

"That's it, you see. What my mother always said, if I didn't get a proper job and proper training I would end up in the poor house. Funny how mothers are often so right."

"I have a publisher interested in a wildlife photo-journal. Big colour, glossy. Twenty thousand print. Expensive."

"To take all my photographs again would take years. That one shot of the old leopard at the waterhole with the quail took me six months of patience. Leopard are mostly nocturnal. Those photographs I gave Lindsay were priceless."

"Did you sign anything?"

"I think so. Yes. A sort of hire and release contract, I think. I don't know. I always trust people. Mother says I'm stupid. She's probably right... Do you think I could have a little more of the roast chicken? Can't roast chicken on two gas rings. Last Sunday my sister-in-law gave me lunch which was very nice of her but I do feel like the poor relation."

"How's the baby?"

"Absolutely fine. Like everything else of Byron's, absolutely fine. Boy's healthy, will probably be good looking, go to Stanmore and take a First at Oxford and end up running his father's bank. My mother is tickled pink with a grandson so that's something. Tell me, Heath, how do you English put up with this weather? Month after month of miserable, cold, grey weather. Very depressing."

"But aren't you English?" laughed Heath.

"I'm African, I'm afraid."

"Why don't you go back?"

"Where to? Zambia won't have me. Rhodesia's in rebellion. Zaire is damn dangerous and South Africa is full of Afrikaners who hate the English. Hannes Potgieter warned me about South Africa. Anyway, I don't like apartheid any more than liberation movements. Both of them kill for power. No, old Africa was just fine. But it's gone."

"Do you think the colonial powers are wrong to pull out?"

"Let history be the answer to that one. What I see is country after country throwing out the pariah system of colonialism and changing it for something ten times worse... Have you seen Josephine recently?"

"Not for a month."

"She works too hard. She's also not happy."

"You're not happy?"

"No I am not. I'm not cut out to live in a row of houses that all look the same. I never did like being part of the herd. I don't want to be brainwashed by television and you journalists with your political correctness you think the public want to hear. I want to be an individual, my own man."

"Go out on your own in business."

"I wouldn't know where to begin and I don't have any money."

"You may with a book."

"Another pipe dream. I've had too many of those. No, the reality is a bedsitter, seventeen pounds eight shillings a week and filthy weather. Some people say I should be grateful. I have a job. Maybe they're right. The worst thing in life is to be shown something better and then have it disappear."

That afternoon, Will wrote the brief letter asking for the return of the photographs.

THE TELEPHONE CALL came to Kevin Smith from *National Geographic*'s office in New York. The man on the line said he was vice-president of the legal department.

"In your agreement with us you stated the photographs belonged to Kevin Smith Publications (Pty), 3rd Floor Bligh House, Bligh Street, Sydney, Australia. I want to see your agreement with the photographer who I understand is one William Edward Langton recently of Mongu in Zambia. If it is a royalty agreement, then we will require proof of payment to said W E Langton."

"Of course we paid him, Mr Lewerstein."

"Ten pounds four shillings and sixpence for thirty thousand pounds' worth of photographs? Better check, Mr Smith, or you'll be the one going to jail for stealing. Do I make myself clear?"

"Perfectly, Mr Lewerstein."

"A normal royalty agreement would pay half the thirty thousand pounds allocated to the photographs to the photographer who must have spent years giving us those fine shots. We would like to have telegraphic confirmation from your bankers within fourteen days that the amount of fifteen thousand pounds has been paid to W E Langton. I presume you will have his address?"

"I don't think we do. That was our problem. The man left Africa."

"Then seeing I have his address and you have his money, we don't have a problem."

The same day Kevin Smith received his phone call, Lindsay Healy received Will Langton's letter.

"You said he wasn't interested in money," stormed Kevin Smith.

"He wasn't. Someone else is behind all this."

"Well, whatever it is we don't have fifteen thousand pounds now or in fourteen days. Running two homes is expensive, Lindsay. You know that. You better get your arse over to London on the cheapest flight you can find on the 'fly now pay later' scheme. Take him his photographs. Screw the man again for all I care but get him to sign for full and final payment and send the bloody letter to New York before real shit hits our fan. We owe a lot of other people money."

"If you had sent him five thousand pounds we'd have got away with it."

"I didn't have five thousand pounds… I've promised to divorce Mahel but we can't even do that without money. How the hell did you get yourself pregnant anyway?"

"You know something, Kevin, you really are a sod."

"True. But you're a bitch. Look what you did to Will Langton."

LINDSAY FOUND Will in his bedsitter the following Saturday morning and gave him the airway bill for the carton of photographs that were waiting at Heathrow airport.

"You'd better come in, Lindsay. The gas heater is on but it doesn't make much difference. Why I wear gloves and a balaclava helmet, even inside the room. In the last century they would call this living in reduced circumstances. I can offer you a glass of sweet sherry, or brown sherry as my mother prefers to call it. Among the English for some reason, drinking sweet sherry is thought to be rather common. I like the stuff. It's also cheap. No, don't take off your overcoat."

"You don't seem surprised to see me."

"No, I'm not."

"Now, the point is, having returned your photographs I need a signature cancelling the royalty agreement we both signed."

"First a drink, Lindsay... No, before we talk about the photographs let's go down to the local pub instead. It'll be warm and they have a good ploughman's lunch, a euphemism for bread and cheese with pickled onions. Apart from Shelley Lane, you're the only person in London who knew the base camp. You even knew my Goliath heron. Let's have a few sherries and a pub lunch and talk about Africa. I don't know which has been colder in England, my body or my soul."

"You haven't found her?"

"No I haven't and I don't think I ever will. People change, Lindsay. Maybe we had a chance those years ago to match our souls, that girl and I. Now it would be too late. Both of us will have been poisoned by life."

They spent the weekend together, Lindsay and Will, sleeping in the one small single bed but never making love.

"What else can I do?" Lindsay said on the Sunday afternoon, her small bag packed and ready for the flight back to Australia. "He's what I know. We're similar. Probably both dishonest. He'll cheat on me as he cheated on her, whether we marry or not, which I doubt. I'll have my affairs when he grows too old to care a lot. I'll have his kid. People don't take marriage seriously anymore. I can go back now and resign and leave him and look for someone else and where will that get me? Another Kevin Smith? I'll be twenty-five next year, the age women begin to lose their power over men, even the good-looking women. If the business goes bang, it's a limited liability company so we will start again. Kevin hasn't signed surety for the company debts. Mahel might have to work which would be a laugh... You think this book deal will make you money?"

"Enough to get out of England, maybe. Some of these deals fade away before you get to them. You want me to come to the airport?"

"No point wasting money."

"Have a good life, Lindsay Healy."

"Don't say that. This time I do want to keep in touch. We had something for a few brief moments beside your big river. At least, I did, I think. You're not sore about the money?"

"Not much point if the company's bankrupt. Can't have what's spent. Maybe without your article I wouldn't have a chance of a book deal... It's possible to rationalise about everything. We can find tears or laughter. Just depends on the way we look at it."

"Thanks, Will."

"You're welcome."

. . .

THE FOLLOWING DAY, while Lindsay was flying back to Australia with a signed, full release from Will Langton witnessed by the girl from the next door bedsitter and her friend, Byron Langton was sitting at his office desk reviewing the six-monthly report from his Swiss bankers. The boom in commodity prices had made him richer than even he had imagined. All his suppliers for copper, chrome and iron ore had signed fixed-priced contracts and his buyers paid the London spot metal price on the day of shipment, the difference, sometimes forty per cent, accruing to Langton Merchant Bank. The newly nationalised Zambian copper mines had been caught on the way down and the way up. Some people in London even said the market had been deliberately manipulated. Whichever the reality, the real wealth flowed into Europe and America, away from newly decolonised Africa.

The only mistake Byron had made was to only buy his brother and Laurie Hall gold bullion when the price had risen from thirty-five US dollars an ounce to three hundred and twelve. Some of the financial papers predicted gold could rise to three thousand dollars due to the growth of inflation in Europe and North America. The figure standing to Will was over two hundred and ten thousand pounds and Laurie seventy thousand, two hundred pounds, this after the Swiss bank had deducted one per cent of the capital sum for storing the gold.

Byron swivelled his chair round to face the back wall. The amount of money would make his brother independent for life and probably unhappy. Laurie Hall would spend it in a couple of years and die of liver failure brought on by alcohol poisoning. More importantly, he had told neither Laurie nor his brother they owned the gold. Quietly, in his mind, he transferred the proceeds back to his own account, postponing, probably forever, the time he would tell his brother.

Byron dismissed the gold and thought about his brother. Despite Will's lack of enthusiasm, the man was honest and certainly intelligent. The transfer from the African commodities desk to London Town Music Limited, and particularly the management of Shelley Lane, would make his brother's life more interesting. To make his conscience less uncomfortable he would increase Will's wage to twenty-six pounds a week.

ON THE TUESDAY EVENING, Will carried the heavy carton of photographs onto a trolley and outside to a taxi he could not afford, giving the man Heathcliff Mortimer's address in Chelsea.

"Bring them to my flat, old boy," Heath had said on the phone. "And if you want my advice, don't mention any of this to your brother."

"Why ever not?"

"Employers like their staff to be beholden to them. Your brother has big ideas for you, Will, but he wants to be in control."

ON THE OTHER side of the world, Lindsay Healy caught a taxi to the flat half-paid for by Kevin Smith who met her at the door.

"Let's have a look," he said without looking at Lindsay. "You sent the original to New York?"

"Yes... In exchange for the photographs, Will agreed to forget the money from National Geographic. They're going to bring out a glossy hardcover. Damian Huntly will publish it."

"How soon?"

"Probably take them a year to reach the shops."

"Good. We can have one out in six months. It'll save our business. I've talked to the shops here and our distributors in Europe and America. That article in *National Geographic* has put us on the map."

"But we don't have the photographs."

"The best of them, we do. Had them copied. One lion looks much like another. We gave him back his damn photographs."

"He'll have the original to compare."

"By then we will be out of the financial shit and a good lawyer can argue for years... You did a bloody good job, Lindsay. Did you have to screw him to get him to sign?"

"No I didn't."

"Why ever not?"

"He didn't want to."

"Wasn't he any good the first time?"

"Kevin, you really are a bastard."

"Come on. We're going out to dinner. Told Mahel I'd be back Monday. Deals that come down like this make me horny."

SHELLEY LANE WOKE with a hangover that hurt every joint in her body. She lay awake unable to get out of bed and pour herself a drink. The accumulation of alcohol mixed in her blood had poisoned her system, swelling the joints of her knees and feet.

"Better suffer, baby. This one's bad," she said in her mind.

The pills were in bottles on the small table next to her bed. After three attempts she found what she wanted, swallowed two pills without water and waited for some of the pain to seep out of her body. There was nothing she remembered of the day before, not even the first drink. She had no idea of the time or the day. After the sedative began to calm her body she took two more pills from a smaller bottle and lay back on her bed. For the first time she noticed that outside her window the sun was shining. Far away she heard the loudhailer from a tourist boat on the Thames. Then her doorbell rang like a sound of thunder.

"Fuck off!" she screamed, jarring her jangled brains to the point of agony. She waited, breathless. Then the bell thundered again into her brain and she lurched out of bed and staggered down the corridor to the horrible door.

"Go to hell!" she screamed again.

"Please, Shelley. I want to talk to someone."

"Who the hell's that?"

"Will Langton."

"Go and screw yourself."

"I need help, Shelley."

"You need help! What the fuck do you think I need?"

"Then open the door."

Pulling back the catches, Shelley flung open the door.

"Shelley, you're naked."

"You think I sleep in my overcoat?... Hell, I feel terrible. Get inside before I really do die; though that wouldn't worry me. Now, what's your bloody problem?"

Will made the coffee while Shelly put on slacks and a sweater. The second lot of pills had taken effect, the upper making her feel a small part better.

"What do you want to talk about?" shouted Shelley rudely in the direction of her kitchen.

"Africa... You're the only one in London who's seen my Africa."

"You got me out of bed to talk about Africa, not about music?"

"Quite frankly, Shelley," said Will, coming back with two cups of coffee and a smile, "I couldn't care a tinker's cuss about music."

"But you're my bloody manager."

"By the way, you look quite cute with nothing on."

"I look like hell and feel like hell... Do you ever drink too much?"

"Sometimes. Shelley, you remember Lindsay Healy?" and he told her the story.

Two hours later, and with the help of more pills from the line of bottles on the side table by her bed, Shelley called a taxi. Together they went to Holland Park and the bedsitter. Shelley found the suitcase under the bed with the guns and pulled them out.

"Come on, lover, you can help."

"What are you doing?" asked Will.

"Packing. You're getting out of this dungeon."

"Where am I going?"

"Back to live with me and you can take that one whichever way you damn well like, Will Langton. Crazily enough, it looks like you need me more than I need you. And if my memory of Africa is right, you can cook."

"I don't think my brother will like this."

"I don't think your brother is getting the offer... You can leave a note for your landlady to keep the deposit. No way we're coming back here."

PART V

1972 TO 1974

15

*F*ive years later a destitute Laurie Hall was sitting in a chair in the lounge of Meikles Hotel, his crossed legs pushed under the low coffee table to hide the holes in the soles of his shoes. Next to him a small green canvas bag, that had once held his squash racket, clean white shorts and shirt and expensive gym shoes, contained his only worldly possessions: three pairs of well-washed underpants, a change of khaki shorts, shirt and an old toothbrush without any toothpaste. Over the top of his clothes rested a large plastic raincoat made from a flimsy, see-through material.

The eyes that stared at the farmers and their wives, farmers with good shoes and packets of cigarettes tucked into the specially large top pockets of their bush jackets, their wives in summer-weight print frocks, the children confident and well fed, saw nothing, the focus looking miles away over their heads, through the walls of the old colonial hotel into the past of failure.

Maybe somebody he knew would come and sit at any one of the three empty seats around his coffee table and buy him a cup of tea.

Six thousand miles away from Salisbury, Rhodesia, Byron Langton was speaking on the phone from London to the bullion manager at the Union Bank of Switzerland in Zurich, giving him precise instructions to sell the two parcels of gold bullion held by the bank under nominee to Langton Merchant Bank and reinvest the proceeds into West German industrial shares with a spread of no more than five thousand pounds into any one share. Account number 2759464 contained one hundred and fifty-two thousand pounds sterling, the original ten thousand pounds investment representing the bonus allocated to Laurie Hall for his work in shooting the crocodiles. The price fetched for the gold bullion was seven hundred and twelve US dollars per ounce, up from the original price of thirty-five dollars.

ACROSS THE ROOM in the Meikles Hotel's lounge, a tall gangling Englishman who, by the rich colour of his skin had spent most of his life in the bush, was watching Laurie Hall. Anthony Scott was twenty-seven years old and the name Ant, by which he was known in the Rhodesian army, belied his height of six foot three inches. There was not an ounce of fat on any part of his body and his sandy hair had been bleached almost white by the African sun.

Laurie Hall had spent the three previous nights sleeping on a wooden bench in Cecil Square, the small park next to Meikles Hotel that had been named after the founder of Rhodesia, Cecil John Rhodes. The January temperature was hot and humid until the rain came down in tropical deluge. Every night, Laurie had pulled the flimsy raincoat most carefully over his tucked up body on the bench, his head on the canvas bag, all covered expertly by the plastic so neither wind nor rain could damage the last few of his possessions. If it had not been for the hunger tearing at his belly, he would have enjoyed the dry warmth inside his cocoon.

The jacarandas in Cecil Square had long shed their pale blue flowers but a host of doves called to the morning as the new sun rose and began to steam off the rainwater from the roads as well as Laurie's raincoat which he hung over the back of the bench in the sun while he sat and looked at the day.

The years after landing in Cape Town from the *Edinburgh Castle* had not been good to Laurie Hall. He had drifted from job to job, drinking whatever he made, a man flushed with discontent. He had gone from a learner assistant on a tobacco farm in Rhodesia to an overseer on the roads, watching a gang of blacks dig the ditches in the blazing hot sun. Once he had panned for gold, finding three gold nuggets that kept him drunk for a week. Whenever possible he tried not to think of Shelley Lane and had long since stopped mentioning her name: no one who met the long-haired, bearded, usually penniless Laurie Hall believed the man could ever have met the famous singer, let alone been her lover. Everyone thought he was telling them lies.

He was thirty-seven years old and looked more like fifty, the only contradiction in his appearance the piercing blue eyes that could still count a herd of buck from a distance of two thousand metres. Thinking clearly of what to do to survive, he planned to raid the dustbins in the alley at the back of the hotel when the daylight went at six o'clock. Trying not to look conspicuous, he watched the surrounding tables changing many times.

In the old days, when he had flown down from Mongu on leave, he had lavishly tipped the waiters and particularly old Guru, the ancient waiter with the red sash and pepper-grey hair who remembered the better times and left the white man sitting in the chair for as long as he wished. When the table next door left their bread rolls uneaten, Guru in clearing the table made room for his tray by moving the plate onto Laurie's table along with the leftover butter and a knife. Laurie's hands shook while he buttered the rolls, trying not to cram the bread into his mouth while he hid the tears of gratitude.

"Do you mind if I sit down?" said Ant Scott, pulling out one of the empty chairs. Laurie looked up at the tall man and choked on the last of his roll. The eyes staring into the back of his head were dark green, the colour of the Atlantic Ocean in winter. Laurie waved at the vacant chair, trying to swallow the last of the bread and keep his holey shoes out of sight under the coffee table. Instinctively, his other hand touched the top of his squash bag to make sure it was there. This giant of a man, he had never seen before.

"Did you hear the news?" asked Ant Scott, sitting down in the chair, his long legs thrust out to the side of the coffee table. When he smiled, small crow's feet appeared at the corners of both eyes, legacy of his years hunting in the bush.

"I don't read the newspaper, or only sometimes," the sometimes when he could find a paper left at the table or left in a dustbin without being fouled by the rubbish.

"There was a major terrorist attack on farms in the northeast border close to Mozambique. They came up out of the valley."

"Who did?"

"The terrorists."

"How do you know?"

"It's my job. Can I buy you some tea or a drink?"

"A beer, please," said Laurie too quickly. Ant raised his hand to Guru showing two fingers together and in less than a minute Laurie was looking at a brown bottle of Castle beer, the sides dripping with condensation, the glass next to it frosted from the refrigerator. Clattering the side of the glass, he poured half the beer, raising a white head in his haste.

"Cheers," he said and brought his head down to the glass to drink, his arm already frozen with anticipation. "Hell, that's good," said Laurie putting down the empty glass still white from foam. The upturned bottle was steady for the second pour.

"When did you last have a beer?" asked Ant.

"Not for a while." Laurie drank the second half of his bottle of beer and put back the empty glass on the table. "You have no idea how good that tasted."

"Oh, I have, Mr Hall."

"So I do know you after all?"

"Not from a bar of soap."

"How do you know my name?"

"I asked Guru."

"Why?"

"Your eyes look a great distance. You've spent many years in the bush. Can I buy you another beer?"

"As many as you like but I can't reciprocate. What I have you see right here. You could say I'm on the bones of my arse. Guru knows. He looks after me."

"I saw... Most bums they kick out of Meikles before the first cup of tea... You can ride a horse, I presume?"

"Yes I can."

"And follow spoor in dry bush?"

"Usually. Leopard are difficult."

"From a horse at a trot?"

"That I never tried."

"You don't want to know my name?"

"Not unless you want me to." Laurie was looking over the man's right shoulder, trying to attract Guru. The taste of alcohol had been delicious.

"Where are you going after here?"

"To the dustbins at the back of the hotel and then the bench to the right of the fountain in Cecil Square."

"What happened, Mr Hall?"

"You really want to hear?"

"An educated man down to park benches must have a tale."

"Are you a writer? Newspaperman?"

"I can't spell. Left school when I was fifteen and roamed the bush for ten years. Then I joined the army. Had skills they wanted. Knew the bush. Like you. Suddenly the likes of us bums are in high demand."

"What do you mean?"

"We're going to have a war on our hands. Sanctions haven't worked to kick the whites out of Rhodesia so the communists have armed the blacks. Probably the Americans have sent in guns as well. Who knows? Doesn't matter, really. But the guns are real. The bush is difficult country to fight. The Shona tribe was never aggressive, Matabele, the remnant Zulu, yes. The Shona farmed and ran cattle and kept to his own business for centuries. He was never a hunter. The likes of you and me are hunters. Why we are going to win the war. I'm raising a group of men to hunt terrorists from horseback. Go where the Land Rovers can't go. Follow the spoor. When I've heard your story maybe I'll ask you to join us."

"Where do you want me to start?"

"At the beginning. Right at the beginning. Two more beers, Guru," he said to the black man now standing at his elbow.

When the man left, Laurie Hall was drunk, drinking on an empty stomach. With the force of long habit he stood up on his feet and bent slowly for the squash bag. Carefully, he walked out through the tables and chairs amid the hum of other people's conversations.

Turning right out of the hotel front door onto the wet pavement he walked back into Cecil Square and found his lonely bench. With the dignity of the drunk, he slowly forced the raincoat out of the bag and over his body. When he slept, he dreamed he was back by the river, at Hannes Potgieter's old base camp. Shelley Lane was there. He was happy in his dream.

IT TOOK Ant Scott a week to check up on the story told to him in Meikles Hotel. It then took him another week to find Laurie Hall. The man who had been known with favour by the head waiters from Quaglino's to the Savoy Grill had finally lost his will to survive.

The alcohol on a three-days empty stomach had given Laurie the cramps and made him vomit even when there was nothing but bile to vomit. The pain from head to toe was excruciating. The few friends he had once had in Salisbury crossed the road when they saw him walking towards them on the same pavement. The only length of anything in his canvas squash bag was the plastic raincoat.

As the sun was greying the morning sky three days after drinking his last pint of beer, Laurie Hall jumped from his wooden seat in Cecil Square, the long raincoat looped over the bough of a jacaranda tree, the end tied round his neck. The plastic gave sufficiently to prevent the snapping of his neck but he hung from the tree, the holey soles of his shoes three inches from the ground, the mourning doves calling in the trees around. A young trooper from the British South African Police, the force started by Cecil John Rhodes, saw the body hanging from the tree.

Laurie Hall came round looking up at the young policeman.

"Shit," he said, "I can't even kill myself properly." The policeman was scooping water from the fountain and forcing Laurie to swallow.

"What's your name?" asked the trooper.

"What's it to you?"

"Routine. It's against the law to kill yourself. You'll have to come to the charge office. Then we'll have the police doctor look at you."

"Do something wrong and everyone wants to know your business. Otherwise you can rot in hell."

"Things are never so bad the next day."

"You're too young to know."

LADY FIONA LANGTON had given Byron three children in exactly the right order, one boy and two girls. She was editor of Langton Publishers and the first volume of Heathcliff Mortimer's *Africa Yesterday, Today and Tomorrow* had sold ten thousand copies in hardback, thanks mainly to good reviews in the *Daily Garnet* and its satellite publications in the provinces. Byron had purchased four provincial newspapers and one in Australia.

The day Ant Scott found Laurie Hall in a police cell, the marks of his attempted hanging still visible around his neck, Byron and his wife were visiting a country estate with a view to establishing a new dynasty now the cash flow in eighty per cent of his companies was positive.

The house outside East Horsley in the county of Surrey would be bought by a company in Lichtenstein which in turn would be owned by nominees of the Union Bank of Switzerland. The company would rent the estate to Langton Merchant Bank for a peppercorn rent with one wing of the old house used by the bank to house the accounts department of the entire Langton financial empire. With one stroke Byron would buy a two thousand-acre country estate with money that had never been subject to tax, the cost of the accounts department would drop forty per cent, the house servants and gardeners would be company employees and tax-deductible and any loss made by farming the estate largely as a shooting lodge for Langton clients would be tax-deductible from banking income. More importantly, the children would grow up the same way Fiona's ancestors had grown up for five hundred years.

Largely, trading from African mineral exports had paid for the estate.

. . .

AT A MILITARY CAMP thirty miles from Hilary Bains's mission station, Sixpence, Fourpence and Onepenny were undergoing weapon training. The drill sergeant was a Russian as were the weapons.

The three trackers had bought as many cattle as their bonus money from the crocodile hunt would allow, their ancient farming methods that had worked for centuries never once suggesting they ask where the cows would find their food, in old Africa there was always grazing and plentiful water. A combination of foot and mouth disease and drought had left the trackers destitute two years before Laurie Hall found himself sleeping on a bench in Cecil Square.

The same skills they had taught Laurie Hall, the skills that had been taught to them by Hannes Potgieter, were needed by the Russians to push the last of the colonials out of Southern Africa.

When the time was right, each tracker would back a group of guerrilla fighters over the Zambezi River into Rhodesia and through the deep bush to the soft targets of white farms and mines, the ZIPRA soldiers of Joshua Nkomo doing the fighting before being led back by the trackers to the safety of Zambia.

For Sixpence, Fourpence and Onepenny it was another job like any other. Before the new job for which they were thankful, none of the three had ever heard of Russia, communism or Joshua Nkomo.

FOR THREE MONTHS Laurie Hall trained in a military camp outside Bulawayo before joining the Horse Scouts at their forward base in the Zambezi Valley. The camp was above the Victoria Falls almost on the Botswana border.

Mongu was over one hundred miles upriver but on the other side of the water. Each trooper in the Horse Scouts was responsible for his own horse. Every one of the animals was salted, having been bitten by the tsetse fly and found immune. The rains had been over for a month but the camp was hot and humid. Laurie's new job was to patrol the riverbank on horseback, looking for hostile spoor and terrorist food and ammunition dumps brought across over the years by civilians in preparation for the second Chimurenga or war of liberation.

The overall troop was commanded by Ant Scott but the horsemen patrolled great distances in pairs. They were scouts, not to make contact with the terrorists unless attacked or they had to intervene.

The irony of having left England in the first place to avoid national service and two years in the British Army was not lost on Laurie Hall. His mind shut out the past and the future. Why the strange trail of life had led him into the valley to hunt down men gave him as little pleasure as trying to hang himself. He was alive and the instinct to stay alive was stronger than the one which wished to kill himself. And to stay alive he needed a job.

Ant Scott had paired off inexperienced young men with strength and older men with experience of the bush. The brawn of one would help the brains of the other, or so his theory went, and he sent his men out into the wilderness.

Mike Barrow was twenty-two years old, a virgin from lack of opportunity and the great-grandson of a pioneer who had helped raise the Union Jack at Fort Salisbury in 1889, pronouncing in the process that all the land of the Shona belonged to the Queen of England through the good offices of Cecil John Rhodes, a self-made imperialist backed by his wealth from diamonds and gold in South Africa. The Queen of England had given him a charter, based on dubious mineral concessions obtained from the local chiefs, to find the legendary gold of King Solomon and the Queen of Sheba in the ancient lands of Ophir, the land of Monomatapa in the heart of darkest Africa. Rhodes had told Mike Barrow's great-grandfather there was more gold in the hinterland than all the gold in the Witwatersrand and he was wrong.

The first night Laurie Hall and Mike Barrow camped next to the river deep in the mopani forest, Laurie started collecting wood for the big fire in the way Will Langton had shown him what to do.

"Major Scott said not to make fires the terrs can target," said Mike Barrow.

"On that score Anthony Scott is an ass," said Laurie Hall, going about his business of collecting thick pieces of fallen wood. "There are more bloody lion, leopard, hyena, jackal and wild dog in this bush than terrs by a multiple of ten thousand to one, but I do have a plan for Moscow's messengers of liberation. And I'll take another bet, young Mike. The poor bloody terrorists exploited by the Great Party of Liberation which will tie their balls in a knot far worse than the British will die in far greater numbers from wild animals than any firefight with our great security forces. You believe Uncle Laurie; build a fire. I've been here before. For a lion we are just part of the food chain. Also, I hate eating cold food when there's game to be shot without a game ranger telling me what to do. In a war, the rules go. We make our own. Now, young Mike, you get the fire prepared while I go off and shoot us something to eat."

"You're going to shoot with an automatic rifle?"

"One single shot. And there's another lesson from my friend Will Langton. Never, but never shoot more than you can eat."

It was almost dark when Mike heard the single shot from upriver. The tree frogs and cicadas fell silent for a brief moment before resuming the croaks and screeches that deafened the night. He waited, clutching his new FN rifle, and as he waited the last of the light went and he could hear fish plopping in the Zambezi River and the grunting of the hippos in the pools they had passed when a half-kilometre from making camp. Up above, the planets were visible, the moon nowhere to be seen, the void of the great universe as black as ink.

Mike Barrow, fourth generation Rhodesian, was too scared to light the fire. After five minutes he wet his pants, the hot liquid spurting down inside his right trouser leg. He waited for two hours without sign or sound of Laurie Hall and then a sickle moon rose up from the bush and the new, small light showed him the shadows of the trees. Even the horses on a long rein had not moved in the night. An owl called from across the river and was answered from the top of the mopani tree to the right of Mike Barrow, raising prickles of primeval fear all over his body. Never before in his life had he felt so much an animal. Briefly, he wondered if the other animals could smell his fear. Mike Barrow waited... In the dark of the bush an animal crashed away in fear followed by the terrible sound of a caught bush pig about to die, rending the night with its agony of death. When he turned away from the snarling and thrashing, Laurie put a vice-grip on his shoulder.

"You don't want to shoot me," said Laurie, calmly. "That's a leopard eating that pig two hundred metres away and you're sitting in the dark, young Mike. Light the bloody fire, old boy, or we'll go the way of that bloody pig."

"Why were you so long?"

"You pissed in your pants?"

"Yes...a long time ago."

"Waiting for the moon... You try and walk through those trees in the dark. Young impala ram. He'll eat well."

Laurie put a match to the dry leaves under the pile of wood and within seconds fire leapt out into the night, showing the trunks of the trees.

"Bring the horses closer, Mike. Closer to the fire. We lose those horses and we might as well be dead. My friend Will Langton tried walking it once... You would have liked to meet Hannes Potgieter."

"Who's he?"

"The fountain of all our knowledge, passed down by generations of Boers, Afrikaners... Haunch of venison cooked over hot coals and brushed by the smoke of the fire. Young Mike, go and rinse out your pants in the river. I do not like the smell of stale urine... And please mind the crocodiles, though luckily there are not as many as there used to be."

Laurie Hall made a tripod from green wood he cut from the undergrowth. Searching, he found a straight sapling and cut the base with his hunting knife, the blade nine inches long and sharp as a razor, the product of his first pay from the army. While he whittled away the bark, he listened to the sounds of the bush, listening subconsciously for the sound of danger. For the moment he was happy. Mike Barrow had taken his rifle to the shallow pool and when he came back Laurie could no longer smell an unflushed public toilet.

With the tripod far enough away from the fire not to burn, Laurie stuck the haunch of venison with the bark-free sapling and propped the meat close enough to the heat of the fire to cook. The rest of the impala ram he began cutting into strips for biltong. Each long strip of bloody meat he hung over the bough of a tree next to the fire where the wood smoke would taint the dried strips of game.

When he had finished with the carcass, Laurie hung it in a tree three feet away from the fire and on the other side of their camp from the river. Mike Barrow sat on a fallen tree, one an elephant had pushed over during the previous year's dry season, and his army pants began to dry out. Being cavalry, they were heavy trousers with leather patches to protect the inside of their legs from saddle sores. Mike had placed a small billycan for coffee next to the fire on a flat piece of ground, two coffee bags floating on top of the river water.

Laurie walked out of the light from the fire, down towards the river. When his eyes were ready, he looked up at the universe and wondered at the myriad of stars; the Milky Way, the second lacy layer of terrestrial light above the nearer stars. A yellow moon shone up the surface of the river, flat and oily black in the night. After ten minutes communing with the unknown universe, he walked back to the fire. Mike Barrow had turned the haunch of venison without being asked and steam was no longer rising from his trousers.

"Why did God make mosquitoes?" asked Mike Barrow.

"Why did he make man, if he did?"

"You don't believe in God?"

"Darwin's theory of evolution is pretty convincing. I don't believe in the instant creation of Adam and Eve. Religion is a crazy way to keep man under control. Threaten him with eternal hellfire and he might behave himself without being watched. A thinking savage? That's dangerous. The laws of nature appeal to me more than the laws of man or the laws of God as written by man. There are many stories in the Bible. The distillation of man's philosophy ever since he could think and imagine himself important enough to merit a God. I'm an agnostic, young Mike. I don't know and most men don't know for certain any more than me. From my experience, too many of those who say they know for certain have an ulterior motive. Try the new liberation theology for a current example. Whenever politicians and priests start agreeing with each other, beware... You can turn the meat again. That's the law of nature. This Rhodesia is overpopulated with man so now we fight each other. England was overcrowded when your great-grandfather came up with Johnson and Selous. Then there were open spaces, millions upon millions of game and less than half a million people. Now there are six or seven million people and it's overcrowded. We English thought the open spaces of Africa would last forever. They didn't. They thought the same in America. In America, they killed off the locals. We didn't. There is something a little immoral when America tells us how badly we are behaving... That coffee ready?... We are all animals, young Mike, and anyone telling you different is a liar."

"You think we will win this war?" asked Mike, passing Laurie a mug of black coffee.

"Of course not."

"Then why are you fighting?"

"Same reason they are. Money... Then maybe I'm sick of this life and want a way out."

"Do you think we should have colonised Africa in the first place?"

"At the time it was a great adventure," said Laurie. "Most of it was empty land claimed by some chief as his hunting ground but never used, never occupied. Is the moral right of it all where you are coming from? Livingstone was bringing his God. So was Moffat. To save the savage from the pits of hell. The empire loved a religious crusade to make conquest right. Priests and politicians with a common goal. Dangerous. According to modern anthropology, backed by some very convincing skeletons, we, that is man, came out of Africa in the first place. With equal insanity you can say we were reclaiming our birthright... I could do with a drink. Man drinks or takes drugs to remove his mind from a world made mad by himself. We don't like the world we created. Most probably we don't even like ourselves. That's why we like wars, Mike Barrow. So we can kill people. And we think by killing other people we will make ourselves feel better."

TWO HUNDRED AND ninety-three miles from the roasting venison, Heathcliff

Mortimer was sitting in a hotel with no running water. Something had gone wrong with the municipal supply. It had gone off that morning, and it was now nine o'clock at night. With his body itching from mosquito bites with nothing to treat them with, Heath had gone down to the bar where he was drinking brandy made from cane spirit. There was no whisky and no soda water in Lusaka, the capital of Zambia.

Zambia, in full compliance with the United Nations resolution on Rhodesia, had closed its border with the rebel state to the south and largely cut off Zambia's road and rail connection to the outside world. Erratic shipments of copper left the mines on the longer route to Lobito in Angola where the liberation armies of Angola regularly cut the Benguela railway line in their war with the colonial Portuguese. Very little was coming into Zambia and very little was going out.

The most visible source of income for the government was the prolific liberation movements in exile fighting the whites in Rhodesia, South Africa, Mozambique, Angola and South West Africa, all sponsored by the Russians and Chinese. The Zambian politicians in Lusaka spent their time flying round the world screaming at the West to reimburse them for their sacrifice in the fight against colonialism.

Heathcliff Mortimer had come to write up the moral indignation of a country raped by the colonial power who in the process had not had the forethought to leave behind an alternative rail and road route to the sea. Heath had shaken his head with wonder and admiration at the ability of the Zambians to keep the British, in particular, feeling guilty. As he was to say in the second volume of his book, before Cecil Rhodes there were no roads, railways and copper mines and no moral indignation for the lack of them. It was an extortionist's dream come true and Heath had smiled at the air-conditioned Mercedes-Benz cars cruising the unswept streets of Lusaka above the broken water supply pipes. He did not have to ask who were the owners of the luxury cars paid for by the British taxpayer to assuage their colonial guilt. Wisely, with an eye to future exploitation, Heath pointed out, the Russians and Chinese gave guns and ammunition.

Down the end of the bar a voluble young black man was entertaining a senior member of the African National Congress of South Africa. They were both laughing and enjoying themselves. They were drinking Scotch whisky from a special bottle hidden by the barman under the counter and Heathcliff Mortimer smiled at the reality of Third World politics.

He ordered another local brandy. It was alcohol, and he had needed to get drunk. Fourteen months from his seventieth birthday was no age to be staying in hot climates without running water. He had tried talking to the barman without success and he was now trying to listen to the conversation of the two black men at the other end of the bar. They were talking in English which he knew they would not do if alone in the bar. It was the prize snobbery of the Third World, showing off the residue of their education. Heath smiled to himself. The two men were making heavy weather out of keeping up their conversation in English. He was bored and a little drunk and picked up his glass and walked down the bar. The worst they could do was tell him to go to hell and the best they could do was allow him to buy a round of Scotch whisky. The greeting when it came was a total surprise.

"Hello, Mr Mortimer. I wondered when you would recognise me, Paul Mwansa. I met you in London through Josephine Langton. Jo and I were going out together. Don't you work for her brother?"

"Yes I do," said Heath thinking on his feet, having not recognised him in the dull light of the bar.

"This is a friend of mine from the ANC. We are helping him fight apartheid."

"That's very good. Can I buy you gentlemen a drink? What are you having?"

"I only drink Scotch," said Paul Mwansa. "So does my friend."

"Mr Barman," called Heath, allowing himself a small smile. "Three Scotch whiskies please. Doubles."

When the new drinks were poured, Heath raised his glass. "To the liberation of Africa," he said.

"That's a very good toast," said the man from the ANC without a name.

"I know it is. Everybody in the whole wide world would like to be liberated. Very few are."

"How is Josephine?" said Paul with the air of old proprietorship.

"Not very well, as a matter of fact."

"Why is that?"

"The Labour Party is out of power in England and Josephine is out of a job and out of a salary and money. She was a junior minister in the Labour government."

"She's still a Member of Parliament?"

"Not anymore. She lost her seat."

"But she must have made some money," said Paul Mwansa.

"Not in England. We take a rather poor view of corruption in our governments. Maybe in the future we will catch up with the rest of the world. I rather hope not. Now, can my paper buy you another drink?"

"Why ever not?" said Paul Mwansa.

'Indeed, why ever not?' said Heath to himself. There was just enough in the bottle for three more drinks.

THREE HUNDRED AND fifty-four miles from Lusaka towards the West, Hilary Bains was fighting another bout of his recurrent malaria. He was so thin that his wife Mary was not sure whether he would live. They had been married almost fourteen years and none of the family were strong. Mary knew it was the river. They were too close to the river, the mosquitoes and the malaria. Malcolm, the boy, was also sick and Penny, the girl, had never been strong growing up in the bush. Hilary thought it was God's way of allowing the family to serve Him through serving the poor and sick, lost in the wilderness of Barotseland, a Barotseland that now only existed as part of Zambia, the old British Protectorate lost in the liberation. None of the Bains's children had ever been outside the mission station, their only education coming from their parents and the books sent to the mission school by the London Missionary Society. They could speak Lozi as well as English and they had never worn shoes. Hilary and Mary believed in leading by example.

Limited medicine had reached the mission from the outside which kept them alive and strong enough to preach the word of God. The new government, mostly, just ignored them. Most of the whites in Zambia had left the country after their farms and businesses were confiscated and handed over to loyal members of UNIP, the ruling party that had won the 'one man one vote' election. The small farm at the mission outside Mongu was so poor that it was left alone, coveted by no one as it scratched at the soil to give the children in the school and the patients in the makeshift hospital one meal a day. The mission was in permanent crisis. For Mary and Hilary, there was work and six hours' sleep and nothing in between, not even recognition by the local authority or the far distant mission in London.

A week after Laurie Hall and Mike Barrow had eaten the haunch of venison, the boy, Malcolm, died of malaria. Mary said it was the will of God but Hilary was not so sure. Recovering enough to bury his only son, the Reverend Hilary Bains, for the first time, realised he had lost his faith. For fear of hurting his wife he kept the revelation to himself. At the age of thirty-eight he had lost his God and with it the meaning to his life. Being the man he was, he blamed no one but himself.

COMRADE JACK HAD BEEN the garden boy of a very nice English family who lived in Bulawayo. For the first fifteen years of his life he had lived in a township outside the city, the place of the killings, the old capital of Lobengula, King of the Matabele, who had been chased out of his royal kraal at Gu-Bulawayo by Cecil John Rhodes before the turn of the twentieth century. Jack had become Jack when he joined the very nice English family who gave him a room at the back of the house, 'boy's' rations of meat, mealie meal, salt, beans and soap plus three pounds a month. There was an outside shower next to the room and a flush toilet, neither of which Jack had seen before. In the old township he had used a 'long drop' for a toilet which constituted a deep hole in the ground, and the communal tap with which to wash himself. Inside the room was a bed with springs and a mattress.

Jack's job was to keep the leaves out of the swimming pool, the weeds out of the flowerbeds, and keep the grass cut to perfection. In the dry season he watered the lawn and the flowers with a long hosepipe.

By the time he was eighteen the young maid from the house next door spent most of her nights on the mattress in Jack's room and the nice English family never seemed to notice. Once a week there was a beer drink in one of the servant's rooms, chosen for when the owner of the house was away. There were ten years of Jack's life spent pleasantly watering the flowers but when UDI came along, Smith's declaration of independence from the British, followed by what Jack heard to be sanctions which meant absolutely nothing to him whatsoever, the nice English family decided to go and live in Australia where, even if they had wished, Jack would not have followed. Because of similar laws of immigration it would have made no difference if the nice English family had decided to go back and live in England. None of this Jack understood but he did understand that no one wanted to buy the house, and though he was told he could stay in the room until the house was sold when the new people would give him a job, there were no 'boy's' rations every week and no three pounds at the end of the month. After three months of being left on his own, Jack was not sure whether the departed nice English family were nice after all. For ten years he had seen them for every day of his life and they were gone, never to be seen again. Unbeknown to Jack, the same thing had happened or was happening all over colonial Africa. The white man was moving out, and fast.

The pretty young maid who had been replaced four times was not so sure of Jack without any food and money and his friends no longer invited him to the beer drink. Sadly, he walked back to the old township where he was recruited to fight to throw out the rest of the whites that had stolen his country.

They had offered him a job, so he went with them to a military training camp in Zambia where he had become Comrade Jack instead of the garden boy. The Russian instructor could not understand or pronounce the Matabele name he had lost at the age of fifteen. Jack had been easier so Jack it was.

In the training camp he was taught the great ideology of communism where everyone was equally rich, and how to use an AK-47 assault rifle, RPG rockets, and how to lay mines under roads. The Russian instructor thought all Africans knew how to live off the bush and survive in the wild so fieldcraft was left off the syllabus.

By the time Sixpence, Fourpence and Onepenny had paddled the freedom fighters across the great width of the Zambezi River, pointing out the crocodiles in the dusk on the sandbanks and the noses and eyes of the submerged hippopotami, Comrade Jack was terrified and refused to let the trackers leave them behind in the bush. At one point Comrade Jack had to point his gun at Onepenny. Comrade Jack was desperate.

In a quick conversation between themselves in Lozi – which by then they knew was understood by nobody else in the raiding party, conversation between Comrade Jack and the trackers being conducted in English – they agreed to stay with the freedom fighters until the time was right to melt away into the bush. Their job had been to deliver the freedom fighters onto enemy soil and not fight the war. The worry was Comrade Jack reporting them when he returned from his raid into the white-owned ranching district three hundred miles southeast from the Victoria Falls. By this time, having seen that Comrade Jack had no bushcraft whatsoever, the trackers thought the chances of the ill-trained soldiers coming back alive were very small. They had vivid memories of Hannes Potgieter, the Boer, in their minds. And Hannes Potgieter had told them there were many Boers in Rhodesia.

The second day had taken them fifteen miles from the river. The water bottles were empty, they had seen a pride of lion at close quarters, fortunately on a kill with full bellies, twice they had been mock-charged by elephant flapping their ears, and the trail they had left behind them was so obvious they might as well have blazed the mopani trees. All through the day, the tsetse fly had hovered over the party making a noise like an engine.

Half an hour before dusk the trackers brought them to a dried-up river, making Comrade Jack look around his command of sixteen soldiers and the trackers with utter despair. The thirst was the worst torture he had ever endured in his life. He wanted to scream when he saw the cheerfulness of the trackers, who were chatting among themselves while they took three small sips from their water bottles that were still half-full. Then they walked off upriver, over the dry white river sand and over the intermittent outcrops of rock. The banks of the river rose on either side of them and the birds and the insects were silent in the extreme heat captured by the bed of the dried-up river.

"Where are you going?" shouted Comrade Jack, pointing his gun at them. The sound of his voice echoed for a long distance down the riverbed, far ahead of the trackers.

"To find water," called back Sixpence.

Not believing the trackers were not running away and leaving them to die of thirst or be eaten by wild animals, Comrade Jack ran after them. Halfway to the trackers, who had stopped and were waiting for him, he fell over one of the outcrops of rock in the riverbed and his gun went off on automatic, shattering the silence of the bush. The trackers had seen Comrade Jack falling and had fallen flat on their stomachs behind another outcrop of rock, the reflex tuned by inept big-game hunters 'from across the seas'. In their ears all three heard the voice of Hannes Potgieter. 'If he trips and falls holding a gun, man, drop to the ground fast', which was just as well as the AK-47 sprayed half a magazine in their direction before it stopped.

Two hundred metres further upriver, they found what they were looking for, a deep hole in the riverbed made by the trunk of an elephant looking for water. With a further foot of sand removed from the hole by Onepenny, sweet water seeped to the surface, and Fourpence used his Russian army issue tin mug to bring up cups of water. He had to lie on the sand and reach to the full length of his arm for the water. If the water had been deeper, they would have tied a stick to the mug. The underground water would last right through the dry season.

By the time the soldiers had rushed to the small waterhole, called up by Comrade Jack, it was almost dark but every man was able to slake his thirst. While the men drank the water, the trackers carefully chose a place by the riverbed for the night's camp. Away from the site, a smooth run of rock ran right across the riverbed into the trees where it rose up to the top of the riverbank.

In the dark of the night, before the moon came up and with the men sleeping the sleep of exhaustion, Sixpence took the reading of south from the Southern Cross as he had been taught so many years before by Hannes Potgieter. From the south line, he judged the direction of northwest. In bare feet, Sixpence led his trackers across the smooth bare rock, making neither sound for the night nor spoor for the morning. When they reached the trees, they melted into the African night and stopped. An hour later, the moon came up, and they moved off through the ghosts of the mopani trees in the direction of home.

. . .

ANT SCOTT, on the Botswana border, had identified the shots as AK-47 automatic fire and left his camp at dawn with a troop of six men. None of his other patrols were near the direction of the gunfire and there had been no return fire.

"Wild animals," he had said to his corporal after waiting in silence for ten minutes.

By twelve o'clock the troop had cut the untidy spoor of a large group of men moving away from the Zambezi River. Ant took the centre and sent three men out on either side of him in the shape of a horn, so when they came up on the terrorists the front of the horns would close round the terrs, cutting off retreat. Ant could have followed the tracks at a gallop but kept the horses down to a trot, watching up ahead. By two o'clock Ant knew the exact position of the terrorists by the startled movement of birds up ahead. The danger call of a crested guinea fowl gave him the first warning, and he brought the horses back to a cautious walk. By hand signal, he sent the points of the horns to circle around up ahead through the mopani forest. The terrs were now making enough noise themselves to camouflage the sound of the horses.

Comrade Jack died without seeing the enemy. The sixteen men and Comrade Jack had just moved out of the forest into the clearing where the grass was knee-high. With calculated efficiency, his fellow freedom fighters were shot down one at a time, the FN rifles of the encircling House Scouts staying on single shot. Some of the men tried to fire back into the surrounding forest, not even hitting the horses which were trained not to run from the sound of gunfire.

Ant camped his men in the cover of the forest and waited through the rest of the day and then through the night. Only the next day did he lead them out into the small clearing to count the seventeen dead men.

"Whoever trained these men should be court-martialled," said Ant. "Better leave them where they are. Pick up the guns, ammunition and those bloody landmines. Poor sods. The animals and birds will eat well for the next three days. Why the bloody hell couldn't the rest of the world have left us alone? Russian guns, Russian boots and Russian water bottles but not a bloody Russian in sight."

LAURIE HALL HEARD the contact and estimated it had lasted less than ten minutes. He had also heard the short burst of AK fire the previous evening. The previous night they had not made a fire and their food had been the dried biltong. It was the first time either of them had heard shots fired in the war and Laurie began to take the process of his survival more seriously. They were patrolling the riverbank and one hour after the contact had fallen silent they found the point of disembarkation and two of the makoris that had brought the terrs across from Zambia.

"No wonder, they didn't last long," said Laurie, surveying the multiple signs of the landing. Both he and Mike Barrow had heard the single shots of the Belgian-made FN rifles well after the sporadic AK fire had stopped. "The remnants will be coming back this way and you and I will wait for them, young Mike. They will find themselves caught between a rock and a hard place. We'll make camp in the mopani forest and listen for them coming back."

Taking the hunting knife with the long blade, Laurie began carving a large hole in the first dugout canoe. Mike kept guard.

That night only one of them slept while the other stood guard. The metal bits had been taken from the mouths of the horses and muffles put on their feet.

THE TRACKERS HAD HEARD the contact and understood what it meant. They had moved slowly through the mopani forest, expertly covering their tracks. The surrounding bush had fallen silent after the gunfire. 'Don't forget if you find one lion hunting there is always another waiting for the buck to run. Usually there are five or six females and the old man waiting for his supper to be killed for him.' The words of Hannes Potgieter were constantly running through the mind of Sixpence as he tried to lead his friends away from death. The Russians had said they would not meet opposition, that the white farmers would be soft targets.

"Better we keep away from the river and go northwest into Botswana," he said. "If I were a Boer, I would have cut the spoor of Comrade Jack and followed it back to the river, using the makoris as bait."

"Can't we run for the river?" said Onepenny.

"Never we go back to that army camp. We will walk back to Mongu and build a hut where we had the base camp. There is fish and game and the vegetables we will start again. There we wait for these people to stop killing each other."

"How do we get across the river?"

"We will find a way."

LAURIE HALL AND MIKE BARROW staked out the canoes for three days but nobody came. By the time they left to return to camp and report what they had found, the trackers were well into the safety of Botswana. Then they cut across the border into Zambia and made once again for the river. They found a small village that knew nothing of the war and were taken across to the other side of the Zambezi.

Three weeks later they found the broken site of the old base camp. The river had cut away the main house, leaving behind wooden stumps and the first three steps that had led up to the deck. The small house that had been the home of Laurie Hall was still standing. Being a rondavel, the water had washed round and away, finding no purchase. The thatch had gone from the roof and the old mattress on the double bed was rotten. The trackers smiled at each other.

"Better we never left," said Fourpence.

The next day at dawn, when Onepenny came out of the rondavel they had slept in, he was attacked by the Goliath heron. The bird gave him a painful nip on the back of his leg. Man and bird stood eyeballing each other, the big bird with one cocked eye looking at Onepenny.

"You are a fine bird," said Onepenny in Lozi. "The bloody heron's still here," he called back to his friends.

In Laurie Hall's tin trunk, the one he had brought out from England on the boat, they found an unopened tin of coffee. The pack of powdered milk had gone as hard as a rock. Next to a small pile of books they found Laurie's box of fishing tackle. By the time the smell of coffee drifted down to the river, Fourpence had caught two fat bream and was casting for the third. The fire that was sending the sweet smell of wood smoke and the coffee would never be allowed to go out. Behind Fourpence in a tall acacia tree, vervet monkeys were trying to see what he was doing, the pert eyes and black-ringed faces popping out from the sanctuary of the tree trunk forgetting their long tails that hung in full view.

The windmill that drew water from the river into a holding tank next to the ruins of the big house had seized up, probably rusted. The fence that guarded the kitchen garden from the baboons and wild pig was broken.

Sixpence, after careful searching, concluded no human had been to the base camp after the great flood. With luck, he concluded, they would be left alone by the rest of mankind. All the crocodile money had gone with nothing to show for it. They were not so young anymore. They would make themselves comfortable and sit in the sun as their ancestors had done as far back as the stories handed down by his grandfather. The new life brought to Africa by the white man was nothing but trouble.

16

*S*helley Lane had not sung a note in public for five years. She now lived with Will Langton rather than Will living with her. The EMI contract had not been renewed, and no one wished to sing the songs she wrote. At thirty-three her career was not only over but most people could no longer remember her name. The thirty per cent share in Music Lane Limited had been sold to Byron Langton for a small amount of money to maintain the last six months of her hedonistic lifestyle. Then it was over and they could no longer afford the Chelsea flat.

Will was working for his brother. The coffee-table book had been reasonably successful and would have sold better without competition from a similar African wildlife book out of Australia. This time Lindsay Healy had not put her name on the book but Will knew quite well who had taken the photographs. When Shelley needed looking after financially, Will went to his brother and asked for a mortgage loan to buy himself a semi-detached house in Wimbledon. He had calculated the net income from the book would be just enough for the deposit on the two-bedroom house; the government having added his royalties to his salary and taxed him sixty-four per cent for the privilege of living in England. Will had asked Heathcliff Mortimer how it could be that someone who neither risked publisher's capital nor spent ten years taking the photographs had run off with two-thirds of his money to give to people less fortunate than himself.

"They are in the majority," Heath had explained patiently. "Democracy takes from the competent and gives to the less competent as they are in the majority. How else can a democratic government get elected?"

"What happens when the competent, as you call them, stop producing?"

"That is what communism and socialism will find out. First, they create a very boring society with everyone down at their level and then they run out of money to give away. Then the whole bloody thing collapses and a new ideology takes its place."

"Which one?"

"It doesn't matter when people are starving. They do exactly what they are told. Look at Africa. In the process and even after the collapse, the likes of your brother laugh their way to the bank."

"How do they get away with it?"

"Their competence is unscrupulous. An unscrupulous businessman can always understand a politician. Both are only in it for themselves whatever the politician says in public. They feed each other, the businessman with party funds, the politician with favours. You were left with a third of your money. The men of big business and politicians leave you enough to make it worth your while working. And don't think your two-thirds went to a worthy cause. It didn't. It went to keep up the system. Go and buy your semi-detached in Wimbledon. What they want you to do. Live in a row like the rest of us like a good little boy and watch television. That way everyone thinks the same and the individual in all of us is exterminated. And best of all, big business produces what we watch on television. These same people are able to control our minds. They tell us when to cry, to laugh, to be up in arms for whichever cause they wish us to follow. They even make us feel we are in control of our democratic governments. The almost perfect manipulation."

"You make it sound very horrible, Heath."

"It's quite all right if you like watching television."

Shelley watched Will become accustomed to his life. The man shrivelled in front of her. At exactly nine minutes past eight every morning, in sunshine, snow or rain, Will Langton left 27 Primrose Lane and walked for ten minutes to Wimbledon station. There he waited on the platform for two minutes to board the eight twenty-one for Waterloo where twenty-three minutes later he got off and walked forward with the other commuters to the Piccadilly Line entrance to the Tube station and walked to the office, in sunshine, snow or rain, and at nine o'clock he walked into the offices of Langton Merchant Bank. He would hang up his umbrella with his bowler hat, overcoat or raincoat depending on the season, and sit down at his desk to address matters that interested him even less than the journey up from Wimbledon.

His brother had not put him on the board of directors which was to no one's surprise. The sinecure of a job enjoyed by Will, the other members of the staff put down to brotherly love.

Having not told his brother after so many years that Will was worth more than half a million pounds, the West German industrial shares having done particularly well on the Frankfurt stock exchange, Byron assuaged the faint residue of his guilt by giving his brother a job and house mortgage Will did not deserve.

Within a few more years Byron would forget the money ever belonged to his brother. If his brother had not been around, like Laurie Hall, Byron would have forgotten all about the guilt a long time ago. Anyway, Will had run off with Shelley Lane which was some consolation. Deliberately, Music Lane Limited had been refusing the copyright of Shelley's music to other musicians until the singer sold her shares. Knowing Shelley was comfortably living in a small house in Wimbledon helped Byron convince himself that he had always done the right thing by her. At the right time he would again release her songs sung by the new, young singers in his stable, one of whom he was having an affair with.

The country estate was everything he wanted, including his children, and his wife was making him money as a publisher. Since Jack Pike had died, Johnny Pike had legitimised his father's empire and taken himself off to elocution lessons. Johnny had both his sons down for Harrow School, the alma mater of Winston Churchill. The Pike family had moved from peep shows and prostitution to the establishment in one generation thanks to Byron Langton's ability to launder their money. It would not be long before Byron agreed to Johnny Pike joining the board of Langton Merchant Bank in which the Pikes had a major shareholding.

There had been a lot of water down the Thames since Johnny Pike had given him LSD to circumvent his national service in the army. For old times' sake, once a month, the two of them met in the Green Dolphin in Greek Street where it had all begun. Every month they drank to having beaten the system.

JOSEPHINE LANGTON STARTED off standing outside South Africa House in the pouring rain. In the same demonstration were three bishops and four Labour Party MPs. The placard Josephine held in her cold hands called for the stopping of forced removals and the dividing of the races into separate areas under the apartheid government of South Africa.

When Byron heard his sister was part of an upbeat demonstration in the Strand, he suggested his editor of the *Daily Garnet* get along a man with a camera and have a picture of the ex-Labour minister, drenched in the rain, with a clergyman on either side, doing her moral duty. The bedraggled picture appeared on the front page of the paper the following morning. The photograph ricocheted round the world which pleased Byron and made his sister out to be a hero. She stood up for the poor blacks starving in the gutters under the jackboot of the Boers who were now no better than the Nazis. Byron was particularly pleased to have his name linked to his sister's as some of the good deed rubbed off onto the proprietor of a popular tabloid. They were both part of a popular cause.

Every word of disgust that flowed from Josephine's mouth vilifying the racist oppression was reported in the *Daily Garnet*, and when she joined the anti-apartheid movement as an executive member, no one was surprised. She was lauded in all the newspapers as a modern crusader for the rights of the oppressed men and women of the world. With the help of the *Daily Garnet* in particular, Josephine raised tens of thousands of pounds for the anti-apartheid movement, often from Labour-dominated county councils who gave away chunks of their ratepayers' money for the good cause, giving Labour a fillip in the opinion polls.

One headline in the *Garnet*, hoisted high on its own rhetoric, said all the whites should be kicked out of Africa. They had no right to be there. They were stealing the black man's birthright. Apartheid and colonialism were a crime against humanity.

The anti-apartheid stance of the *Garnet* made its readers both indignant and righteous in their wholesale agreement. When pictures of smart homes with swimming pools were published showing the way of life of the average white in Africa, the indignation turned to screams. Everyone wanted to give a pound to smash such horrors.

Heathcliff Mortimer was sent off on a special mission to report on South Africa but was not allowed out of the airport at Jan Smuts, Johannesburg, being sent home on the next plane back to London, making him an international celebrity overnight.

Lady Fiona Langton, at her publisher's desk, was delighted by the orders from the retailers for the second volume of the Mortimer journal on Africa which she published the week before.

To Heath's enormous surprise he found himself, as he put it, 'the flavour of the day', a phrase that he was to use constantly in the future. Everywhere in black Africa he was welcomed with gratifying accord, giving him three more major contacts for Langton Merchant Bank.

"Do you agree with your sister's anti-apartheid stance?" he asked Byron over a drink in Byron's office.

"Of course. She needed the job."

THE LETTER from Laurie Hall reached Will Langton in 1973 at the end of a long winter. Laurie had been in the Rhodesian army for over a year and Will was in his third year of catching the nine-minutes-past-eight up to Waterloo every morning. Spring was reluctant and twice retreated under a flurry of snow and ice-cold east winds that found their way deep into the old semi-detached house despite all the precautions. Will had looked at the tatty piece of grass at the back and knew at some stage he would have to buy a lawn mower as both neighbours had complained at the poor state of Will Langton's garden.

He had met both neighbours twice, once when they were invited to visit and once when the gesture of neighbourly goodwill was returned. Will tried the subject of Africa and failed; Shelley, the fact she used to be a singer. Both neighbours thought Will and Shelley were telling tall stories.

Shelley's black hair, that had once had the sheen of a raven's wing, was streaked with grey and her face was blotched from drink and the tablets she had swallowed to compensate for her depression. She was sleeping fourteen hours a day and went for days without getting dressed. They had long since stopped sharing a bedroom. The only rare visitor was Heathcliff Mortimer.

Since Josephine's marriage to the anti-apartheid movement she had kept well clear of her younger brother because he had once lived in Africa as a colonist.

Byron Langton had never wanted to see the semi-detached house and Will's parents in Dorset rarely left Langton Manor, Randolph Langton, the elder brother who ran the farm, even buying their food for them so they would not have to go to the village. Red Langton daily relived the horrors of night bombing and the atomic bomb he had watched fall on Japan. Adelaide waited patiently for the visits from her grandchildren. She was sixty-three years old and walked with great pain from arthritis, mostly sitting by the fire in winter painfully knitting for the grandchildren or sitting in the small conservatory when the sun came out in summer. Her mind dwelt in the years before the war when she was a young woman with a young family to bring up in a world that still knew the difference between right and wrong.

She and Red sat for hours without speaking to each other. The ritual glass of sherry was the highlight of their day.

Laurie's letter described the Rhodesian war as escalating but was so fill of bounce and excitement that it brought Will out of his trance. Will had not felt excited about anything for five years. Coming out of a clear blue sky after so many years of silence, the letter made Will think of a life he had once enjoyed, when getting up in the morning for a cold shower outside under the acacia tree was the first blast in a day full of happiness.

"You want to read a letter from Laurie Hall?" he said to Shelley when he came home that night. The letter had been addressed to him through Byron at the bank.

"No... You got any drink?"

"Shelley, we can't afford it."

"This is a miserable fucking life."

"Laurie's in the Rhodesian army. Horse patrols. Fighting the war."

"Can't we go to the pub just for once? You know that brother of yours is a jerk. I sang him a fortune, and you made him another out of bloody crocodiles and we can't buy a drink. Shit. Life stinks. We don't even fuck anymore."

"Shelley, please?"

Will heard her bedroom door slam shut and sat down to read through the letter once again. Laurie described the bush and the Zambezi Valley like a lover describing his mistress. The smell of wild sage mingled with the strong stench of a herd of buffalo. The splash of fish at night in the big river. The distant echo of game splashing the river water late in the quiet dusk while they drank. The call of so many birds. A dugout canoe poled by a black man standing in the bow. The smell of wood smoke. The cry of the fish eagle. A crimson sunset silhouetting the skyline of the river trees. Grunting hippo in the mud-pools. Flamingos touched in pink flocking up the river, shadowing the moving water with their wings... Africa.

Again he read the letter and again the same paragraph sprang out of the page.

"Will, most probably the war will drag on for years and come to an inconclusive end with both sides sick of fighting. The nationalists will win politically as history always tells us but when it is over they will need us more than ever before. Look to the north. Come independence the West loses interest. The troublesome child is on its own to sink or swim. Nearly all of them have sunk for lack of the knowledge to run a modern state. The communists only gave them guns. So back they go to savagery. The warlord tribes return and happiness is lost... They will try to run it themselves but in the end they will ask for help and the West won't bother to listen. Africa has water round its shores. There will be no starving hordes pouring out of Africa into Europe. The starving will die at home, long before they are any nuisance to the West. The white tribe of Africa, we from Europe who settled here to live generation after generation, must stay dormant quietly, ignoring the insults so that when they turn to us, we will be ready to do our job again, to grow the food economically, manage business without corruption, repair the collapsed infrastructure, provide the security of law and order so an honest man can walk the streets without fear of his life. But it will happen only when the whole of Africa has fallen to its knees amid civil war and corruption, anarchy... With the guns at the walls of the citadel, property here, especially agricultural land in the remote areas, can be bought for very little as the white people fear for their lives. The sugar estate on the Zambezi downriver from Chirundu is no longer functioning. Once owned by Tate & Lyle it is dormant, the sugar mill silent. Some people have bought parts to grow bananas and failed. When the war is over, as all wars are eventually, and the part of man that is sanity prevails, a swathe of land along the river will make the perfect safari camp to show off the last remnants of African game. Will, whatever you have, sell and come back to Africa. The most difficult changes are usually the best."

For seven days, Will made discreet enquiries. The value of the house had risen to compensate for inflation but the amount he borrowed had remained the same. Even after estate agent fees he would double his money on a quick sale. The pension fund seemed a good proposition for Langton Merchant Bank and the insurance company but not for Will Langton unless he worked to the age of sixty-five in the same company. He would retrieve the money deducted from his pay each month but the sum paid on his behalf by the bank went back to the insurance company to reduce Langton Merchant Bank's monthly premiums for the remaining staff. There was a small amount of money in a savings account kept away from Shelley Lane. The money would just be enough to buy a slice of the old sugar estate.

"How long do you want me to give you notice?" he asked his brother.

"Not very long."

"Would today be enough?"

"I think so, Will... If you had wanted to, you could have been a director."

"If I had wanted to. Not your fault, Byron. We all have our own lives to live."

"You're going back to Africa, I presume?"

"Yes, I am."

"Where, for instance?"

"Rhodesia."

"You must be mad. There's a war going on. You don't think Smith can win, do you?"

"No, I don't."

"Then why?"

"Because it is Africa and my Federal residence permit allows me to live in Rhodesia. You do remember the Federation of Rhodesia and Nyasaland?"

"No one else does... When are you leaving?"

"Friday. Tomorrow I go down to Dorset. The house is on the market. I've signed acceptance forms at a low price."

"You should have asked me."

"Probably not."

"Is Shelley going with you?"

"I haven't told her."

"You'll have to do that."

The brothers shook hands, and that was an end to it. For a split second, Byron wanted to tell his brother. Then his business sense took control. The Swiss bank account, 2759464, was under Byron's control and it was better that it stayed that way. The problem pigeonholed in the right place, Byron was never to think about the matter ever again. Anyway, he had done all the work. He had made the money. He had been stupid to imagine any of the money belonged to his brother or Laurie Hall. Most important of all, all the money in 2759464 was tax-free, out of sight and free of any government's restrictions.

"YOU'RE WALKING out on me! Selling the roof over my head!" shouted Shelley Lane.

"Shelley, we haven't lived together in that sense for years. Come with me. London has nothing for either of us."

"What are you going to do?"

"Buy a safari camp... I can't go back to Zambia. Build another base camp in Rhodesia. It's the same river just further down."

"You won't find tourists coming to a war."

"I can live for nothing until it's over."

"Or they shoot you."

"Then I really won't have to worry."

"You are mad, Will Langton... When do we leave?"

"Friday. By air."

"Do you have me on the flight?"

"I had made a reservation for two."

"All right, lover. One more try. You're right, we're both dead here. Whatever happened to all those songs I was going to sing?"

"There's never been anything stopping you."

"Africa... I did enjoy that one trip... You think they'd pay for a few gigs out there?"

"With all the sanctions thrown at them, you'll be a sensation."

"You think I should dye my hair?"

"Yes I do... Try some make-up again, Shelley, you're only thirty-four."

"Am I really?"

Will had to take his eyes from her face. "I'm going down to my folks tomorrow. Back on Wednesday."

"Maybe I'll get myself together for a change. Africa! Has a nice ring to it. I'm going to Africa! You think Laurie will be surprised to see me?"

JOSEPHINE LANGTON KNEW the date better than her own birthday. Twenty-three years before, she had aborted the only child she had ever carried in her womb. She tried to imagine her life with a daughter or a son, even with grandchildren, a family that truly belonged to her. The barren prospects that made up her life were no consolation for a family. The feminist movement of which she was stridently a part had given women all the rights, given them the money and careers to live an independent life. Soon half of them would be so independent they would be living on their own for the rest of their independent lives, husbands divorced or never married, children brought up as strangers by other strangers in day care, the life of family, the family life she had belonged to in Dorset, thrown out on the garbage heap of history, a victory for the suffragettes.

At forty-two, Josephine was no longer certain of the meaning of her life. She had maintained the flat in Westminster, hoping for a by-election she could win for Labour but none had come along. Even the platitudes of her fellow social preachers were ringing hollow in her ears, the substance of her hopes lost in the reality of man and woman, mostly destroyed by their own dishonesty and greed. There were too many lies.

Maybe she should have told Wolfgang Baumann, her teacher and the father of her child, that she was pregnant those many lonely years ago. At eighteen she had been so sure of herself. Everybody told her they could change the world, make it a better place. They never said there was a chance they would make it worse. Josephine shuddered in the mild, evening air as she walked home over Westminster Bridge; someone had walked over her grave.

THE JOURNEY from Sussex to Edinburgh was taken on her own. Lady Fiona Langton, daughter of the Marquis of Bathurst, was going home to look for answers to her life. The three children had been left on the two thousand-acre estate outside East Horsley in the capable hands of an elderly nurse, just as she herself had been left as a child. She had not seen her husband for ten days and there was more chance of him staying in London at 47 Buckingham Court for the weekend than coming down to Surrey. She was thirty-two years old and saw the ravages of multiple childbirth every morning when she looked in the mirror. The children had come upon her so quickly there had been little time to regain her figure. With the children constantly demanding her attention she was constantly tired and running a business publishing books compounded that problem in her life.

Byron had made the move to Surrey sound like the beginning of a great dynasty: the Byron Langton's country seat. She suspected somewhere in his heart he was jealous of his elder brother, Randolph, for being heir to Langton Manor with all its history. Joyously, she had moved the family into the new house thinking her and Byron's offices would now be next to her home. Within a few months she realised the office part of Headling Park was for the tax authorities. Some of the accounts department had been sent down from the Pall Mall offices along with the publishing division, neither of which, according to Byron when she asked, required constant contact with the hub of business in the City of London.

The end of summer was showing dark green in the fields when she arrived at the small railway station on the Bathurst estate, seventy miles from Edinburgh. She had telephoned the Hall from Edinburgh and was pleased to see her father waiting for her at the station. He was alone and hatless and looking at the flowers that were bursting with colour along the side of the platform.

"Ah, there you are," he said, turning round only when the train came to a rackety halt. "Flowers on railway stations make all the difference, don't you think? Nothing like flowers to cheer a man up. Women as well, I believe."

"Daddy, you're wearing different coloured socks again."

"Am I really? Difficult to feel the difference... All you got, gal?" he said, looking at her suitcase. "Better give it to me. Doesn't look right for a woman to be carrying a suitcase. See it a lot these days. Not right, you see. Come along. You can drive the car, Fiona. Never did like driving. You can talk to the horses but you can't talk to cars. Your mother said the same thing."

Halfway down the platform, the Marquis of Bathurst stopped and turned in surprise.

"Where are the children?" he demanded.

"I told you, Daddy, I was coming alone."

"That explains it then. Come along... Did you know my great-grandfather made them put in this railway station?"

"Yes, I did, Daddy."

"Whole branch line from Edinburgh, matter of fact."

Fiona drove them to the Hall in the old Austin following the path of her childhood. Nothing had changed and yet everything had changed.

"Lucky it's not a public holiday." Her father was holding onto the handle of his shooting stick which was standing upright between his legs, the clashing socks now more visible. "Show you what we've done tomorrow. Punch and Judy show. Pony rides. Thinking of a wild animal zoo. Tigers. That sort of thing. Damned if I haven't turned the old Hall into a circus but it pays. Can't afford to keep up a property these days without all those tax deductions. There has to be income to write them off against, what Byron told me and he was right. How is Byron and why isn't he here?"

"I want to talk to you about Byron."

"Don't ask me, gal. You know him far better than I. By the bye, tell him from me. Get out of Lloyd's. Resigned from all my syndicates but it'll take three years to be free of 'em. Claims, you know. Some claims take years to settle. Well, I heard in my club they'll let any Tom, Dick or Harry in as a 'Name'. Foreigners. First, any old colonial which included the Americans which was bad enough. Now any damn foreigner. Didn't like the sound of it. Resigned the lot of 'em. Lately the cheques have been getting less and less but the liability stays the same. Everything I own backs those syndicates. In the days it was an old boys' club we knew what we were doing. You tell Byron from me to get out. Get right out. Now, here we are. Here we are. Don't ask me what's for dinner. Never know. Never knew when your mother was alive. Fact is, didn't ever know. My mother said it didn't matter what you ate but frankly I'm rather fond of cottage pie. We'll take a glass of sherry on the terrace and see if you can't see the new fawn. Born last week he was or is it a she? Can't get close enough, you know. No children, no Byron. Now what is this all about? You think we could keep tigers in Scotland? Leave the suitcase in the car. McKay will put it in your room. Do you know he's been with the family fifty-seven years, or isn't it fifty-eight? Not too heavy. He'll be all right. Now look at that. He's put the sherry glasses out with the decanter. Wherever would we be without a good servant? You had better have two glasses of sherry before you tell me."

"Daddy, Byron's having an affair."

"They all do. He's over forty. First they get their tailor to let out their trousers round the waist, and then they find a young gal. Now, have a glass of sherry."

"What do I do, Daddy?"

"Nothing, of course. Not flaunting it in public, is he?"

"No. It's one of his singers."

"Appearances, Fiona. All that counts. Must keep up appearances. If everything appears all right, it must be."

"I want to divorce him."

"Now, drink this sherry. We don't have divorces in our family, young lady. The gamble of life is going through it and changing horses in midstream is never very wise. Now, does he provide for you and the children?"

"Of course he does."

"Exactly. He's a gentleman, so he would never lay a hand on you in anger."

"No... No, he doesn't."

"The children love their father?"

"Yes, Daddy, but he's having an affair."

"You think he didn't have one before he married you?"

"Probably, I never asked. We loved each other. If he's going off with singers he doesn't love me anymore."

"Your job in life is to bring up your family. Your husband's job is to provide security. Most men go astray and so do most women. No one will tell you that part of it. They don't want to know it happens. The person who thinks the world is perfect is a fool. You keep up a good home and when he's had enough of singers and actresses, he'll be glad to come home. Eventually he will feel guilty and come back with his tail between his legs. Now, have another glass of sherry and forget all about a divorce. You have a perfectly good husband. You try what a lot of these young gals are doing these days and you'll find the next one is a lot worse."

"I feel so hurt."

"Nothing's ever easy... Tell him to get out of Lloyd's... How about some giraffes? Do you think they'll survive in Scotland? Probably not." The Marquis of Bathurst disliked involving himself in other people's lives. To him there was honour, duty and the love of God. The rest of life was incidental.

Fiona Langton had not heard one word her father had said about Lloyd's of London.

HEATHCLIFF MORTIMER HAD RENTED himself a cottage in the hop fields of Kent. The small garden was overgrown with weeds and the house with climbing roses. He was seventy years old and the late summer weather suited him, the deckchair among the apple trees a place to think and snooze and think. A woman from the village came in twice a week to clean up his mess. The pub down the bottom of the carthorse road was refuge from the evenings. The flat in Chelsea stayed empty while he was away. Before he left, he had said goodbye to Will Langton and Shelley Lane, visiting their horrible little semi-detached in Wimbledon. He did not expect to see them ever again. At seventy, he decided, a man said goodbye with an element of certainty.

The cottage, they had told him, was four hundred years old, the doorways making him stoop to go into the house. Man, he concluded, had evolved to a larger size. Whether he had evolved in any other way successfully, Heathcliff Mortimer had his doubts. There was the progress of science that would, in his opinion, create more problems than it solved. And there was the rest of man trying to govern himself.

The book, *The Journal of an Africa Reporter*, was halfway through the third volume. In the first, Heath had written of hope for the new Africa, the post-colonial Third World, where he wrote at the moment he could only see despair. Three of the new dictators, so it was said, who had emerged from the triumph of freedom over colonialism, were reported to eat their opponents, one keeping the body parts in his refrigerator. Instead of hope and progress there was anarchy, fear and starvation as the reward for destroying colonial rule. The Russians and Americans fought each other for control of the carcass, backing any despot who would prattle their ideology. The twentieth century scramble for Africa was no different, he wrote, to the one that had taken place in the nineteenth century, except the two powers that had not taken part in the first one were fighting to kick out the old guard and control Africa for themselves.

The British had sent the missionary, with the chance to be saved by God; the Russians promised communism, the ultimate equality of man; the Americans, democracy, the chance of changing government without resort to arms. Heath was certain that if the men of God had failed to give the poor security and food, the men of communism and democracy would fail. All three philosophies were smokescreens for the greater greed of man. The powers of arms and money, he wrote, not the power of right over wrong, would be the power that would rule in Africa, would, indeed rule the world as it always had done. All the rest was words.

Heath pulled himself out of the deckchair in his apple orchard, the fruit and leaves guarding him from the afternoon sun. He walked the weed-run path into the house to find his desk and write the words of despair that circled in his mind. The Africa Josephine Langton wanted had been lost already.

For two hours, oblivious of sun or home, he wrote on his portable typewriter, the one he had used for twenty years. When he had finished, he left the five sheets of paper beside the typewriter to be read again with a fresh mind.

"Maybe it's just old age," he said out loud to himself. "Maybe every old man is pessimistic of the world... I hope so, Heath, old man."

The summer evening beyond the house was soft with warmth and fragrance. The rich bed of stocks from an old man's garden by the road was sweet perfume in the air, the old man's back to him bent to the garden he tended with love; the last quiet years. The cart road wandered through the green fields and part hedgerows thick with bright red berries. The path was dry. Heath had his gnarled stick for dogs and predators. He walked on in the evening air, lightening his heart, drawing closer to the small village and his nightly destination.

Half a mile from the village he heard the 'chock' of the bat on the ball, the sound coming from afar. There were oak trees over there in the distance and the roof of the white pavilion showing between the trees. It would be a Saturday, he told himself: cricket on the village green, the ultimate stability of England, a civilised game to play, bred by generations of men who claimed the name of civilised life; mad dogs and Englishmen but all of them very, very civilised. Heath smiled to himself and the ball was struck again, the sound from far away followed by the light patter of clapping.

The twenty-minute walk to the Oast House was the contract he made each night with himself, the price he offered for his drinking. The windows of the old stone building were wide open to the summer evening and drifting from inside came the perfect smell of generations of tap beer, the pints pulled from the cellar underneath the small oak bar.

Inside, the gaffer had already poured his pint of mild and bitter. On the old, dark-wood bar, dripping wetly from one side, the beer glass awaited his pleasure. Talking to the gaffer only with his eyes, Heath lifted the heavy glass and tipped it in his mouth, letting the soft gentleness of the beer run down his throat.

"My, but that was good," he said, putting down the glass now a third empty.

"You say that every evening, Mr Mortimer."

"Heath, please. I've been here a week. Heath for short. Now, give me a Southern Comfort to go with the beer, please."

"A pleasure, Mr Mortimer."

Heath shook his head and smiled; the gaffer was too old for first names. Smiling to himself, he took both drinks into the front garden and the bench and table that showed him the length of road he had walked and the small row of village cottages down on his left, window boxes rich in red and yellow nasturtiums.

The second pint with its chaser went down just as well as the first and by the time Heath was happily into his third set of drinks, some of the cricketers had arrived from the finished game dressed in sleeveless white sweaters to tell them apart. The sun had gone behind the oak trees at the back of the Oast House and the scent of flowers was stronger on the air. One man, he heard, had scored fifty runs and was feeling very pleased with himself.

Mildly sad from the alcohol, Heath looked at his gnarled stick resting against the wooden table and mourned his lion-headed cane, left once too often in a bar he could no longer remember. There were no women brought in with the cricketers which also made him sad. Looking at what he had lost was one of the pleasures left in his life.

He guessed the cricketers had batted first and the man after his half-century had bought them drinks in the cricket pavilion. All three of them were approaching the crossroads of drunkenness.

"Well, I'm socialist," said one of them loudly, "and I think we should have gone in with troops and hung Ian Smith for treason. Colonialism's a disgrace."

"Rot," said the man of fifty runs. "Utter rot. Colonialism brought law and order."

"And exploitation."

"You think building a modern state is exploitation?"

"They were slaves. It's the same with apartheid South Africa."

"We provided our colonies with security, an administration free of corruption and vast sums of capital investment."

"Capitalist exploitation, that's what it was."

"There can never be wealth in Africa again without proper management."

"Management's grossly overpaid."

At this point, the fifty-run man got to his feet and began to shout. "You socialists have never done a productive day's work in your bloody lives. You're parasites sucking other people's blood."

"Without the workers your management couldn't do a bloody thing. You don't even know how to get your hands dirty."

"Without us you'd starve."

"Just 'cause you made fifty-three bloody runs for the first time in your bleeding life, doesn't mean you know what you're talking about."

Heath, watching with mild amusement, the possibility of a fight, thought about stopping the verbal dispute with a knowledgeable word or two but instead minded his own business, which was better.

"When the likes of you have bled the wealth creators to death, you'll grovel on the floor to the last man of ability to get you out of your shit."

The socialist brought the punch up with him from the bench and what had started to Heath like a grand game of cricket ended up with the star batsman flat on his back with the gaffer out the door of the Oast House to stop the fight and protect his furniture.

"Never talk no politics or religion in a pub," he said between the socialist standing up and the batsman on the floor. "If you want to know about Africa ask Mr Heathcliff Mortimer over there."

"Please, please," said Heath almost squealing. "Don't bring me into it."

"You the journalist?" said the socialist, turning on Heath.

"Yes I am."

"Well, what do you think about apartheid?"

"Not very much. Not very much. But I have an awful fear that after it is swept away, there will be hunger in post-apartheid South Africa. It would seem you can be free to starve and shoot each other out there or have to put up with colonialism. Now, be a good chap and give your friend a hand up from the floor."

17

*T*he letter Will Langton had written to Horst Kannberg at the Victoria Falls drew no response and Laurie Hall had ridden off into the bush. Through the *Rhodesia Herald*, Will and Shelley had found a cheap room to rent halfway up Second Street. They said they were married. They spent three months waiting for Laurie Hall to come out of the bush and tell them how to go about buying part of the land that had once been a Tate & Lyle sugar estate before the rebel government had taken control from the British government and before the war. They walked long distances around Salisbury where the war had had little effect while the grey streaks grew back into Shelley Lane's hair. They both agreed they were getting on each other's nerves.

"Lover, we've got to get out and about. You don't meet the right people tramping the streets and Laurie always was unreliable. Typical."

"You mean we should spend the royalty cheque," said Will. The cheque for that year's sales of the coffee-table book from Damian Huntly came to twelve pounds seven shillings and eight pence. Once they had come to him every six months but not anymore. He was even surprised Damian Huntly had shipped fifty-three copies. The note with the cheque had also amused him. 'Now you're back in Africa, how about a new book?'

"We'll go down to Bretts," said Will on the spur of the moment. He too had reached the end of his patience.

They had asked the army twice a month for news of Laurie Hall and no amount of enquiries led them to any settlers of land once owned by Tate &

Lyle. Everyone looked blank in the estate agents and told him the Zambezi Valley was a war zone.

Shelley did her best with the make-up but most of her energy had been lost in the walks after their arrival at Salisbury Airport from London. The house had been sold in Wimbledon but Will would not tell her the price.

Will had often noticed that when things are going wrong in life, the wrongs reach the very bottom before they start coming right again. When he took his English royalty cheque to the Standard Bank in Cecil Square where he had originally deposited his Swiss franc-denominated traveller's cheques, he was told that due to United Nations mandatory sanctions the only foreign currencies negotiable in Rhodesia were Swiss francs, Portuguese escudos and South African rands.

"We were going to Bretts tonight," he told the teller with a shrug of resignation.

"Best nightclub in Rhodesia," said the teller, passing back the non-cashable cheque. "Too bad."

"All right, lover," said Shelley outside. "He called the place a nightclub. Chances are they have never heard of me but these are desperate times. I've worked myself up to a good night out and we're going to have one. We've got enough for a couple of beers out of our tight-arse budget?"

"Okay, Shelley, but the bar only opens at five o'clock."

"So we wait until five o'clock. I haven't had a drink for three months so what's another couple of hours?"

The bar and nightclub were downstairs in the basement. At the bottom of the red-carpeted staircase they looked into the nightclub with its bandstand and well-laid tables and turned into the long room with the L shape.

They were the first customers. The barman set up their drinks, two very cold Lion Lagers, in the total silence. The light was dim except at the bar. There were mirrors round the room making it look larger than it was. Every piece of upholstery was a plush red and for the first time in years, Shelley Lane felt at home. She caught her reflection in the mirror. Her face was out of the bright light and reminded her of a face she had known some years before. Part of the light had created the old sheen that had made her black head of hair so different. The smell of the place reminded her of other days. From nowhere, notes of new music played softly in her mind.

"You got a pen?" she asked the barman, and on the back of her cigarette box Shelley drew some lines and filled in the music.

"What's that?" asked Will. His mind had wandered far away in the bush.

"I don't know," said Shelley. "You got any music in this place?" she said to the barman. "You got a show tonight?"

"An Italian singer."

"Any good?"

"Of course. This is Bretts." He pushed a tape into a machine under the bar and the sound of Frank Sinatra filled the empty room.

"Pretty old stuff," said Shelley.

"Sanctions," said the barman. "No foreign exchange. Someone in Bulawayo is re-recording the best of the music we had on record before UDI."

The bar began to fill with people from their offices and Will and Shelley were lost in the swelling crowd, left to their own thoughts, sipping the cold beer and smoking cigarettes. Neither of them spoke to each other.

A small man sat next to Shelley and ordered himself a drink, a regular customer familiar with the barman, looking first at Shelley's reflection in the wall mirror behind the rows of bottles and then at her face still dim in shadow. Shelley, aware of the look, leant forward into the light which picked out the streaks of white hair that mingled with black.

"I'm sorry," he said, laughing, sure of himself again. "For a moment you looked just like the singer Shelley Lane."

"Wait till you hear me sing," said Shelley, joining with his laughter.

A Dean Martin number crooned its way to a close.

"You got that Shelley Lane?" said the small man to the barman. The bar was full of conversation, the low tables around the small room occupied by groups of friends, some of them in uniform. The barman changed the tape and Shelley heard her own voice fill the room.

"Sounded good in those days," she said, leaning across to Will.

"You were the one that stopped. They never threw you out."

"Think this place would give me a job?" she asked.

"Provided you don't go back on the booze."

"Buy me a beer, lover... I can remember your brother that first time. Took to the floor, did Byron, 'I give you Shelley Lane'. I was so in love with the bastard I sang like a canary."

"What are we going to do, Shelley?" asked Will.

"Go back to England, I suppose."

"He called you Shelley," said the small man butting into their conversation.

"Yes he did."

"Are you Shelley Lane, the singer?"

"Would it make any difference to you if I was?"

"She's my favourite singer."

"Thank you. Why don't you buy us a drink? Just imagine buying a drink for your favourite singer. Fact is, we're damn near broke. Came out to buy some land and lover here keeps his hand firmly on the last bit of family capital. You can always pretend and so can I."

Like many rumours started in jest, the word spread around the bar that the singer of the song playing over the sound system was sitting at the bar having a drink. People began turning their heads to look and stare. Shelley's 'Zambezi' songs played along with the rumour and the small man bought them another round of drinks and Will lost control of the situation. The mention of his brother had once again made him wonder what he was doing with Shelley Lane. They were creatures of their own habits, both left behind, both remembering what they had wanted and both knowing it had gone forever with their age. Will looked at her properly for the first time in many years and saw some of what the small man had seen and was now hoping. The lack of three months' drink had removed some of the lines of dissipation. He remembered the night she had felt his knee in the taxi, the time they had first met. She had been using him against Byron, he was as sure then as he was now... Will's mind drifted away. Everyone, he thought, used everyone. There was always an ulterior motive except for his one brief look at truth on the rocks at Dancing Ledge.

A tall middle-aged man, half-bald with the look of a hawk, was making his way through the now crowded room towards the bar while Shelley was chatting to the small man who had bought them their drinks, the small man in love with the idea, however small the chance, that the lady drinking with him was the voice that had lived in his soul so many lonely nights.

Will was more alone in the crowded bar than any night alone at Hannes Potgieter's base camp. Shelley was going to get drunk on someone else's money and he was going to guide her home, his only use in the way of things. Did it matter, he asked himself? Did it matter if he bought the house money into the dying Rhodesia through Switzerland and together they drank it out with the last colonial death rattle? He had been in love with the idea Laurie Hall had written him, no less foolishly than the man at the bar in love with a phantom singer as the Shelley Lane in the song had died years ago... Then he thought again. He had run away three times to Africa, so what was the difference? Maybe they could take him for the Rhodesian army if the war grew worse.

"Shelley," he said. "Let's go home."

"I'm enjoying myself. Come on, Will. We're miserable as it is. Maybe I'll sing for our supper and pretend for a night or two. Relax this once and try and enjoy yourself."

The tall man with the hawk face had reached them at the bar.

"Are you Shelley Lane?" he asked. "I'm the owner of Bretts and a good friend of Laurie Hall. Which one of you is Will Langton?"

"I am," said Will, coming out of his trance.

"Laurie said you were coming out. Will you be my guests for supper?"

"Can you do me a small favour?" said Shelley.

"Anything, Miss Lane."

"My, they are formal in the colonies! This man has been buying us drinks. I'd like him to join us for the evening."

"James," said the owner to the barman. "Put everything Miss Lane orders on my bar account and I will sign it later. Shall we say seven-thirty in the nightclub?" he said to Shelley.

Two hours later, when the photographers were ready in the nightclub and the spotlight turned to Shelley sitting at her table, the owner of Bretts for the price of dinner had his nightclub on the front page of the *Rhodesia Herald* amid the speculation that Shelley Lane would sing at Bretts. As Will said when they were delivered home in a taxi later in the night, 'it's the way of the world'.

In bed, with the lights out, Will asked Shelley why she did not sing.

"Oh, I'm worth more than a dinner. You wait. Mr Bretts or whatever his name is, will pay. Did you note I was not drunk? Come here, lover, I want to make love."

'Who to?' thought Will without making a sound.

Three days later when the landlady knocked on their door, they had decided to go back to England and face up to the rest of their lives. Will had no idea what he was going to do.

Shelley, thinking silently, had concluded a change in 'live-in lover' might improve her circumstances. Will Langton, unlike his brother, was a loser. Everything he had ever done had come to nothing, even the girl he had met by the sea and that story she was sick and tired of hearing. It was like a tap dripping, the reproach in his eyes that she was not the woman he really wanted her to be. She was sure that once they reached London, they would go their separate ways, taking with them a few memories. After three days and nothing from the nightclub she was sure she would never sing again: if they did not want her in the middle of Africa there would be no chance whatsoever in London.

The knock came again on the door. It was ten o'clock in the morning and they were still in bed.

"You got a visitor," called the landlady and left it at that. They both heard her footsteps retreating down the corridor followed by the bang of the kitchen door. The woman had let out all the rooms in the flat, leaving herself the smallest bedroom and the kitchen. No one was allowed in the kitchen.

"Who knows we're here?" said Will with little enthusiasm, pulling on his pants.

When he opened the door, a young boy in army camouflage was standing in the hallway not sure whether he should turn around and leave.

"Are you Will Langton?" asked Mike Barrow. The whole flat had the smell of stale cooking as if no one ever opened the windows and let in the air. It was not the kind of place he expected to find a world-famous singer but Laurie Hall had been specific with his instructions.

They had all heard about Laurie Hall and Shelley Lane and no one in the unit believed a word of what he said. In the bush they respected Laurie Hall but round the campfire the stories the man told were so tall no one, including Ant Scott, believed one word. Their unit of Horse Scouts had been stood down for ten days the previous afternoon. The night before they had all gone to Bretts as was their custom on the first night of leave where the owner told Laurie Hall his old flame, Shelley Lane, was in town. Apparently, and as quoted by the nightclub owner, 'the singer is on the bones of her arse'. Mike Barrow had first heard Shelley Lane singing on the radio when he was at school and she was still singing on the radio five years later and people who did that, in Mike Barrow's mind, did not end up 'on the bones of their arse'.

Ant Scott thought the chance of laying to rest the Shelley Lane tall stories was too good to be lost. He had bet Laurie Hall the price of a lunch for the whole unit. By then all nine of them were drunk, and it was agreed that Meikles Hotel would be the venue where the food was some of the best in town. Laurie had gone off into a world of his own, which all of them put down to the embarrassment of facing his own lie. Ant Scott had to throw down the challenge again before Laurie Hall asked him to repeat what he had said.

"If this woman is really Shelley Lane, invite her to lunch. If it's Shelley Lane, I'll pay for everyone and if it's not, you pick up the bill and never mention her name again."

"Sounds a good idea to me," Laurie had answered with little enthusiasm.

"Better still, make it supper tomorrow night here in Bretts and include the cover charge in the bill."

By the time Will Langton appeared at his bedroom door, Mike Barrow was already feeling Laurie Hall's embarrassment. They had ridden thousands of miles together and Mike had no wish to see his friend made to look a fool. In the army, there was no place to run and the war, they all knew but did not even admit to themselves, was going to last a very long time.

Even when Will Langton took the note from Laurie Hall and seemed to be pleased with what he read, Mike Barrow was sure there was no Shelley Lane among the smell of stale cooking oil cooked too many times. With the note delivered, Mike wanted to get far away from the embarrassment as quickly as possible.

"Hey, where's Laurie?" called Will after reading the note and looking up to see the soldier down the end of the corridor letting himself out of the door to the flat.

"Oh, he's with Lieutenant Scott."

"Who's he?"

"Our CO. Now look, I've delivered the message."

"What time tonight?"

"Didn't it say? I don't know. Whatever time people eat supper in nightclubs." The front door opened and closed and the soldier's footfalls were silent in the corridor, as if the messenger had never even been.

Shelley, reading the note sitting up in bed, agreed the handwriting belonged to Laurie Hall.

"Why the hell didn't he come here?" she asked.

"Don't ask me but then I've never been in the army."

By nine-thirty that night, Bretts was full of drunken laughter and loud voices trying to talk over each other. The only blacks in the place were serving food or drink or cooking in the kitchen and most of the patrons were young men with tans from fighting in the bush. The few young women were sucked up by the crackle of danger that lived at every table, the laughter a little more false than it would have been in peacetime. At the Horse Scouts' table, two tables joined together, there were no women: the word had gone round the room that one of the spare table settings was for Shelley Lane the singer, the singer who had featured on the front page of the *Rhodesia Herald* the previous day.

There had been many hoaxes in Rhodesia during the war and by ten o'clock everyone in the room except Laurie Hall was certain the Shelley Lane story was a management hoax to fill the nightclub which was five deep at the bar. The Italian singer had done her first show to mild applause and gone off miffed. The owner of Bretts, the man with the hawk face and the partially bald head, was seen to look at the bottom of the outside stairs too often. Mike Barrow had sunk into himself in his embarrassment for Laurie Hall who was taking no notice of the looks and comments from the men in his unit. He was staring far away from the smoke and the noise, oblivious to his surroundings.

If Laurie had been asked to voice his last wish before execution it would have been to keep Shelley Lane and his memories out of Bretts nightclub. He had no wish to shatter his dream and cursed his weakness that months before had had him thinking of a tourist camp beside the river and all of them back together again.

At half-past ten the hope that his wish had been fulfilled was shattered by a stir at the reception desk tucked against the bottom of the stairs and the owner moving quickly to greet his new guest. Laurie did not even see Ant look up in surprise and then she was coming towards him between the tables led by the owner and somehow holding Will Langton's hand. She swept towards him like a queen, her make-up perfect, her black hair the perfect sheen he had remembered and lost along with his money, the smile the same, the dark brown eyes set in their almond cases, the white skin tinged with the down of orange-red, the large inviting mouth, the ears like seashells, the long strides filling the skirt like a ship in full sail. In the dim light and cigarette smoke she was quite magnificent.

Shelley watched Laurie Hall stand up from the table and saw the white hunter she had met at Mongu. The army had honed away the surplus fat, the sun had tanned his skin and the crow's feet his smile made were like the devil's wings, the sky-blue eyes springing a host of memories to make her know her power again. For the first time in five years she felt like singing. She let go the protection of Will's hand and felt the power of the strong arms crushing her against his chest.

"Where've you been?" he said to her and then, a too-long pause afterwards, "Will, good to see you. Come and sit down. These are my friends. Everyone, meet Shelley Lane and Will Langton."

Will sat at a chair between two soldiers he had never met before and found himself alone in a room full of people. Food was set in front of him that he had never ordered and a full glass of wine appeared beside his plate. The local Rhodesian wine, the product of sanctions, tasted more like paraffin than alcohol but none of the waiters would take his order for a bottle of beer, the whole nightclub concentrated on Shelley Lane. The woman who in bed that morning had looked her thirty-five years of age had been transformed by the hairdresser and the most expensive dress shop Will had ever entered. After an hour of pleading that followed the letter from Laurie Hall, Will had opened up the capital account, the one that was going to buy his life back on the banks of the Zambezi River. Fascinated and sick to his stomach, Will watched the old magnetism return to the lady he had lived with for five years. She captivated everyone in the room, except Will.

They had fallen together more out of habit than any love or lust, out of mutual protection, two lonely, lost people, lost in a world that for them had fallen apart, shattered by her alcohol and by his loss of Africa. They had tried to force their lives to work together. There had been moments of peace and understanding, the comfort of familiar lives, the need they had for each other made up from their fear of living alone. Shelley Lane had loved his brother, had made love to Laurie Hall. He was her comforter.

Pushing the piece of raw steak around his plate, he ate some of the chips and some of the soggy vegetables and swallowed his glass of wine in two large gulps only to find it full again a moment later. After four glasses, without speaking a word to anyone or anyone speaking a word to him, the roof of his palate was numb and the alcohol from his glass had gone to his head and he watched the people around him as if from a great distance. He was only there to watch. One after the other, the soldiers danced with Shelley Lane but all the time he saw her eyes looking for Laurie Hall. Never once did she even smile his way and sadly, it did not matter.

By midnight the Italian singer had come and gone again. The nightclub was waiting. By one o'clock they were still waiting, and no one had even left the bar. Mostly she danced with Laurie Hall. As he watched them, oblivious to the crowded room, any last idea Will had of living by the Zambezi River disappeared, the dream lost in the reality of Laurie Hall's letter: the man wanted the girl to come back to Africa.

Back at the table Will watched Laurie pick up both of her hands from the table and looked into her eyes.

"Shelley, you remember Victoria Falls? Will you sing for us? The guys would appreciate it. We lost one of our troopers last week. War is ugly. You can make it softer, take them into your world while you sing."

Will watched his lady get up from the table as Laurie signalled the man with the hawk face, the band faded out its number and the couples stood motionless on the dance floor as the owner took the microphone and told the quiet nightclub what they wanted to hear.

The first song she sang was the song she had first sang in public for Byron Langton, and Will more than anyone understood the meaning of 'If You Want To Be Mine'. After the third number from her first album, when the clapping was furious, Will got out of his chair and left the table. At reception, he borrowed a pen from the cloakroom attendant and wrote down his note to Shelley Lane, wishing her a lovely evening but he was tired and going home.

It was the end of March and the main rains were over and outside, when he reached the top of the stairs, the night was warm and clear. There was no one on the streets and he walked to Cecil Square where Laurie Hall, unbeknown to Will Langton, had tried to kill himself. Will turned up Second Street towards the Avenues. Away from the street lights he looked at the heavens; he could see the Southern Cross and hear the voice of Hannes Potgieter telling him how to find south.

Will walked alone, free from human eyes; the jacaranda trees canopied his head. For a brief moment he thought he was going to cry but the wave of sadness passed him by and left him walking in the street.

By lunchtime the following day, Will was still alone in the room. He waited the whole day and the night and the following morning before the note came from Laurie Hall.

"The only apology I can think of is to say Shelley and I were lovers first. I am too pathetic to tell you to your face. You will always be my friend."

Quietly, Will packed his bags and paid the landlady for the extra month. There were two flights a day from Salisbury Airport to Johannesburg in South Africa which was the way Will went home alone.

WITH THE REBUILDING of their youth and Shelley Lane's singing career, Laurie Hall and Shelley Lane agreed to marry and, despite what Will thought on his long flight back to London, the two ex-lovers had not shared the same bed. There had been an argument which was won by Laurie Hall.

"Whether you like it or not, under common law you are married to one of the best men I have ever called a friend. To sleep with you now would be an insult to Will Langton."

"Then what am I supposed to do?" asked Shelley. They had left Bretts nightclub at three in the morning and gone back to the small flat Laurie kept in Baker Avenue, Shelley not wishing to end her evening. She could still hear the wild applause.

"First, we will get married and then make love," said Laurie emphatically.

"Are you proposing to me?" asked Shelly, incredulously.

"Yes. Will you marry me?"

"Do you know you're the first man to actually propose? And when do you intend getting married?"

"As soon as possible. There are licences. Things like that. Tomorrow we'll go and find out."

"Then I'm not going back to Will?"

"No. If he loved you, he would have married you years ago."

"True. So why can't we make love?"

"Because I'm a stupid old romantic."

"Why didn't you ask me before? In London?"

"Because you were the great singer. Rich. I had a little money but no job. Certainly no prospects other than going back into the bush."

"And I'm not a great singer anymore?"

"You're not rich anymore. That's the difference. I don't have to compete with your wealth. You said your career was dead in London. Here you can sing and we can be married and when the war is over, we'll buy that tract of land downstream from Chirundu and run a famous safari camp where all your old fans can come and do penance at the feet of Shelley Lane. You love the bush and the animals. I talked to my CO, Ant Scott, about buying that land and he said that if Will was not interested, he'd put in some money and after the war I could show him how to run a safari camp. I still have a list of Hannes Potgieter's old hunting clients who wanted to shoot game with a gun and not a camera. Let's have a drink and talk, and tomorrow go to the magistrates' court and find out how we get married the simplest way possible. Bretts will give you a three months' contract and there are clubs in Bulawayo and Umtali: the war takes me all over the place so it doesn't matter where you are singing."

"How long's the war going to last, Laurie?"

"Until we win."

By lunchtime the following day all the arrangements had been made and Ant Scott and Mike Barrow had agreed to be witnesses at the registry office ceremony. In the excitement, even Shelley Lane forgot Will Langton sitting in their room on Second Street waiting for her to come home. Only the next day, after a boisterous engagement party at Meikles Hotel, did Shelley ask Laurie to have a note sent to Will telling him what was happening.

Soon after the note was delivered, and five hours before the ceremony was to have taken place in the magistrates' office, Ant Scott received the order recalling his unit. A large force of ZANLA guerrillas owing allegiance to Robert Mugabe had infiltrated across the Zambezi River from Mozambique in the exact area Will had contemplated his safari camp.

As Will's aircraft touched down safely at Heathrow airport in London, Laurie and Mike Barrow were riding side by side into the bush at Mana Pools. The Horse Scouts' orders were to cut the spoor of the guerrilla incursion, find its direction and report by radio to an army base behind the Makuti Hotel at the top of the Zambezi escarpment where the helicopters were waiting with sticks from the RLI, the Rhodesian Light Infantry, waiting to destroy the invaders.

In Salisbury, Shelley Lane sat back in the small bachelor flat in Baker Avenue and wondered what had happened to her life so suddenly. That night she sang again at Bretts to wild applause.

Three nights later Laurie Hall had still not cut the spoor of the Chinese communist-backed army. There was an hour before the light would go and they were starting to look for a place to spend the night. The mopani forest was thick and the screech from the pools, still wet from the rains, was the dominant force over the bush.

"You know what," said Mike Barrow, riding behind Laurie Hall. "We have the sexiest frogs in the world. Just stop and listen to what they say."

"Our job isn't listening to the mating calls of African frogs."

"That's my point, Laurie. Just listen to them. Thousands upon thousands of them and all the males are calling *Fuck-me, Fuck-me*, and all the females are saying *Thank-you, Thank-you*."

"You've got a one-track mind, young Mike."

"Probably. But can you hear what they are saying?"

"Now you mention it."

Walking slowly, the horses moved on between the tall trees. The sun was down behind the trees, sending shadows. Birds called to each other to say where they were going to be in the coming night. Between the trees and the dappling shadows to Laurie's left a shape moved and was gone into the undergrowth that covered an anthill.

"Leopard," said Laurie. "Don't often see them. Usually come out when it's dark. You see him, Mike?"

"No. You sure it was a leopard?"

"Never sure of anything in this kind of light. Dusk is the best time for predators. They can see their prey without being seen. Why the leopard has spots. The pattern the leaves make from the late sun provides perfect camouflage. Every animal has evolved with a means for survival. When the camouflage of the leopard's spots no longer works, he'll become extinct."

"That can't happen," said Mike.

"It can when man cuts down the trees."

"Ah, I see what you mean. But a leopard has no enemies."

"Oh yes he has. Man. Spoilt women like fur coats. And when man has killed off all his fellow creatures in the rush to get rich, he'll die of boredom and sorrow."

"You've been in the bush too long."

"Probably. Maybe not. You know, young Mike, I could have lived here before the white man brought in his guns and his problems. Parked off by the pools with game in abundance. Fish further back in the big river. Never really feeling cold. No one coveting my minuscule possessions. Must have been bloody marvellous."

"Since you got engaged, you've become a romantic."

"It's rather nice... Think we had better stop over there for the night. No fires."

"What about the leopard?"

"He won't bother us. Too much food around."

"Over there, then. I'm hungry. What's the matter, Laurie?"

"Why have all your frogs stopped being sexy?"

The frogs, as one, had gone silent.

"Even the birds aren't calling," whispered Laurie. "We'll get behind the anthill with the leopard."

"Why?"

"Muffle the horses, Mike. Do it quickly but don't make a noise."

With the metal part of the harness wrapped in cloth, Laurie led the animals on foot to behind the anthill. Where the sun had gone down, the sky was crimson red and still the frogs were silent.

The light went ten minutes after they took up a position behind the undergrowth that had fed on the nitrogen in the anthill. The well-schooled horses stood motionless in the beginning of the night. First the stars showed through the tree canopy above their heads. An hour later, a half-moon rose from behind the trees and bathed the bush in a pale light. Twice they heard the guerrillas talking and each time the frogs stopped their chorus. The infiltrators had made camp for the night. Cleverly, and instead of pushing inland after crossing the Zambezi, they had stayed in the thick bush. Laurie felt the taste of bile in his throat: for the first time in his experience, the guerrillas knew what they were doing.

When the wind changed and blew into their faces over the anthill, they both smelt the leopard lying up in the thicket on top of the small hillock. All night long they waited, taking it in turns to sleep and eating the dried meat from their saddlebags, drinking from the water bottles on their belts.

In the first light of dawn, Laurie moved forward. The horses stayed tethered. The light was paling behind the ZANLA camp. Moving with every skill Laurie had learnt at Mongu, they reached the camp with the dawn. Six men were preparing to move out through the thick forest.

Together they each threw a grenade. When the bombs exploded they opened single-shot fire. One guerrilla returned fire before being shot dead by Laurie Hall.

Ten minutes later the cicadas were singing in the long, dry grass.

EVERY NIGHT when Shelley appeared at Bretts the nightclub was full of people trying to forget the bush war. The feeling of wellbeing stopped her drinking before and during her performance. She was content with herself.

After three weeks and with mild surprise she noted her period had not shown on time: the return to singing and her pending marriage had created a change in her metabolism. Every day she expected Laurie to return from the bush and every night she sang harder, trying to draw him back from the danger. There was no word and the soldiers she spoke to said more than once they had stayed on patrol for three months at a time and that the worst attacks came from mosquitoes and tsetse fly. Patrolling the bush was boring and rarely did the two sides ever make contact. The bush was vast and the people few.

After five weeks Shelley was aware that something was happening to her body; the fact dawned with the morning nausea. Asking the club owner for the name of a doctor, the truth was confirmed. She was pregnant. For the first time in her life she was pregnant.

If she told Will Langton, far away in London or Dorset or wherever she had sent him without saying goodbye, he would laugh down the phone. After five years together he would have every right to disclaim any responsibility. If she told Laurie Hall, he would know very well he was not the father. His romantic ideal of celibacy before their marriage would be the cause of it never taking place.

Two days after the doctor's confirmation, Laurie came back from Mana Pools in high spirits. The incursion had been ruthlessly crushed, the helicopter gunships destroying the bands of guerrillas whenever they were found by the ground forces. Away from the thick mopani forests close to the river, the bush was open grassland with intermittent trees. The airborne machine guns chased the running figures down in the long grass: without air-to-ground missiles there was no response.

Laurie's troop had arrived back in the club while she was singing, all of them high from the danger. By the time the evening was over and they were back alone in the Baker Avenue flat they made love, Laurie Hall, sick from the killing, burying his horror in the primal instinct to create new life. For two hours they made love in a fury of fear. By morning Shelley had nothing to say, hoping premature births were more prevalent in the tropics than in the wet and cold of England.

The marriage took place on the Thursday, the reception was planned in

Meikles Hotel. Ant Scott gave Laurie ten days' leave and the nightclub suspended her contract for a week; the publicity caused by her marriage more than compensated the club. Laurie Hall, the white hunter, had married the world-famous singer and newspapers across the world, many of which had thought she had died from alcoholism, featured the romance.

In London, Byron Langton, owner of the copyright to Shelley's music, used the marriage as an excuse to release her records and sell the copyright to another singer. All the newspapers made a major story out of her successful fight with alcoholism, carefully avoiding the fact that Laurie Hall was serving in the rebel Rhodesian army. Somehow the marriage, according to the *Daily Garnet*, took place in Gaborone in Botswana.

Will Langton read the story in one of his brother's newspapers. Three days later he went to the post office in Langton Matravers and sent them a cable at Bretts nightclub. He was probably the only person in England who knew the African nightclub applauding the singer's return to the stage was in Rhodesia and not Botswana. His brother, as always, had slightly twisted the truth.

When Shelley returned to Salisbury from her honeymoon at the Victoria Falls, she read the words of congratulation.

For two days Laurie watched his wife sing from where he sat at the front table in Bretts. He was still surprised and pleased at her unwillingness to drink alcohol.

"Now I have something real to live for, why must I drink?" she told him.

"Ant, myself and young Mike have put in an offer for an old banana plantation thirty miles downriver from Chirundu. My wedding present. They've agreed I can pay off my share after the war when Hall's Safari Camp is making money. We'll make it rival Treetops in Kenya. All the celebrities in the world will flock to the Zambezi to see the animals and hear you sing. Young Mike's father has money which is really the luck of it all. You know, lover, when things start going really right in life you can't go wrong. You think Will Langton will forgive us and pay a visit?"

"I'm not sure about that one. Despite the cable he must feel awful. I wonder if he's found himself a job?"

"The Langtons have money."

"That's not the point."

"I've got to go back on duty tomorrow."

"You will be careful?"

"More careful than ever in my life. What we must do now is have some children."

"With your performance I'd be surprised if I'm not already pregnant. I stopped taking the pill."

"Have you ever seen a man more happy?"

THE PATROL HAD BROUGHT them onto land that would soon be theirs. The old banana trees were tatty, and any fruit had long been eaten by monkeys. The cottage next to the pump house had been destroyed in a guerrilla night attack, killing the farmer and his wife. Ant Scott had negotiated the purchase from the deceased estate. The five-foot diameter flywheel in the pump house had withstood the guerrilla attack and Mike Barrow was sure the pump could be made to work again.

"Those old engines are indestructible," said Mike. "Can use it to pump water to a swimming pool and the lawns we'll spread around the camp. Upmarket. Rich people like cut grass even in the middle of the bush. Makes them feel secure. Are we going to do anything with the banana trees?"

"Transport's the problem," said Laurie. "Too far from Salisbury. South Africa is a whole world away. Bananas are bulky. Probably let them rot. Let's camp further down the river, I fancy fresh meat. Haven't seen a sign of the terrs. Ant was saying ZANLA lost three hundred plus in that last attack."

"You think they'll give up?"

"Everyone gives up in the end. Keep your eyes on the thick riverine bush for kudu. Buggers are difficult to see, they blend in so well. The wind's in our face. A bloody big fire and venison."

"You think the dummy camp site by the fire will work again?" asked Mike.

"Probably not. No, when we've eaten we'll push off further downriver. There'll be a good moon tonight... Another hour before dusk. The kudu'll be around in the bushes waiting to go down to the water when it's safe. Make ourselves some more biltong. Livers and kidneys for breakfast... A man can make himself hungry thinking about food like that. All we need is the redcurrant jam and new-picked peas and we'd feast like kings. That's how it will be in our safari camp. Buffalo kidneys for breakfast and kudu steak for supper. Get a few tame cats to come in each night for the leftover carcass. The Americans and Germans will talk about their Hall Safari for the rest of their lives. I'm going to make a recording of all the night sounds so when they wake at night they'll know what they are hearing. People like to know what's going on. There are some very rich people in this world and all I want is a little part of their money. Probably bore their friends stiff back home but every time they tell the tale they'll be getting a little bit more for the money they gave to us, young Mike. You can only make money in this world with a clear conscience if you give as good as you get. Now, are you looking for kudu or are you not?"

"Oh yes, I am looking. Top of a horse is a fine place to look for them. Heard that said in a film but they were talking about Indians and you can't eat Indians... How many people are we going to have on camp?"

"No more than eight and not less than four. Fifteen hundred US dollars a day. Minimum ten days. They buy their own game licences. We'll give them four animals, from ten days with at least one buff. We'll need some trackers. Just maybe I can find the three we had at base camp."

"Over to your left is a young female kudu," said Mike. "Her big round ears gave her away. You see where I'm looking?"

"Good eyes, young Mike. Got her now. Hold my reins. I want to be on the ground for a clean kill. You know something, I'm turning forty on the 29th March next year and I can still count a herd of springbok a kilometre away? Give me your range on that kudu."

"Three hundred metres."

"My estimate."

Strapped to the rump of his horse in a leather saddle holster was a .375 Brno with a telescopic sight. The FN assault rifle was taken off Laurie's shoulder from a strap and leant against the stump of a tree that had been pushed over by an elephant. Very carefully, Laurie prepared the Brno and took up a shooting position. Drawing his breath evenly, Laurie squeezed the trigger, aiming at the kudu's chest. The crack of the gunshot was followed by the animal running out of the bushes into full view before crashing to the ground, shot through the heart.

"The modern gun and telescope make it too easy," said Laurie, sadly. "The early Boers used muzzleloaders. Now, that would have been shooting. This is slaughter for the pot. Take me an hour to butcher that beast, meantime you can make the fire."

The bloodied meat was hung in a tree near the fire to drip the last of the blood. Later, Laurie would pack the meat into their saddlebags when they moved away from the beacon of their fire that could be seen from high ground in Zambia, from where the ZIPRA guerrillas of Joshua Nkomo operated, backed by the Russians. Another fifty miles downriver was ZANLA territory, infiltrated from Mozambique.

Laurie had cut four good steaks from the rump and was showing them to Mike when Laurie's horse took the first whiff of lion from across the Zambezi River in Zambia. The horse jerked back from the horrors of the pungent smell and knocked the steaks from Laurie's hands onto the ground.

The light was going and the flare of crimson was vivid towards the river where the water flowed on in its endless journey to the sea. The Zambezi was seventy metres from the fire made ready for the meat, the coals hot and glowing. Mike helped pick up the meat covered in dirt.

"I'll dunk them in the river," said Laurie, philosophically. "You always have to wait for the best things in life."

"Use my water bottle," said Mike.

"The river, young Mike. I feel like walking to the river. Look at that sunset. You never see sunsets like that anywhere else in the world. Every shade of red and orange with duck-egg blue between the flaming clouds... I think I'll become a poet."

"Take your FN," said Mike, handing him the gun.

"Hang it over my shoulder so I can carry the meat. Back in less than five minutes."

With Shelley Lane's song from her Zambezi album singing in his mind, Laurie began the short walk to the water. Behind the tall trees that followed the course of the river the rich sunset was shooting lines of colour off the clouds. The smell of wild sage was strong, and the frogs were deafening in their symphony of sex and reproduction, each frog recognising its potential partner amid the cacophony of sound. Laurie followed the track made by the game which took him to the great African river.

The heavy water was constant in its flow, and the last light from the sunset picked out the clumps of weed floating downriver. Over on the Zambian bank four elephant were dousing themselves with water, filling their trunks and squirting the water over their backs, the big ears flapping in sympathy, the water sound reaching Laurie as he walked down the steep bank to the edge of the river, the steaks held out carefully in both hands. Two of the elephant were up to their bellies in the water.

Standing still, looking at the glory of the African night, Laurie watched an owl laboriously fly across the sunset. Then he bent down to the water's edge, kneeling to flush the dust-caked dirt from the meat.

The blow from the crocodile's tail knocked him senseless, sending the meat into the river and dropping the FN from his shoulder. When Laurie regained consciousness he was under water, pushed into a crevice below the bank, the crocodile holding him by the shoulder waiting for him to drown. As he drowned he saw nothing of the past or future, only the futility of the moment.

PART VI

1979 TO 1980

18

Josephine Langton, five years later, in May 1979, was once more out of a job. Socialist Callaghan had been beaten at the polls by Tory Thatcher in the British general election. For thirty-seven months Josephine had been Minister for Commonwealth Aid and Welfare, praised in liberal circles as one of the great British ministers of all time. Her twin brother, Byron, was more candid. In one of his own newspapers he was quoted as saying his saintly sister had given away more of other people's money than anyone else in history. He quoted his protégé, Heathcliff Mortimer's new book, which likened aid to Africa to decanting money down a rathole. Heathcliff Mortimer's latest book, a runaway bestseller, Byron quoted, had gone on to describe the beneficiaries of the minister's largesse as mostly murderers, thieves and tinpot dictators and that every one of the new states, with barely an exception, had ignored their hard-won Westminster constitutions in favour of a one-party state where the looting of the fiscal would be more orderly and more complete with no chance of redress unless it came through the barrel of a gun.

Will Langton had not spoken to his brother or sister for three years. He read about his sister's good deeds and felt proud of her, but they had little in common to talk about. So far as the family was concerned, Will was a failure. He had not spoken to Shelley Lane but heard from the newspapers about the birth of her daughter and the death of her husband. Young Mike Barrow had been shot dead by terrorists before he could report back to Ant Scott. The British and American newspapers said the singer's husband had been a soldier in the rebel Rhodesian army, shot dead by freedom fighters. The press had turned on Shelley Lane and her singing career was over. The report of the marriage ceremony in Gaborone eight months earlier was corrected by the *Daily Garnet* but not before the re-release of Shelley's records had sold out. Byron Langton had, in every sense of the word, 'milked her dry'. As she was no longer of use to him, Byron forgot her as easily as he forgot his mistresses.

Will sold his guns, the guns given to him by Hannes Potgieter, and lived frugally from the proceeds, drifting around London as an itinerant barman. Two years later a further edition of his wildlife book was published, and the public bought more heavily than before. Africa, the Africa of the wild bush, was fast disappearing, along with the game. Elephant and rhinoceros had been decimated. Will's book was a record of what had been and would never be again. Ten per cent of the retail price was donated by the publisher to the World Wildlife Fund. Damian Huntly, the publisher friend of Heathcliff Mortimer, had used the charity to treble his sales.

Heathcliff Mortimer had brought him the royalty cheque. With Heath's drinking habits and Will working behind bars, it had only been a matter of time before they came face-to-face.

"What are you going to do with the money?" Heath asked.

"That's quite a lot of money, Heath."

"More exactly, what are you going to do with the rest of your life?"

"Live it out, I suppose, like everyone else."

"You can start something with that cheque."

"You have something in mind?" asked Will.

"Yes I have. The book sold on nostalgia. There are a lot of people in London who lived in Africa. Probably the ones who bought our book. Start a bar-restaurant with an African theme. Blow up some of your photographs and pitch them round the walls. Get hold of some spears and drums, hunting rifles, old zebra skins, a lion's head. Make the old colonials and the new conservationists pay for their nostalgia in the company of like-minded folk."

"What are you going to call it?" asked Will, trying to make the conversation into a joke.

"The Zambezi Bar, of course. Tell you what, I'll even be your silent partner. We'll find premises close enough to the *Daily Garnet* offices and for once I can make a profit out of my drinking... Will, you're over forty. You really have to do something with your life."

Heathcliff Mortimer's part ownership of a bar was much to his satisfaction. He even continued to rationalise that by drinking he was making a profit. Most nights, instead of going home to his Chelsea flat, he walked down to the Soho bar where most of the conversation was Africa, all in the past, none in the future. As a celebrated Africa hand, Heath found himself the centre of many good conversations, and people who had come into the bar for a drink or two found themselves staying to closing time and going home in a taxi. Heath always went home in a taxi, ordered and paid for by Will who knew how much business his partner brought to the bar.

Colour transparencies had been made of the best African sunsets, blown up to the size of the walls and lit from behind. The result was sundowners in the bush with the sounds of Africa played through loudspeakers. With a boma in the middle of the floor and the smell of roasting impala, no one would have known the difference. Will had drawn the line at a fire and spit roast, but the rest was easily authentic and pure nostalgia for the white Zambians thrown out of their country by a government that had nationalised their farms and businesses. The words had been Africanised to 'indigenisation', 'Africanisation', 'retribution for colonialism', but the result was the same. Along with the ex-Zambians were the ex-Kenyans, the ex-Ugandans and a few old hands from Tanganyika. The war in Rhodesia was reaching a deadly climax and many of the whites were fleeing the country, leaving behind everything they once owned.

For the brief hours these people spent in the Zambezi Bar they were among friends and the cold and sleet outside were driven from their minds as they stared at Will Langton's magnificent photography and listened to the screech of the cicadas and the call of the frogs, heard the familiar bird calls they thought they would never hear again, the night laugh of hyena and the roar of the lion.

Shelley Lane no longer sang in public and he wondered how she was paying her bills but the hurt of sitting in that room in Salisbury waiting for her to come home, the note from Laurie, the lonely journey back to England, were too strong to spark his sympathy. Even with the bar making a financial success he told himself if she had survived so far with the kid, she no longer needed his help and, anyway, she would have long ago found another lover. As best he could, Will put the past women in his life out of his mind and concentrated on the fantasy of his bar and the brief spells of nostalgic happiness he was bringing to so many lonely people.

Heathcliff Mortimer came into the bar half an hour after James Callaghan conceded victory to Margaret Thatcher. The place was full as usual and before he sat down at the bar, three people had asked him if Thatcher would now be able to solve the Rhodesian crisis. He was overweight, drank too much, ate the wrong food, worked long, irregular hours and at the age of seventy-six to his wild surprise there appeared nothing wrong with his health. It was not the result of the general election that made him brush past the questions without giving an answer but a conversation he had overheard in the offices of Langton Merchant Bank between a top executive of the Union Bank of Switzerland and Byron Langton. Part of Heath's training as a journalist had been to stop, wait and listen when something was being said that he or anyone else was not meant to hear.

The babble of conversation in the bar drowned out the insects, the animals and birds, and no one was looking at the stationary sunsets over the Zambezi River. Only the first-time customers looked and listened in awe.

"You want to come and talk to me at the table in the corner?" said Heath to Will.

"Okay, but why, Heath? What's the matter?"

"You remember bringing back a horde of ivory when you first came back to England from Barotseland?"

"Yes. Some belonged to me and some to Hannes. Byron sold it for us. Hell, that was years ago."

"What happened to the proceeds?"

"Nothing much. Byron said that windfall money like that should be gambled on risk investment. I asked him quite a few times what happened to the investment, but he was paying me a good salary, more than I was worth I can tell you that, and when he said that some investments were better than others for the fourth or fifth time, I don't remember really, I assumed he had gambled and lost my money and was too embarrassed to admit his investment eye had gone wrong. Money has never been a big thing with me, you know that."

"You remember all those crocodile skins you shipped across with Laurie Hall before independence?"

"I think that's my point. The money Byron paid Laurie did Laurie more harm than good and when he had spent the lot, no one wanted to know his troubles. Money attracts the wrong kind of people."

"Aside from that, did you know how much money your brother made out of the skins once he had turned them into shoes and handbags?"

"I never asked him. My concern was for the chief to be paid. I didn't want anything to do with the slaughter."

"The chief did very well. Your brother invested his money and made him a rich man. His children went to the best private schools in England and are now proper Englishmen with very proper accents."

"I'm glad to hear some good came out of the slaughter."

"Did you know that when the final profit was calculated by Byron, he gave Laurie a substantial bonus?"

"Nonsense. He would have told Laurie. Laurie was on the bones of his arse until he joined the Rhodesian army."

"Well, I'll tell you something. In August 1965, your brother awarded Laurie a bonus of ten thousand pounds and for your introduction to the business he allocated you thirty thousand pounds."

"Shit. That's a lot of money."

"The money was invested in gold bullion with the Union Bank of Switzerland and sold for an eight hundred per cent profit a few years later. The proceeds were then invested in very difficult to buy German equity stock before the Deutsche Mark made its historic bull run against the pound. At that point the well-invested proceeds of the ivory, yours and Hannes Potgieter's, was added to the equation and far from losing your money, your brother made you a fortune. Because the money was in your name and that of Laurie Hall, but under the signature of your brother to move the investment wherever he wished, he saw the rise in capital and decided to keep quiet, thinking he could take back a bonus he never mentioned and an investment you thought had gone bust. This morning I overheard a conversation between your brother and the bank when they told him the money belonged to one William Edward Langton and the estate of one Laurie Makepeace Hall. Your brother, apparently, was trying to take back the money for himself."

"How did you find out all the detail?"

"I'm a reporter... No, that wasn't the only way. After the man from the UBS had left on a waft of self-righteousness, I confronted your brother. I said I was going to tell you and Shelley Lane, the widow of Laurie Hall. He said I could go to hell."

"He'll fire you."

"He won't."

"Why not?"

"I've got enough dirt on your brother laundering money out of Africa to put him in jail for the rest of his life."

"You say his money is made through crookedness?"

"The seed money, yes. His mentor was the notorious Jack Pike who made the bulk of his money out of prostitution and soft porn."

"What's Johnny Pike to Jack Pike?"

"Father and son. They own forty per cent of Langton Merchant Bank through nominees. Your brother made the second generation legitimate."

"Why hasn't someone done something about it?"

"Don't look at me, Will. I like my Chelsea flat too much and my interest in Southern Comfort is very expensive. If he goes out of business, someone else will help the Mobutus of this world buy their villas in the South of France. Your sister tried a few years back when she finally worked out what was happening to her aid for Africa. She said the blacks could be forgiven but not your brother. She threatened to expose him if he did not stop financing imports to and exports from Africa, the word 'financing' being a nice way to take ten per cent and hide the money in Switzerland. Your brother laughed in her face and she was a minister in the British government. Josephine came to me after that nasty little row with her twin and wanted to know what she could do. I told her nothing. That there was nothing she could do but find a better way of sending aid into Africa that would bypass the crooked politicians and the predators like her brother. You see, your sister when she was very young had an illegal abortion and the Tory Party would have had a field day tearing apart the sanctimonious Labour Party if they had found out. Your brother not only had proof, he had photographs, seeing he organised the abortion with the help of the Pikes. Your brother has a file on just about everyone who might get in his way."

"Josephine was pregnant? By whom?"

"A man called Wolfgang Baumann."

"I remember him. He was her tutor. We had a Christmas together at Langton Manor."

"He never knew. Only Byron."

"Poor Josephine. She'll be so lonely now. Out of office. No husband. No kids."

"That's the point, Will. Everyone has to live with themselves. But if I were you, I'd go and ask your brother for your money."

"And Shelley?"

"I'll tell Shelley," said Heathcliff Mortimer. "You know she never made a penny out of the re-release of her records? She'd sold her share in Music Lane Limited to Byron and Music Lane owns the royalties to her music."

"What's she doing, Heath?"

"You don't want to know."

WILL LIVED in a small flat above the bar and restaurant. Every morning at six he went out to buy fresh vegetables for the restaurant. The dark, cold mornings of winter were giving way to the light of summer and the walk along wet streets more comfortable. In the bad days he forced the images of Africa away from his mind and concentrated on the present. With the help of Heathcliff Mortimer spreading the word, the bar and twelve-table, alcove restaurant had made a profit in the sixth month and presently he was three months ahead with the rent and all the bills had been paid as everything was bought for cash, making Will highly conscious of the price of food. Will did all the buying and handled the meal receipts at the bar. There were two waitresses for the lunch trade and another two for the supper, with a cook preparing both meals. Will did the washing up and a cleaner service came in to do the floors. The rhythm of work and sleep, six days a week, suited Will's mood and the familiar faces that became his regular customers were his friends. He was comfortable and mostly content and with his forty-second birthday coming up later in the month had resigned himself to spending the rest of his life on his own. Wife and children had passed him by.

For a week, Will avoided the issue of confronting his brother as he thought through the result of finding his ownership of so much wealth. Half the fun of the Zambezi Bar was keeping it ticking, making enough to pay the staff an above-average wage with fifteen per cent of all profit split between the cook and the waitresses at the end of each month. Will had good company, a drink when he chose, a meal when he was hungry and a comfortable bed. He had the certain awareness that his graph of happiness would fall with so much money in the bank. The small excitement of cashing up each night to tell the others how the bonus looked would be taken away. The whole point of his own business would be drowned in a flood of wealth. Maybe Shelley needed the money, she had a child, but he had no use for more than he earned from the bar. Every night Heathcliff Mortimer asked if he had seen his brother and every night he shook his head.

"Have you seen Shelley?" Will asked at the end of the first week.

"Yes I have."

"How is she, Heath?"

"Better now. She needed money badly."

"What did you do with the money?"

"Your brother transferred all the money from Switzerland and gave me a cheque made out to Shelley. Fortunately Laurie had made a will so Shelley would get a widow's pension should anything happen to him in the war. Living in England, she was not able to receive the pension from Rhodesia. United Nations mandatory sanctions."

"How much was it, Heath?"

"A little over two hundred thousand pounds."

"Shelley can't control money."

"I know. She agreed to put it all in trust for the girl and only touch the income."

"What was she doing?"

"Forget it, Will. It doesn't matter anymore."

"I want to know."

"Then ask Shelley Lane... Do you still love her?"

"I don't think I ever loved her, Heath. We needed each other for a time."

"She needed you after Laurie died."

"You ever been left in a room where you lived with a woman as the days went while she'd gone off with your best friend? That hurt. Not the love or sex but the crass inability of both of them to think of another person."

"Would you like me to get a cheque for you from Byron? Save you and your brother the embarrassment."

"I'm not sure if I want the money. Do you know how much I have?"

"Over a million. Quite a bit over a million."

"And he was never going to say?"

"Not a word."

"How can a man steal from his brother?"

"To him it was a legitimate business deal. The profit was hidden, and he was the only one who knew the hiding place."

"He'll have to live with himself."

"He doesn't consider anything wrong. Byron had one hell of a row with the chief executive at the Union Bank of Switzerland. Those Swiss banks are getting nervous about their secrecy laws...hiding drug and terrorist money. The man from UBS said yours and Shelley's had a non-British resident trust account number and only the beneficiaries of the trust, both nominated by your brother for tax purposes when he opened the accounts, could receive the money. You will have to talk to the tax lawyer yourself. Shelley's new bankers are working on that one."

"Even now the problems start."

"What are you going to do?"

"As I said before, when I make up my mind I'll let you know... The man must have a twisted mind."

"Who?"

"My brother, Byron. What does he want from all this money? He never goes down to East Horsley. Stays in London with his whores. Had a phone call from Fiona wanting to see me. Don't know how she found out about the bar. The worst thing you can ever do is interfere in other people's private affairs. Said we could talk if we met at Langton Manor but I don't go home anymore. My father is on his knees most of the time praying to God for forgiveness. Thinks the bomb on Japan was all his fault. I could get no sense out of him at all and when Mother went on and on about all the money they had skimped and scraped to send me to Stanmore and what had I done with it and how could she have a son who made a living as a common publican. I love my mother but that was the final straw. Well, not quite. The permanent comparison to one minister of the Crown and one pillar of the city of London drove me out of Dorset and I've not been back. As usual, I send her a bunch of flowers on my birthday for the pain she suffered giving me life and I phone them both on their birthdays... Why do families grow apart? We used to be so close growing up as children. There was always so much family at Langton Manor, especially at Christmas time. Randolph's still all right, but he thinks he's a failure in our mother's eyes by not siring a son. He's the eldest. Langton Manor goes to Randolph and after that it will be Byron and then Gregory, Byron's son. Gregory's eleven now, boarding school at Stanmore prep, and if he saw his father in the street they probably wouldn't recognise each other. And the younger girls, despite living at home, see their grandfather more often than their father. Anyway, Fiona's got her career which is what these women seem to want these days. God knows what it will do to the next generation. There just isn't any family life anymore."

"Man is adaptable," said Heath, draining his glass. "How we evolved from the swamps to living in a concrete box in the sky. Pour me another Southern Comfort. I've got a bit of a thirst tonight."

THREE MONTHS LATER, Heathcliff Mortimer was sitting on the same bar stool thinking back on his life and keeping it to himself. Will understood Heath's evenings of solitude, quiet in a crowd, drinking Southern Comfort, and left him alone.

The day's special was poached cod with a tarragon sauce, both fresh that morning from the market, the cod plentiful and cheap by comparison to meat and poultry. Neither of the waitresses had arrived. The few customers were sitting at the bar. Outside on the street it was broad daylight but inside the lights were on. The same switch that lit up the bush scenes that covered the walls turned on the tape recorder, engulfing the early drinkers in the sounds of Christmas beetles and cicadas with the intermittent bay of a black-backed jackal.

An old man and a much younger woman sat down at one of the tables. The man Will guessed was in his mid-sixties and the woman her mid-thirties. Other customers came to the bar, and he lost sight of them and then

Milly the waitress arrived and he put them out of his mind. Old men with young women were common in London but the expression on the man's face looking at the murals was so rapt that Will knew the man had experienced the real bush. Another nostalgia freak, but it was the way he made his living. Soon the bar sounds of man overcame the night sounds of insects and animals. It was going to be a good night for business. Still Heath ignored the company and Will filled his glass when it was empty without being asked and without saying a word. One raised finger from the level of the wooden bar counter acknowledged the service and like any long friendship they were perfectly at ease without words. The old man's ability to consume Southern Comfort never failed to amaze Will Langton. He could count on one hand the number of times he had seen Heathcliff Mortimer drunk and never in public.

As always at seven-thirty, Will handed over the bar to Milly and went on a round of his tables to ask if everything was all right. The cod was selling fast which was no surprise as the clarity of the eyes of each dead fish had been checked and the skin smelt, with the cook knowing how to poach out the flesh colour in the middle of the cod without overcooking. The tarragon sauce was one of her minor masterpieces.

The old man and his young wife were still at their same table and Will bent to pick up their well-cleaned fish plates and found himself surprised that both his guests, by the sound of their accents, were American. There had been very few Americans in British Colonial Africa and Will wondered if he had come in off the streets by mistake until he remembered the look he had seen the old man give the massively blown-up shots of the Zambezi River at sundown.

"I know that place," said the man, pointing at the wall behind their table. "I recognise that Goliath heron. Belonged to a man called Hannes Potgieter."

Faces change, covered up by age and the drain of colour from skin and hair, but the one thing that mostly never changed was the voice.

"Melvin Raath! What a coincidence... You remember me? I'm Will Langton. You even gave me your address in America. Have it upstairs as a matter of fact. You remember that trip to base camp? That was my first safari with a client. You're in newspapers. Something like that. Hannes said you were the best of all his clients as you truly loved the bush and not just the idea of a trophy on your wall back home."

"Good God, is that really you? What happened, Will?"

"Why? What do you mean? Oh, all this."

"Why aren't you in Africa?"

"They kicked us out, don't you remember? Hannes is dead many years back."

"I know. Why I didn't go back. He left it to you, didn't he?"

"Yes. Well, me and the trackers I suppose."

"This is my daughter, Mary-Lou. She's my youngest. We're going to watch a show in the West End. What time you put up the shutter?"

"Eleven."

"We'll call back after the show. Sounds like you live on the premises. You can buy us a cup of coffee for old times' sake and let an old man talk about the only place he ever felt really at home. Bore my Mary-Lou to shreds but that's a small price for her trip to London."

Will thought of Melvin Raath the rest of the evening, the man who came to Africa and the bush instead of seeking a shrink. Will had been eighteen and the impression the newspaperman left had stayed with Will for twenty-four years. The picture of modern America drawn by Melvin Raath all those years ago had struck the chord which stopped Melvin Raath from being the conventional, educated modern man. There had been something about too many sidewalks, not enough grass and a world that had lost sight of how to make itself happy. Quite a few African hands after spreading their meal or drinks thick with nostalgia had said they would be back but never came. Only the ones close to Soho made it their place to drink. He had barely noticed the girl before going back to take over the bar from Milly. The book of his photographs, described in words by Heathcliff Mortimer, had sold well in London and people talked. Many a barman in the top London hotels knew the photographer owned the Zambezi Bar in Soho. They liked the idea of a fellow barman publishing books and they talked about it to their stray customers who sat at their bars with nothing better to do. London was really a very small place.

The surprise came when Will was cashing up and the Raaths, father and daughter, arrived to claim their cup of coffee.

"What did you see?"

"You won't believe it but that show by your Agatha Christie. *The Mousetrap.* Been running nearly thirty years and the house was sold right out."

"You want to come upstairs for some coffee, Mr Raath? This place is weird when there's only me, I have to turn the lights out on the panels or I feel creepy."

"Homesick, more likely."

"There's nothing worse than feeling homesick for a place you can't go back to, a place that no longer exists. You read about people in history being banished into exile and now I know what they must have felt. Let me put this money in the safe and we'll go upstairs."

That evening, every time Will turned his attention away from Melvin Raath he found the daughter's eyes boring into him. She never spoke and never took her eyes off Will Langton. Even the father noticed.

"You're the first live white hunter my Mary-Lou's met, Will. Have to forgive her. Ever since a toddler, I told Mary-Lou about Africa and to Mary-Lou a white hunter is a whole lot better than a knight in shining armour, don't you say, Mary-Lou?"

To Will's consternation, Mary-Lou said not a word but continued to bore into his brain with her eyes. She had this disconcerting habit of flicking the underneath of the thumbnail with the nail of her second finger. A gun in her hand would have been no less disconcerting. The girl was not unattractive physically, with big breasts pushing firmly into a silk blouse, distinctly showing him the shape of large, round nipples. Will guessed her age as thirty-five or thirty-six.

The father retold story after story of his great days on safari with Hannes Potgieter and the daughter went on clicking her thumbnail. It took an open yawn to send the message that six o'clock in the morning was the time he started work.

"Sorry. I've been talking too much," said Melvin Raath. "Come, Mary-Lou. Will told us he has to do the shopping early in the morning."

"What time do you open?" asked Mary-Lou, the first words she had spoken.

"Eleven-thirty like all other pubs but one around here. The Green Dolphin in Greek Street opens at ten."

She gave him a last look deep into his eyes before going down the stairs in front of her father. Will saw them out of the front door of the restaurant. It was two o'clock in the morning and raining. Luck brought a taxi with the 'For Hire' sign lit within a minute of them standing in the doorway and Will's late-night guests went on their way to Claridge's Hotel.

'Must be richer than ever before,' thought Will, going inside and locking the door. Within minutes of finding his bed he was sound asleep. He had been careful to drink two cups of coffee. For old times' sake and the memory of Hannes Potgieter, he had let the American talk for two hours. The last thought he had before sleep was that the world was very strange.

At eleven the following morning when Will opened the front door to the public, Mary-Lou Raath was standing on the pavement, a dry pavement bathed in sunshine.

"Sorry about Melvin last night. He just likes to talk about Africa."

Having smiled, made the right sounds and overcome the strangeness of a daughter calling her father by his Christian name, Will moved back inside and took up his customary position behind the bar. Cook would not arrive for half an hour but a clean kitchen was ready and waiting, Will finding it easier to clean the place himself rather than relying on outside help. Dishwashers were notoriously late or did not come at all. The dole was a much simpler source of income.

"You got some of that coffee?" asked the girl who had followed him to the bar. "Melvin's coming later."

The only other words she said for an hour were, 'You got a customer,' while he was in the kitchen making her coffee. She sat and watched him and only drank her coffee when it was cold.

Will had three regular single women coming into the bar on their own and all of them had given him the look of availability but none of them had made him awkward. She was still on the same bar stool at half-past two when he closed up for the afternoon.

"When do you open again?" she asked.

"What happened to your dad?" he said, ignoring the question.

At half-past five they both arrived at the same time.

"You ever think of moving to the States?" asked Melvin Raath. "Mary-Lou wants to open a restaurant and says you run the best restaurant she ever saw. What we think is, making a Zambezi Bar in New York only much, much bigger with waiters dressed like askaris with red fez hats and black tassels, a man on the door wearing a lion skin, black man of course, punkahs up in the ceiling. Real Colonial Africa. Get the first one up and running in New York and then we franchise right across the States. Got a whole pile of money waiting to invest and you got the right idea here, Will. Be nice for me, sitting in my own bar thinking I'm back in those good old days in Africa."

"Colonial rule isn't exactly the flavour of the month."

"People say one thing, do another. No one minds anything in America so long as it makes money. Take my word. Instead of scratching a living for the rest of your life I'll make you a rich man. Bet apart from this bar you don't have a cent to your name."

Across town in the offices of Langton Merchant Bank, Byron Langton was thinking. Years ago he had discovered the only person he could talk to properly was himself. The conversation going on in his mind was trying to fuse his brain. He had flown in from Switzerland that afternoon without the one and a half million pounds. The Swiss bank was adamant. The money belonged to his brother.

"It was a tax opportunity," he had shouted. "My brother hasn't ever heard of the money. He was overseas, and I used his name to invest thirty thousand pounds in gold."

"What about the ivory money? That certainly belonged to William Langton. We had to see the will of his partner to combine the money."

"There didn't seem any point in two accounts."

"Swiss law is Swiss law. You gave your brother thirty thousand pounds. Why or for what reason is none of our business. Mr Langton, if everyone who gave anyone money in this world wanted it back again where would we be? My goodness, where would we be?"

"I may have given him thirty thousand pounds. I don't remember. But it was me that made the rest of it."

"I'm sure your brother will appreciate the skill. And Mr Langton, as your overseas bankers, the amount of one and a half million pounds set against your personal assets is rather small. You have become a very wealthy man."

"It's the principle. He didn't make the money, I did."

"We agree, Mr Langton. It's the principle. The money was invested in the name of William Edward Langton and if any money is taken from the trust account, it must be done with his written approval."

"There is absolutely no justice in this world."

"From my experience in Swiss banking I must heartily agree with you."

"What does that mean?"

"Mr Langton, we even banked for the Nazis. We would even bank for the devil if he gave us money to invest."

Sitting at his London desk, the thoughts and arguments swirled in Byron's mind and always he was right and everyone else was wrong: he was the one that made the money; no one else; without the likes of himself there would be no wealth in the world.

Having berated himself for half an hour, Byron rationalised the reality. The money was gone. He would make the best of a bad job. It was six o'clock and his secretary, who had been with him for more years than he could remember, had gone home. Finding the right telephone directory outside at reception, he went back into his office and dialled the Zambezi Bar in Soho.

"Will, old chap, how are you?"

"Who's that?"

"Byron, you bloody fool. Can you come over to the office?"

"Not now, Byron. What's the matter?"

"We have to talk about your investments?"

"What investments, Byron?"

"Oh, don't be so bloody stupid. That old fox Mortimer must have told you. Pickles what's left of his liver most nights at your bar so they tell me."

"Maybe this time, Byron, if you want to see me you come over here. I believe you know the Green Dolphin in Greek Street. We're just around the corner."

"What do you know about the Green Dolphin?"

"I believe it was owned by your partner, Jack Pike. But what you do with your life is up to you provided it doesn't interfere with other people. You might as well bring a cheque."

"Just forms for the bank. Then you deal direct."

"Why not put the forms in the mail?"

"Right. I'll do that."

"By the way, thank you, Byron."

"Oh go and fuck yourself."

"They didn't teach you that at Stanmore."

The receiver was slammed down at the other end and the phone went dead in Will's ear. 'Money does awful things to people,' was all he thought. Three people were looking to order drinks, all of them slightly agitated. Will smiled to himself. A man without a drink when he wanted one was an equally sad thing. "Shit," he said quietly to the row of bottles as he turned to the optic with a glass for a shot of brandy. "What do I do with all that money?"

Finished with the drinks, he went back to Melvin Raath and his daughter at the end of the bar. He carried a double whisky for himself, a double bourbon for Melvin Raath and a Coke for the daughter.

"Cheers," he said. "This one's on me."

"Could you find a reliable manager to run this place?" asked Melvin Raath.

"Probably," said Will. "There are so many ex-Rhodesians coming into London without a job or a penny to their name. Even if they could sell their farms and businesses back home, they can't bring out the money. Everything goes to the war effort. Maybe the Lancaster House talks will bring that to an end but chances are the new government will confiscate white property as they have done everywhere else in Africa."

"Unless they can make some kind of agreement to stop that," said Melvin.

"Point is, Rhodesia was living in the colonial past; the whites with their proverbial heads in the sand. But not all the colonial past was bad. In those days an Englishman was honest as, if he wasn't, they tossed him out of the club. These new refugees from Rhodesia have been trained to run an empire that no longer exists, so running a bar and restaurant will be small beer, if you'll excuse the pun... If they sign the Lancaster House Agreement it will finally end the second empire and Britain will revert back four hundred years to being an insignificant island off the coast of Europe with arguably the worst climate in the world."

"What was the first empire?" asked Mary-Lou.

"America and Canada... When I was born in 1937, the Union Jack flew over one-fifth of the world's surface and one out of four on this earth were subjects of the King-Emperor. And that was the second empire. Africa and Asia, we'll leave behind our language, maybe, and cricket."

"What's cricket?" asked Mary-Lou.

"A game played by Englishmen with a strict set of rules."

After two hours of further conversation, Will was not sure whether they wanted him for the business, the daughter or for Melvin Raath to talk on about his few lost days in Africa.

England, so far as Will was concerned, was riding backwards into the dark. Maybe America would have a glowing sunset. Most importantly, he told himself, he had nothing better to do.

19

Three months later, Byron Langton, in December 1979, was invited to the signing of the Lancaster House Agreement which would end the rebellion in Rhodesia. Having given equal amounts of money to Joshua Nkomo's ZAPU and Robert Mugabe's ZANU, both parties wanted to know where his loyalties lay.

As a newspaper proprietor, Byron had kept a solid distance from his 'clients' who were often not sure whether the party funding was less important than the power of the Langton Press. Like the British at the height of the empire, Byron found fraternisation with his inferiors not only uncomfortable but bad policy. The more aloof, the more mystical the power. Heathcliff Mortimer was sent in his stead.

Byron had enjoyed telling his twin sister Josephine of the invitation, failing to say whence it came and certainly not telling her there were two of them. Josephine had spent considerable energy to resolve the problems of the last British colony in Africa but had not been invited to watch the resolution. She was no longer a minister of the Crown, not even a shadow minister. To complete her ignominy, she had lost her seat in Parliament at the general election won by Margaret Thatcher. She had a pension and a ticket into the wilderness. Her flat in Westminster was as cold as charity. No one even visited her anymore.

Byron chuckled to himself. Except for South Africa which would now feel the pressure, the Anglo-Saxon cabal had rid themselves of African responsibility and would now allow the price of base minerals to drop through the floor. The Africans had inherited a well-planned mess. Africa was to be marginalised and in Chicago, Byron sold short on copper, chrome, manganese and nickel. To add to his certainty of a price drop, the Russians were flooding the world market with anything they could sell in a last attempt to support the Soviet socialist system. Without the fear of Stalin or the incentive of capitalistic greed, Byron's analysis told him that Russia's economy was going to collapse. Switching his long-term investment plan, Byron began buying American stocks with the emphasis on technology. He was convinced that science would solve man's problems, not politics or religion. If it blew them all up the problem would be solved in one big bang, but Byron had faith in the selfishness of men. There was no point in blowing up the competition if it blew you up as well.

At forty-eight, Byron was married to a woman of thirty-eight who no longer turned him on. For years Byron had understood that women over the age of twenty-five rarely caught his eye. The glorious age of women was nineteen to twenty-five, when they were confident and at the summit of their powers to sexually attract men. For Byron the aphrodisiac was money. Poor Fiona would have to understand. She had the beautiful home he rarely visited, three beautiful children that she brought up perfectly, a career in publishing that every career-orientated woman would die for and if she only saw her husband once a month, surely that was a bonus. For Byron, chuckling again to himself, not only was she the perfect wife for him but she also made him money. Most wives cost a fortune. His turned a profit.

During the week, Byron worked at his business without any play but when it came to Fridays and Saturdays, they belonged to the reason he had created so much power and wealth, his pursuit of sexual excitement with the most beautiful partner he could entice out to dinner. Byron Langton liked the chase. He liked women. He liked expensive restaurants. And best of all he loved enticing women into his bed. Never once in his life had he handed over money or a present apart from the best dinner money could buy. Sometimes he failed with his enticement which made the next challenge even more exciting. Even if he now had a paunch and his hair was really going grey, there was nothing a well-tailored suit could not hide and, as he told himself, every woman over thirty coloured her hair so why shouldn't he?

Byron's flat in Knightsbridge, at 47 Buckingham Court, was exactly the same as in the days of Virginia Stepping and Fanny Try except he now owned the building to avoid paying rent. Too many rich people flashed their wealth which from Byron's perspective was quite unnecessary. The more visible a rich man made himself, the more he became a target and Byron had no wish to be a target. Maybe the flashers had inferiority complexes, something from which Byron considered he had never suffered.

Even if he had wished to commute daily to East Horsley, it would have been impractical and the flat at number forty-seven was certainly too small for the whole family. Byron mostly worked fourteen hours every day which left him no time to travel up and down to London. Over the months and years he had simply moved away from his family. Some of his friends commuted and never saw their children awake during the week. Then sometimes he had gone into the office on a Saturday and after that it never seemed worthwhile taking the Tube, standing at Victoria Station and eventually finding his way home to discover the children were going to a party and Fiona had another of her dreary writers staying for the weekend who either fawned over him as the proprietor of the *Garnet* or treated him like an intellectual pygmy. He had far better have stayed in London. He hoped for her sake that Fiona was getting a bit on the side as when it came to sex, neither of them were interested in each other. Familiarity had finally bred a total lack of motivation. So, mostly, he left them alone, retaining his family ties by phone.

The first Friday of the new year had been a tiresome day and only the thought of that night's delicious prospect took him happily back to Buckingham Court for a bath and change. By half-past eight he was standing in front of his mirror in the flat: a man of forty-eight, looking older than he should have been with the shirt tight across his belly and grey hairs definitely showing at his temples. For the umpteenth time a tinge of guilt registered with his age, and then he was telling himself 'what the hell, if you can get away with it', and he went downstairs to look for a cab which the doorman found for his usual pound note in double-quick time. He gave the girl's address and sat back in the taxi, highly content with the prospect of his evening.

"Hello," he said when the door to the communal flat opened ten minutes later. "I'm Byron Langton. Is Marcia ready to go?"

"No, she isn't," said a girl he had never seen before.

"May I come in?"

"No, you can't."

"Marcia does live here? She gave me the address."

"She's eighteen. You're too old. Fact is, you're a dirty old married man. Go and perve around somewhere else. Marcia's my sister."

With what appeared to be an act of moral indignation, the sister slammed the door of the flat and left Byron standing on the mat with a bunch of flowers for which he no longer had a use. Not since he was a boy just out of Stanmore had a door been slammed in his face. Quietly, as he retraced his steps, he gave himself the answer. 'It's over, I'm too old. All that bloody money and I'm too old. What a bloody waste of time.' Being called a dirty old man had hurt because he knew it was the truth. A new, unexpected feeling spread through the melancholy in his mind. He was lonely. For the first time he was lonely. He had never been lonely before.

To his surprise, when he climbed back into his waiting taxi, he gave the driver an address in Westminster. and when he sat back in the seat waiting for the journey to reach its end, he undid two buttons of his shirt front and let out a sigh.

"It had to end sometime," he said out loud. "Eighteen. Shit! She told me she was twenty-four."

Byron rang the second front door that night and waited. He had paid off the taxi downstairs. He could hear someone inside coming to the door and when it opened he smiled.

"You know, sis, we do have the same colour eyes."

"What do you want?"

"To make peace. Maybe to apologise."

"You've been stood up?"

"Matter of fact I have. Turned out to be eighteen and not twenty-four. She lied. Her very righteous sister slammed the door in my face. I brought you some flowers."

"Disgusting."

"The flowers, Jo?"

"You. You're disgusting."

"She said she was the sister but you never know these days."

"Oh what the hell! You'd better come in and I'll put the poor girl's flowers in water."

"How did you know the flowers were for Marcia? You know, I really feel old. Do you feel old, sis? We're exactly the same age."

"That's the second time tonight you've said 'you know'."

"We are ratty tonight. Don't you have any company?"

"Frankly, Byron, I never have company anymore. Men don't find me attractive and after your comment of 'decanting money down a rathole' which the Tories picked up to crucify me in the election, my erstwhile political friends don't call either."

"It wasn't me. The quote was Heath. You have any booze in this flat?"

"That I do. That I do... Would you really have printed those photographs?"

"No. But would you have gone for me for helping your black friends to make some money? I'm sorry Paul Mwansa was assassinated but he really couldn't go on changing sides and get away with it... I'll have a nice big Scotch if you don't mind."

"You deserve to be locked up!"

"It's the system, Josephine. You moralists just don't understand the system. All the political claptrap is just another means of getting the hands on the money."

"Taking those photographs really hurt."

"Johnny Pike had the photographs taken. It was illegal, remember? Still is. Johnny was protecting himself."

"Against whom?"

"Against you."

"I'm sure it was a boy."

"Sis, don't let's go back on that one again."

"You brought it all back with those damn photographs."

"And you were going to ask questions in Parliament about one Langton Merchant Bank. Did one of your African friends try to blackmail you when he found out we were twins?"

"It was Paul Mwansa. Did you have him killed?"

"Not me, sis. Maybe the people I do business with. It's a jungle out there, if you'll excuse the pun. Cheers! Nice Scotch. Are you happy that Britain has given back her last colony in Africa?"

"She hasn't yet. There still has to be a free and fair election. The freedom fighters have to come in to the assembly points and the ceasefire has to hold."

"Oh, it will. My information is both parties have had enough of shooting at each other. They're exhausted. And the election will be free and fair if Robert Mugabe wins. Which he will."

"Why?"

"Because Africa is tribal not political, despite your democratic constitutions. One man one vote, the biggest tribe wins, loots the fiscal, shoots the opposition and makes sure it stays in power for fear of retribution. It's a balls-up and will be for a long time and the people you, Josephine Langton, want to help will be the ones to suffer most. A few will get rich and the rest will starve."

"With your help."

"Don't blame me, sis. Do you really think a man or a woman who can't read, doesn't have a radio and only sees life as it relates to crops and the weather, is going to understand a vote? All you've done is taken away fairly good, mostly uncorrupt colonial management and replaced it with a few politicians whose only purpose in life is to steal. Maybe a few of the top men are honest, but the rest! Sir Roy Welensky, the prime minister of the old federation of the two Rhodesias and Nyasaland, was going to turn Central Africa into a dominion as powerful as Canada. Everything was there. Minerals, a good system of roads and railways, superb farmland that only needed a network of dams to irrigate the crops, a hard-working though illiterate indigenous population and the last generation of Englishmen who were prepared to leave home to become permanent white Africans and provide the management to make the dream come true. Darling sis, you can have all the minerals, the manpower, the money and the markets but if you don't have the fifth 'M', management, it doesn't work. You've taken the management out of Africa and without it, and until it's put back again, it won't work. By your wish to make everyone equal you've starved a whole continent. The problem's not the likes of me making a living according to the free-market system but people like you who made the tragic mistake of believing that everyone in Africa is as good as you. You are a good person, sis, I know that. But I also know that the true likes of you are as rare as hen's teeth. Now, did you hear Will's going to America to go into big business, which he will hate? That young brother of mine has a passion for Africa. Nothing else matters. And he can't go back. Not anymore and not for a long time... Any news of Hilary?"

"As usual not a word... When are you going to stop taking out young girls?"

"As from now. May I have another Scotch?"

"Help yourself."

"Then we're going out to dinner. I have a table booked, remember?"

"The head waiter will never believe his eyes."

"Are you happy, sis?"

"No I am not."

"What can we do about it?"

"I've not the slightest idea but a good meal might be a start. I'm sick of cooking for myself. And the trouble is I'm a lousy cook."

THE SMALL FRENCH restaurant in Hay Street was the place Byron favoured to impress young girls. It was intimate, warm, and the tables were far enough apart from each other for his conversation not to be overheard. Byron knew that seduction started at the ring of the doorbell which is why he had carried the flowers. Women liked to feel very good about themselves before they went to bed with a man the first time. Byron tried to make them feel for an evening that they were the only woman in the world, believing flattery was a power tool.

The owner of the restaurant was an equally good confidence trickster and made his regular customers feel they were so welcome it broke his heart to leave his guests alone at their tables. Byron had a strong suspicion the man was an Irishman masquerading as a Frenchman but it really did not matter: the young girls were all most impressed, having never had a chair moved back for them to sit on in their lives. In a moment of surprise when the man saw Josephine the mask fell but very briefly.

"So nice, Mr Langton, to see you and your wife."

"My twin sister."

"The Honourable Josephine Langton," smiled the proprietor, recovering his full stride. Smiling the sunshine of good favour, he left them with a waiter to take their order.

"That man's good," said Josephine. "Did you see his first impression?"

"I'm afraid I did."

"So did I. Rather depressing." She picked up the foot-wide piece of cardboard given her by the waiter. "Now that's what I call a menu. Seeing you're so bloody rich, Byron, I'll have a dozen Brittany oysters on their little bed of seaweed and crushed ice. And please, just this once, don't put me down as a tax deduction. Oh, and a nice dry German hock. The German whites are better than the French."

The bill when it came later was for two hundred and eleven pounds. Byron never added up bills in restaurants. Taking out his wallet he counted the notes with a ten per cent tip and gave the money to the waiter.

"Maybe another cup of coffee?" he said to the waiter, showing the palm of his hand to Josephine for her agreement.

"Why not?" said Josephine. "After that they can afford an extra cup of coffee. Do you know how many families that would've fed in Africa?"

"The perfect statement of a socialist but the trouble with socialism is it only understands the pursuit of power, never the fundamentals of creating wealth."

"Rubbish."

"The modern favourite is every man was born equal which is just as ludicrous as saying the world is flat. However equal people like to think I am, I would not survive one blow in a boxing ring from Muhammad Ali. Why? He's bigger than me and he has a great boxing talent. The American Declaration of Independence states that all men are born equal before the law. Everyone with a mind less sharp than his neighbour prefers to leave off the last three words and as most of us in this world are stupid, social democracy has used a wrong statement to gain power without being questioned. I do believe a lot of people now think they are just as good as the next man. In America they have tried to legislate such equality. All affirmative action has done for the blacks is piss off the good blacks who are capable of holding down their good jobs through their own ability as everyone now knows they only got the job because they are black. Like the Church with its dogma, socialism can never succeed when it is based on an incorrect premise that every man is equal. Fortunately we are all very different and the insides of our heads are just as different as the outside appearances of our bodies.

"Now, to explain how I see the basic economic fact of the bill just paid. Your only correct argument is the amount and quality of the food we ate, not the size of the bill which would feed post-colonial impoverished Africa. By being stupid enough or lazy enough not to run my own cow and harvest my own oysters, I have created a flow of wealth right from the waiter to the cowhand and the man or woman who cut those delicious oysters from the rocks off France. I am the fool who paid the bill but all the oysters in the food chain benefited from my ability to afford this restaurant. You can't give away money and create sustainable wealth. You have to make a man work for his living and the more people who work successfully in their particular fields, the richer we all become. In Africa, we have created nations of beggars shouting anti-colonialism in the hope we will feel guilty and give their top brass some money."

"People must govern themselves."

"If they know how. The old tribal Africa was a very different kettle of fish to run than a modern state."

"You talk a lot of rubbish, of course everyone is equal to the next person. Sometimes I think you start these arguments just to make me annoyed. You personally rob Africa blind and then have the gall to sit there and tell me Africa's poverty is my fault."

"But it is, sis. The whole damn modern world was too big for them and you tossed them in the deep end without the wherewithal to swim. You think our brother Will could run Langton Merchant Bank or Randolph be a minister of the Crown? Will can't add up and Randolph is embarrassing in company. But they both live good lives. Different lives. Someone has to breed the cows and someone has to serve drinks in a bar. We are all siblings but we are not all equal, thank heaven. Oh, and you and I should do this more often. I enjoyed the evening."

"Better than you would have done with Marcia?"

"Funnily enough, yes. I'd forgotten the pleasure of good conversation."

"Save your flattery for the gullible. Are you going down to East Horsley this weekend?"

"No."

"Are you going to divorce Fiona?"

"No."

"Suddenly we don't have the words to express ourselves," said Josephine sarcastically.

"Are you sad you never married?"

"Not when I see the mess my friends make. People have a short attention span. They don't stick to anything. If the job isn't right, the fault is the boss or the company and they resign. If they have an argument with their wife, they go off and screw someone else and then wonder how they got divorced."

"Social democracy, darling. Everyone's got it too good. There's no financial fear anymore to keep people together."

"You should know."

"Maybe we weren't meant to coop ourselves up in one house for life. I've had the kids. Done my duty to secure the future of my race. After that there's only common interest in the children. Fiona has her own life. Once the sex is over, sis, there's rarely very much left. No, I'll stay married, Fiona suits me fine, we see little of each other and never fight. If she wants something she gives me a ring. Very civilised. Better than sitting head-to-head each night and boring each other stiff."

"Maybe life after all was just an accident... Do you think Fiona's happy?"

"I have not the slightest idea."

"Why don't you ask her?"

"Sis, you, of all people! You're a politician. Have you ever found a person who will tell you what is really in their mind? Either they answer in a way that suits their own purpose or they tell you what they think you want to hear. Man has never told the truth in his life unless it suited him. Only when they find a method of reading people's minds will the shit stop. Only then will people stop telling lies. We compromise. Fiona has compromised. She has her children and her highly successful publishing house and if she doesn't really have a husband in the process, does it matter? When we really get old, we'll have to talk to each other as by then two out of three of the kids will be out of the country and the one that stays behind won't like its parents. Law of averages. Otherwise we'll end up in separate old-age establishments boring stiff a bunch of strangers... You want some more of this coffee?"

"Why not?... They've asked me to rejoin the committee of the anti-apartheid movement."

"Why is it our family is so obsessed with Africa? All except Randolph. The world, my dear sister, is as crooked as a corkscrew. You happily support the AAM, which supports the ANC, which supports uMkhonto we Sizwe, the spear of the nation, whose avowed reason for life is terrorism in all its forms. But if Sinn Fein asked you to join you'd run a mile from them and their IRA, shouting you'd never deal with terrorists let alone support them."

"You're talking rubbish again. South Africa is totally different. Apartheid is morally disgusting and you know it."

"Did you ever hear me say it wasn't?"

"The IRA are a fringe group of murdering bastards. The majority in Northern Ireland is Protestant."

"But not in all of Ireland. If you think the IRA lack popular support you are wrong. The Irish of Celtic descent think that any part of Ireland run by the British is just as morally disgusting as apartheid. You get a good government job in South Africa if you are white and a good government job in Northern Ireland if you are Protestant. In one breath you despise terrorism and in the next you are holding rallies to raise funds to help the ANC."

"But apartheid is wrong."

"So is terrorism, sis. Don't you remember our mother saying two wrongs never made a right? When the new order takes power in South Africa, as I have no doubt it will, they will have gained power through killing people who disagreed with their policy. If you think the means justifies the end, that murder is acceptable as a last resort, go ahead with your crusade but don't let your moral indignation become a gold mine for other people's manipulation. With the end of colonialism in Africa, the one policy agreed upon by Russia and America, who unfortunately in the last century were unable to grab a part of Africa for themselves, the superpowers will turn black against black in their pursuit of hegemony. Russia wanted the colonial powers out and used your same moral indignation to achieve their purpose. Unfortunately for Africa, their purpose was not to uplift the poor of Africa and give them independence, but to gain power for Russia through communism, with a string of one-party puppet states answerable to Moscow. America, on the other hand, had two good reasons for kicking the colonial powers out of Africa and to achieve their ends climbed on top of your same moral high ground to shout their own brand of righteous indignation. And they were good, even making it seem like a crusading liberal America who believed in human rights and equal opportunity. The real reason, history will write, is they wanted the colonial markets of Africa for their own multinationals. Secondly, it gave the white holders of power in America the opportunity at no political cost to scream abuse at whites in Africa who treated their blacks badly, all the time nervously looking over their shoulders at the American civil rights movement. Now all I see in Africa, is America and Russia squaring off to each other through the same string of tinpot dictators that jumped into the power vacuum when the colonials ran out with their tails between their legs. The African leaders are having the party of all parties playing one off against the other... America and Russia are fighting each other right across the globe with surrogate armies because in a nuclear age they dare not fight each other for world hegemony. Everyone's after money, sis. Not nice but how it is. They are all about as morally right as the devil."

"You make everything that is trying to be good so dirty. South Africa has to be changed. No one in his right mind can defend separate development as made into law by South Africa. The laws are an insult to humanity and have to be changed by whatever means in the same way we had to destroy Hitler. You compare the ANC to the IRA. I compare apartheid to Nazi Germany."

"You are right of course, sis. Throughout history the good man has always wanted to fight the good fight. Civilisation against the hordes of Attila the Hun. The Christian followers of Christ against the hordes of Islam. The history of Europe is littered with nationalist uprisings against the conquerors. Strange thing is, both sides thought they were equally right. Rome thought it was right giving Britain a rule of incorruptible law, language, roads, peace, prosperity. The nationalists of Britain were indignant at their loss of power and privilege. And so it has gone on throughout recorded history with everyone chopping each other up, even more crazily in recent Europe, praying for help to the same God to give them deliverance. Fact is, it's all about power and money. Socialism is all about giving the poor enough to stop them revolting. I know that and agree with the principle but I don't run around saying that I'm the last gasp in altruism, everyone has the right to food, shelter, medicine and education whether they work or not, get it for free or pay through the bloody nose. If we had stopped right from the start of man killing each other and destroying everything in sight, there would have been more than enough for all of us centuries ago. Unfortunately, with all the fine words of all the fine people through history, we have not found an equitable way of governing ourselves, of finding our God, of distributing our wealth. We are a very stupid race of people and deserve to live in our permanent mess."

"There has to be a better way," said Josephine as Byron stood up to go.

"And we socialists intend to find a way through the minefield of governance. You just can't have such disparity of rich and poor in the same community side by side."

"Then you must find a way of making all men and women exactly the same. Maybe television will make us all mindless and docile. The last big circus on earth. Only snag I can see is when you achieve your utopia, it will all be so boring people will wish they had never been born."

THE HAND-WRINGING and sunshine smile began again at the door as they were both thanked profusely for their patronage. The owner had called a taxi and held a large umbrella ready for the moment he opened the front door.

"You'll have to run," said the owner, knowing what was on the other side of the door. Byron smiled to himself, hearing the first trace of the Irish brogue. Then the door came open, and they were running through the bucketing rain, the owner holding the big umbrella against the onslaught. Finally inside the taxi it was warm and Byron gave the driver Josephine's address in Westminster.

"I have a theory," said Byron. "If the English weather had not been so terrible there never would have been an empire. The only reason the likes of Will and Hilary got out of this country was to find a pleasant climate."

"This island would be very full."

"Like sheep in a drought, maybe they would have become infertile until nature balanced itself again... Do you miss Parliament?"

"Yes. Very much. My mind is so active, so much energy and nothing to do."

"Politicians have a short shelf life. Try something else. You want a job? Your brains would work on anything. There's a saying in the banking world that you can teach banking to an intelligent person but not intelligence to a banker. It's meant to be one of those jokes to show how clever we bankers are as within the next twenty or thirty years we will have more power than anyone on earth."

"That's the most insidious thought."

"Money can manipulate politicians whatever system you try."

"You should know... Would you really offer me a job?"

"Would you accept?"

"I don't know. Making money for the sake of money seems pointless."

"Oh, sis, you really should hear yourself sometimes. Maybe you can even use some of the money to do some real good. In Africa, a project has to be started by the Langton Merchant Bank and controlled by the bank until it is finished and working. That way no one steals and the people you want to help get something tangible other than the sight of their friendly politicians running around in a top-of-the-range Mercedes-Benz."

"You really think the banks will control the world?"

"The people with money, yes. They always have. That's what the political fight's about. Getting hands on the money to patronise the rest."

"You want to come up for a drink? I'm so full of coffee my eyes are pinging."

"We're both lonely, aren't we?" said Byron after a moment of silence.

"I think so."

The taxi pulled up under the canopy outside Josephine's block of flats. Her key let them into the building. Upstairs in her flat the central heating had the rooms warm and friendly.

"Put your coat in the closet, Byron. I'm going to get out of this bloody dress and feel comfortable. Thank goodness there has never been incest in the family, if you know what I mean! Decanter's on the sideboard in the sitting room. You really think the Americans are hypocrites?... We can go on talking through open doors."

"A nation with thirty-five per cent of the world's gross national product, the world's income that is, and five per cent of its population, can't be a saint. We were no better in the last century, advocating free trade the way the Americans talk about a free-market economy. The trick in our day was all the free trade had to be transported on British ships. Rule Britannia and all that shit. With free markets and no exchange controls, the American multinationals can set up shop to sell to the local market and better still, manufacture with cheap labour, and ship a brand name back to the States which their public buys without the least idea of the sweatshop that made it in Bangladesh. The clothes sell at normal American prices and the profit is outrageous. The real wealth stays in America not Bangladesh, as the American system would never allow a Bangladesh company to market their product in America. With the wealth, America can afford research and development that keeps them ahead in technology so that when the Third World wants a sophisticated product like an aeroplane, they have to save up their dollars and buy American. It's the same old exploitation with a different shine to the ball. In the early nineteenth century we British talked about the spread of Christianity to the heathens and then hoisted the Union Jack when they were all kneeling down with their eyes shut. The Americans learnt fast, or maybe they are the third British Empire. Same people, same language, different accent. The British are just as much a mix of all the

European races, starting with the Italians, then the Saxons, Angles, Vikings, Danes, Normans with a sprinkling of Celts to give it the flair. And I'll tell you something else about Africa. The last thing the Americans want is a viable white tribe that in the end sides with the black tribes of Africa and shows them how to screw the West. Kissinger said white Rhodesia was a minor refugee problem and if they asked nicely, lots of them would get green cards; the best, naturally, and the rest could go home to England. Any well-educated white Afrikaner is welcome in America. The theory is a few white dregs left behind in South Africa will marry into the blacks and leave the rest of the population easy prey to Western manipulation. If there hadn't been colonialism and apartheid the Americans would have invented something else to get the whites out of Africa."

"Now that is rot," said Josephine, coming into the room wearing slacks and a sweater.

"Any generalisation is a lot of rot, sis."

"You can change the direction of an argument in mid-sentence. Did you know that? Ever since you read Plato's dialogues. You were fourteen."

"Was I really? How precocious."

"First, we have to get Nelson Mandela out of jail and hold a free and fair election in South Africa. Then, maybe, we start worrying about the likes of Botha cosying up to the ANC in a cabal to rouse the Third World against the West! The Afrikaners hate the blacks and vice versa."

"Another generation, sis. Just be careful in your quest for justice you don't crash the South African economy and start a real race war... You know I read somewhere the apartheid government has built an electric fence halfway across their Mozambique border and unlike the Berlin Wall, which was built to keep the communists inside the Soviet Empire because the lifestyle was so much better on the other side, the electric fence is to stop the herds in newly independent black Africa wanting to get into white apartheid Africa to get a better life. Somehow there's a contradiction. Could there ever have been wealth in South Africa without apartheid? Has there been any wealth created elsewhere in Africa? An interesting thought. Well, I don't know. I'm just a simple banker. You and lots like you, Jo, genuinely mean well for Africa. Just be careful you don't throw the baby out with the bath water. If I was a black man, I would prefer apartheid Vorster and his ilk to Idi Amin, freedom or no bloody freedom."

"They are both horrible."

"On that we both agree. I talk to Heath a lot when he's not trying to make young brother Will rich. He says a lot of ordinary people are going to die in Africa while the world looks on, saying it's no longer their problem."

"I heard about Will. You want to tell me the truth?"

"I credited him with thirty thousand pounds from the crocodile skins. Turned it into one and a half million. Thought the bugger didn't deserve that kind of money."

"What about the ivory?"

"Same thing. Most of the money came from me."

"Isn't that what good financial advice is all about?"

"There was a tax angle."

"There always is. Not only do you extort silence but you steal money. And you want me to work for you?"

"As I said, businessmen were never angels. We take any deal as far as it will go. Johnny Pike took out insurance and Heath and the Swiss bank made me pay over the profits to Will. Poor man has no idea what to do with it."

"Maybe he should give it to the anti-apartheid movement? The money was made from Africa."

"Interesting, why don't you ask him before he emigrates to America and finds a hedonistic use for his money? Like getting married and having a wife spend it for him."

"You can add cynic to your CV."

"Why is it so often people find the truth cynical?"

"Your wife makes you money."

"Ah, but I'm a banker. Remember, very soon we are going to be running the world and you politicians will be dancing to our tune. I think it was Cecil John Rhodes, of Rhodesia that was, who said that every man has his price. I seem to remember he was talking about Barney Barnato, a Jew, who sold out to Rhodes for money and membership of the Kimberley Club. Naturally Barnato was the only member who was a Jew and Rhodes was chairman of the club. Everyone is corruptible. You just have to find the way... You know this flat really is rather comfortable."

Leaving the 'comfort and the warmth' hanging in the air, Byron sipped his whisky and waited.

"What kind of job would you offer me?" asked Josephine, forcing Byron to think of something else to stop himself smiling. "I mean, I just need something to do."

"Bullshit, sis. You need the money. Remember I'm your twin brother; we cuddled up together in the womb. Your pension's crap. You can't afford this place much longer unless you find a job with a proper salary. The amount British politicians are paid, I'm surprised all of them are not on the take. Something in our schooling I suppose. Just isn't done to be a corrupt civil servant. Business is another matter... Mind if I have another Scotch? Send you round a case tomorrow."

"You did buy dinner."

"Oh yes. I forgot. Well let's see. Public relations would be your portfolio. Making twin brother and his companies politically correct."

"Would I have any influence if I saw you doing something wrong?"

"But of course. Wouldn't make any sense otherwise. The public want to see us as caring. The just side of capitalism. Creating wealth for the benefit of all mankind. The tabloid owner and the businessman on the side of the common man; you see, it's the age of the common man. Politicians have to do the bidding of the average man whether it's good for the country or not. Hence the size of the national debt. We have to be seen to be right, that's all. The right smile on television is worth more to a public figure than the IQ of an Einstein. The image counts. The socialist statement. Making people feel comfortable. I thought sixty thousand pounds a year with a seat on the main board would be fair compensation... You see, sis, I don't think your Labour Party are going to be in power for a very long time. Every time they get back for five years they give away what little progress the previous Tory government has managed to make for the country. You made a right bloody mess of it last time, despite all the good intentions. As I've said to you a thousand times, giving away other people's money is easy. Making the bloody stuff is another story. You have to make a country rich not bone idle... You need a job, sis. I tried to get Will into the business to have some backup but his mind was always wandering around in Africa. You and I could have some very good arguments and both of us would benefit. You'll have to give the Tory government over half your salary, so at least that should make you feel you are doing some personal good. Either that or you join some fancy NGO that spends eighty per cent of its donations on fundraising, salaries and Land Rovers."

"And the anti-apartheid movement?"

"Marvellous. As a director of Langton Merchant Bank you would make us politically correct the day you started."

"Will you subscribe to the AAM?"

"I already do, have done for years."

"You give a lot of money to political organisations."

"Politicians, like revolutionary movements, require money to gain power to gain control of the national exchequer. The seed money is small, the prize a whole country, whoever said you can get somewhere in this world without friends in high places was a bloody liar. Judicious spending on politicians' ambitions is a key part of modern business. We are all really in the same pot, boiling away nicely at a comfortable temperature, scratching each other's backs. Put more exactly, politicians would never become politicians without the business or trade union money that put them into power. The Trade Union Congress have the British Labour Party by the balls after every successful Labour election. When they have put you into power, they want their reward, and most times what they want is death to a competitive modern economy. Look at Britain. Gone from a lion to a pussycat in thirty-five years. And if Thatcher doesn't break the power of the unions this time round, this 'precious stone set in a silver sea' will sink without trace.

"Now, more important to our lives, what are we going to do about Father? He's gone from depression to manic depression. The horrors of war live for a long time afterwards. Each and every war, however righteous, like the war Father waged against Nazi Germany, leaves scars on every soldier, sailor or airman."

"It was the bomb on Japan. There are new drugs in America to help Father's depression."

"Well, I'm afraid to say his religion hasn't saved his mind in this life."

"Maybe we should go down more often. Why don't we drive down tomorrow? You can sleep here and on the way to get your car you can go up to your flat for some clothes."

"Good idea. Let's stop drinking and get some sleep... Maybe we should all spend more time together. When was the family last all together?"

"A long time ago, Byron, in more ways than one."

20

*O*ne of the few joys for old people was seeing their children and Adelaide Langton's joys were few and far between. She was about to turn seventy and her husband in earlier society would have been sent to a lunatic asylum; her eldest son and daughter-in-law, childless and living in their own house on the opposite side of the farm, rarely visited Langton Manor for fear of being verbally attacked by her husband, Group Captain Red Langton, and farming, being what it was, there was always a financial problem with two families trying to live off the proceeds of one farm. At times she even thought of her one-time socialist brother Clifford with fondness, the Uncle Cliff who had made such an impression on the youthful Josephine and driven her towards a life in politics. Even her brother had died, leaving the remnants of Great-Aunt Eve's fortune to his not so young, any longer, mistress. To add to Adelaide's distress, she rarely saw her grandchildren and Gregory, Byron's eldest, was back at Stanmore in the spring and soon he would be a grown man and all of his childhood, when a grandmother could really play a part, would have passed her by. The girls, Penelope and Morag, were now little girls of nine and eleven.

The car that crunched the old, weed-choked gravel outside the front door of Langton Manor was unfamiliar and the portent of bad news. Strange cars visiting two old people just before lunchtime on a Saturday morning were either lost tourists, which never happened in the winter, or more bad news. She had not seen Red that morning; they slept apart in separate bedrooms as the gnashing of what was left of his old teeth stopped her from sleeping, and with his terrible swings of depression, she was never sure of the mood he would wake up in each morning. Despite all their fifty-one, nearly fifty-two years together, she could no longer bear the tirade of agony that spilled from his mouth without fearing she herself would take the same road to insanity.

The car was rather big and expensive, of a type she had never seen before.

Christmas had been a bigger disaster than usual with only Randolph and her daughter-in-law, Anna, sitting round the big table looking at the roast chicken as a turkey would have been far too big for the four of them. Three of her children, four if she included Hilary lost somewhere in Africa, and all her three grandchildren had stayed away, their only brief presence the 'expected' phone calls that had left her feeling hollow. Christmas was the time when she felt the disintegration of her family most. She blocked out of her mind the years when the house had been full of Red's Langton family and her Critchley family for a whole week of boisterous noise, overeating and the marvellous spirit of family. Red said the two wars had destroyed the very soul of England. Maybe he was right. Peering through the small leaden pane in the corner of the drawing room window, afraid to show herself, she watched a man and a woman in heavy coats get out of the expensive car and only when they turned to look up at the old, ivy-clad house did she recognise her own twins, Josephine and Byron, both of them, and the sudden joy lifted the taste of bile that had risen in her throat.

"Red," she called out to an echoing house. "The children are here. *Red*, can you hear me? It's Josephine and Byron and I haven't had my hair done in a month."

"Shit," said Byron, looking up at the ancestral home. "Bloody old pile is falling down. There are more weeds than gravel and the box trees on either side of the front door haven't been cut for years."

"You could spend some of your money fixing it up," said Josephine. "Wasn't that Mother at the window? After Randolph, Langton Manor will be yours or Gregory's."

"No one wants to bury themselves in the country anymore. I'd sell the place."

"You can't sell a house that's been in the family for hundreds of years."

"Why ever not? Being impressed with a man's pedigree went out of the window years ago. When I saw the headmaster about Gregory, he took me round my old house with the new housemaster and most of the boys I spoke to talked with a regional accent like everyone else in England. They want a classless society with the old plum knocked out of the accent. Come on, let's go up and face Mother and Father. I'm freezing out here and it wouldn't surprise me, looking over towards Poole, if it snowed. Often snowed at the end of January when we were growing up... Why didn't you come down for Christmas?"

"My career was over, I was depressed. Didn't want Father looking at me with that look. He hates the socialists. Says they were the ones who took the Great out of Britain. Nonsense of course. You can't go on living in the past that doesn't exist anymore."

They were standing in the porch, looking back over the farm, down along the row of leafless poplar trees standing sentinel on either side of the drive; the great oak to their right, stark in its winter bareness, the tree the first Langton had planted with an acorn hundreds of years ago. A crow was cawing from the rookery but the rest of the Dorset countryside was still and quiet, the clouds above tinged with the yellow threat of snow. The temperature was a few degrees above freezing.

"You think the old toboggans are still in the stables?" asked Byron.

"Probably... You're right. It's going to snow. Pity your kids aren't here." The front door opened. "Hello, Mother! Surprise. The twins have come to visit. Sorry about Christmas."

Adelaide was crying and her throat was choked. Hugging each of her children in turn, she pulled them inside and pushed shut the big door.

"We've made a cosy room by putting a folding door across the middle of the morning room," said Adelaide, drawing her children into the house while she found her composure. "There's a fire. I'll make some tea."

"Where's Dad?" asked Byron.

"Somewhere in the house," said Adelaide. "He lives in the past. The bad parts of the past. Your father is not very well, children, I'm afraid... Byron, where's Fiona and the children?"

"In East Horsley. Sis and I had dinner together last night and had the urge to come and see our parents."

"Wish you'd had the urge more often." The look of reproach was in her eyes. "Red! Red! Where are you? The twins are here... Are you all right, Jo, after the election? What are you going to do?"

"Byron's offered me a job."

"How extraordinary. Red!... Byron, please go and look for your father while we go into the kitchen and make some tea. Better keep on that overcoat. I wear mittens even indoors. The old house is so cold. Do you remember those old days before the war when there was a fire in every room, including the bedrooms? Fires burnt all winter, and the house was never cold or damp; there were so many people. You do remember those days, don't you, Josephine?"

"Yes, Mother... Matter of fact, the older I get the more I remember."

"I do hope Byron finds his father. I worry about your father all the time. It was the bombing, you know. He never got over the bombing. He has nightmares about all those children down below when the whole of Dresden was on fire. And the children in Japan. I'm afraid to say it but your father's going off his head. Nobody comes to visit anymore. Why do people have to change? So worrying. If it hadn't been for the war, we would have lived happily ever after. Your father is a very good man, but the war damaged his brain. He thinks he's going to hell, you see. That part of religion he does believe. Not the part about redemption. He thinks man is doomed to extinction on this earth and we'll all end in the blinding fire of hell for the way we have behaved since Adam and Eve. The devil lives in his tortured mind and tells him the devil has won. Man is doomed. The world is evil. He raves that man under his veneer of civilisation and apparent concern for righteousness is evil to the core, man's very being... Well, it's not easy to listen to that kind of conversation morning, noon and night. But it's my duty to look after him, Josephine, and I will. The good and the bad. There was plenty of good before the war. You see, we'll even drive you children back to London as it's all so depressing. Maybe we humans live too long these days. Dead by forty of physical hard work in the very old days. No time to let the mind deteriorate. Sad thing is, it ruins all those good memories... We'll have some roast beef for supper. Off the farm. Byron likes roast beef. No point in doing a great piece of roast beef for the two of us so I turn it into mince. There are lots of recipes for mince, Jo. I have a special book. Without the freezer and our own beef I don't think we'd eat at all. Have you seen the prices in the shops? I do hope Byron finds your father. Red wanders all over the place but never feels the cold. Says the Lancaster was always cold despite the wool-lined flying gear. Sometimes I think he is still up in that damn aeroplane. Lately, he's been having long conversations on the intercom with Hilary's father, the poor man who came back dead in the tail gunner's turret or whatever they had at the back of those damn planes. We did do our best for Hilary, didn't we, Jo? I worry about Hilary. After his boy died his letters have been so terrible, and he's not a strong man after all those attacks of malaria. He really has given his life to God and helping his fellow man. Malcolm, he called him. Poor Malcolm. Never even saw England. I don't think all those colonies were worth the pain. Better off without them."

By three o'clock it was snowing outside and Byron knew his father had lost his mind. He had found him before lunch in the big greenhouse that his older brother Randolph heated to grow tomatoes in mid-winter for the London hotels. The plants were grown in sand on waist-high benches with liquid nutrients fed to them by drip irrigation. Under the tables were cucumbers that liked the dark and the humidity. The group captain had been sitting on an upturned wooden box.

"Are we going up tonight?" his father asked without the slightest sign of having recognised his son. "The runway will be snowed in. They won't make us take off in the snow. It's going to snow, Adjutant. What do ops say? If I lose another bloody aircraft through bad weather, I'll go up there myself. Would you like a tomato? Come on, we'll go up to the mess. Why they let WAAFs into the mess, I don't know. Women in an officers' mess! We'll win this war but the country will go to the dogs. Mark my word. Did you have a word with the CO about my leave? Four kids at home. You'd love my Adelaide. Best looking gal you've ever seen. Well, you don't have to answer. We're short of pilots. We're always short of bloody pilots and it's going to snow."

With tears in his eyes, Byron had led his father back to the house where the group captain had eaten a large plate of bacon and eggs, four pieces of toast and drunk two cups of coffee.

"There's nothing wrong with his appetite," Adelaide had said.

"Can't fly on an empty stomach," Red had answered. "What happens if we have to bail out? Running around in Jerry country, might not get food for days and their civilians don't like us bomber pilots. Excuse me, I have to visit the bog."

The silence when he left the kitchen table hung in the air for minutes.

"Sometimes he remembers where he is," Adelaide had said.

"How long's it been?" asked Josephine.

"Been coming?" replied her mother. "Five years, I suppose."

"Has he been to a good doctor?" said Byron.

"Oh, we know what it is. Mania. Brought on by manic depression."

"Isn't that dangerous?"

"Some of them are not dangerous."

"Why didn't you tell us?" asked Jo.

"You all have your lives to lead. What was the point? There's nothing you can do."

"I can employ a live-in nurse to help you, Mother," said Byron. "You're the one to worry about. You're the one carrying the burden. From what I've seen, he doesn't know what the hell is going on."

"We'll see," Adelaide said while she moved the dishes across to the double sink where she began to do the washing up.

"He was right about the snow," Byron said at three o'clock. "It's going to be heavy. No flying tonight."

"Don't you make a joke about it, Byron," said his mother.

"Sorry." He was standing next to the fire in the cosy room, looking out of the window at the long terrace and the east side of the old oak tree. The terrace had not been swept of autumn leaves. Byron was wondering if he could put the staff he was going to employ to run Langton Manor on his company's payroll to make their wages deductible against tax. Maybe a storage facility at Langton Manor would constitute a need for staff. After all, storage space in London for old files was prohibitively expensive. By law he had to keep the old files and none of them were ever looked at again. The whole thing had become a financial problem to Byron, like everything else in his life where all problems were solved with money.

From the kitchen, Adelaide heard the banging of the front door knocker. The battery of the doorbell had long ago ceased to work and as nobody called at the manor anymore she had left the dead battery in its socket. Outside it was snowing hard and dusk had fallen. Again the old, brass knocker, stiff with age, was methodically crashing against the old oak door, sending a hollow memory of sound through the hall, down the long stone passage to the kitchen. She knew Red was somewhere in the house but unlikely to answer the door, trapped as he was in the mind of his past. With Josephine, she waited for the noise to go away. Neither of them had heard a car and the old manor house was far from the beaten track.

Back in the cosy room, Byron heard the distant echo from the big front door. He had watched the snow collect on the terrace, now layered in white. The dusk and the snow had taken away the great oak and the trees beyond, bringing his world down to the half room and the small fire. Shivering, as if someone had walked over his grave, he drew the heavy curtains over the cold windows and walked back to the folding room divider. Striding down the passage to the hall, he was in time to hear the fourth series of crashes. The front door had a Yale lock and old-fashioned bolts that were never drawn. Opening the Yale lock, he put it on the catch and gripped the big brass centre handle with both hands and pulled back the old door. Under cover of the silent porch stood a snow-covered figure in overcoat and hat. The hall light showed nothing of a car behind the man, who had the brim of his hat pulled down against the snow. Byron felt the stab of fear and pulled back to slam the door.

"Did I give you a fright, Byron?"

"What are you doing here? Aren't you meant to be in America?"

Will Langton walked past his brother and pushed shut the front door and released the catch on the lock he had helped to install as a young man.

"It's bloody cold... Thought you never left London these days. How's Mum and Dad?"

"Mother's all right. Father's off his rocker... Josephine's here."

"Maybe the pull of family does work after all. There's going to be two feet of snow out there in the morning. You remember that winter of '47? Reminds me of the same thing. Have we still got the toboggans? What happened to the doorbell? That bloody knocker could wake the dead."

"Probably the battery. Mother's in the kitchen with Jo making tea. No staff. Place is like a pigsty."

"Caught a taxi from the station," said Will, looking around. Then he walked to the closet of the hall and took off his heavy overcoat, shook off the snow and hung it with his hat on the stand in front of the big mirror. "Living in Europe makes you as white as the snow. I never like looking at myself in the mirror. Why are you here, Byron? What do you want this time?"

"You have a nasty mind. You should have married Shelley instead of letting her run off with Laurie. You never were any good at holding on to things. So are you going to America?"

"I've just come back, actually."

"Quite the jet-setter with all my money. Some people have all the luck."

"You really are a big shit. How the hell do you live with yourself? What Shelley saw in you is one of the mysteries of my life."

"Power, little brother... Look who's here," he called as they reached the stone-floored kitchen. "My jet-setting younger brother. Just flew in from America."

"Find another teacup for me, Josephine. Will, what are you doing here? What's the matter?"

"The doorbell doesn't work."

"I know, the battery's flat. Give your old mother a kiss and we'll take the tea into the cosy room. Byron, did you put some more coal on the fire?"

"No, Mother."

"Then go and do it. Didn't you know it's snowing outside? My goodness, now what are we going to do for supper?"

"You said the roast beef," said Josephine.

"Did I? Yes, I did. Good. That's settled... All my children at Langton Manor. It's like a little miracle. Would you like some buttered toast, Will? You look very pale. We don't have any biscuits anymore."

"Where's Dad?"

"Somewhere. I'm afraid he thinks he's back in the air force but he does have his good days. Your father's had a very difficult life. Will, you can bring the tea tray? Now, come along. We'll make believe this is Christmas with the whole family together again. Josephine, go and phone Randolph and tell him to bring Anna over for dinner."

"Byron brought down a case of red wine in the boot of his car," said Josephine.

"At least he does some things right," said Will, picking up the tea tray.

"Now I don't want you children quarrelling," said Adelaide. "It's Christmas, remember... We had some lovely Christmases all those years ago. Whatever happened to the time? I can't even imagine myself as a young girl anymore. Everything was so much better before the war. You'd better go and phone Randolph before Anna starts cooking supper. After tea, you boys will go into the dining room and light both the fires. Josephine can help dust the big table and put the hoover over the carpet. We don't have time to clean the family silver but that can't be helped. I cook the beef an extra hour when it's frozen. I have some frozen Brussels sprouts and peas from the garden and the potatoes were put down in deep soil at the side of the woodshed. Byron, you'll need lots of that wood. You'd better go and find your father again. If he's still back in the war, tell him there's no flying tonight because of the snow and the CO has declared a dining-in night for all officers. Seven for seven-thirty... We'll need sherry glasses but as we don't have any sherry, we can use a bottle of Byron's wine."

"I'll ask Randolph for the sherry," said Josephine.

"Better tell him to bring the port for the toast to the King," said Byron.

"Are you being sarcastic?" asked his mother.

"Not this time, Mother. Not this time. We'll put the lack of five courses down to wartime shortages. Excuse me, I'll go and find him."

The room stayed silent, except for the crackling fire. The folding partition snapped shut, and they heard the morning room door open and shut.

"Byron was crying," said Will. "I've never seen him cry before. Not even as kids."

"Byron was very close to your father," said their mother. "He likes to portray a lack of all human feeling but it's an act like so many of us. I often wonder if life is just one big act from start to finish."

AT SIX-THIRTY, Will opened the big front door to his elder brother's knock. Outside it was still snowing hard and everything picked up by the shaft of light through the front door was white. The gravel had disappeared.

"Everybody together, now that is a surprise," said Randolph, drawing his wife into the old house. "I found two bottles of sherry and one bottle of port." The door closed behind him and Anna shivered in the cold.

"How are you, Will?" she asked as the men shook hands.

"Fine thank you. You know where to hang your coats," replied Will. "The cosy room is warm and two fires are blazing in the dining room. Byron's told Dad it's a dining-in night."

"Is he bad?" asked Randolph.

"Thinks he's back in the war. Wanted to know if it's number one dress with miniatures."

"Oh, my God."

"Mother says at least he will come down and eat properly. She hates the thought of him sitting in his room without a fire. Byron's going to send in some servants to look after them. Funny how it turns. For years your parents look after you and then overnight it's the other way. Granda was dependant on Mother and Father at the end of his life."

"That is what families are meant to be all about," said Anna. "Who wants to be looked after by an impersonal state when you can no longer look after yourself? It's part of the whole reason for having children. In this new day and age, children abuse their parents and then tell the state to look after them. I want to know what happens when the state collapses under the burden of looking after everyone else's mother and father. Society will self-destruct. Nothing ever lasts when you rely on other people. Socialism has destroyed the reason for family by creating this so-called welfare state. They may think it looks after the body but it can never look after the soul. It's as cold as charity."

"Better not tell that to Josephine," said Will. "Mother has made us promise we won't fight tonight."

"Aren't you meant to be in America?" said Randolph.

"I was, but I came back again." Will opened the door for them into the morning room where the temperature had begun to rise. When he opened the sliding door, a big log fire greeted them. On the right of the fire stood a six-legged table covered by a silver tray. Cut crystal glasses stood on the unpolished tray and Randolph put down the sherry bottles next to the glasses.

"Where should I put the bottle of port? Behind the curtain? We need a decanter."

"Byron brought a whole case of French red wine," said his mother, accepting the kiss on her cheek.

"That is something. Where are Jo and Byron?"

"In the kitchen."

"And Dad?"

"Seven for seven-thirty," said his mother. "It's only just gone half-past six. We can't even pour a glass of sherry until seven o'clock. Anna, my dear, come and sit by the fire. You look pasty."

"I am. I don't think the English ever grow used to their weather. It's going to snow all night."

"Tomorrow," said Will, "Byron and I are going tobogganing. Want to join us, Randolph?"

"Of course. I took you on your first ride."

"It was Dad."

"Maybe, but I rather think it was me."

AT FIVE MINUTES past seven the folding door was pulled back from the wall and Red Langton joined his family in the warmth of the cosy room. The forty-year-old monkey jacket fitted remarkably well as with the advancing years and lack of proper meals, Red Langton was free of fat. If anything the sleeves were too long, as if his arms had shrunk. The smooth barathea cloth of the dress uniform was faded to a light blue and at one corner moths had made a hole. The pilot's wings on the breast pocket were faded white and the campaign ribbons were indistinguishable from the ribbons of the Distinguished Flying Cross and the Air Force Cross. The small star in the centre of the DFC, which indicated the medal of bravery in action had been won twice, shone where the worn metal showed through the Bakelite coating. The row of miniature medals hung from just under the double line of ribbons. Instead of patent leather shoes, the group captain wore bedroom slippers but the bow tie was as straight as the pilot's wings. The four thick rings of the rank of group captain stood out clearly.

"Now where's the CO?"

The silence pervaded as their father glared round the room. No one spoke. "Never mind. I'll take a glass of sherry." With the glass in one hand and the other behind his back he warmed himself at the fire. After a minute of silence, he took a sip from his glass of sherry. Having assumed the position of senior officer of the night he was not required to talk. Chit-chat with junior officers was frowned upon at formal gatherings.

"Carry on," he said and dipped his head a second time into his sherry. As mess president for the night, he expected to be ignored.

Will Langton was not sure whether to yell or cry until he saw there was nothing any of them could do to bring reality back. The charade continued through three glasses of sherry and their removal to the dining room at exactly seven-thirty led by the mess president. Will was junior officer and designated mess vice-president by his father for the evening requiring, him to propose the toast to the King with the port, decanted by Josephine before the meal into a cut crystal decanter. The group captain then told them they could smoke, his first words of the evening. Five minutes after the royal toast, the group captain said good night to no one in particular, scraped back his chair and left the room.

When the dining room door had closed and the footfalls had faded into the old house, Adelaide smiled at her children. "At least your father had a proper meal. Reminds me of the subterfuge I used with you children when you wouldn't eat your vegetables."

"Will he be all right?" asked Anna.

"Only God will know," said Adelaide, "and I'm not even sure of that anymore. Let's go back to the cosy room and enjoy some more of Byron's generous supply of wine. He was a good husband and a good father to all of you and that is how he must be remembered. Just help me take the debris into the kitchen and then we'll enjoy the wine and each other. I have the premonition this will be the last time we will all be together, except in each other's thoughts. You see, life just moves on, that's all. There's nothing we can do about it. You have your own lives to live. Most of mine has gone. Happiness for me so often is looking back on the happy parts of our lives together and tonight we are all going to be happy."

At a little after eleven o'clock, Adelaide left her children in the cosy room and went up to her lonely bedroom to try to find some sleep. Her life was over. The rest was merely a question of waiting.

The red wine played its final magic and sent her off to sleep where she dreamed she was young again with all the excitement of life's expectant future. Outside the window, the soft white snow fell and fell on the old house.

Downstairs the fire was stoked and Byron pulled the cork from the fourth bottle of red wine. They were all quite tight and liberated from the aura of a ghostly war, none of them fully understanding the end of their parents' lives.

"Randolph, you and Anna best stay the night," said Byron, filling up their glasses. "I have a mind to sleep in Dad's armchair in front of the fire. This is the only warm room in the house. Now, young Will, you'd better tell us why you came back from America in such a hurry."

"Give me another glass of wine," said Will, holding out his glass. "You're right. I'm going to sleep here too and pretend it's a campfire... You've been to

New York, Byron? Well, Melvin Raath and his daughter, Mary-Lou, decided to show me the town my second night in America. The day was cold, but the sun was shining and after a good lunch in some restaurant, Melvin hired a horse and buggy and off we went round Central Park for me to look at America. Over lunch they had offered me a ten per cent free ride in a chain of restaurants he was going to finance and she and I were going to run, all of them to be called 'Zambezi Bar and Restaurant'. The first three to be owned and the rest on franchise. This franchising is a big thing in the States. You prove an idea that makes money and sell the concept and expertise to as many entrepreneurs as you can find and everyone seems to get rich."

"What about all the money I just gave you?" interrupted Byron. "You could have done the deal without this Melvin Raath."

"He was American, and I thought I needed an American partner. I never told them about my new money. They still think I'm practically broke. Anyway, a few yards down the road, he stops the driver and gets us a six-pack of beer and off we go again. Round about four it was getting so damn cold as all those tall buildings put us in shadow, so he paid off the driver and we went into this bar. Looked like any other bar to me and pretty empty but warm. Feeling guilty I hadn't put my hand in my pocket, I ordered three more beers. Then Melvin sees this Negro down the end of the bar and walks out with his daughter, leaving me with three beers to pay for and no time to drink. Being a new boy in New York I didn't want to stay in a strange bar and when I went outside, they were waiting for me on the pavement.

"'What was that about?' I asked Melvin.

"'Don't drink with niggers,' was all he said, which wasn't true as he often drank with the trackers when Hannes Potgieter was alive. So I came home."

"You can't judge a country by one person," said Josephine, holding out her glass to Byron for a refill.

"No, I couldn't. But this one was going to be my partner. They've got some problems in America we don't even know about in Africa."

"But we are not in Africa," said Byron. "We are snowed in in England."

"I'm going back," said Will. "That money you gave me, Byron, was seeded with elephant ivory and crocodile skins. I'm going to return it. I'm going to join Hilary on the mission outside Mongu."

"They won't let you into Zambia," said Byron.

"They will with one and a half million pounds."

WILL WOKE the next morning and swore never again to drink red wine. He was stiff, cold and his mouth felt like the bottom of a well-used birdcage.

The fire had gone out and without double glazing on the windows the cold had come back into the room with a vengeance. Josephine was pulling back the big curtains and outside the windows, snow was thick on the trees, weighing down the evergreens. Randolph was snoring deep in sleep on the sofa and Anna, his wife, was out of the room. Byron was looking at Will across the cold fireplace.

"I love red wine but red wine hates me," Will said for something to say. The look had made him feel uncomfortable.

"Join the club... What was the other reason?"

"What other reason?"

"For leaving America so fast... You're the camping man. Better make up the fire. You'll need to go and fetch some kindling... I don't believe one poor man in a bar could turn you around like that."

"Have you waited all night to ask me that?"

"I'm always curious why people change their minds. All the previous thought and effort is just a waste of time... We would have been better to find a cold bed with lots of blankets."

"I was rather drunk. You make the best you can... She had eyes like gimlets."

"Who?" asked Byron.

"Mary-Lou."

"Now we are getting to the truth."

"Anything you said about America they took as a personal affront."

"As Josephine said last night, you can't judge a country by one person or even two. The woman was after you. They all want to mother you, Will."

"Not all of them. Shit, my knees are stiff. Sorry, Jo. That was a damn good party. Someone find me a box of matches and I'll have the fire going. The ash will still be hot."

"You still want to go tobogganing?" said Randolph, who had just woken up. "Where's Anna?"

"Gone to make tea," said Josephine, pulling back the last heavy curtain. "It's so beautiful outside. Anna said she would look for some aspirins. Do you know it's half-past ten in the morning? In the old days we would all have gone to church."

The thought of their father hung over the silence which was broken by Anna pulling back the partition with one hand while balancing the tray on the other.

"Good morning, everyone," she said. "Mother's taken tea up to Dad and he's quite rational but tired. Doesn't want to get out of bed. Will really is a boy scout. Look at that fire."

"We're all going tobogganing after breakfast," he said, balancing a log in the flames. The tea when it came to him tasted better than all the wine the previous night. When he had finished his second cup of tea, he stood up. "Come on. Let's go and find the toboggans. We'll run the slope from the clifftop down into the dale. The girls can cook breakfast while we pull out the sledges."

"Don't you want an aspirin before you go?" said Anna to the disappearing backs of the three brothers.

WILL HAD PUSHED back his empty breakfast plate. The racing red toboggan was outside the back door with the big yellow sledge that Red Langton had bought for his children before the war, and a fresh cup of tea was steaming at his elbow. He was as excited as a schoolboy. Josephine was seated next to him and all of them were dressed and ready for the snow.

"I'm rejoining the committee of the anti-apartheid movement," she said, now that he had finished his breakfast. "We are looking for donations, Will. Look, Zambia is liberated but South Africa is still in shackles. Can I put you down for a hundred thousand pounds?"

"No."

"Fifty then."

"No," said Will, not even turning to his sister.

"Then ten thousand, for goodness' sake?" said Josephine.

"Not a penny."

"Are you telling me you support apartheid?"

"No, Josephine, I don't. But you are all looking at Africa through your eyes and you can't really see what is going on. Did you know the World Council of Churches gave money to the terrorists in Rhodesia?"

"Of course they did. For humanitarian purposes. Clothing. Medicine. That kind of thing."

"Which freed up the rest of the money to buy guns that will haunt Africa for generations. You can throw an AK-47 in the river mud, pull it out twenty years later and kill someone with it. In Rhodesia, what you call freedom fighters turned their guns on each other in their fight for power. I don't want my money turned into guns by power-hungry despots, however rational they sound to you on their way to power. Yes, some of the people in the liberation movements are genuine. Many of them. You are, Josephine, I know that and never doubted it. It's the wolves in the sheep's clothing that worry me and they have no principles or the slightest concern about the men and women in the villages. Mobutu in Zaire is a ruthless dictator who uses white mercenaries with American backing to keep in power while he robs his people and accumulates money in Swiss banks. Ask our brother, Byron. He makes his fortune out of helping the likes of Mobutu. Maybe South Africa will be different. I hope so for the sake of the people, but in Africa there are far worse things than apartheid, however appalling that may sound. No, I'm going back to Africa to help the people who need to be helped, not a bunch of exiles who want to send their sons to Stanmore on money meant for the benefit of their people."

"But first we must get rid of apartheid."

"You do it your way, Josephine, and I'll do it mine. That was a lovely breakfast. Thank you both for doing the cooking."

At twelve o'clock the sun came out and snow began to fall from the trees. The slope they had known all their lives served them well and after the second run down the hill – Randolph on the racing toboggan face down, the others sitting upright on the big yellow sledge – said there was no strength left in his body to walk back up the hill.

"We should be with Mother," said Josephine.

"I want a long walk after my journey from America," said Will. "You go on in."

The others walked away, pulling the sledges behind them, and left him alone. In front of him the apple orchard was bare and to his right, dollops of snow were sliding off the fir trees. He was due to leave for London early the following day to catch his flight to Johannesburg. The Zambian High Commission had told him to apply for an extension to his visitor's permit in Lusaka. From Johannesburg he would fly to Salisbury and take the train to Victoria Falls. He had sent a cable to Horst Kannberg, his one-time partner, poste restant, please forward, and hoped the smallness of the town would deliver his message. With the political change in Rhodesia, the border was open again. All the telephone lines to Mongu had been out of order for months.

He walked back up the hill towards the cliff and the memories were still as vivid as they had been twenty-three years before. The times with Lindsay Healy and Shelley Lane were unimportant in comparison, a passage of time.

At the top of the cliff he looked down on Dancing Ledge. The swimming pool, cut from the natural rock for war refugees, was still down below and he could see the small cave so important in the years of his childhood. Snow was on the top of the rocks, but nearer the sea the spray had stopped the snow from collecting. The path down to the ledge was visible through the melting snow. The ritual of walking down to where they had met took him ten slow minutes and then he was looking into the dark water of the winter pool.

For half an hour he stared into the empty water but nothing came up to the surface. All the images were in his mind. With a sigh, he turned and once again began the long journey back to Africa. It was how it had been those twenty-three years ago and nothing now was going to make it change. Maybe the girl had never existed.

PART VII

1981 TO 1986

21

*B*y September 1985, five and a half years after Horst Kannberg had taken him on the *Zambezi Queen the Third* upriver to Barotseland, the terrible drought was in its third year. It was the same year that Lloyd's of London underwriters wrote insurance policies against computers becoming obsolete within five years, a crucial contract unknown to Byron Langton at the time. Will had found Hilary at forty-seven an old man and Mary his wife, who was ten years older, a walking skeleton. Even then there had been very little food. The mission was falling down; unpainted walls, the ground bare of grass with underfoot a quarter inch of dry dust. There was no glass in the schoolroom windows and someone had taken off the door for firewood. The only sign of trees were stumps too low to the ground to yield a sliver of firewood and too stubborn to yield up their roots. Soon after Will arrived, the Zambezi River dropped from lack of rain in Angola and even the low draught of the *Zambezi Queen* would have floundered on the rocks amid the white-water rapids. It had taken Will a year of argument and bribery to bring in his first shipment of medicine, powdered milk and protein-rich biscuits. The extension of his visitor's permit had cost him one hundred pounds in English pound notes, the local party official scornful of kwachas, the Zambian currency, which most often halved in value by the week. The man had given Will a six months' extension and every six months had come for his one hundred pounds. Everything brought into the country attracted import duty, whether a gift to the country or not, and twice whole consignments, paid for by Will against a letter of credit after leaving the

British port, were lost on the new, Chinese-built rail link from Dar es Salaam in Tanzania. What had frustrated Will most was that no one seemed to care. The party had its sinecure in a one-party state and that was all that mattered. Finally Will had reverted to importing through the apartheid ports in South Africa, paying extra for the long-distance trucks from South Africa to deliver the lifeblood of the mission.

Before leaving London, Will had redeemed his guns, the ones left to him by Hannes Potgieter, from the pawnshop and sold the Zambezi Bar on terms to the ex-Rhodesian manager. The years of independent rule had not been kind to Zambia.

"What's happened?" Will had asked Hilary Bains a week after his return.

"Oh, it's probably my fault as much as anyone's."

"What do you mean?"

"You see that young girl over there with the baby tied to her back? She's twelve years old and Mary delivered her baby. The baby is a little girl and in twelve years' time, she will have a baby tied to her own back. By then her mother will have given birth to ten or eleven babies of which one may have died. In the old days, before the white man brought in his obstetrics, that young girl would have had a thirty per cent chance of dying in childbirth and if she had lived through the birth, her daughter would have had a twenty per cent chance of reaching puberty. In the last five years we have had a ten per cent per annum increase in the population in my area of Barotseland which means that every seven years – seven years, Will, not seventy – the population is doubling but not the land or the water. With that kind of population explosion you soon don't have enough renewable firewood, and what's left of the game is pushed into the arid areas to die. They blame colonialism for the woes of Africa and they are right because charity like ours has maintained the population explosion while the administrative system of the West, which would have urbanised the majority of the people, has been replaced by ignorant corruption. Don't blame them. There weren't twenty blacks with degrees when the British handed them administration of the country. We are, to quote a phrase you used to use at school, farting against thunder which from a man of the cloth is an uncouth expression. You see, Will, they can't have one thing without the other. They can't have the benefits of our civilisation without the know-how to make the money to pay for it."

"So what's going to happen?" asked Will.

"Famine and war. War and famine. When there is too little for too many they fight over what's left."

"Can we do anything about it?"

"Yes. Bring back a government that maintains the rule of law and isn't corrupt."

In the second week of Will's return to Africa, the trackers had arrived at the run-down mission station. Sixpence conducted the interview in Lozi with Fourpence and Onepenny squatting in the dust, nodding their heads and grinning. There was still no grey in their curly heads or wispy beards. After ten minutes of polite generalities about the weather, the families of the trackers still left in their ancestral village, wives, children and grandchildren, Will cut the conversation short, extracting pained expressions from all three black faces. He had broken the African rules of etiquette.

"What happened to the big bonus from the crocodile hunt?" There was complete silence outside the clinic under the one tree that had not been cut down for firewood. The smiles were wiped from their faces. Will knew the money generated for them by Laurie Hall would have kept their families in food for two generations. They would have gone back to their villages as rich men. "What happened to all that money?"

"The cattle, they died. We were hunters. They sold us bad cattle. The wives and children of our friends were jealous. Our friends were jealous. Somehow the cattle died and then no one jealous. We went back to the base camp where Onepenny dream three nights you coming back. So we wait. We wait many years and each year Onepenny dream three nights in succession you come back. So we wait."

"The house was washed away."

"Hut of Baas Hall not swept away. We build our huts by the river and wait for you to return."

"And if I had not returned?" snapped Will.

"We would have waited. To dream the same dream for three nights certain one day you return. Now you return. Now you give us jobs and tourists come back and we have money to send back to our families."

"There will never be any more tourists."

"Why?" asked Sixpence.

"The airport at Mongu is now tribal grazing and tribal fields. No planes can land."

"They can come up by road."

"The roads have been washed away, and no one has done any repairs since the British resident left Mongu at independence."

"Then they come up by boat like you," said Sixpence, showing a full display of rotten teeth.

"The river is dropping. No rain. A heavy boat with supplies and tourists will not get through the rapids. You can have a job on the mission to pay for your food. I am not going back to base camp."

"What are you doing here? Why you come back?"

"To build a school. To build a hospital. To help the poor people."

"Why?" asked Sixpence. "You are a hunter. We are trackers. That is our job."

After a week the trackers had come to him where he was trying to help Mary in the clinic saying, "We are going back to the base camp to wait for you. We are trackers. Women clean floors."

"I'm not coming back," said Will patiently. "Can't you see?"

"You will," said Sixpence and all three of them shook Will's hand in the African tribal handshake. They were smiling happily. With a blanket each over their shoulders, barefoot, with no food, they set off to cut the Zambezi and make the long walk along the banks of the river to base camp. They had left their rifles hidden in the rondavel built by Laurie Hall yet there was no ammunition left for the guns.

"What do I do with them?" Will asked Mary.

"There is always time in Africa. Time is eternal. They talk to God through their ancestors. They become Christians because they believe Christ will sit them nearer to God in heaven. Time is eternal. These people have always looked upwards to the heavens, not in words to their own selfishness. They believe their ancestors live forever and one day they will become an ancestor to help their children on earth, to speak to their grandchildren in dreams. We Europeans have become so insular we only think of ourselves and our own comfort. Only here, in terrible hardship, can we find our God. They will wait for you, Will Langton, and there is nothing you can do about it. You became part of their lives. Maybe that is the real reason you came back to Africa."

"I came back to help the mission, to return the money that came out of Africa. I am not responsible for the trackers. They had money from us to go back to their village."

"They lost it. To them, you are still responsible for their mortal lives."

"How can a man be permanently responsible for another man?"

"They asked Queen Victoria for protection. The men in Lusaka took away British protection from Barotseland without the Lozis' consent. You gave the trackers protection and took it away without their consent."

"For God's sake, Mary. We whites were kicked out. UNIP, the bloody party, would not renew my concession. They even kicked out the chief. They can't kick us out and still want protection. Shit, this conversation is just bloody silly. I'm going to give them a proper school and a hospital. What more can I bloody do?"

"Will, please don't swear on the mission."

"I'm sorry, Mary. I'm just a little frustrated. I can't seem to get anything done here. All that money in England to spend and nothing happening. I never knew how difficult it would be to give away my money to people who really need it."

"Maybe you should ask God."

"Mary, you know I'm not religious."

"If you lose your God, you lose everything. Find your God again, Will."

PENNY BAINS, the surviving child of Hilary and Mary, came to Will three days after the trackers had left the mission.

"Can I talk to you?" said Penny.

"Of course you can."

"I don't have many people to talk to in English. How do I apply for a British passport?"

"Well, I suppose you go to the British High Commission in Lusaka and fill in some forms. Birth certificate. Parents' birth certificates. Their marriage certificate. Why, Penny?"

"I know it will be terrible for Mother and Father but they can't go on holding me here just because Malcolm died of malaria when he was twelve years old. I'm nineteen now and need a life. Working sunup to sundown with little appreciation and no pay is not my idea of fun. Mum and Dad decided themselves they wanted to be missionaries, not me. I've never even been to school. What I know, and that isn't very much, I learnt through correspondence courses and the few hours my parents could put aside for my education. Zambia is finished. They are wasting their time. The powers that be don't even want us here. Just look at the place."

"That's why I am going to build a new school and a hospital."

"No one will appreciate it and if they do the party will take the credit. I want to get out of Africa and never have to see the place for the rest of my life. Please help me? I don't have a passport or a ngwee to my name, and I'm screaming bored with being taken for granted. If my parents want to find God by working all day and half the night for other people, I don't. I want to have some fun. Is that so wrong in life? ... What did you do at my age?"

"I came to Africa."

"Then it was British. This is a mess and will stay a mess whatever we do on the mission."

"I'll talk to your parents."

"Oh, I've tried that. Everything comes back to God. Frankly, I don't think there is a God, just a system invented by man to make people like my parents throw away their lives to make poor people healthy enough to have a miserable life in poverty and behave themselves while they are suffering for fear of burning in hell. One of the books I've been reading says that people should mind their own business. These people lived far better lives before the British arrived. Sure, they died young but isn't it better for a few to die young and happy than the whole damn lot live in misery? They are multiplying like flies all because of us. We've interfered with the balance of nature."

When the small girl with big brown eyes had gone off on some errand she no longer wished to complete, Will walked away from the scattering of mission buildings towards the few trees left standing in the rapidly arriving desert. Remembering the girl's words for people to 'mind their own business', he was not sure of the right thing to do. He had just arrived back in Africa and was it his business to interfere in the life of a family? Then he thought of the girl in an old print frock that had come out from England in the charity bundle. The girl, who had only just turned nineteen, had not even been wearing shoes. For better or for worse, he made up his mind and went looking for Hilary Bains.

"When did you and Mary last go home on leave?" he said to Hilary.

"Oh, we don't have time for that."

"Given a few months to work out what's going on, I can run the mission. Or rather, the secular side of it. The Missionary Society must allocate you leave."

"They do, I take leave pay and passage money and spend it on the mission."

"Is that fair to your family?"

"Oh, Mary doesn't mind. It was her idea the first time home leave came round. What would we do in England, anyway? This is our house."

"Do the London people visit you?"

"They never have yet. I send them an annual report which is all they want. I gave up asking them for money and since then they are quite happy the way I do things. We are on their map as an operating mission and that's what really counts. You know, you'll have to ask them before you spend all this money you talk about."

"I didn't know that."

"Oh, yes. It's their mission. It belongs to them. They'll want to know if your money can be spent better elsewhere."

A cold premonition went through Will's mind. There was obviously more than one way to wrap Africa up in red tape.

"How can they tell me how to spend my money?"

"You want to spend it on their mission. There are rules, you know. My goodness gracious me, if everyone ran around putting up buildings left, right and centre it would all get quite out of control."

"Doesn't look as though too many people have been running around here recently putting up buildings."

Hilary Bains ignored the jibe. "And I can't possibly leave you in charge of the mission. You're not a missionary. Maybe you should think of doing something else with your money."

"Maybe I should... Do you ever think about your daughter?"

"Of course I do. What on earth has this got to do with Penny?"

"She just asked me how she could get herself a British passport."

"I hope you didn't tell her."

"Of course I did. What did you expect me to say to her? I don't know how to get a passport?"

"Nothing. You should have said nothing. She's still a child."

"Not anymore. But I agree, Hilary. She's your child, and it's none of my business. I'm sorry. I'll just have to get used to the rules. Do you think the good fathers in London will object if I privately import a consignment of medicine for the sick?"

"You won't find that so easy."

"Why ever not?"

"You will require an import permit."

"For emergency medicine?"

"Oh yes. Anything coming in or out of African countries requires a permit. You have to pay the government to import or export anything. They don't like businessmen making money out of the people without the government receiving a tax. How else are they going to pay for the civil service? There has been import duty in England since the year dot. All those brandy smugglers from France. Granda used to tell me stories. Your Granda. Now, Will, I'm sorry. You've taken up enough of my time. There is always so much to do."

"How do I go about applying for an import permit?" Will said to the back of Hilary's cassock.

"I have absolutely no idea."

"Shit," said Will so Hilary was unable to hear. "You can't even give the bloody stuff away without some bureaucrat or NGO getting a cut. The world stinks."

Soon after the somewhat bilious discussion with Hilary Bains, Will realised that if he was going to make any sense out of what he was trying to do he needed viable transport between Barotseland and the rest of the world. After visiting the old airstrip at Mongu, the one for which Laurie Hall had worked so long ago as airport manager, Will saw the only cultivation was at the edge of the old airfield and the only real change was scraggy cattle grazing, or attempting to graze, the barren land instead of the buffalo. Even Will's untrained eye could see there were far too many cows for the available land and that any slaughtered cattle would dress out as skin and bones. Chasing off cows to land an aircraft would be no different to chasing off the game in the days gone by.

The only answer to his problem, he told himself, was to buy an aircraft and learn how to fly. Remembering some of the early conversations with Laurie Hall, he knew the aircraft would have to be twin-engined and the pilot's licence he required would have to give him instrument rating and the ability to fly at night. With the vision of coming down in the bush, even on grass veld, he made a mental note to take an extensive course in aircraft maintenance. How he was to go about the exercise was beyond his immediate comprehension. Will could hear one of his mother's favourite expressions echoing in his ears: 'If you are going to do a job, do it properly', followed by a second of Adelaide Langton's homilies: 'If you want to do a job properly, do it yourself'. He often wondered how many generations in his family had passed down such truths. Having made up his mind to overcome the first obstacle, he found a second hurdle equally a problem. Getting up from the Victoria Falls with his old partner, Horst Kannberg, had been one thing. Getting out of the mission without transport or a workable telephone to call for help, the locals having found a better use for copper telephone wire, was insurmountable. The walk from the old jetty on the Zambezi River, where Horst had left him in a hurry to beat the falling river six weeks ago, had taken a day and he knew the way. There was no chance of him walking to the Zambian capital, Lusaka, or the Victoria Falls without dying on the road, even with all his experience. There were too many starving people who would find his small possessions, particularly his gun and ammunition, riches beyond compare. He began to empathise with young Penny Bains whose big, brown, sad eyes haunted even his dreams.

With the patience of having lived in Africa for so many years, Will waited for the trader to visit Barotseland with his overlander truck that could travel through the bush in the dry season without need of a road, a slow, hot, tsetse-bitten journey that Will at forty-four years of age had hopefully discounted as the option to solve his own problem of moving around. To add to Will's problems, the young Bains girl was looking at Will with eyes that asked for more than a way out of the bush. Or so it seemed, and he hoped he was wrong.

The sporadic rainy season had petered out soon after Will's arrival without a sign of the main rains that swept in with the cyclones from the Mozambique channel. Just before leaving England, Will had first heard of the weather pattern that the scientists were calling El Niño, which was caused by the Pacific Ocean either warming up or cooling down, Will had not paid enough attention to remember which. What he did remember was the forecast that for the next several years the world's weather pattern would change and there would be terrible floods where floods would least be expected and terrible drought in Africa. 'Global warming' was a phrase he had also heard for the first time, and like everyone else on earth burrowing away at his own particular life, he had taken little notice. In England the weather was always bloody awful so what was the difference?

That year the inland waterholes dried up in August, forcing the game to trek to the Zambezi for water and back again for food. For ten miles from the big rivers, there was not a blade of grass or a leaf within reach of an elephant's trunk or the delicate lips of a giraffe. To compound the problem, any tree that was not strong enough to stand up to the weight of a fully grown elephant had been pushed over for the prize of the top green leaves: the tree had been killed. Everyone was waiting for the rains to start building up but day after day the sky was dust blue with the occasional puff of cloud. Nature was preparing a final, dreadful blow to the chaos of post-colonial Africa.

HYMIE GOLDBLATT, the current holder of the trading concession once held by Octavio Goncalves, had been recruited into the South African Communist Party when he was a law student at the University of Cape Town. He had fled South Africa three years earlier, just ahead of the state security police who were fighting the 'total onslaught' of communism that beset apartheid South Africa. One of his fellow advocates had been murdered by the security police the day before and Hymie had been smuggled out of Cape Town into Botswana before arriving in Lusaka where the African National Congress of Nelson Mandela conducted their struggle against apartheid. With no use for his services as a working advocate in Zambia, he sat around in the Zambian capital for months doing nothing. He had never had an intention of going into politics, his membership of the SACP having come about through the persecution of his own people, the

Jews. Through defending four members of the ANC in separate cases, he was one of the few whites in South Africa who understood the depth of persecution brought down on anyone who disagreed with apartheid. He was not even safe in Lusaka from the South African Bureau of State Security and when UNIP, the party that controlled Zambia, told the ANC they were looking for a trader to operate Barotseland, Hymie Goldblatt was offered the concession. Being a man of quick humour, the idea amused Hymie as he knew his great-grandfather, who had fled the Tsar's pogroms in Russia, had made his living in South Africa as an itinerant pedlar, better known in those days as a *smous*. The old man had toiled from Cape Town to the Transvaal with his two horses and cart, selling anything and everything to the isolated farmers, the Boers of South Africa. The horse and cart had eventually given way to the trading company Goldblatt and Sons, which presently generated billions in trade between the outside world and South Africa, everything from steel to maize to sugar, anything in fact that had a buy price slightly less than the sale price. Hymie's younger brother was training under their father to take over the family trading house with its overseas offices in Australia, Hong Kong, Teheran and Israel. And here was Hymie, the heir to the family throne that he had first forsaken for the law, going back to being a *smous*. The only difference in the lifestyle of Hymie and his great-grandfather was the five-ton truck, with the big high wheels, and the horse and cart. Inside, the merchandise was much the same. To complete the irony, most of the goods he sold were bought in South Africa as goods from America and Europe were far too expensive. Hymie was convinced that a government of the people, by the people in South Africa was the cornerstone that would solve some of the problems of sub-Saharan Africa.

By the time he met Will Langton for the first time he was thirty-three years old. By then, to Hymie, whether the future South African government was communist or democratic, it mattered not, so long as the nationalists were removed from power and replaced by a government of all the people. In some ways he was an idealist rather like Will Langton who not only sought his help to get to Lusaka but to bring up the medicines Will wished to buy for the mission. They had all been entertained to dinner by Mary Bains when Hymie had shattered the practicality of Will becoming a qualified pilot.

"First you will be spending more money on transport than medicine and secondly the time and energy you will have to spend to qualify as a pilot could be better spent helping the poor. Believe me, I know. What you need is a reliable transport company that can bring in your precious cargo without them worrying about the condition of the roads. For a price, of course, but a price far less than the drastic scheme you have in mind... Mrs Bains," Hymie had said, "your cooking is superb even if it is not strictly according to my religion. At least, Reverend Bains, we have what you would call the Old Testament in common."

"Do you know of such a transport company in South Africa?" Will had asked.

"Of course. Goldblatt and Sons Transport, a division of Goldblatt and Sons."

"They wouldn't happen to have anything to do with your family?" Will asked with a quiet smile.

"Oh, yes. I can get you a very good price."

"And on the medicines?"

"Undoubtedly."

"I think God has reached out to you, Will," said Hilary and, looking at the trouble in his adopted-brother's eyes, Will was not sure whether Hilary was being serious.

"Can you give me a lift to Lusaka and an introduction to your family?" said Will.

"Can I come too?" said Penny Bains, who right through dinner had not taken her eyes off Hymie Goldblatt.

In the silence that had followed Penny Bains's request, Will had excused himself from the table. They were drinking tea grown on the mission, the bushes guarded from the goats by a thorn-thicket fence that had proved impregnable. Through the big veranda window protected by a gauze screen, he could see the four of them seated at the table, the two paraffin lamps smoking in the still of the night.

The night was cloudless and stars held every point in the pitch-black sky, layer upon layer of unknown light speaking from eternity. Automatically Will took the line from the Southern Cross to the pointer stars and found the true south. Cicadas screeched in the night. The smell of wood-ash was heavy in the air, the elephant-destroyed trees having found their way to the mission. Some way behind the crumbling bungalow that Hilary called his house, an owl was calling to its mate and Will listened for the answering call. When it came, he smiled to himself and walked further away from the house.

Nature was calling to the girl, the most primal call, more powerful than parents' words, and Will had no wish to enter the argument: without that primitive call to reproduce, he surmised, man would long ago have left the planet which set Will to wondering. Did all the talk of life's meaning have anything else to say, he thought? Did God and goodness, the struggle to live a better life, have anything more important to say than the preservation of the species? Was that the only reason for man's pursuit through life: to live, love, reproduce and die? Did man make up the rest and confuse himself? Was it not just that simple? What was one man amid all those stars if he did not reproduce?

Looking back to the earth, Will retraced his steps towards the sophistication of the dining room table. Then he opened the insect-proof frame, covered with gauze that guarded the door.

"Everything's in its place in heaven," said Will. "The night sky is beautiful. Mary, please excuse me for breaking up the evening but my new friend is leaving early in the morning and the long road is rough. For a moment out there in the dark, life was heavy on my shoulders and it has made me tired. The older I get, the less I understand. Rather sad. Once upon a time, I thought I would find out the answers. Goodnight, Mary, Hilary, Penny, Mr Goldblatt."

"Call me Hymie."

"Goodnight, Hymie. I will see you in the morning."

THE ROW BEGAN AT BREAKFAST. The lamps had been removed from the table to the sideboard and the dead insects, drawn to the fatal light the previous evening, had been swept away: even the glass shades had been cleaned of soot. Mary Bains believed godliness and cleanliness went hand in hand. The first rays of sunshine sweeping across the brown compound of the mission caught a wall picture of Christ hanging from his cross. Outside the bungalow, between the house and the schoolroom, long-legged chickens had begun their desperate forage for survival, eternally searching the layer of fine, dry soil that covered the surface of the mission compound. With a cluck of delight an old hen found the scattered dead insects from the paraffin lamp swept over the steps of the veranda, and frantically pecked up the incinerated remains ahead of the seven other mission fowls that half-flew to the meagre source of food. The day was going to be hot with the powder-blue sky almost cloudless.

Will had packed a small bag and was ready to face the heat and dust. The six hundred-kilometre trek through the bush would take them through the Kafue National Park. They would camp out next to the truck four times before reaching Lusaka.

Penny Bains marched in to breakfast with a small bag hanging from her shoulder that had been made for her by the children in the school, the children bringing the reeds to the school from the Zambezi River. The bag was remarkably strong. The sun had been up for ten minutes when she took her usual seat.

"Hymie, please, may I have a lift to Lusaka?"

"What are you going to do in Lusaka?" snapped her father.

"Obtain a British passport and go to England."

"Don't be silly, you don't have any money."

"But I do have my birth certificate, both your birth certificates and your certificate of marriage which I took from the bureau. The British High Commission will provide me with the form to fill in and then I will wait."

"And what are you going to do for money?" laughed Hilary. Mary had stopped eating her breakfast and was staring at her daughter. "Did you have something to do with this, Will? You obviously told her how to obtain a passport. Have you lent my daughter money?"

"No, I have not."

"Will you swear that on the Bible?"

"Of course. But..."

"There are no 'buts' about it. Either you did or you didn't."

"Your daughter never asked me for money but had she done so and with your permission I would have given her passage to England. Mother would happily receive her at Langton Manor, which is your home after all. The girl is English and has a right to see her heritage."

"Are you telling me how to bring up my daughter? Penny, you will come to your senses and put that bag back in your bedroom where it belongs."

"Daddy, I'm nineteen. I am not a missionary and never will be. The British High Commission will be obliged to repatriate a destitute British national and in England they have a welfare system designed to set me on my feet. If Hymie will give me a lift to Lusaka, I will fend for myself."

"Mr Goldblatt, I forbid you to offer my daughter a lift. It's abduction."

"I don't think so, Reverend. I may be a *smous* by practice but I am a lawyer by trade. Under British law, Penny has every right to make her own decisions. Will is her de facto uncle. A lawful chaperone. But what I will do is delay my journey by a day and excuse myself while your family find a solution to your problem. Will, I think you would like to visit your old base camp, or what is left of it. Let us leave this family for the day to come to terms with itself... And may God be with you. A house united shall stand, a house divided shall fall, Reverend, Mary, Penny. Thank you for my breakfast... I know the pain of losing family," he said, turning back from the door. "Until apartheid falls, and that may be longer than my lifetime, I cannot go home for fear of my life. Penny can always fly here and you can always fly to England. Maybe in this life we should all think on the bright side."

The following day in the early dawn, the three of them set off in the five-ton truck, an old Bedford that had come down Africa with overland tourists and broken down beyond the skills of the tour operator. Hymie had bought the vehicle with money lent him by the ANC for the price of the recyclable spare parts: all the profits from his trading went to the ANC to fight apartheid. In the woven reed bag behind the front seat of the truck was a letter from the Reverend Hilary Bains giving his nineteen-year-old daughter permission to apply for a British passport. None of them were sure, not even Advocate Goldblatt, whether parental consent was required after turning eighteen or twenty-one years of age. Having fought through the worst family day since Malcolm died from malaria, Hilary had no wish for the united decision to flounder in the hands of bureaucracy: it would be one thing to find a lift to Lusaka and another to find one back.

Penny was dressed in well-washed and darned shorts that once had been khaki, a top of indeterminate colour and a pair of rough sandals. Her hair, thick and healthy, that had never been washed in anything but cheap soap, reminded Will of a badly made rat's nest. The hair was tied up in a red scarf at the back. Vaguely Will wondered what the girl would look like in the latest London clothes with her hair washed out in shampoo. He was then forty-eight years old and even the family connection didn't stop him from speculating. Uncomfortably, he decided the girl probably had a very good figure and as she was seated in the middle of the bench seat, he carefully ensured that his bare knee kept away from the bare flesh that was twenty-five years younger than himself.

As if to compound his problem, less than an hour out of the mission, Penny turned to him sweetly. "How old are you, Will? Or should I say, Uncle Will?"

"Just Will is fine... Very old, Penny, very old."

"I'm serious."

"So am I. Now, if you ask Hymie his age I'm sure he will have no problem telling the truth... Out of interest, Hymie, did this vehicle ever have a suspension?" In all the jolting and bouncing around it was impossible for Will to keep his knee out of contact with young Penny and he was conscious of the girl enjoying his discomfort.

"She's better fully loaded. They bring them overland down Africa with anything up to fifteen passengers and all the camping gear. There's the three of us and very little stock left over from my trip... Sorry. I'm not sure whether it's better when we detour off the road or hit the potholes. I never average more than fifteen kilometres an hour or the tyres would be blown off their rims. And yes, I do carry spares. Four of them and ten inner tubes. The big acacia thorns are as much of a problem as the potholes."

"Doesn't anyone try and fix the holes?" asked Penny.

"Not since the British left," said Hymie.

"And you support the system?" said Will, innocently.

"I can't argue politics when my kidneys are being punched every fifty metres. Save that question for the campfire and I'll try to give you an answer. Nothing's ever simple in Africa."

There was no air conditioning in the truck and Hymie was forced to lower the windows when the sun came over the trees and pierced the cab. Shortly after, they were forced off what was left of the metalled road onto a long detour that wound through the mopani forest. The next track went round trees pushed over by elephants, and anthills the size of small hills, where the nitrogen-enriched soil had fertilised small thickets. Penny took the red scarf from the back of her hair and put it across her nose and mouth to keep out the dust.

"We used to have an old Land Rover on the mission before it bust," she explained. "I went out with Daddy to the villages. In those days he called on the very sick. Now they have to be brought to him and that usually means they die."

"Can't your Missionary Society send you a replacement vehicle?" asked Hymie.

"Daddy talks about priorities. Fact is, Daddy has a fixation about priorities. Felt it was not right for him to be seen driving around when all the children have pot bellies from lack of nutrition. Will, if you're going to send in medicine to Daddy you should bring in protein-enriched biscuits for the children. I read about the biscuits in *Newsweek*."

"You read *Newsweek* out here?" asked Hymie as he wound the old diesel truck around the big mopani trees following an old track he had probably made himself: unless occasional military traffic passed through the rural areas.

"Every week," answered Penny. "They are six months old but so what? Daddy has a friend from theological college who's now a bishop and sends Daddy all the newspapers and any books he thinks Daddy would like to read."

"Does Hilary know you read *Newsweek*?" asked Will, his curiosity piqued by a girl who had never been to school reading international news magazines.

"Oh, I think so. We don't have TV or even radio anymore. No electricity.

All I have are the papers and the books after dark. One paraffin lamp is enough if you clean the soot off the glass every now and again. I read everything cover to cover including the letters to the press. Some of the books I don't understand but that makes it more interesting."

"How long have you been reading *Newsweek* cover to cover?"

"Since I was eleven, I think it was."

"Good God," said Hymie as they drove on through the heat and dust of the African bush, followed by a cloud of tsetse fly they could even hear above the drone of the diesel engine. The cloud of flies was fooled by the moving truck into thinking it was animal and blood and their only source of reproduction. Some of the flies flew into the cab and were swatted by Will against the windscreen. The chances of contracting sleeping sickness were small but the bite of a tsetse fly was similar to being pierced by a red-hot needle.

They had seen one warthog since leaving the mission and Will was wondering what had happened to the game. The bush was tinder-dry from the poor rain season and the next rains were six months away. For six months, not a drop of rain would fall on the bush. At first, he had felt naked in the bush without his rifle.

"Leave your gun behind, Will," Hymie had told him. "In Africa north of the Limpopo a white man with a gun is suspect. Nkomo's army may have gone home to Zimbabwe but I'm sure it's no secret the ANC and SWAPO are training freedom fighters in Zambia to launch attacks on South West Africa and South Africa. Leave your gun behind. There are more dangerous things in the bush for a white man than wild animals and malaria. Some of the cadres are aggressive having lost friends and relatives to apartheid."

Will surveyed the surrounding bush. A great deal more than a looming drought had come to Zambia since Will had left after independence. There was menace emanating from the bush. The trackers, yesterday at base camp, had probably been right, he thought, when they told him to stay out of the way. 'In Africa,' Fourpence had said, quoting a long-standing African truth, 'you either follow or lead or get the hell out of the way. We stay out the way, baas. You best join us here and stay out the way.' Fourpence had spoken in Lozi, Will suspected intentionally so that Hymie would be unable to understand. Even the new white men could be friends of the Party. 'I have a job to do, Fourpence. To give back something to Africa.' 'Be careful, baas. This Africa is not so good anymore.'

The grinding, low gear fight through the bush went on all day, with Will spelling Hymie as the driver. For the first time in his life, Will Langton was not enjoying a journey through Africa. When they camped at dusk, he gathered a pile of wood for the night's fire which in the old days would have lasted a week. Again, for the first time in Africa, Will was nervous, and he didn't have a gun.

They had driven well off the track to make camp, deep in the mopani forest where their fire would not attract attention. There was no early moon, and the night was black. Before the light had gone, Will had gathered a heap of thick worms with hairy bodies that grew on the boughs of the mopani trees. They were still a day's drive from the Kafue National Park. Will put the worms he had collected in his leather hat on the seat of the truck before making the fire that would burn all night. As darkness fell and Africa contracted to two men and a girl round the campfire, Will felt at ease for the first time that day. When a lion roared deep in the forest, five, ten miles away – it was difficult to judge from so far away – Will relaxed. The small furrow disc he had seen in the back of the truck was now next to the fire, put there by Hymie Goldblatt. First, they made tea and drank it in silence, listening to the cicadas and night birds, Will putting a name to each of their calls. A tin of beans and a tin of sausages sat next to the furrow disc and Hymie was preparing sudza from maize meal in a three-legged iron pot under which he made a separate fire. They sat on low camp chairs. There were no mosquitoes as there was no water for fifty miles. The heat of the day went quickly and left them cool at the start of the night.

"Do you know what you are going to do in England?" Hymie asked Penny wistfully. For the first time, Will realised the loneliness of the man.

"Oh yes. Whether I will find it possible remains to be seen. From what I've read, you always seem to have to know someone and the only people I know in the world are Mummy and Daddy and the two of you around this fire, which rather limits the chances."

"Did you take any examinations through your correspondence courses?" asked Will.

"Not one. How could I? Where was I going to go to write Oxford and Cambridge O levels, let alone A levels? The nearest adjudicator was over three hundred miles away and we didn't even have a car. Doesn't mean I wouldn't pass. On the dummy papers I sent back, all the results were good. You know, I read somewhere that all the knowledge of man is in between the covers of books so all you need is to read. I've had the books. Lots of them. The bishop has a weird catholic taste in books that he sends Daddy and I've read everything from an abridged Gibbon's *Decline and Fall of the Roman Empire* to James Bond. I rather liked James Bond, but I also liked Plato."

"You've read Plato's dialogues?" asked Hymie.

"All of them."

"Did you understand them?"

"Not the first time, silly. Round about the sixth read of the *Republic* it began to make sense."

"You've read Plato's *Republic* six times?"

"More like ten. I told you, there was nothing else to do on the mission except work during the day, read at night and think most of the time. I did a lot of thinking."

"I'll bet you did," said Hymie, stirring the white maize porridge. He had only read the *Republic* once himself, Karl Marx three times, as well as the abridged form of *The Decline and Fall of the Roman Empire*.

Will, watching Hymie stir the sudza pot, felt decidedly uneducated, despite all the family money spent on sending him to school at Stanmore.

"You know the big laugh?" said Penny. "When Socrates was talking to his friends hundreds of years before the birth of Christ he didn't even think much of democracy, let alone a tyranny like communism. A philosopher king was what he wanted. A man who would always do that which was right however politically inconvenient the decision. Of course no such man or woman has ever existed, as far as we know, as anyone with that amount of intelligence would not have taken the job. Maybe Christ tried to be the philosopher king. Who knows? I'm not even sure if I believe in God. Do you believe in God, Hymie?"

"Of course."

"And yet you are a self-confessed, or should I say proclaimed, communist. Isn't that a contradiction? Communism is the farthest end of the spectrum from religion."

"Sometimes the end justifies the means. We have to defeat apartheid. Communism can defeat apartheid. Capitalism is too concerned with profit from the white-managed South Africa."

"My goodness," said Penny, getting up to throw more wood on the fire. "I'm just a little mission girl stuck in the bush but even I can see that white South Africa manages their country better than we do. I'll bet they don't have potholes every fifty metres and pot bellies every child, black or white, in South Africa. Hymie, don't you think these people might just be using you and communism to gain power? It's all about power, Hymie, not right and wrong. They made Socrates drink the poison, remember? In many ways we've retrogressed since those days. Look at mass slaughter in the trenches. Atom bombs on people. The Holocaust."

"And apartheid," said Hymie.

"And we call ourselves civilised," smiled Penny, nineteen years old.

"Indeed we do."

The new wood burst into flame and sent dancing sparks into the trees, their world briefly deepening into the surrounding forest. Will put the furrow disc in the fire and Penny leant to open the two tins of food. For ten minutes they listened to Africa and kept to their thoughts. When the disc was red-hot, Will walked across to the truck and brought the hat full of cleaned mopani worms to the fire and threw them onto the disc where they jumped, sizzling the outside fur away from the worms. Will pushed the gutted worms around the disc with a stick until they were ready and scooped them onto a tin plate.

"Better than shrimps," he said, offering the plate.

"Much better," said Penny, who had never eaten a shrimp in her life.

The tinned beans and sausages were poured into the cooked sudza and stirred. They could see each other's faces by the light of the flickering fire. When the food was dished out onto the plates, they ate in silence.

"What is it you want to do in England, Penny?" asked Hymie, when he had finished his plate of food.

"I'm going to be a writer," she said with total confidence.

"What kind of writer?" asked Will, wondering if Hilary or Mary had ever seen this side of their daughter.

"Articles, books, novels. That sort of thing. Do you think I can be a writer in England? The weather's very cold, isn't it?"

"I may be able to help," said Will, envious of the girl who knew what she wanted to do with the rest of her life. "I have a friend by the name of Heathcliff Mortimer. He must be nearly eighty by now though he never lets anyone know his age. I rather think he will tell you quite quickly whether you can write. Didn't Hilary tell you my brother owns a string of newspapers?"

"He mentioned your mother and father. They were very kind to him."

"Hymie, do you mind if I sleep in the back of the truck? I'm not used to sleeping on the ground anymore. Old age is creeping up."

"Nonsense," said Penny. "You can't be over thirty-five?"

"I shall wish," said Will. "You know, Hymie, I rather think it's going to be easier to introduce Penny to the world of writing than bring medicine to the mission."

As he got up to go to the truck and the mattresses he had seen inside, he wondered what the rear gunner would have thought of his granddaughter if he had not been shot dead in the back of Red Langton's Lancaster bomber. The twist of fate. Maybe the girl would have not read a book in her life. If he had done his national service all those years ago, would he be climbing into the back of someone else's truck in the middle of Africa? If the girl had not been lost to his life? Maybe there was never any permanence or future. Just the present, changing.

He could hear Hymie and the girl still talking as he fell asleep. When he dreamed, he dreamed of Dancing Ledge, looking into the girl-less, empty pool. Opposite, a small boy was crying in the cave.

*B*yron Langton met Penny Bains when she was nineteen years old. It was the year of the great drought in Barotseland, the one Will thought so incorrectly would never grow worse. She was quite a girl.

Africa at the end of 1985 was a basket case. Whoever was in power favoured Moscow rather than Washington, or the other way round. For every government in power there was a government in exile backed by the superpower whose puppet was not in power. When the rebels won, the government went back into the bush and the process started again. The pickings for the winners were the control of the countries' minerals. From Ethiopia in the east to Nigeria in the west, governments came and went at the point of a gun barrel. Byron Langton grew richer by the day, the eternal go-between, the man who could turn the military victory into hard currency so when the new government fell, there were newly rich men who cared little for the suffering of their people. More importantly, they had money to buy more guns. It was callous exploitation and the powers of communism and capitalism fought their surrogate wars with every dirty trick known to man. Byron Langton was a big player in a cast of millions, his real power not the ability to launder money through Switzerland but the files he kept in the walk-in safe that led from his office, the files on Africa's despots and power-seekers started by Heathcliff Mortimer. He was the unjust side of press freedom, the man people feared in democracies: Byron had worked on the principle that any man who reached for power had something to hide. An honest man in Byron's world of 1985 was as difficult to find as a needle in a haystack.

Byron was over fifty when he first met Penny and even his tailor was now unable to hide the paunch that started at his navel. His body was the shape of an avocado pear. Above the paunch were sagging breasts and above those appendages sagging jowls. The once thick brown hair was dirty white, what was left of it. The only resemblance to the good-looking young man who had joined Logan, Smith and Marjoribanks in 1948 was the violet eyes. The eyes, which once had charmed his way to success were calculating, some said ruthless. The only things going for Byron in 1985 were money and power and he was sensible enough to understand the problem. What the young girls looked at when they saw Byron Langton, particularly with his clothes off, was a debauched old man who had not seen his willy in years except through the reflection in a mirror. What Byron saw in young girls was exactly the same as he had always done. The flaw in his libido was that it never grew up, something his long-suffering wife found to her cost from two directions: after the children, he never touched her, and what he did touch stayed below the age of twenty-five. Young girls who had never been bought with more than the price of dinner were the target of his perversion and after the sister's slamming of the door in his face, he always paid for what he was going to get before he got it. Rhodes of Africa, Byron remembered, had always said that every man had his price. For Byron, every young girl had her price if he could only find out what it was. The chase to find the price for his sexual gratification was equally exciting as the days of Stepping and Try, Virginia and Fanny and all their friends. The game was just the same, only the rules had changed, and what Byron had lost in good looks he made up for in knowledge, the real knowledge of people.

TWO PEOPLE HAD COME into Penny's life since she arrived in London four years earlier. In the reed bag she had packed on the mission were a cheque for five hundred pounds signed by Will, letters from Will introducing her to Heathcliff Mortimer, Josephine and the new owner of the Zambezi Bar, and a piece of paper with Adelaide Langton's phone number. The first letter started her writing, the third got her a job as a waitress and the second she was too frightened to use: ex-cabinet ministers were rather impressive.

"What do you want to write, fact or fiction?" Heath had asked.

"Fiction. Definitely fiction."

"Then you don't want to join my newspaper even if I did have a chance in hell of getting you a job." They were seated on Heath's favourite bench overlooking the Thames in the garden of his favourite pub. The early May afternoon was mild and Heath was enjoying the first of his double Southern Comforts and Penny was drinking a lemonade. "You are lucky to find me in England. Your mentor's brother is a hard taskmaster. Did Will give you an introduction to Byron?"

"No he didn't."

Heath thought about this for a moment. "Fiction is the quick way to starve as a writer. You'll need a job. I have shares in a pub-cum-restaurant."

"Zambezi Bar. Will gave me a letter."

"Have you got any fiction of yours I can read?"

"Not yet."

"You haven't started writing?"

"No I haven't."

Heath looked at the sky, making his long mane of white hair flow free from his back. Why did people ask him to do the impossible? "Tell me what you've read in your very short life." If there was a tone of sarcasm in his voice he had done his best to hide it. "Do you have an A level in either English language or English literature?"

"I never went to school. This is the first time I have been off the mission. But I have done some reading," and she began to rattle off titles and authors as they came into her head. Heath had never heard a mix like it in his life. With the list still growing he got up and walked away from the bench into the pub for a refill to his drink. Penny turned to look at his receding back and thought the old man had walked out on her. With the resilience of youth she shrugged and turned back to enjoying the river and London. Some people were frightened of the bush. Some were frightened of the Big City. She was frightened of neither. She had taken full advantage of Hymie's generosity in Lusaka, taken the paid-for ticket to London with a knowing smile and paid nothing more than the looks she gave the men to encourage their indulgence. Obviously, she now reflected, this old generation was past all hope.

When he sat down again with a new drink, she gave the old boy her best smile. Penny Bains liked being a young woman. Until Will had come into her life, she had had no idea of her power.

"Have you somewhere to stay?" asked Heath.

"Oh yes thank you. The man at the bar. Alex. You know him? Will said you own shares in the pub. Alex gave me his room until I find something. He's sleeping on the couch. Don't you drink in your own bar? Will had the flat before he went do-gooding in Mongu."

"I do. I've just come back from Africa... That's how you look at him? A do-gooder?"

"My parents have been do-gooding all their lives and look where that got them. Now they're too scared to come back to England and live with normal people. People in Africa only say they want the missionaries. What they really want is what they can get out of them. Most of the time they're laughing behind their backs at someone born on earth being the son of God. They talk to God through their ancestors. To them it makes more sense as the ancestors have gone on ahead."

"Did you hear much about African folklore? Their history, that kind of thing?"

"For ten years of my life I spoke Lozi better than English. The very young didn't mind my white skin. Then they changed and left me with no friends and nothing else to do but read. I know more about them than they think. I grew up with them, for God's sake, I was ten before I stopped swimming with them bare arse in the Zambezi."

"What about the crocs and bilharzia?"

"We knew where to swim. If the water flows, you won't get bilharzia. One of the kids stood guard on a rock. You can see a bloody crocodile metres away in shallow water... Now that's one thing I do miss. Wouldn't like to swim in that river," she said, pointing ahead. "It's filthy and you can't see the bottom."

"Write me an African story and post it or bring it to my office."

"Don't you have a home?" said Penny, using her eyes.

"Of course."

"Can't I bring it to your home?"

"If you wish to." Then he thought: 'You silly old bugger, Mortimer. The girl's flirting with a septuagenarian and you fell for it. There's no fool like an old fool.' And then he smiled at Penny and wrote out the address of his Chelsea flat.

That evening Alex made a pass at her and she knew that staying in his flat and not in his bed was not going to be a proposition but she needed the job and somewhere to stay. Alex, she guessed, was nearer forty than thirty. 'Ugh!' she thought. 'Why do old men chase after young girls?' The problem was going to be to get rid of her virginity without him realising. Her virginity had to go, that much she knew from books. No woman in literary history had ever had any fun staying a virgin. If she had to close her eyes the first time it was only a small price to pay for a free flat, a job and three meals a day. Surprisingly, the first time with Alex was less painful than she expected and far more fun. She had kept him waiting a month while she went on the pill, learning another good lesson in life: a man kept waiting was easier to manipulate. By the time she let him get into her pants he had bought her clothes, taken her to the theatre and even proposed. She was on a high the day she finished the ten-page story and that was how it happened. The second time Heath met the girl she was no longer a virgin, and it showed. Heath had smiled to himself.

"Sit down and don't talk while I read," said Heath. "You'll have to learn to type." Taking out a red pen, Heath sat at the desk in his small lounge and began to read and correct as he went along. When he had finished, there was more red ink than black and Penny was white in the face. "Your English is dreadful," he said. "There are twenty or more clichés and you can't spell. The grammar is quite funny in parts."

"So what do I do? Give it up?"

"You can see in your mind the pictures you write?"

"Of course."

"Then we will have to teach you English, Penny Bains. You see, you are one of the rare born writers. I can teach you English, that's easy, but I could never have taught you how to write. You can either see those pictures in your mind or you can't. I can't. Why I write flat journalism. Fact rather than fiction. Once you know how to use all the words, you'll paint pictures like a painter."

"You mean you'll help me?" she said, giving him her best smile.

"Yes. And you don't have to look at me like that. Even old men have memories. If we can develop your talent, that will be payment. Take this home and see what I've done with it and then write me another."

That weekend he told Fiona Langton he had found a young girl who could write fiction. They were at the East Horsley estate where he spent one weekend a month when back in England. Byron had stayed in London as usual. Gregory was at boarding school and the two girls were somewhere riding on the estate.

"She's got the same name as your eldest daughter. Penny."

"We call ours Penelope. Byron thinks Penny's a bit common."

"Who else is coming for the weekend?"

"Two writers and an agent. One of them's bringing his wife. When's the next volume of *African Journal* ready, Heath?"

"Soon. Very soon."

The second person that came into Penny's life played a guitar and seduced her on Alex's bed when Alex had gone shopping for the restaurant. The guitar player had been employed to sing songs in the restaurant. His favourite numbers were from an old Shelley Lane album, *Zambezi*. With Will

Langton's blown up photographs lighting up the walls and Shelley Lane's haunting music and words, any African hand trying to eat his supper found a lump in his throat that choked on the food. Penny fell in love with Jonathan Christie during his first song. He was twenty years old, thin as a rake, long black hair down to his shoulders, a nose that any predator bird would have been proud of, a voice like silk that evoked the primal urge to procreate, eyes pale blue and far away gone to the roots of his song, a clean, square jaw and a mouth more sensual than anything Penny had conjured in her mind. The dash for the bedroom was done without a word from either of them.

Jonathan Christie was a travelling singer who sang for a few coins, a place to sleep and sometimes a pint of beer. Alex had made up a bed for him on a bench seat, moving away the restaurant table. The man-boy was so thin he fitted the small width of the leather-covered bench and slept without turning in his sleep, the guitar and a plastic bag of clothes, his only possessions, under the bench. He rose when Alex came down in the morning with the big wicker basket ready for the vegetable market.

"You can go upstairs and take a bath, Penny's still asleep," Alex said to his guitar player. "I'll be gone an hour. Growing tobacco in the old days was easier than running a restaurant, even getting up three times in the night to check the barns in the curing season. Make yourself at home. The customers thought you were great so stay as long as you like."

Which was all very well for Penny in the weeks ahead, servicing one man at night and the one in the morning and all the time writing stories about an African mission. Penny and Jonathan were born for each other; Alex paid the bills. It would have remained the perfect *ménage à trois* if Alex had not dropped the vegetable basket and had it run over by a growler taxi forcing him back to the Zambezi Bar before Jonathan and Penny had finished with his bed. The noise going on upstairs was unmistakable for what it was as Penny was telling God in a loud voice she was coming. By the time Alex ran up the stairs into the flat they were a spent force with no fight left in either of them.

"Get out!" were the two words they understood and by nine o'clock in the morning they were standing outside on the pavement with a guitar in its case, a plastic bag containing male personal effects, the reed basket containing the minimum Penny had been able to salvage amid the barrage of verbal abuse, and just under fifty pence in their pockets. They were both giggling like children. Arm in arm they walked off in the morning sun to face the next part of their lives. Under a lime tree where the scent from the flowers was so strong they could reach out and touch it, they kissed, oblivious to anything except the exquisite scent of the lime flowers. Breaking away, the pale blue eyes looked into the smiling brown of Penny's and they laughed again.

"Did you put your writing in the basket?" he asked.

"I left him the clothes, poor man. Jonathan, we were wicked. Alex was nice."

"And old enough to be your father. Later, you can write him a note thanking him for having you." They laughed again.

"I have an idea," said Penny. "I have a friend who's very old, the one teaching me to write. We'll ask Heath what to do. All we have to do is walk from here to Chelsea. He doesn't get up before noon."

"What do we tell him?" asked Jonathan.

"The truth."

FOR THE FIRST two days Penny sat at the small dining room table writing her story. Heath went about his business, which Penny suspected included a friendly bar, and Jonathan took his guitar round the restaurants looking for work. They slept on the couch in the Chelsea flat where there was always a reserve case of Southern Comfort but very little food. Penny ate cream crackers and cheese she found in the kitchen and drank tea. After a search she found an old bottle of tomato ketchup which she small-dolloped on the crackers. She presumed Jonathan ate on his travels as the money Will had given her in Lusaka had been spent on their nights off at the Zambezi Bar. Alex was tied to his cash business so Jonathan suggested he show Penny more of London than the inside of a bar that reminded her of home. Each day Jonathan went off with his guitar and when Penny had made certain the plastic bag with his clothes was behind the couch, she relaxed and got on with her writing. Her man would get a good job and together they would find a crash pad and be out from under Heathcliff Mortimer's feet.

The lovers were asleep on the couch when Heath came home from his last appointment. Alex was a nice man, but he never had time to talk to his regular customers: the man was more interested in the money than the people. For Heath a good bar owner or barman had to talk and talk well. After the second night he barely noticed the kids fast asleep on the couch, fitted together like a perfect jigsaw puzzle.

On the fourth night he came home thinking he would pour himself a last Southern Comfort to find Penny sitting up alone on the couch.

"He's not coming back, is he, Heath?"

"I brought you some snacks from my last bar. The toast's a bit soggy but the anchovies are nice."

"He's left the plastic bag. It's still behind your couch. It's one o'clock in the morning. There's nothing much in the bag and it all needs washing... His toothbrush has gone."

Heath quietly went to his small cocktail cabinet to the side of the couch, glancing at the plastic bag on the floor. It had the look about it of being left on its own.

"You've spent all Will's money, haven't you?" he asked.

"Every penny. He showed me the theatres. I knew he had no money, so I paid. It didn't seem to matter."

"He made you feel like the only woman in the world?"

"I was the love of his life."

"For the time you were together I'm sure you were."

"You don't think he's coming back." It was a statement more than a question.

"No, Penny, I don't think he's coming back. There are many people in this world who use their charm to get them through life. They are wonderfully pleasant people to have in our lives, but they are usually rather expensive and never reliable. Simply, they live off other people."

"He seemed so sincere."

"The good ones do. Like everything else in life, if you are good at your job, you succeed. Jonathan is good at his job."

"You think he knows what he's doing?"

"Probably. Many I have known like him hone their craft like any other professional. They make people feel good about themselves when they are in the room. They make people feel special. I never heard him sing but I doubt he'll ever be a good singer. The guitar is a prop. The type of clothes, part of the image he wants people to see. He'll go through most of his life like that, having a wonderful time and helping other people too. The good ones know when to move on. Penny Bains, this earth is not the beautiful place we would like it to be. Now, having lost the first but not last great love of your life, I recommend a touch of Southern Comfort. Probably how the drink took its name in the first place. Now, more importantly believe it or not, how was the day's writing?"

"Not bad at first. After I looked in his bag and found the toothbrush missing, not very good. Do you want to read?"

"Not till you've finished."

"You think he's found another woman?"

"Certainly not," lied Heath, handing her the drink he had topped up with water.

THREE DAYS later the plastic bag was still untouched behind the sofa and Penny was hungry. A diet of stale crackers, cheese and old bar snacks was not sufficient. For the first time since arriving in England, she sat down and wrote her parents a letter. How long it would take to reach Mongu was beyond her knowledge: they were certainly too far away to give her any help. To go back to Alex never even crossed her mind. The problem was her clothes, as in her rush to avoid physical confrontation, she had left the new clothes bought for her by Alex and the snappy wardrobe bought out of Will's five hundred pounds in the cupboard, snatching at the reed bag in her panic. Being naked on a bed with another man while the owner screamed at her made her mind concentrate. She had managed to zip up her jeans without catching her pubic hairs as her panties had long fallen off the end of the double bed. She was still buttoning up her top outside on the pavement with the reed bag clutched between her knees. Underneath she was braless too, barefoot as usual but otherwise unharmed. All that was left in the reed bag was the remnants of the charity bundles that she had meant to throw away. Her nipples showed through her one and only top, but this she hoped would be a plus rather than a minus in her quest for a job. Luckily, dirty jeans with knee holes were still in fashion in laid-back London. With a rumbling stomach that needed food, her clothes, hair and face fixed as best she could, Penny stepped out of the foyer of Heathcliff Mortimer's Chelsea flat into a summer's morning in search of her first real job, her conscience telling her the previous job had had more to do with bed than being a waitress.

The first restaurant manager went to the phone to call the Zambezi Bar and check her previous stated place of employment. By the time he came back from a garbled outburst, the pretty girl with the nice nipples was nowhere to be seen. Finally, back in Soho, Penny avoided the girlie clubs and with consummate luck found herself a job in Greek Street at the Green Dolphin, the new manager being well aware that the almost fifty-year-old Johnny Pike liked young girls with big nipples and a tight arse that fitted their jeans to perfection. When this one walked in, he had noticed, the cheeks talked to each other. Penny had seen a paunched old man sitting on his own at the end of the bar who had taken her in from bare feet to protruding nipples with a practised stare that left her feeling naked. Penny, with her mind now concentrated on the man who could give her a job, did not see the old lecher give a nod of his head. Johnny Pike was always looking for something new to keep him amused.

For three days she worked as she was in her bare feet which no one seemed to notice in the rush: few of the men were able to drop their eyes below her navel. She worked the day shift, and every afternoon walked the three miles back to the flat in Chelsea, waiting for her first pay packet to find a place of her own. Tips from the first day had been enough to buy a pair of sandals. From going barefoot in Africa most of her life, the soles of her feet were hard, but not, she thought, hard enough to stop a broken glass on the floor lacerating her feet.

On the fourth day, the paunched old man was back at his seat at the end of the bar. As Penny worked her tables she could feel the old lecher's eyes following her every move. The casual nipple 'pervers' worried her not at all but the old man on his own at the end of the bar had an aura of evil. She knew when he left without turning her head. The frantic lunchtime trade went on and by the time she was ready to leave and walk back to Chelsea, the bad vibrations had gone and been forgotten. That afternoon, to make herself less obvious, she used the day's good tips to buy herself a bra and two pairs of panties. The cook had given her two Cornish pasties to take home and the evening was warm and wonderful.

JOHNNY PIKE HAD NEVER MARRIED as he had never found it necessary. For all the years of his adult life, women came to him, were seduced and sent on their way. He worked on the principle that women enjoyed sex as much as he did and the affair, long or brief, was mutually satisfying. He never once looked at it as the best years of a girl's life, the seven or ten years, sometimes only two or three, when a woman was in control of the sexual attraction. He never thought of the good-time girls ending up on their own with little money or no prospects unless they had used those years wisely to find a productive man, give him three or more children and a mortgage so she would have his support for the rest of her life. Johnny Pike had never had the inclination to bring up children. In fact, he didn't even like children and understood the Victorian dictum that children should be seen and not heard. His friend of over thirty years, Byron Langton, maybe had the best of both worlds with his wife and children in the country and the rest of his life left exactly as before. Old Jack Pike, Johnny Pike's father, had died without seeing a grandson and the old man's last words were the only disturbing note in an otherwise perfect way of life. 'What's the point, so to speak, in cheating your way to wealth and limitless riches if you've got no one to leave it to?' Johnny was an only child.

Old habits die hard and Johnny preferred drinking in the Green Dolphin to the smarter bars in Mayfair, and once a month he met with his friend Byron Langton to have a beer together and talk of younger times. Johnny, who had started Byron on his business way, was proud of his friend and prouder still of himself owning a major share in Langton Merchant Bank. The idea of making money out of other people's greed had always appealed to Johnny Pike, especially when so much greed had been unleashed by bleeding liberals bemoaning the fate of the Third World. Often he and Byron chuckled at the real result of democracy in the world of Britain's old colonies in Africa. Apart from the people starving across the Dark Continent, multiplying at a pace unseen in history, everyone seemed happy. The governments were black, not colonial, the business of digging up the minerals was going better than usual and the Western powers no longer had the cost of running the colonies. If the people now starved, it was not the Western powers' problem. In the years since the Europeans had thrown out their colonies on a high of political correctness, the people of Europe had become rich beyond their wildest dreams. The money was in the products that came from the raw materials, the products of high technology and that money by and large stayed in Europe and America. Johnny had never once been to Africa and had no intention of visiting the continent any time soon.

Johnny had tried to reach the Green Dolphin before the new girl went off duty but business had kept him: running the soft pornography business was time-consuming and with television showing some of the same and competition being legitimate, the sleaze business was not what it used to be. In the new liberal London, everything was out in the open. Men cuddled men in the park. Gamblers gambled through the night. Whores competed with amateurs from all over the world. Dirty pictures were sold on the news stand. Drugs were supposed to be illegal but half the swinging members of the town were permanently high. Anything went so long as it was politically correct with a political lobby to keep it correct and frighten vote-seeking politicians into line. Sipping his first beer while waiting for Byron, Johnny Pike wondered if he should not become a politician. The fun had definitely gone out of the sleaze business once the politicians made it legal, and he wondered if the drug business would one day suffer the same fate. Being a romantic with a distinct perverted quirk, Johnny Pike often thought he would have liked to live in America during the days of prohibition when the morally righteous politicians had made it illegal for a man to take a drink.

Johnny watched his friend push through the door and smiled to himself:

there was even a waddle to Byron's walk with all the fat stuck to the inside of his legs.

"Give me another beer," he said to the barman and turned to greet his friend.

Byron Langton was distinctly jaded. He took the beer and lifted it to his mouth without saying a word. There was something about old friendship when it didn't require an explanation. Byron had eaten too much rich food at lunchtime, entertaining a potential new client, and the heartburn was physically clutching his chest. The two antacid tablets had not taken effect and the beer burnt as it went down his throat. The one thing Byron Langton hated was stop-start drinking. He believed in either getting drunk and sleeping it off or not starting at all. The two men at lunchtime were twenty years his junior and their livers were stronger. They were preparing another revolution in East Africa and needed some working capital. Byron summed them up in his private mind as right royal little shits and thanked his lucky stars that he didn't live in the country they were about to throw into turmoil. They were both Marxist, professed dedicated interest in the proletariat, asked him to raise ten million pounds sterling for the cause, and promised to sell their country's raw materials through Langton Merchant Bank provided the bank paid ten per cent of the FOB price to a nominated account in Switzerland. The two men were spending their money before they even came to power and Byron marvelled at the word of mouth that had led them to Langton Merchant Bank with the knowledge of such words as 'Free On Board'. The eldest one by a few months, as judged by Byron, was a major, his partner-to-be a sergeant, the one having worked out the finances for the commissioned officers to come in on their revolt and the other the NCOs. Byron had learnt from experience not to laugh at bizarre propositions and had phoned Heathcliff Mortimer after the lunch and told him to pack his bags for Africa and find out what chances the major and his sergeant had of pulling off their military coup. There was big risk and big profit in Africa.

The second pull at the beer went down easier and the sucked tablets belatedly began to compete with his heartburn. Two more people came into the Green Dolphin and sat at the opposite end of the bar.

"Not a good day," suggested Johnny, finally breaking the silence.

"What makes me laugh is they like doing business with the British because we are honest." Johnny refrained from asking what he was talking about. "We just make it legal."

"I think it was Cromwell who said it was only treason if you lost."

"Johnny, what the hell are you talking about?"

"Power. Anything's legal if you get away with it ... There's a new girl started on the day shift. Just your type, Byron."

"How do you know my type? This beer tastes flat."

"Because your type is my type, and she had my hormones dancing on the ceiling... She comes from Africa."

"You never went for blacks."

"Her father's a missionary."

"Johnny, you're a pervert. Missionary daughters! I suppose she's nineteen."

"Yes she is. With nipples half an inch long. She doesn't wear a bra."

"You think these two blacks would be happy with lunch but they want to see London's nightlife. Said they want to fuck a white girl. The things I bloody well do to make money. The bloody world's crazy. All the blond Swedes and Germans rush off to Kenya to fuck the black whores and when the blacks get over here, they want to fuck ours. Why can't we all be satisfied with our own women?"

Johnny left that one hanging in the air and ordered two more beers. The trouble with both of them, he thought, was boredom. They had done it all before. Even the new girl had not taken Byron's mind off the perversions of his business.

"You got a club to suggest I can take my clients tonight? I'm sick of that one in Hay Street. All I want to do is go home, get some sleep and wake up without this heartburn... What's the girl's name?"

"Penny something," said Johnny.

"I'd call my daughter Penny only Fiona thinks Penny's common. It's her bloody father. He likes the sound of Penelope running off his tongue. The man's a bloody snob... Did you buy this beer? Cheers. Barman, give us both a chaser. It's going to be another long night."

AFTER THREE SUCCESSIVE nights of the evil eye, Penny Bains asked who was the paunched old man who usually sat at the end of the bar facing the restaurant tables. The manager had changed her shift to the evening, increasing her expenses by a taxi fare to Chelsea at night. The tips were much the same but more than she expected when she took the job, judged on her experience at the Zambezi Bar.

"Johnny Pike?" said Penny, after questioning the manager. "He owns this place? He was in the bar at my interview. Was he the reason I got the job?"

"He's a very wealthy man," said the manager.

"I don't care how much money he's got. He's fat and old and gives me the creeps. I can feel him looking at me with my back turned. Look, I may be young and new to the world but tell that old pervert to keep his eyes off me, let alone anything else. I'm a waitress, not a whore."

"How did you learn all these words on a mission thousands of miles from nowhere?"

"From books. Anything you want to know is in books. I'm going to be a writer. Please, do us all a favour. Tell that old bugger to keep his mind in check. There are more bloody predators in London than lions in Barotseland and there are a lot of bloody lions around Mongu."

"Mongu?"

"My home. Look it up on the map if you can find a dot small enough. Central Africa. You'll find Mongu in Central Africa... My tables are getting agitated. Excuse me."

Half an hour later, Johnny Pike took up his seat at the end of the bar and was joined by the manager who sat with the owner for five minutes before getting on with his job. Penny watched them from the corner of her eye. When she cleared her third table she turned with the dirty plates to take them into the kitchen, a five-pound tip in her pocket. Johnny Pike caught her eye, smiled and winked and for the rest of the evening took not the slightest notice of her.

When she left to go home, her first pay packet was wedged in the front pocket of her jeans and no mention had been made of her losing her job.

Heathcliff Mortimer had left the previous day for East Africa, leaving instructions for her to write and under no circumstances look for somewhere permanent to stay until he returned from his trip. The night shift at the restaurant gave her the whole day to write and read.

She made a cup of tea before sitting down to count her money. Inside the brown envelope was a note which she opened first. 'A man never goes where he is not wanted, a lesson I have learnt throughout my life.' The note was signed by Johnny Pike and when she counted the money, it was exactly double what she expected. Many years later she was to look back and realise that the note was the beginning of her memory bank, the bank that she would use to write her stories: nothing in life was ever predictable. Even before Heathcliff Mortimer returned from Africa, she was talking comfortably to Johnny Pike and never once did he make the slightest pass.

FIVE WEEKS AFTER LEAVING, Heath returned to his flat, exhausted. Penny saw he had lost weight. They smiled happily at seeing each other.

"Penny, pour an old man a drink. I'm too old for chasing around Africa and the new rape of the place makes me sick. You can't believe the corruption where I just came from. First thing, of course, the president made himself president for life. That's a prerequisite for staying alive as every one of them murders his way to power... A little more Southern Comfort and not so much ice. Thank you. It's nice to have someone to chat to at the end of a trip... The man I went to write about has put a ring of steel around his palace, and I mean a palace. He has a taster to test his food and more treasure out of the country than Hitler. All the mineral royalties go to the president paid through contracts with American and French multinationals while the people scratch their living from the soil, their lifestyles little changed from the dawn of history. Foolishly, the president for life has not paid enough of the loot to his soldiers who now think they can do better on their own. So they will kill the despot and steal his throne, the one he had made in France for five million US dollars. The new man in waiting, currently in a safe haven across the river where his own tribe is more numerous in the neighbouring state, has evoked the interest of the West by calling for free and fair elections. The man, of course, is a communist, but he needs all the arms and money he can get to force his way into power. Mark my words, once in power he will find a new way to make himself president for life, like Mugabe in Zimbabwe with his one-party state, a party that no one will dare to compete with if they want a job. Across every divide the Americans and Russians face off against each other, each scared shitless that the other will gain exclusive control of Africa's minerals. So the people starve... Now, be a little darling and pour another drink. Then I want to see everything you have written while I was away."

THE FOLLOWING MONDAY, Penny found a room of her own. Heath needed his own place to think and write. Men like Heathcliff Mortimer, Penny had worked out, lived alone because they wished to live alone and Penny, from her own experience, understood his need for solitude. When he needed company, he went to a bar and left when the company grew boring. She judged he was not a man who had to rely on other people.

The routine became written in stone. Five nights a week she went straight home and slept for eight hours. The first hour in the morning was spent thinking, the next two writing, the next an hour in the park if it wasn't raining, the rest reading newspapers, news magazines and books, before walking to the Green Dolphin to work the night shift. In Africa, Penny, with the help of Heathcliff Mortimer, taught herself to write. Within six months she had written her first novel. Heath asked Fiona Langton to read the manuscript and received a look of disapproval.

"New writers are too expensive to promote," she told Heath. "A writer has to be marketable, preferably famous before they write a book. They have to be able to self-promote, which I doubt would be the case for a missionary's daughter. Really, Heath, at your age."

"Why won't you read it?"

"I wouldn't waste my time."

Penny sent the manuscript to every fiction publisher in England with the same result. No one was in the slightest bit interested and had Heath not told her the book was well worth reading, she would either have committed suicide or given up writing for the rest of her life. As the second year of the terrible African drought began, she completed her second African novel with the same result.

"It's better than the first. Much better," said Heath. "Write another book."

"I'm sick of waiting tables. I want to be an author."

"You are an author, Penny. You just haven't been paid."

"What the hell do I do to get paid?"

"Write another book."

It was soon after receiving Johnny Pike's note in her pay packet the previous summer that she had met Byron Langton. If Byron had bothered to keep up with the life of Hilary Bains, through his marriage and children, he might have asked if there was any connection. He knew the young Hilary had gone off to Africa, which he considered at the time a good thing as he felt the boy was sponging off the family. Once during a visit to Langton Manor he heard mention of the name but as Hilary was of no interest or use to Byron, he paid no attention.

Penny, on the other hand, was fully aware of not only Byron's background with her father but his power in the business of publishing books.

Byron rather enjoyed the game, having found out the girl wished to be a writer. He knew her price from the start and just bided his time, waiting for the inevitable call for help. When her first book did the round of publishers, unbeknown to Penny, the close-knit world of London publishing had been forewarned not to touch the book: somehow, the rights belonged to the Langton publishing empire and no one wanted to upset the reviewer in the *Daily Garnet*. No one in the industry said anything but everyone knew.

Slowly and casually over the next few years, Byron had made himself known to Penny Bains while he bided his time.

The fifth novel, Heath said, would sell a hundred thousand copies in hardback if she had a publisher.

"Can't you find me one, Heath?"

"I've tried. One could almost think it a conspiracy. No one will even look at your books. In your job at the Green Dolphin, have you ever met a man called Byron Langton? Fact is, he's my boss."

"Once or twice a month. He always makes a point of talking to me."

"There's your answer. The bastard likes young girls. If you ask him nicely to look at your new book and accept his invitation to his flat, you'll be a well-paid author within twelve months."

"You mean sleep with him!"

"No. Become his mistress."

"The man's revolting." She was about to tell Heath Byron's relationship to her father but she stopped. "Are people really that disgusting?"

"Oh, yes. Keep him on a string until you sign the contract and dump him when the book's published."

"I think I'll be sick."

"Probably. There's a price to pay for everything, the good and the bad. The world is full of influence, not talent. Most successful people have been a whore at some stage in their lives and that includes all democratic politicians. The press, the so-called freedom of speech press, have the world in their power. There has never been a democratic politician who reached the halls of power without them. At the moment, Byron supports the Conservatives. If they try to interfere with his business or if he thinks they may lose the election, he'll switch his chain of newspapers. I'm as much a whore as any of them. Byron Langton bought me a long time ago and made me comfortable and I've found I like being comfortable. That was my price. Yours is more transient. Close your eyes and think of England."

"You want me to sell myself?"

"If you want to publish, Penny Bains. Many years ago the women found him rather exciting. The more important thing is the books are well worth publishing. If they weren't, I'd tell you to throw them on the fire and look for a husband."

THE ROW OCCURRED six weeks later when Byron Langton paid one of his rare visits to his East Horsley estate. The excuse was Gregory's final sojourn at home before he set off on his gap year. His girls, Penelope and Morag, were also at home and though Byron's only interest in horses was betting on the Derby, he walked to the stables with his daughters to inspect the new ponies he had given them for Christmas. Penelope was fifteen and Morag nearly seventeen and if there was any way to soften up Fiona, it was through their children. The boy, so far as Byron was concerned, was a drip and the girls were going to end up looking like their horses. Byron had the wild hope that when they were older, he would find them more acceptable.

"I want to publish a book recommended strongly by Heathcliff Mortimer," he said to his wife that evening over supper in the dining room. The girls, together with his son, had all gone into town to see a film, and the cook had left a cold buffet on the sideboard. Byron found talking business to his wife a pleasure as the publishing house she ran was highly profitable, a combination of good book choice and good reviews in Byron's now wide-ranging string of newspapers that took in Canada, Australia and many of the provincial cities outside of London, the home of the *Daily Garnet*: the one hand fed the other hand and most of the profit landed up with Byron.

Fiona took the manuscript from her husband and looked at the name of the author.

"Don't be silly, Byron. Heath's been foisting this girl onto me for years. She's the daughter of a white missionary still stuck in Africa and totally unmarketable."

"I want you to read it."

"Byron, you're disgusting. The girl's not twenty-five."

"If you are suggesting what I suspect, then you're disgusting. It's a family matter. The girl is the daughter of Hilary Bains who was unofficially adopted by my parents during the war. His father was my father's tail gunner who came home dead on a flight back from Germany. Hilary's mother was killed in an air raid. Will calls Hilary his adopted brother, though I never went quite that far."

"Then it's nepotism."

"I don't think you will say that when you read the book."

"Don't tell me you've read a manuscript?"

"As a matter of fact, yes. I intended to flip. It's the story of a young girl growing up divorced from her culture and coming back to her roots. It's funny and sad and it gives a shocking exposé of what has become of Western society." Byron went back to eating his cold chicken. "Fiona, will you please read this book?"

"I'll send it out to readers."

"That's good enough."

"Is it really that good?" asked Fiona, her interest roused by her husband's reaction.

"Send it to a reader. Read it yourself. Whatever. You'll publish it, Fiona."

"And you will make a lot of money."

"That's the idea isn't it?"

FIVE WEEKS EARLIER, when Heathcliff Mortimer had written up his African report and taken it to Byron Langton, he brought up the subject of Penny Bains.

"You realise she's the daughter of Hilary Bains?"

"Yes, though I couldn't imagine the Reverend Hilary Bains getting it up, let alone siring a daughter. Anyway, what is Penny Bains to you?"

"I taught her English. She came to me with an introduction from Will."

"Young Will, the do-gooder. I still don't see the connection."

"I want you to publish her book without seducing her. Damn it, Byron, for all intents and purposes you are her uncle. I've checked the publishing market. You let out years ago you didn't want them to publish her books."

"You know something, Heath, you've given me a way round a dilemma. Now, is this report going to make me money? Do I give my major and his sergeant a contribution to their political campaign?"

"The answer's 'yes' on both counts... She's a nice girl."

"That's why I'm going to help her publish her book. And Heath, don't look at me like that. I've told you for years that everyone has their price. I like young girls and she wants to publish her work. It's a perfect match. Better still, now you tell me I'm her uncle, Fiona will think I'm doing it out of kindness to a sibling. She'll know the truth but have a story to salvage her pride. That's Fiona's price. Her pride. Her family name. Provided I don't embarrass my wife, she will bring up the children and provide the social background I require. A man who works hard is entitled to play every now and again. Anyway, what else does a man of my age do for fun? Once the sex urge goes a man might as well shoot himself. Is the book any good?"

"It's going to sell a lot of copies."

"This gets better as it goes along. I have always fancied making real money out of a mistress. By the way, Heath, if you like your comfort, don't tell her I knew her father. I certainly won't. But surely she must know."

"The world is bloody sick."

"No. It's a lot of fun."

. . .

Penny Bains had thought about it for another week and then she took the manuscript with her to work, ready to sell her soul to the devil. For two nights the man she was after did not appear and when he did, there was no willingness on his behalf to start their usual conversation.

For three weeks Byron kept her on the hook, smiling to himself at the girl's frustration, marvelling at the compulsion to give birth to a book. When he was sure the girl would not renege on her side of the bargain, he arrived at the Green Dolphin earlier than usual, before the tables filled up with people wanting to eat. Johnny was due to join him in half an hour's time.

"You want a drink, Penny?" asked Byron, turning on his charm. The body had changed, but the charm had never gone away. "I won't tell Johnny you are drinking on duty and neither will anyone else. Look at your tables. There's nobody there... George," he said, turning to the barman. "Give young Penny a gin and tonic. Now, come and sit down and tell me how you've been doing."

Penny climbed up onto the bar stool and accepted her drink. She was flustered. By the end of her drink she was no further forward with her plan. A second drink was put in front of her on the bar and still no customers were sitting at her tables. There were two other waitresses and both of them were working hard at their tables and the first double gin was going to her head. Johnny Pike joined them at the bar and she found herself sitting in between the two. Still there were no customers sitting at her tables and the others were almost full.

"Looks like you don't need Penny tonight, Johnny," Byron said when Penny was halfway through the second double gin. "We were thinking of going out to dinner. Monday's always a slow night at the Green Dolphin. We were going back to Penny's place to let her change and then coming back into the West End. You won't miss her for one evening. The major and his sergeant will be joining us for dinner and as Penny was brought up in Africa, I thought she would be interested."

"When is the military coup?" asked Johnny Pike.

"Oh, they won't tell me that, will they? Penny, do you have something nice to wear?"

"Yes, I think so," she croaked, the constriction in her throat barely allowing her to speak.

"We have a mutual friend, Penny, Heathcliff Mortimer. He calls himself your literary mentor. Maybe on the way we could pick up this manuscript he's been talking about."

. . .

IN THE ROOM next to the one Penny had lived in for the last three years was a mostly out of work stage director. In the one next to him was a mostly out of work actor. They had shared the top floor or the semi-detached building for most of this time, the stage director coming to London for his pot of gold, seven weeks after Penny had moved off the couch in Heathcliff Mortimer's lounge. There was one common bathroom the size of a cupboard and cooking was done in the rooms on two-plate cookers in alcoves that had once been cupboards. Through the fire escape was a small landing overlooking the back garden and hops grew right up the back of the house to flower in profusion. The landing with all its greenery was just big enough for three chairs with the actor able to put his long legs out in between the chairs. When the sun was out in the summer they spent their spare time talking and drinking cups of tea. They were to be some of the happiest hours of Penny's life, even when she looked back from a much older age. They were young and thirsty for knowledge, with time to talk and dream. All of her first five books were dreamed about on the landing and the help she found in the two young men was as important to her work as the technical learning she got from Heathcliff Mortimer. Most of her money went to feeding the boys when they were out of work, which was most of the time, which was why she had never moved into a flat of her own. The books that had not been sent out to Mongu by the bishop were found by the boys who were able to fill in the gaps of her reading. They all agreed that when she was famous, she would write a play with a plum part for the actor to be directed by the director and then they would go onto films. Throughout the years at the top of the house, both boys had kept out of her bed as they knew a relationship would shatter their peace. To the boys she had explained her publishing predicament and its solution.

"Just watch he doesn't renege," said the director.

"Get it in writing first," said the actor. "There's no such thing as a free lunch."

"So you don't find it disgusting?"

"Everyone lies and cheats these days. No one gives a damn. People only know the difference between right and wrong if what they do succeeds. Make the old fart wear a condom and have a good shower afterwards. The path to glory is littered with shit. Penny, you've tried every other way. Go for it but don't tell your children." The actor stretched out his long legs, the length of the small landing.

"If the end justifies the means, go for it," said the director. "In your Africa the liberation movements killed people who got in the way. Look at South Africa. Don't tell me the terrorist means don't justify the end. How else are they going to get rid of apartheid? The capitalist monopolies have the publishing industry by the throat, the whole damn media for that matter. Get published. Use their sordid system. When you're famous, you can tell them to go to hell. Then you will have a free voice without any clutter. If the freedom fighters in South Africa have to bomb the odd civilian target to rid themselves of a bunch of fascists, what's a friendly fuck in bed? Just make sure you turn out the light. Use your imagination. You're a writer. Use the bastard and get what you want."

THE EVENING with the major and his sergeant went smoothly in a class of restaurant Penny never knew existed. The menu she was shown showed no prices and Byron Langton was the perfect host. The manuscript of *Is This Really Civilisation?* was locked in the boot of Byron's car and Penny was wearing the only dress she possessed, a summer frock that showed off her figure better than she had intended. Byron had waited patiently downstairs while she changed. It had taken half an hour by which time, unbeknown to Penny, Byron had finished a number of pages of her book. At first, the major thought the white flesh was there for him but changed his mind when Byron held her hand on top of the dinner table. Throughout the meal, Penny played the dumb female to avoid joining the conversation on behalf of the starving millions strewn across Africa. Penny knew instinctively there was evil sitting at the table.

From the restaurant they went to a nightclub where two girls even younger than Penny were introduced to the Africans and with the free flowing of the drink, Penny understood Byron Langton was prepared to partly bankroll the major's bid for the presidency of his country. For Penny to realise the spoils of Africa were carved up in Western nightclubs made her determined, by whatever means, to get herself published so she could write the real books about Africa, the ones that would expose the cruelty and corruption, the total indifference to the plight of the African people.

At the end of the evening, the major and the sergeant were sent off with the whores in a taxi and Byron Langton drove her straight back to her home. Politely he got out of his car and saw her to the front door which she opened with her key.

"We'll do this again when I've finished with your book," said Byron.

"You mean you've already read some of it?"

"Yes. Next Wednesday, your night off, I'll collect you here at eight o'clock. Before then, go and buy yourself some evening clothes and have them call me at the bank for payment."

"Why?"

"Because I want you to look nice. Surely, Penny, by now we understand each other. If we don't, then we're both wasting our time. For what it's worth, going out with a much older man who has seen a great deal of this wicked world may give you storylines for your books. Put it down to research. Eight on Wednesday and I'm never late. I hate people who are late. Wastes both people's time. You didn't like my guests tonight?"

"They are a pair of thugs."

On the day Penny Bains received her contract and cheque for ten thousand pounds in advance royalty, she also received a phone call from Byron Langton. She had been working day shifts ever since Byron had asked to see her book.

"Remember, you owe me dinner tonight, Penny Bains. I will pick you up at eight o'clock to celebrate. Congratulations."

All the restaurants they had been to so far were small and out of the way, with food and service beyond anything in the famous hotels. They were run by the owners who all seemed to count her escort as a personal friend. This evening's restaurant, where she had never been taken before, was in Knightsbridge, close to Buckingham Court. At her place at the table for two was a single, perfect blue-white orchid which Byron pinned to her dress. There was no scent to the flower. The cocktail was poured into a glass filled with crushed ice and drunk through a straw. Deliberately, she had never asked Byron the name of the cocktails and never once had he shown off by giving them a name. The five-course meal she guessed had been ordered in advance. Each course found a different wine which was taken away with the empty plates, along with most of the bottles' contents: Penny assumed the kitchen staff drank the rest. They finished a perfect meal and Byron called for his usual cigar and brandy, a coffee liqueur for Penny.

"Are you ready to pay the price?" asked Byron softly, the two violet eyes watching her intently.

"Yes," she whispered, "if that's what you want."

"I never go to a lot of trouble for nothing. You know my flat is a couple of streets down?"

"I know you have a flat in Buckingham Court."

"Was it a good trade? My wife tells me she has ordered a twenty thousand print run. Not bad for hardback. My literary critic at the *Daily Garnet* has read an advance copy. He guarantees me a good column of praise.

I think you are going to be famous. Did you know I made Shelley Lane famous? You'll be all right. Writers last much longer than singers."

"Did you seduce her?"

"Actually, it was the other way round. Worse, she fell in love. She ended up with Will for a while when they were both on the skids. Dumped him for his best friend. Had a baby by the friend who was killed in Rhodesia. There is no accounting for women. People really. Why do they all do it, I ask myself? The gentlemen from Africa you rightly called thugs are presently executing their president by firing squad, unable to see the inevitable picture of their own backs to the same wall. Young, beautiful girls are prized by men beyond treasure, yet everyone knows the ravages of age. We all know and we all fall into the same traps, making life's journey rather pointless, don't you think? What is it all about? Most of what we want is pointless when achieved. I go on making money without a personal purpose for that money. Like a lion who kills the entire herd of buffalo, eats one and leaves the rest to rot. Maybe the creation of wealth is different as others benefit, like the vultures, we destroy as much as we build. There was great wealth in Europe so we fought two wars to knock it down and force ourselves to start all over again. What a strange animal is man, never satisfied, always envious and rarely happy." Byron looked into his glass. "Good food and good wine. I talk too much. Shall we go when I finish my brandy?"

"If you wish."

"Should I not wish? Weeks and weeks of preparation. Have you not got what you, Penny Bains, wanted?"

"Yes I have."

"Then why not me? Why may I not have what I want? I give you a career in writing and you give me a night or two in bed. A rather good trade, I would imagine. All this moral righteousness is for losers, Penny Bains. We both know the price of winning. There is always a price. We have a contract, you and I. Will you honour that contract?"

"Yes," she said quietly for the second time.

"But you find me repulsive?" Penny lowered her eyes away from the question. "Is it my age and corpulence or the methods I use to make money?"

"Both."

"You are honest. Have you not enjoyed any of the time we spent together? Surely there was something you have learnt? A quick, sharp lesson in the perversions of man? Now, I think we must go. My restaurateur friend has a taxi waiting for us. You are not working tomorrow. Fact is, I told the Green Dolphin you have resigned. A rich writer, about to be famous, does not wait tables. All your dues but one have been paid... Are you ready, Penny Bains?"

"Yes, I am."

"So quiet. So unlike you."

The door to number 47 Buckingham Court was thrown open and Penny stepped over the threshold. There was a strong scent of incense which surprised her and the flat was poor for so wealthy a man.

"I have been here since I was your age," said Byron. "The only thing that has changed is me. Look in that mirror and remember yourself at twenty-four. Remember well. It never lasts. Do you want a drink?"

"No."

"The time has come. Sit down, anyway. Make yourself comfortable. I have waited nearly five years."

"You won't hurt me, will you?"

"I tell you what. Go into the bedroom and take off your clothes while I have a small brandy."

For five minutes there was silence in the flat broken by the clock ticking on the mantelpiece.

"Are you naked?" he called through the closed bedroom door.

"For God's sake, Byron. Come and do it."

"You can put your clothes on again and come back in here."

"What the hell's going on?" she said, coming back into the lounge.

"It's all over. You've fulfilled your contract. You see, Penny, the chase is always more exciting than the catch, the hunt better than the kill."

"Would you have published my book if it was no damn good?"

"Certainly not. You would have received a contract and a royalty advance and silence."

"So this was all a charade?"

"Oh, I don't know. I enjoyed proving once again that every person has their price. We are all whores, Penny Bains. Just some of us are more expensive than others. Send me a signed copy. The taxi is still waiting for you downstairs in the street. Have a good life."

23

*A*t the end of 1985, when Penny Bains was signing copies of her book at Harrods, little or no rain had fallen in Central Africa. The main rivers were nowhere in sight. In Zimbabwe, where Mugabe had harangued but not nationalised his commercial farmers, ninety-five per cent of whom were the white settlers he had fought in the bush war, the food situation was not so serious as Zambia, where Kaunda's brand of socialism had chased out his commercial farmers. In both countries, without help from outside, the present subsistence farmers would starve. In the villages, the rickety storage silos built of bush timber were empty of maize cobs.

In Zimbabwe, Mugabe drew from the surplus grown by his commercial farmers, much of the crop grown under irrigation. With the foreign exchange generated by the commercially grown tobacco crop he imported grain from America. In Barotseland, with no such help, the famine had begun to kill.

Perversely, in northwestern Angola the rains had been good and by the end of April 1986, the Zambezi began to swell, rushing precious water past the parched bush where the grass, for as far as the animals could eat and return to water, was grazed to the roots.

The last two truckloads of maize flour sent from Port Elizabeth in South Africa by Goldblatt and Sons, paid for by Will Langton's bankers in Switzerland, had been hijacked in Zambia and looted. There was no grain food left on the mission and the buck, buffalo and bush pig were so emaciated the only food from them would have been skin and bone.

Resigned to their fate, a fate that had been passed down to them through the centuries of Africa's feast and famine, the people sat under the leafless trees and waited to die. For the first time in his life Will Langton knew the agony of permanent, gnawing hunger and there seemed nothing, with all his money, he could do except leave the country to its destiny. The population of man, like the population of animals, was being culled by nature. Once again only the fittest would survive the decimation ensuring the future strength of the gene pool. The clever diligently fished the river and irrigated vegetable patches close to its banks, heaving bucket after bucket of water up the slopes to the plants. Day and night the diligent watched their small patch of vegetables, chasing off the marauding baboons.

After the second hijack, Goldblatt and Sons, the company owned by Hymie Goldblatt's family, refused further transport and no one else in South Africa was prepared to chance a vehicle further into Zambia than the capital, Lusaka. Will watched the river rise from the good rains at the Angolan headwaters and thought of Horst Kannberg. From the mission he sent a message to the trackers still patiently waiting for his return to the half-demolished base camp. Then they waited, Will, Hilary and Mary, watching the steady rise of the Zambezi while their patients, staff and schoolchildren slowly shrunk from hunger.

Horst Kannberg had never seen fit to build a house. The doctors had told Betty Gulliver many years before that she never would have children so there had seemed no point for more than a caravan. Most of the time in Zimbabwe was spent outside of a building and like the Africans, Horst treated his home as a place to sleep. Betty, married to Horst twenty years ago on the *Zambezi Queen the First*, had turned fifty and both of them missed the children they had never had. It was the only cloud above their happiness.

Two years after Will Langton had watched them being married, the Victoria Falls municipality built a campsite for tourists around the launch site of their cruise boat, making them pay a mooring fee for their boat and a campsite fee for their caravan. The compensation was a game fence, an ablution block with constant hot water and a stream of tourists, all of whom wanted a trip upriver on the *Zambezi Queen*. When Mugabe took over the country in 1980, the bush war came to an abrupt halt and within two more years foreign tourists were again enthralled by 'The Smoke that Thunders', the Victoria Falls. In three years, Horst and Betty invested their profits in new boats so that by the time Onepenny and Fourpence had paddled the five hundred kilometres downriver from the base camp, there were three *Zambezi Queens* being lapped by the waters of the Zambezi River. On the bank above the moored boats was the immobilised caravan surrounded by

Betty's garden of ferns and flowers, orchids and palms, and a vegetable garden tightly guarded against baboons and vervet monkeys by a walk-in cage of strong wire mesh. From the tall trees that drank the waters of the Zambezi, the monkeys swung over the game fence and foraged for food among the tourists.

Sixpence had stayed at base camp complaining of old age. His hair, curly and tight, had gone from pepper grey to white. He was probably five years older than the other trackers and his eyes could no longer count a herd of impala at two thousand metres. Over his eyes an opaque film was growing, and he knew that soon he would be blind. With his fishing line and the small garden protected by the thorn trees he would wait for them to return from their journey.

The makori, cut from the trunk of a single tree to give them access to the river and the fish that swam away from the riverbank, was the length of one and a half men stretched flat on the ground. With the verbal message from Will Langton, they used this to go downriver but would abandon it when they reached Baas Horst.

Horst was reading a letter from his brother in Cape Town. It was the middle of July and cool under the jackalberry tree. In midstream he noticed a dugout canoe trying to beat the flow and turn in to shore. One of their parent's relatives, the son of his mother's sister, had written from Riga in Latvia saying the Russian Empire was about to collapse. There was even hope of the properties owned by their grandparents being returned to the family. The two blacks in the makori had fought out of the current and were heading directly for his jetty. All three of his riverboats were on the sunset cruise upriver.

The order on Goldblatt and Sons in Port Elizabeth was fulfilled in seven days. The bags of maize meal were loaded from the five-ton lorry straight onto the deck of the *Zambezi Queen the First* whose adjustable outboard motors were more likely to navigate the rapids. Horst Kannberg filled in the amount of the invoice on Will Langton's cheque in Swiss francs, which included the duty charged by the Zimbabwean government at Beit Bridge and paid in rand by Goldblatt's clearing agent. The cheque already signed by Will Langton on the mission and delivered with a letter by Fourpence was the kind of business enjoyed by Hymie Goldblatt's brother. The cheque would be deposited in his illegal bank account in Switzerland against the day a communist government in South Africa nationalised his business and threw him out of the country.

At the side of the *Zambezi Queen the First*, the same boat designed and built by Will Langton, three tenders each made of four sealed and empty forty-four-gallon drums supported drums of petrol for the voyage up and down the river. The five tons of food were stacked on the lower and upper decks of the boat. With the permanent captain and crewman now under the command of Horst Kannberg, the boat left the jetty and pushed upriver, avoiding the central flow by keeping to the riverbank. Behind, the tenders followed, attached to the steel wire ropes. Both the captain, a Matabele cadre who had fought for Joshua Nkomo in the Rhodesian bush war, and Horst were armed with hunting rifles.

On the third day, the cargo of maize meal reached Katima Mulilo and the Zambian border. Horst showed the Zambian custom's official the letter from Will Langton which he tried to read upside down, all the time glancing at the sacks of maize meal and the drums of petrol. Fourpence and Onepenny were taken away because they didn't have passports. Horst tried to explain the trackers were Zambians who had paddled five hundred kilometres to seek help for starving people.

"Unload your cargo for inspection," said the man, returning the upside down letter. "Bring those drums ashore. You may not bring petrol into Zambia without paying duty. They are confiscated."

"Then we go back to Zimbabwe."

"You have left the Zimbabwe border post. You are in Zambia. Unload those sacks for inspection. There is duty to pay."

"The food is a gift to the people on the mission."

"There is always duty to pay. Unload your cargo for inspection."

"I refuse."

"You have guns under those sacks! You are a South African agent. Your passport is South African."

"I have lived in Zimbabwe over twenty years."

"Unload your cargo or I have you arrested."

"I'm going back to Zimbabwe."

"Do you have Zimbabwe papers to export your maize and petrol?"

"The petrol is for the journey to Mongu. The maize is a gift."

"My friend on the Zimbabwe side will arrest you for stealing food from the people of Zimbabwe. Unload your cargo. Do you have a permit for those guns?" He had pushed on board the *Zambezi Queen* and seen the rifles.

"We have Zimbabwe licences."

"You are in Zambia. Give me the guns."

"No."

The man shouted in Bemba and armed men ran out of the border post and boarded the *Zambezi Queen*.

"Unload the maize for inspection," he said, smiling. The two rifles were removed by the soldiers.

"If you are going to steal food meant for starving people, unload it yourself."

"No. You unload your cargo for inspection."

Three hours later the sacks of maize were piled on the wooden jetty alongside the full drums of petrol. The sun was going down.

"You are not cleared for Zambian water," said the man who said he was a customs official. "You will moor in Zimbabwe water." He was still smiling.

In the morning, the food and petrol had gone from the jetty and when Horst asked for the customs official a new man said he didn't know what Horst Kannberg was talking about. There was one other man at the border post. The soldiers, if they were soldiers, had gone.

THE SCHOOLCHILDREN HAD GONE home to whatever they would find and the last patient had died in the mission hospital. A scrawny chicken that had long since stopped laying eggs had been boiled and boiled to give Mary Bains a few bowls of chicken broth. She was sixty-one years old and dying. By her bedside the Reverend Hilary Bains was reading out loud from his Bible but Will Langton, standing in the open doorway, doubted if she could hear the words of her God. The thin, dirty sheet, dirty from washing without soap, covered her skeletal body and her eyes were shut. Outside, the October sun was scorching the scorched earth and the only sound that came through the open window was the sound of silence. Hilary put down his Bible and stared at his wife. He had lost his son to malaria and now he was going to lose his wife. They had been married for twenty-eight years and never left the home in which she was dying. They waited, Hilary and Will, while the rain clouds outside in the heavens tried to compete with the burning sun as the new season built up the rains. They waited patiently and then she died.

They buried her in the grave dug by Will in the dry brown earth of Africa. At her head stood a wooden cross that would soon be eaten by termites. The sun was down way over behind the distant Zambezi, making the heavens red and scarlet.

"Did God mean us to end like this?" asked Hilary of Will. "Alone? Our life's work come to nothing?"

"Better to ask me 'is there a God?'"

"You don't believe, do you, Will?"

"Not anymore. Maybe I never did. I just don't know."

"But why? There has to be a God."

"There should be, to make any sense, but doesn't all this horror make more sense if there isn't a God? Maybe pain and suffering are real and part of life, not some means of redemption. Didn't man, maybe, in his search for a better life that he has never found on earth conjure up another world in heaven, the perfect world of his mind? In their bid to make life more tolerable on earth, did not the holy men invent a promised land that we would only reach if we behaved ourselves on earth? Did not man need God so desperately that he believed in him to live in his mind to make the pain of living tolerable? And with that image of his God, man wrote down his religion in His Bible, calling it the word of God, every word true, every word to be believed. Believe or be damned. The fires of hell! Better the God of compassion who died for our sins! The wonderful story of Christ!... Oh, how we needed our God. All we had to do was believe in Him. Blind faith in Him... I envy you, Hilary, with your faith, your goodness and your God. Without your God I agree there is nothing much worth living for.

"But then the blue heavens were penetrated by moon rockets and man knew he could journey to the stars. He gazed with new science and understanding into the galaxy. Elsewhere Darwin was proved right, man had evolved from the slime. We even know the make-up of our bodies; galactic dust that has been recycled a billion times... So what happens to an educated man? He cannot accept many parts of his Bible because science has proved it false. Once part of the story has been destroyed the rest just drifts away. We question with certainty the very creation written in the Bible and we are lost in a violent world without the balm of faith. We are animals, Hilary, who have evolved to have the ability to think, to try and understand. We have searched through science to prolong our meagre lives. Probably we will self-destruct because in our searching for the truth of life too many of us question the presence of God. Man has lost his faith and yes, I think he will destroy himself to run away from all the pain and suffering."

"One day you will find your faith again... But now, what are we going to do, Will, you and I?"

"Go back to my base camp and wait for the trackers, they were likely robbed like Goldblatt's trucks. Then, somehow, make ourselves a life. The mission is finished, Hilary. There is nothing further you or I or the Church of England can do about it. You have done your job as did Mary... We have enough petrol in the big tank to reach the base camp with your books and what else has value. We have all done our best, and that is all a man can ever do. Maybe someday we will go back to England. Who knows? Long ago I would have said only God knows. Now I am not even sure of that."

EPILOGUE

*M*any years later Will Langton left the river running strong and returned to England and Langton Matravers. On the anniversary of their first meeting, he took the path from the back of the house, up to the Downs and the cliff path down to Dancing Ledge. He walked to the pool that had been blasted from the rock ledge for the refugees from the Blitz and stood looking into the water. Deep in the pool he could see her image and even though he was an old man he began to cry.

Then he retraced his steps to Langton Manor and took afternoon tea with the Reverend Hilary Bains.

DEAR READER

~

Reviews are the most powerful tools in our kitty when it comes to getting attention for Peter's books. This is where you can come in, as by providing an honest review you will help bring them to the attention of other readers.

If you enjoyed reading *Just the Memory of Love,* and have five minutes to spare, we would really appreciate a review (it can be as short as you like). Your help in spreading the word and keeping Peter's work alive is gratefully received.

Please post your review on the retailer site where you purchased this book.

Thank you so much.
Heather Stretch (Peter's daughter)

PS. We look forward to you joining Peter's growing band of avid readers.

~

GLOSSARY

∾

Bemba – a Zambian tribe of people

CAA – Civil Aviation Authority

FOB – 'Free On Board' is a term in international commercial law

Kak – Afrikaans word for 'shit'

Makori – African dugout canoe

NGO – non-governmental organization

NCO – non-commissioned officer

Pax – slang for passengers in the airline industry

Smous – a Jewish pedlar who traded in outlying and remote country districts in South Africa

Sudza – traditional African maize porridge

PRINCIPAL CHARACTERS

~

The Langtons
Adelaide – Wife of Ethelred
Anna – Randolph's wife
Aunty Eve – Adelaide's aunt on her mother's side
Byron – Son of Red and Adelaide, Josephine's twin brother
Clifford (Uncle Cliff) – Adelaide's brother
Ethelred (Red) – Squire of Langton Manor and group captain
Gregory, Penelope and Morag – Byron's children
Harold Langton – Granda and father to Ethelred
Josephine (Jo) – Daughter of Red and Adelaide, and twin sister to Byron
Lady Fiona Renwick – Byron's wife
Randolph – Eldest son of Red and Adelaide
William (Will) – Son of Red and Adelaide and central character of *Just the Memory of Love*

The Bains
Hilary Bains – Son of Norman and adopted by Red and Adelaide
Malcolm and Penny – Hilary and Mary's children
Mary Bains – Hilary's wife
Norman Bains – Red's tail gunner in the war and Hilary's father

Other Principal Characters

Beatrice Kendle – An English socialite

Betty Gulliver – Horst's wife

Danika – Late wife of Hannes Potgieter

Gloria Kendle – Beatrice Kendle's mother

Heathcliff Mortimer – Newspaper reporter who works for Byron

Horst Kannberg – A Russian aristocratic

Hymie Goldblatt – A Jewish trader in Barotseland

Jack Pike – Johnny Pike's father

Johannes (Hannes) Potgieter – Afrikaner hunter and trader in Zambia

Johnny Pike – Byron Langton's shady business partner

Kevin Smith – Australian publisher

Lawrence (Laurie) Hall – Airport manager at Mongu

Lindsay Healy – Assistant and mistress to Kevin Smith

Madge O'Shea – Byron's secretary

Mahel Smith – Kevin Smith's wife

Melvin Raath – A well-known American reporter

Mike Barrow – Member of the Horse Scouts

Paul Mwansa – One time boyfriend of Josephine and political activist

Shelley Lane – Beautiful and troubled singer who is in love with Byron
Langton

Sixpence, Fourpence and Onepenny – Hannes Potgieter's trackers

The old chief – a local man, chief of his own tribal land, and junior to the
Paramount Chief Mwene Kandala III

Virginia Stepping and Fanny Try – girlfriends of Byron Langton

PLACE NAMES

∾

Barotseland – is the region between Namibia, Botswana, Zimbabwe, Zambia and Angola, and is the homeland of the Lozi people or Barotse

Kasungula (Kazungula) – a small border town in the Southern Province of Zambia, lying on the north bank of the Zambezi River and about seventy kilometres west of Livingstone

Langton Matravers – a village on the Isle of Purbeck in the county of Dorset, southern England

Mongu – the capital of the Western Province of Zambia and formerly-named province, Barotseland

South West Africa – modern-day Namibia, formerly ruled by South Africa

ACKNOWLEDGMENTS

~

With grateful thanks to our *VIP First Readers* for reading *Just the Memory of Love* prior to it's official launch date. They have been fabulous in picking up errors and typos helping us to ensure that your own reading experience of *Just the Memory of Love* has been the best possible. Their time and commitment is particularly appreciated.

Alan McConnochie (South Africa)
Felicity Barker (South Africa)
Marcellé Archer (South Africa)

Thank you
Kamba Publishing